CW01468445

THE SIEGE OF MALTA

THE SIEGE OF MALTA

Many times in her long history Malta has held a key position in the struggle to control the Mediterranean. Her strategic importance has been much discussed again lately. During World War II she withstood the fury of the Nazis. But, four hundred years earlier, she sustained an even more famous and dramatic siege.

For five long months in 1561 a huge Mohammedan force attacked Malta—and was defied, in a great epic of endurance, by the Knights of St. John.

The story of this siege fascinated Sir Walter Scott, who visited the island, gathered material and began writing a novel about it. Scott died before the work reached anything like a finished form. More than a century later, S. Fowler Wright traced Scott's manuscript and notes to New York, and from them wrote this splendid romance, *The Siege of Malta*, now published for the first time in a single volume.

It is a story of high courage and deep faith. At its centre stands the old Grand Master of the Order, La Vallette (after whom Valetta was named), grim and unshakable as though he had been carved from the very Rock of St. Peter. But it is also a story of love undaunted amid fearful perils; of a girl who, rather than be separated from the man she loves, learns to wield a sword, and, escaping by a hairsbreadth from the clutches of the infidel, finally wins even the Grand Master's grudging admiration.

Fowler Wright—or perhaps one should say Fowler Wright and Walter Scott—paint with rich colours on a huge and teeming canvass. Here is a historical novel to stir the blood and stimulate the imagination. And its theme has become strangely relevant again today.

THE SIEGE OF MALTA

by

S. Fowler Wright

Founded on an Unfinished Romance by
Sir Walter Scott

TOM STACEY

First published in Great Britain in 1942 by Frederick Muller Ltd

This edition published 1972 by
Tom Stacey Reprints Ltd
28-29 Maiden Lane, London WC2E 7JP
England

ISBN 0 85468 167 1

Printed in Great Britain by
C. Tinling & Co. Ltd, Prescot and London

FOREWORD

It was in the last year of his life, and in broken health, that Sir Walter Scott visited Malta, with the double purpose of avoiding the rigour of the northern winter and collecting material for a contemplated romance on the siege of Malta. During that time he was without the clerical assistance to which he had become accustomed, and both his Journal and the MS. of this projected book were written with a hand over which he had lost full control.

Lockhart, into whose possession the MS. came at his death, condemned it lightly as illegible nonsense, and that verdict naturally prevailed so long as its author's reputation for judgment and veracity remained unshaken.

But the fact that the entries in the Journal, made during the same period, have been deciphered, created a presumption that the MS. of the *Siege of Malta** would be equally legible; and the further fact that those entries are very far from nonsense and show Scott's intellect to have had, at the least, intermittent vigour (they include saner and more accurate estimates of his business position and prospects that his son-in-law was afterwards to present) suggested the possibility that it might not be wasted labour to discover what the *Siege of Malta* really was.

In the pursuit of this object, I traced the ownership of the MS. and its copyright to Mr. Gabriel Wells, who gave me an opportunity of inspecting it when in New York, and to whom it is a pleasure to express my gratitude, not merely for giving access to it, but for the courteous generosity of his permission to use it as the foundation of this romance.

The original MS. consists of about 75,000 words. It contains the opening scenes, and one or more later episodes, very much as they now appear. Beyond that, it is mainly an account of the Siege of Malta, which it follows to its conclusion. It is frequently inaccurate and repetitions are numerous.

When Scott started home from Naples on his last journey, in the hope of recovered health (Lockhart's suggestion that he hurried back with a premonition that death was near is not merely a doubtful guess, it is clearly disproved by Scott's own statements and by the leisurely nature of the first part of the journey) he sent this MS. to Abbotsford by sea, to await his arrival; and there is at least one reference by which he appeared to regard it as a finished work.

If he did so, it was a mistake; and had it been published in such a form it must have been a grotesque failure. But it is far more

* In his Journal, Scott uses the titles "Siege of Malta" or "Knights of Malta," indifferently, and I have followed this precedent.

probable, as evidenced by its substance and brevity, that he considered it rather as the historical skeleton on which he would construct a complete romance in the leisure of the succeeding summer.

The short months in Malta had been used for the accumulation of historical material, and in this sense the brief MS. which he had written with his half-palsied hand had finished what he required. The opening scenes were sketched out: the historic background was complete. The romance itself could be dictated (as had become his method for creative work during several previous years) in the summer peace of his Abbotsford library.

The probability of this theory is increased by the nature of the defects of the MS. in its present form. Had it a weak or confused plot, it might be more reasonable to accept Lockhart's suggestion that it was an abortion of failing powers. But the more curious fact is that *it has none*. After the opening chapters, Angelica (for instance) is not mentioned at all. She fades out; and Francisco soon follows her into a similar silence. The MS. becomes nothing more than a picturesque account of the siege of Malta, vigorous in parts, but with the defects and repetitions that such a draft, so written and unrevised, would be likely to have. Whatever might have happened had Scott lived for another year, it may be asserted with entire confidence that he would not have published it in its present condition.

Its form being thus, it became natural to examine it carefully for any indications of the plot which Scott had designed to use, and this resulted in the discovery of one slight but probably significant clue.

The account of the visit of the Maltese envoy to Don Manuel, with which the story opens, contains no suggestion that he is other than he professes, unless it be in the remark of a boatman whom he first approaches, that he has the look of a heathen Moor, and in some petulance on Don Manuel's part at the medium of communication that the Grand Master had chosen. Neither of these is at all conclusive, as a genuine Maltese might have given such an impression to an Andalusian boatman, and Don Manuel would have had a similar ground of complaint against the genuine messenger. But in a later part of the MS. there is an incidental allusion to the envoy "*said to have been* a herald at some college of arms," as a man under suspicion of being a traitor to the Maltese cause. It is an allusion without consequence, the herald not being mentioned again, but it is obviously suggestive, and it is on the pregnant implications of that phrase, and the foundations supplied by the master of historical romance, that I have ventured to build this tale.

S. Fowler Wright.

PART I—ST. ELMO

CHAPTER I

THE sun was setting over the broad waters of the Straits of Gibraltar, and its western rays adorned with brilliant colours and violet shades the serrated mass which has in its wild variety one of the most impressive effects of mountain scenery in the world, when a light galley, flying the scarlet sign of the Maltese Cross, and having cast anchor in Vilheyna's harbour, but at some distance from the other shipping which it contained, dropped a small skiff, which pulled rapidly toward the quay.

From the boat a single officer disembarked, and had directed it to return, even before he was approached by the warden of the quay with a courteous but yet somewhat peremptory challenge of whom he was, and what business had brought him there.

It was a tone which may have owed something of its quality to the stranger's appearance, his turban, and the looseness of the white garments he wore, giving him more the aspect of a Turk than a Christian man. But he answered with the assurance of one confident alike in himself and the business on which he came.

"I am from Malta, on a commission from the Grand Master to the Commander of Vilheyna and Aldea Bella, to whom I will thank you to guide me without delay."

"Don Manuel will be at meat in the next hour, which is not a time when he will consent to give audience, unless the matter be one of an urgent kind."

"My commission is here," the pursuivant answered, showing a chain of gold with the insignia of Malta around his neck, "and its urgency would excuse intrusion were he engaged in his private prayers."

The Spaniard, surprised at the boldness of this reply, regarded the speaker with more intentness than before.

"He must surely," he thought, "be either Christian or a most insolent and audacious dog to have landed thus; though I have seldom seen one whom I would have more quickly called by the name of a heathen Moor. But to the Castle he shall go by his own desire, and his reception should not be a dull sight."

Having so resolved, he delayed only to give charge to an assistant officer to take order till his return, and led the way from the harbour and through a fishing village that lay on its eastern side and then by an uphill road to the great castle of Aldea Bella, which stood on a steep height overlooking the bay.

They walked on in the growing dusk until they came within sight of the castle, crowning the head of a deep precipitous valley, the wide sweep of its walls being broken by a succession of turrets, both round and square, after the fashion of the military architecture of that period. The main gate of the castle, to which the road gave access, had the usual defences of barbican, drawbridge and portcullis, which were kept guarded and closed, even in this time of comparative peace, except to those who had a recognized right of entrance.

But as they came to the wide space before the castle which was left bare to prevent the covered approach of a hostile force, they were aware of a solitary figure upon another path, which was converging upon them.

"It appears," the pursuivant's guide remarked, "that you will not need to enter the castle to meet its lord."

A moment later, they stood before the Commander of Vilheyna himself, a tall, grey old man, muscular even in age, clothed in a black cloak which bore neither ornament nor any token of rank, except the scarlet sign of the eight-pointed cross which was embroidered thereon.

Don Manuel's glance passed quickly from the stranger to the servant he knew, with a sharp enquiry of what it meant that they should be there—which did not condescend to the familiarity of a spoken word—and the man answered with the brevity which he knew his master approved: "Lord, this officer comes from Malta."

The Commander turned his gaze upon the pursuivant. "With what tidings?" he asked.

"I am to inform you that the island of Malta is threatened by the instant invasion of the whole force of the Turkish Empire. The Grand Master orders that you shall——"

"You have said enough. I do not need to be told my duty by such as you. Follow me, and be prepared to answer such questions as I may ask at a later hour."

With these words the Commander turned and led the way to she castle, the gravity of the tidings he had received being scarcely sufficient to overcome his resentment at the method by which they had been communicated. "Such," he thought, "is the degradation of the times to which we have come that the Grand Master thinks it no offence to communicate his wishes through such a channel, to one who is little less than himself in the great Order to which we belong; and who is, besides, one of the greatest nobles of Spain. I can recall a time when a knight of the Order would have been the only possible messenger to employ."

It was not until they had passed the entrance and stood in the great hall of the castle that he again showed himself to be conscious of the pursuivant's presence.

"You have told all that you need," he then said, in a tone somewhat more cordial than before but still of a condescending quality, "when you have told me that the Moors are preparing attack. We know enough of the tender mercies of the infidel to understand what their success would mean to our brothers there. But we may be sustained again, as we have been in many earlier perils. I must suppose, beyond that, that you have come to intimate the Grand Master's pleasure that I shall go to his aid with such troops as my revenues can supply or that I can solicit among my friends."

The pursuivant appeared about to reply in a speech of sufficient solemnity when the Commander abruptly checked him: "But I will spare you the trouble of telling me my duty on this occasion, which it is possible that I know better, not only than yourself, but than most of the younger brethren. You must forgive me, sir herald; I am aware that our Order, following the example of many important potentates, has of late entrusted its relations with its own members or foreign states to diplomatists of your character. It is an innovation of which I do not approve, but I will assure you in few words that I shall support the Grand Master with instant speed and with all the resources at my command."

"My lord," the pursuivant replied, with a ceremonious and even humble courtesy, which yet seemed to be of deliberate assumption rather than a natural attitude, "no one conversant with the Maltese Order could entertain doubt that your Lordship would on this occasion, as on every other of the kind, show a brilliant example to the Knights among whom you have ever been an illustrious light. The summons is of routine, as I need not say, and sent indifferently to all."

"So it may be, yet it remains that it is not fitting for such as you to inform me of what my duties to the Order may be. But," he continued in a more courteous tone, "it is the hour of the evening meal, which I will ask you to share, and after which you can tell me more than it is now convenient to hear. . . . Ramegas, will you make this señor's comfort your care?"

He spoke to one little less than himself in age or gravity of demeanour, and who also wore the distinctive dress of the great half-monastic Order to which the Commander belonged. But though also a servant of St. John of Jerusalem, he was not one who ranked among the dignitaries of the Order. He was one of those who were known as Brothers-at-Arms, or Serving Brothers, being men of good birth and repute, but not of such rank or wealth as would avail them to claim the high honours of Malta's Knights. Such men would often attach themselves to one of courage and high conduct among the principals of the Order; and those who did this, like Juan Ramegas, and afterwards distinguished themselves by the standard of their own conduct, might gain reputation and authority far beyond the title that they were permitted to bear: but though Ramegas had thus acquitted himself, yet at his patron's retirement from the sea-warfare upon the Turks, which was now the main occupation of the Maltese knights, to the comparative seclusion of his own Commandery of Aldea Bella, the door of preference within the Order was closed against him. His time was now largely occupied in control of the estates which Don Manuel ruled in the Order's name, and his pride may have been secretly somewhat touched that he should be so completely under the domination of one man's pleasure. . . .

Don Manuel having withdrawn to his own apartment, the pursuivant found himself committed to Ramegas's charge, and under the necessity of introducing himself in a more personal way than the Commander had required or would probably have considered it seemly for him to do.

He gave his name as Rinaldo, and described himself as being an ensign of a noble Florentine family; but having said that, he was quick to turn the conversation adroitly to an account of improvements made upon the fortifications of Malta since Señor Ramegas had last been there, and to the reputed size of the Turkish fleet, which was reported to be taking the sea for the destruction of Malta's knights, until they were interrupted by the loud clang of the bell which announced the bringing-in of the evening meal.

CHAPTER II

Rinaldo found himself directed to a seat beside Ramegas at the upper end of a long board which divided the centre of the hall, and in a place of honour inferior only to the smaller cross-table at the head, which was reserved for Don Manuel himself and those of his own blood.

The Commander of Vilheyna had taken the vows of the Order of St. John Baptist at an early age, and had been prominent for over forty years in the incessant struggle which had been waged between Christian and Infidel, between Charles V and the great Turkish Emperor Soliman, for the control of the Mediterranean. He had been present at the unsuccessful defence of Rhodes, when the Order had been expelled, though not without the honours of war, which their valiant resistance won: he had taken a distinguished part in the expedition which captured Tunis in 1535, and liberated 20,000 Christian slaves. Six years after that he had been present at the disastrous attack upon Algiers, from which Charles had retreated with a mere remnant of his men, leaving his baggage and artillery for a Turkish spoil.

Now—twenty-four years later—Charles V was dead, and his son, Philip II, ruled in a Spain which still increased in dominion, prestige and wealth. But while it gained in Northern Europe and the Atlantic, the course of events had caused a gradual abandonment of the Mediterranean, which had become little better than a Turkish lake.

Soliman still lived. He still warred in Europe, where he had overrun Transylvania and reduced the power of Hungary.

Forty years before, he had captured Rhodes, driving out the Knights of St. John, who had previously held the island for over two centuries. After that, they had been granted—by Charles V—possession of Malta and the adjacent islands for the quitrent of a yearly falcon to the Sicilian crown. With the bitter experience of Rhodes to urge them, they had made the fortifications of Malta strong, and had remained there during the intervening years in an apparent security, making it an eyrie from which they had preyed upon the commerce of the Mohammedan powers.

But now Soliman the Magnificent, as men had begun to call him, designed to repeat in his age the triumph which had adorned his youth. He planned, with the aid of the tributary powers of Egypt and Algiers, to dispatch a fleet and army of ample strength to drive the Knights from the refuge which Charles had given, and to complete the dominion of the Mediterranean.

But through all these changing fortunes of forty years, the Viceroy of Algiers had learnt that he had, upon the opposite coast of Spain, in the person of the Commander of Vilheyna, a ruthless and sleepless foe. This Viceroy of Soliman, Dragut by name, had become of a great and feared repute in the western waters of the Mediterranean, where, since the battle of Djerbeh four years before, there had been no nation of Europe disposed to dispute his power, But the galleys of Don Manuel still sallied out, as occasion offered, to strike some swift and disconcerting blow, and return, before retribution could overtake them, to shelter beneath the security of his fortress guns.

It was in recognition of these relentless and long-continued activities that Don Manuel had recently received from the King of Spain a present of two large and powerful galleys, to replace others which, after facing many years of battle and storm, had become unfit to be put to sea. . . .

Seated at the Commander's right hand, Rinaldo observed his nephew, Francisco, to whom common repute gave a more direct relationship; but since a statute of the former Grand Master, De L'Isle Adam, had forbidden, under penalty of expulsion, that any knight of the Order should openly admit that he had broken his vows of chastity by recognition of children, the relationship of nephew had become so common as to be almost synonymous with a nearer word. It was, at least, clear to all who observed the youth so seated at the side of the older man, that they were of no distant blood.

Young though he was, Francisco had already received the honour of knighthood, and had seen active service on the decks of his uncle's galleys. It was assumed that he would, in due course, himself enter the Order, and take its monastic vows.

It was a destiny to which the sons of the Maltese knights were directed, if not compelled, by the policy on which it had based its power. The estates that the Commanders controlled, originally dowered by—ancestors or others—those who had dedicated themselves to the Order's service, had become of enormous value in all parts of the Christian world, and were now commonly held on the terms of remitting a certain yearly sum to the Treasury at Malta, beyond which they were not required to make account during peaceful days, on the understanding that threat of war, or other crisis, would place their whole resources at the Grand Master's call.

Holding estates on such terms as these, they could make no disposition of them by gift or will to a son, whether so recognized or not. The only method of succession was by submission to the Order's authority, and the acceptance of its monastic vows.

Seated on Don Manuel's other hand, Rinaldo observed the Señorita Angelica, a girl little younger than Francisco, and the Commander's actual niece, being his sister's child.

The least houseboy in the castle well knew that, as surely as Francisco would be regarded as dedicated to the service of the Order of Malta, so Angelica—from the day when, at the age of ten, on her mother's death, she had come under her uncle's authority—had been engaged to enter the Convent of Holy Cross, where she would be able to confer great benefits on her family by a life of prayer.

But, having arranged this from the first, Don Manuel had seemed in no haste to part with her to her pious calling; and the Abbess of Holy Cross was in no doubt that it would be to her own interest to defer to the Commander regarding the time of introducing his niece to the house over which she ruled.

Angelica's entrance to the holy state continued therefore to be spoken of as a settled thing, though no time was mentioned at which she would begin her novitiate. In the meantime, she had remained under the charge of Morayma, a Moorish captive, who had been her nurse at the first and her duenna in recent years.

Rinaldo had leisure enough to observe the members of Don Manuel's household, and, in particular, to let his eyes linger as much as courtesy would permit upon a type of beauty which may have differed from those which he had previously been privileged to observe, for the Commander made it plain both by his silence and by the directions to which he would lead the conversation when he occasionally interposed, that he had no intention of allowing Rinaldo's errand to be discussed in the common hearing of his retainers and of the menials at the lower end of the board.

It was only as the meal drew to its end that he said, in a voice of authority that brought instant silence upon the hall: "We have with us to-night one who brings word that the invasion of Malta, of which there have been many rumours of late, is no less than a certain thing, and the Sultan's fleet may be already upon the sea. At such a need, we can have neither choice nor wish but to go there with our utmost speed, and with all the rescue that we can raise. I will, therefore, that you shall forthwith address your minds to that end, while awaiting further orders from me. . . . Señor Ramegas, you shall remain to take counsel with me hereon."

His words were sufficient to clear the hall in a brief space, the murmur of excited voices only rising outside the doors. When none but Ramegas and Rinaldo remained, he addressed the latter in the tone of authority which he was accustomed to use.

"I may not ask you to tell where my duty lies, which I am not needing to know, but if you have knowledge of the Sultan's latest designs, or of any special cause from which this invasion springs, you have the season to tell me now."

"There has been something of special cause," Rinaldo replied, "though it may surely be said that the very principles on which the Order is founded are such that there can be no peace between it and the Sultan's power; and the species of piracy"—here he paused as he observed that the word was ill received, and substituted another expression—"or rather of sea-warfare as practised by us against the commerce of the Moslem states, could not fail to sustain the traditional enmity which divides the Christian world from the followers of Mahomet; but the immediate cause of the invasion that threatens now is said to be the pressure put upon the Sultan by some odalisques that his seraglio holds.

"It appears that a number of these ladies united the gold that his favour gave in a trading venture that would have brought them fortune had it arrived at its intended harbour.

"They equipped a vessel of the largest size with one of the richest cargoes that have ever been loaded into a single hold. To secure its safety, it was mounted with many guns, and half a thousand janizaries manned its upper decks to secure it from capture, if an enemy should succeed in grappling it on the sea. Its commander was one of the most famous officers in the Sultan's fleet.

"But the Knights of Malta, having obtained secret knowledge of when this vessel would put to sea, had made preparations of equal magnitude. In a word, ship and cargo were captured: the captain was mortally wounded: the crew and janizaries who survived the combat were chained to the benches of Maltese galleys, or sold in the slave-market of Venice.

"The odalisques were furious both at the loss and indignity of this issue of their adventure into the merchant's perilous ways, and they had voices which Soliman could not decline to hear. They were extremely offended on finding that it was not a simple matter to obtain redress from a Master whose power they were taught to believe was absolute in extent as well as in kind.

"There is no doubt that the capture of this vessel was felt by the Sultan to be of the nature of a personal affront, and that it roused him to extremities of effort against the Order of Malta, which he might otherwise have directed toward the more active prosecution of the Hungarian war."

"I have heard something of this before," Don Manuel replied, "though in a less detailed way. Can you tell me further to what extent the Sultan's anger is shown in the force he assembles for Malta's end?"

It was a question to which Rinaldo appeared to have no difficulty in finding a full reply. He said, as Don Manuel knew to be no more than a constant truth, that there could be little happening at Byzantium, even in the palace itself, which would not be betrayed for sufficient gold, such as the Grand Master would not neglect to provide for so great a need; but he went on to describe the counsels the Sultan had received, both from Mustapha, the Egyptian Pasha (now an old man, but of a high military repute, and having been in his youth the general in command when the Knights were driven from Rhodes), and other of his greatest lords, at a secret conference he had called, with such detailed particularity that Don Manuel was led to express some wonder that he could be so fully informed.

"I am somewhat puzzled," he said, "to understand how you can have acquired information so complete, and that even of a conference which, by your own showing, was entirely protected from hearing or observation."

For a moment, the pursuivant appeared to be disconcerted by this criticism, even beyond reasonable expectation; but, if that were so, he recovered himself very quickly, and his explanation was plausible and adroit.

"So I can suppose that it may appear, and had I not thought that personal reference would have approached impertinence, I should have mentioned before that not only have I had, owing to the nature of the office I hold, a full acquaintance with all the information that has reached the Grand Master during the last year, but I have a particular familiarity with the places and individuals of whom I am now speaking, as I was captured by the Turks at the battle of Djerbeh, and was in captivity in Egypt, and afterwards in Byzantium, for nearly three years before my friends were able to effect my ransom."

"May I conclude," Señor Ramegas interposed, with a deferential gesture toward the Commander, as though to speak unasked were in the nature of a liberty in that formidable presence, "that it is to the circumstance of your captivity that you owe the fact that you are somewhat darker in complexion than is common either in this country or your native Florence?"

"I have no doubt that you may," Rinaldo replied very readily, "though, as a fact, those who are native of Malta are sometimes even darker than the hue to which I have been burned by Egyptian suns."

"That is so," Don Manuel confirmed, as one who closes an interruption which had already exceeded its occasion, "for so I have seen it to be. . . . I would now have you proceed."

He addressed a few further questions to Rinaldo concerning the strength and leadership of the Turkish fleet and army, from which he learnt that Mustapha had somewhat reluctantly consented, at the Sultan's urging, to take the military control of the expedition, while the Admiral Piali would command the fleet, and Dragut, with his Barbary corsairs, would bring not only a strong support to the forces that would be engaged in the coming siege, but an experience in Mediterranean warfare, which, by the Sultan's orders, his colleagues were not lightly to overrule.

And then, having learnt all that he wished to know, Don Manuel rose with an abrupt word that he would talk again on the next day.

CHAPTER III

RINALDO found himself in a room which was comfortably, though somewhat austerely, furnished, and of a quality which showed that the rudeness (as he was disposed to view it) of the Commander of Vilheyna did not imply that he would not be regarded as a guest of consideration.

But while he observed this circumstance with satisfaction, he dismissed it promptly from a mind which was fully occupied with more urgent and important things.

"So," he said, half-aloud, but in a tongue which only one in that castle would have been likely to understand, and which we must presume that he had learnt during the years of slavery which had darkened his countenance, "I have played the pursuivant well enough, as I had little doubt that I should. . . . Slave in Egypt! Well, they may prove what it means to be that, if I can shake this fruit to my father's lap, as I have good hope that I shall be able to do. . . . The old Spaniard would learn how to bend his back, and to answer in a more abject way. . . . But the niece is an Allah's dream. It will be soft cushions for her! Worse than she have been sold before now for a Sultan's pet!"

With these singular reflections, Rinaldo stretched himself on the bed and passed into the dreamless slumber of those who have health and youth, and to whom adversity is a distant and unregarded foe.

He was awakened by a beam of light falling across his face from one of the narrow windows of the turret chamber in which he lay, at which he was quick to rise, seeing that the sun was already at some height in the morning sky. He went down, to be met by Señor Ramegas, who invited him to partake of an ample breakfast, at which Don Manuel did not appear, but which was attended by Francisco and brightened by Angelica's presence, with that of the Moorish governess or duenna, who appeared to be her almost inseparable companion.

It was obvious that the absence of the Commander caused a general relaxation of the atmosphere of restraint which Rinaldo had previously experienced. Ramegas was formal still, but it might be described as a more urbane formality and of an added dignity, which did not display itself with the same assurance in Don Manuel's presence. Francisco was, in physical attributes, a striking illustration of the deeply impressed and repeated characteristics of an ancient race. Although not yet come to his full stature or strength, he was a living likeness of what his uncle must have been in his own youth. There was evidence in him already of the same pride, even of the same dignity and gravity, which made his father distinguished among a race which had come at that time to be regarded as among the most arrogant of mankind; but that which in his uncle had become fixed with the hard coldness of ice, had in him the motion and impetuosity of a torrent; and he was aflame this morning with the hardly-restrained excitement of expectation. For he did not doubt that his uncle would permit him to accompany the expedition, and surely in such a position as the dignity of his name required.

Angelica was alive also with excitement of a different kind. Like her cousin, she saw that they were at the end of the quiet life in which the years had seemed so long to the impatience of youth, but had drifted too quickly past in her uncle's estimation, as he had deferred the day when he must part with her for the convent's claim.

Now, she wondered, would she be left in the castle, alone and forgotten amidst the bustle of more urgent and important matters, or would this crisis of events cause Don Manuel to decide that the time had come when the promise should be fulfilled which had been made nearly eight years before?

If so, could she contrive any argument that would persuade him to defer a purpose which she was hopeless to change, as she knew that she had cajoled him during the last three years, though he might suppose that the delay had been his own decision, the weakness of love for her?

She knew his character well enough to realize that he would tolerate no suggestion of breaking a pledge made to the Church—that the mere proposal of such dishonour would probably produce in him an inflexible resolution for its instant consummation, and she knew that, while he lived, she was at his disposal, alike by social custom and the iron bond of the law. She had also a strong affection for him, as she knew that he had for her, and she had not herself till now been in open rebellion against the idea of a convent life, which had not been entirely repugnant, so long as it remained a vague and undated destiny. Apart from a marriage to be negotiated in the Spanish fashion with some stranger of equal rank, what hope had she of a life of similar dignity or responsibility? For she knew

that, even in her novitiate years, the niece of Don Manuel would have an honoured place in the Convent of Holy Cross.

In the end she would be Abbess, when the Abbess died. She would come to an absolute control over the lives of all within the convent walls: a wide authority over the convent lands: an absolute disposal of the convent wealth. There was no other position of equal importance and independence for any woman beneath a queen in the Spain of that day. Yes, it was well enough—as a dream. To take the step to-morrow, in an irrevocable way—well, what was the haste? Let it wait for another year. And beyond that—must we look as far ahead, when the years of our life are few?

"Sir herald," Señor Ramegas remarked from his place at the head of the board, which he had held since the childhood of those who must soon have come to challenge his place had the life of the castle continued its normal course, "if I may say so without offence, which is not meant, you look more closely your part in a peaceful garb than when you appeared last night with a sword girded, and that somewhat of Turkish pattern to Spanish eyes. I have always seen that those of your office had gone unarmed, as is surely meet in such as claim to be secure from capture or ransom, and to stand aside from the strife of swords."

Rinaldo looked at the speaker the while this speech pursued its leisurely course, not in a hostile, but in a somewhat watchful way, as though weighing what it might mean; but his answer was easy and frank, and there was reason in what he said.

"What you say is true, as I do not doubt, for those who move only among men of a Christian kind, where, as I suppose, your observations have lain, but on that galley by which I came—had we fallen in with the Corsair's fleet, and had they boarded our deck, would it have availed me then that I did not fight? Had the galley fallen their prey, would they have sent me home, and by what way? No, it must have been my part to take sword with the rest and drive them back if we could."

"Yes," Ramegas replied, "I can see cause that you should feel thus; though I have heard that the heralds pass without risk between the Christian and heathen hosts in the Eastern wars. But we may both have found that the rule of the sea is of a more turbulent kind. Did you see aught of the Corsair's fleet?"

When he asked that, his thought was of the galleys of the Dey of Algiers, who was the scourge of all who did business in the western waters of the Mediterranean at that time, and so Rinaldo understood it to be.

"No," he said, "though we might have had little fear if we had, unless we had been entirely becalmed, and even then we might have escaped. For our galliot is not only very lightly built and well rigged, but it has twelve oars aside, and there are not, as I am told, more than three or four of the fastest of Dragut's fleet which could over-reach its speed on a quiet sea.

"But we saw nothing of them, the Grand Master having secret knowledge of where they would be, which is a matter I have yet to speak in the Commander's ear. For I was charged, if he should have vessels that he could bring or send at a short date, that I should guide them by such a route that they would reach Malta without being waylaid, which you would not wish them to be."

"As to that," Ramegas answered, "if Dragut be one who is to be engaged in this siege, we may as well fight him soon as on a later day, and I suppose that the two galleys that Don Manuel has would not be easy to take, they having been the King's gift but a short time ago, and perhaps as large and well-found as any ships in this sea; though they may not be equal to those that are built to sail across to the Spanish Main, which are the largest the world has seen. But those, as you know, are built without oars, it being of doubtful gain for a voyage of such length to take so many men as the benches need, or to be low-waisted amid the storms of the wider sea."

"Do you say your vessels could fight the whole strength of the Corsair's fleet?"

"No, I would not say that. And, for that risk, I daresay that Don Manuel will not despise the guidance that you can give."

"Yet, I dare suppose," Rinaldo went on, "that being so newly built, and as well-found as you say, they are too swift to be greatly in fear of any fight that they might think it wiser to shun?"

"I would not boast to that height," Ramegas replied, "though they are as swift as most, or as their kind can be expected to be. They carry sail of a wide spread, and have twenty oars on each side, but they are heavy with guns, and bear crews which are not much short of a thousand men. They have thick walls, and good space for the holding of stores, being, indeed, built rather to fight than fly."

"And how soon should you say that they will be ready to put to sea?"

"It may be no more than two days, as you heard Don Manuel say that he designed that it should, for their seamen are aboard now, and we can send fighting men enough from the castle here and from the country round at a day's call."

"And for stores?"

"They are kept ever ready to sail at a quick need."

"I like not," Francisco interposed, "that we should turn from a straight course to avoid a fleet of a strength that we do not know, with two such ships as we have—and with the good aid of yours." (He addressed the last words to Rinaldo in a tone of rather perfunctory courtesy.) "I should have said that there would be few so bold on these seas that they might not trim sails to another course; and, if we be in this war, it is our part to grieve Dragut at all times, and the most we may."

Rinaldo looked at him with some curiosity as he said this, debating perhaps in his mind whether the speaker were of the courage his words conveyed, or no more than a boastful youth, who had much to learn of the stern lessons of war. He seemed about to speak, but Morayma was quicker than he.

"The Dey," she said, "has a score of ships that are swifter than those two by a mile in five, and could bay them down as the dogs deal with a wolf which may be somewhat larger than they. . . . I pray the Virgin," she added, for she had long since taken the Christian faith, "that you be kept widely apart." She looked with such real affection at Francisco as she said this, that it must have been easy to forgive her boast of the power of her native land.

"You will be less rash than your words intend? You will think that we would see you again?" Angelica asked, with eyes upon her cousin which were so troubled that Morayma thought it somewhat more than should be shown at that time. What (she feared) would Don Manuel think, if he should see such a glance, his niece being pledged for the convent walls?

But whether or not she read the look in a true way, she could not think that it brought response from one whose thoughts were clearly on other things. "You would not have me come back," he said, "with no better boast than a skill in avoiding foes?"

There was something of arrogance in both tone and manner as this was said which caused Rinaldo to look at the speaker again in a doubtful way. It was as though he assumed his return to be beyond doubt, and resented suggestion that it might not be made with all his foemen beneath his feet. From the lips of one so young, who could have had little experience or practise of war—— But, as Rinaldo looked, he was disposed to rebuke his own doubt for a second time. The youth might have his uncle's arrogant style, but Rinaldo thought that he was one whose boast might be made good at the last. There was a quality in him that shone like a bare sword.

Rinaldo thought of a time when he had been a slave who toiled under the constant threat of the driver's lash—when he had been subject to a hundred indignities that it was hard to forget. How would the young Spaniard behave if he were reduced to buying life by endurance of such conditions as those?

But while these thoughts crossed his mind, Angelica answered in a way that showed that she was neither critical of her cousin's manner, nor conscious of rebuke to herself:

"I would have you return, as I think you will, with all the honour that you have the merit to win. For I could not think that you would come back in another way. Yet I would have you use the caution which is said to come with the years, for how can later honour be won, if life be lost on the first day?"

"Your cousin says well in that," Ramegas remarked; "for rashness is ever the snare of youth, and discretion comes at a later year."

Francisco showed no resentment at this admonition, nor did he appear impressed by any wisdom it might contain. He answered with more wit than Rinaldo would have felt sure that he had:

"So the old have said at all times, and who can show they are wrong? Yet how they came alive themselves through the foolish years to be where they are is a thing they do not explain. Their rashness should have destroyed them a hundred times."

"I would take the risk," Angelica surprised their guest by remarking, "with a gay heart, were it twice what it is likely to be, if I were sailing forth on the same track."

"Señorita," Rinaldo said, looking at her in such a way as brought her to blush as she surely had not for any glance or word that had passed between Francisco and her, "I should have said that few would wish to throw down the potent arms which you now bear for a sword which you could not wield."

"You must not think," Morayma interposed in a quick way, "that the Señorita means more than a jesting word, she knowing well the parts in the game of life which are fitting for such as she. Yet I would not have you think that she could not play a more hardy part than her looks can show, having lived a free life in these hills, where she may go in safety and honour by any path that she will, they being all in her uncle's rule, and she has even had some practise in the lighter weapons of war."

"Then," Rinaldo said, with an admiration in his eyes which was of more boldness than was perhaps becoming from a pursuivant to

Don Manuel's niece, "is she doubly armed, which may be held to be less than fair."

Angelica, quickly recovering a self-control which she seldom had occasion to lose, took the explanation upon herself:

"It is true, Señor Rinaldo, that I have some little practice with rapier and poniard, and can send a shaft near the mark at times, but that is not because I am of an Amazon kind. It is because my cousin and I have been reared alone, and must have the same sports or none."

"Yet," Morayma added, as though she thought her own tuition disparaged by the inferences of this explanation, "you must not suppose that they have been taught in the same way. Angelica has no lack of all arts that belong to ladies alone, even to leechcraft and the skill in the healing of wounds which I have been able to give."

"I talked not," Angelica said, "of work but of sport. Yet I would not have you think" (and here her words were for Rinaldo alone) "that I am one who would wish to play a man's part in the dirt and horror of war; but it is possible that a caged bird may look through the bars at times and wish for the open sky."

"Knowing less of hawks," Rinaldo replied, "than it might learn in the next hour."

"Yet some would think that an hour of freedom, and the right to soar to the sun, might be worth more than a longer life in the narrow bars."

"Señorita," Rinaldo replied, "you have said a good word. Yet for such as you there should be the freedom without the fear."

"Which," Ramegas concluded, with gravity, "would be to enter heaven before we die."

Rinaldo became silent. He was not unconscious of the attraction of the girl with whom he had been making exchanges which might have been no more than idle compliment, but were, in fact, of a sincerity which surprised himself, and roused the thought that to cultivate a too friendly feeling for these Spaniards of a day's acquaintance would ill consort with some plans which were private to his own mind.

"You talk," Francisco said, "as though freedom had all the risks, and there were safety and peace in a captive's gyves. If you asked of our galley-slaves, I should say you would get a different answer from that."

Rinaldo did not respond. He seemed to have retired to his own thoughts. But Ramegas replied:

"You confound restraints of two kinds; for they may be born either of hatred or love, or of such confusion of these as may come to no certain flower. For the slave toils in dread of the driver's stripes, and is gyved in a different style from that of the sure peace of the convent walls."

The words seemed to rouse Rinaldo's attention again. He looked across at Angelica as though seeing her in a new and surprising light. As he did so, their eyes met, and hers fell.

"I had not supposed," he began, and then checked his speech. He concluded: "But it is esteemed a high calling in all the lands of the Christian pale." It was clear to all that that was not what he had been commencing to say.

After a pause, during which he appeared to be withdrawn again to his own thoughts, he said: "If, as I suppose, Don Manuel will not require my presence here, I will return to my own ship, awaiting the time when you will be ready to sail."

"I know not," Ramegas replied, "whether the Commander will wish to hear further from you upon the matter you have reported to him, but I am well assured that he will intend that the hospitality of this castle shall be yours while you wait us here."

But Rinaldo excused himself with the plea that, when all was preparation and haste, it must follow that they would be better pleased to have no strangers within the walls, and when Ramegas replied somewhat coldly to that, saying that the castle could not be incommoded by the care of a single guest, be there what bustle there might, he urged pretexts of his own occupations. Yet, being urged by Ramegas, and it being put to him that Don Manuel might consider that he would show a defect of courtesy if his hospitality should be thus contemned, he agreed that he would go aboard at that time, but would return at dusk, at the banquet hour, and remain ashore during the night.

Upon this bargain, somewhat reluctantly made by Rinaldo, who yet could advance no sufficient reason which would explain a more obdurate attitude, the little party broke up and went their several ways.

CHAPTER IV

It was at the height of noon that Don Manuel paced the high battlements of the castle of Aldea Bella, from which he could look down upon the fishing village and the harbour where his galleys lay. The quiet peace of yesterday had been transformed into a scene of activity upon which its master could look with the satisfaction of observing the alacrity with which his orders were being carried out. His plans were complete, his directions given, and he was now able to take a space of leisure for his own reflections.

The two galleys lay at the quay. They were taking in such stores as could be hastily collected and were likely to be of most use to the Maltese garrison in the coming siege. Among these it might be observed that the decks were being loaded with planks and logs and huge baulks of timber, for the Maltese islands were naturally destitute of trees, and every beam used in its fortifications had been imported from other lands; every spar that might need to be renewed on its vessels must be obtained in the same way.

The bustle which Don Manuel's orders had aroused was not confined to the castle and its immediate vicinity. As he paced the battlements he could hear the tocsin ringing in a score of hamlets among the Andalusian hills. As though an actual invasion of the Moors—who had been driven from the land a mere half century before—were impending, he had called the people of the country-side at the need of the Maltese order, to which he belonged, and whose feudatories they were.

As he walked the length of the battlements he came upon Angelica, seated at a projecting corner which overlooked the harbour. She did not appear to observe him at first, her eyes being fixed upon the loading galleys and the smaller, more rakish form of Rinaldo's vessel, which was anchored in the outer bay. She watched them with an expression of misery which he did not miss. With the real though formal kindness with which he had always treated her, he enquired the cause of her grief.

She answered with apparent frankness: "Is it not for Francisco that I should fear? He is unpractised in war, though he knows the ways of the sea, and, as I have heard, he is to go without waiting for you."

The doubt which Morayma had felt when she had seen Angelica's concern at her cousin's coming departure did not enter Don Manuel's mind. It seemed to him that she expressed a woman's natural feeling, though it is not one to which much heed can be given when trumpets call. He sat down on the stone seat beside her as he replied: "He must go, as his fathers went, on the path of danger, without which there is no honour which can be won. He is the one heir of the name I have, yet it is so I would have it be. But the prayers of those who are innocent reach, as I well believe, to the throne of Heaven; and it is such as thou whom the Virgin herself may be prompt to hear.

"I am going myself to the court of Spain, where I will beseech our king for such aid as will be of greater use than could be rendered by my own arm, even were I much younger than I now am; and, after that, I hope to join my brethren, if I can still pass the besiegers' lines.

"I shall go at sunrise to-morrow, and the galleys should be ready to sail, as I suppose, by the next day. I am giving the command of one to Ramegas, and Francisco will have the other. I was but a few months older than he when I was engaged in a fight by which I sunk one of the corsairs' fleet. I remember the grief I had that it should have gone down before we could release the slaves who were chained to the rowers' benches, they being for the most part of Christian blood.

"For yourself, I sent word to the Abbess an hour ago, that she may expect your arrival in two days' time, which will give Morayma space to prepare your needs. You will go in her charge, but she will return when you are settled there. . . . I have delayed your going too long, it having been an old man's weakness to have you here. But now that our lives will be broken apart, and we know not to what end, evil or good, it would be wrong to withhold you more."

The length of this speech had given Angelica time to control the first impulse of protest against a doom which she had dreaded ever since she had heard of the intended expedition the night before. Before Don Manuel had finished, she had realized that to protest would be useless, and might even be worse than that. If there were any way of avoiding a fate from which she rebelled more resolutely as its shadow was closing upon her, it must be found by herself. And what way could there be? There was no one, of whatever rank or degree, to whom she could look for aid. No one would think of listening to any protest with more than inclination to comfort or to persuade. It would appear to all to be a settled, inescapable thing. She thought of the conversation of the morning, and she saw herself as a bird behind bars that she had not the will or the strength to break. Was there really no way? Or, if there were, would it be her courage which would be too small for her need? If the cage-door stood unlatched, would she break loose that she might soar an hour in the sun, before the falcon would strike her down?

As she pondered thus, she became aware that Don Manuel had gone. She had been scarcely conscious of his farewell words, or of the hand that had stroked her hair.

On his part, he had regarded as little that she had heard his decision without response or reply. He was accustomed to issue orders which would be taken in the same silent manner. It did not occur to him as a possible thing that she would resist his will.

After that, she met Francisco, who had just heard of the command that was to be his. He was affectionate in a pre-occupied way, but it was plain that he was excited by the prospect of adventure and the dignity of his new command, to the exclusion of other emotions or any active sympathy with herself. He looked before, not behind. The playmate of his childhood days, the companion of the years that had ended but yesterday, felt that she was shut out of his life. As she saw that the warship's deck would be natural for him to tread, so he would regard the cloister's wall as being natural for her. They must go out to the world by their different roads, for the days of childhood had passed since the Maltese galley had come to anchor within the bay.

She did not suppose that he had lost affection for her, which would re-assert itself under more normal conditions, and of which he would become more aware as the moment of parting came. But, for the time, nearer and more immediate excitements had left her little place in his thoughts. It would be waste of words to tell him that she did not wish to ride with Morayma in two days' time, to enter the gates of the Convent of Holy Cross.

She might tell Morayma, of course. She would be sure of sympathy, and of some measure of understanding. But there would be no power to help. Sympathy alone was something for which she had no use. She was of a character which can better endure disappointment or grief if it be kept silent in the sufferer's heart.

Resolved that she would not go, she would see the last hours of freedom pass, and would go at last, as how many thousand had gone before on the same road? For what else was there to do?

The hours passed in such thoughts until that of the evening meal returned, at which she took her accustomed place, looking pale and sad. It was a contrast to the bright vivacity of her usual expression which would have attracted attention under different conditions, but now it may be doubted whether it were noticed at all amid the excitement and talk of preparation and plan which was around her, like the buzz of a lively hive, till Don Manuel entered the hall, and which scarcely lessened even under the restraint that his presence caused; and if it were noticed by any, was it not natural that she should be grieved at the thought of parting from those who were her nearest and had been her most intimate relatives? So she was left to her own thoughts, in the midst of talk to which she gave little heed—and to a growing consciousness that she had somewhat more than her share of Rinaldo's eyes.

And with the consciousness, curiosity stirred. She had, in fact, felt a certain intimacy of understanding, of a strange, exciting novelty to her sheltered life, since the exchanges of the breakfast-table, in which, with that feminine instinct which rarely sleeps or errs, she had known that she had attracted his admiration, and could go further if she should have the will for so bold a game.

And with that consciousness of the interest she had aroused, there came a lively consideration of what Rinaldo was, and a curiosity to know much more than she did.

He had the name of a noble Florentine family—that was well. He was a herald, and so could scarcely claim equality with the niece of Vilheyna's lord. He was a trusted envoy of the Maltese Order, and in command (she had understood) of the galley in which he came. So much was clear; but she felt with the same instinctive certainty that there was much more to know. She had perceived on the previous night, as Don Manuel had failed to do, that the pursuivant's humility of word and manner were little more than a perfunctory deference. He was at ease in himself, or, if there were any awkwardness at all, it was not that of one who is embarrassed by contact with higher rank, but rather that of one who assumes obsequiousness which it is not his habit to use. She felt that there was a mystery here which she would have been glad to solve, and the puzzle kept him before her mind.

Having this imagination, she watched Rinaldo's conversation as he was questioned again by Don Manuel during the meal, for her uncle had many things on which he desired to be more fully informed to enable him to put the needs of Malta before the King; and it seemed to her that, though Rinaldo answered adroitly and well, and with the same manner of deference that he had shown on the previous day, yet he was watching his words, as though he might say the wrong thing if he were not constantly wary of speech. If Don Manuel observed this, he may have thought it to have sprung from no more than the timidity of one who was so much his inferior both in rank and age, but Angelica was sure that it had a different cause. "He is a prince in disguise, and is in fear lest he say something by which his rank will become known." She thought of nobles who had been exiled from Elizabeth's court, or from that of the King of France. But he was not of such race. Of that she was sure. He might be Italian, as he declared. But she was doubtful of that. Perhaps Hungarian? She knew less of the nobles of Eastern lands. They might (she supposed) be as dark as he. Could he be one who had lost his crown as Soliman's army had spread over Hungary and Transylvania during the last forty years, like an advancing plague? Perhaps his father had been a king who had died by the Sultan's sword. Now he sought revenge, fighting the Turkish power where he could do it the greatest harm, but keeping his name concealed till he should raise it to such a height as it held before. Yet why then assume a pursuivant's part? It was that which she could not guess. But she remembered that Ramegas had said that he was armed like a Turk when he landed first. Who, she wondered in vain, could he really be?

Doubtless, she told herself at the last, he was no more nor less than he said. She made childish mystery in a heart which would know nothing of life, beyond what it could build in a world of dreams. So she would cheat herself, and the hours go by; and the shadow of convent walls was advancing to close her in. And as she thought thus, she became aware that her uncle had risen, and was addressing the hall in sombre words, which were yet lit with a high resolve.

"You have heard, my friends," he said, "of this new affront which the infidels have advanced against the Order of Malta and the Cross of God. They seek our destruction with the same undying ferocity with which they assaulted Rhodes twenty-three years ago, and now, as then, we must defend ourselves in the power of the same Blessed Sign in which our fathers were believers and found their strength.

"Touching earthly valour, we may be loth to compare ourselves to those warriors of immortal fame, but we have been sworn by the same oath to defend the Cross with the best blood that our bodies hold. We may therefore look up to God with the same confident hope that His blessing will point our swords. And in such hope, and no vain confidence of earthly might, we take our arms in the great name of Him, whom these, His enemies, have denied and would now defy.

"And touching the summons of the Grand Master to me, his unworthy brother, you already know the orders that I have given, by which the two galleys that are mine through the gift of my Royal Master the King will sail at the first possible hour, with all the stores and men that they are fitted to bear.

"But I would not that you should think that when I have done that I have finished all that is within my will or my power. At this summons I have now had, all the wealth I own, all the revenues I control, I surrender to the use of the great Order of the Maltese Knights, for it is to no less than that that we are sworn at so great a need."

He paused a moment, and there was a deep murmur of assent and approbation from those who heard, and who were in too much reverence of him who spoke to applaud in a freer way. He went on in a lower voice, that rose again to a final intensity, as it struck a more personal note:

"We will now break up this sad festival, knowing too well that we shall not assemble here again with unbroken ranks, for there is much to be done, and it would be wrong to linger with wine-cups now.

"I go with the morning light to throw myself at the feet of my gracious Sovereign, to solicit his further aid; but I trust it will not be long before I am among you all on the field of war. And for that arch-corsair Dragut, who calls himself Viceroy of Algiers, whom we know as the enemy of our own coasts, and who has sent a message of defiance to myself, I will say this, that there is no knight of our Order by whom he has been either loved or feared. The sword I wear is still that with which I broke his helm at Golitta's siege, and if we meet again he may find that age has been no more kind to himself than it has to me.

"And here, my friends, is a health to the Christian knight, be he whom he may, who shall meet him first."

He filled his own cup as he spoke, and as the toast was drunk the feelings of the assembly broke out at last in a shout that was unrestrained.

Don Manuel raised his hand in a gesture which was at once recognition and dismissal, and left the hall without further words.

Angelica had not been unmoved, even among her own private

troubles, by the tone, stern, melancholy, and at times pathetic, in which her uncle had spoken, with a depth of feeling she had never known him to show before. But through it all the puzzle of Rinaldo continued to vex her mind. In what thoughts had he been so absorbed as Don Manuel spoke that he had failed to make the sacred sign which had been done almost mechanically by all besides at the mention of the name of God? Why had he appeared to hesitate for a moment as the toast was called, so that he had been later than others to fill and raise the cup? Had he not moved his lips in silence before he drank, as though he added invocation or prayer to that which the others heard? Was it, perhaps, his own vow that he would meet the infidel chief, and did he hesitate to drink to himself, as it might seem to him that he had been invited to do?

With such thoughts contending in a confused way with the despair that darkened her mind, Angelica went to her rest. It has been said that, if a woman's curiosity be directed upon a man, she is half-way to the mood in which she will seek his love. Angelica would have been surprised if it had been proposed to her that she could think of Rinaldo in such a way. She would have felt that any tendencies she might have were for one of a nearer blood, who had shown within the last hours that he had no such feeling for her.

Yet it was Rinaldo's dark, handsome, enigmatic face, his slender athletic form, that were on the darkness before her eyes. They were his words that were in her mind: "The potent arms which you now bear—You have said a good word—For such as you there should be the freedom without the fear." She had always been treated with the respect due to her rank. She had taken as her natural right the regard which youth and beauty receive. But here was something different from the deference which domestics pay. Something new in kind, of which she could do with more—which she was never likely to have.

Why must she be held in two days from now within the narrow compass of convent walls, while her cousin would have all the freedom of sea and air and a galley's deck? She had no love for the game of war. She was not of a masculine mind. But she longed for life—to do, and not merely to be. Her mind shrank from the thought of the Convent of Holy Cross. It was like being laid in a coffin while you yet lived.

If she could have gone to Malta, she felt that she could be useful there—perhaps as much as one who could handle a sword. She had learnt much from Morayma in nursing and the curing of wounds, which had ever been a woman's province among the Moors, and in which Morayma had more than a common skill. But to ask her uncle would, she knew, be a useless attempt. There could be no greater shame to his mind than a broken pledge; and the fact that he had given the pledge, which it was her part to pay, would not weigh with him at all. It was the custom throughout the land. Has a guardian no rights? Shall the old not judge for the young? So he would say, if he should condescend to argue at all. But to move him would, she knew, be most utterly vain. To make such request would do no more than to disturb and anger his mind at a time when he had cares and troubles enough without another from her. She had too much sense, and perhaps too much regard for him, to make such useless attempt.

But suppose—a sudden hope leapt to her heart, and her pulses beat—suppose when he had gone—suppose Francisco could be cajoled to let her go on the *Santa Martha* with him? Three times of four she had had her way in their differences of the past. She would persist or persuade. But not in such a matter as this. It was a wild hope! Such a hope as may seem good in the night, but will shrink to a smaller size in the cold light of day. Yet, for the moment, a hope it was, and it gave sleep, and changed her dreams to a gayer colour than they would otherwise have been likely to have.

CHAPTER V

ANGELICA waked with the ease of youth when the dawn was no more than a line of light along the eastern horizon of the Mediterranean. She looked down from her turret-window upon a harbour which was already astir. Boats moved over the water in the growing light. There was bustle and loading of stores where the two great galleys lay warped along the side of the quay. It seemed that men had not slept at all under the urgency of the preparations that Don Manuel's instructions required. She distinguished Señor Ramegas giving orders upon the quay.

Further out, she saw Rinaldo's galley, the *Flying Hawk*, with the Maltese cross fluttering at its peak: the eight-pointed cross, red on its ground of white, which had been the terror of the infidel through five hundred years of a war that had never ceased. The *Flying Hawk* had its own reputation too. It was not of a weight to face the largest Turkish galleys, but it had a speed which rendered it careless of them. In the five years since it had been built in a Venetian dockyard it had a record of raids and captures, of battles with galliots of its own kind, which it would not have been easy to match.

Angelica looked and was bitter of heart that a mere difference of sex should hold her back from part or place in the great adventure which these preparations forecast. Bitterer still, perhaps, in her secret mind, in the deep instincts of womanhood, that she was destined to a life which would be frustrated in its more natural purpose, in the fulfilment of the very difference which held her separate from the busy crowd that she watched below.

It would be no use till her uncle had gone, but then, though she could deceive herself into no more than a little hope, she would try what could be done when she had only Ramegas and Francisco to cross her will.

She went down to breakfast at a later hour, and felt a new depression when she saw that Rinaldo's seat was empty and was told that he had already gone.

"He has consented," Ramegas said, "to aid us by taking some stores on board which must else have gone on our own decks, which will be burdened enough without them. But, for some reason, which must be a better one than he gave, he will not have the *Flying Hawk* warped to the quay. It must all go out in barges, and be hauled aboard where he now lies. When he had consented to this, he went in haste, as though he feared it might be put in hand before he would be there to control. It might be thought that the *Flying Hawk* were his own babe, instead of a boat that has had five years' buffets of storm and shot, and of which he has no more than charge for this voyage. It would not be hurt by a bump, if a hawser broke."

Angelica was not interested in the bruises that Rinaldo's galley was not to get. She asked: "Will he be here again for this night?"

"No. He said he would stay aboard. We must sail to-morrow at dawn, or, to be more exact, at an hour before."

Angelica made no answer to that. What was she to him, that he should dally to say good-bye or come back for so small a cause? What, also, was he to her? It seemed that nothing was all he could ever be. Yet she would have been glad to have had him to talk to now; and for him, perhaps, to say such things to her again as it would be easy to bear in mind. But she saw that that dream was done.

And while she put this folly back from her mind, Don Manuel came to the meal, which it was seldom that he would share, it being his habit to eat alone at this hour. But now he would have all the time that he could to talk to Ramegas and Francisco, as he was taking horse in an hour from then, and Angelica found that she could be silent, and none would notice at all. She felt that she had already gone out of their lives.

She had thought that a short respite from what she feared might be won in another way, when it occurred to her that she might go with Don Manuel to Seville, and to this she almost gained his consent.

"Uncle," she said, "it is four years since I have seen Seville, and I would gladly do so again. And the King I have never seen. Would it not be well that you should present me to him? They say he never forgets any whom he has once met either for evil or good. Who can say that I might not be grieved on a far day that I had missed such a chance as this?"

Don Manuel thought, and was not averse. He saw that there was a shrewd reason in what she said. An abbess might have times when she would have petition to make to a king's throne. It may be well to be able to say you are known of him.

Angelica, watching his face, thought that her point was won.

"I see no reason against that, if it will give you joy," he said, in the way of distant kindness he had, "and it would mean but a short delay in that which you have to do. You shall surely come, if you will; though I shall be in haste for one end, and—nay, but it is useless to think, for I am not like to return here. I am more likely to sail from Cadiz, when I have put the case to the King."

"Yet," Angelica urged, "I could return alone. I could take Morayma, if you desire. It is but twenty Spanish leagues to Seville."

"It is not to be thought. I ride with but two knaves, whom I must have with me where I may go. Morayma will have much to do here. Could she leave in an hour's time? I am grieved, but it cannot be."

"Yet it is a safe road——", Angelica began, but she let the word drop, for she saw that his attention was gone. He was talking to Francisco as though he did not know she was there. It would be useless to ask again. . . . And, after all, it would have spoiled her chance of a larger hope.

So Don Manuel bade her a kind farewell, which would yet have been kinder had he had fewer calls upon his emotions in other ways, and rode off on a steed which was still powerful and proud, though, like himself, it had seen days when it had been more supple of limb, and had thought him a lighter weight; and on the next day he came to the King's court at Seville.

Seville was a great city at this time, very splendid and gay. It was the frequent home of the Spanish kings, and though Spain was losing strength every year, she still seemed to be of an impregnable power.

It was more than fifty years since she had driven the Moors out of the southern end of the land. She sought to make it one of her own blood, and was now doing herself more harm than good by the severity of her Inquisition against the Jews. It was less than fifty years ahead that she would complete her ruin by driving out all her subjects of Moorish blood, being 600,000 of the best that she had.

But, at this time, the Spanish monarchy was of a great and very arrogant power, and Seville, which was the favourite residence of its kings, was magnificent in its palaces and splendid with silk and gold.

There was the glorious cathedral, which had been building for more than a century, and completed forty years ago. There was La Lonja, the great Exchange, which had been built by the present King. There was La-Torre-del-Oro, a building of still greater significance, which had been erected to receive the cargoes of gold which every year the galleons brought in to Cadiz from the mines of the Spanish Main.

There also was the Palace of Pilate, where the dukes of Alcala lived, and which was said to be an exact replica of that which had been built in Jerusalem by the Roman governor; and, strangest and loveliest of all, there was still the Moorish royal palace, the Alcazar, now become the southern residence of the kings of Spain.

Philip II received Don Manuel with the royal courtesy and munificence which it was his habit to offer to all visitors of importance. There may never have been a more accessible monarch nor one whose courtesies were of smaller worth. He had just returned from Madrid, where he had parted from Count Egmont, the prince of Gavre, after entertaining him with the lavishness which befitted his rank, and showering more substantial favours upon him. Yet he may even then have been contriving within his heart the murder which was soon to follow. He knew, already, more of the contemplated assault upon Malta than Don Manuel would have been able to tell him, and had used it with Egmont as the reason why he was unable to pay a visit to the Netherlands which (he said) he had been eager to undertake.

Now he praised the energy and devotion which the lord of Vilheyna had shown at this crisis of the fortunes of the great Order to which he belonged. He gave promises of support of the most lavish kinds, which he might mean or not, for in either event it would be his policy to give them in an equal profusion. He urged Don Manuel to convey these assurances to the Grand Master, which he was naturally eager to do.

As the news at the Spanish court indicated that the besiegers might already be surrounding the Maltese island, with such a fleet that the entry of a single vessel to its harbour would be a precarious enterprise before Don Manuel could be expected to arrive before it, he decided to proceed to Sicily in a frigate of that country which was sailing from Cadiz, and to complete his journey by such means as should seem most prudent, in the light of what he would be able to learn on arrival there.

CHAPTER VI

After Don Manuel's departure, Angelica saw that the decisive hour of her life had come. By the break of dawn, the two galleys would have sailed away, and, if she were left behind, she would be doomed to the convent life to which she was more averse as its shadow fell more imminently upon her. While it had seemed a distant and yet inescapable certainty, she had endured it mainly by refusing it the tribute of thought, as one in health may reject the terror of death, though reason cannot doubt that it must be faced at last. But at the near threat of some fatal malady—at the possibility that it may be avoided—or overcome—how different will the feelings be!

So with Angelica had the vague avoided terror become real and near; and, at this extremity, the resignation with which the inevitable might have been faced had broken down as the possibility of escape, however faint, had invaded her mind.

Now she saw two possible sources of flight: to persuade Señor Ramegas to take her on the *Santa Anna* to Malta, or Francisco upon the *Santa Martha*, of which he was to have command, though under the authority of the older and more experienced captain.

But when she considered the possibility of persuading Ramegas to the granting of such permission, her reason told her that it was no more than a baseless hope. Even if she could obtain his sympathy for such a project (which was unlikely enough) his sense of fealty to her uncle would forbid the possibility that he should assist her to defy his authority in such a manner. And even if he could have been persuaded to do so, she saw that it was not fair to petition for that which would involve his own certain disgrace. For Don Manuel was not one who would hear excuse if his authority were defied.

The better, if not the only, chance lay in persuading Francisco that she would not take the veil—or, at least, not at this time—and that she was resolved to help the need of Malta in an extremity in which even women must have some functions they could fulfil.

She considered also boarding his ship at the last hour, and announcing that she was resolved to go, without asking his consent, but the thought that there would be no cabin reserved for her use, no female companion such as she designed to have, and the fear above all that she might be put ashore with the ignominy of force, if Ramegas should be consulted on such an issue, deterred her effectually. For, in her more feminine way, her pride was no less than that of Francisco or Don Manuel himself. She might brave danger, she might face the unknown with courage; but the fear of failure and ridicule were less easy to overcome.

In the same spirit, she saw that, if she should fail in resolution or power of persuasion now: if the ships should sail at the dawn and she should still be under the castle roof, she would surely go to the Convent of Holy Cross on the next day without showing that it was not cheerfully or even willingly done. It would be intolerable to her pride to remain there in passive, futile rebellion until, sooner or later, her uncle should come again and compel her to that which she had tried in vain to avoid.

On this determination she sought her cousin, and found that it would not be easy to make a favourable opportunity for the interview she desired. Two days before, she could have had his society at any hour. But how great was the difference that that time had made!

She sought him at last on the deck of the *Santa Martha*, through the crowded haste of the quay, to be told, after a time of enquiry that had produced only doubtful or contradictory answers, that he was with Señor Ramegas in the cabin of the other ship, so that she must wait his return, having no wish to go to him there.

And when he came he was in haste and a ruffled mood, for Ramegas had told him of more than one error into which he had fallen through inexperience and slowness to consult one who was his superior officer now, and had made it clear that their ranks held something more than a nominal difference. He had to learn that, though he was Don Manuel's nephew, Admiral of the Fleet was a position he had not yet gained.

"Francisco, can we talk somewhere alone?"

"What is it now?" he exclaimed, with an impatience which, to his cousin at least, he would rarely show. "I have much to do. We sail before dawn."

Angelica thought it best to be straight and bold. "I am coming with you," she said. "I want a cabin for my use, and one for a maid whom I shall bring."

A moment before, she had had the sense of being forgotten or pushed aside, which she had experienced at the morning meal, but there was no doubt that she had his attention now.

"Coming with us! How can you do that? It is to-morrow you are riding to Holy Cross."

"But that can wait. It has done so for eight years. Should not all help at this great need at which Malta lies? There is work for women as well as men in a leaguered town."

"Have you our uncle's word that you come?"

"He had much else of which he must think. I would not vex him with smaller things."

"You will vex him more if you come here when he thinks you at Holy Cross. As to cabins, do you know that we are to bear more than eight hundred men on this ship, and that it is laden with stores? And every hour I hear of more that must come. The men of most rank must lie in a crowded way. The slaves must sleep where they pull.

"Does Señor Ramegas know this? Then you must talk to him. I am nothing here. He would have me ask whether I am to go out by the stern."

"It would be useless to ask him. You must know that. Francis, I cannot go to that tomb at so great a time. I must come with you."

Francisco heard the pleading note in his cousin's voice and considered her request in a more serious way. As he did so, he regained the self-control that he had been near to lose as he came from Ramegas' cabin a few minutes before.

"I would have you here," he said, "with a blithe heart, but I see not how. If we would do this, and let there be wrath at a later day, yet I see not how to contrive. If I should find a cabin for you, there would be those who must be turned out, and they would not keep their tongues still for an hour.

"There are some who are sore now, and have taken tales to Señor Ramegas of how I would have them lie, which I must change, though I know not how.

"It could not be done without the knowledge coming to him and, as I think, it will be better to ask him now. He would not endure that we plan it without his will. You should ask him first. It is a small chance, or else none."

"Well," she said, "I will do that." She had no hope, but she saw that there was no other way.

She went on to the *Santa Anna* and found its commander upon the poop. He observed her at once, seeming to have more leisure than her cousin, and to be aware of all that went on without disturbing the calm of his own mind. He met her with grave rebuke that she should have come seeking him thus.

"Was there none you could send? Did you not know you should not be here?" But when she said she wished to speak to him alone he took her to his own cabin and listened calmly to what she said.

She came out a few minutes later with but one thought in her mind—to keep back tears from the sight of the men among whom she must make her way. Ramegas had been patient and kind. A child's folly had hindered his work, but he was too self-controlled to show anger for that. Also, she was a child of whom he was fond, and Don Manuel's niece. But the thing itself was too foolish for more than a kind rebuke. He had thought her to have more sense, and that her duty would be more plain to her eyes.

When she went, he called to one he could trust to follow her back to the castle gate.

Angelica had passed through a rough crowd, and some things which were not meant for her eyes and had not been pleasant to see. But except for the slaves who were already being labelled and chained to the benches where they must row till the voyage should end, they had mostly been men she knew. And the galley-slaves had been far beneath, in the low waist of the ship.

She saw well that she would have been queen of her cousin's ship, having all the comfort she could, among hundreds who would have run at her word. And the voyage to Malta would not be long. She would still have gone if she could; but she saw that it would not be. She had done no more than to give others a cause for jest, and to soil her pride.

When she had regained her room, and could be private to her own mood, she looked out on the harbour with eyes that were bright with tears. They were tears of anger and shame, of one who was not used to defeat. She saw Rinaldo's galley anchored far out in the bay. Why had she not asked it of him? His galley would not be so crowded of men. There might be more comfort there. "*The potent arms that you now bear.*" She had a confident thought that he would not refuse to help her up the side of the ship. But she knew it to be a thing that she could not do. She did not trust him enough—or, at least, not in the right way.

CHAPTER VII

It was in the later day that Morayma came to Angelica, where she still sat apart in a mood of rebellion against the fate that was closing her in. The call of sea and wind and the wide freedom of life became louder and more alluring as it seemed more hopeless that she could accept its charm. She had all the hunger of youth and she looked down on a meal which was to lie for a lifetime untasted before her eyes. At least, so it seemed to her. The Abbess of Holy Cross, had she been in a confessional mood, might have told her that the plate was not always bare.

"Señor Francisco," Morayma said, "has sent for some things he needs but lacks time to fetch. There is a yellow scarf which he says you have."

"Yes. It is in my chest. It has been there since the masquerade. I will get it now."

She went to a coffer in which she kept such clothes as she seldom wore. After turning out much that it held, she came to the scarf she sought. It was last winter that she had dressed herself as a page for the Twelfth-day masque, which her uncle had chidden somewhat at first, and then praised her, as making a pretty boy. There was not much that might not be done on that night. She had borrowed her cousin's doublet and hose; a suit that had become small for him, though it had been ample for her. The clothes were still there.

As she looked at them now, a thought came which she put away, but which would come back to her mind. "There is none," she thought, "that would guess, if my hair were shed." Then she thought: "But I should be shamed if they did." And after that: "But I am slim enough, and I stride well. I see not how they should know."

She said aloud: "It is a wild thought. It is a thing I shall never try. . . . I should need a sword, if I did."

She might be sure that it was a thing she would never try, yet she went to her cousin's room and found the rapier he mostly wore when he was dressed in a formal way. He had left it for a heavier sword, now that he went to the grim business of war, so it was there with the belt and dagger to which it belonged, all of which she took to her own room, with some other things which were of a man's kind.

She had some gold saved, which her uncle would give her freely at times, and this she put in a hollow belt that ran round the inside of the doublet, where it was drawn close at the waist, and was well concealed. She did not know what her need might be, but she knew that to have gold at hand is best for those who wander about. There was a pouch also hanging upon the belt, at the dagger's guard, and she put some smaller money in that for an instant need.

"It is what," she said to herself, "I shall never dare; but it can be no loss to have ordered well if my mind change at the last, as it will not do."

It was in this mood she remained till the day went down and the darkness came, though her hands had not been idle the while, and after that, as the space of escape narrowed towards its last hour, she came to a mood that was both active and bold, and though it might change with another day, it might do more before then than could be undone by too late a fear.

Through the hours of night there was coming and going of men between castle and quay, and the castle gates were not closed, nor its lights dimmed. At two hours before dawn it was easy for one who walked out with assurance enough to pass unchallenged and unobserved; and it was at about that time that an old fisherman, grounding his skiff on his own beach—to which he had returned from taking some goods to Rinaldo's galley—was aware of a young gentleman who stood at the water's edge, and asked him, in a voice that was somewhat husky and low, if he would earn some coins by pulling out again to the *Flying Hawk.*

Vaguely, for he was a tired man, Pedro heard a familiar sound in the voice and, had there been better light, he would more certainly have recognized Francisco's clothes and given a closer look to one who wore them with doubtful right. As it was, he thought only of time and toil.

"Señor," he said, "it will be a hard pull, and the time is short, for they weigh anchor in much less than an hour. But I will do what I can."

"There is time, if you pull well. If you get me aboard I will give you something more than I said. There is this to take."

She handed him a valise which she had found heavy enough, though it was not large. The beach at this place had a good slope, and the boat could come well ashore, but as she got aboard she wetted one leg to the knee, at which she was less than pleased. Pedro had settled more than he knew, for she had resolved that he should be the test of whether her disguise would prevail. As he knew her voice as well as herself, it had seemed a sufficient ordeal to pass, and as he pulled over the dark waters of the bay, she had a better confidence that none would guess that she was not that which she appeared, which did much to control her fear of what her greeting might be when she had climbed to the galley's deck.

They passed close enough under the stern of the *Santa Anna* to hear the voices of those who were casting the hawsers clear, and when they drew into the shadow of the *Flying Hawk* they heard the noise of men who sang at the capstan bars, and the bow anchor was already awash. Pedro pulled round to the low waist of the ship, and when he hailed that he had a gentleman to be put aboard, the rope-ladder was cast, with less pause to ask for whom it might be required than there might have been in the light of day, or at any moment than that, for the sheet-anchor was hard apeak, and as it came clear of the sea-bottom the galley must fall away with the wind. The oarsmen had their long sweeps ready to pull, and Angelica found that she must be agile to seize the swaying ropes before the boat would be backed away. The valise was handled in such a sort that it was by no more than a good chance that it did not fall to the sea.

Pedro pulled away in some wonder and doubt of what he had done, for, as Angelica gave him that he had earned, she had been careless to speak in her own voice, saying farewell. It seemed a wild thought at the first, but when he heard, at a later hour, that the Señorita could not be found, he had little doubt of what he had done, about which he had sufficient sense to keep quiet. He had not seen her, he said, with an oath which his conscience allowed; for who can see in the dark?

Angelica was led by the light of lanterns that swung from the masts, and the first faint efforts of dawn, along a raised plank from which she could look down on the benches of those who were chained to the oarsman's task. She had to keep her footing with care as the ship came loose to the wind, and she heard strange-tongued cries from those who controlled the oarsmen by word and lash, bidding them dip their sweeps to a task which must be sustained till the voyage's end.

She had asked for Captain Rinaldo, not knowing if that were the proper designation to apply to the pursuivant who was also (as she understood) in command of the vessel by which he came. The seaman whom she addressed, who appeared to be of the rank of a quartermaster or boatswain, but whose features were hard to see in the wavering light, had replied in a foreign tongue, which might be Maltese for any better knowledge she had, and had led her toward the poop. He had, in fact, understood no word except "*capitan*," which conveyed all that she needed to say, and her dress and manner were sufficient to indicate the part of the vessel to which she would most naturally be assigned.

When she had climbed to the high poop, she saw Rinaldo there, but the man, having led her so far, either had other work of an urgent nature upon his hands, or he did not think it necessary, or perhaps wise, to interrupt the captain in his task of guiding the ship through the harbour-mouth. He pointed to Rinaldo, with some more words of the foreign tongue he had used before, and hurried away. Angelica stood in the shadow of a short mizzen-mast which rose from the poop deck. She saw Rinaldo in the light of a lantern which hung over the stern. He was clothed in somewhat looser garments than he had worn when he came ashore, and had a curved sword at his side. She was not sufficiently familiar with the equipment or crew of a Maltese warship to judge the meaning of all she saw, but was aware of a barbaric tone in her new surroundings beyond anything she had expected to meet. It was exotic, even intoxicating, in its first effect, as though she were privileged to walk in safety in Algiers or Egypt, where no Christian, other than the ingratiating ubiquitous Greek, could hope to enter, save in the heavy gyves of a slave.

Finding herself unobserved or unregarded by those around, she turned her attention to the dim forms of her uncle's galleys, coming up behind with spreading widths of canvas which hid at times the lights of the castle which she had left for so wild a path. As she looked back in a tumult of contending thoughts, she was aware of Rinaldo's voice at her side.

There was now a broadening line of dove-grey light on the rim of the eastern sky, foretelling a quiet and misty dawn. She could not see his face clearly, and he less of hers, she being in shadow and her back turned to what light there was.

"May I ask to whom I have the honour to speak?"

The words were courteous, but the tone had an inflection of satire, at which her heart stirred to a sudden fear; but it was a question she had expected, and for which she had an answer prepared.

"I must ask your grace for the way I have come aboard without leave. My name is Garcio—Don Garcio of Murcia—I am near of blood to Don Manuel, and came to give such aid as I could. I did not arrive till his galleys were near to sail, and they were so thronged that I thought it best to ask if you could find me space here."

There was no answer to this, and she added: "If I have taken too great a freedom, I have no doubt Señor Ramegas will find means to bring me to his own vessel. Or I could pace the deck here, if your cabins are full below. You would not mind that?"

She did not want to face Ramegas, but it appeared best to speak in a bold way, and, at the worst, he could not put back for her. She felt that the die had fallen now, and it might not have been unwelcome to have found herself among friends again, and to discard a dress which had served its use. Yet it was not easily to be thought that Rinaldo would be reluctant to welcome any who might come as a volunteer to the defence of the threatened isle, or to refuse hospitality on a ship which the Knights of Malta owned.

"We will speak of this at a later hour." As Rinaldo said this, he moved away without inviting reply. There had been a subtle note of ironic mockery in his voice, at which her heart stirred again to that first instinct of fear.

Yet she was of too fine a blood to be lightly frightened without a cause, and her reason told her that there could be no need for alarm. Even if he had guessed who she was—which she was not quick to believe—she must be in safety enough, with the Maltese flag over her head, and its own envoy in charge. She did not forget that she was the niece of one of the Commanders of the great Order to which the galley belonged. One who was next in rank to the Grand Master, La Valette himself.

Perhaps it was just because Rinaldo had not guessed who she was that he had dared to speak in that mocking tone. He might think her to claim a rank that she did not own. He might even think her a spy. But, even so, she need have no fear. The truth would be her secure defence. Had she been really alone she might have stirred to a sharper fear. But she looked at the two great ships that were but three furlongs behind, drawing out of the harbour now, the *Santa Martha* slightly in advance on the starboard side, and she knew that Ramegas—her cousin—and a hundred others upon those decks could speak for her of who she was. She looked at the beauty of sea and sky in the growing light with a mind that was more at ease than it had been since Rinaldo's coming had broken the peace of the castle life, as a stone drops in a pool.

And the scene was one of beauty and quiet peace, though it might be pregnant with menace of coming war, as the three galleys, like wide-winged birds, with white gleams of foam at their sides from the measured strokes of the oars, left the dark coastline of Spain behind, and moved outward toward the dawn.

The two galleys of Don Manuel, which had been built at Cadiz, and were the gift of the Spanish king, were each of a length of two hundred feet, being among the largest ships of their kind that were then afloat. The waist was low, where the rowers sat, and they would be drenched in a windy storm, and might even be glad of their chains at such times, without which they had been sucked away by a falling wave; but poop and bow were built high, having several decks. They were like castles, bristling with cannon, crowded with men.

They were built somewhat broad of beam and round of bow, speed being less regarded than strength, and space for armaments and for a large regiment of fighting men. But they carried three masts, and could show a spread of sail that was high and wide. They had twenty oars on either side, each being pulled by three men. With a good wind they could do ten knots an hour, if not more.

The *Flying Hawk* was a smaller ship of a different kind. It was lean and swift. It had some height of poop, and there were gun-decks there, where it showed teeth that were strong and sharp. But the bow was lower and pointed keenly ahead, like a falcon's beak. It had cannon there on a single deck, long brass swivel-mounted guns that could be trained ahead on a flying prey. It had great grappling-hooks hung out on either side of the prow, that could be used to grip the bulwarks of a ship that might be too shy to close with less persuasion than that. With the sharp-pointing prow, they showed like the beak and claws of the deadly bird that it claimed to be.

It had but twelve oars aside, with two rowers to each, but it could make as good speed with those on a calm sea as could the greater galleys with six-score rowers that pulled on their longer oars; and with a fair wind, it could do nigh three knots to their two.

Angelica looked at it now, gliding forward with less than its full effort of sail, and with its oars stilled for a time, that it might not draw too far ahead of her uncle's galleys, which might be said to be panting behind, and she thought it to be a ship which it would be easy to love. She was at peace with herself and with all she saw, when a man stood at her elbow and spoke to her in a tongue which she did not know, but which had some sound of that which Morayma used when she met one of her own race.

The man had on a red cap, and his jacket and drawers were linen, not over-white, which might be excused on a ship that was scarcely clear of the harbour-bar, and was still busy with a crowd of men who were carrying stores to the hold, coiling cables away, and removing raffle from off the decks.

When she answered in Spanish, and he saw that she did not understand him, he found enough words of that tongue to say that Captain Hassan wished to speak to the Señor.

"Captain Hassan?" she asked, in some surprise, thinking that this must be another officer to whom Rinaldo had referred her business; but she followed the man across the deck, and it was to Rinaldo that she was led.

He looked at her in a cold way, and there was no friendliness in his voice, as he asked:

"Señor Garcio, you are, as I understand from yourself, of a wealthy house? You are one for whom a good ransom might well be paid? Should we say of two thousand crowns, or perhaps more?"

"Yes," she said in some wonder and doubt how to reply to this most unexpected query. "What of that?"

"It may be well for you that you have such friends. You were not asked to come here, and musi look for the fate of those who adventure with rashness thus."

Angelica was more puzzled than alarmed by the threat which the words contained. She still thought that, if all else should fail, she had but to reveal who she was, and her safety, at least, was sure. She looked at the Maltese flag overhead, and at the two great galleys that were scarce a gunshot away, and there was no more than a foolish jest in the words she heard.

"Captain Rinaldo," she said, "you talk in a strange way. I am on a Maltese ship, and it is Malta I come to aid. Do the Knights of Malta think that to hold their friends to ransom will aid their cause? Why, all Europe would cry them shame."

"Señor, I know not what the Knights of Malta may do. I am not of their Order, nor was I put in command when this galley was sent to sea."

"Then I will speak to who is."

"If you would do that, you must call the dead."

"Do you tell me that the Captain died, and that you, being no more than the Grand Master's envoy at first, have taken his power?"

"The Grand Master's envoy is on the third bench from the fore, on the starboard side. It is he over whom the driver is standing now with his whip raised, which he will feel the first time that his oar lags, as it is soon that it will."

"I cannot tell what you mean."

"Yet it is simple to see. You are speaking to Captain Hassan, of whom it is likely you may have heard. Six days ago, I was in command of a part of my father's fleet. I fell in with this galley, which I have long lusted to take. Being six to one, we were able to gain it with little loss, having hemmed it round. I took it by the board, for I would not batter it with our guns, more than by the shooting down of some spars to reduce its speed, which were soon repaired.

"My vessels lie with their yards aback but fifty miles off Iviza's coast, and I lead Don Manuel's ships to that place, as two cows that the butcher needs.

"Yet I will not say I have done all that I meant, for I thought that the Lord of Vilheyna would have been the best part of the prey which I took some venture to have. He would have pleased my father better than all, for he had longed to bait him for many years; since, in fact, he broke his helm at Golitta's siege, though he might have borne no malice for that. It was some words that Don Manuel said at that time which he must learn to repent. My father will not be content that either shall die till he have him impaled at his galley's stern, for he has a stake there, as you may know, which is seldom vacant of some Christian to whom he may talk at will.

"There is a chance that he may honour you in that way, but it is the larger odds that he will let you go at a good price, thinking you are too feeble and mean for that which he will keep for his major foes."

Angelica heard this with a mind that was stunned by a horror that left it numb, as the pain of a wound delays till the first shock is spent.

She did not doubt it was true; nor to whom it was that she spoke. It was to Hassan, the son-in-law of Dragut, who was the Sultan's Viceroy of Algiers, the scourge of the Mediterranean for the last thirty years, the best naval commander who supported the Turkish power. And Hassan, Barbarossa's son, was his most dreaded lieutenant, to whom he had given his daughter in reward for a former act of audacity such as that which had brought her here. At least—it was her own folly that brought her here!

She looked back at her uncle's ships, striving to make pace with the swifter vessel, and thinking that every knot they gained made it more sure that they would arrive at Malta before the Turks could obstruct their way to the harbour mouth, and she felt, illogically enough, as though she had betrayed them to the doom that they strained to reach. And yet, if she could warn. . . . And what way could there be to that? She saw—she could have admired at another time in another mood—the superb audacity which had anchored that galley in Aldea Bella bay, with its benches of Christian slaves: slaves too closely watched, too entirely cowed by their ruthless owners, to be able to give alarm, perhaps too terror-weakened to have used such an opportunity had it come.

But now she saw only the eyes which had looked at her so differently two mornings before—which were now cruel with derisive scorn. Was she to watch impotent here while her cousin and all her uncle's power were lured to slaughter or slavery at the Corsair's will? What would be her own fate when the truth were known, which she could not hope that she would be long able to hide?

Desperation brought its own courage. If she had abandoned her womanhood for this pit of horror and shame, was she to forget also the manhood that she assumed? The sword that she yet wore?

They were alone on the high deck, in an ample space, for Captain Hassan was not one on whom others would intrude unless they knew that they were required. Bitter passion and pride, and the wild hope that she might do something to break the trap to which her friends were now led, urged the sudden movement that brought her rapier clear of its sheath. She would have struck, in the revulsion of that instant's despair, be the consequences what they might, but he was as nimble as she. The curved scimitar leapt to light.

"Back!" he cried. "Stand away!" to the running crew. "Do I need aid for such a boy's bodkin as that?"

Angelica thrust twice with a fury replacing strength. Then she knew that her rapier was snapped off at the hilt. The scimitar skimmed over her head, which it did not cut.

"You are more worth," Captain Hassan remarked, "while you yet live. Yet I see not why you should idle here. You may look again at the pursuivant that you thought me to be. He will not last for an hour. When he faints, they will cast him over the side, and his place will be bare for you."

She looked at the bench to which he had pointed before. Standing at the poop-rail, she looked down on the face of a man who was at the extremity of exhaustion and the desperation of a great dread. His bench companion was a huge negro, with a green turban about his head, who pulled strongly and must, indeed, have been doing three-fourths of the work, but the oars were beyond the power of a single man.

The pursuivant, the real Rinaldo, pulled with the knowledge that, if the oar should fail to keep its place with the rest, the lash would descend on a back that was already swollen and raw and in a torture of pain every time that it bent for the next stroke. Nature may do much under the stimulus of such fear, but there is a limit it cannot pass. As Angelica looked, the man's body sank limply forward upon the oar. The lash descended in vain upon a back that quivered but did not rise. The oar fouled the one that came forward from those who pulled on the bench behind. There was confusion and loss of stroke till the negro lifted it clear.

The driver called two men forward to strike off the chains of the swooning man. He shouted also for one of the slaves who were held in reserve for such a need to be brought to supply his place.

Angelica saw the pursuivant's senseless form lifted over the bench, and dragged to the vessel's side. She realized abruptly that he was to be thrown overboard while he still lived. She had known, all her life, that such things were but daily events in the merciless Mediterranean warfare that had been waged for five hundred years between the Christian and Moslem powers. For the moment she forgot her own peril, even the threat that she was to take the vacated place. She turned to Hassan with a cry in which horror and appeal had an equal part.

"Oh, not that! You can't let them throw him over. He isn't dead."

"Señor," was the cold reply, "the man had no ransom to pay."

There was no mercy in Hassan's heart, for he had known the misery of a slave himself, all the bitterness and the blows, as he had toiled in Malta at the fortifications of St. Elmo, while his captors had refused to discuss any possible ransom, so that he was only released at last when Dragut made capture of a Commander of the Maltese Order, and both parties had been glad to effect exchange.

The pursuivant's body was flung over the side, to tumble for a moment and disappear among the swirling foam of the oars; but Captain Hassan's attention had left it before it fell.

Something in Angelica's voice, in the urgency of that appealing cry, in which she had forgotten the pose of manhood she had assumed, awaked memory and brought his eyes upon her with a new sharpness, even as he lifted the pipe to his mouth, the shrill note of which had been intended to summon those who would have chained her in the vacant place, and put back the wretch who was now being driven toward the bench.

"Now," he said, "you may call me fool if you will. Allah be thanked for the better light! Did not Morayma say you could use the sword? But she left the doublet unsaid. There will be no slave-bench for you—Señor Garcio. You shall have the cabin beside my own."

"I see you know who I am. There is no occasion to mock. And the sword I had was no more than a fragile thing. It might have snapped in your own hand. But if you treat me with honour, you may be sure there will be exchange or ransom agreed."

She was conscious, amid the horror of the murder she had just seen, and a host of contending fears, of some satisfaction, even relief, in the fact that he knew her for whom she was, and that the true issue alone need concern her now. She could feel confidence once again in the great name that was hers, and that might, she thought, be some protection, even in this pit to which she had slipped. Fear she must have; but, for the moment, at least, she faced him with a courage that ruled her fear. And as she heard his reply, she had need of all that she could gather from her own spirit or her race's pride.

"You will be held in honour enough. You need have no doubt about that, for it is there that your value lies. But it will be time to talk of ransom when it is asked, if at all. My father may think you a gift that our Sultan will not disdain to take from his hand; though I do not say you should look for that, for the years of the Protector of the Faithful are more than few, and it is said that his seraglio is already beyond his need. My father may think that I have done well, and that I may claim a rose for my own wreath, if I will."

Angelica checked a reply that was near her lips. It seemed that she gained coolness as well as courage from the extremity of danger which was not hers alone, but that of all who were aboard those following ships. If there were a way that they could be warned in time! She saw that the more quietly she accepted the doom that his words implied, the more freedom she was likely to have, and on the retention of such freedom must rest any hope that she could communicate with those who were now being guided to the waiting trap. She said only:

"I had no rest during last night. Will you show me the cabin I am to have?"

He saw that she accepted the position in a very quiet and sensible way, and though he might not have cared had she wept or pleaded or stormed, there being those at call who had the expertness of use in dealing with such cases as hers, yet her attitude proved her friend in securing a different treatment from that which she would have been likely to have.

"Come this way," he said, and led down a short companion-way to the poop-cabins beneath their feet. She recognized in the curt order that she was now something less than either the Señorita

Angelica of Vilheyna, or the Señor Garcio that she had claimed to be; but it was something gained that she was being led to the best quarters that the galley held, rather than to the hard slavery of the oar, which she would have had no strength to endure.

"There is no need," he said, as they entered the cabin in which his meals were served, "that it should be known who you are at this time, and will be better not, in two ways."

The room in which they stood was surprisingly large, though its height was little more than six feet. It was on the port side, and as they entered, looking toward the rudder, there were portholes facing them, and on their right hand, through one of which, as the ship dipped to the waves, Angelica had a glimpse of the *Santa Anna*. She saw the length of its starboard side, and the lifted oars gleam in the sun. She had some comfort in this nearness of friends, and a brave and yet fearful thought that their safety might be dependent upon herself. "I must warn them," she thought, "while there is time, though my life go."

While she thought this, Captain Hassan had called to a Moorish boy, and had led the way to the further of two doors which opened at their left hand.

"You will prepare this cabin," he said, in his own tongue, "for Señor Garcio's use, bringing his baggage here from the deck, and from now you will serve meals for two."

Angelica saw that she was in the sternmost of two sleeping-cabins which opened into each other and into the larger one, the suite of three taking the whole width of the stern. The Knights of Malta might crowd their fighting galleys with men, but they had spacious accommodation provided for the one, whether of themselves or not, who was likely to have command. There would be comfort for him and for one other, wife or *amie*, whom he might bring aboard on a safe voyage.

"You will live here," Hassan went on, when the boy had gone, speaking in Spanish again, "till we come to port, and my father will order all. You may think that you can call to your friends, but you know more than I, if you know how. For even could you swim such a length through the waves (which it would be random to think), you would be shot from these decks as you rose from the first dive, nor would your friends haul a yard that they might come by your way, for they will not pick up that which a consort drowns."

Angelica feared, as he said this, that he might have observed a moment's change in her face, for to swim to her uncle's ships had been a faint hope that had already come to her mind, though it had also filled it with fear. For, having been born at the sea's side, and of a race that had been less often on land than a ship's deck, she had learnt to swim, which she could do well, though she had never put her strength to a test such as this would be sure to be.

"If you are wise," he went on, "you will put such thoughts from your mind, for your own peace. You can bar these doors or not, as you will. While I live, you will be troubled by none till this voyage is through. And you can drive that toy" (looking at the dagger that hung from her belt) "into my back at a likely time, if your folly rise to that height; but it will be no avail to your friends nor to yourself. If you should do that, you might pray for a quick death in the next hour. There are three hundred men on this ship, besides slaves, and no woman at all. They would have no mercy on one who had wrought my death; and what they would do, should they find that which you are, I may guess but I will not say. You might be glad at the last to be impaled on the stake you will have seen at the helmsman's side, which your friends of Malta have used to the torture of those of the True Faith, as its stains attest, but which will bear Christian fruit from this day."

"I am not of those," she said, "who slay sleeping men or who will strike at the back, as I think you know."

"Are you not? There are few, either women or men, who will not do that at an urgent fear, unless they are faint of heart, which I do not think that you are. I will trust your sense as a better pledge."

"You may trust what you will. While you leave me at peace, I shall not desire evil to you. I can see that it might be to fall into more difficult hands."

"Then we are agreed for this time." He went back to the deck.

Angelica remained in the larger cabin, which was furnished in the style of the Italian luxury of that time, having much of novelty to one who had been brought up in the austere atmosphere of Andalusian grandeur, while the boy Alim prepared her own cabin, fitting with soft cushions and silk coverings a deep-sided berth, which was more fit for a woman's ease than the man she proposed to be.

When he had gone, she lay down in the berth, though without discarding her clothes, for, having had no rest during the previous night, she was physically and mentally exhausted by the experiences through which she had gone. Now, while adversity threatened but paused to strike, she lay for some time devising plans by which she might reach her friends who were so near, and so much more numerous and powerful than these men by whom she was held. But her thoughts showed her no more than the strength of the trap into which she had walked, in a blind way; and, after a time, with the resilient spirit of youth, she passed into dreamless sleep, from which she waked in a mood of buoyant hope, having little cause, beyond the fact that there appeared to be a short space of days during which she need have no imminent fear.

She entered the larger cabin to find a table laden with food, and bearing signs that Captain Hassan had eaten and gone. She ate and drank with some zest, during which she was even aware of some doubt whether she would be back in the walls of Andrea Bella, if the choice could be hers, considering that it must be about the hour when she would have been setting out for the Convent of Holy Cross.

Having eaten, and observing that the air was somewhat oppressive in the low-roofed cabin, she found courage enough to seek the sun and wind that the deck would give. If she were to be Don Garcio till the voyage should end, she need not deny herself such freedom as could be expected to be attached thereto. Captain Hassan walked the deck, watching the ship's response to a gusty and changeful wind. He did not regard her at all.

She looked down at the bare-backed slaves who toiled under the constant fear of the driver's lash, and her mood sobered again to the depth of the peril in which she lay. The man who had been put in Rinaldo's place had a broad red weal across the white of his back. He did not look very strong. Probably he, too, would go overside, if he had no ransom to pay. Many did. Others had strength to endure, and, in the end, the toil would become almost easy for them.

It was a cruel custom, doing no good to either side, Christian or Infidel, in its result. The galleys of each were pulled by the war-taken slaves of the alien race. They might equally well have each pulled on their own oars, but so the custom had been; slaves died, or were exchanged if they were of sufficient rank; ransoms were paid and repaid. It cancelled out more or less, as it had done since the days of Carthage and Rome. So long had the custom endured, and so long might it last, till the end of time.

Captain Hassan had occupation for his own mind. A cold wind came from the north. The galleys sailed close-hauled to the wind, and the oars pulled under the urgent threats of the drivers' whips. Captain Hassan had no care for his own ship. He could sail two points nearer the wind than the round-hulled vessels that came behind. He felt like a dog that brings slow-moving cattle to the place where they are appointed to die. If there should be a further rise in the wind—if there should be storm in the night, such as would break them apart—it might be the loss of almost all that he had so audaciously attempted to gain.

Angelica felt the chill of that Alpine wind which the Southerner hates to feel, either on water or land. She saw the grey of the sky and the rising sea. She saw that the galleys that held her friends were more distant then they had been on the earlier day. There was no comfort in that.

She watched them awhile over the stern-rail, and when she turned to go below, after she had been spattered by the spray of a heavy wave, she saw that she was standing beside the stake of which Captain Hassan had warned her that she might make closer acquaintance if she should do him hurt. It was a strong, upright stake, about five feet high, firmly fixed in the deck, and having a sharp point. A man being seated thereon, and the stake being thrust in so far that he would not fall off, but no more, might live, it was said, for as much as four days, while the stake would be driven in by his own weight till it should come to a vital part.

It was a form of execution very popular in Asia and Eastern Europe at that time. It resembled crucifixion in that a man might be able to think and talk for a long time after the executioner's work was done; but it was unlike in that a man could not be taken down, and his life saved. After he had once been fixed on the stake a slow death was his certain fate.

There were corsairs at that time, both Christian and Turk—between which there was little to choose in the modes of warfare they used—who would have a victim impaled by the ship's helm as a constant thing, saying that they must have someone with whom to talk while they steered.

Angelica had heard of such things, which she knew were done, but it is different to see. It was but a bare stake, which had been scrubbed clean of all but some stains that were darker than the grain of the wood. There was nothing frightful in that, nor had she much fear that she would come herself to an end so foul, yet it was not pleasant to see.

She went to her own cabin, and watched for a time, through a stern port-hole, the ships where, if she could reach them, her safety lay.

Lacking air, she tried to open it, but found that it was secured beyond her strength, and, as she thought, on the outside. She went to the starboard port-hole and found that it was easy to set it wide, which she was glad to do, that side being away from the wind. She wondered whether the port-hole astern had been secured so that she should not signal at a place which her friends could see, and whether it might have been done in the last hour, while she was on the deck. She had a fear that she might be watched more than she knew, and resolved to be wary to hide her thoughts.

The ships lay-to during the night, resting their oars, and after the darkness fell, and when she had barred both her doors, she watched the triple masthead lights of the two ships that, at one time, were but a short distance away. She supposed that she could go on deck if she would, by no more than opening her own door; and if she were once in the sea, she thought that she would not be easy to follow or stay. But the night was dark, the waves high. She had little hope that she could do more than drown herself, if she should attempt such a swim; and though she saw that she might have no better chance till it would be too late, she could not make the resolve. She slept for that night, and waked in an April dawn to find that the ships were moving again. The wind had veered to the south of west: the sea was more quiet: the *Santa Anna* and *Santa Martha* came with a full strength of sail: the oars flashed in the foam. With a wind which was dead astern, as it now was, their speed was not greatly less than that of the *Flying Hawk:* they sought to recover the time that had been lost as they lay-to in the night. They made haste to their doom.

Angelica looked, and called herself coward that she had let the night go without an effort to reach their decks. She saw that her life was a small thing beside the stake for which it would be cast in the scale. She might not succeed, but it was a thing that she ought to try. Rather, that she ought to have tried; for there could be no chance now, unless it should come with another night.

Captain Hassan clearly thought it to be an impossible thing. But he might not guess how well she could swim. There were few Spanish ladies at that day who could have lived in the water at all. Few, indeed, who would have made such an attempt as she now pondered and feared, and yet thought it likely that she could do if she should have sufficient courage to try.

Yet Captain Hassan might be right. To swim in the dark to the side of a moving ship was a thing she had never tried. She thought of herself as struggling vainly among the moving blades of the oars. They were not always out. But they might be put out at any time, even while she were swimming toward the ships.

Even if they had not to be faced, she must so contrive that she must come close to the moving side, amid the darkness and tossing waves, and her cries must be heard, or something seized by which she could climb, or in a moment it would have slipped away, and she be left to a hopeless death. She should have tried while they lay-to, however rough was the sea. It was the one chance she had, and her cowardice had let it go.

As she reproached herself thus, there was a sound of distant guns that came over the sea. She looked out, and far to south there were flashes at times where sea and sky met in a vagueness of morning mist.

The firing was not heavy, but came often from single guns. It was most likely that of flight and pursuit. The dawn had come to one of the pitiless Mediterranean hawks, and had shown it a pigeon near. It was only a detail of the ruthless warfare that never ceased on the inland sea, over which merchant vessels, hugging the land, glad of the coming night, would scurry from coast to coast, as a rabbit dashes across a field where foxes prowl.

There was some signalling between Don Manuel's ships and the *Flying Hawk*, as though they discussed whether they should endeavour to intervene, but it came to nothing. They went on as before. Had they been drawn into such a strife, it might have been hard for Hassan to conceal the side to which he belonged, but it is likely that he would have continued the part he had chosen to play, even to the point of sinking a galley of his own land, rather than lose the greater prey that he had brought so near to the trap.

But they did not turn for a chase which they might have been too slow to reach, even had it been a Christian vessel that was in jeopard of loss, as to which they may have known more than Angelica was able to see. They held their course all that day, the wind continuing fair under a sky that was warm and blue. The sea became a bright mirror that held the sky.

In the afternoon the *Flying Hawk* steered a more northerly course. It must have seemed a cautious route to those who followed, leaving Algiers as far away as they well could, unless they would go round the Balearic Isles, which had been far out of the course that they ought to make. The day ended without event. The night came, and though she could make no more than a vague guess, having little knowledge of navigation or of distances on the sea, it seemed to Angelica that they could not be far from the place where the trap was set. All the day she had vexed her mind with vain plans by which she should have made a warning signal to those who followed, but she could think of none that would be likely to be understood, though they might lead to her own death. She had leisure enough, for she appeared to be disregarded by all around. The boy Alim was alert to observe her needs, but she did not know his tongue, nor he hers. If he thought her to be other than what she seemed, he made no sign. Captain Hassan gave her no notice at all: his mind, we may suppose, was on larger things.

They met no ships during these two days that were more than a flicker of distant sails, such as would fade away almost as soon as they showed on the horizon, for they were too formidable in their own aspect to invite the weak to a closer view. Curiosity would have been a fatal vice in a merchant-captain of that day, and indifference would have led to the same end by a road nearly as short. They lived longest who were most timid of mood, and would fly from peril while it was no more than a speck on the distant sea.

On the second night, Angelica lay at ease in the soft berth, though she kept her clothes on as before, for there was good reason to rest while she could, if she were to adventure that on which it was hard to resolve, but which yet would not leave her mind.

She rose after a time and looked out on a night that was dark and still. There was no moon, and the stars were few. The two sets of triple mast-head lights followed at some distance apart. Perhaps they were further away than they had been during the day, but one was much in advance. They came on with some spread of canvas, but their oars were drawn in; for no weight of lashes will give men the strength to pull without rest and sleep, and the galleys did not carry a reserve of slaves sufficient for complete relief shifts during the night.

She said to herself: "It must be tried now, if at all. If I stay here, I shall be no more than a bartered slave, of such shame as I partly guess, and do not wish to know more; and I shall have the further shame in my own heart that I have not tried to do what I could. If I try and fail, I have lost no more than a life which is near to wreck, and all else will be as though I had never come. But if I succeed, I have saved my uncle's galleys from being seized and my friends from death. I shall have done more for Malta, besides, than I ever thought when I made that my excuse to come by a wilful way."

And as she thought thus, she saw that the fact that one galley was in advance gave her a double chance, for if she should fail in boarding the first, the second would still be coming in the right way; and she saw also that the distance they might be behind did not matter as much as she had been inclined to think at first. For if she could leave the ship unobserved, she could wait rather than tire herself in an effort to swim to them, doing little more than to keep herself afloat till they should be nearer to her.

Having resolved upon this, she lost no more time, but addressed her mind to the trouble of getting clear of the ship. She prayed to

St. Christopher first, he being the patron saint of her house, as well as the right one to guide her through a dark flood, and crossed herself with the three names of God, and stood awhile with a hand that trembled upon the bar of the door, listening for any sound there might be before she consented to draw it back.

She knew that Captain Hassan was in the cabin beside her own, where she must hope that he slept, and so, after she had drawn the bolt back, hearing no sound, she crossed the larger cabin on quiet feet, from which she had drawn the shoes that she would not need. She should have cast more of her clothes, but had been loth to do this, not knowing what she would be able to get again, and was glad to silence a wiser thought with the fear that if she should be stopped by any upon the ship, and were not fully clad, it would be harder to deceive them as to what she proposed to do.

She went through the larger cabin, dimly lit by a lantern which swung from the roof, and up the companion ladder, which had no light but the stars, for she must first mount the poop before she could get down to the low waist of the ship. On the poop deck she stood awhile in the dark shadow of the mast, on the further side from that on which its lantern was hung.

She saw—through the helmhouse window—Salim, Hassan's chief mate, a turbaned Turk with a beard that spread as loosely as the clothes he wore, standing beside the helmsman, to whom he talked as he pointed northward into the night.

Seeing that he was not looking her way, she crossed to the head of the ladder that descended to the waist of the ship. She could observe no motion. She heard no sound except the voices of the watch on the forward deck, which came clearly through the night air, but she knew that she would not be noticed by them.

Thinking that she increased her risk by delay, she descended to the oarsmen's level. She came to a vague awareness of men who lay under the stars, sprawling asleep in their chains. The overseers dozed or slept in their places alike, for they were nearly as wearied as those they drove. They must snatch sleep when they could, waking at once if the boatswain's pipe should call them to action again.

The big negro, who had partnered Rinaldo until he died, half waked as someone stumbled against his feet. He heard a splash, such as might be made by a leaping fish. He raised his head, but there was no further sound. He looked at the dim forms of those who were sleeping around, and then up at the quiet stars, and turned to slumber again.

CHAPTER VIII

SHE came to the first of the galleys on its windward side. It rose above her, a monster of moving gloom. Its masts, its wide spread of sail which towered to an incredible height among distant stars, were leaning somewhat away. So was the smooth side that slipped from her clutching hands as it slid past with such terrible speed. There was nothing to which she could hold. No one answered her cries. The whole ship seemed asleep. Only, as she came under the stern, and looked up in a last despair, high above she saw Francisco's face, on which the light shone from a stern-hung lantern, as he leaned over the rail. He was puzzled by what he heard. Did mermaids call from the sea? And it was strange that the sound should recall Angelica's voice, the more so that it had a note of pleading and fear such as he had never heard from her lips. But the sound went with the wind, where he supposed that its birth had been.

She saw the towering vessel recede, and she felt that her life was done. By instinct she kept afloat, though she did not doubt that the waste of waters would be her tomb. In that minute's despair, as she saw the ship go by, she almost lost the little chance that was still hers, for when she looked for the second galley, she waked to the realization that it was coming up fast, and was not in line behind, but would pass some hundred yards further south.

She knew it to be the last chance of life that was hers, and she struck out again with all the strength that she still had.

How foolish she had been not to cast some of her clothes! Even the belt, with its slender burden of gold, was still round her waist. She could not wait now to endeavour to get it free. She could only exhaust her breath in the effort to reach the ship before it should pass for ever. She did not even call as she swam.

The wide shadow of sail made a black lake of the water to which she came while there was still half the length of the ship to pass, but the hull leaned over her now. At its waterline it was further away, taking some strokes to reach, and there was again nothing to clutch. It slid past her desperate, groping hands. It was at the corner of the stern, at the last second of hope, that her chance came, in a wooden cornice across the stern. Had she been on the starboard side, it would have been lifted high from her reach, but with the ship leaning as it did from the wind, it came down at times, where she was, to the water's edge.

When she looked down in the daylight hours, she was surprised that she had done that climb with such ease in the dark, but she had been bred on the hills, and there had been no more than a steady breeze which, with the way the ship heeled thereto, had been less hindrance than help. In fact, she remembered little of what she did until she had pulled herself over the bulwark rail, and was aware of a curt crisp voice that asked:

"Now who may you be that come thus where you have no business to be?"

She confronted the small truculent form of Señor Antonio, the Genoese seaman who had been captain of the *Santa Anna* before Ramegas came aboard. He stood with his legs apart, and his left hand bearing down the sword-hilt, so that its blade stuck upwards jauntily at his back. Angelica had seen him once or more at her uncle's board, enough to know who he was, but they had not exchanged twenty words. He was not likely to know her in such a light as that in which she stood now, making a pool of water upon the deck.

"I am—I have swum here from the *Flying Hawk*. I must see Señor Ramegas at once."

"You must be content to see me. Why did they throw you out from the *Flying Hawk?*"

"I was not thrown. I came to bring news of weight."

"Well, you are small enough. You must tell me more."

Antonio thought it an improbable tale. He supposed that he saw one who had been cast out to drown for sufficient cause, and who would now save his life, if he could, on another deck. He expected to hear lies. But he saw that, if the tale were true, it was a bold thing to have done, and he had a belief that most of the world's valour is in the hearts of its smaller men. The slimness of the dripping form that had climbed over his rail caused him to show more patience then he would have given to one of a larger bulk. So he said: "You are small enough. You must tell me more."

"Captain Antonio, it is no time for delay of words, and I am too cold to stand longer here. The *Flying Hawk* is in the hands of the Moors."

He had expected a perjured tale, but not such a wild statement as that. Yet he had lived a life which had taught him to be quickly prepared for most improbable things.

"You will be hanged," he said, "if you lie. Will you say it twice?"

Angelica laughed, which she had not done in the last two days, though she shivered as she stood in the cold of the night-wind. She had been warned of evils enough since she left her home, including impaling, which is not a death to prefer; but to be threatened with hanging on the *Santa Anna* was an addition she had not foreseen.

"I will say it till you are tired. But I shall not be hanged on my uncle's ship, be it false or true. Señor Ramegas will explain that. We lose time standing here."

Antonio might strut through life with his head back and his plumed hat on the left side, but he was shrewd and discreet, or he would not have stood where he then did.

"You have been warned enough," he said. "Follow me."

They crossed a deck which was similar to that of the *Flying Hawk*, but of twice the width, and they descended to a passage which had the doors of cabins on either side. Antonio tapped upon one, calling his own name, and the voice of Ramegas invited him to come in. Angelica, hearing it, felt that she had come at last to a safe place. She could have cried on his neck.

Ramegas was awake and dressed, though it was night, and was not his watch. He was one who had always been sparing of sleep.

He thought of himself as a man of action rather than business affairs, and now he was gravely glad that a time had come when he might prove to the world that he was no less than his secret dream; yet the custom of stewardship was still his, and he sat at a table which was strewn with records and bills of accounts from which he made schedules of the men and stores that were under his charge, and the extent of the succour which he was bringing to Malta in Don Manuel's name.

His eyes passed Captain Antonio to rest on the slim, drenched form, in Francisco's clothes, that came in behind. She knew that she was recognized at the first glance, and would have come quickly forward, but he raised his hand, waving her back. He had hardly allowed the instant of first surprise to change the settled gravity of his eyes.

"Señor," Captain Antonio began, "here is one who comes up from the sea with a tale that the Moors have captured the *Flying Hawk*. I thought——"

"You have done well. But you should hold your watch till the truth be known. I will deal with this."

Captain Antonio showed his discretion again. Without further words he went back to the deck, where his duty lay. He looked at the *Flying Hawk*, running before the wind with its topsail reefed so that its consorts might not be left in the rear. It was within range of the heavier guns that the *Santa Martha* carried on her forward decks, though beyond gunshot of the *Santa Anna*, which was further away. Its oars were not out, and it was evident that it was making no effort to draw apart, which its greater speed would have made it easy to do. It could not hope to fight the two great galleys if the truth should be shown when the morning came. It was absurd to suppose that Moors would have captured it and make no attempt to part company from the heavier vessels. Besides, how could that have occurred unobserved? From where could they have come? Captain Antonio had no difficulty in concluding that the tale had been a bold lie to secure audience with Señor Ramegas, for whom he recognized that it had been well chosen, and had succeeded with speed. His conceit was chafed that he should have been the subject of such a trick, but he had seen the instant of recognition in Ramegas' eyes. He felt that he had done well to conduct Angelica below without more opposition than he had shown. And whatever mystery there might be, he felt it was one that he would soon know.

He looked again at the *Flying Hawk*, and then at a long brass culverin, swivel-mounted, upon the poop, that was so placed on that topmost deck that it could be swung round for forward fire with no more than a slight luff of the ship, even though the mark should be straight ahead. He gave an order that the gunner should be called to his place.

He gave order to trim a yard. There would be nothing to rouse suspicion in that. Why should they be behind the *Santa Martha*, as they were now?

Beyond that, he waited till Señor Ramegas should come on deck. If the tale were true, he felt that that time would not be greatly deferred.

When he had left the cabin below, Ramegas said: "You had better tell me from where you came."

"I swam from the *Flying Hawk*. You will give me clothes of some kind, and show me where I can change, unless you wish me to die. Then I will tell you all. But I tell you this first, for it may be that it should not wait. Rinaldo is not Rinaldo at all. He is Hassan, Dragut's son-in-law, of Tunis. The ship has a crew of Moors. There are no Christians there but those who pull at the oars."

"Is this sober truth, or no more than a girl's guess? The Maltese are a swarthy race."

"I saw the true Rinaldo cast into the sea, being yet alive. Do you think I have swum here, barely saving my life, which I thought to lose, to bring you a doubtful tale?"

"Yet I see not to what end——"

"That is what I am coming to say. It is why I am here now. The fleet of Algiers lies await, fifty miles off Iviza isle. It is to that trap you are being led."

As she said this, Ramegas had ceased to doubt that the tale was true. The fact that she had seen a man thrown overboard alive showed that it was more than the conceit of a frightened girl.

"I doubted that man," he said, "from the first. Yet I could not see what could be wrong, it being a Maltese boat, as was known by a score that I trusted well. But you must not stand thus. Come with me."

He led her to his own cabin, for there was no better place to which she could be taken at once on that crowded ship. He gave her a loose robe and some other garments of which she could make use till her own should be dried.

"How you came to be on that ship," he said, "can be told at a better time. But if this be true, as I do not doubt, you have done a great thing, at your life's risk. I praise the saints that you have come through, taking no harm."

He said no more beyond that, asking no further questions, not even how Hassan came to be in control of the *Flying Hawk*, for his mind was on the main issue he had to face. It seemed that it was soon to be proved whether he were fit for the command he held.

He stood in thought for a moment beside the litter of papers and parchments that he had ceased to heed, and then went on deck. He had decided that the tale he had heard was true, and that he must act on that presumption without weakness or doubt, though he saw that, if he should make mistake, he would be ruined indeed. But he had known Angelica for eight years, and he did not think her to be one who would speak or act as she had on no more than a doubtful guess.

He said to Antonio: "Have you checked our course? How far do we lie from Iviza now?"

Captain Antonio might have been more careful had the course not been set by the *Flying Hawk*. He had been content to keep that vessel in sight during his watch, and had felt that was as far as his duty lay. But there was no need to say that. He had sailed those seas so long that it was said that he could tell where he might be by the very scent of the air.

"We should be twenty leagues south," he said, "or it may be more, but not much."

"Then we are near trapped. The *Flying Hawk* is in the hands of the Moors, as it has been from when it sailed into Aldea Bella bay. Hassan, Dragut's son, has the command, so it is said. He is leading us to where the Algiers fleet lies await."

Antonio stood with his legs well apart. He threw up his head, and his jaw set, so that he looked pleased, in a grim way.

"Then you would say it is time to run. Shall we put about, with no foe in sight, or what will you have us do?"

He looked up at the quiet gravity of the man who held a command which he would have been glad to have, thinking that he would soon know of what sort he would prove to be.

Ramegas looked down at him. "We must sink him first, if we cannot lay him aboard, unless he show heels that we cannot catch."

"That is how I would have it be. Shall we creep near, and challenge him when our guns are trained?"

"We will draw as near as we may, but we will not challenge a treasoned foe. We will send a broadside among her masts, which may be useful to hold her here while we have further to say. But we may find she is too wary to let us close."

Ramegas turned to the helmsman as he said this. He said: "Bring her up to the wind. I would have you cross the track of the *Santa Martha*, and close in on the weather side." He turned to Captain Antonio again. "Have the guns manned, and the slaves roused, and ready to row, but show no more lights than you cannot spare. I would have waited the dawn, but the time is short. And they may take alarm if they guess we had warning brought."

Antonio saw that he was second to one who could plan in a cool and resolute mind. For as they brought the *Santa Anna* across her consort's stern, the stir and movement of lights, which they could not entirely avoid as their preparations were made, would be hidden from any eyes that might watch from the *Flying Hawk*. He issued such orders as waked the ship to a sudden life, and though the bustle that followed thereon might be concealed from the *Flying Hawk*, it was plain enough to the nearer eyes of those on the *Santa Martha's* deck. They were soon about to know what it might mean, and to receive the letter an arrow brought as the *Santa Anna* crossed their stern, at a distance of no more than a galley's length; after which she fell off from the wind again, sailing at their side, but somewhat faster than they, for there had been further spreading of sail while they had come up astern.

Francisco read a note that was brief and clear:

"The *Flying Hawk* is in the hands of the Moors. She leads us to where the Algiers fleet lies await. We must take a more southern course, but will sink her first, if she do not fly. Support me when you have read this, with all the speed that you can, and have your guns manned. I need not tell you beyond that.

"RAMEGAS."

He read this by the lantern's light, and he looked again at the *Santa Anna*, which was shaking out all the sail she had; and as he looked he saw her oars come over the side. It was a strange thing to learn in that sudden way, but he did not doubt its truth, nor fail to see that every second was of a golden weight, now that Ramegas' ship had made it clear what she would do.

The *Santa Martha* waked to life at a trumpet's sound. Her oars came overside. Lights shone, and men shouted and ran at the battle-summons that they had been trained to know. Francisco did not mean that his first fight should find him far in the rear.

He looked at the *Flying Hawk*, and saw that her oars also were out, and at the same moment the flashes of sudden light were a tempest along her side. The thunder of half her guns sounded across the sea. She had not waited to be attacked, but had been the first to fire, even as she gathered speed for her flight.

The next moment the *Santa Anna*, showing no sign of hurt from the shot that had battered about her bows, luffed somewhat, and a blaze of light leaped out from her guns. As the *Flying Hawk* lit the darkness again with backward flashes of light from decks that were somewhat more distant now, the *Santa Anna* replied with all the weight of her port-side guns. But even as her broadside deafened the night, her foremast, which had been struck by a shot from the first discharge of the *Flying Hawk*, and had now taken the strain as the bow came up into the wind for the port guns to bear, gave a loud crack, and leaned, for a long moment, with all its spread of canvas and weight of cordage and spars, before it snapped off, at a height of about six feet from the deck, and fell outward and somewhat astern, cumbering the main shrouds and causing the port-side oars to be drawn inward in haste.

It was plain that the *Santa Anna* would make no speed, nor could she be handled with ease, till she had broken clear from the wreckage which dragged like a sea-anchor along her side.

Hassan, watching from a deck where a man died at his feet,

joyous of heart as he would ever be when a battle came, though with some cause for wrath both at his own folly and fate's caprice, had an audacious thought that he would put about and use his forward guns at a shortened range on a wreckage which, in the dim light of the stars, he may have thought to be somewhat worse than it was. Even to board might not have been beyond his attempt, for, though his force might have been little better than one to three, he had a high belief in the fighting quality of the pirate crew, which was of the pick of his father's fleet; and the evidence of that fallen mast showed that he had gunners who did not fail.

But the thought died as it rose, his foes being not one, but two. For as the *Santa Anna* lost speed, her consort came up on her starboard side. She came past with a spread of all the sail that she had to a freshening wind. The whips cracked over the rowers' backs. The oars moved rhythmically and fast. As they glided by, Francisco leaned over the rail, and called to know what the damage was. Ramegas answered with words that the wind carried away. Antonio, better practised in the science of shouting at sea, could be partly heard. Between the bursting din of the guns which were now firing each for itself, as their crews could reload and train them again, his voice came clearly enough, though only to a fragment of what he said: "Hold them in play, if you can, till we get it clear."

The *Santa Martha*, straining to equal the speed of the *Flying Hawk*, put her helm down till she had interposed her own bulk between the crippled ship and her smaller, but perhaps deadlier, foe. For the first time her guns entered the fight, making the night louder than before and adding to the heavy drifts of sulphurous smoke which increased its gloom. The gun flashes stabbed into a darkness they could not lift.

Francisco saw that the *Flying Hawk* was drawing further away. He had a ruthless thought which showed him true to the stern creed of those who had striven for so many inconclusive centuries for the control of the central sea of the civilized world.

It was the traditional custom of both sides to avoid attack on the galley-slaves, being so largely recruited from those of their own blood. But now Francisco saw that the *Flying Hawk* was drawing surely away. If he luffed, to give her the weight of more than his forward guns, it would be for the last time, unless that broadside could check her speed. He had been taught that no price for victory was too high: no excuse for failure was good enough, if a possibility had been left untried. He ordered that every gun should be trained on the starboard oars of the *Flying Hawk*.

They were to be directed upon the oars, not the men; but the range was already long, the gunnery of that time not exact, and some of the gunners were unused to the pieces they had to work, for Don Manuel's galleys were new ships, which had not been in action before. Some of the shots went wide, but enough found their mark to shatter the starboard oars, and to scatter death among rowers who were also struck by the kicking fragments of the smashed oars that they were pulling as the broadside came.

For a moment Francisco thought that the fight was won. The *Flying Hawk* floundered upon the sea, like a duck with a broken leg. Being lighter, and the swifter sailer, she still kept ahead, but the distance shortened as the chase left the *Santa Anna* behind. Had not the wind increased at this time to half a gale, it is likely that Captain Hassan would have fought his last fight, or had a second spell of slavery which might have been even worse than that from which he had been delivered so hardly before. As it was, the *Santa Martha* soon found that the *Flying Hawk* was beyond the reach of her guns. But having struggled to that distance away, it seemed that she could do no more. She changed her course more than once, as though she would dodge pursuit in the light of a growing dawn. She spat backwards with bursts of fire that seemed no more than a demonstration of futile rage, the shots falling short, though not much.

But Captain Hassan was not one to waste powder with no better purpose than that. He fired that the sound might be carried on the wind to the ears of a fleet which should not be far distant now. He had changed the course of his flight point by point to the north with the same object, until the broadening dawn showed the long line of Formentera upon the northern horizon.

Francisco saw it as well. He looked back to see the *Santa Anna* far to the south. She had cleared her deck, and was sailing freely again, steering an easterly course. Urgently, she signalled for his return.

Reluctantly he gave the order which he should have done half an hour before, shaping his yards for a south-easterly course, and letting the chase go; and, as he did so, the yards of the *Flying Hawk* came round to the same point and she followed upon his track.

He had some cause to doubt the wisdom of his pursuit when he saw that, and still more when he saw, where the dawn-light curved to the north, making a horizon of lemon sky, the dark specks that were the Algerian fleet coming out from Formentera's easterly point, behind which they may have been at anchor during the night.

CHAPTER IX

MALTA stirred like a threatened hive.

The Knights of St. John had been preparing for this hour by excavation of solid rock, by battery and barricade, ever since Charles V had given them the islands, forty years before. Every year, as Christian power had declined and that of Islam advanced in Eastern Europe by land and sea, it had become a darker and more imminent menace; and the same causes that had brought it near had decreased their power to hold it longer at bay. Christians had ceased to think of the tomb of Christ, or of the breaking of infidel power, being at issue among themselves. Those who had adventurous rather than pious minds turned their eyes to the west, to the wealth and empire of a new world which had the lure of the hardly-known.

When Charles V gave the Maltese islands to the homeless Knights of St. John he asked no more rent than a yearly falcon to be paid to the Sicilian power. The terms seemed easy enough. Being assured that the ancient laws of the islands would be sustained, the people of Malta had accepted the arrangement with short demur. It may have seemed that the Knights received a princely gift, at no price.

But Charles knew what he did, and the Knights of Malta were well aware. Should a wolf-hound give thanks that he is kennelled where he can get his fangs to the throat of the prowler around the flock?

The Knights of Malta were recruited from the most noble blood of every nation throughout the west. They drew revenues from all lands. And now that Palestine had been lost, and their Jerusalem hospitals gone, their sole object was to make war on the Turks. Charles did no more than make an eyrie for hawks, from which they would vex his foes. The form of the yearly rent may be taken as a symbol of what he did.

But meanwhile, as the years passed and the power of Islam increased, the number of the Knights became less and their revenues shrank. An English king, taking the lands of his own Church, was not likely to leave theirs.

It had been intended to build a rampart of stone such as would have made an outer wall of defence of an almost impregnable kind, but this had been abandoned after a calculation of its cost had shown that it could not have been completed without larger funds than the Order could hope to raise.

Of late years there had been few new knights from the nobles of the more Protestant lands. In five hundred names there is but one—that of the Grand Master's secretary, Sir Oliver Starkey—which has an English sound. Yet the knights had been strongly established in England once, and a Grand Master had come from that land.

And of the knights who were now arriving from all parts of Europe at the call of this final need, many, like Don Manuel, were elderly men. The Grand Master himself, John la Valette (as he would shorten his name) was near the end of his life. He was a hard-faced, bearded man, with a long straight nose, upright and sturdy enough, and still able to use a sword, though becoming slightly corpulent under his belt. He ruled all in a just but merciless way, trusting more to fear than to love.

It was said by all that he was the right man for the crisis that now came. He was a hawk that would be hard to dislodge from the eyrie where he had chosen to dwell.

Now he toiled with servants and slaves that the fort of St. Elmo might be made strong before the Turks should arrive. He was not deterred by the stiffness that comes with years, nor by the dignity of the great office he held. He put his shoulder beneath a beam.

Seeing him do that, his knights could not refuse to toil in the same way. Every day that the Turks delayed to arrive, the defences grew. Every day brought fresh succour of knights who came at their Order's call, and of volunteers who would strike a blow for the Christian cause, or sought the excitement of war. They came daily in fishing vessels, or half-decked boats that made the run from Messina when the seas were kind, and at times in larger galleys. The Sicilian vessels came in a watchful fear, ready to turn and bolt at the first horizon sight of the coming Turk. Having landed their cargoes, they were in a great haste to be gone.

The Grand Master had asked aid from Sicily, both of stores and men, as he had a right to do in return for that falcon he yearly paid, for to attack Malta was to affront Sicily, and Spain beyond that.

The Viceroy of Sicily replied with words of goodwill. He had asked instructions of his master, Philip of Spain, without which he was powerless to move. Doubtless these instructions would accord with the dignity of the Spanish crown, and the insolent unbelievers would be chastised.

Actually, the Viceroy was unsure what Philip would say, except that there would be no lack of fair and promising words, which he would seldom stint; and he was in even more doubt as to what he would wish him to do. For the time, he did nothing at all, beyond writing long reports to Madrid, which he knew that Philip would wish to have. He knew that they would be fully read and very carefully filed away.

So it was, when April changed into May, and the watchman upon St. Elmo's wall saw that two great galleys came from the west. They came fast, with a fair wind in their sails, and their oars out, but as they drew near, and signalled that they would have a pilot to guide them in, it could be seen that they had been battered, either by storm or war. Their lower sails were tattered and holed, and the foremast of the one had been broken off within a few feet of the deck. Their masthead flags were the Maltese Cross and the haughty symbol of Spain.

They came from a running, day-long fight with the swifter vessels of the Algiers fleet, which had been smaller than they, but had vexed them much, as dogs may trouble a bear. They were glad to be nearing port, for they had taken many shots where the water washes the hull, such as were not easy to plug, and the pumps of the *Santa Martha* were clanking upon the deck.

Angelica stood on the *Santa Anna's* poop in her boy's clothes, and her name was Garcio still; for Ramegas said: "You have done that in which I will have no part, either to hinder or aid. You go now where no women are, and where none should be. And you do this, being pledged, as you know, to the Convent of Holy Cross. It is for Don Manuel to resolve, and I must leave it to him. You have saved his ships at a great peril of life, and he must be grateful for that. But I cannot even guess what he will say.

"I must tell the Grand Master of whom you are, and the whole tale, for I owe my duty to him. Also, if I were silent, and it should be otherwise probed, it might be read in a worse way. But, beyond that, you will be Don Garcio still, having chosen your name, and there being no clothes here of a woman's kind that you could wear if you would.

"Even Francisco I shall not tell. You can do that or not, when you will meet him after you land, but he will hear nothing from me."

Angelica heard this and was well content. She could speak to whom she chose, and at her own time. Ramegas could not prevent this, if he would. While he would know who she was (and the Grand Master as well) she did not doubt she would walk secure.

And, so far, she had had her will, for the Convent of Holy Cross was distant a thousand miles, and she was coming to Malta now.

The harbour which they approached, which was to be called Valletta in later years, was one of the best in the world as far as it was then known. It was deep and large and sheltered from every wind, and it was divided internally in a very curious way. There were, indeed, two harbours, divided by a tongue of land, having the entrances on either side of its point. The entrances were narrow and the harbours widened within. The eastern harbour was in some ways the better, and it was that which the Knights used. But they had built a star-shaped fort, which they had named St. Elmo, on the point of land which separated the two, and while that was held, the western harbour would be useless to any foe. Behind it, the tongue of land rose in a hill of rock that was solid and bare.

It was at the construction of a ravelin to this fort on its western side that the defenders toiled against time, and the Grand Master was overseeing the work. So the pilot said when Ramegas asked where he could be most quickly found.

Learning that, Ramegas decided that he would take a boat, and go straight to the Grand Master to make report, not waiting until the galleys were docked, to which others could give atttention as well as he.

He hailed Francisco to tell him what he intended to do, and saying that he and Captain Antonio would be left in charge of the ships.

He decided to take Angelica with him, for he thought it best that she should be near himself till her status should be agreed, and it was partly of her that he had to make his report.

So the *Santa Anna* lay-to as they came to the harbour mouth, and dropped a boat which pulled for St. Elmo's beach, and the two galleys went on, the *Santa Anna* following in the wake of Francisco's ship.

They passed St. Elmo on their right, with a shore beyond the fort that was straight and steep; but the harbour widened upon the left, where two spurs of land ran out, long and wide, with a deep basin of water between.

At the end of the first of these spurs the castle of St. Angelo stood, where the Order of the Knights of Malta had centred its power. If that should fall, there would be nothing left it would be worth while to save; and while it stood, the Turks could not say that their purpose was won. Behind the castle at the broadening bend of the spur, was the old town known as the Bourg.

The further spur of land on the other side of the basin had been fortified also and had been named the Sanglea, its ridge being crowned by St. Michael's fort, and behind it a new town called Bermola had grown.

All the shipping was now docked or anchored within the basin between these spurs, and since there had been rumour that the Turks would come, the entrance had been secured with an iron chain of a monstrous size. The two ends, at St. Angelo and Sanglea, were secured on platforms of rock, and the chain could be lowered at will for the ships to go out or in.

It was easy to see that, while St. Elmo was held, both harbours would be closed to the attacking fleet; but if it should fall, though they would have gained access to both, and would have made the western one entirely their own, yet the Knights might do well enough, providing that they could hold the two tongues of land, St. Angelo and Sanglea, with the harbour-basin that lay between, and the two little towns behind.

So in the last days, besides setting up the great chain at the harbour-mouth, they had cut deeper the trenches around the Bourg on the landward side, which had not been easy to do, for the whole island was solid rock, and they had added a terreplein to the ramparts on the further side of Sanglea, and had established a three-gun battery outside St. Angelo, down at the water's edge, the use of which would be seen at a later date.

La Valette had not been sparing of toil, and he would not be sparing of blood when the time came. He meant that, while its Knights lived, the flag of Malta should fly, and that, if they must go to God with a tale of failure to tell, they should not fear the condemnation of those who fight the battle of life and faith in a lukewarm way.

And so, having made St. Angelo as safe as he could, he turned to St. Elmo next, seeking to build it so strong that the Turks would break their teeth on that at which they might make the first bite.

CHAPTER X

THE galleys went on to find their safety behind the harbour boom, and Ramegas landed on St. Elmo's shore with Angelica at his side.

He did not have to seek the Grand Master, who had seen his approach, and met him upon the beach. He wore a wide-plumed hat, and a doublet and hose of indigo velvet, dark and rich, and finely cut, but now soiled, and having been torn in places and since stitched, showing the uses to which it had been put in the last days, yet it did not seem that he had been labouring much on this, for his ruff was white and clean, as was the lace at his wrists. But he was not one of those who need care for clothes, having his dignity in himself.

He listened while Ramegas said who he was, and explained that Don Manuel would follow after he had pleaded the Order's cause at the Court of Spain.

La Valette said no more than: "He may be kept there." Few men would ever hear what he thought of Philip of Spain. So far, he had got eight hundred Spanish soldiers, for which he owed Philip little thanks, for they had been stationed in Sicily at the Spanish charge, and transferred to him on condition that the Order should find them pay, with some aid that the Pope gave. Philip, on his parsimonious side, would find means of advantaging his purse, even in a war that was truly his.

But La Valette cared nothing for the character of Philip of Spain, be it bad or good. He had to get what he could (if anything) from him for Malta's aid, and he knew that he would not improve that chance by speaking contempt aloud, which might be repeated by one of Philip's ten thousand spies. He went on:

"They look to be the best ships that we have. It will be a good aid. From their look I should say you have fallen in with the Algiers fleet. But where is the *Flying Hawk?* I trust she has not been lost."

Angelica, looking at the man with a woman's eyes, felt that it might go ill if her fate were to be decided by him. She felt that he could be ruthless, even to the taking of life, and put it out of his mind in a second's time. He was not one whom a woman could wheedle or coax, though she were fairer than the Mother of God. Yet she supposed that he would be just in an austere way.

In fact, he had but one thought. She had seen that a faint warmth, like a winter sunlight, had come into his voice as he said: "It will be a good aid."

Ramegas told the whole tale, with a brevity that the Grand Master approved. He added: "We have little of which to boast, yet we have sunk one of their lighter craft, which became too bold, and came under the full weight of our guns, so that the *Santa Martha* was able to ram it, after its rudder was shot away. And there are others that must run to Tripoli or Algiers to refit before they can vex us here."

"You have done well to break that trap. How were you first warned?"

"It is that to which I must come. It is that we owe to Don Garcio here, as she is called——"

La Valette waked at the name. It was like to that of the Viceroy of Sicily, Garcio of Toledo, who had promised to send his son to Malta, that he might aid in its defence and gain a knowledge of war. It was a gesture of support, having a value beyond that of a single sword. The Grand Master looked keenly at Angelica, who showed no resemblance to the strongly marked and swarthy features of the Castilian knight, and being puzzled by what he saw, he said nothing. He returned his attention to Ramegas, from whom he heard a tale of a different kind. He said to him, not looking at Angelica again:

"You have done well. She being Don Manuel's niece, the matter is domestic to him. He is sufficient to discipline his own house. Until he come, so that she bring no disorder within our walls, she may keep the name and part which she had chosen to bear. Only Oliver must not be misled. I will have true records, or none. Beyond him, none will know, unless you speak of yourselves. It is to Sir Oliver Starkey you should report. He is at St. Angelo now. He would be easy to find, but I will send one with you who will be known at the gate, where the guard are watchful for spies."

He turned to an attendant to whom, being a Piedmontese, he spoke in the Italian tongue, and went back to the scarp of the demi-lune, which he meant to have completed before the Turkish sails should be sighted by those who watched on St. Angelo's tower.

Señor Ramegas took boat again, and they rowed round the head of St. Elmo's point (for it was on the western side, overlooking the Marsa Muscetto, as the western harbour was named, that the new ravelin was being built, so that its entrance might be more surely closed to the Turkish ships) and came into the harbour that was filled with shipping, and gave approach to castle and town, and so landed beneath St. Angelo's walls.

St. Elmo was no more than a fort, or place of gun-platforms and ramparts of stone, where such shelter as its garrison had was contrived rather to save their heads from a dropping shot than to comfort their resting hours. But St. Angelo was a high-walled castle, containing noble chambers which had been cut from the solid rock, appointed as was fitting to the palace of the Grand Master of one of the noblest Orders that the world contained.

Men of many races and diverse tongues might be met at that day in Rome or Venice, in Paris or Cologne, but there was no such variety to be seen in the world's breadth as passed each other on St. Angelo's stairs, or crowded the audience-hall to which the Señors Ramegas and Garcio were now led; for Knights of the Order from all parts of the Christian world had been gathered here by the urgent call that the Grand Master had sent out, some of whom had seen little of Malta and less of each other before they came. The tongues of Provence and Germany, of Italy and Castile, contended with the more frequent Latin, which the most part of the knights could speak, though their diverse accents made it more easy to use than to understand.

But different as they might be in costume, and colour, and tongue, they were alike in the faith they held and the purpose for which they came: alike in that they were all about to be tested in the bitter ordeal of one of the most merciless struggles of East and West that the world had seen, and that the whole world would now pause to watch; as though the fate of Islam and Christianity, the future of three continents, were brought to final decision in that island arena situated so centrally in their midst.

And though they came thus to a test which they would not all equally endure, so that there would be many changes of place and repute in the coming days, and though they walked under a shadow of death from which few would escape to the life of another year, it could be observed that there was among them a confident and very resolute spirit, which might prove itself to be not less than equal to that which it came to meet. It was in such a mood that their predecessors had gathered for the defence of Rhodes forty years before; and though they had failed at last, they had been able to withdraw with safety and all the honours of war, and with the valour of their Order become a boast through the breadth of Europe for what they did. They were resolved that the record of Malta should not be less, and their hope was to make it more.

"You may wait, if you will," the usher said, with the curtness of a worried man who had much to endure. "You can observe how it is. Sir Oliver cannot see all. There are these who are before you."

Señor Ramegas answered with a cold pride, the humility which he kept for Don Manuel and the Grand Master being about all that he had: "If you will inform Sir Oliver Starkey that I am here, I do not see that you have a duty beyond that, nor that you need tender opinion as to whom he will see, nor of what I shall think fitting to do if I should be long delayed in this hall."

The usher, who was born in Auvergne, went without further words, though with some inward curses at Spanish pride, to announce his presence to the Grand Master's secretary, though he did not think it necessary to communicate the result on his return.

Señor Ramegas stood impassive for five inwardly impatient minutes, which gave his companion time to observe the rich paintings on ceiling and walls, and all the luxurious dignity of the hall of waiting, as well as the various groups of its human occupants, before the heavy curtain at the head of the hall was lifted somewhat aside, and a slender man, approaching to middle age, and being plainly but very neatly dressed, stood for a moment glancing over the hall with eyes that observed all, but did not rest on any whom he was not anxious to see.

After a second's pause he came straight to where Ramegas and Angelica stood, moving with a light step, which was quick yet without appearance of haste.

"Señor Ramegas," he said, "as I presume? Malta greets you with thanks for yourself and the aid you bring. I would talk with you at more leisure than some will need. Will you delay, of your courtesy, while I deal with those whose business may be more quickly disposed? It will be but a short while."

He spoke in Spanish, and even with an Andalusian idiom which Ramegas had not expected to hear; for he could talk, as he could correspond, in any language of Europe, and in some that were further away, though he did most in Latin, as was the diplomatic use of that time, in which tongue he had grown even accustomed to think. He spoke quietly, as one who was dealing with ease with whatever work he might have to do. He went back, having placated a man who would have become vexed, and in a short further time the usher bowed with somewhat more respect than before, to say that Sir Oliver was at leisure and would be pleased to see Señor Ramegas, if he would follow the way he led.

Sir Oliver Starkey was at this time of a most high repute throughout the western world, for a learning which could be equalled by few, whether in ancient and modern tongues, or in the sciences of the day. He had held a Commandery of the Order in England till the English king (Henry VIII, now dead) had confiscated it for the Crown's use, and he had come to Malta to take an appointment which scholarship and ability equally fitted him to hold.

He controlled the wide correspondence of an Order which held property in every country in Europe, and had envoys at every Catholic court. In all its affairs outside Malta itself, La Valette had given him an absolute trust and an almost absolute power.

Now he gathered the scattered strength of the Order, both in money and men, and the stores of munitions and food which would be needed for the coming siege.

He worked now, as his custom was, in a room which was narrow and long, being the library of the Order, and having shelves along its one side loaded from floor to ceiling with books that were mainly of theological or historical kinds, with classics in ancient tongues, and some on fortifications, and the art of war both by sea and land. On the other side was a row of windows, narrow and high, that gave a wide view of hills and harbour and of the ocean beyond.

Sir Oliver sat at a wide table which was drawn from wall to window across the narrowness of this room. It was finely carved in dark oak, and its top was inlaid with crimson leather, in which were upholstered also the chairs, ample and soft, of the outer side, in which visitors of consideration were invited to sit.

Behind him, four scribes worked with diligence, on separate tables that were piled with manuscripts and letters and bound books of account, but Sir Oliver's own table was clear.

Sir Oliver rose as his visitors entered, and extended a hand to Señor Ramegas with a formal courtesy, which he had not previously used, and as though he had not seen him before.

He looked at Angelica, as expecting naturally that she would be presented to him, which Ramegas made no motion to do. Ramegas looked at the scribes, who continued their work without appearing to observe those who entered, and said:

"Most of that of which we shall have to speak will be open to all who are in your trust, but there will be one matter which should be private to us alone."

Sir Oliver looked at Angelica again, as though he connected her with this request in an agile mind. She had a feeling that he saw through her disguise, and yet without surprise, and in a way which she could not resent.

"If you will be seated," he said, "you can speak with all privacy here, if you use no Latin; and, beyond that, you should avoid the German and Roumanian tongues."

"I am unlikely," Ramegas replied, "to use those that I do not know, and Latin I will be careful to shun.

"I come to give you account of that which I have brought in Don Manuel's name, and would know first how much you will wish to learn, for I would not talk beyond that which you are willing to hear."

"I would hear all, if I may. I am told that your galleys have come showing the scars of a fight you have had with the Algiers fleet, and that the *Flying Hawk* is a lost ship, which I was sorry to hear.

"Before the close of the day, I will thank your care, if you can let me have tale of the men you have, of whatever rank or degree, with a separate schedule of slaves, and also a record of all stores you have brought to our aid.

"For I have two galleys preparing now, which should sail for Palermo to-morrow, at prime of day, and which I hope to see here returned before the Turks will arrive, and bringing good cargoes of things which we still need; and I may alter the requisition I make when I have seen the succour you have been able to bring."

Sir Oliver did not say that the galleys would have sailed ten days before that, had he not lacked credit or gold sufficient to purchase more than he had already bought, either of powder or food; but he had now heard from the ambassador of the Order at the Papal Court, that Pope Pius IV had given 10,000 crowns as a donation to meet their need, on which he could draw at once, it being in the hands of goldsmiths in Rome; and when he had read that dispatch, he had not let an hour pass before the galleys were warned to be ready to put to sea.

Señor Ramegas replied that there were documents already prepared giving all such detail, which could be in Sir John's hands as soon as he should return to his ship, and could send them up. On his side, he would be glad to know whether, or to what extent, his men must remain aboard, where they were too crowded for comfort or health, as Sir John would know.

Sir Oliver was prepared for that question, and had disposition already made. Some could be lodged at once in the town. Others would have accommodation found with little further delay. It was likely, when the siege would commence, that the galleys would be emptied of men, they not being of any avail against such a fleet as the Turks would be sure to bring. There were, in fact, only five that belonged to the Order, now that the *Flying Hawk* had been lost, so that there would be seven in all, with a flotilla of smaller vessels, which would lie securely behind the great chain, and beneath the protection of the castle guns, their crews being employed ashore.

For Señor Ramegas, when he could leave his ship, and for Don Manuel's nephew, there would be such lodging found as their position required, allowance being made for the crowded state both of castle and town.

After Sir Oliver had said this he looked at Angelica, and added: "But there was more, as I understood, that you had to say, there being nothing private in this for any who are of our part."

Being reminded thus of matters from which the conversation had turned aside, Señor Ramegas narrated the full circumstances of the voyage, including the escapade of Don Manuel's niece, and the part she had afterwards played in bringing warning of the peril into which they were being led.

As this narrative proceeded, Sir Oliver listened with an impassive face, but with an attention that missed no word. It had not gone far before he reached for a quill-pen, and began to make occasional notes, but of a brevity which did not delay what was being said.

When he heard how Angelica had swum from ship to ship in the night, and had climbed the stern of the *Santa Anna*, he spoke for the first time:

"It was bravely done. Malta owes the Señorita her thanks for that deed."

He looked at Angelica in a way at which she felt pleasure and a new pride. For the first time since she had left her home, she saw kindness in a man's eyes when they were turned to herself. But her pleasure had deeper sources than that, for it had been a glance which respected her in a new way.

She had lived a secure, protected life, destined to one of its permanent backwaters, which she was to have entered in the leisured manner which was characteristic of the whole pattern by which she would live and die. She had been surrounded by formidable powers, but, if she left them unchallenged, their terrors were not for her. Such thunders as she might hear would be distant and overhead.

Don Manuel's regard for her was genuine, and may have been deeper than he was aware, but she was to him no other than a pretty affectionate toy, who should accept without criticism or protest his dispositions on her behalf.

She might not doubt that Ramegas also was fond of her in his own way, but she was primarily his master's ward. His duty was to Don Manuel, not to her; and the claims of duty controlled his mind. If he knew what Don Manuel would have him do on her account, her wishes would not turn the scale by a feather's weight.

She had had admiration from the false Rinaldo, and of a kind that she had liked, and which had also been new. "*The potent arms which you now bear.*" She remembered his look as he had said that. She sometimes thought of it in the night. In fact, she thought of him somewhat more than it may have been wisdom to do. For though he had trapped her, and threatened her liberty and honour—which she had no reason to think that he would have scrupled to sell for the best price he could get—yet she had walked into that trap, which had certainly not been set for her; and, be his intentions what they might, he had done her no wrong, and in the end she had trumped his trick. She could afford to look at all that in a generous mood.

Yet his admiration had been of a different quality from that of Sir Oliver. Rather than herself, it had admired the womanhood that was hers; and her instinct told her that such admiration, pleasant though it might be, was consistent with an oriental contempt even of that womanhood to which the roses of its homage were lightly flung.

But Sir Oliver had looked at her with the eyes of a friend.

He turned to Ramegas to ask: "You say the Grand Master has ordered that she shall keep this pretence, which has served its turn?"

"It was to be known to you, but no other, till Don Manuel's pleasure can be enquired."

Angelica did not think that that was exactly what the Grand Master had said; and, whether it were or not, she felt that Sir Oliver did not approve; but, even if she were right about that, it was clear that La Valette's decision would not be questioned aloud by him.

"Unless," he said, "Don Manuel be soon here, the matter may be resolved in a way which cannot be changed at this time."

Angelica, with a somewhat fearful satisfaction, had had the same thought in her mind ever since she had climbed the stern of the *Santa Anna*.

He went on: "We should be glad of all aid, whether of ladies or knights, which is offered by those who are of courage and a good will." He asked her: "Have you any skill in the nursing of wounds?"

"I have been taught much," she said, "after the manner practised among the Moors, but I have done little, not having been where there was need."

"You may alter that, if you remain here. Can you write a fair hand?"

"I can write, though not well, in the Spanish style."

"Señor Ramegas, if you will leave Don Garcio to my care, I

will find lodging suitable and secure, which it might not be easy to do without assistance from me, the town being as it is, and this disguise having to be maintained for some days, if not more."

Ramegas rose at that, taking it as an intimation that the interview was at an end. He said that he would be pleased to leave Angelica in Sir Oliver's care. He went, feeling that he was relieved of a burden he had been sorry to have, and that all would now be done in the best manner till Don Manuel should come.

Sir Oliver looked at Angelica in a contemplative way when he had gone, which did not disturb her ease, for she felt that she had come at last to one who sought only to help.

"We are an Order," he said, "as you know, to which no women belong. But there is no lack in the town."

She did not entirely follow his thought. She said: "I see not why I should continue to wear this garb, which has served the use which it had."

"Yet it has been so resolved. You could not have the lodging which I intend, were it to be known what you are." He added: "You must have many needs. You could have brought little away when you passed from ship to ship as you did." His mind considered the event again. "You did much for Malta, in truth. It should be recorded on our annals, to give you praise. Yet I know not. It might be that which you would not wish to be widely shown. It shall wait for this time."

She observed that, as with her uncle and Ramegas, as with La Valette, it seemed natural to Sir Oliver to suppose that the interests of the Order supplied the dominant impulse from which heroic action would come. Even Francisco had shown something of that inspiration when he had received his command. Candour caused her to say: "Malta owes me less thanks than you are urgent to see. It was not for that cause that I took the great risk which I did. But I thought of my uncle's ships, and of those I knew, who were being drawn to a trap that they did not heed. Also, I saved myself."

She smiled as she said that, thinking that she had motive and troubles enough of her own, and could be excused that those of Malta had been out of her mind. Their eyes met in a laughter of understanding which was common to both, so that they were better friends than before.

"That," he said, "may all be as you will; yet it was a brave deed, such as many would not have tried, whether of women or men. I should not have done so myself, as I suppose; or, if I had, I should surely have failed."

"You think it was more than it was, for I am practised to swim."

She had risen the while they talked, and as he looked at her he said: "You will need a sword."

She laughed again. "It is useless to me. I have learnt that."

"Well," he said, "I am not of much avail with one myself. Yet one you must have; for if your belt be empty, as it now is, it will draw eyes which should pass you by."

The four scribes had continued their work during this time, not lifting their eyes, nor regarding what might go on, which it was not their business to do. Now Sir Oliver spoke to one in his own tongue, who, after he had listened and replied two or three times, rose and left the apartment by a door at its farther end.

"There is a chamber," Sir Oliver said, when he had gone, "where you may find more than you would be likely to hope; but I will ask, of courtesy not of right, that you make no mention to any if it should appear that a woman may have used it before."

He gave no more explanation than that, and went on to ask: "Do you lack gold? For there must be things you will need, which can be bought in the town."

She said no, she was not lacking in coin.

"Then, if you will be guided by me, you will tell Olrig, on his return, if you can talk in the Latin tongue, or permit me to do so on your behalf, how you have swum from a corsair's ship and have nothing, even of change of linen, such as one of your rank must need, and instruct him to procure all, which he will be glad to do at my word."

As he spoke, Olrig returned, and having received these instructions in a tongue which was foreign to Angelica, and she having given him a sum of money which Sir Oliver advised, he was next instructed to conduct Señor Garcia to the chamber, the keys of which Sir Oliver had previously sent him to fetch.

A short corridor led to a winding stair of stone which, after several doors had been passed, ascended to one which Olrig opened with the two keys he bore.

Angelica, observing that the room had been double-locked, may be excused, after her experiences of the last few days, if she had a moment's thought that she was being led to nothing better than an altered form of imprisonment, but her memory of Sir Oliver rebuked the doubt, the appearance of the interior of the chamber was reassuring, and any lingering apprehension ceased as Olrig laid the keys down for her own disposal and withdrew with a polite ntimation, which she imperfectly understood (it being in the Latin tongue) that His Excellency desired that Señor Garcio should regard the contents of the chamber as being entirely at his own disposal.

Angelica looked round, and was puzzled but well-content. Her privacy was, at least, her own; for in addition to the keys which she now controlled, she observed that the door, itself of stout and iron-bound oak, was furnished with two long and heavy bolts which could be dropped into sockets in the stone paving of the floor.

Apart from that, it was a woman's room, and one of a soft and luxurious kind, very different from the dignified simplicity of her own apartment in her uncle's castle. And it was not merely a room which was intended for feminine use, it was one which a woman had recently and (it seemed) abruptly left. Her most intimate possessions, even articles in daily use, were scattered about, as though they represented a recent toilet, nor was there any depth of dust upon them, such as would indicate that they had lain undisturbed for more than a few days at the most.

So, in fact, it had been. The Knights of St. John were a celibate religious order, and the upper chambers of the castle of St. Angelo were among the last places where a woman should have been expected to be. But the vows of celibacy, which were founded at least as much on the policy of protecting the property of the Order from private inheritance as monastic ideal, had been variously and sometimes loosely interpreted by the Commanders of the Order during succeeding centuries, and while the character of the Order had gradually changed from that of ministrants to sick and indigent pilgrims in Palestine to that of ruthless warriors who opposed their own lives as a bulwark of Christendom against the advance of the pagan power, yet it had kept itself comparatively, though not absolutely, free from the luxurious corruptions which had contributed, like an internal cancer, to the destruction of the Order of the Knights Templars, which had once been its rival in power and wealth and valour and equal in devotion to the Christian cause.

The present Grand Master, who had held office only since 1557, was known to be of a stern integrity in his interpretation of the Order's vows. But he had not been able to eradicate all the weaknesses of human nature, nor the results of the more tolerant methods of his predecessors, among the Knights he ruled. Inflexible in discipline in regard to all that came under his notice, there may still have been matters which he thought it inexpedient to go out of his way to see. There must have been many things that he did not know.

When the threat of Turkish invasion required that Malta should be organized and stript for the stark business of war, there must have been many who scurried away, either from fear of the event itself, or of consequence to themselves which the disclosure of their presence would bring, as insects run from beneath a suddenly lifted stone.

There were women, more than a few, who had found residence in the town (and one, it appeared, some use of the apartment which had been allotted to Commander La Cerda), who had made hurried departures on their own volitions, or with the impetus of hints of humiliation, if not of actual chastisement, should they further delay.

What had occasioned the sudden vacation of the chamber which he had now allocated to Angelica's use, was best known to Sir Oliver, who, while he would have concealed nothing had he been asked by the Grand Master, had yet thought it beyond his duty, or an abstract wisdom, to divert La Valette from more important considerations with a tale which would at least have incensed him further against La Cerda, who had already incurred his disapprobation from a separate cause.

It seemed enough to Sir Oliver, amid a hundred superior urgencies, that he had secured that that chamber should be so abruptly vacated, and it was now by a very fortunate chance that he was able to allot it to such an occupant that its contents would seem natural, when (as he supposed) the secret of Don Garcio's sex would be honourably revealed. He may, amid the pressure of more important things, have found a moment to congratulate himself on the prudence that had kept it locked since its previous denizen had departed, and so avoided the wider scandal which would have followed its investigation.

Be that as it may, it was for Angelica a very fortunate chance. She found herself securely and comfortably lodged; and as Sir Oliver Starkey offered to utilize her services in such clerical work as she could undertake for himself in the moment's emergency, she had occupation which may have been more useful in diverting attention from herself than important in its assistance to him.

She was content, from day to day, to sit in Sir Oliver's room, using a copyist's pen, and observing the hundred persons and activities of which he was the controlling centre, and only shadowed by the doubt of what would happen when Don Manuel should arrive and learn how his wishes had been disregarded and his authority defied.

But the days passed, and Don Manuel did not come; and on the 18th of May, as she sat at her table in Sir Oliver's room, there came, from the castle-roof over her head, the deep boom of a single gun. It came again—and again. A moment later, a gun from St. Elmo's battery answered in the same way. Men listened, and lost a breath. It was the signal that the Turkish fleet had been sighted from St. Angelo's tower.

CHAPTER XI

Angelica heard the gun, the signal of fate and death, and the fear that she might be compelled to return to seek the seclusion of Holy Cross faded finally from her mind. Whether or not Don Manuel would succeed in joining his brethren before the investment would be complete, she supposed that he would not wish her to take the risks of leaving, even were a suitable escort available, now that the Turkish fleet had actually arrived. For good or evil, for joy or sorrow, it seemed that she would be there till the siege should end in a day of triumph, or in such a way that she could hope for no better fate than that of a Turkish slave.

Yet, for the next two days after the sound of that warning gun, it seemed that there was no change at all. The Turks did not appear at the harbour-mouth; the Knights toiled at the completion of their defences neither more nor less than they had done before. Angelica remembered the sense that she had had of being forgotten and pushed aside when the news had first been brought to Aldea Bella, and wondered if her position would be very different now.

In the last fortnight she had seen Juan Ramegas once, when he had called upon Sir Oliver, though he had not spoken to her. She had not seen Francisco at all. She knew that, though the great galleys in which they had come were now laid up and moored under the protection of the castle guns, he had been given command of one of the smaller and swifter Maltese galliots, similar to the *Flying Hawk*, which still put to sea, patrolling the Sicilian route by which supplies and recruits would continue to reach the island until the investment should be complete.

Even when she had ventured at times into the narrow, climbing, stone-paved streets of the town no one had spoken or looked at her with curious eyes. There was so much of strangeness in the far-gathered crowd that nothing was strange at all.

And on the afternoon after the cannon had sounded that threefold warning note, she sat copying a schedule which Sir Oliver Starkey had been altering from day to day as new recruits had come in, and which he had now put into final form, to remain as his careful record of the forces with which the Christian nations of Europe were content, after many weeks of warning, that the Knights of Malta should face the full weight of the Turkish power.

It was a schedule which concerned itself less with differences of race than of language, of which three were spoken in France and two in Spain at that time. It began with a list of those of the Order itself, distinguishing between those who were "Knights of Justice"—that is, in their own right, having that rank, apart from the Order, in their own lands—and the serving-brothers, such as Ramegas, who were of a second rank. This is the list she wrote:

	Knights	*Esquires*
Provence	61	15
Auvergne	25	14
France	57	24
Italy	164	5
Aragon	85	2
England	1	0
Germany	13	1
Castile	68	6
	474	67
		474
		541
Hired Spanish troops		800
Garrison troops of St. Angelo		90
Ditto of St. Elmo		60
Grand Master's household and guard		150
Artillerymen		120
Crews of galleys still in commission		700
Volunteers from Sicily, Italy, Genoa, Piedmont and other countries		875
Total of Regular Troops		3336
Add Militia enrolled:		
From the Bourg	500	
„ Burmola & Sanglea	300	
„ the rest of the island	4560	5360
		8696

"The militia" were the whole male population of Malta, who were of sufficient vigour to lift a sword, and their fighting value only the test could prove.

The Turkish fleet, consisting of one hundred and thirty-nine oared galleys and about fifty sailing vessels of various other designations, after cruising for some time round the southern coast of the island, selected the Marsa Scirocco, a wide bay at the south-eastern corner of the island, and landed there, and in the Marsa Scala and St. Thomas's Bay, without opposition, an army of 29,000 men, which was intended to attack St. Angelo on the land side, while the fleet bombarded it from the sea. The Algerian fleet was still to come.

A Council which the Grand Master had called a few days earlier had made a decision, in which his own view had overridden that of other equally experienced soldiers, and on which the course of subsequent events must have radically depended.

The old town of Citta Notabile, in the centre of the island, with its decrepit castle and almost defenceless walls, was not to be abandoned, neither was the Maltese militia to be concentrated within or around the defences of St. Angelo. St. Angelo was to depend upon its own garrison: the bulk of the Maltese militia was to remain at large upon the island. If the whole force of the Turkish attack should be directed upon Citta Notabile the militia must defend it as best they could; if upon St. Angelo, they should vex the rear of the infidels to the extent of their power.

The Turkish army, landing as it did on the south-eastern side of the island, therefore found itself opposed by no organized force capable of engaging it upon the field of battle, neither did it survey an abandoned territory from which the inhabitants had been withdrawn; but it was surrounded by the watchful, lurking hostility of the island militia. It raided inland in a great force, and saw no sign of human life and little of human occupation: it ventured small parties, seeking information or plunder or the filling of water-casks, and they did not return.

It wasted the country around its encampment and gained little, for the land was stony and poor. The goat-herds had driven their flocks to the remoter hills. The imported Sicilian draught-oxen—which had become numerous since the arrival of the Knights had resulted in much additional building throughout the island—were hidden or removed from before the advance of the marauding forces; but of these a sufficient number were captured to ensure the transportation of baggage and, in particular, of the heavy artillery, when the army should be ready to advance either to the attack of St. Angelo or to occupy the interior of the island.

Such was the position when Piali, the admiral of the Turkish fleet, came ashore from his galley to attend a Council of War which Mustapha had called that they might agree upon a plan of action in which the sea and land forces would co-operate for the defeat of the common foe.

Piali was a man of uncertain nationality and nameless birth, brought to the position he now held by the caprice of fortune and the Soldan's whim. Thirty years before Soliman the Magnificent, riding over a victorious Hungarian battle-field, had reined his horse to avoid a living babe that was crawling among the slain.

The Soldan looked down and was met by the black eyes of a child who looked boldly and curiously up at the splendid vision above him.

"Let the child live," Soliman said. "Pick him up."

He ordered that Piali should be reared with his own household. When he was grown, he gave him one of his own granddaughters for a wife.

Having no nationality of his own, Piali may have done well to take to the sea. With the Sultan's favour, he rose rapidly to the high position he now held. He was not of the disposition of those who may not hear the summons if fortune should try the door. He fought his ships in the same way.

His body, most probably born from hardship and poverty, had grown to an almost giant coarseness and strength amid the softer surroundings of the Sultan's court. It showed signs already that it would become gross if he should live toward middle age. But now it was impelled by an abundant vitality.

His manner was arrogant and over-bearing. He was impatient of opposition. He came to meet Mustapha knowing his own mind, which he would be certain to speak. He was without subtlety, and might have said that he had no occasion for the practice of guile.

Mustapha was a man of different breed. He stroked the white beard of age, and though his step was still vigorous, and his eye bright, he looked more fit for the Council Chamber than the rough hazards of war. Craft and lies were the familiar weapons by which he had guarded himself through the perils of many years, and come to the lordship of Egypt which he now held. To speak his thoughts would have seemed to him no better than the act of a clumsy fool. He had the reputation of being a very fortunate and able leader of men, cautious, and yet prompt and bold to take advantage of any favourable chance. He was the most popular general in the Turkish empire, it being said that he counted the lives of his men as a miser will tale his gold, and that he would not send them rashly to death for a doubtful gain. It was he, forty years before, under Soliman's orders, who had captured Rhodes from the Knights. If he had shown reluctance to undertake this new command, and expressed doubts of its success, it did not follow that he would not be resolute to prosecute it, nor inwardly sanguine of its results. He had merely taken the precaution of being able to say afterwards, if it should fail, that it had been against his own judgment, and only undertaken in loyalty to his imperial master's will. If he should intend to meet Piali's plans with the same subtlety of precaution, he would have an opponent who would be very unlikely to perceive or avoid the trap.

The Council consisted of about a dozen of the principal military and naval commanders, but the discussion which ensued was between Mustapha and Piali only, to which the others listened in a rarely broken silence. To Mustapha, their importance lay in the fact that they might be after-witnesses of the things he said.

They sat in a circle, cross-legged on the rich softness of a carpet spread over the open ground, and a strong guard was stationed round them, but out of hearing, to make the privacy of the discussion more certain than would be possible in pavilion walls. They spoke between intervals, during which they smoked in an impressive silence. Even Piali knew that, if he should appear to speak without pauses of thought, he would lose the respect and confidence of those who heard.

"It would seem," Mustapha began, "that there are two courses between which we must make a choice. We may proceed first to make the island our own, which it can have no force to resist, outside the strong forts where the Knights have centred their power; or we can proceed at once to invest them there, both by land and sea, taking no account at the first of those who are loose in other parts of the isle, except that we must slay such as molest our rear."

"There is a thing," Piali replied, "which we must heed before either of those. I must have a harbour where I can lodge my fleet."

"Have you not harbours enough?" Mustapha inquired.

"I have none where I should be secure from a seaward foe."

"Where do you seek to be?"

"There is a fort at St. Elmo's point, which is of so small a size that it does not hold more than three score of men. If we destroy that, we have safe entrance to the best harbour there is, with a mouth of no greater breadth than we can secure by strong batteries on both sides, so that we can lie there without fear, or sally forth as we will."

Mustapha considered this in a silent gravity before he asked again: "Are you secure from the winds as you now are?"

"I am well enough from the winds, there being choice of anchorage in more places than one. I am thinking of seaward foes."

"Of whom we have word of none?"

"Of whom we may hear when it will be too late to gain the safety I seek. We may have all Christendom on our heads at a near day."

Mustapha was silent again. It was a risk which he thought small. He knew too much of the jealousies and divisions of the Christian powers to expect any concerted action from them—and if it came he thought it would be by a slow way, of which they would have warning enough. It was unlikely—but it was a possible thing, and if the Turkish fleet were to be forced to fight because it had no secure harbour in which to lie, and then, if it should have the worse, destroyed because it had no safe harbour to which to retreat, he did not intend that he should be blamed therefor.

"Are you assured," he asked, "that St. Elmo can be taken with speed, and at a light cost?"

"It can be taken with speed, and at a cost which will not be too high for the gain it brings."

Mustapha did not dissent. He smoked in silence again.

"I would," he said at length, "that Dragut were here."

"And so," Piali said, "he should be."

Mustapha did not feel moved to deny that. He said: "He should be here any day now. You know the charge that we have."

Piali was silenced in turn, and with less of deliberate choice. When he spoke it was to argue with no change of will but somewhat less arrogance than before.

"That was meant for the conduct of the main attack, as I think. We are not meant to sit still, doing nought while our foes thrive, because Dragut is slow to come. Suppose he should not come for a long time? Are we to waste all the strength we have? This is such a thing as may be well done to make ready for when he shall be here."

The firman that Soliman had given appointed Mustapha to the chief command, but it left Piali in control of the sea-forces, after he had put the army ashore. It directed both to await the arrival of Dragut, the Viceroy of the Barbary coast, and to take no decisive action without seeking counsel with him.

Mustapha, at least, saw clearly why that instruction had been given. Piali might be a bold seaman, and one whom the Sultan loved, but Soliman could not think him to be an equal admiral to the Algerian corsair, who, when he was not drunk with rum, to the scandal of all True Believers of stricter habits, had a genius for naval warfare which had done far more than could be credited to any other single commander during the past thirty years to convert the Mediterranean to a Moslem lake. Boastful, truculent, quarrelsome, drunken he might be; but his name was such that his mere presence at a naval battle was enough to give assurance of victory to his friends and dishearten his boldest foes.

"I am an old man," Mustapha said, "somewhat stricken in years, and the blood runs coldly in aged veins. I will not shrink to confess that I might have so interpreted the instructions we have received that I should have delayed to choose the place of our first assault until we had Dragut here, to join his counsel to ours.

"I might also have been too simple to doubt that the great fleet you have would be sufficient to hold these seas, even without that of Algiers, which cannot be far from our aid, until such time as we shall have resolved the siege and you can anchor in what harbour you will."

"Do you say that my fleet should be equal to face the whole Christian power, which may be stirred by this assault on an Order which is derived from all their nations alike, and that I should be careless to do that with no harbour to which I could retire at a great need?"

"I should not say that. I say you have less to fear, for they are in division amongst themselves. The English queen (whose ships are the most spiteful of all) will be content that we vex her foes. The Baltic League will not send the worst ships they have; they will not sell a spar, as I think, nor a coil of rope (unless they first have the value paid), to give an Order support which owns the headship of Rome, with whom they have more bitter and nearer feud than can be their hatred of us, for it is not here that their trade lies. We have Spain to fear, but her King is cautious and slow. He has nearer foes, and his fleet must guard the far land where he gets his gold. He will not weaken his power there for this barren isle. He will send many words and, it may be, a few men."

"Then what," Piali asked, "would you do?"

"I have not said you are wrong. I have but said that the old are inclined to the surer way.

"I had thought that the island could be overrun in a short time. There are but scattered houses of no defence, and a town in the midst with such walls, so it is said, as our batteries would lay flat. There would be great slaughter, or taking of slaves in a full net.

Also, there would be plunder of sorts, though it is a poor land, and unlike to Rhodes, from which we sent many galleys laden with spoil even while that war was not won.

"Or if the people who are now scattered over the land should flee to St. Angelo's walls and we not be able to cut them off, as it is like that many would do, whether by the hills or along the coast, I suppose that the Knights would gain little by that. They may have men enough for the walls they defend. They must all drink, it is said, from cisterns which the rains fill. They have store-houses of corn which are well stocked, as our spies say, yet they must count to a time when they will come to the end and may not welcome that they will have more to feed.

"They may look to hold out till there will arrive strong aid from Europe at last. I do not say you are wrong in that. They may count the days. Have you thought that they may have built St. Elmo to that very end, that we may waste our own days on assault of such a fort as may fall and leave them little worse than they were before?"

"Have you thought," Piali replied, his wits being alert enough in a simple way, "that they may have left the Maltese loose for the same end, that we may chase them from shore to shore, while we gain naught that will avail us at last, and the days go by?"

Mustapha, who had thought of that, among many more difficult things, did not count it worth while to give a direct reply.

"I can see plainly," he said, "that you are bent on your own plan, and though I may have some doubt of what our lord would have had us do before Dragut come, yet I know well that there must be common purpose and good accord between two leaders placed as we now are. It may be that I am somewhat old and not swift to resolve in a bold way. If this fort be so easy to take, as you say it is, you shall have the harbour you will.

"We will survey it to-morrow morn, both by land and sea, that we may combine in such assault as you judge best."

The conference broke up at that word, leaving them both content, though there was little between them either of trust or goodwill; for Mustapha, who saw the advantage, if not the necessity, of capturing St. Elmo as clearly as Piali, but was less confident of an easy success, was satisfied that, if it should fail, the doubts he had uttered would be recalled to the minds of all who had heard, and it would be said that his wisdom had been overridden by the impetuous folly of the younger man. He saw also that, if the attack were to be commenced at that point, it could not be too sudden and swift, and though he had insured himself from the first against the worst penalties of failure, by declining to advocate that the siege should be attempted at all, and by appearing to excuse himself from accepting the chief command, so that Soliman had to thrust it upon him, yet it did not follow that, having so undertaken, he was not resolved to bring it to a successful end, and confident that he would not fail.

As for Piali, so that he had his own way, he was careless of how it came.

"The old rascal," he said to his captains as they walked back to their waiting boats, "would wander over the island till the summer is done, and at the end he would have slaughtered some peasants, and as many goats as would feed his host for two days, or perhaps three.

"He would go back boasting of what he had done, and saying that he had seen that St. Angelo was too strong to take by assault, and that he had spared the lives of his men, as though there were any merit in that. What, in Allah's name, are their lives for?

"But in war you must ever strike at a vital spot, and it is never too costly to win. St. Elmo is but a small fort. We will have it down in two days, and you will enter a harbour where you can lie without fear, though all the fleets of Christendom were cannonading without."

His captains made no answer to that, for the idea was pleasing enough; and they had learned that he was one who loved the sound of his own voice much more than to listen to theirs.

CHAPTER XII

THE same morning that the Turkish Council of War was held Francisco stood on the poop of the *Curse of Islam* (that being the name of the galliot of which he had been given command) which was patrolling about half a mile to the north of St. Elmo's point.

The *Curse of Islam* was built in the style of the *Flying Hawk*, and was as swift but much smaller than she. It had but one mast, and was of light draught so that it could enter inlets and shallow bays without fear that it could be followed by larger ships. Small as it was, it had fourteen oars on each side, for it was in speed that its use alike with its safety lay, whether it were hunting Turkish merchant vessels that it could plunder and sink, or running from their fighting ships that it would be too weak to endure.

Now it tacked against a light north-east wind, so that it might keep out from the shore. Its oars were in, and it moved lazily over a quiet sea, as though it drowsed in the heat of the sunny noon; but it was watchful on every side, that it might be ready to aid its friends or to avoid being cut off from the land if Turkish galleys should approach by a coastward way.

For though Piali had anchored the larger part of his fleet in the Marsa Scirocco and in St. Thomas's Bay, he had spread a swarm of his smaller galleys and other vessels around the islands, so that it might be said that the whole Maltese group were already invested in a loose way. He had over one hundred and eighty ships of all sizes under his control, with crews of more than nine thousand men, and now that they had landed the army and stores they brought, they were light and lean, and very hungry for prey.

Nor did they fish in an empty sea, for there were still Knights of the Order and volunteers of various ranks arriving in Sicily to assist the defence, and the Sicilian coast not being much more than sixty miles distant, and the Maltese boatmen bold and knowing shallows and currents, and often making the night their friend, were still bringing them across, and would continue to do so for several weeks, each side becoming more expert to chase or avoid their foes.

In these first days it was a game of death which was played on both sides in a clumsy, beginner's way, but Turkish galliots of the lighter kind were lurking in many of the inlets around the coast, ready to sally out on a careless prey, or for their guns to do mischief to any who should approach from the landward side.

The *Curse of Islam* put her bow into the wind, and began to glide again on the starboard tack through the peace of the summer sea, when there came a noise of guns from the north-west, and not, as it seemed to those who listened, at a great distance away, though they could see nothing, the coast in that part being hidden beyond the point of St. George's Bay, nor could they be sure whether the firing came from the land or the sea.

But Francisco did not wait to listen a second time. He felt as one who had ranged the woods for three days without sight or sound of the prey he sought, though he knew that every moment might see it leap from the thicket, and that it was round him on every side. The *Curse of Islam* shook out her wings. Her oars flashed overside, and she leapt, as they smote the foam, like an unleashed dog.

Francisco went forward to see that the guns on the forward deck would be ready, and Captain Antonio stood at his side He had no duty there. He had come as a volunteer, rather than be idle on land. He watched Francisco with a critical eye. He listened to the sound of guns that became louder as the seconds passed. He had discretion enough to keep a shut mouth, and had his reward when Francisco asked: "Now what would you take it to be?"

"I should opine," Captain Antonio replied, "that the craft are small and are propelled by oars, for they approach fast, and that without favour of wind.

"They carry no cannon on either side and cannot be further distance apart than can be crossed by an arquebus ball, for it is that weapon which we have heard.

"You will have noticed that there were five shots, or it may be six, almost as one, and then after a pause that was somewhat long, there was such a chorus of shots again. I suppose that to mean that the pursuers rest oars at times, that the arquebusiers may not be spoilt in their aim by a lifting prow.

"It is most like that we shall be friendly to those who flee, but, be that as it may, it is a game that we shall decide, for we shall meet them, as I think, almost bow to bow as we are rounding the cape."

"I have no doubt," Francisco said, "you have guessed well." But as he spoke, there came the deep boom of a heavy gun, and another thereafter, showing that, if the guess were good, it had not come to the end of the tale.

Yet, as far as it went, it had been good enough, for as they rounded the cape they came in sight of a half-decked boat that fled before one about twice as large as itself, which had a single mast and a spread of sail that was of little aid, the wind blowing as it did. But behind these there were three galliots coming up, showing the black flag with the green turban thereon and the golden scimitar gleaming below, which was the battle-ensign of the Turkish navy at that time, these symbols being as near to the portrayal of a created thing as the second commandment of Moses would allow a Moslem to go.

The fleeing boat, depending on the strength of its oars alone, had crept over during the night and the earlier day from the Sicilian shore, aiming to make a landing in St. Paul's Bay, where it was thought that, as yet, no Turks would be likely to be. It was manned by six Maltese oarsmen who did not row with their backs to the bow, as is the more common style, but stood upright, looking ahead, and pushed rather than pulled the boat with the full weight of their bodies on every stroke. Don Manuel and his two servants sat in the stern, and there was a Maltese seaman who steered, making ten in all. The boat was flat-bottomed and shallow of draught, being adapted for coastal work rather than open stretches of sea, though the hardy Maltese boatmen would often use such craft for crossing to Sicily when the winds were kind.

It had come without incident, or sight of more than a distant sail, till it had rounded the curve of St. Paul's Bay, where they had thought to run into a cove which had an easy beach for the boat, and thence make cautious way overland toward St. Angelo, avoiding any advance of the Turkish army, which would have been easy to do among hills where all men were their friends, either to guide or warn.

But as they came to the full sight of the bay, they saw that at which their oars paused in a sudden fear, so that there was a moment when the boat drifted on at its own will.

"Back, men, back," an old seaman called, who was the owner of the boat, and who pushed on one of the bow oars, with his son at his side. But even as the oars were lifted to strike the water again, he altered his word: "It is too late. We are seen. There is no hope but ahead. Push, men, or our lives will pay."

What they had seen was no less than half a dozen Turkish ships of the smaller kinds that had made resort of that bay, and were anchored, more or less, at its upper end. They were not all alert to make chase, some of their men being ashore. They were, in fact, seeking water, of which there was here a little stream entering the sea, which was worth regard in an island where springs were few and most men drank that which had been stored in cisterns after the rain.

Being in a land of foes they had sent a strong party ashore, with the water-casks that they sought to fill, and the two largest galliots had trained their guns to command the beach.

The boatmen felt as a rat might do on finding itself in the very kennel of some careless dog, which stretches and yawns and has no thought of a prey. It will dart back, if it can, before its coming has been observed.

But as the seamen paused in that first panic of doubt they knew that they were too late to draw back, for they had been already seen by the watch on the nearest ship. There was an outbreak of cries. Being perceived, there was no hope in retreat. Their safety lay, as they thought, as far off as within the range of St. Elmo's guns. To reach them, they must pull across the front of St. Paul's Bay, in full sight of their foes, and then continue along the coast, keeping ahead if they could.

The boatmen pressed on the oars, while the corsair vessel that was nearest, and had first called the alarm, showed that it would soon be in hot pursuit.

Its sail rose to the wind: its oars came overside: its anchor cable was cut.

Its sail might be little use, with the wind blowing the way it did, but its oars were nearly twice the number of those on the Maltese boat, and each was pulled by two men. Against that, its size was much more, but it was built for speed, which the Maltese boat was not. The Turks looked for an easy prey.

Don Manuel sat in the stern. He was clothed in steel and his sword lay across his knees. He said nothing, watching the pursuit with a sombre and haughty gaze that held some hatred, and some contempt, but no fear.

He could see that it was an unequal chase and that the Turkish vessel might almost reach to cross their bows before they could have a straight course ahead. Yet they must converge as they did, for if they should steer a course which would take them more out to sea, they would be further at last from the land where their safety lay. The Turks came fast. They were eager and fresh. The Maltese had been rowing for many hours. But life is a great stake. They were inured to the work they did. Their strength was neither wasted nor spared. The oars moved as one. When they crossed the corsair's bows they were still some hundreds of yards apart.

As they did so the Turks lay on their oars, steadying their deck that the arquebusiers might take a good aim. The arquebus was a heavy weapon, clumsy and slow. It was like a cannon for the use of a single man. When he had loaded it, he must set up a tripod on which he could rest it while he was taking aim. A slow-match would ignite its powder at last. There would be noise, if no more. The lighter, deadlier musket was still to come.

Now a volley came too low, or fell short. Looking back, Don Manuel saw the water spurt upward where it was struck by the heavy balls. His expression altered to that of a somewhat greater contempt than before. He thought that if they would stop often enough for that foolish firework display there might be a good chance of escape, which he had not greatly hoped until then.

He was of a generation which had been reluctant to admit the power of the new weapons or that they had ended the reign of steel. At that time a knight's age might be fairly guessed by the amount of armour he wore.

The Turkish vessel came on again, and though the boatmen strove with their utmost strength, the distance steadily shortened between them. The corsairs had seen the steel-clad form in the stern, and they toiled now for a prize of worth. The Knights of Malta were almost always men of rank and wealth in their own lands, and their ransoms were fixed at rates which were equally high.

Now the corsair's oars lifted again. It steadied somewhat as it lost speed, and the arquebuses were levelled a second time. But now the volley did not fall short: a ball glanced off one of Don Manuel's ailettes and splintered the gunwale of the boat. He stretched out a jarred arm with the satisfaction of finding it would still be equal to using a sword, and observed at that same instant that one of the foremost oarsmen had fallen forward. As he did so, the old man at his side also abandoned his oar and stooped over to lift him up.

Don Manuel rose in a quick wrath. "Boniface," he called, "is this a time to regard the dead? I have seen you in bygone days when a bullet——"

"But not through a son's heart."

"Even so, he has gone the sooner to God. We have our duties who still live. You must let him lie."

Don Manuel's voice was kindly but stern. It was, indeed, evident that it was no time to grieve for the dead, which would be to involve all in the common end. As he spoke he took the steersman's place, so that he could go forward to the oar of the dying man, whose father resumed his labour.

There was urgent need now, for the boat had lost speed in this momentary confusion, which more than offset the delay caused to their pursuers when the rowers paused for the arquebusiers to fire

Flight would have become hopeless, but for the fact that they now approached a place of shallows and outlying rocks, where they were able to take advantage of a narrow channel through which the corsair's vessel could not venture to follow but must take a course further out to sea, by which it lost half a mile, if not more.

With this timely assistance the chase was repeated on the same lines as before, with the pursuers further behind but closing more rapidly upon the Maltese craft, for the boatmen were finding it beyond human capacity to maintain the exertions with which they began their flight. And at the same time, as though to destroy the last faint hope of escape in despairing hearts, another of the Turkish galleys, a much larger vessel which had stood further out to sea, was now coming up rapidly behind, and opened fire with two of its forward guns on the fleeing boat.

They were not struck at this time, though a plunging ball, dividing the waves, passed them so closely that they were drenched by its scattered spray. And as they became aware of this fresh menace they became conscious also of a hope, which induced Don Manuel to urge them to renewed exertions.

"Push hard," he exclaimed, "there is help ahead."

For at the end of the spur of land which formed the eastern side of the cape which still hid them from the *Curse of Islam* and deprived them of knowledge of that approaching support, there was a group of Maltese soldiers who watched the chase, and in their midst a battery of two mortars which had been placed there by the Knights to defend the point. These mortars were clumsy weapons, even by the standards of that time, but capable of taking a heavy charge, being of stone and hollowed out of the solid rock. They were loaded with liberal charges of powder, and wooden tompions were then laid over their mouths, on which would be piled an assortment of cannon-balls, stones, and bars and fragments of iron. They were discharged by means of slow-matches, such as would allow time, after their ignition, for their crews to retreat to safety. Their fire could not be accurate nor their range great, as they threw their missiles high into the air, from which they would descend with a force which might not only bring death and wounds to those unable to avoid it on narrow, unsheltered decks, but might well prove sufficient to sink vessels of considerable size.

It was evident that the drama of flight and death was now nearing its climax, and that climax may be taken, alike in its incidence and in the ruthless spirit which inspired its antagonists, as symbolic of the arger struggle which was to come.

The boatmen, with a renewed vigour of hope, which became a mere desperation should they look back at the nearness of the pursuit, rowed straight for the protection of the battery.

The Turkish corsair saw the menace of those loaded mortars, but, like a hawk too intent upon an almost captured prey to heed that it is chasing it to the very foot of a man whom it would otherwise have avoided in terror, could not resolve to leave a capture so nearly made.

"They dare not fire," the Turkish captain exclaimed, "for we are too close to their friends. They could not direct their discharge so that it could descend on one ship, and not both; and those of their part might take the more hurt, their boat being weaker than ours."

"If they follow to within the range," the captain of the battery said, "and we see that our friends cannot escape, we must not scruple to fire, for it is much better that all should sink than that the Turks should sail safely off, having taken their prey."

"Boniface," Don Manuel called from the stern, "if they lay us aboard, I must charge you to send a pistol-shot through that case in the bows where our powder lies, for we shall go to God by a clean road, and not as having been first mauled by these infidel dogs."

"So I will," the old man answered. "So I will at the last need. But you will pardon me if I delay until then, for life is dear to us all."

"You may delay till then, but be sure at the last, if the need come; for if they will not lay off the chase we shall find the land too distant to gain."

And then, as though to mock them with a second mirage of rescue, too distant for real avail, the *Curse of Islam* appeared round the head of the cape, coming on at a great pace, for it could make more use of the wind, and as they approached one another, though not in a direct line, it had the effect of advancing even faster than it actually did.

It was yet too distant for Francisco to see whom the boat held, but the meaning of all was too clear to misunderstand. He gave an instant order that they should steer straight to the rescue of the Maltese boat, but to train their guns upon the galley that came up further behind, it being a clear mark, with no danger that a shot would go where they would not wish.

So they fired, though at a long range, and their coming cannot be said to have been without result, for the galley, seeing the *Curse of Islam* approach in so bold a way, supposed her to be no more than the first of a Christian squadron which might appear at the next minute around the headland, and so put her helm up, and made off, signalling to her consorts who were further away that they should do the like.

But as though the guns of the *Curse of Islam* had been the overture for a concert of hell, the next moment was loud with thunder, and livid with flame.

Don Manuel had seen that the Turkish vessel was close behind. Her commander had called for a supreme effort from the oarsmen, and whether willing or under threat of the lash, they pulled so that the ship leapt ahead, and this time it was distanced by no answering spurt, for the Maltese rowers could do no more.

Don Manuel saw the prow of the approaching vessel almost over his head. He rose up from the useless rudder. He shouted to Boniface that the time to fire the powder had come; and then, with his bare sword in his hand, and forgetting he was somewhat stiff with the passing of years, he reached up to the bowsprit above his head and swung himself on to the corsair's deck.

It was a moment before that, that the captain of the battery had realized that the Maltese boatmen were doomed, and that only vengeance remained. There was no mercy given, nor often asked in the warfare between Christian and Moslem at that day. The ferocity of the conflict was only tempered by hopes of ransom or of the price that a slave would fetch; and even these considerations were often forgotten when men were roused to a lust for blood.

The flashes of the two great mortars leapt up to the sky: their thunders deafened the air. Like Mount Etna's deadly hail, the heavy missiles flung upward by that giant discharge came rushing down from a blackened sky. They struck the water, sending high columns into the air. They crashed down on a deck where a crowd of turbaned pirates shouted and smote at one armoured figure that fought grimly its final fight. More than one went through the deck to shatter the hull below.

The *Curse of Islam* had no more to do than to send a broadside into a sinking vessel, the decks of which were already awash as it came up. The Maltese boat was floating bottom upwards, a shattered wreck.

Francisco looked down on a sea that was strewn with wreckage, and in which there were men that swam round like drowning rats, having little hope of a better fate.

They picked up five, who were all Turks, of whom they kept four for the labour of the oars, and threw one back, who had a wound which it would have been trouble to heal.

They saw nothing of the Maltese, nor of Don Manuel, who would have sunk with his armour's weight, had he not been already slain.

Francisco sailed back, not knowing whom he had been too late to save.

CHAPTER XIII

ANGELICA still wrote, though in a room which, for the moment, had no occupant but herself. It had an aspect of leisured learning, of wealth and secure peace. The high shelves, laden with calf and vellum-bound volumes, lettered most often in vermilion or gold, were in shadow, but the high sunlight of a morning that neared its noon patterned the softly carpeted floor through windows that showed a few white cumulus clouds moving majestically across the deep blue of the summer sky.

But as she wrote she had heard for the past two hours the low thunder of distant guns. It came from the south, where the Turkish army advanced on a wide front and was opposed by the Maltese militia and as many knights as there were good horses to mount, or the Grand Master would allow to go out of the lines.

She could not tell how the battle went, but she knew that the Turks came on, for as the hours passed the noise grew. The guns were louder, and their volume increased in another way, as though the battle were more generally joined.

Also, in the last half hour, there had been a sound of guns from the north, as though it came from the sea. It had been little at first, but now there came a two-fold explosion of sound that was almost one, which was the firing of the stone mortars upon the beach, and soon after that the sound of cannon firing at once, which was the broadside by which the *Curse of Islam* had sunk her foe.

Angelica was not short of a task, for Sir Oliver Starkey was one who liked his records to be exact.

He must have the name of every man who would be stationed within the lines and the place he would hold. There must be space to record his wounds, or the day he would die, and perhaps a few words beyond that. There must be provision for record if he should be transferred to another front.

In all this Sir Oliver went his own way, being a man of very orderly mind, yet there was a special reason for the care which was shown in the stationing of the garrisons both of castle and town. For to give an order that would have been understood by all the four thousand men that were gathered there it would have been needful to speak in more than a dozen tongues.

It was a difficulty which had been faced by the previous Grand Master, De Lisle Adam, when the Turks had threatened attack many years before. He had arranged his knights so that those adjacent should be such as would be nearest of tongue to themselves; and though the additions to the fortifications which had been made since that day had strengthened the places once esteemed the most dangerous, and therefore of the greatest honour, so that they might now be the most difficult to assault, yet La Valette had considered it expedient to adopt his predecessor's plan, by which, when it was known, none could say that they were favoured or treated less than the first.

The Italians, under Sir Peter del Monte—who was destined to survive the siege and become Grand Master himself—stretched southward, around the Sanglea and St. Michael's fort.

On the outward side of the Bourg, which had once been protected by no more than a low wall and a shallow ditch but which was now very strongly fortified, were placed the three *Langues* of Provence, Auvergne and France, with the Genoese volunteers in a corner which would otherwise have been too weakly supplied with men.

The Knights of Arragon, with Catalonia and Navarre, defended the bastion which faced north-east, from the end of the French line toward the head of Calcara Bay; and beyond them Castile, Portugal, Germany, England held the northern bastion in that order, from the end of the Arragon line to St. Angelo's seaward walls.

But the German ranks were no more than a tithe of what they had been before division entered the Christian Church, and England, which had been chosen before to defend that outer corner where St. Angelo looked toward the sea, was now represented by no more than a single name, that of Sir Oliver Starkey himself.

This position was met by allocating to this point a number of volunteers of various nationalities and a part of the Spanish troops which had been hired from Sicily, and it was to this body that the name of Don Garcio of Murcia had been attached.

So far, if Angelica's instinct had not erred, no one had guessed that she was other than she appeared. Sir Oliver had been scrupulous to treat her in every way as though she were a young noble of Spain who, though not of the Order, had come to assist the defence, and had been no more than consistent with this in entering Don Garcio's name among those who would be stationed beneath himself. When Don Manuel should appear, as he might any day be expected to do, it would be time enough for the truth to be shown, and the responsibility would have become his. Meanwhile, Sir Oliver was careful to do or omit nothing which might attract attention or rouse suspicion in any mind.

The noon hours passed, and there was no interruption in the quiet room, except that a young page brought refreshment of wine and meat on a silver tray, as it was his habit to do, and two of Sir Oliver's scribes returned and resumed work at their own desks.

Angelica was accustomed to regard them with the smiling but distant courtesy which becomes natural among those who cannot speak the same tongue. Here, as when she passed through the more public rooms of the castle or went abroad, the cosmopolitan atmosphere of the assembled champions of Christianity, with their endless diversities of physique and manners and dress, and with their babel of tongues, was her sufficient protection against the curiosity out of which suspicion is born.

Within the castle she had encountered no women at all, though there were naturally many among the Maltese in the town, and some of these had been employed during the last days in the hard toil of improving the fortifications on which their lives would depend at last.

Now the hours passed, while the noise of conflict increased until it was plain to hear that it was no further away than the outer wall of the town. The noise of firearms was mingled with another sound that came from the mouths of men. But they died as the afternoon waned, and some time after that Sir Oliver entered the room.

He spoke first to the two scribes in their own tongues, giving them such instructions as caused them to rise and leave. He stood for a minute's space looking at Angelica in a thoughtful way. She went on with a steady pen, not lifting her eyes, until he said: "Don Garcio, there is something here you may like to see."

She looked up at that, and observed that he had in his hand an armlet of gold and rose, gaily embroidered in silk, and not looking to be of a Christian kind.

He came and sat on the side of her desk in an easy way, holding it out for her to see.

"Are they words?" she said, looking at a strange scroll, which was not formed of any letters she knew.

"They are words," he said, "and very easy to read for such as know the Arabic tongue. A knight of Navarre, Sir John de Morgut, sent it to me an hour ago, asking that I should read it for him. He took it from the arm of an infidel knight—who was very splendidly dressed—whom his lance had slain."

His words reminded her of that which was most moment to know. "Has all gone well," she asked, "in the day's strife?"

"It has gone well enough, as I hear, though it has not been my part to see. The Turks are about our gates. They came close at one time, but they have paid a full price for that, such as they will not be eager to pay again.

"They have made their advance, yet I should say that we have done well enough. We did not think to hold them off in the open field."

He added, as though thinking that her question might hide a personal fear: "You are safe here. I do not know what the end may be, but it will not come in a day, nor a week from now."

"I had no such thought. Be they here for a short time or a long, I suppose that the Cross will fly from towers that they will not take."

Sir Oliver, listening to this confident reply, appeared to check something that he had been about to say. When he spoke, after a pause, he said: "I suppose you are of your uncle's blood at the last, though you may be gentler of manner and speech, as is but natural to think, and that is what I should have supposed you would say. Yet it is of that that I came to speak, for there are things that should be said now, if at all. . . . I will tell you what these words are that you cannot read: '*I do not come to Malta for honour or wealth, but I am seeking to save my soul.*' You will see that neither wealth nor honour is his, for he has been slain by a Christian lance on the third day, having done nothing at all, and that he has saved his soul is a thing we cannot believe. We suppose that it is in hell at this hour."

"Why do you show me this?"

"Because you have come to a strife which is not as are those when Christians with Christians strive, though they may be such as a woman cannot avoid too far; but this is one in which it is believed on both sides that we fight in the cause of God against those whom He would have us hate, and for whom pity is sin.

"We know well that we have the true cause—God pity us if we should be wrong in that!—but we know that we are not wrong. . . . I am not telling you to doubt that, but to understand that they are as sure as we.

"Should we fail to sustain our part, there will be none left living within these walls. You may thank God for a quick death, which you may not get. And I must tell you that our defence is not sure. If we have no help from the Christian lands—and as yet we have had fair words, but no more—to hold these walls against such hordes as have come may be beyond human power. We do not complain of that, nor do we regard it with any faintness of heart. We are here to die. Before which time we propose that the infidel deaths will be more than few.

"Yet it is different for you, who should not have come. And there is yet time to go back. If Don Manuel were here, or if he were sure to arrive, I would have said nothing of this, for you are his charge. But he has not come, nor can we say that he ever will.

"Only at this noon, a boat has been sunk carrying some knight who was seeking to join our ranks. I do not say, nor suppose that it was he. But the danger to those who will attempt to reach us from now may be increased beyond what we can guess.

"First and last, he may not come.

"But there is a vessel leaving to-night, a felucca that is built only for speed, in which the nephew of the Grand Master will sail for Palermo to urge the Viceroy that he shall be more swift to our aid. You would be safe on that ship, and I could commend you to the care of good friends that I have there, so that you would have nothing further to dread."

"Sir Oliver," Angelica replied, "you speak from a kindness which is needful to thank, but it is as you would not do to the man that I ape to be. If I ask you one thing, will you answer in a true way?"

"Yes," he said, "so I will, by my knighthood's oath."

"If I accept the offer you make, after I have come as I have, will it be to augment my honour, or else my shame?"

Sir Oliver was silent for some time after this question was put.

"You have asked," he said at last, "a hard thing, which all might not resolve alike; yet if I answer with truth, as you have adjured me to do, I must say, by the Passion of God, that it will be to your greater honour to remain here, if you can be equal to that which comes, as I think you will."

"That is what I supposed you would say. And on your part, will it be to Malta an aid rather than a burden that I remain?"

"When I think what you have already done in our cause, I should call it a likely aid."

"Then I will not go on that ship."

"Yet you should give thought to the dangers that are ahead, which you may suppose less than they are. There are things that you have not seen."

"I have seen a man thrown overboard while he yet lived, for no fault but his failing strength. Are there worse matters than that?"

"Yes. I should say there are. Yet, as I hope, they may not come in your way, if you are resolved that you will not go."

"You asked me, when first I came, if I had any skill in the healing of wounds, and I answered yes. Was there purpose in what you asked?"

"There was purpose, but it is not a skill which can be put to use at this time. . . . As you know, we are an Order which was first of a healing kind, and all we who have taken John Baptist's vows are of some skill in such arts, though they are such as, for the most part, are not used. Yet we have good spitals within the town, which are served by such of our brethren as have vocation therefor. There are no women within its walls. If you go as you now are, you may find it to be a secret you cannot keep, and might be greatly mis-thought if it should be discovered when you are without friends at a short call, and the truth held to be no more than a wanton's lie.

"Nor, as I think, could you serve there if your sex were known, being alone among men, and it being against our custom, if not our vows, that women should be of those who work in an infirmary that our Order has built. Or, at least, I suppose you would not be allowed, except in a much greater need than we now have.

"But that which I came in truth to ask you was this: if Don Manuel shall still delay to arrive, and you stay here, is it well that you should continue this disguise which you now wear? Or shall I speak to the Grand Master thereon that the truth be shown?

"You must consider that men may die at such times as these. Who and what you are is known to none but Ramegas and me; even your cousin is not aware. If our witness were not at hand, who would believe your tale?"

"I suppose that it might be believed by those who are themselves of good conduct and faith."

"So it might. It would be to prove at your cost. And even then. . . ."

"There is the Grand Master himself."

"So there is. But did he greatly heed what was said, as one who would hold it clearly in mind?"

"So I should have supposed. But, in truth, I cannot tell that. Is he one who will lightly forget?"

"He will not forget that which it is for our Order's good that he know. But, at this pass, his mind is set on one thing, that the Cross shall still fly from our towers. Except it bear upon that, you may talk what wisdom you will, or of things of price, and he will not hear."

"If you bring it back to his mind, what will he be most likely to say?"

"I cannot warn you of that. He may send you away, as he did a month ago all who were old or sick, or whom he thought would be less worth than their food, even those who were native born.

He showed no mercy in that. He would heed no plea. But I think he would let you stay."

"Yet it is a risk which I will not choose. I think rather to wear this dress, as I have his order to do, until my uncle come, or there be more gain by a change than I see now. . . . Could I keep the chamber I have, if it were known who I am?"

"I should say no to that."

"Then, by your leave, I will stay as I am for the time."

Sir Oliver did not say she was wrong. He looked a doubt, and would surely have said more, but, at that moment, the Grand Master entered the room.

His good friend, the Viceroy of Sicily, had given him some advice at the first, though, being servant to Philip of Spain, he had not been able to give him much else. The advice was that he was worth more to Malta than a sword's point, and that he should guard his life with a great care, keeping away from the front of strife as a duty he owed to Malta and God Himself, though it might be bitter to do.

Seeing him now, it was easy to doubt whether that advice had fallen on heedful ears, for though he wore no arms of offence (which he may have thrown aside in the last hour) his back and breast were of steel, and he was fouled with dirt on his right side, as one who had been down in the ditch or had rubbed a wall.

He had not come now to his own place, for since the first rumour of the Turkish attack he had left the castle and taken a lodging within the town, which had been a gesture to give confidence to those who dwelt there and to hearten them to strengthen their walls while there was time.

"Sir Oliver," he said, "you are well found. I have dispositions to change."

"Is all well? I thought the strife was done for this day."

"So it is, beyond doubt. But I will have no more of this open war. I will trust to stone. There are those gone I am grieved to lose."

Sir Oliver looked a moment's surprise, for he had supposed that the Grand Master would have given the life of every man that he had, as freely as one will empty a purse which can be filled on the next day, had he thought it to Malta's gain.

So he would. But his mind was also as that of one who will not pay out a coin unless assured that it is buying its utmost worth.

All the morning the Turkish army had made its advance over some miles of land that was scanty of trees, but of an uneven surface, and divided into many small fields surrounded by low walls of stone.

Against their advance the Maltese militia—ably commanded by Marshal Couppier, a famous knight of Auvergne—had opposed a guerrilla warfare, firing from behind the shelter of every wall and falling back in time to avoid too close an encounter with numbers which would have overwhelmed them by five to one.

In this way they had inflicted much loss and suffered little. The masses of the Turkish infantry had offered a mark which was not easy to miss: the stone walls had been their friends, both when they had used them to lean their arquebuses for steady aim, and to cover them when they slipped away.

A force of mounted Maltese knights, under Sir Melchior d'Egueras, knowing the ground, had been able to charge the lighter ranks of the Turkish cavalry and break them with a great loss.

In the whole of the two days' fighting up to this evening of Sunday, May 20th, the total losses on the Maltese side were four score of all ranks, and it was estimated that those of the Turks must have been over fifteen hundred, at which it might seem that even La Valette would be well content.

But the Turks, not being satisfied to advance to the village of St. Catherine, which lay midway between St. Angelo and their former camp, and which was to be their headquarters through many subsequent weeks, finding that, whatever loss they suffered, their advance was not seriously contested, had become somewhat too bold. With fierce cries of *Allah!* some regiments of janissaries, being the very flower of the Turkish army, had carried their horse-hair banners even up to the bastions of the Bourg, the crest of which was planted with the crowding pennons of over a hundred knights of the three *langues* of France, Provence and Auvergne.

Louder than the fanatic cries with which the infidel host had rushed to assault the wall, cannon and arquebus opened such a fire upon them as left no more than the options of flight or death, between which many found it too late to choose. It was then that the Grand Master himself had leapt down into the ditch, leading a charge by which he had secured that those who limped in a flying rear, expecting Paradise, might be sent to their certain hell.

It was there that a large part of that total of fifteen hundred had learnt the lesson of death, and the Grand Master, calling back his knights lest they should pursue too far for their safe return, and wiping a bloody sword (for his weight had not been enough to keep him behind the line) had reflected upon the heavy loss which must be the lot of those who offer their human flesh against the cold denial of granite walls.

So as he walked away from the bastion of the Bourg, he had said in his heart: "My knights shall ride out no more. I will trust to stone."

Now he said: "Couppier is falling back into the hills, as I have ordered before. He will make Notabile his base; but if they come there, they will find him gone. He can lead them a long race, as I think, and cause more loss than he is likely to take; but, be that as it may, I cannot have all Malta within these walls.

"It is of d'Egueras I came to speak. He shall ride out no more. I can put my knights to a better use. But I must find him other command, for he is near to the best I have. I will make him Chief of St. Elmo's fort, for de Broglio is not fit for so hard a charge. He is past his prime. I would have you make out the commission now."

Sir Oliver sat down at the word. He took parchment. He dipped a quill. But he was slow to commence to write.

"De Broglio," he said, "is a gallant knight and of great repute."

"You speak of days that are dead. He is old and fat."

"He is well loved of the knights."

"I cannot alter for that. I must have the best man there. I will have St. Elmo held till it is no more than a ruined grave, if it be there that they press attack, as I think they will."

"You can make him deputy, if you prefer. They are not men who will jar."

"Yes. It is a good thought. You can make it out in that way."

So the old knight was left at his post, to gain some more honour which it might be said that he did not need, and a wound that would not be easy to heal (of which he had more than enough in his younger days); and d'Eguaras was appointed his aide, and having got down from his horse for the last time, he crossed to St. Elmo with sixty knights of the Order in boats during the midnight hour, so that the garrison had been doubled when the dawn came, and that with knights of the greatest names that the breadth of Europe could boast.

Having disposed of that, the Grand Master went on to give instructions on other appointments that must be made. He talked in the Latin tongue, so that Angelica, by whom it could be read better than heard, did not understand much that was said, and though she looked up when the names of Ramegas and Don Francisco came into the talk, yet the eyes of the two men were not turned to her, and she judged that she was outside their thoughts.

La Valette went in some haste at last, for he had ordered that all who could should attend at evensong in San Lorenzo Church, where he purposed, after the service was done, to address his knights, exhorting them to be equal to the great occasion to which they came, speaking in the Latin tongue, which should be commonly understood, and which he was well able to do. So he hastened away, having other things that must be done before that. And Angelica went to the church with Sir Oliver at the due time, and found it crowded, so that they must stand in an aisle and be jostled by those who still pressed in at the doors, till it was trouble to breathe.

There were no more than sentries and an occasional guard along the lines of defence at this time, for there was no doubt that the Turks had had enough for the day, and had fallen back on St. Catherine and a line level therewith. They would not try storming forts again till their artillery had been brought up, after the loss they had had.

Angelica stood at one time within a few yards of her cousin's side and his eyes met hers in an idle way. It was with an effort akin to pain that she controlled her own glance that it should not respond; for the sight of one she had known so well brought back all that had been theirs so few weeks before; the distant peace of Aldea Bella, that was now so lost and far that to think that they would see it again might be held an unlikely thing.

His eyes saw her and went heedlessly on, which might not have been had she still worn the clothes that were his; but she had laid them aside, partly from discretion, lest they should be recognized by any of those who had come in her uncle's ships, and more surely because they had been through the sea-water and soiled by climbing on a ship's stern. The fact that she went in a false guise had not made her careless of what she wore.

She thought that Francisco had changed in another way, his face having become somewhat harder for all its youth, and his eyes sterner than they had been when he had had no care but to hunt in the Andalusian hills. They had both come to a school where much must be learnt in a short time.

There were few who heard the Grand Master's words, women or men, who would be alive when the summer failed. But they would all have lived in a great day.

Thinking of Francisco as she walked back, and debating in her mind whether she should make herself known to him or wait Don Manuel's coming, caused her to recall the conversation between the Grand Master and Sir Oliver, in which she had heard his name.

"I have been little," she said, "with those who have talked in the Latin tongue, though I can read it well enough, as you know; and there was no cause that I should give heed to words which were not for me. But I thought I heard the Grand Master mention Señor Ramegas, and my cousin thereafter. Am I wrong to ask what was said?"

She had to say this again, for Sir Oliver had his own thoughts and had not been heedful to her. But when he listened, he said:

"Not at all. It is what you should know. As to Señor Ramegas, it was no more than this. He should fight, as you know, under Don Manuel's pennon, being esquire to him. But Don Manuel is not here. Señor Ramegas is of gentle blood, of mature years and of very good repute, especially on the sea, though he is neither a Knight of Justice, nor has he brought us the wealth by which is bought a place in our highest rank.

"But the Grand Master would not put him to shame by placing him under another knight; and these are days when a man must be judged for what he is rather than by any title he bear. So I have orders to draw a commission by which he will have charge of the shipping which we have laid up within the boom, both while it is anchored there and if it should have occasion to sally out."

"You mean that he will be Admiral of the whole Fleet?"

"You may call it so if you will. But you will see that it may be little more than an idle charge, for in a few days, at the most, the boom may be let down for the last time, and the few ships that we have be anchored beneath our guns till the siege is done.

"Yet if there should be occasion to use the ships at a sudden chance, the Grand Master would have one in command who is both bold and discreet and of sea-craft already proved."

"He will be well pleased," Angelica said, "and so, for his sake, am I; for he was always kind to me, though he would have ordered me to the rack at my uncle's word, and thought that I should be glad to go. It is all duty with him—duty and pride. But I wonder what you will do with Captain Antonio, who was on his ship. He is one at which it is easy to laugh, yet I should call him a good man in command, and one who knows much of the sea and of how a ship can be fought in the best way."

"He is a good man, for whom a use will be found. But he is not one who could be put in command of knights, being of plebeian blood; for that is not our way, as you know."

Sir Oliver, being English-bred, had a thought that it might sometimes be well if that rule were less strictly observed; but there are things which it is better to think than to say, and even of its truth he was less than sure.

The Spanish navy, clashing with that of England in West Indian seas, must have a hidalgo on its quarter-deck, or, by preference, a noble of higher rank, even though he might be a better judge of a lace cuff than a tarry rope. The English seamen were dogs in their own phrase, but they held their own, and enough more to suggest that they might be the better led.

Yet Sir Oliver, moving among men who were gathered from those of all Europe who were of a traditional pride of race, could observe also that breeding may be more than an idle word. Gentle nurture may not be barren in its results. Pride may be a sharp spur.

But Sir Oliver said nothing of what he thought, and Angelica's interest in the plebian Genoese was of a transient kind. She went on to enquire what station Francisco had been appointed to hold, if the *Curse of Islam* were to be idle against the quay.

"That is another matter that the Grand Master has wisely resolved. For, as you know, the honours of our Order are not passed from father to son, we having celibate vows, so that there is none of our knights who can have a son bearing his own name. And though Don Francisco is entered upon our rolls as one destined to take the vows when he is of a full age, yet it should be, both of courtesy and of use, when his uncle is here.

"Therefore, to avoid question of whether he should raise Don Manuel's pennon, or less than that, or in what degree he should serve, or whether he should take the vows in haste, on a day when there is much else to be done, the Grand Master has given him a separate command, and one suited to the eagerness of his youth, for it is one where he should be alert at all hours.

"He will have charge of the battery which has been placed below St. Angelo, at the water's edge, of which the purpose is to defend the great boom which guards the inner harbour where our ships will lie up."

"It is a post of great danger, or so it sounds?"

"It is a post of honour which, had it no danger, it would be unlikely to be. Those who would avoid danger should not be here. . . . Yet it may not be so at the first. For it is the inner basin it must defend, and that cannot be assailed till the outer harbour is won; and that is ours while St. Elmo stands; and I should say it is there, or else at the outer bastions of the Bourg, that the first weight of attack will fall."

Angelica thought of where this battery must be, which she had not seen. She was not yet as clear as she would later become as to the location of the fortified area, for she had walked little abroad except into the town, but she thought that it must be near the angle which it was Sir Oliver's part to defend—that of the English who, except himself, were not there.

"It is a post to which our station is near?"

"It is closer than that. The place where the battery is now put is before the western salient of the position we hold. We should overshoot it toward the sea, and it would be our place to defend it from such attack, its own guns being pointed across our front to defend the boom which, itself, is somewhat beyond our view.

"It is exposed on the shore front, being beyond our walls. It is a battery newly made, after we had fixed the great boom: for its defence is a vital need."

Angelica asked no more about that, for she was answered enough. She saw that the way in which her cousin was handling the *Curse of Islam* must have been well approved for him to have been chosen for such command, he being so young. She saw also that it was likely that he had bought his own death. Yet the battery could not be attacked as yet. She must use that thought for what comfort she could.

She waked from her thoughts to the knowledge that Sir Oliver was speaking to her again.

"As you know," he said, "I have men under my command who are drawn from all lands, those of my own not being here, where many have left the faith, and those who have been steadfast have lost the lands they had. Now if, as I speak to any, it should seem to you that I am using my own tongue, it is not a thing at which to look twice, nor to remember when you have gone away."

She was puzzled at first, and then thought that she understood. "You may trust me," she said, "in that."

"So I do, or I had not spoken at all."

The fact was that there were a few English who were there under foreign names, being of the Catholic faith, and willing to help the Order at such a need; but they feared (in which they may have been wrong) that, if there should be proof of this, they would lose any lands they had, and their families might suffer alike. For the Order of St. John had been scourged enough when her father was on the throne, but Elizabeth had gone further than he, stripping any Knight of St. John that she could find in her realm till he was as bare as a new-born babe. Yet, as she watched Malta's defence, there is reason to think that she half-turned to another mood.

But these men went to their nameless graves, having no earthly honour for what they did.

CHAPTER XIV

Mustapha Pasha sat his horse on the summit of Mount Calcara, from which a large part of the island of Malta could be surveyed. His chief officers were grouped around, for he had come to resolve how the attack on St. Elmo could best be made.

Like a map he saw the two great harbours spread out below, with the high tongue of land on which Valletta now stands, but which was known as Mount Sceberras then, a barren desolate rock, dividing their entrances, with St. Elmo's fort at its point. He saw that Piali was right in so far that neither harbour could be entered at all while St. Elmo stood, and it was true that it was not a large fort. It should be easy to take.

If it were down, the further north-western harbour, which was now empty, would give a safe retreat for the whole of the Turkish fleet; and the south-eastern one would be free for them to enter at a less risk, so that St. Angelo might be attacked both by land and sea.

He looked down on St. Angelo itself, with keen experienced eyes, being old in war and in all the lore of the taking of towns. He saw that to have St. Elmo would be little more than a wasting of life unless it should be a way to open the gate to the larger gain. He saw that the shape of the occupied harbour, with its out-jutting spurs of land and the basin between, in which the fleet had been moored, favoured defence, and his army had learnt something the day before of the strength of that defence on the landward side. Still, towns and castles had been taken before. Ships had been burnt in the harbours in which they lay. And it was said that there was a weak point in the bastioned wall that was the main defence of the Bourg. He looked round at a manacled man, who was guarded some paces behind, and called for him to be brought to his side.

Two days before, a party of a dozen of the Maltese knights had ridden out to destroy stragglers or scouts who might come too far from the Turkish lines. They had some success at first, but in the end they had been ambushed themselves by a force of Turkish infantry which had opened a heavy fire upon them from the shelter of the low stone walls, which were a continual feature of the more cultivated parts of the island. Leaning their arquebuses, which were longer and carried somewhat further than the Christian weapons, upon the walls, they were able to shoot with considerable accuracy, and the knights, having nothing to oppose but their lances, which were of little use on that broken ground, turned quickly to ride away.

There was a French knight among them, de la Riviere, who would have got clear, but looking back he saw a brother of Portugal, d'Elberne by name, fall from his horse. He was dragged by the stirrup for a time, after which the horse shook him off and fled in the haste of fear. Riviere turned and rode back.

Doing this, he drew the Turkish fire upon himself from all sides but he was not struck. He got down to find that he had returned to the aid of a dead man. D'Elberne was shot through the head: he could do nothing for him. He mounted again to ride off, and as he did so a bullet brought his horse down. He was roughly thrown and the weight of his arms made him slow to rise. When he did so, he found himself surrounded by Turks, who called on him to yield. So he must, having no choice.

He might have hoped for ransom or exchange, but he was taken before Mustapha, who thought he could be better used in another way. He was asked to tell of the strength of the Christian army, where it had mounted its guns, where its defences were weak and where strong. When he refused, he was put on the rack, and under that persuasion he began to talk. He gave much detailed information, including that the best place at which to attack the town was the station held by the Knights of Castile.

Mustapha, having learnt so much, thought it might be worth while to bring him along and hear more. Probably the taste of the rack he had already had would be sufficiently clear in his mind to render it needless to do more than hint at a second application.

"Where," he asked, "is that point which the Knights of Castile now hold in so weak a way?"

La Riviere showed no slackness to point it out. Indeed, what use would there have been in that? Over the wall the pennons of Castile blew in the wind. They could have been seen at a nearer view.

Mustapha looked long. He wished to be quite sure. But he was too old in war to be left in doubt. The Castile pennons floated over the curtain, bastion-flanked, where the Bourg line rested on the head of Calcara bay, showing no weakness at all. He saw that he had been fooled and mocked.

He turned round to the manacled prisoner, and a cruel fury was in his eyes. Few could have more control over face and voice than Mustapha Pasha when he dealt with men of his own race, and he would be subtle to hide his mind. Those who knew him best might doubt their power to guess whom he approved or whom he counted his foe. But there was no need of concealment here. His lip lifted to show yellow teeth over his beard. He spoke no word, but raised the baton he carried, and brought it down with all his force across the eyes of the French knight. Piali, standing by, gave a great laugh. He was amused that Mustapha had been beguiled, but he felt no kindness to Riviere for that. He carried a heavy staff when he climbed the hills, on which a man cannot balance himself as easily as he has learned to do on his own deck. He brought it down on the captive's head with more force than Mustapha had used, being much stronger than he. Riviere fell at the blow. Being stunned, he did not know that the whole group of officers were belabouring him in turn, each emulating the rest in the strength of the blow he dealt.

Battered so, he was soon dead.

Mustapha said: "Let him be. We will have him back on the rack. He shall give better truth before I have done."

But, by God's good mercy, he spoke too late.

CHAPTER XV

THE Turkish artillery was said at this time to be the best in the world, which there is no reason to doubt. It had proved its worth on a score of battlefields in Eastern Europe: it had breached the walls of a score of towns. It was well served, its gunners being trained in the hard school of continual war.

Piali, looking down on St. Elmo's fort from Calcara's height, counted that it would be his in five days, if not less. It would be bombarded from the sea, where his galleys would be out of range of the Castle guns. He would build a battery on Mount Sceberras, which would bombard it from the land, and though that ridge was within the danger of St. Angelo's guns firing across the harbour, he thought that he could make his battery safe from them by erecting it somewhat on the further side of the ridge, which sloped down to St. Elmo in front and to the two harbours on either side, somewhat in the shape of the smooth back of a beast.

So it was agreed to be tried, and the battery was commenced with an effort that did not slacken when it had been found that it would be harder than was supposed at the first, and was taking a larger toll of the lives of men.

For it was found that the mountain was solid rock, into which it was too hard to dig, and having no soil on its face. It was rock which they could not easily trench. They must labour at first under the fire of St. Elmo's guns, and there was no surrounding material with which they might construct any defence. Every fascine, every earth-filled gabion, had to be dragged over the hills.

They built on the western side of the slope, which hid them, as they had designed, from St. Angelo's guns, but this had a defect which they should have foreseen, as perhaps they did. Had they planted their guns on the ridge's crest they would have been exposed to long-range fire from the castle, to which they could have replied in the same way, but they would also have commanded the water between the castle and fort and could have sunk any boat which had ventured to cross the harbour to comfort St. Elmo's garrison with reinforcements or other aid. As it was, the Grand Master could learn how they did and send them such support as he would.

The Turks toiled at this work for three days, under a constant fire from St. Elmo, to which they could make no reply. They may have worked the faster that they were erecting shelter for their lives, but the whole siege was destined to be carried on in a desperation either of haste or delay; the Grand Master fighting for time and looking northward for the succour of a Christian continent that had paused to observe the strife, which it made no movement to aid, and the Turks toiling to make an end before such aid should appear.

During these days the Turks had less help from the fleet than Piali had thought to give, for it was found that the St. Elmo guns could outrange all but a few of the longest culverins that the galleys bore; and while they could have no support from the land, to have allowed his ships to close in would have been to risk them overmuch for any hurt they would be likely to do.

St. Elmo was a star-shaped fort, having four salients, the landward side being broken into bastion form by small rounded flanks. On the seaward side it had a high cavalier, with an intervening ditch, the guns of which could either fire out to sea, or landward, over the lower fort. On the western side, overlooking Marsa Muscetto harbour, was the detached ravelin, or lunette, which the knights had been building during the last days before the Turkish fleet came into sight.

The fort was small, and there might well be a confident hope in the Turkish ranks that it would not endure many hours when they should have prepared their attack; but it had somewhat more strength than appeared from the same cause that had hindered the construction of the opposing battery: the site being of solid rock, the Knights, being in less haste than the Turks, when they had first commenced to build it, had sought less to erect it upon the granite their mattocks met than to excavate it therefrom.

Yet the Turkish gunners thought it would be a simple matter to lay it flat when, their emplacements being ready on the morning of Thursday the 24th, they brought up ten heavy guns and trained them upon the fort.

These guns, which the ox-teams pulled, were all mounted on wheels, and were the best and newest of the siege artillery of that day, having been reckoned equal not merely to blowing St. Elmo down but to the reduction of St. Angelo itself. When the Grand Master knew that they were being pointed the way they were, he was well-content, let their effect on St. Elmo be what it might. Not that he was indifferent to that. But he counted days till relief should come. He did not mean that the Order should leave Malta as it had left Rhodes. And though St. Elmo were blown to the sky, while St. Angelo stood it was plain that they would not be shifted at all.

The Turkish battery consisted of ten guns of a like pattern, each throwing a solid ball of eighty pounds weight, and three columbines of somewhat older and lighter make, throwing a sixty-pound shot; and, in addition to these, there was a single basilisk, a monstrous cannon throwing a ball of one hundred and twenty pounds, but for this the gunners had little love, for it was slow and cumbrous to work, and frequently needing repair, having very complicated parts, both for directing its fire and for controlling recoil.

The battery itself could not be seen by those who crowded St. Angelo's walls to watch, but, as the guns opened, the flashes shone over the ridge, followed by the heavy thunder of their discharge; and, for the first time, St. Elmo answered with every gun she could bring to bear.

For till then, her guns had been used in a spasmodic way, firing at times at any mark that might show or sweeping the battery position after a lull, such as would cause the Turks to grow careless and bold, and so assist to their own deaths; for though there was a large store of powder and shot, both in castle and fort, yet there was a limit to what should be fired away at less than a certain mark.

But now St. Elmo replied in an intensity of desperation as the iron tempest hammered her splintering stones; and meanwhile the day, which had opened with some light rain, became misty and dull under a low grey sky. Black clouds of sulphurous smoke hung over battery and fort, and would not shift in the windless air. The gun-flashes showed more brightly as they pierced the inferno from which they came.

As the day passed the mist thickened, and in the growing gloom the guns faltered and ceased.

It was after that, in the late afternoon, that Angelica sat alone in Sir Oliver's room, where she might most often be found, for it was not only that it was there that her work and her duty lay: it was there that she felt at peace, as one being among friends and secure.

So she worked more than she need, as giving a reason for where she was—when most men would be abroad—and Sir Oliver, sending his scribes right and left as occasion came, gave no such errands to her, which might be explained by the rank she claimed and the dress she wore; and that she was of a different sort from them was very easy to see.

She was of changing moods at this time, having much loneliness, from which would rise a timid fear of what she had done and a great doubt of what its end would be likely to be in this place which was staged for death, and among men of strange nations and famous names, who had taken celibate vows, and most of whom were much older than she. For besides Sir Oliver, who was kind but full of greater affairs, she had no confident friend, so that she was tempted from hour to hour to seek Francisco and tell him all, and yet had a doubt of how much sympathy or blame she would have, which held her back, for it could always be done on the next day.

Yet she had finer moods in which she was less aware of herself or of her own weakness and fear, and more of the great drama in which she moved and in which a small part had become hers; for she saw that she had come to one of the great days of the world, which was to judge how Christian Europe was yet to fare against the rising tide of the Turkish power.

For though the Moors had been thrown from Spain fifty years before, yet, almost from the same day, the dark-skinned infidels had advanced over Eastern Europe like a creeping tide which there was no power that could stay. And the Christian lands had become weak with the blight of internal strife; and while they blasphemed their faith with tortures of stake and rack, the cloud advanced, and was little heeded except by those who were near to the place where its shadow fell. And furthest of all, the English Elizabeth, ruthless, bold and mean, called it a blessing of God that the Turks were active against the Catholic lands.

And so now, in this island arena, in the very centre of all, the test came, when a band of knights—who were not of one country, but had gathered from all parts of the Christian lands to be over-matched by the great host of their infidel foes—strove to keep the Cross afloat over their walls a sufficient time to bring the rescue that had been pledged, and that Europe was well able to give. . . .

It was an hour when the daylight should still have been full in this later May, but the mist had become so dense that Angelica had called for the cresset-candles to be lighted along the walls, when the curtains at the main entrance were flung apart, and a knight whom she did not know strode into the room.

He was richly and gaily attired, wearing light armour of damascened steel, but not enough to hide the under colours of trunk and hose, yellow and olive-green, elaborately embroidered and pinked in a somewhat fantastic way. He had the manner of one who can give orders in the assurance that he need not wait to see them obeyed.

He glanced along the room, and asked abruptly: "Is Sir Oliver here?"

Angelica was annoyed at the manner in which this question was put, showing neither the quality of courtesy which was due to her in her true person, nor that which she had assumed, but character and training combined to prevent her from answering in the same way. She said coldly: "That is to be seen."

The reply drew the knight's gaze on herself in a way she could have spared, though she took it with composure enough. Anger gave place as he looked to a change of mood, bringing a more courteous tone. They were both puzzled by whom they met. Angelica observed that he had walked in as though the Castle were his, but she did not know that there was anyone besides the Grand Master of whom she need stand in dread.

"I would know," he said, "where Sir Oliver Starkey may best be found. Or if he will return here in a short time."

"I must know to whom I speak before answering that. It is not usual to enter here without your name being first announced."

"I am La Cerda," he said, as though that explained all. "I would know by whom I am asked." The tone had become reserved, but unsure. He was more puzzled than she as to whom it would be who answered him thus in the Andalusian tongue, and it was hard to guess who might be met in the Malta of that day.

"I am Don Garcio of Murcia."

"You are . . .? I know Murcia well." La Cerda did not look less puzzled than before. Angelica had sufficient discretion to keep silent, making it difficult for him to ask more, and at that moment Sir Oliver returned.

His appearance recalled to La Cerda's mind the purpose for which he came. It was a question about a horse's food, which it appeared that money had been unable to get.

When the Grand Master had seen that the advance of the Turkish army would divide St. Angelo from the little army which he had decided to leave loose in the island, he had given a general order that the knights' horses were to be left outside, so that Marshal Couppier might mount as many of his men as their number would allow. These horses would increase the mobility of the Maltese militia, while they would have been of no use in the town. Most of the knights had surrendered them without demur, though it may be supposed that they were not pleased. But La Cerda had thought that such orders were not for him; or, at least, not to be applied to a horse that was his, and which he valued and loved. He had ridden in and put the horse, as before, in the stable where he lodged in the town. And now he had been told by his groom that he could get neither corn nor hay. They were rationed by Sir Oliver Starkey's order, and a proffer of money had been of no avail.

"I know well," he said, striving to speak with a courtesy which it was not easy to feel, "that things are done at such times as these such as are not meant, orders being applied in a wrong way, and so I came to yourself."

Sir Oliver, listening in his own way, which was quiet and cool, thought that there might be another explanation than that. He might have come himself because his pride would not risk a rebuff which his squire would know. It was trouble of a kind with which he must often deal. La Cerda had a great power in his own land. He was used to command, as were half the knights who had now come from the ends of Europe to serve as little more than privates in this defence. And in spite of, or perhaps because of that, the Grand Master was resolved that the obedience he exacted, the discipline he maintained, should be of the strictest kind. It was as though he had to command a regiment, each of whom was a general in his own right. If he should be lax at all, where would it end? It would not be easy to tell.

Sir Oliver did not give a direct reply. He said: "I have been your friend before now."

The remark recalled the incident of a month ago, when La Cerda's mistress had left the turret chamber, to be embarked without the Grand Master's eyes being turned her way. La Cerda saw the implication of that, but the reminder was another cause of wrath brought to his mind, and the knowledge that there might be more trouble ahead, of a kind which Sir Oliver was not likely to guess.

"So you were," he said, "and it had my thanks. But that there should have been cause! And to think that I was one of those who gave him votes that he could have had no hope to obtain! And what are we now but the leather beneath his feet?"

La Cerda spoke of that which all knew. For when De Lisle Adam had died there had been stronger candidates for the Grand Master's place, and no one had thought of La Valette as a likely man. La Cerda would have called his own the much better claim, though he had not attempted to win the prize. But those who have strong friends may have strong foes. Rival factions quarrelled and strove, and yet all agreed that the Order was so reduced and in so dangerous a pass that the Grand Master must be one who would be accepted by all. And so, at last, they had compromised the claims of rivals too haughty to give way to each other, by the unanimous election of a member of whom few had thought at the first, as would often happen in the election of Popes at that time, from the same cause. And La Valette had found, to the amazement of others, and no doubt his own, that, having come to give his vote to a man of more wealth and much wider fame, he was the Grand Master himself.

"I would not say that. He regards us all as himself, being vowed to a cause which is much greater than we."

"So we are agreed. That is why we are here. It will be death for most, if not all. Yet that is a poor reason why we should have no joy while we live."

"Need we argue on that?"

"I will say no more beyond this, that I have been wroth at times that I should have so meanly withdrawn. I am, as you know, of a wide rule. In my own land there is none who will cross my will. I come here, offering life and wealth, and I find that my very chamber is not secure. I was told that I must cast off the *amie* who shared my bed."

"My lord," Sir Oliver replied in a patient way, rather as one who would wait till the other had spent his words than as having any aim to convince, "you will allow that we have taken celibate vows?"

"We are vowed that we will not wed. To ask more is to ask too much. I am not alone when I say that. Do you think there would be many to blame, should you put the chamber where Venetia lodged to the same use, as I daresay that you do?"

The words were randomly said, but as he spoke them his eyes fell on the slight figure of the young noble (if such he were) who had given a name which was hard to place, and the idea, which was after the custom of the time, though not of the stricter code La Valette sought to enforce, suddenly took shape as a very probable thing.

"But perhaps," he added boldly, "I say too much, speaking of that which I should not see."

Sir Oliver showed no surprise, nor any sign of offence. He answered in the same cool and patient tone as before: "You may say as you will, for my manner of life is known. But you came to speak of a horse, as I understood, and we have wandered therefrom."

"I ask no more than an order for fodder and corn, which the beast needs."

"You ask something which I am unable to give."

"What! Shall it starve?"

"Surely, no. It can be sent to the stalls here, where it will be fed with the rest."

"Then there are other horses allowed here?"

"There are horses that did not go out of the town."

"And there is this one that has come back. Why should it not be fed at my own place? I will pay what charges you set."

"I cannot offer more than I do. It is a horse that should not be here."

"I will not consent. I will speak to Valette."

"You can do as you will. It will be less trouble to me. But I do not think you are wise."

"Would he not be wroth that you have offered as much as you already have?"

Sir Oliver's eyebrows were slightly raised as he replied, but his voice kept the same level tone. "Do you think I exceed my trust? I should tell him what I have offered, and why. But I conceive that it is my part to see that he is not disturbed by the smaller things, when he had shown me his mind."

La Cerda made no answer to that. He stood in an evident indecision, wisdom fighting with pride. Perhaps it was because his eyes fell on Angelica again that Sir Oliver spoke now in a different tone, though he gave no sign that he saw.

"My lord," he said, in a brief way, "I have given more time to this than I should. I came here, having many matters upon my hands, which were not meant for delay. I ask your pardon. You must do as you will; but I cannot talk more."

He added in mitigation of the curtness of this rebuff: "It is this mist which is spreading over both land and sea which is causing fresh orders to be sent out, such as I have the Grand Master's instructions to draw. It is a matter which should not wait."

He had, in fact, a cipher letter of much secrecy to prepare, which was to be sent to Marshal Couppier through the Turkish lines during the night, if the mist should hold, though he was too discreet to say that, even in his own room. But the mention of the mist brought another thought to La Cerda's mind, on which he had already made his opinion known to his friends while the wine was passed and on which many agreed. He spoke now with the impulse of an anger that rose from another cause.

"The mist will hold during the night. So I am told by those who know these seas better than I. It is a saint's boon to us, if there were wisdom to use the chance. I would see St. Elmo blown up before dawn, so that there should not a stone stand, and every man could be brought safely away. There will not be one alive in two days from now if they are left there. They will be lost for no gain, and our foes heartened by a success that they should not have. But he asks counsel of none, or if he does, he goes his own way in the next hour. Does he think we are babes in war, because he was made Grand Master the way he was?"

Sir Oliver listened to this with an impassive face. He might have resented the tone of the allusion to the Master they were all sworn to obey, but he knew that La Cerda gave voice to an opinion which many held who had no grievance to warp their minds, and who, as La Cerda had truly said, were not children in war.

"It is a matter," he began, "which can be argued another way. If you will think——"

La Cerda broke in: "I have heard it argued enough, but there is one thing you cannot change. We have a strong fortress here, and we send our knights to one that is weak, where they will be more easy to slay. And when they are dead, as it is sure that they will soon be, we must defend these walls with a lesser force and against foes whom we have taught that we can overcome."

Angelica moved with a purpose that they should turn and see what she alone had observed. For, as the words were said, the Grand Master had stood at the door, and his face was black with wrath. And yet, though that which he had heard might be cause enough, she doubted that it were all, for she had thought his looks had been much the same as he had come in, and he was not one who would be likely to listen behind a curtain which he delayed to lift.

Now he advanced into the room, and though his anger was plain to see, yet when he spoke it was with restraint, and with the dignity which he did not lose, even when he toiled with his hands to make St. Elmo's ravelin strong.

"I may be the worst Master that this Order has ever had, but I should be more feeble of mind than I am if I did not know that there can be but one leader in time of war, though he may hear the counsel of all. And while I live, and am Master here, if I find but one who shall murmur against my rule, or who obeys me with lagging feet while this siege shall last, I will hang him within that hour, though he be of my own blood.

"As to St. Elmo, it will stand, as I think, till it have asked a price which even those who may take it at last will think somewhat too high; and if it fall, it will be to the shame of all Christian lands."

He paused, and went on in an even quieter voice than before: "There were no more than two killed and a few hurt at the cannonading to-day, and the fort has suffered little that can not be mended before the dawn. So De Broglio makes report. We had, it seems, the more accurate range, and have done more harm than we took, though I would not say that to-morrow will end in the same way.

"The dead, and those who are sore hurt, will be brought over during the night, and will be replaced, that the garrison shall not be less as the days go by.

"I send the best men that I have, and you will be one to-night. You will be ready within three hours. Nor should you take this amiss, for I send one whom I know to be a most valiant knight."

La Cerda listened with a set jaw, but said nothing at all. When he was out in the air, striding back to his own lodging, he said, half-aloud, when there could be no one to hear: "So he would have my death for that word. . . . Yet it may turn out in another way."

When he entered his own door he gave command for the horse to be sent to the castle stalls, and within three hours he was in a boat which felt its way through the mist to St. Elmo's point.

CHAPTER XVI

WHEN La Cerda had gone, the Grand Master said: "He goes with bitter heart, thinking that he is sent to a sure death, and that, when I do that, I abuse my power. Yet I suppose that we shall all go by the same road before the winter is here. . . . Garcio has sent his reply!"

"The *Bay of Naples* is in?"

"Yes. Salvago brings fair words, and this scroll." He looked round as he spoke to see who might be there to overhear what was said, but Angelica had withdrawn, thinking that his words would not be directed to her, and not wishing to be recalled to his mind with consequences which were not easy to guess.

Sir Oliver took the scroll and read, after a preamble of compliment which was in the custom of the time, and meant nothing at all, though its absence would have meant much:

> "You charge me that I have not sent an army by this day such as could have made it vain for the Turks to land, and turned them empty away, as you say that I pledged to do; but for this I cannot take a reproach, even had it been in my power to muster so large a host in so narrow a time, for I must recall that which you cannot have overthought, to wit, that you were to send ships as I men, which you will not say was beyond your power.
>
> "Yet, on my side, I assemble strength. By mid-June, by the fifteenth day, being but three weeks from now, if your navy be here with speed, I trust to send such a force as will grieve them sore and draw them from round your walls.
>
> "Nor do I doubt that you can show them a bold repulse till that rescue shall come, having such walls as you have, and so goodly stored, and with such valiance of knights, of whom it may be said without vaunt that they are the flower of the lands of Christ."

There was more beyond that, but it was in those words that the core of the letter lay.

Sir Oliver read it without heat, for its purport did not surprise

E

him at all, though the excuse it made had not been forethought, even by him.

"It is a lie," he said, "wearing a true cloak."

"And I have thought Garcio friend!"

"And so I think that he is. Is there better by word of mouth?"

"He toils ever to serve our need. They put up prayers to the saints, morn and eve, in Del Gesu church."

"The scroll may be for Philip's eyes rather than ours."

"So I have no doubt that it is. Do you see the meaning of that?"

"I see that we must trust to our own arms, under the high favour of God. But I have thought that from the first. I put no trust in the King of Spain."

"In which you may think more than is true, being English-born. Even those of your race who are yet of a constant faith have little love for that land."

Sir Oliver did not dispute that. He asked: "Has Salvago brought the grenades?"

"I have not asked. We may suppose that he has. He says that there are two score of our knights, and many hundreds of volunteers at Palermo, and nearer places along the coast, who are waiting to cross to our aid, and it is likely that they will be here before dawn if this mist be far spread. I am of a mind to raise the boom, and have ready our swifter ships that they may sally out if it lift, and be a guard to the harbour mouth. . . . Oliver, you must send one to St. Elmo, by the boat that crosses to-night, who will take message by word of mouth, telling De Broglio and D'Egueras both that no rescue is near and that they must hold those walls to the last stone and the last man; they must be held to the last hour that they can, leaving the count of the cost to me. . . . Have you one you can surely trust? You must go yourself if you doubt that. You would return before dawn. You may say what you will of Spain, so that it be clear that it has not come from my mouth, and will not go beyond them. . . . But they must hold that fort, though it were against the fiery legions of Hell.

"If there come no succour at all, we may fall at last, but I have in mind that we shall so fall as to shame the world which is called by the name of Christ."

"Well," Sir Oliver said, "we are not fallen as yet. I will go myself unless I can send one of whom I am wholly sure. But I must know first if the bombs have come."

La Valette said: "All that I can trust to you. I will order the ships." He went out.

Sir Oliver summoned aid. He saw that there was much to be done. He sent messengers right and left. He thought that he must go to St. Elmo himself, and he would have all things arranged so that he would not be missed. Few men guessed how much rested upon himself, but he might soon be missed if he were not there. He had little leisure to think of what La Cerda had hinted or said, yet he gave it a thought, and from that thought an idea came which he rejected at first, but when he weighed it a second time it had a better look than before.

After that, when his room was clear, he summoned a page. "Ask Don Garcio if he will come here on an urgent cause."

The page knocked on Angelica's door and had no response. After a time he decided that she was not there, and did what she had told him for such a case, and by which he had found her before. He went to the turret-roof, where she was making a habit to walk, rather than to wander too much in the streets of the crowded town.

She looked up to a clear sky in which the stars were brighter because moon-rise was yet distant by two hours. The mist lay low on the water and drifted somewhat, rising at times like a sea round the turret walls. At times, at some places, it would lie so thinly that she could see the slow movements of lights upon the harbour waters beneath, where ships moved, as they did that night, not only there but across the open spaces of sea, groping through the gloom with a double fear, lest a light shown or a warning bell might bring foes as ruthless as shoal or rock, and of a more active hate.

For Salvago had been right when he had told that many would come from Sicily during the night, in the kindly cloak of the mist, which would have been called a peril in time of peace. They came in boats of all kinds, in small swift galleys, but most of all in the light feluccas such as Salvago had used, which were built only for speed, carrying no arms of weight, but being long and low, with rowers' benches along the whole deck from bow to rudder, and a wide lateen sail to give support to the oars when the wind was good.

There were few that failed to come safely through, for the most part of the Turkish fleet lay at anchor in Marsa Scirocco Bay, and even the lighter galleys, ever hunting for prey, were loth to venture far in such mist and in waters they did not know. And so, when the mist rose at the dawn, and with no more than some distant booming of guns and one or two running fights which had little fruit, there were forty-two Knights of St. John and about seven hundred of other sorts who had landed, either on St. Angelo's quay or at other places along the coast, showing that there were men in the world of that day who would give their lives for a cause, having a better blood than moved in the cold hearts of its kings. . . .

Angelica heard the words "for an urgent cause," and did not doubt what it must mean. La Valette had spoken of her to Sir Oliver, or else he to him; or perhaps Don Manuel had come on the ship that had just arrived. She did not know whether she would be glad of that, but it was with a sense of crisis that she went down, which was not removed by the question that Sir Oliver asked.

"You were with La Cerda before I came. Did he doubt who you are?"

"He had a doubt, as I thought, but was not sure."

"It is a doubt that should not be there, for your own peace. We may give him cause to see that it is not as he would be likely to guess. I have a message which must be sent to St. Elmo to-night. If I kept a woman here, should I choose her for such an errand as that?"

Angelica laughed, being quick to see what he meant, and in a great relief that he had nothing different to say.

"I suppose not. But I must suppose that that is what you purpose to do. I am very willing to go."

"You must go in La Cerda's boat, and will be back before dawn. You will go on a mission of great import and trust, but which it will be simple to do. You must put laughter aside, and listen to me with great care.

"I shall give you no writing but this." (He handed her a short note which read: "The bearer of this will bring an order from the Grand Master; and what else he may say is from myself, even as though it were writ here." He took this back when she had read it, signed and sealed it, and gave it to her again.) "The order and the message are for the two Governors of St. Elmo, whom you must ask to see together, which will be accorded with ease, the superscription of that which you bear showing that it is to be delivered to them.

"The Grand Master's order which you will then give is no more than they have been instructed before, that they must hold their ground to the last stone and the last hour, not counting the cost, which will be for his thought rather than theirs.

"But you will add this, as coming from me alone: The Viceroy (whose name you have taken for yours, though not as of Toledo by a good chance) has pledged himself that he will be here by mid-June, with a strong host to our aid; but they will give no credence to that, for he has made a condition which we shall not keep, as he knows well.

"His letter is so written, as I suppose, that it may please his master, your Spanish king, to whom a copy will be on the way before now. And who would trust Philip of Spain (you must not be vexed that I say what is known to all) must be as simple as a nun's prayer.

"You will tell them that when Don Garcio was here, about a month before now, and he was promising all the aid we could need, he asked that he might have our galleys if we should ever be besieged as we are; for, he said with truth, they would only be laid up here, they not being of a number that could face such a fleet as the Turks would send; while, if they were added to those he has, they would be very useful to him.

"To this the Grand Master agreed, for it had a fair sound, and he knew that it would please the Viceroy more than a little, he being one who cares more for sea-power than for anything that the land can yield, and he was willing to do him all the pleasure he could, both because he was seeking help at his hand and that they had been friends from an old time.

"Had Don Garcio come, and with such an array as he ought to have brought, or had he sent it under other command, it is certain that the galleys would have been his.

"Indeed, there are two that he now has, for they have been cruising and had orders already given that they should put into Messina rather than here, which they have done, and their captains are instructed to serve the Viceroy's will as though they were ordered by us.

"But what he now professes that we had pledged is that we should deliver the whole fleet to his hand before he should be active toward our help, which was neither required on their side nor is it now possible for us to do. For we cannot send the ships without crews, and with enough men for the oars, either free or slaves, and it would be what we cannot spare, with the Turks already about our walls, and in the number of which you know. Also, if the ships are laid up we may use their guns to make stronger our walls of stone.

"So you may say that it is my thought (but not using the Grand Master's name) that this is no more than a false word put in to provide excuse at a later day, against an expected default on their side. I say that the fifteenth of June will come and go, and there will be no help from your Spanish king, neither will he allow Don Garcio to expend any large sum in our cause, such as must be found if an army is to be gathered, and fully furnished, and shipped here, when the hope of Turkish spoil is not great, they not being in their own land.

"And if we say that the Viceroy is the Grand Master's friend, and perhaps ours, then it is only more sure how this letter should be read; for he must be writing in a way which he would not do of his own will.

"In a word, you may say that the Grand Master sent his own nephew to Palermo, and Commander Salvago of Genoa also, to urge that Sicily should be speedy to our relief, and to learn the truth of what to expect, whether sweet or sour, and this is what he has got. Which is to say that King Philip will not spend his crowns in our cause unless he be more assured that we cannot defend ourselves than he is now; or we must contrive to die in no more than a gradual way, that he may have time to observe."

"I know not," Angelica replied, "if you are right concerning our king, of whom my uncle is used to speak in a different way, but I shall carry your words, while I hope they may be wrong, as we all must."

"We may hope what we will," Sir Oliver replied, "but you will find that what I say will be lightly believed, even though one to whom you will speak was born in your own land. . . . Have you a good cloak for the night?"

"Yes. I have all I need."

"Then I will meet you upon the quay. By which time I hope to have something to send of a better kind."

He was right on that point, for he learnt within an hour's time that the *Bay of Naples* had brought the consignment of bombs which he had been anxious to have. These were made of porcelain, and fitted with wildfire of such a kind that it stuck where it might be scattered when the crock burst, giving torturing burns, if not death, to those among whom it fell. These bombs, which were made to be flung by hand, had been accounted very terrible weapons before gunpowder had confused the making of munitions throughout the world, and were still widely used. They were made at the great arsenal at Venice, and when La Valette had ordered two thousand of them, the lord of the arsenal, being friendly to him, had put the order in hand, and even sent the bombs on as far as Palermo, before any payment was made; but beyond that he could not be expected to go, for, if he did, it was likely that the Grand Master, being at so urgent a need, would prefer others in payment whose goods were held back for the sight of gold. And though the Order had a reputation for wealth, and for paying the bonds it gave, yet if the Turks should be victors at this time, and Malta lost, it was not certain but that it would be destroyed; nor would it be easy to guess where it might be found by one who had a debt to collect. Even great kings, being rulers of settled realms, did not always find credit easy to get when they were at war in those days, and Philip of Spain himself, at a later time, when he willed to assemble an armada to attack the coasts of the English queen, was to be delayed for a full year (to its ruin at last) because the Baltic merchants would not give him a spar, nor a coil of hemp, till they had his cash in their tills.

The master of the arsenal at Venice had given orders that these bombs should be at the Grand Master's orders, either if the cash were paid or if Don Garcio would give a pledge in the name of the King of Spain. But the Viceroy replied, with the fair words that he used to all, that he had no power except he wrote to Seville, which was a matter of time; and the Grand Master could not spare such a sum from more urgent needs till he had the gift of the Papal crowns, after which Sir Oliver had only waited for a safe chance to get the bombs over the sea, for it would have been evil indeed had they fallen a prey to the Turks, and been flung at last from the wrong hands.

But now the *Bay of Naples* had brought them safely to port, and Sir Oliver would send six score of them to St. Elmo on this night (not risking a larger supply at once, for fear it might not endure, and that there should be no means of getting them back), and these cases were brought to the quay from which the boats, being three in all, would put out into the mist.

La Cerda came to the quay with some retinue of his household servants, who bore his effects, but these were lighter than might have been supposed by one who knew his estate and the luxury in which he was accustomed to live, for he had said to the one esquire whom he was taking with him (as he had no choice but to do): "Gaston, we go, as I suppose, to the deaths of fools, for such are the ends of those who let life slip for less than the full price that they should be able to ask. But there is nothing better to do, for my honour has been caught in a net which I cannot otherwise break; and you and I must eat of the same dish. So we travel light, for we shall be soon back, if at all, and in such a plight, if I know war, that what we take will be left behind.

"But if you should take a wound, though it be but a broken tooth or a skinned heel, you may claim to be sent back, and I tell you before you ask that you will have a warrant from me, for I think that both you and I will be of more use alive for the defence of St. Angelo's walls than dead in St. Elmo's ditch, as we are more likely to be.

"The Grand Master is an honest and valiant man (as I have told you before), and while he lives our flag will fly, as I think; but he has neither practice nor skill in the crafts of war, nor will he listen to those who are more subtle of mind."

He added, half aloud, as one who would have his thought heard but does not invite reply: "If any man should say he has the brains of a hen they would do the bird a great wrong." And being one who liked to distribute his wit, and perceiving, by the torches' light, that there was a discreet smile on the somewhat stolid face of the squire, he entered the waiting boat gaily enough, though he was one who valued life more than a knight of St. John should be expected to do, and in spite of certain things he had left behind.

As the oars dipped and the boat slid into the mist, to be followed by one bringing the knights' pennon-lances and sundry baggage and stores, and another bringing the wild-fire bombs, La Cerda was so much occupied by his own thoughts that he gave little regard to his companions, who were two knights (the one busy with Latin prayers, and the other looking eagerly forward into the mist, with his sword lying across his knees), and the slight, cloaked form of the secretary who had roused his curiosity in Sir Oliver's room.

But as the boat grounded on St. Elmo's beach, where a flame of torches guided them to the land, and he splashed ashore, he looked back into the face of one on whom the torch-light shone, as she moved to jump from the bow in more caution than he, and there was a moment when he did not doubt that he looked into the face of a girl, and one of more beauty than most. But the next moment she leapt into the water, and came to land lightly enough, and he saw that it was the young noble (as he called himself, and as he appeared to be) with whom he had some words in Sir Oliver's room. He thought him girlish again, as he had done before, but, beyond that, Angelica's appearance in that place had the effect which Sir Oliver had foreseen. Indeed, La Cerda's thought went beyond the fact on the road it had been meant that it should take, for he supposed that Don Garcio of Murcia (but of what family could he be?) had been numbered like himself among the reinforcements for St. Elmo's garrison, and that that had come from the mere chance that he had been in Sir Oliver's room when the Grand Master appeared. "Does he send all to their deaths here on whom his eyes happen to fall," he wondered, "or was it because the youth overheard what was said to me, and Valette thought he would be best out of the way?"

But he did not dwell on this thought, for the next moment he was surrounded by knights he knew, being one who had many friends. Also, he was a man of a great repute, and they were glad that he should be raising his pennon beside their own; and, beyond that, he had the name of one who was not without some love for himself and was both wary and shrewd, so that it would seem to all that his presence there made the fort's defence to be a sound measure of war.

But, in fact, they were in good heart enough, for most of them had been prepared for a desperate strife, and this first day that the Turkish battery had opened fire they had suffered much less than their expectations had been, which was partly because the gunners had been at fault in their range at times, and partly that the fort was so deeply delved from the living rock, and most of all because the mist had come up from the sea while the day was still young.

La Cerda went off with his friends; and Angelica, when she said that she had come from the Grand Master with a message for the Governor's ears, was led by a different way, along a covered passage which flambeaux lit, and came to a chamber within the rock where De Broglio was seated alone.

She saw a short, corpulent man who was past his prime, and with the front of one who ate too much, and drank more. He looked half-soldier, half-monk, and both in a jovial way. He had a fringe of white hair, but his eyebrows were heavy and black over eyes of the same colour, which were still bright and alert. He feared little on earth, and nothing either in heaven or hell, which may have been why he was somewhat more at home with a jest than a prayer. Now he sat at ease, after toil, with a tankard beside his hand, and with his trunk-hose unbuttoned to give his belly more space than it had had during the day.

Angelica might suppose that he would not have received her in that way had he known her for what she was, but she had learnt in the last three weeks that there were many things which had been beyond the horizon of her previous life, which must now be accepted without surprise if she were to sustain her part in a natural way.

De Broglio took the letter in a careless hand. He must know first who his visitor was, and have his comfort assured: "The boat," he said, "can wait well enough. There is no need to stand thus. There is no hurt in a bench, be your legs as young as they may. And Sir John should be abed before you can get back. He should not require your answer before the dawn."

Angelica had a moment's doubt as to whom he might mean, and how much of herself he might be likely to know, but it was no more than a baseless fear, such as must come often to those who wear a disguise; for, as the conversation went on, she found that when he talked of Sir John, it was the Grand Master he meant, he having known La Valette in much earlier days, so that he would always be Sir John to him, and sometimes John alone in a careless phrase.

He did not press the point when he found that Don Garcio was not disposed to drink, for he was easy with others, as with himself; but he explained that he was driven to much consumption of wine while he had been in St. Elmo's fort, the only water supply being from a well they had sunk, and that being brackish at times, which was not surprising, they being so close to the shore.

He read the letter at last, and said: "It is a message to the Governors that you bring? Well, you must be content with one less, except you have more patience than you first showed. D'Egueras is in the ravelin, or the mist. He counts sentries, and sets them far out from the wall, where they will get an ague before the dawn. It is very well, though I have told him that the Turks will not come at this time, for I know their ways. And, if they should, they would do no good to themselves. We have but to keep a good watch on the walls. The loss would be to those who should try climbing the scarp, which is a thing I have never loved, either by darkness or day. But it was a kind thought of Sir John to send D'Egueras to me. He is in all places at once. He is one who is never still. My shoulders cannot ache while he is here, for they have no load."

He read the scroll while he talked thus, and laid it down with a look on his face as of one who deals in a good-humoured way with the fussing of fools.

"Now what," he asked, "has Sir John to say that is of such moment that it must be brought thus in the night? And what is Oliver's word, that is not from him?"

Angelica gave the message with which she had been charged, but with a sense that it had been set on too high a note, the passionate intensity of La Valette's mood seeming to be rebuffed in a careless, almost contemptuous way, as one may humour a child.

"The Grand Master will have," she said, "that St. Elmo be held to the last stone and the last man, not regarding the cost, which is for his casting alone."

"Well," de Broglio said, stretching his hand for another drink, "you can tell him to lose no sleep over that, nor to shorten yours. For what else are we here? Does he think we shall clear out in the night, or ask Piali to dine? But that is John's way. I warrant there has not been a jest from his lips since Mustapha came, nor perhaps from when he put on his Grand Master's robes, it is six years since. Not that there is much loss in that, for he jests ill."

There was a twinkling amusement in the glance he gave Angelica as he said this, making it easy to forget that they were in a little separate fort upon which the whole might of the Turkish army was being turned, both from land and sea; but his next words showed that his humour was not the obtuseness of one too stupid to see the danger in which he stood.

"As to the last man, if Sir John will be counselled by me (which I do not say that he needs) it will come to the last stone before that, for he must keep us supplied. You can tell him that we should have a somewhat greater force than we have now—not to work the guns, for which we have more than enough, but to repel assaults, which may soon be made in great force. And you can tell him that I will find shelter for all he sends, for we are still delving the rock. We cannot burrow too low when our walls shake, as they will when they have been battered enough; and, besides that, it is better that men should work than sit idly, waiting their time to die.

"And he can send as he will, either by night or day (as we can send the wounded to him) so long as the Turks mount their guns only on the west side of the hill, as Piali is doing now. You can say that we have not much to fear while he is directing the siege. He is an ox, with an ox's brains. Had he more wit where to mount a gun, he could do us tenfold the harm that we are likely to suffer now.

"But if Sir John would give us all the aid that he can, he should throw up the mouths of his longer guns and fire over the hill. He is not likely to hit more than the mountain, which will not mind, but he will cause the infidel rogues to feel an itch on their right sides. They will ever be looking up, and they cannot do us much harm while they are jumping about. . . . And now what has Oliver got to say more?"

"Sir Oliver would have you know that the *Bay of Naples* is back. It sailed, as I suppose you will know, bearing the Grand Master's nephew, and——"

"It sailed for some wild-fire bombs! Has it brought those?"

"Yes. Sir Oliver——"

"That should have been said first. Not that they will be needed to-night. But they will be worth more than another hundred of men."

"There were some brought over to-night."

"Oliver is a good man. I would drink to him now, but I have taken enough, and I would not be caught in the wrong mood at a sudden chance, such as may come ever in time of war. Now you shall tell me the talk of nephews and knights, and of what Sir John thinks, but he dare not say."

"The Grand Master sent his nephew and Commander Salvago to the Viceroy to set out the great force of the Turks, and the urgent strait in which Malta is placed thereby, and to enquire by which day he could be assured that relief would come.

"He has replied with a written word, naming the fifteenth of June as the day on which he will have an army upon our shores——"

"Which I am to be assured that he will not do?"

"He says that there was a condition that our ships should be sent to him, for which he still waits."

De Broglio met this statement with a burst of laughter that filled the room.

"Was Sir John wroth? I would have gone helmless to-morrow to see his face when he read that."

"He did not look pleased, but I have no message on that from him. Sir Oliver says that we can hope little from Sicily or from Spain, at least at this time. We are to depend on ourselves; for he reads the letter in that way, and he thought that you ought to know."

"You have a discreet tongue for one in whom the disease of youth is so rank. Oliver chooses well. I will not tempt you to say more than you have heard, but you can tell him from me that (beyond the jest of the ships, which it was worth your trouble to bring, at a time which is too sober and dull) I have learnt nothing I did not know. Reynard thinks that Heaven should be pleased enough that he nets heretics in the Holland towns without killing infidels here, which it is more expensive to do. *Nolite confidere in principibus*. If he come at all, he will wait till there have been much slaughter on either side, so that there will be less for him to do and more honour to be won at a bargain rate. We should build nothing on him."

Angelica understood easily enough that whom he called Reynard must be her Spanish king, of whom, as she had said to Sir Oliver before, her uncle had been used to speak in a different way, but she used the discretion on which she had just been complimented, giving no answer at all.

She said that the boat would be waiting to take her back, and if the Governor had no further message to send——

De Broglio said no to that. He said he gave thanks for the bombs, praising appropriate saints. For the rest, Sir John could be assured that the Turks would not find it easy to come over St. Elmo's walls, "for," he concluded, "we are in more comfort being alone."

Angelica parted with the ceremonies of courtesy which she had observed to be practised among the Maltese knights, to which she received a jovial informality of response, and a regret that she could not make a more leisurely stay.

As she was about to leave, she was aware of the sound of a guitar in the adjoining apartment, which was the dormitory of a company of the Spanish soldiers who had been hired from the Sicilian Viceroy, and a song rose in her own tongue:

"Love is the same in every clime,
  In Afric heat or Arctic snow.
Love was the same at every time,
  But only of our own we know;
And when we——"

De Broglio, seeing that she had paused to listen, interrupted with the observation: "You will be able to inform Sir John that we are cheerful of spirit, and—and instant in prayer."

CHAPTER XVII

THE report that Angelica brought back from St. Elmo was satisfactory enough; though, had she seen others of the garrison, she might have met with some who would have talked in a different tone.

But, indeed, De Broglio's matter-of-course attitude (which treated death as a daily event of no more consequence than a meal) may have been of even greater avail than the higher ideality of D'Egueras (who would talk of the surrender of life as of a supreme sacrifice in a sacred cause) in giving courage and confidence to the heroic company of those who looked up the long slope of Sceberras to the hundredfold assembly of their pitiless and implacable foe. And even to say that De Broglio was deficient in ideality is to go beyond proof, he being of those who will never speak of themselves, or of what they think, so that we must guess what we will from that which their lives show, with the chance that we may guess wrong.

It was clear that the St. Elmo garrison was yet confident in the strength of its walls and in a mood to repel attack in a resolute way; and there was cause for good heart and hope in St. Angelo also, as the night advanced, and frequent small parties of knights and volunteers came in from the sea, giving a greater effect of numbers than if they had come at once in a single ship, or in two. But this was offset as the morning dawned by the news that a Greek renegade, Ulichiali, a pirate who stood high in the confidence and regard of the Turks, had joined them from Alexandria on the previous day (though he had been able to do no more than anchor beyond St. Paul's Bay till the mist cleared), with six galleys which were heavily armed, and crowded with such men as a corsair is likely to have on board.

The Turkish battery did not open next morning against St. Elmo in the first hour, for Piali had been less than satisfied with its performance on the previous day. He was anxious that St. Elmo should fall before Dragut could arrive, so that the full credit should come to himself; and he had been disconcerted already when he had found that the fleet could not operate against it with much effect. It was now realized also that though the fort was intended primarily to defend the harbours from sea-attack, yet it was so designed, its heaviest guns being mounted on a high cavalier on the seaward side, that it could bring them all to bear against a landward assault, as they could be turned and fired over the inner fort, which was less lofty than they.

The idea of attacking it as it were from the rear, on the landward side, became therefore more formidable at a closer view than Piali had supposed when he had advocated it at the first. Not that he was in any doubt as to the result, the disparity of force being too great; and he was resolved, if all else should fail, that it should be taken by storm before Dragut should come, though it might be at the cost of a thousand slain.

With these thoughts in his mind, he had ordered that the battery should not open on the second day, even though the mist should have cleared, until he should be there himself to direct its fire; and, being eager to make an end, he was there at an early hour.

The Turkish cannon were heavier than those that were mounted upon the fort, but the mounds which had been built for their protection were less strong than its walls of stone, so that they had suffered more on the first day; but this damage had been well repaired in the night, and a shattered gun-carriage replaced, so that the whole of the fourteen cannon were able to open at once, directing their fire upon the cavalier with the intention of silencing the heavier artillery of the fort.

St. Elmo's guns, which had been silent till then, replied from every angle at which they could be brought to bear on the Turkish battery, and those who watched from St. Angelo's walls saw their separate flashes, and the clouds of sulphurous smoke gathering ever blacker in a still air, as they had done on the day before.

But the Grand Master had not been deaf to the request that De Broglio had sent, and St. Angelo opened fire also, with two long culverins which were mounted upon its battlements, and were intended to sweep the harbour against any hostile ships which might pass its mouth.

Now they were tilted aloft, and threw their balls across the harbour to the opposite hill. They had no better target than the smoke that hung over the Turkish battery and the gun-flashes that could be seen at times. They fired short at first, striking the near side of the hill, but after that they got the range and found that they could fire over the crest, though it was not to be thought that they would do much hurt, not seeing where their shots fell.

More than once the balls bounded down the far side of the hill, falling at last into the harbour beyond with a useless splash, and the Turks watched them and laughed. But after that there came one that may be said to have paid for all. It fell on the battery mound, where it had been built of some blocks of stone. The stone it struck was flung in fragments around, and when the dust cleared, the Admiral Piali lay a senseless heap, for a splinter had struck his head.

Later in the day there came a rumour to St. Angelo that Piali was dead, at which there was rejoicing beyond the cause, for he lay in his tent with nothing worse than a broken head. But the event gave St. Elmo a respite of something less than a week, for Mustapha, taking control, ordered that, though the bombardment should be kept up, there should be no effort beyond that to obtain the fort till Dragut should arrive.

For a short space of days the event paused, with no more than cannonading at times, some sharp-shooting on both sides, and constant skirmishing along the rear of the Turkish positions, where Marshal Couppier gave them rest neither by dark nor day.

A doubt rose at this time as to whether the attack on St. Elmo were to be pressed as had first appeared, or whether the resolute front which had been shown to the first assault might have caused Mustapha, now that Piali was stilled, to decide on concentration upon the castle itself without wasting further time on the smaller objective.

The people of St. Angelo and the Bourg moved as those who look up to a black cloud which delays to burst, not knowing where it will fall but seeing that the near tempest is sure. Each day a few wounded or dead were brought in from beyond the walls or in boats from St. Elmo's point, and were tended or buried with more of care or ritual than would be thought sufficient at a later time, and each day La Valette counted a gain to him, thinking that it must bring them nearer to that on which the Christian States would become active for his relief; but on the fifth day there was a great salvo of artillery from the Turkish fleet, telling that Dragut had arrived, and giving him the welcome due to his name and the strength he brought.

He came up from the south, with thirteen galleys and two galliots under his flag, from which he landed fifteen hundred men, keeping their crews and rowers aboard, for he would not reduce the fighting strength of his fleet, in which he took more pride than in the provinces that he ruled ashore.

They were all of the same style, ships that were swift and lean and fanged, having little space for cargo below, they being no more than a pack of hunting wolves, the carnivora of the sea.

Dragut came ashore at once, and when he heard that Piali was hurt, he said that Allah was great, which those who heard could take as they would, for he cared for none.

He was met by Mustapha very courteously on the shore, and taken to his tent, where they talked for some time, finding that they could agree well enough, for their opinion of Piali was the same, though it was Dragut who gave it words.

As to attacking St. Elmo, he said it had been folly at first. They should have overrun the island, driving Marshal Couppier into the sea, and then attacked St. Angelo with their whole force. He said the ships could find harbours enough. He scoffed at the idea that Europe would gather a fleet that would be strong enough to offer battle.

"Will they come," he asked, "from England or Spain, or the Baltic seas? They would take a year to agree about that, if they ever should. We should be home months before. It is no more than a fool's fear."

But when he saw the battery that Piali had set up his contempt broke out into ribald jests. There was in Dragut, whether sober or drunk, a furious energy that was never still, and before which opposition melted away. He had, beyond that, an instinct for the essential which approached genius.

He saw that, if they were to withdraw the battery from before St. Elmo, it would be a confession of divided counsel if not of failure, of which all Europe would hear in the next week. He also saw that they would need the heavy guns that were planted there if they were to attempt to batter through the walls of Burmola or the Bourg.

Therefore they must continue the assault till St. Elmo should fall, on which he agreed with Piali that it should be the work of no more than a few days, but he did not think that his methods would have brought that result. He saw that to attack St. Elmo without speedy success would be just what the Grand Master would have them do. "Shall we be," he asked, "no more than a tail that Valette wags as he will?" He saw that to make St. Elmo's reduction sure it must be cut off from the Castle's support, and that their guns must command the harbour for that. There was no avail in a battery that skulked on the further side of the hill to avoid St. Angelo's guns. He had not landed a day before excavations were being made on the crest of Sceberras, and material being dragged up to make a higher and stronger battery there, which could reply to St. Angelo's guns and sink any boats that should attempt to cross to St. Elmo's point. On the further side of the entrance to the northern harbour he landed men from the fleet, who built a four-gun battery there to bombard St. Elmo from the other side. They had heavy guns and good gunners enough, and he was determined that they should be used to the full. He directed all with his own presence, and his own voice, toiling as one who counted the hours. Some of the Turkish galleys were deprived of their larger guns, and (to silence complaint) he even brought ashore one long serpent-handled culverin from his own ship, which it gave him no joy to do.

Two days later, while the new batteries were still incomplete, the spirit which Dragut had brought to the attack was demonstrated in another way. During the night of June 2nd-3rd, two of his corsair followers crept down, by the light of a clouded moon, till they were under the walls of the ravelin, where it looked out over Marsa Mucetto harbour-mouth, toward the new battery which Dragut planned to erect on the further side.

They listened, and all was still. It was a side from which St. Elmo had yet no fear of attack: its guns had not yet found a target on which to fire. One of the men climbed on the shoulders of the other, and looked in at a gun embrasure. The silence was unbroken. The moonlight shone on a platform of stone that appeared to be empty of human life. Unseen, unheard, the men stole back to tell what they had found. An hour later, a regiment crept down Sceberras' slope through the night.

The ravelin was no more than an isolated lunette, connected with the main fort by a covered way. During the night it had a garrison of twenty men, who should have kept a good watch. That there were those among them who slept when they should have waked appears sure. But, beyond that, nothing is known, for the whole garrison died.

They did not all die in their sleep. There was alarm given which was too late to avail. The night became loud with voices and the clangour of swords. But the Turks had swarmed up the wall before that, and were ten to one. Having slain all that the ravelin held, they tried to enter the fort itself by the covered way.

But St. Elmo was roused by then. There was strife in the narrow passage, fierce and short, and the Turks gave up what it had become useless to try. But if they could not win the fort, neither could the Christians win the ravelin back. It showed the Turkish flag when the dawn came, as it would continue to do, and its two guns had been turned, and now pointed towards the fort.

It was a poor tale for the Grand Master to hear.

CHAPTER XVIII

"It is vain talk," La Cerda said. "You are like the Grand Master himself in that. You will shut your eyes and think you avoid a fact which you do not see. There is but one course, if we are to recover our loss, as any soldier would say."

"You mean," D'Egueras replied, "that that is a name which I do not bear?"

"Not at all," La Cerda parried, seeing that he had gone too far. "You are a soldier of great repute, as is known to all. Therefore I say you must see the truth unless your eyes are shut by your own resolve."

"Had you had your will, you had blown up the whole fort before now."

"So I would. I have been plain about that. But I would have stayed my hand had I thought the Turks would try such folly as you would now do on our side. If you want to die a vain death, there is no surer way than to stand under a wall from which bombs are thrown, and some boiling pitch, and a few trifles besides. And that might be sound warfare if done by the Turks which were plain folly for us. We have not the men. Even the Grand Master would see that."

"He would see what is seen by all, that you would blow the ravelin up as a step toward that which you have urged from the first. You would blow up all if you could. . . . But you are one who did not toil at the work!"

"Well, it is not for us to decide. I may give advice by the favour of those who hear; but, I thank St. Peter, the decision is not for me."

La Cerda looked at De Broglio as he said this, as though to remind the Lieutenant-Governor that there was one there with more authority than his own. The gesture was lost on D'Egueras, who was not of a jealous kind. He cared for naught but the cause in which he laboured and fought.

De Broglio had said nothing till now. He sat, as he had done when he gave Angelica audience a week before, with his hose comfortably loose, and a tankard beside his hand.

"Nay," he said, "you are both wiser than I. That is why John did not leave me in sole command. I am past my prime. You are more versed in the new science of war, which I did not learn."

He said this with twinkling eyes, not as one who was angered or mocked, but with the tone of one who jests among friends. He added: "But at this time, I should say, if I must, that you are both wrong." He reached for the tankard again. "And if you will have patience awhile, I will tell you why."

D'Egueras had spoken with a passion, and proposed a plan, which were both easy to understand. He blamed himself, more than he need, that the ravelin had been lost. It was no failure of his, though the over-care he had taken at times to watch that the sentries were not asleep, and to augment the patrols, may actually have tended to produce the catastrophe which had now come by causing others to feel that there was no need to be watchful in the same way. Whatever else might go wrong, it might have been thought, there was no fear that a watch would fail while D'Egueras was in command. But it could not be expected that he would recognize, or find consolation in that.

Yet so it had been, and D'Egueras, blaming himself, had proposed to call for volunteers whom he would lead in an endeavour to recover the lost outwork at point of sword, to which La Cerda had retorted that it would end in waste of life, and no more: the only way to undo the reverse they had had was to undermine the outwork and blow it up, sending the Turks which it now contained to their own place without further loss on the Christian side.

D'Egueras rejected the proposal at once, as coming from one whom he thought deficient, if not in valour, yet in completeness of devotion to the cause which had called them together there; and also because he was reluctant to see the ravelin destroyed. He was one of those who had followed the Grand Master's example, working at its erection with his own hands. He knew the cost and the toil. So far, it had been no use. There had been no attack from the side it covered. Its two guns had not been used. To-morrow, Dragut's new battery would assume form on the opposite shore, and would be an objective on which to fire; but to-day it was in the hands of the Turks, who were turning its guns upon those who had laboured to place them there. He did not want it destroyed. He wanted it recovered into the hands of those to whom it belonged.

Looking back on an event that is past, we may see that the hope of Malta was not dimmed, though all the toil that had built that outwork in the last days had been so utterly vain; for it lay in the valour of those whose hands had toiled at the work, and that valour remained, as was shown by the venture that D'Egueras was proposing now.

La Cerda had not toiled at the work. He had no sentimental regard for the ravelin. It was to him a small outwork, mounting two guns, neither more nor less. He looked at the matter in a cool way. He considered that the Turks would have filled it with men, and that they would be surely alert, both by night and day, being so close to their foes. It had a glacis which would not be easy to climb against such a greeting as they would be certain to get. The Turks could afford loss of men much better than the Knights of Malta could do. It was plain folly, look at it any way that you would. He thought D'Egueras to be less soldier than monk, and he knew that his own strength was in the opposite scale. Therefore D'Egueras should listen to him, which he would not do.

De Broglio looked at the angry men, and spoke to La Cerda first:

"If I have understood what I have heard you saying at times, you do not think that this fort can be long held, nor even for a short time without more loss of life than that time is worth. Thinking thus, how can you advise that which would be slow to complete?"

"Because, though you are right that I would blow up the whole fort if the decision rested with me, and withdraw while we can cross the harbour in peace (which we shall not do in two days from now), yet, as it has otherwise been resolved, I would hold out here in the best manner we may, and do our foes the most damage we can, according to the skilful usage of war."

"Well, we are agreed upon that. But have you thought that we must tunnel the solid rock, and how long will that take? If we could work in a soft soil, or a crumbling rock, I would say well. But as it is, and with the secrecy which must be observed, I do not think we shall tunnel them, nor they us, before this bout will be through in another way."

D'Egueras, who was impatiently striding the narrow room, as the Governor gave this opinion in his own leisurely style, turned sharply round at that word.

"Do you mean to say that this fort will not be held? Are you another who talks of flight? I had not thought it of you!"

De Broglio declined to be roused by this outburst.

"Did I talk of flight?" he asked. "I should have thought my words were plain. If you say that this fort can be held against the whole force of the Turkish arms, then I should say you are blind in he way of those who refuse to see. I should say La Cerda here is right about that. It is what even Sir John cannot think, unless he have lost the wits he had in his younger days.

"I should say that we are here to kill Turks, and to draw their fire. He will have us kill all we can, and hold out to the last hour. He will have St. Elmo make such defence that when it fall it will be a shame to the Christian lands that have watched us die.

"If there must be such exhibit made, he will have St. Elmo and not St. Angelo fall; so that, if Europe be roused at last, there will be something left for them to save."

He reached for another drink as he ended this speech. Wiping his mouth, he said placidly, as one considering a matter in which he had no concern: "You may say that John is a hard man, as he ever was at the core, but you need not call him a fool." He turned his glance to D'Egueras as he went on: "And that is why, while I am Governor here, I will have no call for volunteers to climb the lunette walls. We are not here to be killed as we do that, but to kill Turks who climb ours. We must endure (being ever reinforced from the other side) till they get somewhat too bold, or weary of the delay, and are tempted to make assault, for it may be then that our hour will come."

He went on after another pause, which his hearers did not interrupt, he having given them both something of which to think, as he put that in a plain way which must have been vaguely in many minds.

"And that is why he will have been a wild man when he heard that the ravelin is already lost. I would have given much to hear what was said. I suppose he will have cursed us after the wording of sundry psalms. He will have said that that is what comes of leaving a fat old man in control, who is past the vigour of youth. Well, he may be right about that. He can call me back if he will, and I shall get more sleep than I do now.

"Yet he may think that where I sit down, I am not easy to move. He would not think that I talk of flight because I see how he may have planned that he will leave us to die.

"But be that as it may, he will see that his plan is wrecked if St. Elmo can be taken with ease. He should withdraw now, rather than that."

He turned to La Cerda, as he concluded in a way which may have been more unexpected than anything he had said before:

"Now I will tell you what I have resolved. I will send you back. You will go back in my name, asking the Grand Master that he call a Council, as I think it is within our right that we ask, at which it shall be resolved whether St. Elmo shall be longer held, the ravelin being already lost, or if we shall withdraw while it can still safely be done.

"You can put the case for that better than most, and you may stand up to him in a bolder way. And if, after all is said, it be resolved that we hold it still, we shall know to what end it is that we must endure beyond hope of quarter at last, by the settled usage of war."

La Cerda, as he heard this, looked as a man who feels that he should be pleased, but is not sure that he is.

He asked: "Am I best for that? He will be wroth, seeing me back. It was for such a word that he sent me here."

"Yes. I should call you best. I know none besides who could do more than say Amen to the first speech he might make, let them grumble here as they may.

"He may fume awhile, but what can he say? You will have written word that you come from me."

"Well," La Cerda said, "if I have your order I have no choice but to go. When shall it be?"

"I will have letter writ so that you can put off at the matin hour. You should get some sleep before then, for afterwards you will do talking enough. I am for bed myself now."

La Cerda went out at that hint. So did D'Egueras, who would make another round of the walls.

De Broglio did but loosen his clothes, and lay down in such a form that he could be about again at a quick need. He smiled somewhat to himself, thinking of how mad La Valette would be when La Cerda should return with such a message from him. "But," he thought, "I know John. If he be crossed, he will be more set on his own way. He will bear all down. And they will know the purpose for which he sends them to death, which will make them the better men.

"Also, when it is done with purpose agreed, he will send support with less niggard hand than he have done yet; and—by the death of Peter!—I need it now."

For he had met Dragut before.

CHAPTER XIX

"A MAN of law," Sir Oliver observed, "might say it is less than proved, yet it is beyond doubt to my mind. I have not mentioned it to his son, as I sought first to gather all the assurance I could; but I have questioned Captain Antonio, who was a volunteer on the *Curse of Islam's* deck at the time."

"And what," Señor Ramegas asked, "does he say?"

"He says that, as they came in sight of the chase, there was one wearing knightly arms who climbed from the smaller boat over the bow of the corsair ship, as it ran it down."

"Could it be said that Don Francisco sank the ship, his father being on board?"

"It appears not. Or that, at least, Antonio will not allow. His tale is that the Christian knight had fallen some time before, either from the crowding swords of his foes, or from the fire of the mortars which descended upon the decks, which had nigh sunk the ship before the *Curse of Islam* could use her guns.

"When they came up, they looked down on a deck over which the sea washed. They saw Moors who swarmed up the ropes or were already a-swim. Their guns did no more than to shatter a sinking deck, giving death to the corsair crew by a shorter road."

"It is a thing that Don Francisco must know. Will you tell it yourself, or shall I?"

"I will leave that to you," Sir Oliver said, "by your good will. For you know him better, and also have somewhat more leisure than I. But there are certain matters arising herefrom with which our Order must deal, and concerning which Don Francisco should see me at a near date; though it may be resolved, for the most, if not all, that they may be left somewhat aside till we come to a quieter time."

Sir Oliver paused a moment, as though he would have said more, and then stayed his words; but as Ramegas answered only that Don Francisco would wait upon him without doubt, when he had informed him of what was supposed, and then rose as though there were no more to be said, he added: "There is another matter which cannot be left, if we agree that Don Manuel is no longer alive."

Ramegas did not profess failure to understand what was meant, but he said no more than: "It is the señorita you have in mind?"

"Yes."

Sir Oliver, wishing to know what attitude Ramegas might take to that matter, or what suggestion would come from him, found that he confronted a silent man. Seeing that the conversation must die or be sustained further by him, he asked: "Should you say that she will accept her cousin's control? He has done well since he came here, but he is one I have scarcely seen."

"He is one of whom I can speak nothing but good, he being Don Manuel's son. I cannot say beyond that."

Sir Oliver thought that he had said nothing at all, and yet that he had implied much concerning which he had not been asked. For he judged Ramegas to mean that if Don Manuel were dead, it did not follow that the responsibility for his family should fall upon him, which was not far from the truth.

To say that Ramegas was glad to hear of Don Manuel's death would be unjust to one who had been a loyal servant to him, to whom duty was a stern and imminent god, and whose conscience was in good repair.

But he had a pride which had not chafed the less at the lowly office of serving-brother because he had been scrupulous to fulfil its obligations. He had had some liking for Don Manuel, and more respect; but it would have been no pleasure to give up the important separate command which he now held to take a place beneath the Commander's pennon on St. Angelo's outer wall, as Don Manuel might have expected that he would do.

Sir Oliver recognized that there was truth in the implication that his obligation was personal to Don Manuel, and did not outlast the separation of death. The very nature of a celibate order precluded the establishment of inherited rights or responsibilities. It had become exceptional (following a statute of De L'Isle Adam thereon, of fifty years before) for any Knight of the Order to have a recognized son, though the number of "nephews" who joined their ranks at this emergency suggests that this may at times have been a euphemistic rather than an accurate description of their relationship.

Juan Ramegas was not indifferent to the fortunes of Don Manuel's niece. In a sufficient emergency he would have ministered to her security, even her comfort, in a kind and conscientious way. But if Don Manuel were dead, and his service over to him, it must not be understood that he had a remaining duty to her.

For this time he did not regard her as being in any need. He had rendered her to the Grand Master's charge, who had delivered her to that of Sir Oliver Starkey. Beyond that, her cousin was here, who was also of Don Manuel's blood. How could she concern him now? Her escapade, which he disapproved in a grave and tolerant way, was no longer his responsibility. Sir Oliver should see that without the crudity of definition. So his silence implied, as he meant that it should.

Sir Oliver understood him and let him go. Finding leisure among a multiplicity of urgencies, which would have distracted one of less orderly mind, he determined to speak to Angelica himself.

Making a prompt opportunity to have her alone, he said: "I have news for you which is not good; but it is needful for you to hear."

He saw that she became somewhat paler, though she made no guess at the truth. She had a vague fear that Don Manuel had learnt where she was and was exercising his authority to have her sent back, and to the Convent of Holy Cross, even though he were not come himself. She had formed a sound opinion that, if Don Manuel should make such request, she would have no support from the Grand Master against him: he would not give her two thoughts. It would be: "Send her away," and his regard would turn at once to the one issue that filled his mind.

Even apart from Don Manuel she was not assured that he would not dispose of her with so off-hand a word, if she should be brought to his notice again. She had for warning the fate of the lady who had occupied her chamber before, of whom she knew little but that La Cerda's position as a Commander of the Order had not been sufficient to keep her, as it was clear that he had wished to do. And St. Angelo was not yet so isolated that return to Sicily had become impossible. If such a crisis should come, she had only one hope, which was in Sir Oliver Starkey himself. She saw that, though he might have little power to influence La Valette on any matter on which he had a fixed mind, yet the Grand Master gave him so large a trust that there were a hundred details on which he would endorse anything that Sir Oliver might propose, or leave him authority to decide as he would; and she could but hope that she might be regarded as one of these lesser things. For though she did not look on the Secretary as one who was weak of will, or would be easy to cajole, she felt that she would have sympathy from him, of which she was less assured when she thought of any others who might have power over her life, and she had an instinctive certainty that he liked her well.

Now she thought that the crisis had come, and, if the news were not good, it must mean that she would be thwarted or shamed, unless she could find both courage and wit which would be sufficient to face the hour.

So she paled somewhat, but remained quiet, her mind wary and alert as Sir Oliver went on:

"It is not certainly known, but it is feared that Don Manuel has come to the harm either of capture or death in endeavour to reach these shores, for it was known to several of those who have joined our ranks during the last days that he had left Messina to cross the strait, and, by the time they give, and by the fact that no other is missed at that date, it is nigh to sure that he was on a boat that a corsair rammed on the day when the Turks first advanced hereon."

"Was it that which the *Curse of Islam* thereafter sank?"

"So it is thought. . . . I did not know that you had heard of that, or would have it in mind."

"It is likely I should, my cousin having command. If it befell thus, my uncle was soon avenged, and by him whose best right it was."

She did not doubt the truth of the tale, having confidence in the sober judgment of him from whose lips it came. Sorrow was confused in her mind with fear, and doubt, and relief, so that it was uncertain which would prevail.

If Don Manuel were dead, it was the end of the one actual authority she had known since she was too young for clear memory to have remained; she could not tell at once how she would stand, or what new difficulties might arise, but she felt that the shadow of Holy Cross was lifted somewhat away.

Sir Oliver went on: "I have not only to tell you this because you should know of one who is close of blood, but because you must consider how you now stand. You will recall that the Grand Master allowed that you should stay here till Don Manuel should arrive, you being under his charge rather than ours."

"Have you talked to Señor Ramegas of this?"

"Yes. But an hour ago. I understood that he feels that his part is done."

"So I should say that it is. Does Francisco know?"

"He may have told him by now."

"Will he talk of me?"

"I suppose not of himself, and Don Francisco is unlikely to ask. If I understand aright, he will suppose you to be afar, and in convent walls."

"So he does. Am I now free to do as I will?"

"That would be saying too much."

"Need the Grand Master know? Can I have time to think what I will do?"

"The Grand Master has heard that we fear Don Manuel is lost. He may think of you, and give what orders he will. If he does not, I do not say that I need call it to mind, your uncle's end being less than sure. Yet on that I can give no pledge. . . . I suppose that you will now wish that your cousin should know you are here and in what guise, you being left as you are."

"Will you leave that to me?"

"You would rather tell him yourself?"

"Yes. In my own way, if at all. I would think first. Is there occasion for haste?"

"I would not say that. You are safe here for this time. But things may change with the days in a quick way. You do not need to be told that."

While they had spoken the noise of gunfire had been continuous in their ears, for though Dragut had not got all his new batteries complete, he had ordered that there should be no respite for St. Elmo's garrison, and all the guns of Piali's battery, and some others, were bombarding the fort, which was replying with every one it could bring to bear.

But now the floor shook and a nearer din came from the castle roof, for St. Angelo was joining the concert with the long culverins she had used before, firing upon those who were building the new battery on Sceberras' ridge. There was no need of more words to tell her of the peril of the place to which she had come at the urge of a headstrong will.

"I should be glad if you would leave this to me, at least till we speak again."

"I may do that. But I would ask you this, for your own good. Have you estate apart from your uncle's grace?"

"I have Segura lands in my own right, which I may claim when I am of sufficient age, and the revenues would, in the meantime, have come to his charge. I was to endow the Convent of Holy Cross with these lands, and in return I was to be Abbess at a far day. That was how my uncle had bargained, as I believe, but I suppose that can be ended now."

"So I should conclude; though it may involve questions of law which are less simple than you suppose."

He questioned her as to the stewards and men of law who handled Don Manuel's own affairs, and found them to be the same who dealt with those which he held in the Order's name. He said that, with her consent, which she lightly gave, he would write to them that her rights should be watched with care. He said: "We will talk again on a near day. I think your cousin should know you are here in this guise, even though it should be single to him."

He turned to other affairs, which were of greater moment than that. For the time she saw that there would be nothing said, unless it were of her will. She felt sorrow as she thought of Don Manuel's end, for he had ever been kind to her in a distant way. She felt freedom also, and with it some measure of fear, for she had little practice of how to walk in the open ways of the world, and being garbed as she was, in a way which she was loth to longer maintain, and doubtful how she could cast aside, either to remain or to go. But she put fear aside with a very resolute will. She thought she would meet Francisco and tell him all; and then concluded, as she always did when she thought of that, that it could be done just as well on the next day.

And while she thought of these things and doubted what she would do, or to which end she would be likely to come, the batteries thundered without. And a boat from St. Elmo struck boldly across the harbour, which was not yet under the menace of Turkish guns, and La Cerda sat in the stern, being less than pleased with the mission on which he came, but resolved that he would do his charge in a manner fitting to the name he bore, and that La Valette should not silence his words, though he might conceive himself to be as great as the Pope of Rome.

CHAPTER XX

Venetia, raising long, softly-rounded arms over a pale-gold head in a yawn of weariness, such as may be born as surely and less tolerably from idleness as from toil, wondered whether she should be called a fool.

It was a question which she had seldom felt occasion to ask in the twenty years during which the chances of changeful times, her own sharp wits, and a judicious trafficking in the beauty of her supple, milk-washed body (but there was no milk to be had here, either for glance or gold!) had raised her from Genoa's shore-side slums to the exalted, almost respectable, position of the acknowledged mistress of a Knight-Commander of the high Order of St. John—one who was unable to give any woman a more legal name.

A year ago she did not doubt that she was the winner of a splendid prize. La Cerda was a prince in his own land. When the call to Malta had come, and he had said she should not be left behind, it would have seemed a monstrous folly to thwart his will. He was too great for her to doubt his power to protect his own. The talk of Turkish siege had sounded a vague improbable menace, such as was seldom absent from the horizons of those days. There was always the war of yesterday, or that which to-morrow would bring: war advancing over one frontier, or receding across another from a wasted land. It was amid such disorders that the chances had come which had raised her, step by step, to La Cerda's side. Her present name was one that her mother (hanged fifteen years before with sufficient cause) would not have known. Genoa was a city of which she would seldom talk. She had very plausible tales to tell of her early Venetian days, which may be left aside, being untrue. She had come to Malta to find, from the first day, that she was to be kept, if at all, as a hidden toy. She was to be kept like a bird in a gilded cage. Now the cage remained, but the gilt was less easy to see.

Should she have gone when she had the chance? When she had been hurried out of the turret-room she had made her own, in such furtive haste that she had left half her less valuable possessions behind?

She had been pleased at the time when La Cerda swore that he would not let her be sent away, either for fiend or saint: when his gold had been freely spent to find another who would take her place on the ship, and to cause the eyes of the guards to be turned aside.

But it had been irksome to be hidden since that day in this upper room. It had been well enough for La Cerda, who could walk abroad when he would, and then come to take his pleasure with her. That time had been bad enough; but now La Cerda had gone. . . . She asked herself again, had she been a fool to come? A greater fool not to have gone when she could?

La Cerda had warned her to lie close till his return—and Giles said that it was a score to one that that return would never be. Those who were now in St. Elmo's fort were not likely to come back alive. He said that was the common talk. And he also warned her against being seen, telling frightening tales.

Two days ago there had been a quarrel between two knights in which one had been badly hurt, so that it had come to the Grand Master's ears. They had fought, it was said, for the favour of a wanton who had not been expelled, she being a native, born in the town. It was the kind of trouble which would be likely to rise in a place full of armed men who waited for an attack which delayed to come.

The knights had been condemned to a penance suited to their degree: the woman had been publicly whipped. Giles had made the most of that tale. He had hinted that silence may ask a price. She thought that he would be likely to grow bolder as the days passed, if La Cerda did not return. If he should never return? Might not Giles consider her to be at his mercy then?

Well, she had been in worse holes before now, out of which her wits had won free. More than that, she had sometimes found that from danger she could snatch gain. There had been the governor of San Pietro jail. . . . That was how her fortune began. If she had not been caught with a wallet which was not hers, she might be on Genoa streets still. And yet that was less than a likely thing, she being what she was.

She might wish that she had never come, and that she were riding now, hawk on wrist, over the summer fields, as she had been able to do during the last year, that being a sport she loved; but she did not waste much thought in a vain regret. Like her hawk, in her thoughts, she flew high.

If La Cerda's life should be lost indeed, where could she make a friend who would be of avail to protect her now? She had no mind to be whipped. It was an experience she had never had, though she had been near it at times. She thought of La Valette. If she could seduce the Grand Master it would be a triumph indeed. But she considered him—what she had seen, and much more she had heard, and the certain fact that he was not young—in a mind that was shrewd and cool, and she decided that it would be too risky to try, except at a desperate need. Perhaps if the Turks should be driven out. . . . In the moment of triumph, when mind and body relaxed? But not now.

Then there was Sir Oliver Starkey, who had been her friend to the extent that he had been willing that she should go in a quiet way, and that without any purpose of gain to himself that she had been able to see. She considered him with a baffled mind, concluding that the enigma came of his barbarous blood. He was English, a race of whom she had seen little, but it was known that they came from a land of unlifting fog, by which their blood was not wholly thawed.

Well, it might be worth while to try. Not that she sought adventure or would take a chance that she might avoid. She had no thought of romance. It was cold business to her and, perhaps, greed. But she had had to fight for the right to live since she had been able to talk, or before, as did all in the underworld to which she was born. We must allow something for that. And she had fought better than most or, at least, to greater avail.

Now she stretched herself on the silk-soft couch that her wits had won, seeming to rest in an idle sensuous ease, without forethought or care. Even though she rested alone, she gave no sign that she hated the single house-top room to which she was confined by La Cerda's order and her own caution: no sign of the wary wakeful mind that sought to probe the future on every side. For it had been one of her first and most vital lessons of life that the face must not betray thought. . . .

Her thoughts paused at the sound of a quick step that was ascending the stair. She had keen ears. Was it——? Yes, she was sure. Her feet slid to the floor. With a cry of pleasure that was not wholly pretence, she moved quickly forward as La Cerda entered the room.

"You have come back?" she asked, as his kisses paused. "You will stay now? You will not be going again?"

"I do not know what will be. I cannot say. For the time, I wait here."

She asked no more, hearing the note of irritation in his voice, and being wise in her own ways. She supposed she would soon know. She understood the pride that was reluctant to be ordered about, which must have been felt by many of the Maltese knights, they being what they were in their own lands, except that they were inspired by the high occasion to which they came.

Her question recalled to his mind the angered annoyance of the reply he had given to Sir Oliver's first surprised query when they had met. "Why am I here? I do ever what I am told. I go forward and back. I carry notes."

He had learnt that the Grand Master had crossed to the Sanglea. He was inspecting the defences of St. Michael's fort. The loss of St. Elmo's ravelin had roused a restless rnxiety lest nearer and more vital points might be equally liable to surprise.

La Cerda had agreed with Sir Oliver, after the occasion of his coming was understood, that it would be best to return to his own lodging until La Valette should have had time to read the letter he brought and decide what he would do.

"I suppose," Sir Oliver had said, "there will be council called, and you can then say what you will. I should advise, if you will not take it amiss, that you should say nothing till then in a private way."

"You may be assured I shall not," he had replied, taking no offence. He wished to keep Sir Oliver's goodwill, for he was not sure that he might not find it needful to ask of him a greater favour than he had had before, and to admit that he had deceived him then. For, in the ordinary course, he would not have been allocated to St. Elmo's garrison without his household retinue fighting with him at the same place. Sir Oliver had been somewhat puzzled at the time that he had submitted to the Grand Master's order to go in a three hours' space, and a single boat, without raising that question at all, which would have been no more than to claim custom and right; but the fact was that he had seen that he could not have taken Venetia there, and had been content that the event fell as it did, so that his household was not broken up. Now, among other vexations that contended to distract his mind, it was not the least that he might be required to return to St. Elmo with all his train, and must then dispose of the girl as he best could.

It was a position which was not likely to make him less vehement in urging that St. Elmo should not be longer held; but he saw the wisdom of Sir Oliver's hint that he should not further disclose his mind till the Council met, if the Grand Master should consent for it to be called.

As they parted there had been the same thought in both their minds, that it was a fortunate chance that La Valette was away, so that he would read what De Broglio had written before he should meet his messenger face to face.

CHAPTER XXI

"As I see it," Sir Oliver said, "it does not rest upon that. If you will that St. Elmo be longer held, you will prevail at this time. But, beyond that, where do we stand, if it fall on the next day?"

"There is no cause that it should! Had I here but fifty knights of those with whom I had the honour to fight at Rhodes, being then but a youth and the least among famous names!"

Sir Oliver was quiet and exact. "I should say that is about the number we have, though they are not young at this day. . . . But I should also say we have other knights whose valour may not be less, and who are of equal resolve. . . . I did not propose that it need fall on the next day. I only say that we must be prepared against that, if we over-ride those who would blow it up. . . . Let the blame be where it will, we cannot deny that the outwork has been lost in an easy way."

The Grand Master did not deny the reason of this. He said: "It must be held by every means that we have. It were better to blow it up than that it should lightly fall. I need not be told that. I have a mind to go there myself."

"As to that, I should say, if I may, that your place is here."

"My place is that of the most need. Had I been there, do you think I had let the ravelin go? Yet I would not be less than just. There must be blame, though it should be no more than portioned among the dead, and we know not how. All our work in an hour!"

Sir Oliver was silent, understanding the emotion of the older man. And what use was there in words? What could be said?

La Valette paced the room for a time, striving for self-control. Then he asked, in a quieter way: "If I let this Council be held, can you tell me how the voting will go?"

"Yes, I am sure of that. I have been over the names. We can have sufficient support, let La Cerda say what he will."

"Then you advise that we call it now?" The question showed how much the Grand Master was disturbed in mind, for he would rarely ask or welcome advice on such matters as that. He added: "I would have no doubt. It must be held at all risks."

"That," Sir Oliver replied, "is why I would have it called. For after we have carried the vote, which I am assured that we shall, those who have been on our side, and have become hot in debate, will be more eager to prove their case than they are now. They will go with a better will."

"Then let it be called with speed. Can it be in two hours from now?"

"Yes. It can be that."

"Then, in God's name, let it be."

The Grand Master went out, and Sir Oliver sent messages right and left to the Commanders of the Order who were within call, being all that the island held, except those who were with Marshal Couppier, or in St. Elmo itself, to assemble for an urgent Council of War; so that La Cerda, having had a pleasant hour with his mistress, was fetched away at a quicker word than he had expected to have.

Yet he went in less haste than he might, for he did not intend to open his mind in random arguments before the Council should be sat down in an orderly way, and he had a hope that the Grand Master would state his case first, leaving him to a later reply, for he knew the weight of that which is last said, and he would rather have the Grand Master's words to attack than that his own should be exposed before the others had been advanced.

But in that matter he found that La Valette was as subtle of tactics as himself, and with more power to prevail, for when the assembly was set, the Grand Master rose at once, and, without reading De Broglio's note, he said briefly that it appeared that there were some in St. Elmo's fort who did not think that it should be held, and that its Governor, feeling that all should be of one mind, either to stay or to come away, had sent the noble Chevalier La Cerda to state the case of those who did not wish to remain; and he had therefore called a Council of War, as De Broglio had asked him to do, that the will of the Order regarding St. Elmo might be known beyond single responsibility, or the probability of later dispute. He would therefore ask La Cerda to state his case, so that they would have the objections of those who did not wish to continue the defence set out in the best way.

He said this in the Latin tongue, which was familiar to all those who were there, though in differing degrees, and in which he was fluent, and could be eloquent if he were sufficiently moved, and La Cerda saw that he had no escape but that he must rise at once, and reply in the same tongue, in which he was less expert.

Yet he put his case well enough, being curt and direct, and saying that which he truly believed, and which he knew to have support from the accepted rules and usage of war.

"I would have you know," he said, "that I am not here of my will. I was ordered to come. Nor do I wish to speak now, as it is required that I do. But, being constrained, I will say what I think, who am, as you may allow, of some knowledge and practice, and perhaps of some slight repute, in the exercise and methods of war.

"You are told that I speak for others who are of one mind. It is not I who had said that. You have been told that it is the Governor's own report. The knights who have been sent to defend the fort are not less brave than ourselves. They came here, as we all did, to protect the isle that is ours, with such courage and strength as we have, and with our lives as the stake we throw.

"The Grand Master would not say that when he chose the knights whose pennons were to appear on St. Elmo's wall he preferred such as were of doubted courage, or poor repute, even if any such among us would have been easy to find.

"But now, having been there for two weeks, what they say is this (and I do not disguise that I am of one mind with them): St. Elmo is a small fort. It is needless to tell you its size or the guns it bears. They are known to all. It has endured attack for these weeks while St. Angelo has looked on, during which time it has faced the whole might of the Turkish arms. How has it done that? Every day the dead and wounded have been brought off, and new men have been sent, who are to be there till they also fall. They do not complain of that, if it be for sufficient cause, such as will avail at the last.

"But to what end can we look? So far we have held the fort as a sick man may be kept alive, having fresh physic at every hour.

"But those hours are nigh done. Since Dragut came there are new batteries rising on every side. In two days from now, if not less, we shall send no more men to its aid, neither shall we bring the wounded away. It will be cut off, and how long then will it endure an army which is a thousand to ten, and the fire of a hundred guns?

"I say it will be down in three days, either by yielding its flag, when all of us who are there will be Turkish slaves at the best (for what terms could we hope to make, being so cornered apart?), or, if we fight on after hope is gone, those can expect no mercy who may be left alive when the Turks come over the wall, they having continued defence of an untenable post, for such (as I need not say) is the rule of war at all times, and in every land.

"Now to defend it thus we would not complain, though it is

much to ask (for the bravest will choose to fight where there is a hope, however slender and faint, that he may be alive on the last day), if sufficient cause could be shown, but we see none.

"We are to be slain, as it seems to us—I will use plain words, as must be right in such an issue as this—for no more than a stubborn whim, which will not own what all others can see.

"We are to defend walls that are weak, while St. Angelo's walls are strong. We are to face the whole army of Malta's foes, being no more than some scores, while there are thousands here who look on.

"And all this to no end but that, when they have slain us all, and the fort is theirs, the Turks may boast a success which they will not have if greater wisdom prevail.

"If St. Elmo were the strongest wall, or the last that we have, we would defend it still, and would not scruple to die.

"But the matter is not thus. For here are walls that are stronger and better held; and it is here that we ought to be."

He paused a moment to consider whether he had put the whole case, and seeking a final word that could be used with convincing force; and Gonzales de Medrano, a noble knight of Castile, who had won much fame in the Spanish wars, asked without rising: "Then what, by your advice, should we now resolve?"

He asked as one with an open mind, who would not decide till the whole case had been fairly put.

Sir Oliver, watching all, had his first doubt (which was not much) as to how the voting would go, for he knew that Medrano could sway half the Spanish knights, if not more.

La Cerda gave a plain question a plain reply. "I would blow up the fort, so that they get no more than a heap of stones, which are cheap on this isle. I would withdraw our men while we yet can, with such stores as we may be able to save. The Turks will find their new batteries are of no avail when we are not there. St. Elmo will have delayed them the most it can, and at a cost which is less than theirs. If we do not, I tell you that it cannot stand for three days. It is annihilation of our own knights which we contrive to ensure, and for the Turks a triumph they need not have."

La Cerda sat down at that, and Medrano said: "It is fairly put," looking round as he did so to other knights, who appeared to be of the same mind, and then to the Grand Master, as the one who should make reply.

La Valette saw that all men waited for him to speak, which he was not reluctant to do.

He spoke with more freedom of phrase than La Cerda had been

able to use, and though there may have been more of passion and less of reason in what he said, he had the art of moving men with his words, and he had one argument (if such it could be called) which he kept to the last and by which he felt that he must prevail.

"Brothers," he said, "you have heard what is proposed, that we should blow up our fort, it being otherwise lost, as we are to believe, by the mathematics of war.

"And, if we do that, we may be advised in another week that St. Angelo here should not be held against so great an army as we shall then face, and, by these same reckonings of skill, we shall be advised to make such terms as we can, which may be no worse than that they will let us depart with the honours of war, and even our baggage, if we should stand out to that point.

"Well, you may do that if you will, but you will not find that I sit here or have a part in such shame.

"We know how we stand. It is as Sicily's fief that we hold this isle, and, behind Sicily, there is the great empire of Spain, within whose shelter we rightly lie. We are weak and few, and against us are gathered Turkey and Egypt, and all the Barbary coast. There was time enough for Spain to have had an army here by which they would not have landed at all, being met on the beach in such a sort that they would have sailed away from a prey that they could not take.

"We have promise now that a strong aid will be here by the middle month, as to which we shall see at that time, but till it come (as I say that it must at last) we must hold our walls by our own strength, and John Baptist's name, and the high mercy of God.

"When I saw how we should be left for a time I said that I would not venture my knights against the infidel hordes, for I could spare them less than I could be comforted by the foes they slew. I said: 'I will trust to stone.' I meant that the Turks should come to our walls, where they will be likely to die.

"So I said, and I have not changed. I will trust to every stone that we have. If we can hold St. Elmo for a time during which they will assault it with all their power, it is time gained during which St. Angelo stands secure, and while St. Angelo stands they have gained naught, let St. Elmo end as it may.

"But if we blow it up, it is of no avail from that hour. Why, it is for that they strive! It would be to do their work, for which they should shed their blood in a larger way than we ours, as must ever be when there are stone walls to be stormed. Did we toil to build it for that?

"You will say there is the ravelin gone in an easy way. I will say nothing to that, lest I say too much. For I would be just, and when I think thereof I am moved by a bitter wrath.

"But the fort shall not fall at so cheap a price. You can be certain of that. For I will go myself, whether with those who will volunteer, or with none. For I will order no more. I will send no man to death which I do not share. But I intend that the Cross shall fly from St. Elmo's walls till it fall at a bitter cost, if so be that it shall fall at last. And I will defend that wall to the last hour, though I stand alone."

The Grand Master paused, not as one who had finished speech, but as though emotion hindered his words, and in the moment's silence a babel of voices rose, protesting that he could not be spared, that his place was there, and that there was no knight who would not go, whether at his order, or alone.

Amid the hubbub, Medrano rose. "Grand Master," he cried in a clear high voice that cut through the din, "may I say a few words, by your leave, before you reproach us more with that which we have not thought?"

As it was seen that he stood, there was silence among the Spanish knights, which spread through the hall as his voice rose. La Valette stood silent, as though doubtful whether he would not do better to say more, but Sir Oliver's hand was upon his arm.

"It is enough," he said, "we must hear them now." And on that La Valette sat down, saying that Sir Gonzales should next be heard.

CHAPTER XXII

Gonzales de Medrano was one of those fortunate individuals who are not only born to positions of wealth and dignity, but appear to have been particularly adapted by nature for the part which they are called to play in the drama of human life.

Handsome of face and form, combining mental ability and vigour of body with a strength and nobility of character sufficient to withstand the temptations of luxury and ambition, exact in the obligations of honour, generous to his equals, considerate to those who served him, he bore without absurdity the name of "the faultless knight," which had been bestowed upon him by the general voice of his compatriots. Exemplifying in his person and his career the profound truth of the precept that to him that hath shall be given, he yet appeared to have escaped the danger of those of whom all men speak well, and if, at this time, there might have appeared to a detached observer something of arrogance in his manner, of assumption that others would be silent to hear him, it would be contradicted by his deliberate courtesies, and was unnoticed by those around, who, even in that assemblage of princely knights, would give him deference as his natural due.

"We have," he said, "as I see it, a simple issue on which to decide, and one on which we must promptly pronounce with a voice which we cannot change. For in a space of few days, at the most, St. Elmo will be so ringed by its foes that it may be outside our power either to succour or to withdraw.

"We have heard the case for evacuation fairly stated, and well; and I suppose we should all agree that it is so strong that it may be held by those whose valour is of a proved worth and who are masters of the chess-board of war.

"Yet we have heard that it is a course which our Grand Master will not approve, preferring rather to go himself to its last defence, to which we surely could not consent, for his is a life which we may not spare, neither is it to our Order's welfare (which must be first with us all) that our foes should be able to boast they have brought him down.

"We have heard the reasons also upon his side, which are strong alike, and, coming from him whom we have chosen our Order's head, they are such, I think, as we cannot refuse.

"Yet, there is this, I think, on which all will rightly agree, that it were better that the fort should be blown up by our own hands than that it should be stormed on a near day; so I will submit my advice either that it be destroyed in the next hour, or that it be sustained with a much larger force than it now has, it being agreed that we may be near our last chance to send safely across either munitions or men."

La Valette interposed: "There is always the night."

"There is the night," Medrano agreed; "but the moon is now near its full, and apart even from that, if we were placed as the Turks are, we could devise ways to vex those who should seek to cross when their batteries cover both harbour and landing-beach, as they are designing to do, and we cannot rely that their sleights will be less than ours.

"I say that, if we seek to hold St. Elmo at all we should send strong inforcement this night, and to that end, and that the most time may be gained during which our walls here may be left in peace, I will offer this: I will go with not less than two hundred men, and with fifty knights——" he glanced over the board at his sure friend, De La Motte, who nodded slightly, and he corrected his words—"we will go, De La Motte and I, on one bargain alone, that the Grand Master shall here remain, he having all matters in charge, and being one that we cannot spare. Now who will join us in this, or will say where we are wrong?"

He looked round, and was met with a clamour of assenting cries. At that moment he could have had the names of four-fifths of those who were there, though some of them might have blamed their choice in a cooler hour, and the few that were more cautious or faint of heart were content to sit still and be overthought.

Sir Oliver saw that the end they sought had been reached, though the meeting had not gone quite as he thought it would. He was adroit to contrive that it should break up without the taking of formal vote, so that it should appear that all were agreed, as they mostly were.

The Grand Master said no more of going himself, though it had been meant at the time.

He saw that his will was won, but that did not make him the more complacent toward those who had ventured to cross it. He walked down the room, and faced La Cerda with a look on his face which approached contempt. He said only: "In five minutes from now, there will be a reply written for you to take back to the fort, concerning which you will lose no time."

Having said this, he turned aside, without giving any time for reply.

La Cerda stood motionless, only showing that he had heard by the frowning anger that darkened his eyes.

It was, indeed, a vexation to him in a way that the Grand Master could not guess. He had not supposed that it would be necessary to return after the Council in such haste that he would be unable to visit his lodging again. He had told Venetia that he would be back in two hours, if not less.

There had been hints of dissatisfaction, even of trouble, in some things she had said, which he had been intending to probe, but which must now be left to a time which would be unlikely to come. And he saw, beyond that, that whatever honour there might be for others at last in St. Elmo's defence, there could be little for him.

There was one other who saw that as clearly as he, and who felt that it should be said.

Medrano stood at his side.

"You had a strong case," he said, "which you put with reason and right. Are you among those who go back?"

"I am ordered there."

Medrano thought that the Grand Master had done wrongly in that. He should have left La Cerda to go back as a volunteer, if at all. But he kept that in his own mind.

"It is hard," he said, "for you; for you must now toil to prove that yourself was wrong. And" (a smile lit his face) "I will tell you this. I am not sure that you were. . . .

"Yet, the Grand Master standing out as he did, I thought that he would get his way in the end, and that it would be best that opposition should not become strong, so that we should go, if we must, with a common will."

"We go," La Cerda answered, "to a vain death for a stubborn fool."

The smile left Medrano's eyes. "We die once," he said easily—"and, as yet, we live."

He walked on, thinking that La Valette had not handled all in the best way. He had a disposition to make men wroth. He roused opposition that he might have saved himself by a gentler word. Yet, if he roused men thus, he was of a mood that would bear them down.

Medrano saw that La Valette had got his way at this time (by his own aid) as a more moderate man might have found it less easy to do. Well, let that be as it might, he had this adventure to fill his mind, it being, as he saw, likely to be the last of a life that he had good causes to love.

He went to seek Sir Oliver that he might be assured that there would be no lack of provisions for the men he would lead, or of munitions transported during the night.

He found him busy with many cares, but with a moment's leisure for him.

"There will be more volunteers," Sir Oliver said, "than the numbers you plan to take, both among soldiers and knights. Will you have these ignored and your force assigned in the customed way, or will you choose among them?"

"I will have none come but of his free choice, whether soldier or knight, for I think we go to a certain death, which is beyond the expectation of war."

"Then shall we meet here at a later hour, when I will have the lists of those who offer fairly set out, which names I am having taken now in the outer hall?

"If they be too many (as they will), you can then make your election therefrom."

"Yes, I will do that. I suppose you will have much of transport to arrange for so large a force, and for the arms and provisions that we must have, of which I would not risk that we go short, but I would not have a great part of our stores lost. If you allow that we may last for a month, you allow too long, unless there be relief from Spain before then, on which I would stake no more than a small coin. And when you cast up what you should need, I would have you think that men do not eat after they die, by which there may be many who will be supplied if you send food for one day."

Sir Oliver looked his surprise. "Do you think that they will assault so soon? I had thought that they would bombard for two days, or for three, after their batteries are complete."

"I have a hope that it may be longer than that. Yet perhaps I have said enough."

He went away after that to order his own affairs, and came back at the hour agreed. He found Sir Oliver alone, except for a young secretary, Don Garcio, to whom he had not spoken before, and who was now seated at Sir Oliver's side. There were many papers upon the table, at which he was invited also to sit.

"I have here," Sir Oliver said, "the lists of the knights who have volunteered, being over two hundred, and of a few serving-brothers thereafter, with other volunteers, who are of noble blood, from among whom we are to take fifty in all.

"Of the soldiers, there is also too long a list, among whom De La Motte is now making a choice, having assembled them to that end."

Sir Oliver had had a double list prepared, so that Medrano could retain that which he passed to him. He gave the duplicate to Angelica to mark the names of those who were chosen to go.

Medrano turned over the list, ticking a name here and there, and calling it out.

"I have rendered you," Sir Oliver said, "the full list, that you may see the companions you might have if you would, but there are some there whom it would not be well to select, they being of more use on this side."

"Well," Medrano said, "there must be some such, and if I call their names, you must say no."

They had agreed on thirty or forty names when he came to the list of those who were not knights of the Order, and he saw that there were some there that he did not know. He called the name of John de Sola, a Navarese, whom he knew, and to whom he gave fame as he made the choice.

"I do not know these," he said, "but I would be fair to all sides. They must be brave men to have come forward thus, not having the obligations of knights. I will take the first six." He paused with his quill raised to tick them off, and looked at Sir Oliver's secretary. He asked: "Is your name here?"

Angelica said simply: "No."

Medrano said: "It is very well. You are too young for this bout."

The words were free of any tone of sarcasm or reproach, and Angelica felt that had her name been there, he would have passed it over, but yet that she was somewhat disparaged by the fact that it was not on the list.

She heard Sir Oliver say: "Don Garcio is one I cannot spare from my side." But her own thought wandered to the resolve that she had already made, that she would see Francisco that night and tell him all. She would not go longer in a guise by which she was not a woman at all and was still less than a man. This question only made it more plain that she must discard a dress that had served its turn when it brought her clear of the shadow of Holy Cross.

Her thoughts came sharply back to the present scene as she heard Medrano call another name for her to tick: "*Don Francisco de Valheyna*." She felt a sudden fear, if he should go thus to death, and with nothing said. . . . Her emotion found voice in a sharp cry that told her distress, before she was aware, and regained control.

"Oh," she had said, "not him!"

Medrano looked his surprise. He asked: "And why not? Are we women here?" hitting the mark with a random arrow he did not mean. But the distress in her voice had a puzzling sound. He asked Sir Oliver: "Is there cause that he should not go? What does he do?"

"He now commands the battery which has been set up to protect the great boom."

"There are many knights could do that. By your leave, I will tick his name. I have heard him spoken of well, as was likely to be, he being of Don Manuel's blood."

He watched Angelica as he said this, wondering what that exclamation might mean.

She looked at Sir Oliver in an appeal which would not venture to further words.

For a moment he gave no sign, and there was silence among the three. Then Sir Oliver said: "I would ask you, of your grace, to omit that name, and to forget that it had been asked. For should you guess at a cause, it is likely that you would guess wrong."

"It is little," Sir Gonzales answered, "either to grant or forget, for I know well that you would not ask without cause."

He went on choosing the names.

CHAPTER XXIII

"You should be back in three hours," Sir Oliver said, "for we must all work till the dawn, there being much to dispose when so many go; so that you should rest while you may."

"I was not seeking to rest. It was Don Francisco I thought to see."

"You can do that if you will. But you must still work through the night. It is not a time when we can spare ourselves or put forward our private ends."

"I shall not mind that. I am not easy to tire."

"So I have seen. It is the high boast of youth, which is soon tamed. . . . What is the haste on this night?"

"I must change from how I now am. . . . I had Sir Gonzales' scorn."

"Are you fretted for that? . . . Have you thought what will be changed, and in what way, because your cousin will know who you are?"

"I would I were more clear! But it is plain that I may not see him at all, if I shall longer delay. . . . I suppose he will know of my uncle's death?"

"Yes. He will have been told that. But I have not seen him myself, as I meant, having had no leisure from larger things."

Sir Oliver let her go without further words, thinking that she did right, though the issue was less than clear. He perceived that the resolution to acquaint her cousin with her presence there, and in what guise, which she had delayed day after day in a mood of doubt, had become urgent with the sudden realization that he might pass at any time out of her reach into the near shadow of death; and that the impulse had been strengthened by Medrano's question, which showed her that she was come to a time when she must either be a woman known, or act the part of a man.

She went up to her own chamber and changed quickly into the suit she wore when she walked the streets. It was of velvet, poplar-green, and heavy for the time of year, at which silks and satins were in larger use, but it made her less slim than she would have been in a thinner dress, and it would have been hard to find one at which men would have looked with surprise in the Malta of that day, where they had gathered from many lands.

She put a feathered cap of the same stuff on her black curls, and belted the sword and dagger that she must wear, but had no passion to use. As she did this, she stood before a gilt Venetian cheval-mirror (the chamber being furnished in the Italian style of that day), and was not displeased by what she saw.

"I make," she said, "a fair boy, but it is not for that I have come here; nor is it a part I can play well."

She knew where her cousin could be found, for all those who had volunteered had said where they would remain after the sixth hour, so that they could be assembled with speed. It would be at the battery where he held his command.

She had to leave the castle and pass along the harbour shore under its seaward guns, and, as she did so, the sun was low over Sceberras ridge, showing a dusky glow through the black clouds of smoke that slowly drifted to sea from St. Elmo's point, and were ever reinforced as the batteries fired, not in a constant discharge, but seeking a mark where they could damage the works the Turks were toiling to build or slay them if they were exposed in a careless way.

The guns she sought were set on the open shore, and men still toiled with pick and shovel to give them better defence. They were but three, and they did not point outward, being set at the corner overlooking the mouth of the inlet between St. Angelo and the Sanglea, within which all the shipping was moored.

The entrance to this inner harbour was of a width of about three hundred yards and had been closed by a floating boom. This was formed of a gigantic chain, fastened by great anchors fluked in the solid rock. It was supported on a barrier of oak beams, which had been constructed with cross-pieces, like a huge floating ladder. These beams were themselves floated on rows of empty casks, covered with tar. The colossal cable was wound round a number of windlasses on the St. Angelo side.

The three guns which had been given to Francisco's charge pointed over this boom. A rampart, still being erected along the shore, was designed to cover them from gun-fire from the seaward harbour, and high overhead were the outward-pointing guns of St. Angelo, on that section of the wall which had been assigned for the defence of the English knights, before the days when the failure of a princess of Arragon to give a male heir to the Tudor king had caused that monarch to break with Rome, whose Pope would not sanction her divorce against the anger of Spain.

Angelica saw her cousin, as she approached, directing the building operations upon the rampart, which on other days he had not scrupled to share, but now he had arrayed himself in his gayest attire, as had most of the knights who had volunteered to cross to St. Elmo that night, for they understood that communications were likely to be cut off, and while they were prepared to face the probability that they would be quickly destroyed by the overwhelming strength of the Turks, they were not disposed to die in a draggled guise.

She had scarcely seen him before she was aware of another, whom she had not been thinking to meet. Captain Antonio stood at her cousin's side, and while she paused for a moment, thinking what it might mean, striving to recall how much he might know or guess, and of half a mind to turn away for a better time, he was the first to perceive her presence, and quick to recognize who she was, as he had known her before.

She was, in fact, interrupting a conversation in which the captain was imparting the wisdom of a somewhat varied experience respecting the placing of gabions, on which Francisco might have known more than he did, and not much; and there was a shadow of impatience in the mind of the younger man, for, among many virtues, that of taking advice with humility was not one which was likely to have been inherited by Don Manuel's son.

"Why, here comes," Captain Antonio said, "Señor Ramegas' young friend (by which he should be yours too), who brought us news in a wet way. But he has moulted since to a gayer dress, and has gained some flesh."

For the Captain's memory was of a boy's form, standing drenched in the lantern's light on the poop of the *Santa Anna*, to which the clothes clung.

Francisco said: "He is strange to me. I do not think Ramegas can know him well. What can he want here?"

Captain Antonio's words meant nothing to him, for, by the way matters had gone, he had heard little of the way by which Ramegas had learnt that the *Flying Hawk* was in a corsair's hands, and what he had heard had not dwelt in his mind.

Angelica saw she was known. She would have gone back if she could, but it was too late. She did not wish that Francisco should recognize her in Antonio's presence, and she saw a danger that the captain, suspecting nothing, might yet talk in a way which would connect her with the *Flying Hawk* and Vilheyna from which all the ships came, bringing such association of thoughts to her cousin's mind as might pierce her disguise before she should disclose it herself, which she did not desire. He might be led to recall how she had tried to gain a place on his own ship, and so guess her at once to be what she was.

She saw that she must be quick and bold, and also instant to invent a reason for coming thus, and her wits, which were seldom dull, made no trouble of that.

She greeted Captain Antonio as one she had met before, and was glad to see; but turned quickly toward her cousin to say: "You are Don Francisco of Vilheyna, as I presume? Sir Oliver Starkey gives you the Order's thanks for your offer to join the force of those who go to St. Elmo to-night, and I am here to express regret that Sir Gonzales could choose no more than fifty in all, which were completed too soon for the inclusion of all whom it would have been an honour for him to lead."

It was fairly composed for a speech which had so little substance of fact, and of which she had not thought half a minute before, yet it had an odd sound, even to her ears, and to those of Francisco also, though he knew little more than herself of the island's ways.

He had not supposed that his offer of service would be regarded in such a way. If he were not chosen (of which he had had a good hope) he had supposed that he would have been left to guess that as the hours passed. So, in fact, it would have been. Sir Oliver had enough to do in calling the chosen knights, and marshalling transport, and controlling all that must be sent during the night. But her words had the effect she desired, that her cousin did not regard her as closely as what he heard, being vexed at that.

But Captain Antonio heard with a more experienced mind, and one also that was more detached, and to him the words had a false sound, though he could not guess where they were wrong.

"Could you say," he asked, "how many have made offer to go?"

"There were more," she answered, "than two hundred of noble blood." She knew that there was no secret in that.

"Then," he said, "there will be seven score, or it may be eight, to whom you have yet to go."

She was puzzled for a second's space, and then saw that he challenged the truth of what she said, though it might be, as yet, in a doubtful way. She turned his point aside with as quick a wit as before.

"Those," she said, "who have made offer are of the Order sworn, except only a few, of whom Don Francisco is one. And there are special thanks due to those who have so offered their lives, having much less of obligation thereto."

Captain Antonio had no answer to that, and it seemed that

Francisco had scarcely heard. He was vexed that his offer had been refused, having hoped, in a sanguine mind, that it might have proved a path to something better than death. He had the impatience of youth, and felt that he wasted his days in an idle way, being in charge of no more than three guns which might never be used. Why, as things were, the Turks might never enter the outer harbour at all! Even should St. Elmo be lost, they might make their assault on St. Angelo from the landward side, as it was natural for an army to do, and he might be idle there till the Spaniards should come (as he did not doubt that they would) and he have done nothing at all!

Captain Antonio looked up at his commander (for Francisco was a head taller than he and some inches beyond), and understood his mind very well. He had his own cause to be vexed, for he had hoped that the command of the battery might be his, if Francisco had gone, but he had the patience which comes with years. He said: "Do you gloom for that? I should say you were born under a very fortunate star.

"For, from your first days on the sea, you have been so controlled that you have avoided peril and won praise. Even at the first chance you might have been led to the midst of the corsair fleet, where no fighting would have availed. You had been killed or slaved by this day. But you were saved from that by Don Garcio here, who went dangered and wet, and you dry.

"And after that you have a running fight with the Barbary ships, from which you come clear in an honoured way.

"And then, for your uncle's sake, and through his not being here, you must have the *Curse of Islam's* command, from which you win honour again, having little jeopard therewith, and have the fortune to venge his loss.

"And now you have gained the name of one who had volunteered for a place of death, and you will yet live, for which you should waste no grief.

"But when I say you should thank your star, I say it most for the command that you now have and for the same reason for which you fret.

"For I have seen many wars, and great names eclipsed, and crescent fames that have been clouded or come to full, but there is one thing that has never changed. The men who lead at the first will not be there when the triumph sounds and the bells ring. They will be forgotten or cursed. They will be shamed or else dead. It will be those who were unconsidered at first who will lead the host on the last day.

"For those who are in the first charge have the longer chances to die. Those who must marshal the battle at first must stake their fame on a time when there is nothing ready or ranged. Those who lead on a later day may have larger reserves; their under-captains will be weeded out and of surer worth; they will have had time to learn where their foes are strong or where they are weak. They may come to honour or death, being of two where one must. But those who led at the first, on both sides, will have come down before them.

"But here you stand, doing your part (which is naught as yet) while others blunder or bleed, making places above you bare, and in the last days. . . . Need I put it plainer than that?"

"It is plain enough," Francisco answered, "but it is not a chivalrous thought, showing honour at little worth from the mouths of men. I would not climb by such steps."

He answered without much heed, for he had found that Captain Antonio had a will to talk more than he was always desirous to hear, and his attention was more given to Don Garcio, who stood as though unsure whether he had something further to say.

Angelica had fought an impulse to go. Circumstance offered excuse in the fact that she had not found Francisco alone, and she was still in a fearing doubt of what might follow the revelation of whom she was, which she also thought that he should be quicker to see. But the moment came when she must decide; for when Antonio ceased his talk, she could not continue to stand there without showing cause. She could not have guessed whether her courage would stand or fall till she heard herself say: "Don Francisco, there is another matter. May I see you somewhat apart?"

Francisco heard this request without surprise, the thought coming that Sir Oliver might have something to say about his father's affairs. Apart from that, he would have been willing to talk, for Angelica's voice brought recollections that vexed his mind. He felt it was not the first time they had met, but could not recall where it had happened before. He had heard nothing from Ramegas of the circumstances under which Angelica had come aboard the *Santa Anna*, but Antonio had made a tale from which he would have expected something different from this slight and handsome boy, richly dressed, and speaking as one in the confidence of the Grand Master's secretary, though he might have been puzzled to say what there was to occasion surprise. Now he said: "I have no cause to stay longer here. Will you walk my way?"

At which they went off side by side, leaving Captain Antonio in charge of the silent guns.

CHAPTER XXIV

FRANCISCO took the way by which Angelica had come, as though he were returning with her. Having a doubt as they turned to the castle gate whether he might not have misunderstood her to mean that he was required there, she asked: "Is your lodging far?"

"I lodged with Señor Ramegas in the town at first, but I have a place in the castle now, so that I may be near my charge."

"We shall be alone there?"

"Yes," he said, wondering that she did not begin at once what she had to say. "Is it so private as that?"

"It is a small thing, but it is important to me."

That was not what he had expected to hear. He said only: "Well, we shall be soon there."

He led to a little chamber, much smaller than that which Angelica had, of which there were many within the castle, which was adapted to the accommodation of many knights of a noble blood, such as would expect to be lodged apart, in however straitened a way. Angelica saw that it must be quite close to her own, though it was not so high, and was approached by a different stair. She marvelled, without much cause, that they had not met before that.

The room had a narrow bed, a table, a chair, and two chests. They were all made of oak, heavy and strong. There was a silver mirror upon the wall. The furniture filled the narrow room, so that the space to stand was not much. There was some litter of her cousin's clothes, and other things, cast about in a man's way, recalling thoughts of his room as she had known it before.

He offered her the one chair, which she did not heed. "Francisco," she asked, "do you not know who I am?"

"Why, no," he said, though he was puzzled by her voice, and an impossible thought which he put aside, "not beyond what I am told."

"I am Angelica."

He did not, or else he would not believe, and when she said again: "I am your cousin, Angelica," he answered curtly: "I will thank you to jest with another name."

"Why, so I have," she said, with the sudden laughter which was always await to break through a crisis of words, "I have played with that of Don Garcio, with which the Viceroy has more business than

I, as I did not think when I made it my choice. . . . But if you doubt, you can ask Señor Ramegas, or Sir Oliver, or the Grand Master himself, if he have space in his mind for so small a thing."

But he did not doubt. Conviction came at a laugh's sound. Seeing her now, he was amazed that he had not known her before. She looked to his opened eyes as a girl transparently pranked in a male attire, through which all must see at a second glance. That came of the fact that he had known her before, and that he saw what he looked to see. It edged his words, as he asked: "Will you say how you fell to this shame?"

She answered sharply to that: "I have fallen to none."

Through the next minutes they changed angry words, quarrelling as they had often done when they were boy and girl in her uncle's home.

It was a strife of words in which there was loss and gain on both sides, for she made him see some reason in what he had first concluded to be a monstrous, unbelievable thing; and he gave her an alarm, such as she had not felt before, by the reaction he showed, and by the assertion he made that she had not escaped the shadow of Holy Cross, which had been the one thing she had counted her certain gain, unless (he said) it should prove that they would not receive her now, as he was inclined to suppose. "For," he said, "you must see you can never wed, for no knight of honour would call you clean, you having been where you have; of which, if you do not know what tales will be made, you have much to learn."

She said to that: "You talk as though you know much, who are little elder than I. I may have no liking to wed, though I will not be tied to a life of prayer; but, if I were so disposed, you might find you were wrong for a second time."

She looked at him with confident angry eyes as she said this, showing no weakness of doubt, but her heart sank that there should be such words from him, from whom she had hoped (though she knew it had been with a leaven of doubt) that she would have support, or even admiration for that which she had had the courage and wit to do.

She felt that, had he taken it in another way, she would have been equal either to go on as she was, or to reveal herself without shame; but when he said next, "We must think how you can best be got off in a private way," her anger rose to a flame that broke them apart.

She said: "Have I asked your aid? Do you think I am ward of yours? But I have overstayed, having promised Sir Oliver, with whom I have to work through the night."

She turned quickly and went, none the slower because he called after her "*Angelica!*" which it was plainly foolish to do.

He saw no more of her for that night, but in the morning he sought audience with Sir Oliver, who met him alone, seeming to have leisure enough, and showing no sign that his hours of sleep had been only two.

"I have a matter of which to talk," he said, "concerning your uncle's affairs, and to know (but at your own time) whether it is your purpose to join the noble Order to which you now give your support, and to take our vows. But as your cousin sought you last night, I can suppose that it is of her you have come to talk, so, by your leave, we will speak of that first."

"Then she has told you of that?"

"She has told me naught. But it was with my consent that she came."

"I come for your counsel and aid, that we may return her with such honour as we may save."

Sir Oliver looked grave, and then smiled. "Which, you would suggest, is not much?"

The question annoyed Francisco, being put in that way. He realized that, whatever he might think of his cousin's folly, he would not lightly allow it from other lips. Yet it would have been absurd to resent a question which had its roots in his own words, and the tone in which they were said.

"We know what she has done, which we cannot gloss. I spoke as among friends."

"Which you may account me to be. You would have her to return home at once, if a safe route could be found?"

"Yes. Or direct to Holy Cross, if they would consent to receive her now. They could hide much, if they would."

"They would receive her with joy, she having so large a dower. But how would you make her go?"

"What else can she do? She cannot stay here. She must be made to see that. Is she not for me to control, now that my uncle is dead?"

"As I think, no. But I shall be better advised upon that when I have letters from Spain which should be soon here."

Sir Oliver considered it a folly of youth to have thought that the Convent would have made any difficulty in receiving Don Manuel's niece, even had her fault been ten times more than it had, but he said less, seeing much of the father (whom he had esteemed) in the son's manner and words, and judging that he was of a very sensitive pride.

Francisco felt that Sir Oliver's judgment was not entirely attuned to his own. He even had a vague doubt as to the motives which might actuate the older man, which was less than distrust, but may have united with a consciousness of his own inexperience in dealing with such a matter in disposing him to disclose his own mind no further. He added: "If I have no surety of power, what would you advise me to do?"

"I cannot answer that in a word; beyond that I would advise that you do naught till you have considered its end.

"But I will tell you how the matter now stands, as I see it to be, and you may deduce therefrom what you will, according as you place your own pride against your cousin's welfare or peace, or in what you may suppose that her peace will lie; and you should also weigh how far you could bend her will.

"There is one thing sure. She should not have come. There is another, that if she stay, it must be to a perilous end.

"But here she is, in a boy's dress; and if you would change that, either of her will or without, you should sum the cost, which you may find that it is not easy to do.

"You say you would send her home. If you would do that, it must be with the Grand Master's consent. I do not say that that would be hard to gain. If the matter be brought back to his mind he may have her expelled. He may do that as being best for herself; but, even so, he may not be over tender to regard her honour or shame. Or he may think she is useful here, and if he think that, you will not move him by any plea. He cares for Malta alone.

"But if she go now, and against her will, she is shamed by a foolish prank, at the least, such as will be thwarted and void, even if (as you have reason to fear) there be nothing talked in a worse way.

"If she stay, should she cast the dress which she now wears? She is here, where no woman should be. It is a secret, as I think, which is guessed by none. She could not stay in these walls were the truth known.

"She could stay in the town, of course, where there are Maltese women enough, though they are not of her kind. It might be best; but I do not think it could be done without common talk."

"Do you mean," Francisco asked in an amazed way, though he had seen the force of some things to which he had not given much thought before, "that it should be allowed to go on?"

"I would suggest that it may be for her to decide, and if she will keep disguise, that she should know she has watchful friends."

Francisco was not quick to convince. "It may be discovered," he said, "by other eyes; and how will it look then?"

"It can be shown, at the worst, that she is here by the Grand Master's direction, which has not ceased; and it can be shown also how she came by her simple device, for Señor Ramegas is witness of all. And we could then make it her praise that she had done more for Malta than most can claim, when she saved your ships from the Moors."

Francisco rose. He remembered, none too soon, that Sir Oliver was a busy man, and that they had talked at length. He said, with some formal stiffness which might become dignity as his years grew: "I must give it thought. I must thank you for that you have been my cousin's friend at a difficult need."

He went away, still convinced that Angelica had shamed both herself and him by a folly almost too monstrous for words, which it must be hard to forgive; and yet somewhat inclined from that view by the observation that Sir Oliver was disposed to regard it in a more lenient way. But it was not his name that was to be so risked on the tides of chance!

Sir Oliver found a moment's leisure to consider his departing visitor, before turning his thoughts elsewhere. "Spanish pride!" he thought, with a smile, "yet he may go far." But then he thought that there could be few there who would go to more than a near grave.

CHAPTER XXV

THE day passed with no great event, except that a few died, which must have been of some moment to them, but was less in the neat records entered up by Sir Oliver's scribes.

Piali's battery fired at times, but those which Dragut was building on other sites were silent, their teeth being less than grown. There was a gentle steady breeze from the south-west, moving the smoke of the Turkish battery sluggishly toward St. Elmo, where it piled up against that which overhung there, and thence drifted in slow streamers over the sea. Sullen and seldom, St. Elmo's guns boomed reply, and the black smoke thickened over the walls.

During the day the Turks observed that there was a crowding of pennons upon those walls, for the fifty knights who had come in the darker hours must erect their own beside the others already there. The Turks had watched those pennons with care, for when a knight died, or was wounded so that he could not remain, his pennon would be removed, so that they could count the fallen and make a list of their names.

Now they knew that they had been reinforced by a fifty more. They did not know that St. Elmo held a further two hundred Spanish soldiers besides in its crowded walls, nor would they have cared if they had. Dragut would have said that the net was filled with a better haul. The Turks dragged guns over the hill. They brought up powder, which they would not do till the last day, lest it should be fired by a chance shot; they delved in rock: they piled dirt: they heaped sacks of wool. If some died as they worked from St. Elmo's fire, it mattered nothing. They were easy to clear away. There was no shortage of Turks, nor was there fear that they could be translated to Paradise beyond the resources of pleasant fruits and houris' arms that would wait them there.

In St. Elmo the troops who had been transported during the last night slept, as they had been ordered to do; and in the Commander's chamber Medrano urged the plan which had been in his mind when he had told Sir Oliver that there would be many for whom a day's provisions would be enough, but of which he had been too cautious to speak, even in the Secretary's room.

De Broglio pondered awhile. He said: "It is what they will not expect. It is good in that. But you must think that you may blunt your blades with the Turks you kill, and they will not be greatly less. There can be but one end."

"So I suppose," Medrano answered. "It is what we can do before that, if I am not counting too high."

Medrano's plan was no more than to sally out in a sudden way and do the Turkish batteries all the evil they could.

Piali and Dragut had been alike on one point, that when they had chosen the places on which they would set their guns they had feared only the counter-fire which they would get from the fort. With the great army they had, and knowing that St. Elmo's defenders could be counted only in scores, they had not thought that they would venture outside their walls.

Being arrogant in the great numbers they led they had established their batteries somewhat closer to the fort then they might otherwise have thought it prudent to do, and had piled their mounds only in the very front of the guns, leaving the battery flanks naked of stake or ditch.

Medrano said: "I have little doubt that they can be reached by a sudden rush, and if we can be three minutes therein, we need ask no more: after that we must get back as we can, about which we need not despair."

"Well," De Broglio said, "you are surely mad, as we all are. I do not blame you for that. You shall have your way.

"But I will tell you this. I am not coming myself, for my place is here. And, besides that, I am so fat that I could not run either forward or back. Neither shall D'Egueras come, for he is one that I will not lose. And if I would give him leave, I should say that he has worn out his legs watching if sentries sleep, from which, since we lost the lunette, he will never rest.

"Nor shall La Cerda go out, for the old fox" (by which he meant La Valette, as they all knew) "has made him his tool, and, having used him thus, he should not have sent him back. But John is one who looks straight ahead and can see nothing beside.

"In short, you can go yourselves, right and left, you and La Motte here, and you will make slaughter and aid us much, as I do not doubt. If you tumble their guns you will gain us time, and it is for that you are here: and if you do not return we shall be as strong as before you came."

Medrano said: "That is well," and having his plans made, and having agreed with De La Motte what they would both do, he went to rest while he could and slept sound. But he awakened before the dawn, and, while the light was yet dim, they led out their men, he and La Motte, each having twenty-five knights or others of noble blood and a hundred soldiers of Spain, who may have been no less valiant than they. They went out with their swords alone (the soldiers carrying bucklers, they not having breast-plates of steel) so that they could run lightly; and he led those of his part toward the battery that Piali had built, La Motte taking the left hand course to Dragut's new battery that was on the very crest of the ridge, and somewhat on the St. Angelo side.

La Cerda stood on the battlement of the fort, looking upward into the mist that covered Sceberras' side. Beneath him was the depth of the ditch, with its opposite scarp almost as high as himself, for (excepting the cavalier) St. Elmo had been cut out of the ground rather than raised therefrom.

Even the counter-scarp was not easy to see, for there was a light sea-mist that increased the dimness of dawn, and there had been so little wind in the night that the smoke of battle still darkened the heavy air. The sally-parties had left the fort on the seaward front, for there was no nearer exit unless they should cross the ditch, and they kept to St. Angelo's side, though it was a longer way, lest they should alarm the Turks in the ravelin, if they should go under their wall.

Away on his left hand La Cerda heard the steps of men that he could not see, and once a low voice of command. The steps died and a silence came, every second of which he knew to be pregnant with human fate.

Medrano's order had been that they should approach slowly at first, seeking silence rather than speed, and saving their breaths on an uphill way, but if alarm came they were to run forward at once at their utmost speed. Every second now that the stillness endured must mean that they were nearer success. . . . La Cerda hardly knew what he wished to be.

It was an audacious attempt, such as may sometimes attain its end by the very boldness with which it defies the sounder precepts of war. The Turks might be careless to watch, being so secure in their strength: the batteries might be weakly held, their main supports camping more to the rear. But if they were alert, and in probable force, they could meet the attacking party with such a fire as would be their end: at the best, it must soon retire and expect annihilation as it ran back.

Yet, if this silence endured for three minutes more, they might do that which they sought, even though they should all die in the hour. . . . Was the Grand Master right? Was it wise to drive men thus, till they made resolve to cast their lives away in a desperate chance, they being as few as they were? Might it be said (he allowed this in a mind that sought to judge every side) that the defence of Malta with such a force was so hopeless, by every rule, that the desperate risk might be said to be the more prudent choice, being the small chance against none?

Even so, there was no justice in the way in which the Grand Master had met the advice of those who were more practised in war, and no less valiant than he. . . . Would the silence ever endure? Had they lost their way in the mist? That could not be true of both parties alike. . . . There was the sound of a shot from the left. That must be from Dragut's new battery on the east. De La Motte must have been discovered first, though he had somewhat further to go. . . . Confused cries of alarm. . . . Shots that were almost continuous now. . . . And now, over all, the shout of many voices at once, *St. John! St. John!* the battle-cry of the Order rose, in proof that they had cast concealment aside, and were running forward to the attack.

Louder, but more confused, the noise of conflict came to those who watched on St. Elmo's wall. La Cerda forgot all but his natural sympathies with men of his cause and blood as he turned to De Broglio at his side to say: "They hold their own, if not more." For it was plain that the noise of battle was not refluent toward those who heard.

"Ay," the Commander replied, "so they would at the first, but it cannot last. Medrano is mad, as we all are. . . . So you see: who are sane, and look on."

The words were said without meaning offence and La Cerda took them in the right way. He knew that De Broglio was without malice and quarrelled with none. He answered: "I do more than look on. I am here alike."

"Ay, so you are, and it is harder for you."

La Cerda made no answer to that. He thought that De Broglio saw the end as clearly as he, and that his remark might have been applied to himself with an equal truth. Yet what could seem hard to a fat man who jested and smiled and surveyed all in a twinkling way?

As he was silent, De Broglio spoke again: "I have seen a madman walk on a roof's ridge and he did not fall, for which I suppose that he lacked wit."

He got no answer to that, for, as he spoke, it seemed that the fort shook. A sheet of upward fire vanquished the gloom from where Piali's battery stood; and instantly, as the gloom returned, there came the thunder that follows flame.

"Dragut," De Broglio said, in a cheerful tone, "will not curse for that, though they all die." He would rather have seen it come from the new battery on the crest, but he had been taught in childhood that that which Heaven put on his plate should be taken with gratitude, or, at least, without grumbling words. "It will be a week longer," he concluded, "before they will try the wall. . . . I would they were safe back. They are men too good for a nameless death, which the most will have."

De La Motte's party were the first to return. They had been both led and withdrawn in a very soldierly way, as might be expected from the leadership of one of so great repute, and it was by no fault of theirs that they had done no more than they did.

The fact was that Dragut had planned that the great bombardment should commence on the coming day, and he did not mean that it should last long. He meant to show Piali (now getting about again with a bandaged head) how such things should be done. Having brought artillery enough to break St. Angelo's walls, and an army to storm there-through, it was absurd that they should be delayed for a week (which was now three) by the little fort on St. Elmo's point. Meaning to make a quick end, he was not easy to please with three times the guns that Piali had thought enough. He brought up more through the night. De La Motte had advanced upon a battery that was alert with labour and thronged with men.

When the first shot had shown that silence would no longer avail he had charged the battery in a very bold and resolute way. For a brief moment it had been won. There had been some slaughter among the confusion of those who surely had not expected a morning call of that kind: some damage done to the battery, though not more than could be shortly repaired. One gun, being on its own wheels, had even been turned about and fired with deadly effect into the regiment of Turks that was rushing upon them from their camp, which was at no distance away.

But La Motte saw that, for the first purpose he had, the surprise had failed. It remained for him to bring off his men, if he could, with a lighter loss than they had caused to their foes. The mist helped him in this, though it was not much, and was now lifting somewhat to a seaward breeze. As the mass of the infidel host rushed on to retake the battery in an overwhelming force, he spread out his men in a wide line for their retreat so that they should not make a bunched mark to the battery fire; but the Turkish gunners were either slain, or found, on getting back to their guns, that they were obstructed by the eagerness of some of their own men who had run in pursuit of the Christian dogs, and after that they could not get a good view through the mist, and the end was that when La Motte called the muster of those that he had led out an hour before, he found that he had not left behind more than a few, who were dead, for he had brought his wounded away, even carrying those who were sore hurt. It was an example of what may be done by coolness and skill, even when the die has seemed to fall on the wrong side.

But Medrano had come to a different scene. Piali's battery, which he had thought sufficient to flatten the fort, and which, till now, had done all the bombarding which it had endured, was not Dragut's toy. He spoke of it with some contempt. He was not busy during the night to mount it with extra guns. It lay quiet; and those who were on guard sat in a ring throwing dice, and having all their thoughts on a gambling game. But for the sound of the shot when La Motte's party was first perceived, Medrano might have contrived an entire surprise. As it was, he found himself at the first rush in possession of the battery, with scarcely a blow struck, except at the backs of those who made no scruple to fly.

That was what he had hoped, and his plans were made and his orders given, so that all knew what must be done. There were five who stayed at his side, but six score continued advance as though they were seeking to find the Turkish army that they might give battle to it alone. They had to go but a short way before they found as much of it, or more than they would be likely to long endure.

Suddenly roused from sleep, bewildered by the sudden attack they might be, but the Turkish soldiers of that day were among the best in the world, as their conquests proved. They came on, five to one, and were met with a fury alike their own, for the Christians fought as though there were death in a backward step, and this was not from valour alone, or from their fierce hatred of pagan foes, being indeed of a literal truth. For while they had advanced to the Turkish camp, Medrano and his five companions had searched for where the battery powder was stored. They found it in a vault which had been hollowed into the rock to protect it from the danger of being struck by St. Elmo's fire. They did not lose time bringing it out, for it would do very well where it was. They laid a train of powder thereto, and lighted a slow-match, giving themselves time to run forward to where their comrades strove. The Christians fought with the knowledge that every backward step took them nearer to the explosion which was designed, and that they must hold their ground till it came, lest the Turks should get there first, and put out the match.

Medrano looked down at the lighted match, and along the hill to where sword and scimitar clashed in a strife that could not long be sustained.

"Well," he said, with a smile, "we shall not lose life for a little price. . . . But they can do with six more."

He drew out his sword, and would have run forward into the line of strife, when John de Sola cried out and pointed down the side of the hill. A hundred men may hold five hundred back for a time in a stubborn way but there is a limit to how far they can spread their front. Turks ran up the hill, and would be there before the explosion would be likely to come.

Medrano turned and ran down to hold them in play. Four men followed, but John de Sola stood still.

The hillside was somewhat steep at that place. Medrano and his companions covered the ground fast. The first Turks they met paused, or were tumbled back. But it was a position that could not endure for a minute's space. The Turks were coming in dozens from every side. At the best, if they should hold them back (which they could not do), they would be certainly slain. De Sola stooped to the match. He set the powder alight.

Medrano drove his sword through the throat of a man whose sight failed in the sudden glare, which he had the misfortune to face, and, at the same instant, they were flung forward in one heap. He was half-conscious of deafening noise, out of which he rose in a black smoke, while around him shards of iron and fragments of rock fell from the sky.

He had no more orders to give. After the explosion, every man would know that he had nothing to do but to get back if he could.

He could not tell where the Turks were. He could not see three paces away. He supposed they had fallen or run. He recovered his sword, which had left his hand. He went at a slant, somewhat down the hill, thinking to get as de from the main line of pursuit, and that to pass under the ravelin might not be beyond the chance of a single man. He saw that there was a hope of life, now he had come through to this point, which he was not willing to miss.

"If this smoke," he said, "will but lie. . . . By Mary's grace, the wind blows it now in the right way."

As he spoke, a man came stumbling blindly down the hill.

Medrano stood still, with a ready sword. The man was small, and no weapon was in his hand. As he passed, Medrano saw that he was one of his own men, by his Spanish dress. He called after him: "Have a care. That is not the way."

The man made no reply. Medrano heard the noise of his fall. He followed, and looked on one who was vainly trying to rise. His leg was bleeding and torn, but he might not know how much it was hurt, for he had been struck on the face by a falling rock, and his sight was gone for that time.

Medrano knew the man. A common soldier of small valour, and less repute, whom he would not have picked, but De La Motte had known less. He gave him a helping hand. "Can you walk?" The man limped with his aid for a short space, and collapsed again. Terror of what would be his end in the infidels' hands (which it was not foolish to dread) could no longer give strength to the weakened limb.

"I can no more," he said. "I am sped."

Medrano looked down at the man, and his shoulder lifted in a slight gesture that might be contempt, or perhaps despair, but its meaning must be left for each to read as he will.

"Nay," he said, "it is two or none by my count." He threw the damaged form, from which it seemed that conscious life had now gone, over his left shoulder, so that his sword-arm might be left free. He went on under the pall of the friendly smoke.

Sometime after it was thought that the last straggler had wandered in, and he had been counted among the lost, Medrano came to St. Elmo's gate, bearing a dying man to explain his delay. Was it strange that men called him the faultless knight?

CHAPTER XXVI

An hour after De La Motte's return, De Broglio sat in his own room, writing a report which he thought the Grand Master would be pleased to read, though its main event had been loud enough to be known without the help of any missive from him.

He would have written before, but wished to make his record complete, and he had only then given up hope that Medrano would return.

He looked up as La Cerda entered the room. "If you go up to the wall," he said, "you will get a good view of a Turkish flag."

"Why, do they attack?" De Broglio's tone was unperturbed as he reached for his sword-belt, letting the letter lie.

"I would not say that. You must see to believe. They have a battery at the door. It is too weird for a war."

De Broglio answered nothing to that. He went up through a crowd of knights who talked and disputed among themselves, but gave way as they saw who came, and he looked at a Turkish flag which hung over the counter-scarp, not thirty yards away.

What had happened may be ascribed, like the loss of the ravelin during the previous week, in part to the boldness of the Turks, and in part to the unaccountable chances of war.

As the noise of the explosion had died, Medrano's men, such as were not dead or too sorely hurt, had commenced to run back, knowing that they had done their work, and that it only remained that they should so contrive, if they could, that they would be alive to boast on the next day. The Turks did not delay in pursuit. They followed, ten to one by now, if not more, under a murk of smoke, which the wind moved somewhat more slowly than their own legs, but in the same direction toward the fort.

Those who fled inclined somewhat over the ridge of the hill to its eastern slope, as they had to enter the fort on that side, and those who were close in pursuit followed the same way, slaying all they could overtake, till they came to where they could be seen by those who watched on St. Elmo's wall. They were betrayed by the smoke, which now lay or drifted in heavy patches around the fort, with clear spaces between, into one of which they ran before they were well aware, and a heavy arquebus fire drove them back with some loss, and made a rescue for such of the flyers as had been able to keep in front to that point.

But meanwhile another party of Turks who were more behind had failed to keep the track of the chase, and had come straight on, being wrapt in the thickest smoke, and were abruptly checked when they found they were on the edge of the counter-scarp of St. Elmo's fort.

They stood in such murk that the garrison of the fort (most of whom were now crowding the eastern wall, where they had opened fire on the pursuit) did not know they were there.

In an instant, the possibility of the moment was seen, and the word was passed back to the Turkish camp. In much less than an hour's time, when the smoke cleared, it was seen that a heavy barricade had been built up on the edge of the counter-scarp; gabions of earth, rocks and beams, and even broken pieces of guns that the explosion had blown apart, had been dragged by a hundred hands, and piled loosely along the edge. Bags of wool were added in the next hour. It was a barrier against which even gun-fire would not avail, for, having so large a start, it could be built up faster than it could be shot down. For the rest of the siege no man could look over that side of St. Elmo's wall without the risk that a bullet would find his head from the sharpshooters that would lurk behind the opposing barrier, making loop-holes so well concealed that they would be hard to discern till the death-shot came, and a wisp of rising smoke would show where the arquebus had been pointed through.

De Broglio had to add twice to his letter before it went, once to say that so little had the sally availed in driving the besiegers back that it had brought them up to the very wall of the fort, and again to say that Medrano was come in, having taken no hurt.

But as to the first, he wrote: "We have still the ditch, and this barrier they have built may avail them no more than does the ravelin on the further side, and having them thus at our door tends to keep all alert to watch and prepared for a quick call, so we may be content, thinking what Piali's words are likely to be as he surveys the battery which he thought enough to have brought us down." Concerning Medrano he wrote: "I am more pleased by his return than irked that the Turks have approached so nigh. He is one whom men will follow with willing feet, and if this siege should go on till I age too much, as it seems that you would wish it to do, or if you would heed advice, as you never will, you would give him the place I have. He is whole, except that his back will ache for some days, he having brought in a man of less than a ducat's worth, being too broken to mend; and it seems that a scimitar slashed his sleeve, which he must get someone to stitch."

The Grand Master read this letter, and was not entirely content, but, after talking with Sir Oliver he decided that the loss of the battery would have done more harm to the Turks than it could be to their avail to have piled a barrier on the other side of the ditch, where they would (he supposed) be discommoded by the fire of the fort, and to which position they would not find it easy to bring their cannon down the slope, which would be exposed to the fire of the cavalier. He considered that it would not be simple for them to snipe those on St. Elmo's walls without exposing themselves to the same fate, which was partly true, but the difference was that they had abundance of men, while those in the fort were few, so that it was a game they could better afford to play, but for which it is likely that they would not have gone there at all. St. Elmo's defence defied the science of war, as it was then taught. La Cerda had some cause when he said: "It is too weird for a war."

But as to Medrano, La Valette read the report, and was not shaken in his belief that he had the right man to govern the fort, about which, at first, he had been unsure.

"Should I put one in such charge who would waste his strength on a wounded man!" he exclaimed. To which Sir Oliver replied: "Had he had that charge on his mind, he would have let the man lie."

Yet Sir Oliver did not deny that De Broglio was the right man for that post, as he had said at the first, and he observed that the Grand Master was not aggrieved because his reports were freely worded toward himself, which he did not appear to see, for it was for Malta only he cared, and those who guarded St. Elmo's walls could say what they would concerning himself, so long as they did not say that they wanted to come away.

In the Turkish camp, the three leaders met in Mustapha's tent, where the Egyptian Pasha stroked his beard, and bit it at times with his yellow teeth, as he watched the quarrels of his two naval colleagues, putting in a suave word to turn the edge of Piali's clumsy anger or Dragut's jesting contempt, and being well content that their difference left the power of final decision so entirely to him, while either would be willing, in case of failure, to agree with him that the other deserved the blame.

Piali wished that he had lain in his tent for a day more, but would have it that it was Dragut's fault that the battery had not been more strongly and vigilantly held, and when he was pressed as to whether its defence had been stronger in the first days before Dragut came, and finding that he was confronted by one whom he could not overbear by loudness of voice, and the truculence of his own bulk, he shifted ground, and said that the loss would not have occurred had he remained in control, for St. Elmo would not have stood to that day.

"You slow the fire," he said, "from the battery I had built, while there must be two others set up; and because you would do that, you say you are a better soldier than I. Very well, I will say we must have four, and I shall be better than you; unless you shall say we must have eight, which will prove you better again."

"Nay, but you could still say sixteen. You should not omit that." Dragut looked at him with a twinkling in his small rum-reddened eyes, which was itself an insult the Sultan's favourite was not accustomed to meet. He spoke to him as one humours a child. He asked: "What would you have done before now?"

"I would have stormed its walls, as I was planning to do."

"And what now?"

"I would storm it in a day's time, as we quickly can."

"Have you counted the cost of that?"

"It is a cost we can pay. We have men enough. We sit here while the weeks pass, as we should not do. If we cannot cut the calf's throat, how shall we deal with the cow?"

"It was not I who resolved that the calf must be slaughtered first. I was not here. But when I saw you had tied it up, I said you would be a jest if you let it go, or if you bungled the knife. . . . Have you seen the storm of a fort that is stoutly built?"

Piali made no answer to that, for his life had been in the harem walls, and after that on the sea.

Dragut went on: "It is what I have; and I will tell you this. If you assault now, you will take the fort at a great loss, if you take it at all, of which I am less than sure, for all the great numbers you have, and they of a valiance I do not doubt. If you take it not, you are shamed, it being so small a thing; and if you do, you will only show that it could have been had for less loss on a better day.

"I tell you, if you do that, I will go afloat. Neither shall any man of mine be among those who attempt the walls, though my guns you can still have."

Mustapha interposed too quickly for Piali to make reply: "Dragut, the battery being gone, what would you counsel now?"

The corsair turned to the old general, and his voice changed, as though he now spoke to one of his own kind, after being vexed by a boy.

"The battery is gone, as we know, but I should say that the sally failed despite that, for it was the new one which we have built on the crest which it was of most moment to them to have overset, and it is no more damaged than a day will mend. By to-morrow's dawn we shall have our guns pointed so that we can sink any boat that St. Angelo sends to their relief, or to take them off.

"We shall then have gained what I have said from the first that we must do. We shall have them herded apart.

"After that, I would bombard them from every side with the guns we have set up, and with others which we must find to replace those that are gone. I would bombard them for a full week. I would beat them flat. If they do not yield before then, and if there be any that still live, they will be easy to storm. I would so deal that none shall escape alive, either to land or sea. I would have those who watch from St. Angelo's walls see what their own end is most likely to be if they do not yield upon terms while they yet can.

"But I say, if we make assault while they are strong, and we should be thrown back from their walls, we have brought shame on our own heads and shall rouse a stir in the Christian lands which may bring them aid, even to the coming of Spain."

"Well," Mustapha said, as one who reflects, and turning to Piali, as taking counsel with him, though his resolution was set, "a week is not long. We may bombard them for that time, and make their end sure." And then, lest he should make querulous reply, for he saw that the quarrel had gone as far as it safely could, he went on to ask what was the extent of the damage that the explosion had caused.

Piali said that the great basilisk was beyond repair, or at least beyond any resources they had, but some of the other guns were less wronged. They had been rolled about, but they could be mounted again.

Mustapha stroked his beard, and turned to Dragut to say: "It will be well that we repair them with speed, and that we bring up further guns to that point, so that it be even more strong than before, for it will hearten the Christian dogs if they think that the explosion did us great harm."

Dragut did not dispute that, though he saw that Mustapha's purpose was to make Piali content, for the reason was good, and, in fact, he had little care whether Piali were petted or vexed. He regarded him no more, when his talk had ceased, than a fly that he had brushed from his face.

Mustapha played the peacemaker here, but it was done without good will to those which he kept apart. He enjoyed their wrangles which he sought ever to keep alive, so long as they did not go to too great a length, but he watched through all that they should come to such decisions at last that the war would be carried on in the best way.

Medrano's raid had so much result that the assault that Dragut had planned was put off for a full week, and it was possible to communicate with St. Angelo in safety during the following day, but on the next morning the dawn had not fully come when Dragut's batteries opened upon the fort, including that which he had planted on the further side of the western harbour-mouth, to which St. Elmo replied with all the guns that it had. St. Angelo's two culverins also joined the concert again, though the range was too long for them to be aimed at a sure mark, and in the afternoon Piali's battery added its voice to the din.

CHAPTER XXVII

The record of the next week can be quickly told, but it was slow to those who must live through the waiting hours. From morn to night the batteries thundered, and did not cease. There was no doubt that Dragut knew how to place his guns. The fort was hammered from every side. Rock-built as it was, it seemed to cower under the ceaseless hail, as though its battered sides shrank and were near collapse. One by one the great stones of its parapets cracked or were splintered away.

And, as the days passed, its own fire lessened; one by one its guns ceased, till such shots as came were separate, single flashes from the canopy of smoke which now lay over it night and day. It seemed to spit back viciously, impotently, now here, now there, toward the relentless ring of its foes.

And, as the days passed, there was a gradual lessening of the crowds which had watched the duel of death from St. Angelo's walls, till a time came when they would often be bare of all but those who had their duty thereon. What was there to observe but a monotony of smoke through which the gun flashes could be frequently seen? What to hear but the rumbling thunder which did not cease, and was deafened with a regular but less frequent monotony by the louder fire of the castle's guns, which seemed no more than a protest, impotent and absurd, at the agony of a friend that they could not rescue: a vain barking against a foe that they could not reach.

That was how it was in the castle and town. In St. Elmo, men knew a more urgent suspense, waiting an assault which, at any moment, might bring all to a quicker end, but not more sure than that which must come at last from the metal hail that beat ever against their walls. Many would have been glad had they heard the wild war-cries of the infidel host, and been summoned to face the rush of their crowding hordes.

The soldiers diced long, they slept much; they ate and talked, changing memories and tales. They sharpened weapons which had been sharpened before. There were times when they sang: others when they disputed about the mysteries of an invisible world. But there was little of that, for they were free from speculation and doubt. They were men who knew: they were told, and believed.

The knights believed also; although, knowing somewhat more, they had more to doubt. There were those among them who were very frequent in prayer. Yet most would have agreed that they had little need to fear either the devil's wiles or the wrath of God. Having come to die in His name, and to slay those who blasphemed His Triune Mystery with obscene words, surely they could have a confident hope that He would look on any weakness or sin (such as is natural to the sons of men) with a very lenient eye?

As the days passed the isolation of St. Elmo increased. Dragut's guns swept the outer harbour now, so that it was impossible to communicate through the day, and though at first there was some traffic during the darker hours, and a further supply of the wild-fire bombs was sent over without event, this security did not last, for the Turks devised a system of drifting flares by which the water might chance to be lit up anywhere and at any time, so that a boat that had been slipping silently through the gloom would find itself in a glare of light, and such a mark for the Turkish guns as they would not be likely to miss.

When a boat had been sunk in this way, with the loss of a dozen lives, apart from those of the wounded men which it had been bringing away, it became evident that such transits must cease, except at a vital need. Up to that time the bodies of the knights who died had been taken up to St. Angelo for burial in the grounds of the Convent Church, but from now St. Elmo must dispose of its dead as it best could.

The Turkish fleet grew bolder now that the Maltese galleys could not leave their inner harbour without coming under the fire of Dragut's batteries, and while the weather was kind, a squadron of them blockaded the harbour-mouth, so that such communication with Sicily as was still maintained was from other parts of the coast, and that at peril enough, for the whole circuit of the island was now patrolled by the corsair ships.

Yet the Grand Master got away another letter to Garcio, telling of the urgent need in which Malta lay and urging that he should send relief at the first hour that he could. This was sent through the Turkish lines to Marshal Couppier, who arranged its despatch; for though their army was now camped from Sceberras to Marsa Scala, so that St. Angelo was cut off from the militia which had been left loose in the inland, the investment was not so close that a man might not have a good hope to creep through in the night.

Meanwhile Marshal Couppier did his part, harassing the outposts of the Turkish positions and cutting off any parties that might wander apart or try the chance of a sudden raid. He took prisoners as he could, saving their lives from no impulse of mercy, of which there was little on either side in this war, but that they might become counters of exchange to redeem any Christians who might be caught in their turn. The Grand Master, though he had forbidden that any should sally beyond the walls of the town, relaxed this rule somewhat, lest inaction should diminish the confidence of his knights, and he also secured some prisoners, who were saved in the same provident way.

And each day Dragut pushed forward further, with barricade and trench, so that St. Elmo was at the same time more nearly menaced and more entirely cut off.

It was on the third day of this bombardment that Venetia's discontent and disgust of mind commenced to demonstrate themselves in active consequences.

She had lived from her earliest years in a world in which safety depended less upon the care of others than her own wary alertness of mind and activity of body. She had learnt to beware of a trap even before its jaws have commenced to close. Malta itself was a major trap which she did not like. La Cerda's house might easily prove to be a minor, but more immediate one, which it was her first need to avoid.

It was not only that he had gone to a place from which few returned. Since the Council of War he had been the talk of the town, as one who had advised a surrender which had been repudiated by the Grand Master and other more valiant knights, so that the Grand Master had openly insulted him as the Council rose. This talk had not failed to penetrate to La Cerda's household nor to reach Venetia's very watchful ears. She did not think the less of Le Cerda for that. She did not care whether he had been right or wrong, and had it been his sole concern to keep his own skin unscratched she would not have blamed him at all. But she saw that his power to protect her, which had shown its limitations before, must be less now, even should he return, which was a dubious hope. If he did not return, she had to consider how long his household would hold together and what would be the consequences to herself should it be dissolved.

Any day the news of his death might come, and though she knew that the hire of the house was paid, and that the house-steward, Giles, had sufficient money for their present needs, she knew also that they were in a state of siege, in which the power of money and the rights of property may be overruled in tyrannical ways.

The house which La Cerda had hired was one of the best in the town. There were great knights who had arrived later than he who were lodged in garrets, or who slept where scullions had slept before. The present position was unusual in that, owing to the sudden way in which La Cerda had been sent, he had not taken his followers with him, as it would have been natural and customary for him to do. He could have repaired this had he willed, but he had deliberately allowed it to be overlooked, possibly because he had had no willingness in going at all, but more probably because he had not wished her own presence to be disclosed.

Considering this led to another thought. Sir Oliver Starkey had a reputation for detailed organization that all men knew. It was said that he missed nothing, however small. He had shown a spirit of some leniency, if not exactly of toleration, toward herself, on an earlier day. He had said she must go, but he had allowed it to be privately managed. Was it possible that he knew where she now was, and that La Cerda had prevailed upon him that the household should not be disturbed, so that open scandal should not arise? Was it possible, even, that Sir Oliver had assented thereto lest his previous leniency should be exposed, and be displeasing to La Valette?

In this guess she was partly right, for Sir Oliver was aware that La Cerda had gone with a single squire, and that four other men of fighting worth, who had been under his roof, were still there and still stationed upon the wall where his pennon had first been flown. He had felt no inclination to interfere because, of his own will, he would not have sent La Cerda at all. The Grand Master had done that, and if La Cerda obeyed him only in a literal and limited way (for which he could have shown some excuse in the haste of his first dispatch), Sir Oliver saw no occasion to interpose to make trouble more.

She was partly wrong, for he had no suspicion that she had remained in Malta, nor would he have cared had the Grand Master, or the whole world, known what he had done, having thought it best at the time and being content with the tribunal of his own mind.

But the doubt was hers, and may have influenced what she did at a later time.

She was like a rat that considers a threatened hole. It has smelt cats. It has seen a trap. It has become watchful for poisoned food or the dreaded tar. Yet it is in no panic of mind, for it has some confidence in itself, as a combatant in a strife of ten thousand years which has never been lost or won.

She did not think that it was needful as yet to leave a hole where she lay snug for the risk of a harder bed. But she would survey retreats. She must know where other holes could be found at a sharp need. She would go abroad. She would make friends if she could. Well, how was she to do that?

She decided that the house would be easy to leave, but she saw that she could not walk the streets in the dress of a Sicilian lady, and that of the gayer kind. For she looked over all the garments that she had, which were more than few, and they gave her no help. The sombre domino which she had once worn in Mantuan streets, when there had been urgent cause for disguise, would have been welcome now. But even that would have been of little avail. To walk the streets unobserved she must be a Maltese woman, or else a man.

She did not care which it might be. She cared for safety alone. Had it been better for that, she would have walked bare with an equal will. But she could not see that either would be easy to do.

The Maltese women were dark-skinned. They were black of hair and brow. Most of them were much broader than she. When she mirrored her pale-gold hair, and the flower-soft face that she could change so swiftly to be gay, or impudent, or pathetic, less with her changing moods than as she wished it to be, she saw that the disguise would call for more than a change of attire. And in all she did there was one danger to keep in mind. She must not disguise herself beyond possibility of explanation, or sure identification by those to whom she could still appeal at a last need. It is bad to be whipped for a wanton, but it is far worse to be hanged for a spy.

And with these doubts there was a difficulty that outweighed them all. In all the house there was no woman except herself, and no woman's clothes except hers, so that they would not be easy to steal.

She considered the men that the house held, most of whom knew she was there, if not all. But they had been ordered by La Cerda to keep her concealed, and their loyalty was to him. She saw little of them, except the house-steward, Giles, who waited upon her himself, serving her meals, and doing the duties her chamber required, as La Cerda had straitly charged him to undertake.

He was a man of meagre frame, who had left his youth. He was not old to himself, but he was to her. His right eye had been lost on a dagger's point. His left arm (he said) was of little use, a sinew having been cut across. For these hurts, and his little frame, he stood excused from the war. But to one who watched him move at his work he appeared hardy and strong.

Venetia understood him well, for he was like herself, though of lower kind. He would be traitor to any for the best price he could get, which need not be much. She knew well what he wanted of her, which she had sold to others before. But she thought that she had made it worth a better price than she had taken at first. Now she saw two difficulties, even if she had been disposed to go to market with him. The one was that he did not think to be bought: he thought himself able to buy with his own coin, which was silence, and nothing more. He had begun to talk of the risk he ran (which was next to none) by not denouncing her to the Grand Master, if La Cerda should not return, and she be discovered at last.

The second reason was that he was not a man she could trust, nor did she think he would trust her. He would be likely to take all she could give, and then mock at what he had promised before. To help her to get free from that house was the one thing he would not be likely to do.

Thinking of him, drew her mind to the fact that he was more of her size than any other that the house held, and she determined to try his clothes, of which she was not therefore bound to make use, but if they were not too loose a fit it might be profit to know.

She saw no great risk about that, for he went out at times to such market as was still held in the town, trusting none but himself when there was silver to spend. She knew his times, he being the sort who are most at peace when they have established routine. She tried his hose and found it too large, but not beyond what she could adjust or a loose cloak would conceal, such as may be worn in the night.

In the afternoon she abstracted some clothes from his room, such as he did not constantly wear and would not be likely to miss. She put these on when the darkness came, and went down through a silent house and into the narrow street, without being seen or so much as a bolt drawn.

When the Knights had come to Malta more than thirty years before, the houses of the Bourg had been small and mean and of one type, which was nearer that of the Afric Moors than the Christian lands. The Knights had built for themselves, as their wealth allowed and according to the fashions of the countries from which they came. They had scattered châteaux over the island, which were now deserted, and in constant danger of plunder and fire. They had largely rebuilt the Bourg, while the native population had spread to Bermolo and the Sanglea. The house which La Cerda hired was built in the French style of that time. It showed a blank wall to the street, and heavy wooden gates therein, one of which had a smaller door in itself, somewhat raised from the ground, through which a single person might pass, and in this door was a grille through which the porter could survey any who pulled the bell. If a man were admitted there he would see a porter's room at his side, and beyond that a large paved yard, around which the house was built, its windows opening on three sides of the square. As the revenues of the Order had shrunk, this house had been divided into three, each opening on the central yard and having a common exit to the street.

In these days, when the walls must be always manned, there was little difference between night and day. Men passed in and out at all hours as their occasions required. The night-porter, who served all, nodded at his post. The smaller door was not barred. Those who passed with a quiet assured air might have no more than a casual glance.

La Cerda's house was the central one, facing the gates. It had a great door which had once been the main one of the whole mansion. It had an iron lantern, which would have been lit even the week before. But Sir Oliver had ordered that there should be saving of oil during the shortness of summer nights. The only light was the one over the great gate that could also do something to illumine the narrow street. Master Giles' hat and cloak would have passed Venetia out had she had a more careful glance than the porter gave, and when she came back in three hours he gave her no notice at all, having seen her pass out before.

She came back without mishap, though she had had one or two frights, which might make her less willing to adventure again in the same way. But she had heard talk, and she knew now that it was the common opinion that St. Elmo was near its end. It was cut off from support, and the steady cannonade from dawn to dark was now beating it flat. Any time it might be rushed by the Turks. The doubt was whether it could last for another day. No one knew how many of the garrison were already dead, or might yet endure, but they were all regarded as doomed alike. Venetia had been reared in a hard school, in which miracles did not occur, and mistakes of judgment were paid in prompt and physical ways. She put La Cerda out of her mind as already dead.

She concluded that she was in a hole which might be turned inside out at an early day, and she was resolved that when that should occur she would be some distance apart. Even had La Cerda's steward been of a loyal kind, she might have come to the same resolve, but, as it was, she had more excuse.

She spent the day in considering the position, and decided that there must be some among the hundreds of knights who were now idling within castle and town who would be glad of the companionship of one of her sex and sort, if it could be safely arranged. Her business must be to dress herself up again in Master Giles' clothes (but more carefully than at the first attempt), and go boldly out to make acquaintances, among whom she must find one whose conversation or repute made it likely that she could reveal herself with a good result. She told herself that she must aim high. She had proved before that audacity is a good card. There were great princes among the knights who (she supposed) would miss the pleasures which she regarded as inseparable from their estates, more keenly than humbler and (possibly) more continent knights. She knew several languages, or, at least, sufficient of them for the kind of talk that was natural to her, but she reminded herself that ignorance, whether real or pretence, might protect her better than proficiency till she had learnt more of those she might meet than she would like them to do of her.

If she could make such a friend—if she could even locate one to whom she would feel it safe to reveal herself at a later day—she might remain, for a short time, at the least, in La Cerda's house, for if he should return, she would not wish to have lost the position she held, unless she had something secured of a better worth.

She saw that she could not leave the house, in whatever garb, during the day, unless she were prepared to risk the probability that she would be observed. She must choose the dark hours, and those during which Master Giles slept, even though that might somewhat limit the probabilities of whom she might meet when she walked abroad. She saw also that the house-steward's clothes would limit her in another way. It was a time when a man's status, and even his occupation, were still shown by the clothes he wore, though this custom had less of legal requirement, and was less exactly observed in most parts of Europe, than had been the case in an earlier century. Still, even in the medley of race and dress that now jostled in St. Angelo's streets, there were distinctions that all would know. Knights of the Order might be variously attired, but the materials would be coloured and rich. Silks and satins, brocade and lace, speak a language that all can read. The plain stuff of a steward's doublet, the dull colour of his outer cloak, with its hood falling behind his neck, or pulled forward for rain or sun, was of a different class, and those who were so variously attired would not be likely to fall to intimate speech, though they should lounge on the same wall, or sit side by side at a tavern board, either of which they would be unlikely to do.

Venetia would have preferred a dress of a different kind, but she had a practical mind which lost no sleep over that which it could not get. The steward's hood had its use. It could be pulled forward sufficiently to hide her hair, and it would give her a character that she could claim at need—that of La Cerda's steward, which would be better than none, and would lead, at the worst, to enquiry which would end at the right address rather than the hangman's rope, which would be the likeliest end if she were suspect, and could not establish herself in a quick way. That it would save her from the whipping-post was less sure, but it was a risk that she had to take, and she had found before now that her wits were good.

Very coolly, when Master Giles was abroad, she moved in deserted rooms, taking and adapting what she would have for the night, and secreting it beneath her own bed.

"If he miss aught," she said to herself, "he must look round. Things are misplaced at times." She did not think he would be quick to suspect the truth and, if he did, well, she must deal with that when it came! If she were only, she thought, in Sicily once again, in the great mansion in Cerda there, or in La Cerda's Lombardy home! It would mean no more than a pout or an easy tear, and it would be the steward's back that would be bared for the whip. But there was little satisfaction in that, for it made it more clear that the man would not dare to act as he did if he were not very sure that La Cerda was near his end.

So she waited till the night came and went out with no more trouble than before, and walked in streets that were not crowded as in the day, but yet seldom empty or still, and learned much with alert eyes, such as the gutter had bred, but saw no one she could safely accost, nor any chance she could turn to her own gain, till she grew tired as she was in a street that ran down to the water-side, near to where the great boom closed the inner harbour under the shade of the castle-wall. And so she turned into a wine-shop there, which, in these times, did not close with the night, and sat down on a bench which had a table in front and a wall behind, and was far enough from the lamp to make it likely that she would see more of others than they of her.

She had not been there long when another customer entered, seeming to be a young gentleman of good rank or estate, richly attired, somewhat in the fashion of Spain, and sat down at a table facing the door, so that he could observe those who came in.

The light was not good, but Venetia observed that he had a face in which youth and beauty were so securely enthroned that Time itself might appear unequal to their defeat. "I could be," she thought, with a degree of truth which would have surprised herself, "as good a man, were I but pranked in the same style," though she would not have said that green velvet would be the colour for her.

The young gentleman did not appear as one who had come there to drink, or to sit at ease, but watched the door, as for an expected friend, the while Venetia considered his suitability for the purpose she had in mind. But on this point she found that a conclusion was not easy to reach. He was obviously noble and rich, having that aspect in a community where most were of higher rank than their appearance allowed. She thought it likely that he would be generous and kind, with other good qualities which she appreciated in others, though she excused them in herself. He was handsome also, to which she was not indifferent, though she had learnt that such preferences must be subordinated to the exigent realities of life. Yet she inclined to him to a degree which surprised herself, for her general preference was for larger men. Her practised eyes decided that there was here a combination of innocence, inexperience, and youthful vitality, of which it should be easy to make a prey. Her greatest doubt was whether she might not be more capable of seducing him than he of protecting her.

She did not think him to be one who had taken the Order's vows, not only regarding his youth but because she knew that there was a Statute of the Order which forbade them frequenting a public inn; though it would be too much to say that it was always observed.

On the whole she was disposed to a further investigation, and would probably have devised some pretext of approach had she not thought it more prudent to wait awhile, to see whether he would be joined by others and of what sort. She had learnt that much may be seen and heard by those who sit on a tavern bench and keep silent themselves.

It was only a few minutes later that she had reason to congratulate herself on her caution, when a little man with a somewhat jaunty manner, dressed as a mariner of the better sort, pushed open the swinging door, glanced round at the two occupants of the low-ceilinged room, and crossed briskly towards the young gentleman, who recognized him, but not quite as though he were an expected friend.

He was not single in that. Venetia's hand went to her hood, which she pulled somewhat more forward over her face. "Who," she asked herself, "would have thought to see Tony here?" She congratulated herself on the caution which had kept her silent till then and became additionally curious and alert.

Captain Antonio spoke as one who has no secrets to hide, and

Venetia heard none the worse because it was a voice she had known before.

"Don Francisco would have me say that he will be here in a short time, for I go now to relieve his post."

Angelica gave a short answer to that. "He should have come before now."

The Captain, who was mainly ignorant of the relations between the two, did not improve Don Garcio's temper when he replied: "Well, as I suppose, so he could. But he would know first that he would not be wasting his legs."

Angelica replied with a smile, but there was anger in her eyes: "He will do that if he is slow to come, for I shall not stay. . . . Did he really send you for that?"

The Captain became aware that he had gone somewhat beyond the truth, and had also exhibited himself in an undignified light, as one who played the messenger to save Francisco's legs. He replied with more exactness than he had felt needful before: "I have not turned aside, having to pass here, as I go to relieve his post. He will remain at the guns till I arrive, and I had undertaken to let you know this as I crossed the street."

"Well," Angelica said, being only partly appeased, "I will wait awhile. But it is after the hour he said."

Venetia listened with some interest to this conversation, which was exchanged in the Italian tongue, being that which was native both to Captain Antonio and herself, but which the Spaniard had used as one educated thereto. She saw that she had come to a place at which two gentlemen of some importance had arranged a meeting during the night, which suggested intrigue or quarrel, for, at this time, though all must have their hours of duty upon the walls, and be otherwise ready against a sudden alarm, yet, while St. Angelo waited attack, there was enough of leisure for all to transact their affairs in the daylight hours, and too much for most, excepting those who were of monastic mood, and practised the sword of prayer.

Having delivered his message, the Captain went out, with the brisk and jaunty air by which Venetia remembered him in a certain place in Genoa which she did not wish to recall, as she did also by his habit of depressing his sword-hilt in his left hand so that the blade rose behind as he walked, like the tail of a game-cock bantam, from which it must have come down as he passed out through the swinging door.

Venetia owed most that she had become (which she valued at more than the Grand Master would have allowed) to her watchful eyes, and to a lesson she early learned, that there may be much profit from knowledge of men who quarrel or plot: they may give gold either for active aid or the easy service of silent lips.

Now she poured herself another glass from the bottle of light Italian wine that she had ordered when she came in. She drank a little, letting the most part stand. She watched Angelica with eyes which could not be seen under her hood, and was satisfied that little notice was being taken of her. After a short time, she leaned back somewhat sideways against the arm of the bench, as one who slumbered rather than sat awake, but having chosen her posture so that she might see well.

She watched Angelica with the patience of a waiting cat, and Angelica watched the door with an impatience which grew as the minutes passed. It seemed that she was about to rise and leave, when Francisco entered, and, after a quick careless glance round the dim-lit room, crossed it to take a seat opposite to hers. "Why," Venetia thought with surprise, "they are two birds of one nest!" For there was between them the elusive likeness which may often be seen in two of the same blood, though it may be hard to define; and Angelica's dress made this more obvious, though it made her look the younger somewhat beyond the fact.

Venetia watched, hearing much that was said, and being puzzled by that, so that she would have liked to hear more. But though Francisco was not of the disposition to give much heed to those beneath him in rank, and regarded the somnolent form in the steward's cloak about as much as the bench upon which it sat, Angelica (having more at stake) was of a more cautious mind. Her tone was lower, and the use of her own name brought a warning protest, after which their words were less audible than before. Also, they spoke in the Andalusian tongue, which Venetia knew, but not well.

Yet, as she watched, there was once that she guessed the truth, thinking: "It was said in a woman's way: it is what she is." But she put the thought out of her mind, as being fantastic in itself, and doubtless arising from the knowledge of her own disguise. Also, whatever might be puzzling in the conversation she overheard, it was not that of lovers who met in a secret way. Rather, it might be that (she thought) of those who were rivals in love. Certainly, as the talk went on, it took a more quarrelsome tone, and once or twice Angelica's voice was raised in an angry word. "That," she said, "you never shall by my will. You shall find it no gain if you do!"

Venetia could not hear beyond that, till there came a mention of a

Sir Oliver, who could hardly be other than the Grand Master's secretary, the name being uncommon in Malta at that time. She thought now that she could understand the nature of the dispute, if the one who had come in last were resentful that the other should be a suitor for a sister's hand. But that was not likely if, as she had supposed, they were of one blood; nor was it consistent with the fact that neither of them was likely to have a sister there.

But the next moment she put aside speculation of what the meeting might mean, to consider that to which it was likely to lead. "Here," she thought, "is duel toward," for the younger man (who was more facing to her) had spoken in a way which the other was not likely to take, if his pride were what she had thought as he came in.

"Francis," the younger said, more loudly than he had spoken before, "what you say is a foul lie, which I will not endure."

But this outburst seemed to subdue, rather than to rouse resentment in him to whom it was addressed. He spoke in a quieter tone.

"You take it as more than I meant. But if you go on as you are. . . ."

"I may bring all to a good end. But what you will not see is that it is the only way there now is. I must go on, for I cannot go backward nor turn aside. I must go on till the war end, or the siege is done. . . . And I had thought that I should have had more comfort from you."

As he said this, he rose, as though the conversation were done, or he were too wroth to say more. The one who had been called Francis rose also, but in a slower way, as though ill-content that they should part thus. "Where," he asked, "would you go now?"

"I am going back. I have wasted time enough here. I have work at the dawn."

"I am coming to the castle also, having left Captain Antonio in charge."

"We had better enter apart."

"I do not see——"

"But I do. If you will not wait awhile, then I must."

"I must wait if you put it thus." The last words were sullenly said, as Francisco resumed his seat. The last exchanges had been easy both to hear and to understand, as the two had stood, and spoken aloud. Now they parted without sign of intimacy, or the formalities which distance requires.

Venetia thought again, looking at Angelica's back as she went out: "He is like a girl. . . . I am not sure. . . . It is absurd. It is that which I do myself from which the idea is born. . . . Yet it is a game that more than one may find cause to play in this monkish town."

She tried to recall such parts of the conversation as she had heard, lest it should hold a clue which she had not caught, and was only puzzled the more. She looked at Francisco, sitting in a frowning irritation, which he had no care to conceal, and thought: "If she be woman in truth, she is no mistress of his, for their talk was not of that kind. But if it be so, he must be aware, for they are acquainted well, and, as I think, of one blood."

She saw that if she had made a right guess there might be profit, even protection, for herself if she could use her knowledge in the right way. But that would depend upon the circumstances of the case and the rank and influence of those who were most concerned, which, for her purpose, must not be too low, nor too high.

She had no mind to entangle herself in the troubles of others to no gain, thinking she had enough of her own; and her past experiences had taught her to be wary of those who were placed too high to be pulled down. There had been one (she recalled) who had been found floating in Genoa harbour with a knife-wound in the back, because she had not understood when the eyes must be blind, and the tongue still.

Well, she must find out first how these Spaniards were called, and what position they held, which should not be too hard. She looked at Francisco, debating whether she should make a direct attempt. He was young, and she would have been bold enough had she been able to make advance in a woman's way. The shyness might have been on his side, and she would have had some hope she could break it down. But she thought him proud also, and that, against any advance from a stranger not of his own rank, he would be likely to draw off with a more certain reserve than that of an older man.

Wearing the garb she did, she felt unsure how to proceed. She moved somewhat, as one who wakes, yawning under her hood. Sitting upright, she refilled her glass.

For the first time, Francisco gave her a straight look. Keeping her voice husky and low, for she knew that to be a part of her disguise which it was least easy to wear, she said: "It is cold for May. It is the wind from the north. I should say that there will be rain before dawn."

Francisco stared at her, but made no answer at all, unless it were in that which he promptly did, which was to get up, and go out.

She had gained nothing by that, and went home in some doubt as to whether she had not been wasting her time.

CHAPTER XXVIII

VENETIA regained her room without becoming aware that any suspicion had been aroused, and on the next night she went out again.

The day had been without incident, except for the almost continuous sound of the Turkish batteries, still pounding St. Elmo with a monotony which it could not for ever endure, and some talk she overheard from some of the men as they came in from a spell of duty upon the wall. There had been movements observed in the infidel camp by which it was supposed that they were preparing to attack the Bourg as soon as St. Elmo fell. It was assumed, without words, that it was very near to its end. It was said that, if any should remain alive at the last, they must fall into the enemy's hands, for what escape could they have either by land or sea?

Venetia had taken a familiar word from the steward more indifferently than she might have done had her mind not been active on her own plans, and, misreading this, he had become more insolent than before, giving her warning she did not need that the hour of crisis might be with her at any moment.

She had resolved to follow up the knowledge she had gained in the last night, but when she considered how this was to be done she saw the full peril in which she stood. She knew that Don Francisco had command somewhere upon the water-front, which Captain Antonio shared, and that it was so placed that the tavern in which they had met was on the way between it and the castle gate. She knew that Francisco and the other, woman or man, of whose name she was less sure, both had lodging within the castle. But how could this knowledge avail? Could she venture within the castle in the poor disguise which was the best she had been able to get? Should she attempt to search the outer line of defence, where none but those who had duty there would be likely to go, and especially in the night? Where she would be most suspect as a probable spy, and where it would be most difficult to give a plausible explanation of what she sought?

They were not alternatives to be lightly seized, but as she had pondered during the day she had resolved that, unless fortune should prove a capricious friend, one of these she would do. Among some baser qualities, she had courage and wit. "I will not wait," she thought, "till I am caught at a sharper need, or am so placed that I have not this house on which to retire." And so, where a woman of weaker will would have let the days pass in the poor hope of La Cerda's return, trusting to any wiles that she had to meet the troubles that came on their own days, she went out to make her fate again, as she had done more than once before when she had thought herself to be in the jaws of a closing trap.

Her plan was simple and bold. She would first find out more, if she could, of who these young Spaniards were, and if they were of a quality sufficient to serve her need, of which she had no great doubt, having learned to judge such points in a merciless school; and if she were satisfied upon that, she would seek out whichever of them might be the more easy to reach, asking to speak apart, and reveal sufficient of what she was, and in what strait, to gain a protection to which she might go at once, or else flee at a further need, either through pity, or her own sale, with the argument in reserve that she might know something of a secret of theirs, which she would only use at the last, and if she had cause to think it a card that it would be prudent to play.

At the worst, she resolved that she would use Sir Oliver Starkey's name. Even if she were caught for a spy, and her sex stripped, they would not refuse to refer to him, if she made a tale of the right kind, and she did not think him as hard as the Grand Master, or most of the Commanders of the Order, would be likely to be, if they had to deal with her in a public way. A whipping would be the worst thing she would have to fear, if the truth of who she was should be laid bare, but of that she had a great dread, having seen the lash laid upon other backs, and knowing, beyond that, that she would be worth a poor price in the market in which she dealt, while she carried such scars. But she hoped for better fortune than that, having learnt that those who advance boldly upon a danger they clearly see will often find it withdraw, as though it like better to snare such as are looking another way.

She wandered about for some time with alert ears, but being careful not to loiter in such a style as would draw eyes she would not have too closely upon herself. She learned several things of no present use, and, by a direct question addressed to a Spanish soldier, who looked to be of a dull kind, such as would take most things at their outward show, that Don Francisco (unless there should be two of that name, which was a small risk) commanded the battery that had been set up to protect the boom.

She thought that was enough. She knew his name, she knew

his office, she knew him by sight. If she came to talk with him, she had resolved what to say. If she were obstructed by others, she must profess that she had a message which was only for him. She knew where the battery must be, having walked the town in better days, before it had been emptied of such as the Grand Master had thought to be worth much less than the food they took. She made her way there.

She came to a place where there was little light at this time except that, here and there, a lantern flickered above the guns; for there was but a low moon, which the great bulk of the castle hid. But though the light was dim there was wakeful watch on all sides. There might be little fear of attack from the sea while St. Elmo stood, but the Grand Master was ever warning his knights against the risk of surprise, which he feared in a restless way since the tales had come of St. Elmo's ravelin lost, and the counter-scarp gone, both of which would have been saved by a better watch.

She was challenged as she approached, with a levelled halberd across her breast, and a call for a countersign which she did not know.

She answered in a voice which she tried to keep husky and low, so that it should be nearer to that of Master Giles than her own, but yet in an easy confident way: "I know nothing of that, but I have come on an errand to Don Francisco, having a word for his own ear."

The man drew his halberd somewhat aside, but stood himself in her way. He lifted a lantern, seeking to see more of her face than she was anxious to show. "And from whom," he asked, "may the word be?"

"I am steward to the Chevalier La Cerda," she said, avoiding a more direct answer, "it is on his business I come."

"Do you say that you come from him?"

She avoided the trap, if such it were. "No, for he is away at St. Elmo now. It is for that I must move myself, seeing that his affairs are secured while he is busied apart."

The sentinel took this answer well enough. He said: "Then you are out of luck, for, at this hour, he is not here." He added: "You can see Captain Antonio, if you will. But you must wait. You cannot pass beyond this."

"No," she said, in some haste, "that would be vain, for I have no business with him."

To make herself known to Antonio would have consequences hard to foresee. It was to disclose her origin in a Genoese street, which even La Cerda did not suspect—and other matters appertaining thereto.

She turned toward the castle with a first impulse to follow Francisco there; but was it likely that he would be awake, and accessible at that hour? She remembered the time at which Captain Antonio had been taking charge on the previous night, and concluded that it was within the past two hours that Don Francisco had left, and would most probably have sought his own bed. When she thought of Angelica, she saw that it was equally improbable that she would be about at that time, and in her case she did not even know for what name to enquire!

She thought of the Grand Master's guards, who would be stationed around the gate, and she saw the folly of attempting entrance to the castle during the night in such disguise and with no better pretext than she now had.

For this night, she saw that she had done all she could, though it might not be much, and her steps quickened to return as she perceived that a faint light of dawn had invaded the eastern sky.

CHAPTER XXIX

Master Giles Bonhomme waked with the dawn, or perhaps somewhat before. The common talk that St. Elmo must fall in the next hours had not avoided his ears, and he saw that he must be prepared for his own part, if there should be word of La Cerda's death, which (for all he knew) might have been before now. For who could expect to endure under that pall of smoke that was like a halo of hell, through which the gun shots stabbed inward from every side?

Well, if his lord died, he had his own plans to pursue, and certain profits to make, which were not large, for his position was not of a first importance in La Cerda's household (except only in Malta), but they were important to him and, being mostly of an illicit kind, they would be enough to engage his mind. When he thought of Venetia, he resolved, as he had done from the first, that he would have no trouble for her. He would denounce her to the Grand Master immediately that he should be informed of La Cerda's death.

But that plan could remain private to his own mind. All that it was necessary for her to know was that he had that power which, for the present, he did not use; and he had already hinted of that plainly enough for one of her wit to understand and to consider it well.

It was a restraint on his part for which he had resolved to have such payment as she could give, and he had only delayed to take it before now, because he must first be well assured that La Cerda would not return, and because he had a little fear of the girl herself, which he was reluctant to own, but which had not been easy to overcome. Yet he saw that such fear was absurd, she being the kind she was, of which he knew much more than she guessed, for he had picked the lock of a secret casket which she concealed in her chest, and had read things at which La Cerda would not have looked, even had she forgotten to turn the key.

But he saw that, if he delayed more, it might be a deal spoiled, for the market might be closed and the wares gone. And as he longed for her now with a lust which was strong and starved, and which he had no care to subdue, he resolved that he would no longer defer. He rose and dressed in a hasty way and went up to her room.

It might be barred on the inner side, but that was less likely than not, and if it were, she would open soon enough at his call, if he made pretext, as it would be easy to do.

The door gave at once as he pushed the pin, and he entered quietly. He looked round the silent room, and at a bed in which he supposed that she still slept; but he could not see that, for its curtain was partly drawn. For the purpose he had, she could not be in a better place.

He stood a moment, resolving what he should first say, and what mood he would have to face, for he knew that her feeling to him was little short of an active hate. But if he paused, there was no doubt that he would go on now to the end he sought, having no scruple at all. He had at his belt one of those poniards which were common in Italy at that time, having a three-edged blade and a good point. He would show her that, if reason were not enough, or he might let her feel an inch of its point, which should be more than enough, if she should prove to be in a kicking mood. She would not be one to lose life for a virtue that was seven years gone, if it could be said to be that which she ever had. And as he stood thus, he was surprised to hear a short quick step on the stair, and turned to face Venetia, as she entered the room.

They looked at one another in one silent moment of common surprise, which Venetia was the first to break. "What," she boldly asked, "are you doing here at this hour?"

"I would ask first what you do in that guise, and in a cloak which you must have pilfered from me?"

"Pilfered!" she exclaimed with contempt, for she saw that this could best be sustained in a bold way, and she was one whose courage rose when a climax of conflict came, "why, are you not my lord's and all that you have? . . . If I soil your cloak, will he not give you a dozen more? Unless he pay you another way, if I complain of the hour at which you intrude here."

The steward put her words aside with an equal sneer. "You speak as one who still lives in a past day. It is of that that I came to talk. We shall not see our master again, and we must think for ourselves."

"Well," she said, with a smile that gave no key to her thoughts, "so I have—and so I do now."

"Then you must think that I hide you at a great risk, which I can end in an hour. If I go to the Grand Master and let him know you are here I win safety and praise; and he would be doubly glad because it is his will, as is common talk, to bring our master to shame. He would have you whipped without stint, to teach other knights that they shall not break their vows and insult God, Whose favour they greatly need, by having harlots within the walls."

"Yes," she said, with the same smile, "so he would. I have thought of that too."

"But I do not wish to do that. I would keep you close, though the peril rise. I would be friends, as your safety needs. But you must do me what pleasure you can, and it is for that I have come now."

"Nay," she said, "you are wrong there. I am not your meat. . . . You have thought of much, but there is one thing you have missed. The Grand Master will not care about you. When our lord is back, if he find that I have miscarried thus by your fault, do you think that your back will pay? You will wish it had when you hang by the heels over Cerda's wall. . . . You must consider he loves me well. And he will be wild wroth, knowing that I have been hurt for the Grand Master's quarrel with him. He cannot injure Valette, but he will look round for one on whom his anger may fall, and you will be useful then."

She said this with the smile that she would not change, and the steward did not look pleased, for she spoke the fear which had kept him idle till now, and it had a real sound as she put it thus in a very confident way. But his reason still told him that the nearer risk was to keep her hidden a longer time, and it added now that he had gone too far for a safe retreat. After this she would bring him down, let him do what he would, if La Cerda should come back to his former power.

"It is idle talk," he said, "for it will not be. Our lord will be dead, if he yet live, as is less than sure. You must choose which you will. I must put you down, or the Grand Master will be told all in the next hour."

As he spoke he had changed his position somewhat, so that he was now nearer the door than she, which she had not opposed, for she saw that this was an issue which could not be altered by flight.

"If I did your will," she asked, as one who will look at all sides, "what warrant have I that you would not betray me still?"

He protested against that with ready oaths, though it was exactly what he was intending to do. If she disbelieved, she gave no sign. They were both of sorts that were common in that day, and perhaps in most; owing little respect for any law, whether God's or man's; ruled alone by their own cautions or lusts; and coming, as chance might lead, either to high estate or the hangman's hands.

"If you had your will," she said, as one who still halts in a doubt, "how could I avoid that my lord should know at last, if he return, as I think he will?"

That was an easier question to put aside, and it seemed to him that it showed surrender was near. Indeed, what choice could she have? "That," he answered, "is very simple to say. For who should tell, except you or I? Which of us will accuse ourselves thus?" And then he added, thinking it no more than a final argument to remove the last reluctance in her own mind, "you may tell yourself that you have no choice, I coming armed as I do."

He touched the poniard at his belt as he said this, and made a step toward her from which she did not retreat.

"Nay," she said, and the smile broke into a little laugh that she knew well how to use at will, "if you play it thus, you solve all."

She let him advance upon her, standing in a passive way, as though he must do all, and she naught. He did not know, as they came close, that she drew the poniard with a stealthy hand, till he felt the pain as she pushed it upward to find his heart.

CHAPTER XXX

VENETIA rose from a short but desperate flurry upon the floor, during which her hands had covered the mouth of a dying man, that he should not scream. Now he lay limp and still.

She looked down upon a floor that was soaked in blood, and was glad that it was not hers. "It is ill," she thought, "that men do not die without making so foul a mess." She thought, as she often would, that she could have made the world in a better way. Then she thanked the good-tempered saints that the soaked garments she wore had been the steward's rather than hers. Had he come up after she had changed to her own clothes, the pity would have been more than it was.

She wiped a long scratch on her hand, which his teeth had grazed, and wished it were more hurt. "Well," she said, and she smiled with truer mirth than before, "it will suit the tale."

She had no cause to delay now, for her plans had been made while she had held him in talk, but she saw that there was no haste. It was too early to go abroad, and there was no danger while she was here. No one would come to her room, which was high and apart, and only the steward's was at the stair-foot. The noise would not have frightened a cat. He would not be missed for some hours, and then it would only be thought that he had gone out. There would be little curiosity quickly astir in that womanless house, where each went his own way in the lack of their natural lord. She had only to keep the door barred, against the small chance of someone climbing the stair with word or question for her, and she could take her own time. She had rid herself of one fear, and betrayal's risk, and she had a far simpler and, in some ways, truer tale than before if she should be tripped in her next hope. For she had resolved to seek protection elsewhere, telling as much of the truth as it might seem helpful to do, and she saw that she could attempt this now without cutting entirely loose from the anchorage which, a few weeks before, had seemed so delectable and secure. For she would say that she killed the steward to save herself from a foul assault which he had made in the night, and after that she had lost her head (as she was never likely to do) and had fled blindly away. The fact that he would be found in her room would support her tale, and what other cause could she have to stab one who was her lord's servant and hers?

Because she was *amie* to one whose vows were such that he could not wed, and their love so great that they had come together to Malta's siege, did it follow that her honour was less to her than if she were wed by the Church's rule? The relationship was so frequent at this time, and especially among the military monks who were gathered in Malta now, that such a plea would be likely to win support. She thought that she was much safer than before (and especially so against her whipping-post dread), providing only that, if she were accused, she should not deny that the deed was hers, which would place her on trial of fact, with a likely loss of belief in anything she might later say.

She knew the value of truth, and would use all that she could; but she saw that it might be improved, which she was active to do. She dragged the body somewhat nearer the bed, but not much, being very cautious lest she should make a change which could be afterwards guessed. She decided to say that he staggered back when he was stabbed, but holding still to her arm, so that he had pulled her from off the bed. She took off the blood-soaked cloak, which had been his, and cast it on the floor between him and the bed, as though he had worn it when he came in, and then thrown it off, as he might be likely to do. She took a linen shift which she wore at night, and tore it down at the neck, after which she dropped it upon the blood, and then threw it aside on the floor. She did other things which would be slow to recount, working with quick hands and a lively wit. When she had done, she had made a tale in the room that none who entered could fail to read, and that had (she thought) as much of truth as one tale should require, if not more.

She looked at a pouch of silver that had balanced the poniard in the dead man's belt, and bit her lip in a doubt. She knew it ought to be left, but it was hard to resolve, and the more so because she guessed that it would be emptied by others if not by her. She took a few pieces only at last, for it was known that the steward walked with a full purse, and there was too much at stake to be pawned for a small gain. She thought: "If I am to say that I fled in haste, I should not be too long; but if I am not to walk the streets at a lengthened risk, I should not be too early away. Yet it must be allowed that I had to dress! I am so feared" (she smiled to herself) "that there are none but men in the house, after he that was left in charge has approached me thus, that I do not know what I do. How can I tie points with a shaking hand?"

As she thought this, she put on the clothes that she would be most loth to lose, and that would show her flower-fair beauty of youth in its softest way. She hid some jewels, sewing them where they would not be found except by a search that would leave her bare. Then she went boldly down to the steward's room and took the hooded cloak which was his daily wear when he went abroad, and a poke which he might carry if he would market himself. She filled this with some things which she would be most certain to need, or which she could not resolve to leave in a room to which she did not think to return; and, when she thought that the best time had arrived, she went out with more assurance than she might have felt if she had not practised before in the darker hours.

CHAPTER XXXI

It has been well said that there are few things that we cannot win, if they be pursued with a ruthless will; but it is not till they are gained that God will show us the price, which we shall have no choice but to pay. So Angelica found it now. She had won clear, as it seemed, from a life of prayer that had no pleasure for her, and here she was, with her legs in a boy's hose, where they had no business to be, and where it seemed they must remain for the time, about which she had little joy. There have been a few women, at sundry times, who have played the man from a free choice, even to going unguessed to the camp and the battle-front, but she did not think herself to be of their sort. She felt strangely alone, being cut off at once from her own kind and the natural challenge of men. Being neither woman nor man, she felt less than either, rather than equal to both. She had come to the midst of a man's game, which she saw to be of a great kind, but it was one at which she made a poor play.

She might have been in a different mood had she had Francisco's support instead of a fretful reproach, which charged her ever with having shamed a name that they both bore. They met and quarrelled, and came apart, and she had not even the consolation of knowing that her bitter words had power to give a wound that would ache at a later hour, though his pride turned in a blind way from pain that he was not willing to own.

Feeling herself to be cut off from her own kind, and that she was regarded thus, her mouth, which was made for softer uses than that, set in a hard line as she resolved that she would show those who scorned that she could be equal to the part she took. Had she not saved her uncle's galleys in a good way, though it might never be put to her name in the talk of men?

It was the morning the steward died that Sir Oliver, looking at a list of names which she had made out of those who had volunteered to go to St. Elmo if a chance of mist should allow the sending of further support, had seen that of Don Garcio there among, and had raised questioning brows as he had dipped his quill to erase it with a thick line. What, he wondered, would the end of this folly be?

And was the folly all hers, or had he allowed himself a certain portion therein?

It was about the same time that Angelica passed her cousin in the crowd of the castle hall, and was wroth that, as she thought, he saw her and would not speak; forgetting that it had been her own caution that had first proposed that they should keep apart where they were commonly known and their meetings would be observed. She went up to her own chamber, hearing a step behind as she ascended the winding stair, and thought that he had changed his mind and was following her thus—for who else would it be likely to be?—but would not look round lest he should think her somewhat too quick to forgive.

But as she got higher, the footsteps gained upon hers, and she knew that they were lighter than his of whom she had first thought; and then she had a doubt of who could follow her thus, and would not look round lest it should seem to show fear.

She had a thought for a bolt which could be quickly dropped into its place as she closed her door, which she had been speedy to use in the first days, as she had been careful also to lock it when she went out. But she had felt more secure as the days had passed and none had disturbed her there, and the key had been heavy and would have looked foolish had it been hanged at her belt, and was awkward to hide in doublet or hose, so she had ceased using the lock unless she went abroad for a long hour.

Now she had to control a timid mood, that she should not hasten her last steps; but she did this, and called herself fool for the doubt she had, as she pushed the door wide, and then turned to face whoever followed her thus.

She found, as will often be, that when she faced her fear it was soon gone. She looked at one in a steward's dress, who halted as she turned, being then no more than three steps below. She saw a lifted head, and a hood thrown back enough to disclose a girl's face raised in appeal. She did not doubt it was that, from the first moment she looked. To make a doubt of her sex when the hood was up, Venetia would have needed more disguise than she then had, but that was not her present design. Cloak and hood had fulfilled their use, having brought her there. She had passed the guard by the simple ruse of falling into the rear of those who had better right. She had lingered in the hall long enough to overhear one who had spoken to Angelica, and had heard the name she was called. So far all had gone well.

Now she looked up at one of whom she was still in doubt, whether she feigned like herself, or showed the form of a slender boy, on which much would depend as to the game which it would be profit to play. Angelica looked down upon her with the right hand on the door's jamb, and her left at a dagger's hilt, meaning no menace by that, but it was a trick of habit she had gained in the last days, giving her some comfort to feel it was there and reminding her of the manhood she had assumed, to which she must train her moods.

"Will you say who you are, and why you follow me thus?"

"I am chased by men, one of whom I have killed at my honour's need. I would have protection, and to be hidden by one who will do me no further wrong."

Angelica looked down on her for a moment without reply. She considered a surprising demand with eyes that were grave and intent, so that Venetia had a doubt of the kind of answer she would be likely to get. Then she laughed, short and clear, in a way she had at such times.

"Why," she said, "it seems it is habit here! . . . Well, you may come in. . . . I am not one to betray; but I think I should know more."

She stood back, holding the door wide. Venetia entered a room which had been her own a few weeks away. Angelica dropped the heavy bolt into its socket in the stone floor.

"Now," she said, "if any seek, they must learn to knock. Tell me who you are, and why you have come here."

She sat down on the bedside, or rather leaned there-against, it being too high for the bending of knees, and watched her visitor cast off the hooded cloak, showing herself as the woman she was; for she had not sought to give herself any inner disguise, which had not been of her present plan, apart from her desire to bring away all she could of her clothes, which she might find it hard to replace to her own content in the Malta of that hour.

Angelica looked at a beauty which she thought to be more than her own, on which she was wrong, besides that it was such as would sooner fade. "Why," she asked, "did you come here?"

Venetia's wit found a reason as plausible as the truth, and having a better sound. "It was my own chamber," she said, "where I left much. . . . Some of which" (she looked around as she spoke) "is still here."

Angelica had heard enough of what had been to understand the meaning of that. "Then," she said, "you are La Cerda's friend, who was said to have gone away." She added: "I have not stirred what was not mine beyond that which I could not choose. It is yours to take."

Venetia, seated now on a wooden stool, lifted noon-blue eyes that had learned to plead from her gutter days. "But I would take naught. I would stay here, if I may, having no safety besides."

She was still unsure whether it were boy or girl to whom she must make appeal, though she would have picked the truth at a forced guess, the doubt hindering her in the choice of the tricks that would be prudent to play, and it was one which Angelica's reply did not resolve. Her voice was not unfriendly but had a definite note as she said: "By your leave, if you ask my aid, you must tell me more."

Venetia answered that as she must. She told a tale that was mainly true, both because she was too shrewd to float a bubble lie which must soon burst, and that the truth did not sound so ill when it was well told, as she could be trusted to do.

Angelica said little, either to interrupt, or in comment when it was told. She had her own problem to face. She could turn the girl out, telling her that she would not or could not help; but she was reluctant to think of that, both from a chivalry of mood which would have been hers at all times, and in a different setting from this, and also because she saw some likeness to her own case. They were both women, trespassing in a place which men had made for themselves alone, and furtively at bay, with more hope from their own wits than from those among whom they had dared to come. The danger of which Venetia told might be hers on another night, and she in flight from the same fear. The few friends she had, and by whom she was kept secure, might all be dead before there would come a time when she could go free. . . . But then she saw that she could not keep the girl here without disclosing herself. She must show who she was to a woman she had not known for an hour, and was not sure that she knew now. She could not tell where that knowledge might go, or what results it might bring which she would not have. She was lonely enough to feel that she might be glad of a friend of her own kind, but it remained a gamble that she would have been willing to miss.

"I would not say you were wrong," she said at length, "but will it not be urged that you could have called aid, had you cried aloud?"

"There was none (if any at all) who could have heard, except soldiers of common kind, who would have taken orders from him, or, had they put him aside, thinking La Cerda dead, they might have been worse than he. That is truth, but I would not say that I thought all sides, being in so sudden and sharp a fear."

"Then, if you did no more than a woman should, being so caught, will it not be folly to hide? By your leave, if I tell Sir Oliver all, I should say you might be held guiltless of any wrong, he being very patient and just, and having more rule in his hands than some who make a greater pageant of power."

"So it might, if the talk would be of the morning's work. But you must recall that I am here with no right, having been expelled by an order Sir Oliver wrote in haste, lest the Grand Master should have dealt in a worse way. And with La Cerda not here, who should be my guard, and a man's death on my hands. . . ."

There was reason here that Angelica could not deny. She saw that she might not refuse such refuge as she could give to this girl who came to her (as it seemed) in a jeopard so like her own, and she might even be said to have the better right to the room in which they now met; and to do that, for loss or gain, she must give her confidence too.

"Well," she said, "you can stay for this time, where, if you came unseen, none will be likely to look. But you must lie close, barring the door when I am not here and giving entrance to none. It will be a dull life if it last long."

"It is change of cage, and no more. I would I were back in a larger land."

"So I should say you may be, if you will, at an early day. I must find what is talked of your steward's death, which cannot long be unfound, and it will be easy for me to hear. Then, as I think, we must let La Cerda know all, if he be alive, as he was a few hours ago by report which was sent during the night, which had a full list of the slain."

She said this with a mind to test the truth of Venetia's tale as far as she might before her own confession were made, but it brought nothing to shake her trust.

"If he yet live, I would well that he knew all by the swiftest means. My best hope is in him."

This was said with a sincerity which it was not easy to doubt, and, as she heard, Angelica put her last suspicion aside.

"I must get you food," she said, "which will not be hard, though you may have to wait for a time. When I come back I will knock twice, and pause, and then once again. We shall be safe if you open only to that. . . . And if we are both to be here for a time, you must know that I am not to be killed for the steward's cause, being as much woman as you."

Venetia learned this with little surprise, but was not sure whether she were more vexed or glad. She said: "I was guessing that," being too adroit to say when the guess began. She thought at once, now the guess was sure, that Sir Oliver must have turned her out of that room because he could find it a nearer use. She said, in an innocent way, as though being simply glad she had come to a safe harbour at last: "I suppose Sir Oliver will do much for you. You will be *amie* to him?"

Angelica did not know how to take this, which she did not like. She looked at Venetia with grave eyes, which she could not read. "Sir Oliver," she said, in a cold voice, "is my good friend, as I think."

Venetia did not doubt that she heard a lie; or, at the most, that she had erred no more than to guess the wrong name. She looked like a hurt child as she said: "Oh, well, if you trust me no more! . . . I suppose it is the whip that we all dread."

She faced puzzled eyes in which comprehension dawned with a moment's anger, that contempt chased. "I have no such fears. Do you know who I am?" Then laughter came, in Angelica's sudden way. "But Captain Antonio did say he would have me hanged! I must give you that."

Venetia saw that she had guessed too far on a blind road. She said: "Oh, you are sure! But we may come to that if we change hands to the Turks, as we are likely to do. We should be soon out of here if our wits do not make a default that our backs will pay!"

Angelica went out without further words. She was sure that the girl had not meant that at the first, but it bore enough cargo of truth to show her that their fates might not be so far apart as her pride had thought. She was led to recall the peril in which she had stood when she had been the prey of the *Flying Hawk*, and the threats that Captain Hassan had made. She was in a position in which a friend of her own sex might have more uses than one. She was largely ignorant of the world's ways, character and pride having to take the place of knowledge to bear her through; but she knew that La Cerda's *amie* would be regarded as one who might sit at the boards of kings, while she held her place at his side. She thought of Venetia as one who might see many things that she was likely to miss. She might be a comrade it would be good to have. She even thought her one she might learn to like. But as to trusting, she was less sure.

CHAPTER XXXII

One by one St. Elmo's guns ceased. Hour by hour its fire became more fitful and weak, and hour by hour the Turkish batteries pushed advance. New mounds were piled, new trenches slanted ahead. New guns were hauled up from the fleet, of which Dragut would never say that he had enough. St. Angelo could be left alone. It could look idly on, watching till St. Elmo would be no more than a blackened grave of those who had been sent to its vain defence. They could wait their turn, and as they watched they could guess how it would be likely to end. Built of stone it might be, with deep roots in the living rock, but as the days passed Dragut's boast that it should be beaten flat did not seem to be called too high.

Piali would have attacked days before. He said: "You waste powder and time. All it needs is one rush, and it is there that our flag would float in an hour from now."

Dragut said: "So it might. But it would be your men who would rush, and not mine, who are of most use when alive. What are guns for? I make sure." And so the week went, and under a pall of smoke that had ceased to lift the guns stabbed inward until the hard walls shook and crumbled slowly away.

But on the morning of the 15th of June, being the day on which the Viceroy had promised the relief which did not appear, the Turkish leaders stood together on Sceberras, somewhat back on the highest slope, and Dragut turned to Mustapha Pasha to say: "You can rush it now, if you will; as I think, it is fit to fall."

Mustapha stroked his beard, and looked down on a scene as black and foul as though it were one of the boiling cauldrons of hell. "Nay," he said, "you shall take the praise. I will make no claim at the last. You shall order all."

Dragut looked at him, with a laugh that was half a sneer, for he cared not who saw his thoughts, but he cared no more for Mustapha's wiles, being that much greater than he. He saw that if St. Angelo should fall at the last, Mustapha's honour was sure, being first in command of that which would have brought all Europe to shame, the Knights being of every land; but, if that should fail, there would be no help in a minor boast. So he cared not at all to make claim for any detail that might succeed, only watching that, should it fail, he could put the blame on another's head. Dragut said: "If I take charge, I can dispose all as I will? I can choose my troops?" And that being agreed, he was well content. All his life he had been Allah's curse on the misbelievers from Ceuta to Grecian isles, jovial, reckless, astute, breaking the Prophet's laws as cheerfully as he slaughtered those who refused the faith. He had made a name in his own way through which he could make light of the tricks of state. Let Mustapha plot in the night. He was content that there was good liquor for him. . . . Within an hour the Turkish army was on the move to make an end of its cornered prey.

De Broglio heard and was glad. For seven days he had waited for this to be, watching the battered sides of his crumbling walls and writing the tale of the dead.

"So," he had grumbled, "they kill us, when it is time that we should kill them. And all this because Sir John must butt in, and give Piali a broken skull! Though I will be fair about that. It was what I had asked him to do. . . . Do I call Piali a fool? I would not say that. He is well enough on the sea. I have seen him fight his ships in a stout way. He is not the serpent who blandished Eve. . . . But Dragut and I (if we may be put in one breath), we are old in war. We know the use of a wall, and how a fosse will feed on the lives of men."

During these days he had spared the lives of those he had, to the utmost that care would do. He would only allow such men to be on the walls as were working the guns, or who were stationed to watch. He had plans of defence complete, and held half his force at all times ready for instant call, but yet under cover in the foundations of the fort till the alarm should be blown. He had given stations to every knight, ranging them with three soldiers between, so that there would be no place which could be lost, but a pennon's honour must fall therewith.

He had given Medrano charge of defence where the wall had been breached the worst. "I do not say that others might not be themselves of an equal worth, whether in valour or skill," he had said, "but there is none by whose side men will stand with as firm a will, so it is there he must be." He gave d'Egueras the wall facing the lost ravelin, saying that, as he could never get it out of his thoughts, he had best be there; and he divided the command of the remaining circuit between La Motte, La Cerda, and other knights of good name. He gave La Cerda as high a place as the rest, that his honour might not be slurred, but he had a surer care not to place him where the worst assault would be likely to be, seeing what would be said if this post should be first to be driven in. "As for me," he said, with a booted leg on the board, and a tankard beside his hand, "I will have no place, being somewhat past the great deeds that you will all be likely to do. I will potter round. It is all for which I am yet fit. Except, I can take the praise if your valour shall throw them back. I am not too old to do that." He chuckled to himself as he rose with a twinge of pain in a stiffened knee, and went to talk to the Spanish soldiers, who formed an actual majority of the garrison at this time, and who must do their part as well as those of knightlier names (and with less hope of reward or honour therefor) if the assault were to be repulsed, which he assured them, as one who was old in observation of war, that they could do if they would.

"For while we are sufficient to line the wall, though they be a hundred to one, it is no advantage to them. They can reach us by the ladders they plant, and no other way, and no faster than they can mount in their single rows, to be thrown back as they show their heads, which you should be equal to do. And you may like to know that those ladders will be too short. Do I know why? Not at all. But they always are. I have seen sieges enough, and the attempted storming of walls, both from within and without, and I can tell you no more beyond that, that they always are. It may be that they are made by men so valiant of heart that they think the wall to be somewhat less than it is; it may be they seek excuse that they may turn back, without aid from those who are standing above: it may be that they would spare wood. I can but tell you that so it is. The ladders will be too short. And if there should be any of such a length that men may climb to the top, I have seen that it is better to be of those who bash their heads as they show over the edge, than of those who come up to that end.

"Not that I would have you think that the wall will be easy to hold, for while you throw back the assault you must be exposed to missiles from every side, which you will be too busy to heed. But you will find that, if you are bold and sure, there will be many yet alive when the night comes, and some with a whole skin, and the Turks will have gone back, having lost ten to our one; but if you blench from the wall for any peril of shots that come from those that will throng the hill, they will swarm over the wall in such force that our swords will be vain to slay, and we shall be all sped in one heap.

"I tell you it will be hard to hold; but it can be done, and I think it will, you being the good men that you are. If I had my way they would be here in the next hour, but they must go to hell by a slower road."

So he had talked; and if the fanatic passion, at once racial and religious, which inspired many of Malta's knights, was a more powerful influence to them, yet to the common soldiers, who must share in that desperate defence without their exaltation of spirit, De Broglio's cheerful unperturbed demeanour, his cool appraisement of the possibilities of the position, may have been a more potent power. For he had a reputation alike for courage and discretion, for common sense and for common wit; and, beyond these, he was known for a practical soldier of long and varied experience, in whom unlearned men would trust more readily than in the aloof theorists of war, and who would talk to them in a different way.

To Medrano, as they examined the gap in the south-east curtain, upon which the fire of Dragut's main battery had been concentrated for the past three days, while bursts of barbaric music, mingling with many noises from the infidel camp, told that the day of storm was upon them at last, he said other things.

"You will observe that they do not creep up? That they scorn surprise? That is Dragut's way. He will swagger and boast, and they say he has fought his best fights when he was so drunk that he was glad to hold to a neighbour's arm. That may leave the truth somewhat behind, though he is of a riotous blood, and war is to him a sport such as would make him drunk on a great day without the prompting of wine.

"Yet he is not to be valued low; for he wins all, being inspired in his own kind, though John would say it is a fiend that invades his soul. It may be Lucifer's self, by the deeds he has done to affront the standards of Christ, but we have no concern about that, it being beyond our control. What we have to regard (as I need not be saying to you) is that he shall not add an affront the more. And I have some slight hope, even of that, though I suppose Sir John has cast us to drown, either in this tide or the next; for the walls endure in the main, though they be somewhat ragged and split, and men of a better heart I have never led."

Gonzales de Medrano, bareheaded as yet, but otherwise in armour of proof, handsome and splendid in his damascened steel, looked somewhat down on the grosser, slovenly figure of his commander, on soiled leather and a battered breastplate which could have been bettered by half the men-at-arms that the fort held. Was it in unison, he wondered, in a mind which was always alertly observant of the panorama of surrounding life—was it typical of the man who was content to be seen in such guise? "I suppose," De Broglio had said, "that Sir John has cast us to drown, either in this tide or the next"; and with that thought in his mind he went round to range the defence as good-humoured and unperturbed as though he ordered a meal. He professed no religious fervour, no passion of patriotism, no extremity of racial hate. Was his courage no more than the stupidity of routine? It was Medrano's curse that he looked out and afar, that he was aware of that which was around and ahead. He loved life, which had given much, and had promised more. But it must be lived, if at all, in a splendid way. It was that necessity which had brought him here, as he thought, to a sure death. . . . Perhaps the key to De Broglio's mind was in what he had said of the fiendly power that was held to account for the battle-genius of the drunken corsair, and its frequent successes against the banners of Christian knights: "We have no concern about that, it being beyond our control." He was content to do that which lay in his own hands, leaving the ordering of the world, even including his own fate, to the various powers, Divine or human, whose responsibilities they certainly were. In the same mood, he was careless of what he wore, for he did not think of himself, nor were his eyes on any present or future fame. He was a soldier by use, having no doubt that he fought in a good cause, and if the Grand Master sent him to death, it was for Sir John to make good at the throne of God, which it might be supposed that he would not be backward to do.

Medrano, knowing himself to have the greater honour in the mouths of men, and supposing that he would have the greater fame in the after days (which he had been at more pains to secure), wondered in the clarity of thought which may come to those who see death no more than an hour apart, which of their souls would be of the greater weight in the scales of God, and saw reason to doubt.

While these thoughts moved in his mind, he answered De Broglio's words in a different way.

"You think we may stand the storm for this bout? It is hard to guess. We have walls; but they have, as against us, an almost numberless force and are of a fighting fury that all men know. Yet it is to be thought that they must fight without hope of honour or praise, from the very numbers in which they come; and we can take some pleasure in that. For if the fort fall, it is no more than all men will look to see. There is no glory for them. But if they fail they will have their measure of shame, at which they must vomit much."

"Well," De Broglio said, "you are right enough, and, be that as it may, it is our part to keep them out to the last hour that we can, both for the cause we serve and that our throats may remain uncut. Yet," he continued with twinkling eyes, "there will be one in their camp who will find it good for a sore head if our walls stand, or the talk that passes between the lines has somewhat less than the tenth part of truth which is the measure on which we can mostly count without being tripped by a likely lie."

He spoke of Piali, whose quarrels with Dragut had grown in the mouths of men till it was said that only Mustapha's protesting presence had kept the daggers of the two admirals clean of each other's blood. He went on to survey the defence of other parts of the fort, leaving Medrano to his own thoughts, which were sombre but not ignoble, as he pursued the doubt of whether, in God's sight, he might not be of baser clay than De Broglio, whom no men were ever likely to praise as the perfect knight, either in life or death. But he thought of Sir Lancelot in the old romance, and how he had wept like a beaten child when it had been proved that, in God's sight, he was the greatest of Arthur's knights. He saw that to any man it must be an appalling woe rather than a platform of pride, if he should be shown that all his fellow-men were more base than himself. And after that he crossed himself and prayed briefly to St. John and his own saint, and turned his eyes to the curtain of battery-smoke through which there came a growing and mingled sound of drums and cymbals and clashing arms, and the high shouting of men who scorned death in the Prophet's name.

It was an advance of which more could be seen as yet from St. Angelo's walls, now thronged by a watchful crowd who could do no more than look on at an arena of strife over which the smoke of battle would close more densely as the hours went by, so that they would hear rather than see the day-long agony of that inferno of smoke, and outcry, and flickering flame.

They could see something at first of the dense lines of the Turkish regiments moving forward down the length of Sceberras height, and St. Angelo's two cannons, being all there were of sufficient range, opened fire upon them with some effect; but to the most he could, Dragut moved his men along the western slope of the ridge. And, beyond that distant, futile cannonade, there was nothing now that the Grand Master could do. He had cast the die for this day when he had withstood La Cerda two weeks before. He stood now with a group of the Commanders of the Order around him, watching that which he had ordered to be, and with no comfort beyond the thought, as the hours went by, that St. Elmo had not fallen as yet, or the noise of conflict could not endure in the style it did.

He looked outward also to where the smoke of battle drifted seaward in slow long wreaths to the north, on a light wind which died as the day waned. He sought with little hope for the relief fleet which Don Garcio should have sent that day. But the sea was empty and quiet, till the sun sank, and a sea-mist rose in the windless air. As it thickened, the sounds of conflict grew less constant, and then less loud, till they ceased at last, leaving men to guess the meaning of that. Was St. Elmo a grave? There were few who could have courage to hope that it still stood, knowing what they did of the strength of the Turkish army which had gathered round it to take a prey.

As the night came, making a double cloak with the mist, the Grand Master ordered that a boat should venture across, so that the truth should be known at last, whether evil or good; but it had left the quay but a short time when one came with a letter bearing D'Egueras' seal, which the Grand Master opened, and read aloud to as many as could find space around him to hear.

> "We have endured," he read, "for this day, by the high purpose of God, but I know not what the morning will bring. There is truce made for the hours of night, that the Turks may remove their wounded and slain, which are strewn thickly around our walls.
>
> "You must send either succour during the night, or boats to bear us away. Our loss is two score of knights, and about three hundred of other sorts. There are not three score of all conditions who now remain, not having taken a wound. De Broglio is alive, but sore hurt. Medrano is dead. I am wounded, but can endure. By this mercy of mist, which I take to be the direct action of God, you may get off the most wounded and slain while the darkness holds, and those, also, if you will, who are yet whole. But I would know your purpose with speed, that I may order all in the best way. You must know that, as we are now placed, we cannot longer endure."

There was a postscript to this letter which read:

> "There is a tale that Dragut is slain, which the Saints grant! It may go beyond truth, as when Captain Piali was hurt before, but it is like that it has some substance of fact, for a time came when it seemed that the heart went out of those who had pressed us to such a point that we were becoming too few to man the whole length of the wall. When we thought it vain to hope that we should endure more, it seemed that those who were round us on

every side were become less willing to die, so that they drew back, first at this place, and then at that, till a truce was blown at the last, so that, for this night, they will have no foot on our walls."

The Grand Master looked up as he finished the reading of this letter, and there was exaltation in his eyes, and in the voice in which he addressed the assembled knights.

"Behold," he said, "the most high mercy of God, Who does not desert His own, they being of sufficient valour, and the faith without which all else is a broken reed. I trust that Dragut is no more than a dying man, who will yet have space to see the Hell to which he most surely goes.

"Nor can we doubt that this mist is also of the seeing purpose of God, and will not hinder us that we send relief to our comrades who are so sorely beset.

"De Miranda, it is to you that I next must look. You shall assemble a hundred men, of those whose names Sir Oliver already holds as being ready to go. You must embark in the next hour, for who can say how long the mist will lie as it now does?

"Sir Oliver, you shall send instant reply to this scroll, saying that they are to be of good heart, for a strong succour will be theirs at a later hour. And you can say also that they must have ready all who have taken disabling wounds and are not too broken to move, that they may be brought back in the same boats, with such also of the dead as there may be space to embark, that they may be buried as Christian knights."

Those who listened observed that the idea of evacuating the ruined fort had been swept aside without discussion or pause, and if any doubted the wisdom of further defence, they lacked resolution to advance their views against the mood the Grand Master showed, remembering the bitter controversy there had been before, and how arrogantly he had borne it down.

They who had travailled in strife through that day were not to be rescued alive, but were to find comfort in the fact that new comrades would be sent to join in to-morrow's deaths. Yet what did the Grand Master require beyond what they were pledged to give? Chastity—obedience—poverty—to all these they were vowed, their lives having become their Order's, and not their own. But even these vows had been found capable of some differences of interpretation during the later centuries of wealth and ease through which the Order had passed. Poverty? What could that mean to those who controlled the riches the Order owned, except that their wealth must be for its use at sufficient need? Chastity? Was not the plain intention that they should avoid the obligations of legal marriage, or of children such as could claim their names, or any rights they held in the wealth which should be the Order's at last? Obedience? That was certainly the Grand Master's due; but they might still have some rights of argument, of contention, even of bargaining before this obedience were paid. Now they found themselves required to interpret their vows in a harder way, which all were not equally ready to do. It may have been well for Malta, if not for them, that they had a Grand Master who had put his hand to the plough, and would keep the furrow straight, though it should lead to the gates of death.

Yet those who would now go to prolong a hopeless defence would not be sent by duress, but were such as had put down their own names, and others were less directly concerned. Also, it must have been plain to all that it was not a time for debate. That which was done, whether to reinforce or to bring away, must be completed while mist and darkness were joined to give it sufficient cloak, or it would be disaster indeed if the frail boats should be exposed to the fire of the Turkish batteries; or if St. Elmo should be isolated for another day while still containing no more nor less than its remnant of wearied and wounded men. The Grand Master met no word of protest. There was no comment beyond the silent gravity of those who heard his decision.

Yet he must have been conscious of the meaning of that, for he followed Sir Oliver to his own room, which he paced restlessly while the first orders were issued which would assemble the volunteers, and bring the boats to the outer quay, and when this had been quickly done, and Sir Oliver sat down to write the letter which would send the necessary instructions to those who still lived in St. Elmo's walls, he said abruptly: "Oliver, tell me the truth from your own heart. Do you hold me wrong?"

For a moment Sir Oliver paused with a lifted pen. He was considering what the question might mean, rather than what his answer would be. He decided that the Grand Master asked only for the satisfaction or assurance of his own mind. His purpose had not faltered nor changed. If he should be told that his obstinacy was a rank folly, and nothing more, he might be roused to passion, perhaps distress, but he would not change the orders which were even now going forth. Sir Oliver had no cause to vex him thus to no gain, for he did not think it a folly beyond defence. When he spoke, he gave frank reply:

"I do not hold you are wrong. I am not sure. It is a matter which will be judged at last by its own end. A week ago, had it rested with me, I should have blown up the fort and brought its garrison off, as we could have done then. I might do the same to-night. Yet I should have been wrong then; and I might be wrong now. For it is plain that, for the past week, the Turks have spent their strength there, and have left us free, and now they have made assault and have failed, which must have been to them a great cost, both of munitions and men; and if you should blow up the fort this night you would have done far better than to have done so a week before. But as to whether it should be done now—we know our own loss, but less, as yet, of that which our foes have felt, or of what heart they are now in; and there is this rumour of Dragut's death—it may prove that it can be held for a longer day, but it is not easy to guess."

The Grand Master made no reply. He went on pacing the room, as one who had retired to his own thoughts. Sir Oliver turned to the letter he had to write, and his glance fell on the list of volunteers who were now being called up. He added: "There is one thing that we should clearly observe. The men who now go are not of the militia of this island, nor are they of the hired soldiers of Spain. They are the most choice of our own knights, of whom the total number is few. They are the best we have, and if they go they will not return. There are few things surer than that. We cannot look for another mist at the right hour to bring off those who remain, even should they outlast assault on another day. When we face the storm of our own walls, they will not be here to our aid; for we send them all to a sure death."

"And for what else did they come? Are their vows naught?" the Grand Master burst out in a voice of protest, but less as though he argued with Sir Oliver than his own soul. "The better men that we send the more stoutly will they maintain. I have good hopes they will hold it long. . . . But the command is too much for a wounded man. I will send Montserrat to take control. There could be none better than he." After a moment of silence he added, in a voice that had become quiet and grave: "Oliver, men can say of me what they will at the last, so that the Order endure. I know I am loved of few. It is not for that I am here; but, as I think, by the choice of God for a settled end."

He went out at that, and Sir Oliver's room, which had been private to them for a time, became busy again as those that he had sent out on various errands returned for fresh instructions from him.

There were few in St. Angelo's Castle who would not wake through that night.

Angelica was among those who came. She asked Sir Oliver, at the first chance that she had: "May I see the list of those who are called?"

He answered what he rightly guessed to be in her mind. "You need not trouble for that. Your name is not there. I had struck it out."

She looked a relief which may be thought natural enough, but which left him a puzzled doubt. Why had she put it down, if she were not seeking to go? Was it to be explained by the instability of her sex? That what had been pleasing at some distance away, did not attract when it must be faced in the next hour? Or did it mean that her cousin had wounded her at the first (which was likely enough), and had now become active to heal the hurt (which it was harder to think)? So he questioned, having no key to the truth, and then he was more startled by that which she asked next.

"I hear that you have a letter to send, which the messenger who came is unfit to bear."

"That is so. It was brought by a wounded man, who will not return. What of that?"

"May it be taken by me?"

"I should say no. There are others who are more fit. Why do you wish that?"

She faced him with pleading eyes. "If you would not ask? But I have a cause of much weight. There can be none fitter than I, who have been before."

"Yes. But it was not as it will be now."

"There can be no risk," she said stubbornly. "Not in this mist. And there is a truce for the night, so it is said."

"There will be a limited truce; but I was not thinking of that. A battle may not be pleasant to view, while men die and kill by every manner they may. But it is harder to look on the sight it leaves when the dust sinks, and the trumpets die. . . . Would you still go, being warned?"

"It is what I have asked."

"Well, so you shall. You should do your part, being here. It may be well to show that you have been of use, if the Grand Master should perceive your disguise, of which he seems to have had no thought after the first. . . . You will give this letter sealed to D'Egueras' hand, and will tell him that the reinforcements which are mentioned therein are coming in twenty boats in no more than an hour from now, for which he should be quickly prepared, so that they can bring back the wounded and dead, of whom there may be more than will be embarked at one time. He should send message back by them, or else sooner by you, of any needs that we may supply while the darkness holds. You should observe all you may, and bring fuller report than can be sent in a written word. . . . Are you ready now?"

"Yes, I can go now."

She took the letter, and after a short ascent to her room which might have been for no more than the cloak which must be worn against the mist and the night-air, she went down to the quay, where the boat that had come from St. Elmo was still moored, being no more than a little skiff that had brought the wounded messenger, and two men who had pushed the oars.

It had some freedom of rope, so that it must be brought in a few feet, which those who lay on its thwarts, being hailed, made no motion to do. A man of the quay-guard hauled it against the steps, and stirred the sleeping men with his foot, at which one arose in a weary way and put an oar overside, showing a bandaged hand.

His comrade did not stir. A lantern's light cast on his face showed an unnatural pallor amid a bristle of coarse black hair. Being raised, it could be seen that he had taken a wound between the shoulder and neck, which had been staunched and bound, but, as he had slipped on the thwart in his heavy sleep, the padding had come away and it had started bleeding anew. He must be lifted out. There would be no more help from him now.

Angelica saw that there was no one there who would be free to take his place without higher orders than hers. It was no time to delay. She had pushed an oar before then, and it was clear that she must do it again. She reached for that which the man had loosed, and found that where she put down her hand it was sticky and wet. She smelt blood. She found that she was on a seat which had been drenched from the open wound. Well, she was there by her own choice, and it was surely there she must stay. She put the oar overside.

As they moved into the mist, she said, more to make talk to the silent figure behind than because it mattered to her: "He must have been badly hurt. He was not fit to have come."

The man did not hear, or found understanding hard. He asked, in bad Italian, what she had said. When it was repeated, he replied: "There are few who have not taken a wound, and they are not to be spared on such an errand as this. When you have seen. . . ."

His voice fell. He began to push with a slow, long stroke in a weary way, as though against a sea that made progress hard. There was mist on the sea, as there had been when she had made this passage before, and again the stars showed at times, the mist lying low and being thin in places, like a garment worn into holes.

To Angelica they were lost at once, but she saw that the boatman was now keenly alert. He watched the water and looked up at the stars when the chances came. He watched her stroke, which, tired though he might be, was less strong and regular than his own, and paused at times with a lifted oar, that the boat might be brought to a true course.

After a time he grew more vigilant, listening intently for any sound which might come from the other shore, which they should be nearing now. Once he would have them rest their oars for some moments, drifting backward upon the current, when he must have heard what he sought for; after that he pushed in a more assured way, till they approached a dark shadow of land, which they skirted for a short time and so came to St. Elmo's quay.

CHAPTER XXXIII

St. Elmo lay under the triple palls of night and mist and the smoke of a day-long strife. It was a lazar within, and a shambles without, where its trenches were littered with Turkish wounded and dead. There were places where they lay heaped. Among these the lanterns moved, for the infidels toiled to bear them away while the night endured and the short hours remained of a truce that the dawn would end.

Inside the walls the few that remained whole, worn with the long hours of excitement and strife, must still toil through the night at a hundred tasks which it was vital to perform before day should renew the war.

D'Egueras, striving to bring all to such order as might yet be, found that he had less than three score of men of all conditions and ranks who were not dead or had not taken a wound. He disposed of these as he best could, thinking first of how defence could be made for the next day, unless the Grand Master should direct them to withdraw during the night from the breached and battered walls. After what he had seen that day even he was disposed to think that it might be best to blow the fort up in the night, though he had turned with wrath from such talk before. But now it might be said that it had done the most that it had ever could. He did not know with precision that the Turks would count the tale before dawn of more than a thousand either crippled or dead, but he knew that the loss they had suffered was very great. Having done them that harm it would surely be better to withdraw, leaving them no more than a shattered shell, than to be taken by storm on the next day. So he thought, as he waited to learn the Grand Master's will.

He read the letter Angelica brought, with a mind that was too tired for much emotion to stir. He said only: "Montserrat is a good knight under whom I will gladly serve." He gave orders for those who had lived through that day with wounds which left them able to walk, that they should help those who were sorely hurt, that these should be ready to embark with the least delay. It was an office for which he had no sound men whom he was able to spare. To these last he gave promise that they should have hours of rest when the reliefs should arrive. He had less hope for himself, seeing that he would have much talking to do when Monsterrat and he should meet. He was wounded, where his shoulder had been struck with a flying fragment of rock, of which he took little heed.

It was no more than a wide blackness of bruise, for the piece of stone that had knocked him down had come with a flat side, giving a species of wound that was common in this war. The cannon-ball of the day, being solid and round, could not damage more than came in its path, except it shattered that upon which it fell. In itself, at long range, it was not over-greatly feared. As it lost pace it might come bouncing along the ground at no more speed than could be dodged by an agile man as he would avoid the bound of a clumsy dog. But when it fell upon metal or stone with shattering force, it might do as much harm as a bursting shell.

It was so that Dragut had taken a wound, by the talk that came, no one could say from where, during these hours of truce. It came in the guise of many conflicting lies, out of which some truth might be dredged with a careful net.

He had always been reckless in self-exposure, holding that life is lived by a destined plan; and he had a fixed belief that it was part of that plan that he should be Allah's evil to Christian lands, making their seamen slaves and their commerce a prey. He had proved his faith, in a fierce rollicking drunken style, till he had become lord of all the African lands from the edge of Egypt to the frontiers of Spain, and he had gone far to make the Mediterranean a Moslem lake, as it would continue to be for twenty years after his death, till the gathered fleets of all Europe should make an end of that curse to the sound of Lepanto's guns. And all these years, in a jovial drunken fury of cruel strife, his scimitar had shone and reddened in the front of a score of battles, on firm land or the swaying deck, and he had not felt so much as the hurt of a scratched skin.

He had been no more careful on this day than his custom was, and if he remained somewhat in the rear at the first, it was only that he might have a broad view of the operations that he directed from the rise of Sceberras' slope. He had ordered that the main attack should be against the length of the landward side, where the fort had been greatly reduced by the fire of the Turkish guns, most of which had been directed thereon. From the captured ravelin there was to be little more than a feint attack, its nearness being of little real advantage against the strength of undamaged walls that were higher than it, while that nearness would avail of itself to hold a part of the defending force immobile, they not knowing how soon or in what strength it might unmask attack from its hiding walls.

By this disposition he had also planned that the new battery which he had built on the opposite shore of the northern harbour (where it is called Dragut's Point to this day) should be able to continue its fire without fear of a misdirected shot falling among its friends, as there was to be no assault from that side.

As the attack proceeded and the hours passed with a dreadful slaughter on either side but no decisive result, he had become dissatisfied with the work of this battery, which he had directed to concentrate its fire upon the cavalier of the fort, and, with his usual impetuosity, he had ordered a boat and proceeded to cross the northern harbour, so that he might direct its guns with better effect—if necessary with his own hands, as he would often do when afloat—being a gunner of much skill, and with such fortune at times that was widely believed that he had the aid of unearthly powers.

There was a quarter of a mile of water dividing Dragut's Point from the fort, and those who worked the guns there might well think themselves out of the danger of that day, and the more so because the fire of the cavalier was concentrated upon Sceberras' slope, where it took a harvest of death from the regiments of advancing Turks; but De Broglio, who knew that most gunners will work more coolly and take better aim if they are assured that they are out of danger themselves, had ordered that one of the longer guns of the cavalier should be turned at times on the distant battery, so that it should not be too sure of its own peace. And this being well served it chanced that, as Dragut was pointing one of the battery guns with his own hands, a shot struck the top of the wall which had been erected for its defence, scattering a dozen fragments of stone and raising a cloud of dust. When it sank, it could be seen that Dragut lay among other men who were wounded or dead, and when they raised him up it was not easy to see to which he belonged. He bled from a cut head, and on his right side the ribs had been driven in. But he still breathed, and became conscious after a time, asking to be taken back to his own tent.

So it was done, and there he lay between life and death, and as the news spread, the assault, which had been pressed till that time and might have prevailed in another hour, slackened and failed, for its driving force had become still.

Christian men compared his fall with that of Piali before, both of whom had been struck by the scattered stones from a ball that fell from afar, when it might have seemed that their danger was next to none. They saw the guidance of God. The Moslems may be excused that they saw the work of more fiendly powers; yet Dragut would have agreed in so far that he would have said that it showed how vain is the forethought and care of men, and that he had done well to contemn danger through all his life, knowing that it would be lost at the destined time and not a moment before.

"You may tell Sir Oliver," D'Egueras said, "that it seems sure that Dragut is down, though there is a doubt if he be no more than hurt or already dead. It was doubtless by the ruling mercy of God, for we were sore pressed."

Angelica said she would so report. She made no more than needed reply. She was somewhat sick at things she had seen by the light of lantern and torch as she had come to the fort, having had occasion to recall what Sir Oliver had said of that which is left when the dust sinks and the trumpets die. It would be worse in the cold light of the summer dawn, which was not more than three hours away. She should have been gone before then, but she had in mind her own purpose for which she came, in which she was resolved that she would not fail. She thought of the Italian poem which was much read at this time, of how Beatrice had been given courage of God, by which she could walk unmoved through the pits of Hell, and she was aware of a kindred need.

"Am I free to walk as I will," she asked, "within the range of the fort, now that my errand is done?" It would have been simpler to say that she would see La Cerda, having a message for him, but she was in danger enough without that which might have drawn the lightning around her head.

D'Egueras turned his tired eyes upon her, regarding her for the first time in a personal way. He asked: "Do you go back or stay here?"

"I was to go back at once if you had urgent message to send, or else with the boats that will take the wounded away."

"There may be things which should be brought while the mist allows, but I know not what. It was not my part. There shall be search. I know that we have powder enough; and nost else for as long as we shall endure. I should say that Sir Oliver knows better than I what our stores should lack. . . . Could you push a boat without aid? Could you find St. Angelo's quay in this dark?"

"I might handle a boat, if it be lightly built; it is less sure that I could find St. Angelo's quay."

"We have few men who have strength for that at this hour, and less than none we can spare. You must wait till the boats arrive."

She repeated the question that was unanswered as yet. "I can walk at will in the fort's bounds?"

"You can give some help to the hurt. There is none should be idle here. If you are challenged by any who think you strange to the fort, the password is *esto perpetua*, as it will be till to-morrow noon."

Angelica went at that, while she could. She was not unwilling to give aid to those who were in a pitiful need, but she had to do that which had brought her there. She must find La Cerda, if possible by what would seem a chance meeting, and have some words with him which no others would hear.

She learned casually, from a Spanish soldier to whom she gave some help in washing a wounded knee, that the knight she sought was now in command of the southern wall. It was not the post he had first held; but as the hours passed, and men died or withdrew with a wound to staunch, there had been need for others to take defence of the wall where the assault was most strong, and so it had fallen to him. Angelica knew nothing of that, but was glad to hear that he was alive and, as she supposed, unhurt.

La Cerda paced a wall, where he was in charge of a small guard which he had permitted to lie at ease, and perhaps sleep. There was little to fear, for the Turks could be trusted to keep such a truce as was then made and, in any event, he could have waked alarm before any could scale the wall. He had fought well during the day and had said that he could endure for the night. He had not reported a wound. But he was in a pain too great for it to be easy for him to rest or to keep still.

He had pain both of body and mind. For he had seen that he must fight and (he supposed) die, without honour or praise, whether the fort should fall that day or endure. He had said that it could not be held, and he was to fight to prove himself wrong. He could only be right if the Turks should break in and put all who lived to the sword, as they would be most likely to do.

Well, he had fought his best, as his part was; and he still lived, where most of the best were dead. There was Medrano for one. He had died in the breach where the worst fighting had been. For the ladders were too short for the unbroken parts of the wall, as De Broglio had foretold. But at the place where Medrano had held command the wall was battered to half its height, and the Turks had swarmed up, though they had been slain till their dead bodies had become a mound that made the ascent easy and short. Medrano, better guarded than most by his armour of Milan steel, had held his place while others fell at his side or were replaced by those less weary than they. He had taken so many wounds that none could say by whose hand he had died at last. It was in that breach that De Broglio also fell, even as the assault was losing its force, and it could be seen that the fort was saved for that day. He had pushed stoutly in, when he heard that Medrano was down, and though somewhat scanty of breath, he had shown a skill in using the sword that was too much for the most of those who must face its point, though it might lack the grace of fence that the schools would teach at that time. He lay now among those who were sorely hurt, having taken a body-wound from a Turkish pike which made breathing hard. . . .

La Cerda had no wound to show from a foeman's hand, but he had been hurt in another way. He had been directing those who had been flinging the hoops of fire, which were a weapon of clumsy sound but which had been of more avail even than the wild-fire bombs in swelling the tale of death among the Turks who had ever crowded the ditch and clambered against the wall. They were hoops of wood, soaked with oil, and decked with inflammable rags. They were set alight, and then taken in large tongs made for this work, and flung far out over the wall. They were so large that they might fall around three men in a close rank, and would set the light linen garments of the Turkish soldiers on fire, so that they would be sure of such torturing wounds before they could struggle clear of the flaming hoop and put their own garments out, that they were most like to end in a slow death.

La Cerda had been directing how these hoops might best be thrown from the wall to discourage those who fought up to the breach where Medrano stood, when he came too carelessly near, and his arm was scorched by the caprice of a back-blown flame. He had endured then, as the hour required, and had said nothing since, but the pain did not lessen, he rather growing more conscious thereof, as he paced the wall in the dreadful quiet of a night that was heavy with fate and death, and often loud with outlandish cries, as the Turks lifted those who had not been utterly slain, or as the wounded that they delayed to relieve cried out in pain or a bitter thirst.

La Cerda, in this mood of anguish and wrath, was accosted by one whom he could not know in a light which was next to none, but who seemed no more than a slender boy, with a voice in which the manhood was hard to hear, though it was quiet and assured.

"Is it the Chevalier La Cerda to whom I speak?"

"Yes, I am he. What of that?" He spoke in a curt way, as one who would be left to his own thoughts.

"I would speak with you where we cannot be heard."

"Being whom, and for why?"

"I am Don Garcio, whom you once met in Sir Oliver's room.

I come to tell you of that which it is urgent that you should know."

"Well, we are alone here. The men sleep. I would I could do the same. If the Grand Master be stubborn still, and will not clear the fort while the night allows, I know not how we shall endure through the next day. We shall be slain in our sleep. What news do you bring to men who are marked for death that an old fool may not be told he is wrong?"

"It is an issue I cannot judge; but I can tell you that there is strong support now embarking to cross, and the wounded are to be taken back in the same boats."

"Then there can be no weight in aught else you can show, except I am to return."

"Yet you must know, for if it be nothing to you, it is much to me. Venetia is in hiding in my chamber, which once was hers, and the Provost-Marshal is searching the town."

"Fiends in hell! How got he the scent of her?"

"She stabbed your steward, by whom she says that her honour was put to siege, so that it could be saved in no other way."

"The foul impudent cur! Is it thus they affront my name while I am caged here? And do they blame her for that?"

"I know not that there is much jeopard for her. At least, Sir Oliver says that she might come clear, the tale being guessed much as she would have it to be. But the Grand Master will have her found, except (as there is other guess) she may have escaped to the Turkish lines, being no more than a spy, and she having stabbed your steward when he would have discovered her guilt. Such is common talk, which is false, as we know; but the Grand Master is set to resolve whether she be in hiding or not."

"Does Sir Oliver know?"

"He knows nothing as yet, or I were not here."

"Do you think she will be found where she now is?"

"I cannot say. She will not stay by my will. There is proclamation made that there will be death for any who give her harbour after to-morrow noon."

"She cannot ask that you risk that. She must advance to her own defence. On the facts you give she should not have greatly to fear; and the Order will not wish to do me too much despite, let the Grand Master hate me the most he may. I will write forthwith, both to Sir Oliver and to her. That I might be there to defend my own!"

He roused a drowsing soldier, sending him with word to La Motte that he should relieve him for half an hour, which it had been agreed that he should be ready to do. He turned to Angelica to ask: "How long can you remain here?"

"I can remain long enough. But I must tell you that I cannot give your letter to Sir Oliver's hand, except she assent thereto."

"Do you not want her to go?"

"That I do!" There was a sincerity in this exclamation which it was not easy to doubt.

"Then why would you . . .?"

"She has my pledged word. She is in a great fear. She will not be revealed except you be there to defend her part."

"She is a coward by that word. Yet she did well when she stabbed Giles. I have known a new mood with each hour. You may find her changed when you get back."

"Not in this." Angelica thought she already knew what was fundamental to Venetia, and could divide it from such moods as she might put on for the pleasure or vexation of the man to whom she belonged.

La Cerda cursed by several devils and saints, and the places where they are said to abide. Then he had a new thought. He asked: "She has held your room for two nights; and now, if you put her forth, it must be on her terms?"

Angelica's sudden laughter startled the night.

Into La Cerda's mind there came an unlikely doubt that had once entered before. He wished much for a better moon.

Angelica's laugh was soon done, for she saw, in an instant's time, that it might prove a poor jest. She said shortly: "She had no welcome from me."

"How did she chance to come? Did she know you before?"

"No. But she knew the room."

La Cerda saw that there was reason in that. He saw also that he might be in debt to one to whom his courtesy had been less than it should. He said, in a different tone: "It seems that we owe you thanks. But I must deal now. Did you say that the wounded are free to leave at this hour!"

"That is how I was told. I should say that the boats may be here now." So it seemed that it was, by the sounds that came through the mist. As she spoke they were aware of a tall figure that stood at their sides.

La Motte's voice, formal and grave, and giving little sign of the weariness that he felt, announced that he would take charge of the wall, so that La Cerda was free to go.

"It seems," La Cerda said, "that I do not return, for the wounded are now to leave."

"The wounded?" La Motte asked, in a toneless way.

La Cerda's answer was curt. "Yes; I have a hurt arm."

"It is well for you." La Motte's voice was as level as it had been before. La Cerda went in doubt of whether he heard an insult, or the word of a friend. Angelica kept to his side. It might be of much moment to her to know what was done, and to take her own part if the need should come.

What she told was the truth, and no more; but there were two vexations it left unsaid. Venetia had become a most unwelcome addition to the few to whom Angelica's secret was known, and her promise that it should not be told was a bond of doubtful worth. Also, Francisco and Venetia had met, and had talked in a way that she did not like but could not resent; for what was it to her? She judged that Venetia sought no more nor less than to cajole him into providing harbourage or escape if La Cerda should fail; and she was half angered and half amazed that Francisco should seem so ready to swallow the hook. She told herself that she feared only lest he should give the girl aid that would bring him to the Grand Master's wrath, which was reason enough, though it was no more than she had done herself to that hour. But she found that all her fears had pointed the same way. She must get La Cerda to intervene.

CHAPTER XXXIV

La Cerda led the way to the boats. He had brought little with him when he came, and in his pain of body and tumult of mind he had no care to take it away. His squire had been dead for two days. He left his pennon displayed on the wall, as he would not have done had he withdrawn at a quieter time. There would be many pennons of the wounded and dead that would be taken down when the dawn came, to be replaced by those that had come for their turn of death.

He did not go to D'Egueras for permission to leave, as he might have done to De Broglio had he still been in command and as it was his clear duty to do. He disliked the Deputy-Governor, who had a kindred feeling for him, and he had some doubt of whether permission might be refused, or deferred, which he would not risk.

By this omission he came near to a rebuff that his pride would have found it hard to endure, for D'Egueras, being a man of ink-horn and pen, and exact even in that extremity of fatigue and loss, had found time to have an order prepared giving a list of those, both living and dead, who were to be sent back during the night. The boats that were sent were more than enough for the reinforcements they brought, dead and wounded men taking more space than those who are hale. They were emptied at once as they came to the quay, except some that were heavy with stores. All was done in haste, lest the morning should come, or the mist lift, before they should be within the safety of St. Angelo's walls. When La Cerda arrived, some of the boats were already filled and pushing away. There was an officer on the quay who checked all those who embarked from a list he had. Those who had come to land were already employed in bearing the litters of wounded men to the water-side.

La Cerda would have entered a boat which was less than full when the officer interposed. He was courteous, but he would not yield. Without D'Egueras' order he would allow no one to leave. If La Cerda (as he said) would not come out of the boat, then it must be kept at the quay till the Deputy-Governor had been informed.

La Cerda saw that he was wrong and yet it was hard for his pride to yield. It might have ended in a worse way had not De Broglio's litter come down while the wrangle was on and somewhat loud on La Cerda's side.

De Broglio, from a confusion of evil dreams, had been returned to an awareness of painful life by the jolts that his litter got as it descended the steps that led to the quay. He knew La Cerda's voice, and heard enough to guess more. He told his bearers to halt. He learned enough of the truth to decide that La Cerda should go.

The officer, a punctilious man, whose own temper had been somewhat roused by debate, was not quick to give way, even then. He had written orders, and against them only the word of a man who was near death and in the act of giving up his command.

But De Broglio was not one who was easy to thwart, he being a genial man but not weak. He had life enough for a jest and a shrewd word.

"Why," he said, "you must know I am in command till I leave here. I am not yet in the boat. I am on the quay. The Chevalier La Cerda shall precede me now, having my express command to that end. When I am in the boat I will say no more."

So La Cerda remained in the boat and Angelica followed, the officer saying nothing to her, either because he had instructions thereon or that he felt no disposition to argue anew. La Cerda had his way for the time, but the fact remained that his name was not on the roll of those who should have returned, which would be on Sir Oliver's desk in the next hour.

The boat came safely to St. Angelo's quay, though not without risk of harm, for the Turks could not fail to hear the noise of those who landed and went, they being free of the southern trench by the terms of the truce they made, and as that truce was of no more than a local kind and did not cover the harbour waters at all, they sent word to the batteries on Sceberras' side, and these fired at times into the mist, aiming in a blind way at where they thought the Christian boats were most likely to be. There was none hit, by the protection of watchful saints, but a shot struck the water so near the bow of De Broglio's boat that Angelica, being on the forward thwart, was drenched by the wave it flung.

Her cloak, which had been fouled before by the boatman's blood, was no better for this, and at another time her first thought might have been to cast it off and to have cleansed herself and make other amends, but now she thought only that she must keep to La Cerda's side as they went on to the castle through the great crowd of those who had assembled to meet the boats.

The torches were dimmed at this time by a pale forecast of dawn, and the castle, when they had passed the guard at the inner gate, seemed empty, unless there were those therein who slept through the night, as few did.

As they came to the main hall, Angelica, being a pace ahead, stopped and stood in La Cerda's way. "What," she asked, "would you do now?"

"I would see Venetia first."

"So I suppose you should. It is a room you will know. She will be asleep now, by a likely guess. You must knock twice, and once again after a pause. That is the signal we have. . . . I will go to Sir Oliver first, for I must make my report to him. How much may I say of this, by your leave?"

"You may say all; for she could not be longer hid. And now I am here it cannot be told too soon."

La Cerda showed more wisdom in this than he always would. For he saw that his own position would be improved if it should appear that he had given no countenance to Venetia being taken away, but had come back with the object of bringing her forth. And if his own position were clear in this, he might do more for her at a later hour in the accusation she had to meet. If, after requiring her to face what she had done, he showed that he believed her account, and that his faith was constant in her, it might avail much. He could not hope that she would be allowed to remain, but if she were acquitted of special guilt it might mean no more than that she would be held in some present restraint, and sent back to Sicily at the first chance, where she could remain on his estate and he could join her at last, if he should have the fortune to keep his life to the war's end.

"Well," Angelica said, "I can do that, for my pledge to her was that she should not be betrayed while you were not present to be her guard."

So it was; for Venetia had been somewhat subtle in that. She cared nothing for Angelica's risk, but she cared much for herself. She saw that, if she were caught at last (as she did not intend), it was of moment that she should be able to explain why she had not come boldly forth if she were unconscious of guilt. She would say then: "I waited only my lord's return, having no courage among hostile men, unless he should give me support. I meant always that I would tell at that time." She would be able to show that she had fled to the only woman of her own rank (or what she professed it to be) that St. Angelo held, for she did not propose to keep Angelica's secret a moment longer than it was profit to her. And Angelica, whose word would be of more value than hers, must support this, admitting that she had only asked to be hidden away till La Cerda's return.

This was only against the chance that she would be discovered and seized. She did not think to see La Cerda ever again, so that it made no difference beyond that. She thought that all in St. Elmo were doomed to death at that time, as they mostly were.

Angelica added: "I may be more than a short time, for Sir Oliver will have his care on other things besides this, but I suppose you will not mind that, having much to hear and to say. I will come as soon as I can, and will knock in the way we have."

They parted at that, he going up the stair that he had learnt to know in the days of more ease, before the Turkish galleys had left their berths in the Golden Horn, and she going to Sir Oliver's room.

She found Olrig there, and learned that the Grand Master's secretary had retired about half an hour before, giving instructions that he should not be called for four hours, unless there were urgent need. She was so used to finding that Sir Oliver was to be reached at all times of crisis or strain, seeming as one who was never weary by night or day, that she had not considered that this might be, as she saw now that she should have done.

She saw that it would be too long to leave La Cerda without word, even should she be able to get Sir Oliver's leisure to hear her tale as soon as he should be wakened again. Also, she was unwilling to be kept so long from her own room, being soiled and wet as she was. "I will go at once," she thought, "getting there not long after himself, and tell them of this delay."

As she went she thought that it might prove the better course of events, for she had resolved that La Cerda should know what she was and give his own promise of silence, as he could not lightly refuse. She thought that if he and Venetia should be together again it would not long be a secret between those two, and she had a shrewd thought that Venetia would be more likely to respect her own pledge if it had been given in La Cerda's hearing, or spoken of when they were present together. It was, at least, essential that she should know what of disclosure she was likely to have to face.

So she made her way to the room that she called hers at a quick pace, but she found that there would be no occasion to knock, for, as she climbed the stairs, she could see that the door stood wide. From within, there came a clashing of swords, and then she heard La Cerda's voice in a loud oath, which changed to an exclamation of pain.

CHAPTER XXXV

La Cerda had gone up the stairs in some conflict of moods. He was glad that he would be seeing Venetia again, she being to him a dear toy, if no more. He was not of a jealous kind, beyond what a Sicilian noble might be expected to be, but he was in a doubt which had some excuse, though he saw it could not go beyond that. Don Garcio was to him a quiet-toned, and yet confident, boy, whom he judged as having courage and pride, and yet he could not think of him as one who would use a sword. He wondered how he would act if he should be challenged thereto, for which he thought he might have cause before all should end.

He had said, while they were in the boat: "I fear you may have been discommoded more than you should, a lady taking your chamber thus. I trust that you have not been without other resort." And Don Garcio, whose face he had been unable to see, had seemed to be unprepared for reply. He had said: "Oh, I—I do well enough." And then: "It has needed care to avoid that any should suspect she is there." That was true enough; but it might be taken as an excuse that they had made common use of one room, which had to be explained away as it best could. Still, it appeared that Venetia had gone there of her own choice, being in a perilous need and having sought a room where she had been hidden before. It was hard to judge till he should have speech with her. The cause that was said to have brought her there did not suggest that she was careless of her own honour or unequal to its defence. . . . Yet Don Garcio's directions suggested that she would give access, without demur, at any hour of the night. He had enough doubt to go up with a light step, thinking that she should have no reason to pause through hearing a heavier tread than Don Garcio's would be likely to be. He would knock in the secret way, and see what the response would be before she could guess it was he, and whether her first recognition of him would show confusion or joy.

So he did; and he heard a low voice in the room, for which he had not been prepared. But he heard also the lifted bolt, and the door opened without delay.

As it widened he saw that it was held by a young knight, richly dressed in the Spanish style, whom he did not know. Behind him, Venetia lay in the bed where he had often seen her before. She saw him at once and gave a welcoming cry; but there had been a first moment when her face had shown a surprise that he did not like, for, instant though it had been, he had thought it akin to fear.

The face of the young knight had changed also, with more cause, and in a more open way. He had looked unconcerned as he drew the door wide, showing that he had expected Don Garcio, or some other, and had been willing to let him in. When he saw that a stranger was there, he stepped quickly forward, barring the way to the room.

La Cerda took a step in, as though he would have pushed him aside. "I would know," he said, "what you do here?"

Francisco's reply was quick to come. "I would know that of you."

"Why," La Cerda exclaimed, "is the chamber yours and the lady alike? It was what I had not known until now."

"It is my cousin's room, to which no one has right but she."

It was an unfortunate word, which Francisco did not observe that he had used, as was natural enough. It was no less natural that La Cerda misunderstood. He had had a passing doubt of Angelica's sex at a cooler time, but he did not think of that now.

"It is a kinship," he said, "of which I was not aware. But it seems that she keeps a most common room in the night."

Venetia was forth of the bed by this time. "You misread," she said in an urgent voice, "he was not speaking of me."

She called to one who had ceased to hear. He had tried to push Francisco backward to enter the room, and it would have been hard to say which sword was the first out.

Venetia looked on with the eyes of an angry cat. She was not of the sort to rush between meeting blades. She might have said that this was not because she lacked courage but because she was not barren of wit. Also, she had too much wit to cry out, even for that folly to cease, though she saw that it might be ruin to them as well as to herself, with which last she was most concerned. But she knew that it may make the difference of death to cause a man's mind to swerve, for so much as an instant's space, in such a bout as that which she now saw.

The two fought with the fury of those who are roused by a jealous hate and are both sure that the right is theirs. Francisco did not know that La Cerda had the name of the best swordsman in Sicily. (In fact, he did not know who he was.) Nor, in the mood that was his, would he have cared if he had. He had the impetuous courage of youth, and some belief in his own skill. He had some gain in the fact that he fought with a weary man.

La Cerda, turning aside the first fury of attack with a skilful blade, found that he would have enough to do to guard his own life at the first. Well, he thought, he would have wisdom to wait. He had proved before that his defence was not easy to pierce; and when an opponent became weary of the attempt, and fear would come to his heart as he found he was always foiled, then he would be apt to become wild in attack, and would be simple to overcome.

So the swords clashed for a time in the narrow space of the room, where there was little chance either to draw back or to swerve aside, but it did not come to the end which La Cerda planned. For Francisco made a thrust that was sudden and very hard, thinking to make an end as he had turned La Cerda's sword somewhat aside, but his opponent was quick to regain his guard. He deflected the thrust so far that it passed his side, and the point drove into the arm of a chair beside which he stood. Francisco wrenched sideward to get it free, and the blade snapped. He leaped backward beside the bed, his sword being no more than two feet of a broken blade, and drew his dagger out in his other hand.

La Cerda, in quick pursuit, found Venetia in his way, somewhat on his left side, for she respected his sword. "Leon," she cried, in an urgent passionate voice, "will you ruin all? Will you heed naught?" And as he only swore and pushed her aside, for he was in a state of body and mind in which it was harder to think than to act in a blind way, as habit or instinct led, she seized his left arm. Her grasp was hard, for her strength was far more than her aspect showed. The small fingers pressed deep into the burnt flesh, and it was then that he cried out at the sudden pain, so that Angelica heard before she entered the room.

Angelica looked at the scene of interrupted violence with cooler eyes than those upon whom she came would be likely to have, but she found little pleasure in what she saw or what she thought it to mean. Her first question turned to that which was of most moment to her.

"Francis," she asked, "what should you do here at this hour?"

He had come out from beside the bed, on which he had thrown down the broken sword, and had put his dagger back. It was clear, for the time, that the fight was done.

"Why," he said, in an awkward way, which may have come from some shortness of breath or another cause, "I heard you had gone to St. Elmo alone and had not returned. I came here to learn what I could, and if you were back, being anxious at the delay."

Angelica looked at him in a sombre silence, biting her lip. She wondered what had been going on in that room which La Cerda had seen, fearing more than the truth was.

She looked at La Cerda, who was now seated on the chair, in the arm of which the broken blade was still stuck. He looked ill, being exhausted with weariness, and passion and pain. He had felt faint in the first anguish that Venetia's grasp had caused, and had feared that he was about to swoon.

Venetia was at his side now, in her tender mood. She talked to him in rapid words that were so low that they could only partly be heard.

Angelica considered what she should say.

She wished no evil to any there, even to Venetia, providing only that she could separate her from Francisco, which (however little he might be to her) she thought it duty, as it would certainly be pleasure, to do. She saw nothing but added trouble if La Cerda should quarrel respecting the girl, and perhaps cast her off, thinking that she had been faithless to him.

She turned to La Cerda to say: "Sir Oliver cannot be seen for some hours. When he is about, I will come for you again. You had better rest here till then, where none is likely to knock, and, if they do, you need not open except to me.

"But there is one thing you should know first. I am not Don Garcio. I am the Señorita Angelica of Vilheyna and of Segura, where my lands are. I came to help in this siege, in a dress which I have found that I cannot cast.

"Perhaps you will understand, when you know this, why Venetia has found safety here, which, in other rooms in these towers, it had been much harder to do."

Venetia was silent now, watching her with intent eyes, as though she would have read her mind. La Cerda had recovered more of his wits and his self-control than he had had when he sat down.

"That," he said, "can be lightly believed, for I can say now that it is no more than I have suspicioned at times. You have been a good friend, to whom I owe more thanks than I had concluded before. . . . But I may still ask if this knight came here with no right in the morning hours or if he had warrant from you."

"Don Francisco," she said, "is my near cousin, and natural friend." She would have left it there, but saw that La Cerda waited for more, and added: "Is that not enough? Then he had warrant from me. . . ." She turned to Francisco to say: "Francis, we had better go for this time." She looked back at La Cerda, who was still seated in the chair, with Venetia kneeling at his left side. On the other, the broken sword was against his sleeve. She laughed in her sudden way. "You should take more heed, or you may find that my cousin's blade has a sharp edge."

La Cerda stared, in a moment's surprise, at words that had the sound of a threat. Then his eyes followed hers and he understood. "Yes," he said, "we must draw it forth." He saw that he had almost been foolish enough to take her words in a wrong way, yet the impression remained, as though she had warned him that it was for herself (and not for Venetia) that her cousin's sword would be quickly drawn, and the last suspicion of Venetia's faith passed from his mind.

Angelica went down the stairs in no mood for talk, and they were near the foot before Don Francisco, who had his own reasons for wrath, broke the silence to say: "You came at a good time."

"At a good time!" she exclaimed bitterly. "Do you not see how I am shamed? That he will think I am mistress to you? That is what you have done this night."

"Nay," he protested, "I said naught. There had been no harm had you said no more."

"So you think. You said naught, for you could not see. I will allow that. But you should not have been there, as you know well. Will you leave her now, or have you not had trouble enough?"

Francisco left the last question aside. He said: "You may say your will, but it can all be put in one word. You should not be here. I told you that at the first, and when you find where it has led you blame me."

"I blame you where you are wrong, as we both know."

He made no answer to that. He noticed, none too soon, in a light that was now near to the full day, how her eyes were dark from the lack of sleep, and her dress had been soiled and stained.

"What have you there?" he asked. "It is like to blood."

"You need not fret for that. It is not mine."

His imagination stirred to wonder what she had seen during the night, through what dangers she might have come, and what it could mean that her cloak should be so stained as it was. There was something of the old comradeship of Vilheyna days in his voice as he said: "You will have nowhere to go, having given your room to them. Will you come to mine?"

It was where they had talked once before, when she had been

willing to go. But she said now: "It is there I shall never be. You should know that. We are apart from this hour."

As she said this, which she did not mean, though it proved true, she turned sharply away. He did not follow, feeling that they had quarrelled enough, as they mostly did, if not at first, at the end. His thoughts turned to one whom he believed to have softer moods, and such as were more plastic to his. Why had La Cerda returned at the wrong hour, and just as they had agreed that he never would? Was Angelica to be thanked for that? He would have said that thank was the wrong word. Why had she come here, where she had no business to be?

CHAPTER XXXVI

Angelica finished her tale, and Sir Oliver remained silent, his hand restless about his chin. He did not look pleased, but she had a hope that he was not angry with her.

"The Chevalier La Cerda," she said, "has been firm, from when he was first told, that she must give herself up for the steward's death, which came from her, as she does not deny. He will have told her by now, which she may not like, for she seems to have more fear than I think she should. Can I say that she will not have greatly to dread?"

"If her tale stand," Sir Oliver replied, "she should not have greatly to dread from that cause. You can tell her that. And for La Cerda keeping her here, it is his matter rather than hers. She should not be chastened for that. But you must say that the judgment will not be mine. I will tell you this, which you need not mention again. I know more of her than she will be likely to show you. She has fooled me once—or La Cerda rather than she. But it will not be twice. By my will she will not remain here, either in castle or town. I would as soon that she should be sold to the Turks, for which she is quite fit."

Angelica spoke for one she had no reason to love, thinking she had heard a merciless word and one that was less than fair.

"I know not what she has done, and I suppose it is a gutter from which she comes, though that is more than some men will see; but I know something of what she is, and you must let me say that I think you wrong. She is like a hunted beast, being insecure among men. But were she set in a sure place she might have virtues that others lack."

Angelica did not know that her thought was born from the perilled chances of her own life in its last months, though she might have come through them in ways that Venetia would not have tried, they having more difference of blood than she was able to see. She spoke for herself, and for all women who walked in peril of laws that they did not make and customs which were less for their peace than for the pleasure or gain of men.

Sir Oliver was not vexed but unmoved. "It seems," he said

with a smile, "that she outpaces her trade, cajoling those who are not men. But what you say is no more than that Eve had not sinned if the tree of knowledge had not been there. . . . You can tell La Cerda that I will see him now, and alone. The girl can stay where she is till you hear more, which will not be long. For when I have talked to him I shall not delay to acquaint the Grand Master with all, and we know that his ways are prompt. But he should be in a merciful mood, for the news is good. Dragut is sore hurt, if he be not dead. It is said that a galliot sailed at dawn, at its utmost speed, to bring his son-in-law from Algiers, with whom he would speak before death, and who will take his command. He is one of whom you know more than I."

"Captain Hassan?" she said. "Yes, we have met before." She smiled at something that came back to her mind, as she had not done at the time. Where would she be now if she had not left his ship in the night? She was to have been one of his wives, if Dragut were in a generous mood and could forego the price she would bring in the Byzantium trade! Her mind was capricious in a vivid memory of how she had stepped over the sleeping slaves as she had made her way to the lower waist of the ship. Well, if the Turks should take Malta at last, she might come to no better end. She might even meet Hassan again, and be paid by him—how?—for the way she had wrecked his plan.

"Besides that," Sir Oliver went on, "it seems that Mustapha has taken control from Piali's hands. He has surveyed the fort and doubtless counted the slain, and he has resolved that the assault shall not be resumed. The batteries are to be reinforced and to open again. That is sure, for the troops are drawn backward to where they were before Dragut's advance. It is no more than time gained, but that is the aim we have; so there is to be thanksgiving at three hours after noon, which will be service also for Medrano and other knights whose bodies have been brought here in the night. . . . But you should not be there. You should take the rest you need when we shall have got this woman away."

Angelica went at that, and found La Cerda asleep; but, being wakened, he rose at once. He had talked with Venetia, and become assured both that she was faithful to him and not worthy of any blame for the blow she struck. He was confident that, if he should offer to find a ship at his own risk and charge to send her to Cerda, to his estate there, his friends in the Order would not let it be worse than that, even if the Grand Master were hard to rule. He saw some gain even in the fact that La Valette was known to be unfriendly to him. For himself he had hope of life, now that he was clear of St. Elmo's walls. He rose with a resolve that he would hold his temper in check, being prudent in speech, even if he should be chafed by the words of others whom he thought in his heart to be less than he, of whom the Grand Master was one. He went to meet Sir Oliver in that mood, and Venetia and Angelica stayed to wait his return, or for those who would come (as she had a fear) to take Venetia away.

"Leon," she said, "is resolved he can bring me clear. I would I were not less sure. What did Sir Oliver say?"

"He said the judgment was not with him. But, for himself, he thought you had little guilt, either for staying here, or the man you slew."

"Well," she said, "it seems you are all agreed, but it is not your backs that will bleed if your guess be wrong."

She lay stretched on the bed in an easeful style, but with regard for the crown of her pale-gold hair, which she had just dressed in a mode of innocent youth, making her less than her years, though they were still few. Her eyes were on the door at times, for she felt like a trapped rat. She wondered what Angelica would do now if she should resolve to fly. But she concluded that she would not get far beyond the foot of the stair, even in Master Giles' hood, now that everyone was alert and aware of the disguise in which she had fled. And she saw that her case would not be helped if she should now be held in attempted flight, for it was to be urged that she had only waited La Cerda's return to explain all.

Why could he not have been killed where so many were, she asked, with a savage anger at heart? It was not how she had meant matters to be; and now that the crisis came she had a fear lest her wits had failed to protect her skin, to which they had been equal till now.

And he had come at so wrong a time! Though, she admitted in thought, it might have been far worse had it been half an hour later, for Francisco had entered but a few minutes before, and she knew what she had meant to have done, whether he may have had the same expectation or not.

"Your cousin," she said, "has a quick sword. It is not often, if talk be true, that Leon is held so long."

"Yes," Angelica said, "he can fence well."

"So he may; but that is a different thing from when points are bare."

"That I found. I thought once I was equal to him, if not more. But when I tried, it was soon done. I should not be here now, but that I was not worth Captain Hassan's trouble to kill." It seemed that Sir Oliver's words had brought one back to her mind, of whom she had been ceasing to think. She added: "But he had the better sword and is far stronger than I."

Venetia went on with her own thought. "He has a great name in his own land?"

"Who? Captain Hassan? Oh, Francisco. You may say that, of course. There is no name in Spain that is more than ours, except only the King."

"You should not be here in that guise. You could wed whom you will, with so great a name, and with the lands that you have. But with these men, who are mostly monks, what have you to do?"

"That has a sound of sense," Angelica allowed, having seen it clearly enough before now, "but I am so placed that it is hard to draw back without shame, or to go on."

"So you say; but I think, if your place were mine, I should have no trouble at all."

Angelica considered that and saw that it was true. But it was not helpful to her.

Venetia had a surprising doubt as to whether, if Angelica were in her place, she might not also do better than she herself. Francisco had a great name, and a pride which was even greater than that. But he was also of a fine honour, an abysmal innocence (as she thought), and very sensitive to her own charms. Suppose La Cerda should still be killed in the war? Suppose (as she thought likely enough) he should be sent back to St. Elmo, when the Grand Master should learn that he had come away as he had? Was it possible that this game should be played in another way than that which she knew so well? That she would have made the mistake of her life in that next half-hour, if Leon had not come when he did?

If Francisco should be kept to his present command, she thought that few had a better chance of outlasting the war. She had that quality of audacity which had raised many, both men and women, from the gutters of city streets to high places of rank and power. Might she not yet come to be something more than the toy of a monkish knight? She was not afraid that she should fail as one of the first ladies in Spain. The doubt did not enter her mind.

An hour passed, and another. La Cerda did not return, nor did others come. Venetia grumbled and yawned, finding suspense hard, though her mind was active enough, planning what she would say or do in a score of different events, and what replies she should give if she should be questioned in sundry ways. A true tale may be hard to tell without fault, but Venetia had more difficult burdens than that. She had a fictitious past, which must be sustained without fail if she should be examined on that, which experience warned her was likely enough; and that, perhaps, with La Cerda there, so that all must conform to many tales she had told to him. She knew how a whole chain of true witness may fail if it be linked with a lonely lie. But she had confidence in herself that she would not be trapped, nor justly condemned, on the evidence she would give. She had most fear of the temper of those in whose hands she would be likely to be.

Angelica yawned with more reason and less suspense. But she was sombre of mood after her quarrel with Francisco and had a bitter feeling that he had been disloyal to her, which went beyond reason's bounds; for what loyalty could she claim, beyond that which was required by a kindred blood? It would have been more had they come to Malta together in a comradely way, but he had said from the first she should not be there, as most would agree. But she was exhausted, even to the extremity of her vital youth, by excitement and lack of rest. She was conscious of one desire beyond all, that Venetia should be gone.

But La Cerda did not return. It seemed that they might remain quiet and forgotten there till the day of doom; and at last Angelica could endure it no more. "I will find," she said, "what has occurred, for it is foolish to wait here as we do."

"So you may, but I am held, as you know. I can only hope that you will not be long gone."

"You can be at ease about that," Angelica replied, and was no worse than her word, for that which she went to hear could be quickly told.

She learned that, almost as she had gone from Sir Oliver's room, there had been an officer there, in the uniform of the Grand Master's guards. He said that he sought the Chevalier La Cerda, having an order for his arrest, but he could nowhere be found. Could His Excellency help him in that?

It was a title to which Sir Oliver had no claim, but the man, who would be sent on the Grand Master's business more than once in each day, among those who might be princes in their own lands, and of many dignities and titles he did not know, had found that to call them all as of the highest degree was a safe rule and sometimes of profit to him. Sir Oliver, who was addressed in many titles and tongues, and had no care what they might be, answered only: "Well, you will see him soon enough, I suppose, if you wait here. But you must show the warrant you have."

So he did; and Sir Oliver found that it was in good form, having been issued by the Grand Master himself, and that but two hours before. He was vexed that it had been done thus, while he had been dealing with the event in a different way, but he showed nothing of that. In the next minute La Cerda came.

Sir Oliver showed him the warrant at once. "You will acquit me," he said, "of any knowledge of this when I made appointment to see you here. But you are charged, as you will observe, of leaving St. Elmo without leave (which may be right or wrong, as you will know better than I), and for the moment, as you will agree, the warrant must be obeyed. But I will see the Grand Master at once, and will use what persuasion I have that it may end in a better way."

La Cerda said: "It is utter lie. I came in De Broglio's boat, which I had his express order to do."

"Well," Sir Oliver said, "I am glad of that, which is much as I should have supposed it to be. But you should know that your name is not on the list of those who were ordered to leave, which I have here, and which you can see if you will. I had observed it before, but left it to be cleared at a better time."

"It will be easy to prove," La Cerda said. "I should say that most men will see now that he goes too far."

They both knew that the Grand Master was meant, though he was not named. Sir Oliver made no reply. La Cerda added, in another tone: "But I can see that I owe you thanks, and perhaps more than I have given before."

He went out with the officer after that, with no word of the purpose for which he came, which he judged then could best be left for Sir Oliver to deal with all in his own way.

Sir Oliver had gone to seek the Grand Master at once, but he had not been easy to reach. He was aware of the great need of sustained vigilance round the wide girth of his own defences, as the weeks passed and the Turkish army left them alone, and he had a dream in the night that the Sanglea had been lost, captured by sudden storm. He considered, when he awoke, that that would be a likely thing for the Turks to attempt, and that they might have planned to do it while the eyes and thoughts of all would be turned to St. Elmo's strife. He thought that the dream might be no less than direct warning of God, and he resolved to pay a visit to the Sanglea in the next hours, to surprise the truth of how the walls were kept by the Italian knights who were stationed there.

He took a boat across the inner harbour, having told his purpose to none, and discovered slackness which stirred him to a great wrath, and confirmed his belief that the dream had been no less than a warning from those who were not willing that Malta should fall into heathen hands. He was rowed back by way of the great boom, and landed at the battery which was to be its defence, where he found Captain Antonio in charge, and with an alertness at which he was better pleased.

When Sir Oliver found him at last he was in no mood to listen to him. His mind was on the thanksgiving service that was about to be held and on the discourse which he intended to give.

"Oliver," he said, at the first sound of La Cerda's name, "when I ordered the warrant should be made out, I thought there would be protest from you. Why you should give more heed to one who is traitor and coward than you can spare for much better men is beyond reason of mine, but for once I must ask you to stand aside and let me deal."

"By your leave," Sir Oliver replied, not allowing himself to be vexed or rebuffed by a manner which La Valette would often show to others but rarely to him, "there is one thing I must say, for your own honour is nearly risked, and much more than that. For if it be shown at last that you have had La Cerda imprisoned without a cause, it will give him more sympathy and support than he has now, which you would not wittingly do."

"If I should imprison any without a cause," the Grand Master replied, in a more temperate voice than before, "I should be unworthy of the high office I hold, nor could I look for the favour of Those above, which is more than the strength or wisdom of men. But I can see that you speak, as you seldom will, without knowledge of fact.

"There was a note from D'Egueras himself, by one of the last boats, and addressed for my own hand, in which he reports that La Cerda, having suffered no wound, and being in command of the southern wall, had summoned one to relieve his charge and had not returned. It was supposed that, having asked no leave, he had left in one of the boats, about which D'Egueras would make fuller enquiry than he had then been able to do; but he thought I should know with speed, thinking that he would be active at once to stir opposition to my will that St. Elmo should still be held."

"I was not likely to know what I was not told. The letter, as D'Egueras is well aware, should first have been sent to my hand, and much trouble might have been spared."

"He may have thought you too much his friend."

"I am not that. I am not his foe. But it is for Malta my care is spent."

"Then you should leave this, with no wasting of further words.

Would you have such a man loose, to work more harm than before with those who are faint of heart, or fractious of mood?"

"I would not have him jailed for a wrong cause. Though I had not D'Egueras' note, I could have told you much more. It is untrue that he had no wound, and the cause with which he would be concerned was not St. Elmo at all, but that he should find her by whom his steward was slain."

"I had forgot that! That he should have hidden his harlot here! Oliver, it is such men and such ways that would bring our Cross to the dust, to be trodden by heathen feet."

"Then, if you feel thus, would you aim a random blow, which will go astray? Suppose he came by De Broglio's own command, in the same boat?"

"Do you know that?"

"It is what he says; and I am inclined to believe."

The Grand Master pondered this in a mind which was astute enough, though it was stubborn at times, and deaf to that which it was not anxious to hear. He saw that he might make a mistake which would defeat his own ends. Yet the tale might be false, which he would prefer to believe, and it should be easy to prove.

"Oliver," he said, "we will test this in the next hour." He went on to say that he had already resolved to visit the wounded that had been brought over during the night, before he went to the Church. He would meet Sir Oliver there, and they would question De Broglio, and learn what the truth was. "And if he die (for it is said that he is sore hurt), you will be witness for me, for men will believe that you would not condemn La Cerda for less than a certain fault."

This being agreed, Sir Oliver went back to his own room, arriving there while Angelica was enquiring what had occurred, of which he told more.

"We shall see De Broglio," he said, "in the next hour; and, in the meantime, it will be best that the girl shall remain quiet where she now is, for it seems to me that on De Broglio's answer much will depend. If the Grand Master should find that a mistake has been made, he may be in a mood to bring easy accord, and I shall propose to him that La Cerda, with all his household, have leave to go, which I should say he will be willing to do, and for which means could be found on an early day."

Angelica could not deny that this counsel was good, though she was loth that Venetia should be on her hands for a longer time. Also, she remembered that a proclamation had been made threatening death to all who should harbour her after the noon of that day, which was very near. And she felt that she had had trouble enough without having to defend herself from that charge.

"She shall stay if you will," she said, "for it is what I cannot deny, owing you all I do. But will you bear me out if she be discovered, and not through you?"

"You shall have no jeopard for that. You shall have it now, under my own seal, that she is in your charge by my order and will, till new disposition be made at a later hour."

He wrote this as he spoke, and Angelica made no further demur, but went back to tell Venetia what she had learnt.

Venetia heard, and said few words in reply, nor did she show any emotion at all, which was a danger-signal with her, as Angelica would have known if they had been together a longer time. For, when Venetia was alarmed, she would become wary and quiet, like a wild thing among foes. She might smile or frown, or be sweet or bitter of speech, but it would show no more of herself or her own thoughts than if she acted part in a play.

Now she thought that La Cerda's day must be done, either to help her or himself. She did not think it mattered much what De Broglio might have said, or say now (which she supposed might not be the same, for she knew nothing of him), but she supposed that the Grand Master was of a fixed will to bring La Cerda down, and was not lacking in power. Sir Oliver had not known what would occur, for the Grand Master went his own way, without confiding in him. It was clear that he was not in control, and it would be folly to trust him more, even if it were sure that his words were meant.

If La Cerda were in jail on an accusation which might bring him to quick death in a time of war, where would his mistress be, if they should discover her now, with a charge of murder against her name? If the charge against him were false, was there any comfort in that? Would it not show that a false charge was enough, against one whom the Grand Master's anger was hot?

That which had been counselled by others for her relief had always looked more like a trap to her. She would not have talked as she had, but that she had believed that he would not return. "Now," she thought, "we are to be drowned in the same boat if I stay here. I must trust none but my own wits if I am yet to win free. And, at the worst, if I be caught as I try to flee, can I not say that when I heard the arrest of him whom I love and trust, I was seized with a panic fear . . .?

"You are worn," she said, "and too tired to stand, you should rest now, for there is no more can be done."

Angelica did not deny that. She lay down on the bed, and was quickly asleep. Venetia watched her awhile, and resolved that she would not wake though a bolt should fall.

She had leisure for what she planned, so that she could first eat a good meal from the store of food which Angelica had brought for her use, and then she searched through Angelica's clothes, making the best disguise for herself that she could among them. She waited, after packing all she could lightly bear, till she heard the sound of the organ-music from the Church which told that the service of thanksgiving and burial had begun. She judged that her chance was then, for between those who must man the walls, and those who could be crowding the Church, she thought that the castle would be empty enough. She drew the door-bolt with a cautious hand, but Angelica did not stir. She went out from the room in an unhurried way, as one who knew where she was, and where she would go. She went down to Francisco's room, meeting none on the way. She had enquired of him as to how it stood, and remembered with such care that she could now enter without doubt. It was only that it might be locked that she had had reason to fear, and that was unlikely enough, for she knew that it was not custom among the knights to so fasten their doors except when they were within, and would be alone, either for sleep or prayer. She looked round on a room which was of inferior comfort and smaller than either of those which had been her prisons before. But she did not intend to remain there after Francisco should return. She intended that he should find her better and surer harbour than that.

Angelica slept undisturbed either by the sounds of music and chanting that came at times from the church, or the distant booming of guns which began much at the same time, telling that the bombardment of St. Elmo's garrison had become active again, and that they replied with such guns as they were still able to work.

The service was long at the church, for the bodies of the knights who had been killed must be buried with a full mass, and each in his own *langue*, the great church having been so built that it contained a separate chapel of burial for each country from which they came. And before this, after a chanting of psalms and a time of prayer, the Grand Master gave his discourse, the theme of which was that men might fail, but God did not desert His own. When he spoke of the failure of men, it might be thought either that he glanced at the promised relief of Spain that delayed to come, or that he would rebuke those who would have been unwilling to continue St. Elmo's defence. When he spoke of the sure rescue of God, his thought was on the mist which had risen during the night, without which it had been impossible to send reliefs or to bring off those who were most hurt. There could be little doubt that Mustapha would have renewed the assault with fresh troops at the dawn had he known the fort to contain none but those who had been exhausted, and more wounded than not, by the strife of the day before; nor could it be thought they would have repelled such an assault for another day, they having been brought as low as they were.

It seemed to many who heard that it was so put that men must either deny their faith, or admit that the mist had shown that St. Elmo's defence had the approval of God, and His active support. It was not a hard gospel for those who remained within St. Angelo's bounds, and saw that their own walls remained free from attack, and only loosely contained, while the weeks went by, and the Turkish army reduced its strength, both in munitions and men. But it was different for those who had been sent to a death that was nearly sure, for whom the distant music was drowned by the thunder of Turkish guns.

CHAPTER XXXVII

Both the booming of guns and the organ-music had ceased when Angelica waked in the late twilight and saw, with a sense of relief preceding surprise, that Venetia was not there.

She found the door was unbarred, and concluded, with reason enough, that she had been fetched while she slept, by Sir Oliver's order or as a result of information given by him; and that, as she had not waked, she had been left in peace by those who had no mission to her.

She dropped the bolt with a pleasant sense of having regained a privacy that she had been vexed to lose, and seeing that night was near and having no reluctance for further rest, she threw off the clothes that she had been wearing till then and slept till the morning came.

It was not till she waked again that she discovered that not only had Venetia gone but other things with which she was less willing to part, including garments, at which she had a new doubt, and then thought, by the sun's height, that Sir Oliver would be back at work, and if she went to him she would soon know.

She found him as willing to talk to her as she could have wished, for he put other matters aside at once, and ordered that his room should be private till he should call.

"I supposed," he said, "that you would sleep long, which I would not break, but there are some matters on which your witness may help me now."

"I should not have thought. . . ."

"Yet so it is. La Cerda——"

"Has he not been set free?"

"No. It is of him I have to enquire. When he was charged that he had left his post without leave, he replied that he had De Broglio's order for what he did. When I told the Grand Master this, he sought to have justice done, and he went with me to the hospital where the wounded lie. We gained little by that, for De Broglio has been near death since his wound was searched, and, except for one moment at first, he did not seem conscious of what was said." (The one moment, on which Sir Oliver did not think well to be more explicit, had been when La Valette approached the ped, and, at the first sound of his voice, De Broglio had opened his eyes, and said, clearly enough to be heard by several around: "Ah, John, shall I cheat you yet of the death you had meant for me?" Men who heard might have thought that he accused the Grand Master of having placed him in St. Elmo's command to ensure his death, as the issue of some old feud which was only known to them two, but that his tone had been that of one who mentions a jest. And after that, his eyes were closed and it seemed that he did not hear.)

"So it seemed," Sir Oliver went on, "that La Cerda's defence must lack proof; but I have thought that you came at the same time and may know something of this, though the chance is small."

"We were together and I heard all. It was on De Broglio's order he came."

Sir Oliver looked relieved at that, thinking that it gave him the means of bringing this affair to a quick end, and perhaps having some natural satisfaction in the fact that the Grand Master would be proved wrong, rather than he; and though this satisfaction was somewhat less when he had the full tale, for it showed beyond doubt that La Cerda had been determined to come away before the chance of De Broglio's presence had given him the authority on which he now built his defence, yet he still thought that the way in which he had been arrested without fuller enquiry would be held by most to be evidence of the Grand Master's prejudice rather than of a rule that was wise and just, and he had a hope that he might make La Valette see this, so that he might be in a mood to bring all to a simple end by letting both La Cerda and his mistress go.

"It will be well," he said, "that you should meet the Grand Master here, telling him not only of this, but of how Venetia has been hidden in your own room. It is a thing he must know, and though you may not welcome that it should be recalled to his mind who you are, yet I do not see how we can avoid that; and having this other matter on hand, he may take it in a good way.

"But I do not wish that she should be apprehended by the Provost-Marshal before the Grand Master shall have considered the matter more, nor can I be party to her concealment now that I know where she is hid. You must tell her she must be ready at any time to meet the Grand Master here, and with such a tale as will stand test, if she is to hope that she may go free."

"I cannot do that. Do you not know she is gone?"

"Do you mean she has left your room of her own will, or been taken away?"

"She was gone while I slept, and my door left without bar."

"Then you know naught beyond that?"

"I have missed such clothes that I think she went in disguise, and so of her own will."

"She is a very pestilent fool."

Sir Oliver spoke with more passion than he was accustomed to show. He saw the neatness of his own plans dishevelled by the one party to these events whom he was not careful to save, and that against her own good, simply, as he supposed, because she was of those who must always find it hard to accept law, or to trust the justice of any into whose hands they may fall. She had done after her own kind, though how far she had gone on that road was beyond his guess, and it was clear that La Cerda's affairs could not be closed with the completeness which he had planned a moment before.

But the question of his imprisonment still remained, and a promise that the Grand Master had made that he should be brought to justice without delay had a double edge, while De Broglio was not able to speak.

"You must bear witness in this," he said, "for, as I see it, you cannot remain still without shame; and I would prefer, for your own peace, that you tell the Grand Master in this room, rather than in public assize."

Angelica did not agree about that. While it had seemed that it would be Venetia of whom she must give account, she had seen it plainly enough, for she could not say that she had kept her in her own room without prejudice to Venetia's repute, which might reduce the credence with which her tale would be heard, nor would her own part in the matter be clear, while she called herself by Don Garcio's name.

But if there were no more to be told than what she had seen and heard at St. Elmo's quay, she thought that she could better sustain the character which she was now accustomed to wear in witness in open court, than if she should have the Grand Master's attention closely drawn to herself, with chance of query of what she was, or even recollection of how he had seen her first.

But she found that Sir Oliver could show cause that she should come to another view. "For you must think," he said, "that if you give witness in the court that our Order holds, it must be under oath, and with declaration of who you are, and even if you would bear false witness thereon, you might be questioned in ways which would be hard to endure. . . . Does La Cerda know your true name?"

"Yes; and Venetia alike."

"That is worse "

"It was needful to tell. . . . But is my witness required? There were others who heard. There was the officer on the quay, with whom he quarrelled while in the boat. He could not forget nor deny."

Sir Oliver agreed about that, for his only defence for having allowed La Cerda to go when he was not on the list would be that he had De Broglio's order therefor. That his evidence would be otherwise unfavourable to La Cerda was equally sure, but he was not overmuch concerned about that, having no zeal to protect him beyond the truth.

"He might be brought," he said, "in the night, and your public witness excused. But I must still think that the Grand Master should be first informed of what you can tell, and that in a private way. Beyond that, I cannot consent, now that she has foolishly fled, that your harbouring of the woman should remain privy to me. As to the Provost-Marshal, I should say that he may discover it for himself, if he can. But the Grand Master should know all, both as his due and lest he should hear of it in a lying way. Also, now that there are more that have knowledge of who you are, and some being less than your certain friends, he should be made fully aware of how you are still here; for if he have it from me in the right way, he may be more your friend than you are timid to fear."

Angelica did not dispute that Sir Oliver should do this, being in a mood to accept what came in a dull way, and, apart from that, she had trust in him, and she had also found that when he was once resolved he was hard to turn. He was one who could see all sides, making him at times slower to act than would be those of a single view, but he was not weak of will when his purpose formed.

"You will do," she said, "as you think well. I knew it would be vexation to me, when she first entered my room. I would have thrown her out with a good will, but it was yet that which I could not do."

"It would have been wiser than what you did."

Angelica did not dispute that. She went back to the room that was hers again, meeting Olrig upon the way, who told her that her friend, Don Francisco, must have been looking for her, as he had seen him coming down her own stairs. She had a moment's pleasure at that, thinking that he had come to make accord of the quarrel of yesterday, but was puzzled also, for it was not a time when she was likely to be there, for she would work in Sir Oliver's room during the morning hours. She was going now to the town, by his leave, to purchase such clothes as the damage that hers had taken during the night—and Venetia's discriminate thefts—had rendered needful to get, which she had now confidence to do for herself, and for which she did not regard Olrig's choice as to be preferred to her own.

She thought with some satisfaction that Francisco must have had an urgent wish to see her alone that he should have made attempt at that hour, and then in explanation that he must choose a time when he was not on duty at his command. But when she came to look round her room, she had a thought of another kind. He had not come to see her, but to remove some things that Venetia had not ventured to carry away, not wishing to seem to be burdened when she had walked through the castle halls. She had had a fear before that it was to him that Venetia had fled. But it is different to know.

CHAPTER XXXVIII

Mustapha Pasha looked down on St. Elmo's fort and his eyes were cruel and fierce. He had more than the lust of an eagle who takes a prey. He had a cold anger and hate toward those who had repulsed his army's assault and brought shame on the banners of Islam that no success of to-morrow could wipe away.

A walled place must always be taken with waste of life, if it be stoutly held, and whether it be worth the price of storm must be pondered with care. That was true, even if success were a fruit you could surely pluck, as it had seemed to be here. But to squander strength in a vain attempt—that was a fault which no sophistry could condone, and one that, in a lifetime of many wars, he had avoided till now. It must be either the general's or the army's shame, and in this case it might be put to both doors.

He was glad that he had left the immediate command in the hands of those colleagues who had been given to him by the wisdom of Soliman, who had doubtless thought that he would be the better for the counsel of younger and more vigorous men. Well, they had had their turn. Piali's blind bull-courage, and Dragut's wilier impetuosities, had failed alike. It was time that the cooler methods of long experience should take control and prevail.

So he thought. But while he might be content that the repulse should be coupled with Dragut's name, his own judgment did not blame him for an assault which he might have ordered himself and which he had not expected to fail. He saw now that they had undervalued the defence of these obstinate Christian dogs. Had he not warned Soliman at the first that they would have to meet the very flower of the Christian lands. . . .? They should have bombarded for another week, till the fort would have been no more than a heap of stones; "and yet," he said bitterly, repeating Piali's words in a way which would be remembered by those who heard, "if it be so hard to slaughter the calf, how shall we cut the throat of the cow?"

He ordered more guns to be brought up, more gabions to be piled. He pushed forward his batteries on every side. If there must be some loss of life before their protections were made secure, it would be much less than had been spent in that vain assault, and it led to a surer end. From early dawn to the late dusk of the next day, the batteries did not pause. The iron hail battered ceaselessly on the splintering, falling stones. The guns came closer; and still closer during the night.

So it was again on the next day, and after that, at the darkest hour, a boat slipped away with muffled oars and came safely to St. Angelo's quay. It brought a letter from the new governor of St. Elmo, Melchior de Montserrat, saying first that, as to the officer whom the Grand Master required, he regretted that he could not be sent, being dead. He enclosed a list of the casualties of the last two days, that the Grand Master might know the strength that he still had. He enclosed also a petition, signed by fifty-three knights, on which he desired to express no opinion himself, only giving assurance that all were loyal and in good heart, and that whatever instructions might come would be bravely obeyed.

Sir Oliver read it with care. He said to himself: "He will not be pleased. Yet it is fairly put, and must be answered alike. He cannot say that La Cerda's hand is in this."

He went to the Grand Master, to whom it was clear that it must be instantly shown, and La Valette would have answered at once in his own hand, but Sir Oliver, being patient and firmly resolved, was able to get his way at last, so that a Council of the Commanders was called. "For," he said, "you have had your will to this day, and none can say you have erred, and you have La Cerda jailed, with a good pretext enough. But if you decide this for yourself, and you are wrong, as the event prove, you will be blamed on all sides, and all who have opposed at the first, and are now stilled, will be vocal again. If you are still resolved, let it be handled so that there shall be some who will have been persuaded to say Amen."

So the Council was quickly called, and the petition read out, of which the substance was this, after the forms of loyalty had been done, and the core came:

> "If it be your will that we shall remain here to our deaths, which cannot be long delayed (for the fort is now shattered on every side, except we lurk in the lowest chambers beneath the ground), we do not complain, having respect for our vows. But we humbly petition this, that we may sally forth and die in a knightly way, working mischief among our foes. For, as it is, we are destroyed by bombardment to which we cannot largely reply, the cavalier being wrecked as it is, and its guns down. So that it is we who bleed, and they laugh.

"But if we have license to sally forth, we have some hope that our swords will reduce them before we die."

The Grand Master heard the reading of that which he knew before and watched the faces of those who heard. When he spoke, it was in a more temperate style than he had used when St. Elmo had been cause of debate on a former day.

"Brothers," he said, "you have heard the petition of those who will be agreed by all to be loyal and valiant men. And we may be agreed on this too, that it is a petition we cannot grant. For if St. Elmo be so flattened and rent that it can no longer repulse attack, then we should withdraw those who yet live to the protecting strength of our walls, and that while there is still time to convey them here, which, even now, it might not be simple to do.

"So that there is one question remains, and no more. Is it indeed truth that St. Elmo's walls have fallen beyond further defence?

"We have the witness of those who are there, which is not lightly to be contemned; but we know also that it is not three days since the whole might of the Turkish arms was thrown back from those walls with such slaughter and shame as all Europe will hear with pride. Now we see that they do not assault again. They prowl round like a pack of wolves that have not the heart to spring, having been so chastened before.

"If they should be tempted to make attack and thrown back for another time, it would be great glory and gain to the Cross of Christ, which it is our honour to bear, and beside which our lives are no more than a dust which the winds will strew.

"Yet I would assume naught as against the witness of those who see. I would send three of ourselves, who can cross this night with a good hope that they can safely return (for the moon is late), and if they agree without internal dissent that the fort cannot be longer held, they shall have commission under my own seal to order that its garrison prepare at once to be brought away, having first set its powder alight, that nothing fall into heathen hands."

The Commanders agreed to this without much debate, for even those who would have abandoned the fort before must admit now that it had been used to do a sore hurt to the Turkish arms; and the plan itself had a fair sound. Moreover, they so far prevailed that two of the commission were men of no special valour, nor likely to go far on a desperate road, but the Grand Master cared nothing for that, having secured that De Castriot should be the last, and he being a knight who would be loth to fight with three foes if he could find four. For he had said that the commissioners must be in agreement among themselves if the fort were to be given up, as he did not mean it to be. His thought was that, when the garrison knew beyond hope that their lives would last so long as they kept the Turks out but no more, they would yet make a hard fight before they would let them in.

And so, with a mind at ease, when the Council had broken apart, he turned to a tale which Sir Oliver had told him two days before, and with which he had pledged his word that he would not deal without thought in a sudden way.

"As to the wanton," he said now, "she must be found, when she will have a sore back, if no more; but he who harbours her for another day shall hang without grace, though he be the best knight that we have, and so you shall make it known.

"For the rest, I would not fret for a small thing, and, if there be fault, it is mostly mine; for I will own I was told at first, and it left my mind. Nor would I see the name of Don Manuel brought to scorn, for he was a good knight, and my early friend.

"It seems that his house has bred one of a pert sort, whom it will be needful to tame, but the part is not mine; and I have your warrant that she is chaste, and has worked no mischief among my knights.

"I have in mind that I will send to the Viceroy again, by a boat which will leave Melletia three nights from now, as Marshal Couppier will arrange. She can go by that, if not in a safe way, yet with lighter risk than if she should longer remain, for I suppose we have darker hours to face than we have yet seen."

"Where will you have her go?"

"I will recommend her to him whose name (or one like to it) she has too lightly assumed. He will do her the honour her own requires, and find escort, either by land or sea, that she be returned to the place she should not have quit. You can assure her that, when Palermo is reached, she will have no more cause for alarm."

"I should say that she will not be greatly feared of that risk, but she will be loth to be sent away as being compelled, and so shamed."

"That is well, for she will be lessoned thereby."

"Will you see her before this be lastly resolved?"

"I will see her, though not to bicker thereon. For, the officer on whose witness La Cerda trusts being dead, as Montserrat writes, I will hear her tale of that night."

Sir Oliver, who knew when speech was of no avail and, besides that, was less than sure that the Grand Master was wrong, said no more; and, when he saw Angelica next, he told her that she must be prepared to meet the Grand Master at any time that he might be at leisure to hear her tale.

"He is resolved," he went on, "that you shall return to Spain, which he says you should not have quit, and, Don Manuel being dead, he takes it upon himself to see that you are despatched in the best way that can be contrived, which will mean that you will be transferred to the other side of the isle either through the Turkish lines in the night or by a boat that will trust the moon and the shallow channels along the coast, after which you will be on such ship as can show speed on the sea. It is a risk which it may be said that you came to take, but after Palermo is reached you will have no cause to dread more, being within the protection of Spain."

"How soon is this intended to be?"

"In three nights from now."

"Is it because Venetia hid in my room?"

"No. The Grand Master made little of that, you having made your report to me within the time the proclamation allowed."

"She has not been found?"

"Not that I know. But she will gain nothing by this second escape. She is like to be whipped, if no worse. She is said to be known as one of a wanton trade before she came to La Cerda's bed."

"I suppose she cannot be hid long?"

"It is hard to think; and the more so that there will be new proclamation made that the utmost judgment will be enforced without grace against whoever shall hide her more, whether high or low."

Sir Oliver looked at Angelica as he spoke, and saw fear in her eyes. There was a sharpness in his tone that was not frequent with him as he asked: "You are not hiding her more? You would not engage in such folly as that?"

"No, there is a point where my folly ends—and she is one for whom I have little love."

"Have you any thought of where she is now, or in whose hands?"

It was then that Angelica learned to lie. "No. For I was asleep when she went, and it was a thing of which she had not spoken before. Why do you ask that?"

"Because, when I spoke of judgment on who should harbour her more, you looked somewhat troubled and pale, as though with a sudden fear."

"I was amazed, as I still am, that while her own guilt is held in doubt, or as of minor degree, there should be a worse fate for who may do no more than give her shelter and food."

"That is because you do not observe the terms on which a fortress must be controlled at a time of war. That which is venial of itself may be offence of the rankest growth if it be done in defiance of order proclaimed."

Angelica felt that there were answers to that which were best unsaid. She replied only: "Yet it had a hard sound. . . . May she not have crossed to the Turkish lines for a spy's pay?"

"I should call her too shrewd for that, unless she were pricked by a most sharp fear. The Turks would use whip or rack for a Christian's pay, thinking that they would then get the truth by a short road and one cheaper than gold."

"Well, I wish her less ill than that; but I wish her far."

She went at that, fearing that she might say too much if she stayed, and left Sir Oliver assured that she was not hiding the girl, but puzzled in a shrewd mind as to why she should be perturbed by the threat of judgment against those who should take her in, or so urgent to wish her farther away.

Angelica went to her own thoughts, which were grey enough.

CHAPTER XXXIX

THE governor led the way, carrying a lantern himself, for he did not wish that the conversation should be overheard as he showed the three commissioners the extent to which his guns had been shattered and overcast and the state of his crumbling walls.

They came back to his own room by a passage which led near to the well from which the garrison drank, and there was a sound of splashing, as though articles of weight were being cast therein, one after one, in a regular way.

De Castriot, who had said little till now, paused to listen. "What," he asked, "may that be?"

"It is round-shot," Montserrat answered, "which we shall not be able to use. I have it cast into the well lest it fall into other hands and be used in a worse way."

"May it be stayed for an hour?"

"To what end?"

"Because it is not yet resolved whether the fort be longer held. If but in courtesy to ourselves. . . ."

"You misapprehend. But it can be stayed for that time."

Montserrat gave the order required, and led them on to his own room. When they were private there, he addressed them at once, without waiting for them to speak.

"Signors," he said, "you have seen with your own eyes; and I have said nothing, leaving you to judge of yourselves. As to the purpose for which you came, I shall say no more, not being asked. I was sent here to defend this fort, and that, while I live, and my orders remain, I shall continue to do.

"As to the shot which I was casting away, you must consider this. We cannot use all that we have, though we should be here, and the Turks kept out, for another week; for the most of our guns are too wrecked to fire. If we withdraw from the fort (as I see not how we could do, even now, except by sudden, very perilous flight with much likely loss) it is sure that we should not take the round-shot away, preferring things of more worth and less weight. If we blow up the fort, the shot might be found to be none the worse, if it were not buried too deep to dig. I would have it thrown to the one place where it will surely remain, and not be used to batter St. Angelo's walls.

"It is the part of one who commands to consider all, and to judge well. If the fact that I have ordered the round-shot to be cast away be held to show that I am unfit for the place I hold, there are knights enough who are used to commands in their own lands who would be likely to do better than I, and the change should be quickly made."

The first commissioner, a grave, grey-bearded man, past the vigour of youth, and one who looked less soldier than priest, was the first to reply.

"You may say what you will," he said, "with the name you have, both for valour and skill in war. The casting down of that shot was a prudence which we do not misread; but I would charge you by your own vows, and the cause we serve, that you speak with freedom, and fully of all, for we would have all the guidance we can. You spoke a moment ago of the Turks being kept out for another week. Is that the most that can fairly be hoped, if the fort be held?"

"If you constrain me thus," Montserrat answered, "I will say what I think, which I had not intended to do. We can hold this fort for some days if they are content to hammer our walls and no more, in the sense that, by that time, we shall not be all dead. But Mustapha knows his trade, and will storm again before then: and when they rush us will be the end."

"Then you would withdraw while you can?"

"That is not for me to resolve. I suppose we shall not die, being behind walls that are less than flat, without slaying more Turks than our numbers are; and that, and the way that we waste their time while St. Angelo stands secure, may be reason that we remain. But I will tell you two things, one being for either scale, so that you may weigh all when you make resolve.

"The first is that to withdraw is not as simple as may be supposed, even in darkness of night, for the Turks are alert for that. Their spies crouch in shadows beneath the walls: their boats, being swift and light, hover in the water around. It is most like that they know you are here now. If we should attempt to move many boats, even to-night, we should be quickly grieved by their fire. And their batteries come closer with every day. To-morrow noon I suppose that our landing-stage will be under fire, and all the water around, and we should withdraw at a great loss. I should say that to-night is the last chance we shall have, which will be soon gone.

"And the second is this. The Turks have no name for mercy

in storming of town or fort, even when it be held by the rules of war; but it may be said that we are not in that case. We are rather in that of those who prolong defence of a post that is outnumbered or overcome and who yield too late, as thinking first to inflict all the loss they may and then to save their own lives. But those lives are forfeit by rule of war in all lands.

"If they storm this fort, you must expect that it will be the end of all that its walls contain, for they will let loose all the ferocity which is theirs, being moved thereto, both to avenge the long tale of their own dead, and to give warning of what St. Angelo may expect if its defence be prolonged to a like extreme.

"You should understand that we who are here will maintain the strife to the last moment we may, but our end is sure. . . . Unless only," he added, "that the Viceroy shall send relief in a large way, so that the Turks must lift their attack, which we may expect if we will."

The second commissioner, a small wizened man, very wise in the healing art (which was not closely pursued by all the Knights of St. John at this time), but whose fitness for the office he held was to be explained, if at all, by those who proposed his name, answered at once, as stating what must be clear to all:

"The case being so, it is not to be thought that you should remain, to be no more than a Turkish prey. We lose time while we talk, and the night goes. For, as I suppose, we are sent for no other cause than that it should not be said that you have withdrawn of your own will, but as having orders from us."

The first commissioner agreed, though in a less resolute way. "I would not," he said, "go to that length, for our orders are that we shall think of Malta alone, and not of the lives of men, but, as I see it, St. Elmo has done its part, having inflicted upon the foemen of Christ a great loss and a greater shame. Why then should we yield our comrades to useless death and allow the Moslems to boast of a late success? Let the fort be so set that it shall be blown to the skies with those who shall be first to trespass within its walls. But let us get off all the men we may while the darkness holds."

"I am the least among three," De Castriot said, "but it seems that I am of the better heart, and the better concept of why we came. We are not here to make excuses for flight, but to resolve if this fort have yet strength to resist the Turk, which I say it has; and I should say that to the latest hour that its walls can stand, for we must resist if we are to overcome at the last, with every stone that we have, as our Grand Master has made it clear, whether we think to endure till we have the succour of Spain, or till the infidel host shall lose patience and sail away."

"It has a brave sound," the first commissioner said, "yet you might reflect that St. Angelo has many stones, yet few men; and those behind walls that are higher than these, and of triple strength."

"We may better think that the Saracen host has been thrown back once from these walls, with a slaughter they will not forget to a far day. Now they lie nursing their courage, which is yet not enough for them to come for another meal from the same dish. We should use the hours without weakness of doubt that we may prepare for them a worse time when they come again, that this fort may be a name of fear in the infidel lands for a hundred years, as it is most likely to be."

De Montserrat listened to this talk with a dumb face. He was resolved, having answered what he was asked, that he would say no more. He observed that the two other commissioners were unmoved by the passion that stirred De Castriot's speech. They looked at one another, and their eyes said that, though folly be bravely brayed, it is folly still.

"What you urge," the physician said, "would be of a good sound, though it might lead to no more than heroic deaths, if these were not the weakest walls that we have. But we say that there are good men here who will be lost for no equal good, and who could be of greater avail if they were within St. Angelo's bounds."

"You talk," his colleague went on, "as though we were sent here to devise defence or to take over control. But our mission is less than that. We have to resolve if St. Elmo can still be held, for which it is plainly unfit, its guns being overset and its walls crumbling away, as our eyes have seen, and it being alone amidst an army that is as forty to one, if it approach in its utmost power."

"Yet I have said what I have, which I will not change, so we may spare our words at this time," De Castriot said, "as it is clear that we shall not agree."

"Yet must our judgment prevail, being two to one."

"But that is not so at all, for our commission is clear. We can order retreat if we accord to that end, which we shall not do."

"Do you think," the physician exclaimed, "you can override us both?"

"I think we must make report to the Grand Master that we cannot agree."

"Do you reflect that it is not ourselves but our brothers that we leave here to a useless death?"

"I shall not leave them at all, by my will. I will raise such as respect their vows, by the Grand Master's leave, and bring them here that they may await the Turkish attack, giving them a worse day than they had before."

"Signors," Montserrat interrupted, "you can dispute this in the boat (though I would recommend that your voices be lower than they now are) or when you are in St. Angelo's walls, but you will risk yourselves to no gain if you stay here."

He led them back to the boat, having a desire to be alone with his own thoughts. He parted with De Castriot in a very cordial way. "There are few," he said, "I would rather have at my side in the coming days; but, as I suppose, I shall not see you again."

He was right in that, as in all, for though De Castriot meant his words, and was active when he returned to collect the names of such knights as would be willing to go to their comrades aid, yet it came to naught, for the next day it was seen that the Turkish batteries were advanced too far for such rescue to reach. Even in the dimness of summer night the boats could not hope but that they would be sunk as they neared the land.

All that day and the next the Turkish guns poured their fire into a fort that was now cut off upon every side.

CHAPTER XL

THE Grand Master listened to Angelica's witness concerning Venetia, and also how she had sought La Cerda and been the cause that he came away, and of how De Broglio had interposed at the quay. He asked few questions, and those fairly enough. She told all to that point, having little to hide; but she said nothing of her cousin's duel with La Cerda or of his being found in her room, on which she was not likely to be asked, it being outside any knowledge that either the Grand Master or Sir Oliver had. Nor did she say that, after Venetia left, some of her things had gone on the next day.

At the end the Grand Master said: "Oliver, I was too hasty in this, as I will not hide. I say not that La Cerda was hardly served, for he was guilty of will. He would have come, if he could, though De Broglio had been further away. But being wrongly charged by my fault, I will not alter the count now I know more. He shall go free for this time, taking his place with the knights of his own land, so soon as he shall be fit therefor, in defence of the Sanglea wall."

He said "when he is fit therefor" because there could be no doubt now of La Cerda's hurt, which may have influenced his mind to the decision to which he came. The burnt arm, having been left too long to itself, except where Venetia's fingers had pressed, had taken so ill a course that it was said to be more likely that it must come off than that it could be healed by all the art which St. Angelo held, which was perhaps the best in the world at this time.

"There is one thing," he went on, "of which La Cerda is cleared through his arrest, of which he may so far be glad. He had no hand in the woman's second escape, of which he had else been very shrewdly suspect. We may hope that she is outside our lines, to such fate as we need not enquire; for I cannot think that any would find her harbourage here; or, if they should, there will be no mercy for them."

He turned his eyes on Angelica for the first time in a personal way. "You had a look of Don Manuel once," he said, "as you made your account, recalling him as he was when we were at the siege of Rhodes, and were boys but little older than you. It was but as a passing shadow across your face, which I might not have seen had you been in a better dress."

He paused a moment, as though his memory went back to forgotten things. He went on: "Sir Oliver gives me good report, as I should have expected of one of so fine a blood. . . . You saved our ships at a peril that few would dare. . . . If you feared that I would send you back as being found in garments of shame, you were largely wrong. But this is no place where a woman should seek to be."

"Yet," she said, with a new confidence, born of the manner in which he spoke, "I would stay if I may."

He looked at her with a puzzled gaze, and intently, as though he must read her mind. "Will you tell me why?"

It was a question which she could have answered a week before, but she could not now, having a reason he must not guess. She said, after a pause in which she found it hard to sustain his eyes: "You care for Malta alone. If I stay, I will do what I can; and you say I have served you once. Why should it not be again?"

As she spoke, the dull booming of the guns that battered at St. Elmo was in their ears. It was a sound that only ceased with the night. The doomed fort was isolated now, waiting its end, with the men he had sent to death, and would not withdraw while there had been time. Now it was too late: there was nothing left but to watch till the end should come.

"Yes," he said, with a sigh that was not for her, "I care for Malta alone. Men will say that, at the best. At the worst—— I know not what they may say. But it is to God I must stand or fall." He fell silent, and then said: "Oliver, life is not much, but death is a lesser thing." He appeared to become conscious of Angelica again. "Oliver," he said, "I will leave this to you. She may stay or go. But," he turned his eyes to Angelica, and they had resumed the implacable resolution which set all softer feelings aside, "it is your own word. I care for Malta alone. If you stay I will use you thus, and I warn you now."

Having said that, he went out to join those who watched on the highest wall, though there was nothing to see but the sudden flashes of guns and the murk of smoke that lay over St. Elmo and Sceberras ridge, and drifted somewhat to sea. He had got a letter to Marshal Couppier through the Turkish lines, charging him to give no rest to the Turkish rear, but what help was there in that? The Maltese militia were a force brave enough, but unskilled. They harrassed the Turks without respite and with a hatred that was no less than that of the knights, for they fought not only for faith and race but for their children and homes, but they could not stand against the trained regiments of spahis and janissaries who had spent their lives in the art of war. They vexed the skirts of the Turkish camp, sniping by night and day. They made bold and sudden attacks at places where they could scatter among the hills before they could be faced by too large a force. But they could not reach to St. Elmo's aid or hinder its siege. Before the main force of the Turkish arms they were no more than gnats to be brushed away, or, at the most, as having a waspish sting. . . .

It was the early dawn of Friday, the 22nd of June, when Mustapha ordered advance upon St. Elmo again. He had given charge of the operations to Ulichiali, the Greek-born pirate whose lean Egyptian galleys, merciless to the weak and swift to fly from the strong, had been a ten-years' curse in Levantine seas. In this he pursued his usual policy of providing other shoulders than his for any blame of failure that might arise. The Greek was eager to take control, being jealous of the authority Piali and Dragut had received, which had been greater than his, and regarding the assault as one which would come to easy success, the fort being so battered and scarred and its garrison known to be few, among which there were many wounded and spent. Besides that, it seemed that its guns had been almost stilled; for, during the past two days, it had made so faint a reply to the Turkish fire as was next to none. Either its guns must be broken down, or its powder spent, or its garrison must be mostly dead.

It was thought by some that Mustapha had been too cautious in the length of this final pause: had he continued the assault the fort would have been his in an hour at the dawn of the second day.

It was the weakness of this belief that the Turkish troops advanced in the expectation of reward to be lightly won. They did not look for a desperate strife, or that their own lives should be hardly staked: they came to make end of a dying prey.

Yet they came in a great force, moving up on every side, with the batteries firing over their heads at a fort which might have been empty and dead, but that the pennons of many knights were still displayed on its walls and the Cross of Malta was over all. The Turks had ladders this time of the right length, and they thought to be up them with little strife. Ulichiali, watching all from a safe rear, thought that a white flag would soon flutter over the wall, and had given command that, if it did, the batteries should not cease; for, he said, the time for mercy was past.

Montserrat stood on the ruined wall and looked at the shouting infidel host, the noise of which and of the barbaric music which cheered their ranks deadened the duller thunder of the guns that were still firing above their rear. "They make a brave show," he thought, "but they will be somewhat surprised, and there must be many there who will not live to the next hour." But he said nothing of this to those who stood round, for he was not a man who loved words, and they could see it as well as he.

He had not seemed one who would inspire a hopeless defence when he had first come, saying little, and some of the orders he gave showed that he had no assurance that the fort could be held for another week. It might have been thought by any to whom his record was not known that the Grand Master had chosen with less than his usual wisdom, or as being unwilling to lose one more of his greatest knights. But as men observed the disposition he made they perceived that they were part of a careful plan, which was to encourage the Turks to assault again and to persuade them that they would have little resistance to meet.

There were at this time within the fort about a hundred and fifty men who had not taken a wound, including the hundred that Montserrat had brought, and about two hundred who had been more or less hurt but were able to serve. He set these men to such hours of labour as they could endure without too much fatigue to be fit to fight at a short call. They toiled to build inner defences where the walls were worst breached, so that the Turks might swarm in, and find, when they thought they were near to win all, that they had come to a deadly trap and a welcome of boiling pitch.

Also, he had the cannon closely surveyed, and remounted such as were not shattered beyond repair, but he would not use them again lest the Turks should be aware of the strength that remained, and also lest they should draw the fire of opposing batteries on themselves till they were dismounted again. The Turkish round-shot battered the walls where the breaches showed, and the silent hidden cannon were left alone. Now they were loaded with stones and small fragments of iron, but they were silent still, waiting till the advancing host, which was expecting no more than a thin volley of bullets from such arquebusiers as the Christians could still muster to line their walls, should be nearer and more largely exposed. There was a good distribution of wild-fire bombs, of which Montserrat had brought over a new supply, and the great hoops were ready to be set alight and flung over the wall at all points where its weakness might tempt attack.

But for the fluttering pennons along the wall the advancing army might have thought that they came to capture an empty shell from which the garrison had already fled; but they were more like to those who handle a bee which they think dead till they feel its sting. For as the first lines of the storming troops were about to deploy under the walls, some having already advanced to that point in column of march, a trumpet sounded within the fort. It was but one flourish, brief and high, and as it died the silent walls burst to a halo of outward flame. It was seen by those who watched on St. Angelo's walls, telling them that, though St. Elmo might be in no better case than that of a cornered rat, it had still the strength and the will to bite hard at those who came round it to make an end. After that the smoke of battle closed blackly above that cauldron of bitter strife, as it had done seven days before, and only the confused noise that came over the harbour waters at the caprice of a shifting wind told the watchers that it refused to fall as the hours went by. There were times that were loud with the cries of men, when the Turks assaulted the wall, as they often did during the day, and others, in the spaces between, when there was no sound but that of the guns that were never still. So it was, during the length of the summer day; but with the night, the noise fell. . . .

After that the Grand Master came to Sir Oliver's room. "I must know," he said, "if St. Elmo stands, but the boatmen say that it is vain to approach the quay. They would be certainly sunk, and what use is there in that? I must have one who can swim well, and can land unseen."

"That," Sir Oliver replied, "should not be too hard to find."

"Yet is is not easy at all. It is near a mile, if not more, both to come and go. I have made enquiry of many knights who would not decline, but the most of them could not swim, though it were but a short way, being inland born; nor could they be sure in the dark to find a quay that they do not know."

"There must be Maltese of the town who would call it a little thing. They have a common repute that they swim well."

"So it is, and so I suppose it must be; but I would have preferred one of ourselves, or, at least, one who would be able to talk a tongue in which Montserrat can reply. I thought there would be one of whom you would be likely to know."

His eyes fell on Angelica as he spoke, and their expression changed, as though he saw what he sought.

"Now," he said, "if you—— It is what you have done before in a worse way!"

"I should say," Sir Oliver remarked, "that there could be others found who are more fit."

"But," the Grand Master went on, "I do not know that there are." He said to Angelica: "You have been there before. You have been twice?"

"Yes," she said, "that was so." Beyond that, she was not quick to reply.

"You could swim so far," he queried again, "both to go and return, while the darkness holds . . .? It would be no gain for you to stay there, nor to drown on the way back."

"Yes, I suppose I could."

"There might be a boat sent out which would meet you upon the way."

"In the night?" she asked. "I should not trust greatly to that."

"I could make enquiry," Sir Oliver said, "among the Spanish soldiers upon the wall. There may be one who can speak and can also swim."

"And how long would that take? The night is short and soon sped." He looked at Angelica again as he said: "It was on such terms that you had leave to remain. I warned you that I would not spare you at all."

"Yet in such a matter as this——" Sir Oliver began; but she interrupted him now, having made her resolve.

"It is a thing I can do, and no more than the bargain was."

"You will go forthwith?" the Grand Master asked, in a style that was half query and half command.

"Yes."

"You will approach the fort with all care, not knowing but that it may now be in infidel hands, and with such caution as is required by the watch that our friends will keep within if they be still there, lest you be slain as a Turkish foe. You will bring full report if it still stand, and in what guise of defence. But if it be still held, and its flags fly, you shall tell those who have slaughtered Turks for a full day that their part is done. If you are back while there is still night in the sky, we will make bold to send over sufficient boats, when the moon is down, even at a great risk, to bring off those who remain. But I must first know that the fort endures, and that they would not row to no more than a useless death."

"Then," she said, "it seems by that that it is a matter of urgent haste."

"So I say. Can you swim fast?"

"I can swim fast at that need." She got up to go. "I must somewhat prepare. I shall not be long."

The Grand Master looked well content. "She is of a good race," he said, "and I am assured that she will not fail. I did well when I resolved that she should remain." He added: "God rules all." But it was not clear whether he gave the praise in the right place or made boast of a strong ally.

"Do you think we can bring them off?" Sir Oliver asked, in a doubtful tone.

"I have a very confident hope. I would not that our faith should fall behind the sure succour we have. . . . Do you doubt?"

"I should call it too late. But I have been wrong before now. We shall know more when Don Garcio brings his report."

"Don Garc—— . . .? Yes, I recall. It is how she is called."

"It is the only name that I use."

"It is the more prudent way. I will do the same." As he spoke Angelica returned to the room. She was in no mood to delay now. Imagination had the support of what she had seen in the fort at the end of the last assault. If they had kept out the Turks for another day of the same kind. . . . She saw that she could not be there too soon, having a better message to take than had been her portion before.

Sir Oliver had not been idle the while he talked. He had written a brief line to the effect that the bearer, Don Garcio, might be trusted in all he said as from the Grand Master himself, and this he read out, and wrapped in an oilskin case, that it might not be soaked in the flood.

"I have written no more," he said, "lest by evil chance it should reach the hand of our foes, when it will tell naught. But I would counsel you none the less, if you be in any danger of being snared, that you destroy it in good time, that none may see what you do. For if this letter be read they will go to all lengths to obtain knowledge of what message you bear, and it will be much the same if you should be seen to cast it away. So that, at the worst, you should be prepared with a likely lie, such as may save yourself and yet will do us no ill. But it will be much better than that if you are so wary and wise that you do not fall to their danger at all, as I have good hope you will be."

She wore no more than the close-fitting singlet and drawers—which were the usual inner garments of men at that day—below a cloak which would bring her unremarked to the waterside. Sir Oliver walked with her himself to that point, for what was done could not be too secret from all. Even within the walls there was talk of spies, and wonder at times that the Turks learned so quickly of the events of each hour, even to trivial things.

"You could go down with the tide," he said, "in an hour's time, which would be your aid, though it is not much in these seas."

"No, I will not delay."

She had the thought in her mind of those who might have endured through the day, and to whom she was to go this time with a word of slender, belated hope, rather than to tell them that they had done so well that they were to continue to strive and die.

The night was quiet and warm. There was a thin declining moon which the clouds hid, but which gave a faint light, showing the dark outline of the opposite shore. The clouds were broken at times, disveiling uncertain stars.

"I would," she said, "there were more light. But I may be glad of darkness before I land."

Sir Oliver thought he heard a note of fear in her voice, which the thought of that landing brought, and he was more doubtful than he had been at first of the wisdom of the Grand Master's choice.

"It is not too late," he said, "to decline that which most would say that you should not have been asked to do. I am of small doubt that boatmen could be found who would call it a little thing. The Grand Master had made enquiry only among his knights. Are you not afraid, now you face the attempt?"

"No," she replied, "not overmuch. I am not afraid of the sea. It is less than I did before at another need. It is less risk. . . . When I land, I shall do well enough. I know the approach."

"I will have those I can trust await here with a dry cloak."

"Then I will be careful of where I come."

She dived in without further words, and struck out in a steady way, turning once, when she was a short distance out, to see how the quay looked from that view, so that she should have no doubt where she would land on her return. The water was warm enough. She was not afraid that her strength would fail, nor that she would go greatly astray. The ridge of Sceberras showed darkly beneath the veiled light of the moon. The stars would be guides enough, if they would be no less than they were then, between fluctuant clouds. She swam lightly and fast, breaking waters that were level and quiet. . . . There came a time when she was glad that the stars were few, and that the clouded moon was hid by the height of land, so that St. Elmo's point was black where it met the sea. . . . Her hand felt up the wet face of the rock, which sank sheer so that there was no footing to gain; but it shelved backward not more than two feet over her head, so that, with a short effort, she came to land. She had not dared to land at the quay, and she moved now with more caution than speed. Lights flickered around the fort, and barbaric shouts came at times on the quiet air of the night. Yet, in fact, she had little to dread but her own fears. The fort had been held till the darkness came, and now there was truce till dawn, as there had been five days before, that the Turks might succour the wounded and count the slain.

She entered with no demur, being accepted at once by a guard at the fort gate who seemed to have no briskness in what he did. There must have been valour enough in those who still lived in St. Elmo's walls, but there was no hope. There was a truce made, so that it seemed that they would be allowed to live through the night. They had no thought that they could endure for another day. And even so—there would be no doubt of the end. The hour struck. D'Egueras, who had given much time to prayer since the last assault, was with those who now prayed through the night. There were some twenty of these, of whom none had less than a bandaged wound.

Angelica, begging the loan of a cloak before she should come to a full light, which was a boon easy to grant, for there were more cloaks in St. Elmo now than living shoulders to put them on, heard the hymn which the monkish knights, who had fought all day against what must seem no less than unbelievable odds, were now raising to Mary's praise.

"Patens cœli janua,
Salus infirmorum,
Videamus Regem,
In aula Sanctorum."

It seemed a prayer which she would be very likely to grant.

Angelica was led to the room where she had seen De Broglio when she first came. Montserrat did not wake nor pray. He slept on a bench. On the table he had cast down a sword that was blunted and stained; and another, sharp and clean, was lying nearer his hand. His heavier armour was taken off, but he slept in clothes which were formal and rich and had made a brave show when he put them on. Now they were rent and stained, and the most part of one sleeve had been torn away, but when he waked, which he did at the first word, he was quiet and grave, as he had ever been since he came. He read the letter that Angelica brought, and listened to what she said with an expression that did not change.

After he heard, he pondered awhile, and then said slowly, as one who would have his words remembered with care: "I will write naught. Sir Oliver was right about that." He broke off what he had meant to say to enquire: "What did he say? Did he approve ıe Grand Master's plan?"

"He said little while I was there."

"Which meant much. . . . You will say that, having still some advantage of walls and by the use of some deadly tricks, and of the valour of cornered men, and no less by the high favour of God, we have held our own for this day, with such slaughter of those who came as the Grand Master will joy to hear. I should say we have slain more than was done at the former assault, for they came at first with less care. But, for ourselves, we are mostly dead or maimed, as you may see yourself if you are in no haste to return.

"As to taking us off, you need not hide that we should be willing to go, but it is yet an attempt which will have no sanction from me, for I hold it vain. It is a thing which the truce does not protect, and the Turkish guns are now trained on the water around the quay."

He paused and pondered again, and then asked: "Is he bent to do this at the last in his stubborn way?"

Angelica recalled what she had heard. She thought that La Valette would not easily abandon his present plan, and she thought that, however desperate it might be (which she could not properly judge), it ought to be tried. It seemed dreadful to her that all who still lived in the fort should be left without hope to a cruel death.

"He seemed," she said, "fixed in resolve."

"So he would be." He fell silent again, as though he would examine the question on every side. Then he said, with the same slow gravity as before, but as one who had weighed all and could speak in a final way:

"You shall say that we are at the end of our strength, and will be glad to be taken off as we should have been content to remain. But, for to-night, it will be too late to arrange. To-morrow night, if the fort stand until then, and if the attempt is to be made at all, it is in all ways the better chance; the more so as the Turks will expect it less, having seen that we let this night go, and knowing to what straits we have fallen now.

"I do not say that we shall endure through another day, yet I do not say that we may not, having seen all that I have; for, when I let this be known, it will recruit hope, which can be a great spur, and, while we fought through this day, we had little, or less than that. . . . I will announce that the rescue comes, for I must serve the orders you bring, but you will say in plain words that I do not approve, nor shall I blame if the Grand Master adjust his mind when he shall have taken more counsel thereon, for I think the attempt will fail, with the loss of some who might live to a further day."

He asked: "You can remember that? It need not be twice said?"

And then: "The boats will not put off till you return . . .? If that be so, there is no haste. You can give us aid for an hour, if not two. . . . What can you do best? Why, you can give water to those who thirst. You will find corners where they have crawled, or they may lie where they fell. There is none to tend or to nurse, where we are all wounded or near to death." Her eyes followed his to where the hose about his ankle was darkly stained, which she had not noticed before. "But I would not be too quick to staunch blood, nor to stir those who are plainly sped. There will be no mercy in that."

The words revealed that he saw the end beyond doubt, as he had done at first when he had ordered that the round-shot should be cast into the well. But he showed no sign of feeling thereon, unless it were that he had talked more than his habit was. He lay down again, and Angelica went out, seeing that he had finished with her. . . . He heard the sound of singing which rose again from the little chapel within the fort. "Men go," he thought, "by many roads to one inn, where the night's lodging is sure, but who can speak for the next day?" He thought thus, having faltered somewhat in faith since the Lutheran heresy had shaken the foundations on which he supposed that the Church had stood, of which he had spoken to none. Then he thought: "Why should we draw others to useless deaths? The boats would be smashed before they could reach the quay. That at least may be saved, for I suppose that we shall not last till the noon is high." Then he muttered a prayer which held comfort still, having been learnt from his mother's lips; and after that he slept well.

CHAPTER XLI

In the first dimness of dawn, the Turks assaulted again, bringing fresh troops, and having resolved that the time had come when they could make an end against men who were wearied and few.

But, before then, Montserrat had been round the fort arousing all who were not too injured to stand and strive, with a word of new hope if they could but endure for another day; so that they overcame fatigue and the stiffening of wounds, and went in little bands to the weakest parts of the wall, and loaded the single gun that they were still able to work, and laid bombs and the hoops of fire where they would be ready to throw. Also, De Montserrat gave orders that the pennons of the knights who had fallen during the previous day should not be withdrawn, but that they should be somewhat shifted about, so that their weakness should not be known nor the trick guessed.

The new troops advanced in a bold and confident way and set their ladders against the wall. They were not easy to thwart, for they had no more to overcome than three or four score men who were little fitted to fight, but they were met by these men with a courage which was blended of despair and a new hope, and in so stubborn a way that they drew off at the last, leaving many dead in the ditch; and after that a rumour spread in their ranks that the Christians had landed secret reinforcements during the night, and that the fort was no nearer to fall than it had been on the previous day.

The sound of the renewed bombardment was pleasant in the Grand Master's ears. It seemed that the Turks had ceased assault after one day's repulse, as they had done a week before. The fort could endure the battering of round-shot for another day, and at night he did not doubt that, with Heaven's aid, he would bring off those who remained. He ordered Senor Ramegas to prepare a sufficient number of boats, leaving the details to him, as a man he had found fit for the trust he held.

Ramegas considered the instructions he received, against which he did not protest, for who could urge that no attempt should be made to rescue comrades who were so desperately placed? But he thought it a forlorn hope, with only one slender chance of success, if they could surprise the Turks when they were careless and unaware. He considered also, from the report that Angelica had made, that the men to be brought off alive, whether wounded or whole, could not fill many boats, but, if a relief should land, and there should be a skirmish ashore, he would need some force to hold a clear line while he brought the wounded men to the quay. He ordered that nine boats should be prepared, with as much secrecy as such an order allowed, each of which was to carry ten or a dozen men, whom he picked with care from the fleet, or from the Maltese boatmen to whom the harbour was known, including such seamen as were arquebusiers of skill. They were to be ready, with muffled oars, to leave as soon as the darkness fell, and to proceed down the nearer shore, only crossing to St. Elmo when they came to the harbour mouth.

It was noon when Ulichiali assaulted again, and the Christians, after some hours of respite and rest, manned the wall for the last struggle which, as they hoped, they would have to face, and endured again for a time. But their numbers failed, one by one, which was an end they could not help, till it was plain to all that they were at their last hour; and then, as by a miracle, the attack slackened and then withdrew.

They could look round, as the bombardment resumed, and count those who remained, and there were scarce a score who had any strength either to stand or strive. They must stand from now, if at all, less by any valour of theirs than by the forbearance of most merciless foes. Or was it by the over-ruling mercy of God that there might yet be a remnant saved?

They might be glad that this respite came, from whatever cause and however short, but they would have found no pleasure in the words with which Mustapha, coming up himself to the place from which Ulichiali controlled the attack (well in the rear, for the Greek-born pirate had neither Piali's headlong courage nor Dragut's fatalistic audacity) had told him abruptly to call it off, having heard from a renegade spy, who swam at times, at a great risk, from the Sanglea shore to that of the Turkish camp, that there was talk of preparing boats which were to take off the garrison, if they should endure through a further day.

Now he said: "Let them be. Will you draw the last bait from the trap?" So it was by Mustapha's design that the Christian flag still flew from St. Elmo's wall when the darkness came. . . .

The Grand Master, seeing that the hours passed, and the fort stood, was confirmed in belief that some of those who had been its defence would be brought off in the night, giving him a last boast against the Turkish arms, which had been foiled so long by a fort so weak that it would be said, by all the canons of war, that it should have been reduced in a day from when Piali's battery had been made ready to open fire.

"To-morrow," the Grand Master said, "being the twenty-fourth of the month, is John Baptist's day. It may well be that he will show his power and favour to those who exalt his name, bringing our brothers safely away and making mock of the heathen power."

In the fort (where D'Egueras lay dead, having done with prayers for this time) Montserrat lay with a deep wound from which his life was ebbing quickly away; for he had taken a thrust when his sword failed in the last scuffle by which the Turks were kept to their own side of the wall.

He was faint of speech, and his sight was dim. He knew that his time was short, and he found that thought was hard to control, being urgent to wander apart to its own dreams, and a brother-knight, who was sorely hurt, but to whom duty was more than life, would have shrived his soul. But he put him aside, having, as he conceived, a more urgent duty than that, and gave command that all who were yet fit should leave their posts and be assembled where he was laid.

There were no more than could be held in a small room, being a bare score, and when they had come he spoke so that most could hear:

"I have called you together here because it is vain to hope that you can longer defend the wall, being too few for another bout. So, if they venture again, you may let them do as they will, which you cannot stay. But if they leave you alone till the night fall (as they seem likely to do, though I can make no more than an evil guess as to the meaning of that), then you may look for the coming of boats in the darkest hour, when the moon is down. You should then be ready to leave with speed, taking all who are not dead.

"But if the boats do not come, or are beaten back, then my counsel and orders are that all who can, not being too weakened or maimed, shall leave this fort before dawn and swim, if their strength allow, to the far side of the harbour-mouth. And for those who remain perforce, my orders are that they do not resist when the Turks come with the dawn, as they are most likely to do, but be found engaged in the taking of food or other peaceful affairs, when they are more likely to save their lives than if they be found with a futile sword."

He said this with some pauses at times, and it seemed that he would have said more but his strength failed, or his awareness of where he lay. He died in the next hour, leaving the name of a good knight, as he surely was. . . .

The night came, to the hour of the setting moon, and the Grand Master stood on the quay as the nine boats were manned with ten or twelve good seamen in each, and pushed off into a darkness that was more relieved by the stars than they would have wished it to be. He gave Ramegas a strait charge that he should bring away not only all that lived, but the pennons of those knights who had shown them there, whether living or dead, with the flags of Malta and Spain that were over all.

The boats, moving with noiseless oars, passed out of sight, and there was a long time during which those who waited for their return could count the silence as proof that they had not been espied by a watchful foe. But when hope had come to a good height, there was the sound of a single cannon from the point where St. Elmo lay, and after that a burst of heavy fire, as though the fort were bombarded with all the batteries that the Turks had set up. But this quickly fell to a rumble of fewer guns, and then to single shots, and then ceased. It was hard to guess what it might mean and harder to think that its meaning might be good for the boats, but after a time they were to be seen returning toward the quay. There were seven now, and they came unhurt, with no more than a wounded man. They said that they had been close to St. Elmo's quay, the boat of Senor Ramegas and another being somewhat ahead, when a single cannon had been discharged from the shore, upon which the trumpeter upon the Captain's boat had blown the signal for them to retire, which they had done when it was sounded a second time, having his strict orders that they should withdraw in haste if such a signal should blow. They had been followed by many shots, which had gone astray in the night, but of the two leading boats they had seen no more.

So it had been; they having come clear of a trap which would have ended all if it had not been sprung too soon. For the Turks, knowing that the boats would come, and finding little danger left from the fort if they should leave it alone, had brought up their cannon very close to the water's edge, and so trained, while the light held, that they were assured that no boat would live long if it should come near the shore. But a certain gunner, having good eyes, had seen the foremost boat coming out of the night while it was still some distance away, and, being too eager to hurt his foes, he had blown his match and put it to the gun before he had received orders to fire (for which he would lose his head on the next day), and the shot, being well-aimed, struck the foremost boat, smashing its side, so that those it held were soon in the sea.

Señor Ramegas had seen that, if the Turks were alert, there would be no hope that they could bring off those that the fort held, though he had said little of what he thought, for there was no gain in making those faint of heart who must bring it to proof. He had given such orders as might enable some to escape if the worst should be, and had meant his own boat to be first of all, but the eagerness of the second boat had taken it somewhat ahead. When he saw that it was hit by the first shot, while still some way from the shore, he knew that they could do no more than bring up their boats to be sunk by the Turks who, besides, if they should land, would be a hundred to one; so he bade his trumpeter sound the retire, while he ordered his own boat to push on that they might rescue those who were now overset in the sea.

Of these, they hauled two to safety over their side, and might have sought more but that their own bows were stove in with a glancing shot, after which they could do no more than crowd to the stern and so lift the broken bows somewhat out of the sea, and bail hard till they were glad to beach the boat at the nearest point on the opposite shore.

The Grand Master must take what comfort he could from the fact that he had lost but one boat and one crew. He could not blame Ramegas that he had ordered retreat, for the thing was too plain, and the more so that he had made his own courage clear by pushing forward to rescue those he could from the sunk boat.

But St. Elmo was lost at dawn of John Baptist's day, with all it held, except that there were nine who had entered the sea at that bitter need and found strength to swim the breadth of the harbour-mouth. They did this in the night, after they had seen the boats driven away, and knew that no hope of rescue remained.

The Turks entered a fort that made no further defence, for Montserrat's orders were obeyed, and so they kept nine or ten of those who had been too feeble, or unable to swim, making them slaves for the bench. They slew all who were wounded to death or whom they thought too hurt to be worth their care.

But Dragut died in his tent as the green banner rose over St. Elmo's walls, for which St. John could be thanked, if for little else on that day.

Mustapha stood in the taken fort, and he was a wroth man as he saw how weak it had been, and how weakly held at the last, and as he thought of the long tale of the Turkish dead and the weeks they had wasted around its walls. It was said afterwards that the loss to the Turkish arms, first and last, in this siege was not less than eight thousand men, though it may be that many of these were not too hurt to be of service again.

He asked again how they thought to deal with the cow, if to butcher the calf had been a work of such toil and blood, and being eager to take revenge for his own loss, though it were but barren abuse of the dead, he collected the bodies of those knights who had died in the last days and ordered that their heads be cut off, and their bodies cut down and across, making a mock of the faith they held. When this had been done, he had the bodies cast into the sea at such times as the tide would bear them to St. Angelo's quay.

He gained nothing by that, for La Valette's wrath, as the bodies were brought ashore, was too fierce to be stilled till some reprisal was made. He ordered that, for every body the tide might bring, the head of a Turkish prisoner should be cut off and fired over to Sceberras ridge from a cannon's mouth; and after this had been done for a few times the bodies ceased to arrive.

On the next day, the Turkish fleet, with those of Alexandria and Algiers, being nearly eight score of great vessels in all, sailed round the coast from Marsa Scirocco bay and anchored in the new harbour that had become free for their use. Their crews landed upon the shore, making a camp which was under the shelter of many guns of the fleet, so that they felt strong and secure. They found cisterns from which they could drink that were not far from the shore, and were well content with the new quarters that they had gained. But they were in another mood on the next day, for Marshal Couppier had poisoned the wells, which was not guessed till the water had been drunk by half the crews that were there, and not less than eight hundred died.

The war grew more bitter on either side from the hour when St. Elmo fell, and in the old inland city, where Marshal Couppier's headquarters were—to which at the time the Turks did not attempt to invade, feeling that they needed their whole force to contain St. Angelo's walls—there was order made that a Turk should be hanged each noon at the market-cross, that the people might be somewhat cheered to see that the infidel vermin were one less than the day before.

PART II—ST. ANGELO

CHAPTER I

"You are one," Captain Antonio said, "for whom I would do much. If it would not ruffle your pride, I would call you friend. But there is a length to which you cannot ask me to go. I will not be hanged for that slut."

Francisco controlled his anger in a way which, had he considered it, might have been surprise to himself. It was an evidence of the strait in which he stood, which he was coming to see, and which a quarrel with the Genoese sailor would not relieve. But it was the most he could do to reply in temperate words.

"I must ask you to take that back, after which we can talk of that which is on your mind."

"Why, so I do, if you wish," Antonio replied, in a ready way. "I will call her La Cerda's mistress, or what you will, but you must allow for this, that I have known her before."

"I should say that you do not know her at all."

"Well, so you may. It is a thing I have never sought. So of what she is, or is not, I will say no more, except that she is one for whom I am loth to hang."

"So you have said once before. But you are not asked. Do you know where she is now?"

"I could make a most excellent guess."

"So might the Provost-Marshal himself and guess wrong. They cannot hang you for that."

"Yet if there be signs littered before my eyes——"

"Which you have no occasion to see."

"Which it might be said that I have. . . . And it is not for myself that I fear alone. For who does that which I must say that I do not know that you do—he is in a most perilous pass, for the Grand Master is one that not only the Turks may dread."

"Yet he may threaten that which he would not dare, or for which his strength would be too weak at a test. I am more in my own land than was he in his, and there are Spanish knights who would be my friends, should he seek to abuse his power."

"Do you think that? It is a test that you should not try. You would go down like a straw. . . . Even La Cerda is more than most in his own land."

"He was not long held. He was soon free."

"So he was. But it was said that the Grand Master did it himself, both to bind and loose, his friends looking another way. . . . They say that there is none but one to whom the Grand Master will give more than a moment's heed when his mind is set; and your friend that was has his ear, as the talk goes. It is Sir Oliver that I mean, as it may be needless to say. But you have quarrelled now with your friend, so that there would be little comfort in that, even were there more at the most."

"I know little of what you mean. I have quarrelled with none."

"Well, you should know of that better than I. . . . But I had observed that you do not meet since you took—I will say since you took what was there from his own room, and came away with a shortened sword."

"It was not broken as you suppose: the point caught by chance in a chair's arm."

"I have never doubted your word. But I may conclude that the point was bare."

"You must conclude as you will, but it was not pointed at him; nor did he draw upon me, as he never would."

"You may be right there, for I should say that he is not one whose sword would be quickly out. Yet I have a doubt when I say that, for I should not think him one who is poorly dowered either with courage or pride. . . . There have been times when I have thought that he would make a better maid than some are. But when I have seen how Sir Oliver sends him forth in most perilous ways I have put it by. I suppose that there are so few here wearing shift or gown that our eyes can no longer compare in a true way. . . . But I have vexed you again, and I know not why? I will be resolved to say naught, and to see no more. I will not even know that your sword snapped. For I am resolved of two things beyond that. I will neither hang for her nor will I quarrel with you."

Francisco felt that their words could not end in that way. He had found Captain Antonio, though not of his rank or race, and though they were of many alien habits and thoughts, yet to be a man of some good parts, and with the will of a loyal friend, and he had became aware that his friends were few. He was young, and of a reserve which was partly shyness and partly pride. The Knights of Malta, for the most, were much older men. He had been brought up to regard the Order as the first cause for which men must live and be very willing to die. To that extent he was one with the spirit that drew them there from ease and honour in many lands, to be at the Grand Master's command and to die for Malta's defence. But, beyond that, he had little in common with most of those among whom he moved, and though he might have made some friends of the right kind had he been placed on the wall amid the knights of his own land, yet, being in command of a battery that stood somewhat apart, and having to keep station there for long hours of each day, he knew little more of the knights of Castile who were lined on the eastern wall than when he had landed two months before.

He felt, rather than thought, that it would be a fool's part to let Antonio sulk, and the little Captain's face showed more offence than his words held. Yet he did not ask for a full confidence which, indeed, he might have good cause not to desire. Francisco answered with such measure of frankness as Antonio might be likely to take in the right way.

"If you had asked, I would not have held it from you, though it is not to be widely told. It was La Cerda drew upon me, Don Garcio not being there. When he came he made peace, being my friend in that, for I was reduced to two feet of blade and such aid as a dagger gives. . . . But it was true that the sword had snapped as I told you before. It was a mischance of the narrow room."

"Well," Antonio replied, "I did not doubt what you said. Nor do I ask what she did in the bedchamber of the one, nor why the other should have drawn upon you. But I may conclude that he is less than your friend; and it is a fact I cannot fail to observe that since the day you have walked aside of where Don Garcio goes, while I had thought before that you used some contrivance to meet. . . . I have no concern with the cause of this, but I must suppose that, if you were in the Grand Master's peril for aught you do, the Knights of Sicily would be dumb, and there might be those of your own land who would say no more, and I would rather see you with more friends and to need them less."

"So would I," Francisco replied, "and it is a friend's thought, and I must thank you for that. Yet I do not feel in more peril than I may lightly endure, for even if that should be laid bare of which it is agreed that we shall not speak, you must not disregard that I have not taken the Order's vows, to which it cannot be held that I should therefore conform in their monkish way, nor am I in the Grand Master's danger to that degree."

"That is true; and it is what, at such a pass, you would be certain to say. But I should be loth that my own life should hang on so thin a thread. For it is time of war, and you are under his rule, and I should say that the Grand Master's regard for any logic of speech would be of less than a groat's worth when his wrath is high."

"He has such repute," Francisco agreed; "but my uncle called him a friend, and I would not think him to be without some recollection of that. And it might be thought that there are foes enough over the wall, even for him, that he need not be stubborn to vex his friends."

This conversation took place three weeks from John Baptist's day, when St. Elmo fell. Francisco had become slow to leave the battery now and quick to return, even though Antonio might be in charge, for none knew when or where the Turks might attack next, either by water or land. Now their fleet was anchored in the harbour waters over Scebarras ridge, and the whole army was camped round the landward walls. St. Angelo could no longer hear the sound of guns which were pointed another way, and look across at an agony which it did not feel. The shots shook their own walls and battered the houses within the town.

The hardest part must now be sustained by those who manned the fort of St. Michael which stood on the Sanglea spur, and the outer walls of the Sanglea, for the inlet which was its southern side was neither deep nor of great breadth, and the Turkish batteries rose on the height of the opposite shore and Turkish troops swarmed at its landward end. But the Turks were now on all sides, and so closely drawn both by land and sea that there was no point at which instant watch must not be kept; none from which peril might not suddenly rise to a deadly height; none which was safe from the risk of a flying death.

Compassed thus, there was a show of reason in Francisco's complaint that even La Valette might be content with the count of his outer foes, and shun the making of more from those who would be his friends.

The Turks blew what boast they could of St. Elmo's fall. They loaded the wreckage of thirty guns into a galley which would bear them as trophies to Byzantium's quay. If Dragut were dead (which could not be denied), De Broglio was dead too, having spoken no further word since he made the Grand Master his parting jape. The

Turks made a list of the great knights who had died in defence of St. Elmo's wall, and it was better reading to them than it would be in the Christian lands.

Had the Viceroy yet sent the relief which should have come on John Baptist's day? He would have said yes, which the Grand Master would have denied. He should have sent a great fleet, and an army which would have enabled Couppier to draw the Turks from St. Angelo's walls to guard their own heads on an open field. He read orders from his master, the Spanish king, which were not meant to be clear to any except himself and, if he read them aright, they were such as he did not like.

He had pledged his word to Valette, and he knew where his honour lay. It was Spain's honour alike. Yet could he go against the King's will?

He ordered that the two galleys which had belonged to the Maltese knights should put to sea, and he added two which flew the ensign of Spain. He filled them with volunteers, who crowded Sicily at this time, seeking to aid Malta's defence from love of race, or love of God, or of what we will.

He put the four galleys under command of Don Juan de Cardona, a good knight, with written orders that he should approach the island in such a way as would be most likely to avoid the Turkish fleet, and to learn whether St. Elmo yet stood.

If it had fallen, he was to bring back the troops, for what use would there be in so small a force, if the strife went ill, and the Turks were already crowding round St. Angelo's walls? But if St. Elmo stood, and the Turks had the worse loss, he was to land them during the night, and leave promise of more to come.

Cardona read this order and may have thought it good, or may have cursed those whom he would not name. There is no record of that. But he sailed his galleys under cloak of night, to cast anchor outside Pietro Negri, and there he landed a knight who learnt that St. Elmo had fallen some days before.

There is some doubt of his name, by which we lack that of a valiant man, but he was one who had come to Sicily with the purpose of aiding the Christian cause, and having now landed in Malta, he had no mind to go back. He returned to Cardona's ship, where he lied in God's name, and we may suppose that the saints were glad. He said that St. Elmo stood and the Cross prevailed. Cardona did not question that which he may have been hoping to hear. He landed forty knights and seven hundred other soldiers of sundry sorts. He sailed back to Palermo with empty decks, having avoided the Turks again, and bringing a tale which he held for true, though it was soon changed by other reports.

The men who had landed thus in the night did that which made sport of the rules of war, as courage so often will. They marched where they wished to go, and so passed through the Turkish lines in a silent file, entering St. Angelo's gate without sound of a hostile shot, the Turks not having kept a good watch against that which was unlikely to be.

The Grand Master was glad of the aid that came and saw that its meaning was clear. For the time he had got all that he would from the crown of Spain. He did not despond for that, but he observed that he must prepare for a lengthened siege. He went over his stores. When he had done that, he made an order that Turkish prisoners were not to be taken, as food would be needed for better mouths. There had been little of quarter or mercy on either side before now, but there was none from this day. To each side their foes came to be held as no more than pestilent rats, till the last should be slain or gone, and Cross or Crescent should float in the only peace that either side could conceive in a single land. . . .

The news of St. Elmo's fall spread through the lands of Christ, and there were many of every faith whose hearts were heavy thereat. Even the English Queen, though it was by her will that those of the Order of St. John had been chased away, forgot the bitter Protestant feud, and ordered that there should be prayer for the Maltese knights in all the churches of which she was called the head.

Caring nothing for Christian prayers, Mustapha Pasha tightened his lines of siege and made his batteries strong.

CHAPTER II

THERE was no station in St. Angelo's girth, either by water or land, that was not fronted by active foes. The weakest point, as Mustapha saw, and Valette would have agreed, was the Sanglea, with St. Michael's fort at its highest point both because it was separated by the inner harbour from St. Angelo and the Bourg, and because of the shallowness of the inlet which protected its southern side.

It was against the Sanglea that Mustapha now directed his heaviest guns, and planned that which he expected to be decisive attack; while the Grand Master, warned both by his own military knowledge and by the report of a Greek-born engineer, Lascaris, who had deserted to the Christian ranks from a high post in the infidel army, that it was there that the first fury of storm would beat, laboured with an energy that seemed to increase with the passing days to strengthen barricades and make bastions firm; so that, while they were battered by Turkish shot, the defence, now here, now there, grew more formidable with every hour.

So that he should attack St. Michael both by land and water, and yet not risk his boats beneath St. Angelo's guns, Mustapha had a number of these, of the largest size, dragged on rollers over Scebarras ridge; and against this threat (which Lascaris may have betrayed) the Grand Master barricaded the mouth of the shallow inlet with piles; to which Mustapha replied by searching out men who could swim well, that they might ply axes at the right moment to break them down. . . .

Hearing its need, La Cerda came to the Sanglea, where his station was. He might have been excused for a further time, having an arm that he would not use for a long space, if it should heal at all, which was less than sure. But he would not be held slack in the cause for which he had come, so long as he were not driven too hard on what he thought to be the wrong road.

Admiral Sir Peter del Monte was in chief command at Sanglea, having the Italian knights under his rule. La Cerda reported to him that he was fit and willing to take his place on the wall.

Sir Peter, a discreet man, of that type of valour which makes no foes, and who was to be Grand Master himself at a later day, looked at a swathed arm, and said: "It is not what I had guessed, had I not heard it from you."

"But my sword arm," La Cerda said, "is still good."

Sir Peter thought of several things he might say, of which he said none. What he did say was: "If you are so resolved, I must not deny, having too urgent a need: and you are one I am glad to have."

La Cerda set his pennon on St. Michael's wall on the next day, having no mind that any should say that he loitered at such a time nursing a wound. He had a bitter wrath against La Valette, whom he would gladly have slain at a quieter time.

He charged him in his heart with Venetia's loss and perhaps her death. For he was convinced that she had had no purpose of flight when he had left her, a few hours before she was gone. That he thought (and was right in part) was the result of Valette's harshness to him. She had fled in panic, when she had heard that he was arrested without a cause—had fled to what fate, and where? It might be to death or torture or unspeakable shames at the infidels' hands. And he held Valette to be guilty of this by his intolerance of the natural conditions of human life; as also by the arrogance with which he imposed his power upon those who were of nobler blood than himself, and of higher rank in their own lands: and who might, by whatever scale of judgment, be better men; and also by the stubborn military folly of which he had made him the victim first, and then unjustly confined him without trial or question asked, which had been the final cause of Venetia's flight.

His attachment to her might have no spiritual profundities, no intellectual support, but it was real in its own way. He loved her for what she was, as well as what he supposed her to be. At the least, she was a possession he valued much. She was the most costly of all the gay material things: castles and woods, horses and hawks, tapestries and jewelled clothes, which had embroidered his life till now.

And Valette had taken his mistress, as he had taken his horse, and had even done these things without courtesy of request, in an unmannerly way, like the boor that he surely was. He had assaulted his honour too, which might have been as hard to forgive had not La Cerda felt that his loss was less under that count. It stood, he thought, too secure for Valette to have pulled it down. Yet even there he had a wound that he felt more than a burnt arm, it being the pain of that which drove him to take the wall when most would have said that he was unfit to serve.

For it is certain that he did not go thus to the wall because his passion for slaying Turks was beyond control (as might have happened to some of the Order's knights), nor did he think St. Michael's peril to be so nicely poised that it would stand or fall by his single arm. He went that he might assert his valour in all men's sight, and be esteemed among the Italian knights who were his natural friends.

The last hour he had had with Venetia, when Angelica left them alone, had assured him both of her loyalty to himself and of her innocence of any different offence. He would have sought her now, to the delay of his pennon's flaunt, as well from obstinacy as regard, but that he was not sure that it was what she would thank him to do.

If he found her, could he protect? It was a bitter question to have to ask himself, and take a doubtful reply.

If he should find her, and did not disclose her hiding, it was doubtful that he could do her any avail, while the search itself might be watched by those who would make it their aid to find her for other ends. And if any were giving her harbour now in the town, to disclose what they had done would be to put them in the way of a likely death.

If she had escaped, whether to Christian or Turk, whether by land or sea, he could do nothing to aid her more. If she were still in the town she would hear of him, though he might know nothing of her, and she might find safer means of letting him know of any need that was hers than he could find to reach her.

These things were simple to see, but they did not content his mind. It is always harder to remain still than to act, even though action and wisdom may not lie in the same bed. He must learn what he could, and for this there were three to whom he could talk, though in different ways.

He would see Sir Oliver and Don Garcio (as he supposed she must still be called), and Don Francisco, whom he had ceased to suspect. He had La Valette and the Provost-Marshal further back in his mind.

He went to Sir Oliver first, who received him with courtesy though without warmth, being a tired man, and burdened with matters for which he felt greater concern than for any troubles which (he would have said) La Cerda had brought on to his own back.

"You will admit," La Cerda said, "that she was one whom it was my part to protect, having brought her here."

"It may have been your part," Sir Oliver replied, "but it was not mine. Yet I did something in that, and perhaps more than I should; and I think, had she not fled as she did, I should have sent her hence with a whole skin."

"With a whole skin!" La Cerda exclaimed, taking the phrase in a more literal way than it may have been meant, "would you say that she risked that? Why what, in the devil's name, or in the Grand Master's if you prefer, had she done but what her honour required? I should say that some have been sainted for less than that. . . . And does he think that she can be shamed and my honour stand? It is poor reward that Sir John gives to those who put all aside that they might come here at the greatest peril that well could be."

"You speak," Sir Oliver more quietly replied, "beyond reason and beyond fact. You have not been without cause for wrath, and there are matters in which I have not been less than your friend, as perhaps you see.

"But I must remind you first that she was kept here by a trick, after I had secured that she should be sent safely away. That was an affront to me, of which I might say more than I have yet done, and you may see how your honour came clear in that (if I may say it without offence) more than I have been able to do.

"And, beyond that, when a man is slain at a dagger's point, in a place apart, it is required in all lawful lands that he by whom it is done (and a woman cannot be in a better case) shall come forward to show that there was sufficient cause. What has she done? She has replied by hiding and flight, as one who protests her guilt. Yet, had she been found, she would have had fair trial of all, as I may say that she will now.

"But the last thing I must say is that you use the Grand Master's name as it is not reason to do (I say naught of our vows, of which each must judge), for we did not come here as doing favour to him, but as being joined in a common cause; of which, by our own votes, we had made him head."

"Yes. We were demented in that."

"I must differ there. I say he is the man for this hour, and a better would not be easy to find."

"Well, he is friend to you."

"He is more than that. He is Malta's shield."

"So he should be. We will not quarrel for that. I came not to ask of him. Have you tidings of her?"

"I can answer freely in that, having had none. We may hope that she has fled far. But if I knew more, I might have said less, rather than told it to you. I cannot counsel more as a friend than when I say you should put her out of your thoughts. This is not randomly said, for it is like I know more of her than you ever will

I say not this of myself but of the office I hold. It is my business to know."

There were angry words on La Cerda's lips, which he did not speak. He remembered that he had come there resolved that he would not injure his cause (or else hers) because patience failed, as he had done before then.

"But I will tell you this," Sir Oliver went on; "if you find a man who is giving her harbour now, you will meet one who is next neighbour to death, for orders may not be lightly flouted in time of war. I had that in mind when I said that I hoped she had fled away."

"You would let me know without pause, if she were found?"

"Yes. It would be your due."

"Then I can ask nothing more."

He rose with these words, feeling that it would be waste to speak more, and aware that Sir Oliver would be very willing for him to go. He resolved that, should she be found, as he thought it likely she would, he would test his strength to the last friend he had before he would see her shamed or death come to those who had been her aid. . . .

She lay on a bed at this time, having excuse that there was little else for her to do. She had learnt that La Cerda was released from any charge the Grand Master had made, and that he was walking abroad, though with an arm that was thickly wrapped, at which she bit a petulant lip. Would he neither prevail nor die? A protector who could no longer protect was no use to her. She cursed the day that she had lost sight of Sicily's shore. "I lie here," she said to herself, "and the food is poor. And if it were better, I dare not eat as I would. I must starve or grow fat as I lie here. . . . Yet it might be changed for a worse jail. . . ." She thought of La Cerda again and wished he were dead, which would solve much. For she had other plans that went well.

CHAPTER III

La Cerda met Angelica in the hall.

"Don Garcio," he asked, with more courtesy than he would have given to whom she professed to be, "may I speak with you apart?"

"Yes," she said, with a readiness which she would have found it hard to assume, "we can talk here, if you will. . . . But will you do me the kindness to recollect that I am that which you called me now?"

As she spoke, she had turned to a window-seat in an alcove near, which was so placed that those who were seated there could not be secretly overheard. She had no quarrel with La Cerda, whom she might rather have felt to be somewhat in her own case, and in an alliance of which she could not make him aware, but the tone and gesture of his address had been such as would be given more naturally to a woman than to another knight, and her first thought had been to restrain that and to draw him quietly apart. It was only when they were seated that she recalled that there were things which she knew or guessed that he must not suspect, but by that time the frankness of her first response had assured him that she had no reserve on her mind, and that her sole fear had been that he might make disclosure of whom she was, which her first words confirmed.

"I would be sure," she said, "that you would not reveal——"

"It was needless to ask, for that which you did being for Venetia, and therefore for me, we are bound alike to hold the confidence which you thereby gave."

"I did not doubt," she replied, "that you would regard it thus; but I had rather in mind that more is disclosed by inadvertence than by design." She did not add that she would not trust Venetia a yard away, let him protest as he might. If Venetia kept a closed mouth, it must be that she could open it to no gain, or that it had been shut for another than her.

"It shall be my care," he said, "that I do not err in that wise. . . . It was from your room, as I understand, that Venetia went. May I ask if you have either knowledge or guess as to where she may be now, which, though you might withhold from others, you would not cover from me?"

"She went while I slept, having said nothing of her intent. I have not heard from her since."

"Do you think she went out alone, or was she taken or lured?"

"As I think, she went of herself, and with a good will, for she had unbolted the door, and she had dressed with some leisure and care, taking some things of mine which she must have preferred."

"It was freely done," La Cerda allowed. "She may have thought it was for your own peace that you should have no knowledge of where she went."

Angelica agreed about that, thinking it might have even more reason that he supposed. She said: "Well, she took naught that I grudge, and her need was surely the more." She turned the course of her words to ask of his hurt, which he answered was well enough. He looked at her for herself at this time, and had a wonder of what she did. He could not think that she had come with no more resolve than to be her cousin's mistress in that inferno of bitter war, nor did it consort either with the way in which he had seen her to risk her life in active affairs, nor with Sir Oliver's knowledge of whom she was and that she was allowed to remain. Yet Sir Oliver (he reminded himself) had been more lenient to Venetia than the Grand Master might have approved. It was a puzzle it might be profit to solve, with Venetia in jeopard, and in a case that seemed somewhat alike, and yet it might be that which his honour would not allow.

"I would," he said, "that you could have shown me more than you do. But I can see that she went in a secret way. I owe you thanks, which I will pay if occasion come."

He went with no other courtesy of retreat than he would have shown to a knight of his own rank, being much younger than he.

Angelica reflected that she had revealed no more than she had told Sir Oliver at the first, and that La Cerda had no share in her own guess, of which she supposed that she must be glad.

CHAPTER IV

La Cerda had resolved that there was one more to whom he should have something to say, though with less expectation that there was knowledge of Venetia to be gained. Still, he told himself, he had gained nothing where he had gone in more hope, and the third attempt might well result in a contrary way.

He was rebuffed at his first effort to meet Francisco, being told that he was seldom seen in the castle now, and that his chamber was given up to another knight.

"Well," he thought, "I suppose there is one above that will do better for him, when he has the time to come here." But that thought was confused by what he heard in the next breath.

"Don Francisco will not leave his battery more than he must, the Turks being round on all sides, and none knowing when they may assault the boom which it is his special duty to guard, but I should say that he has less cause to come here than he once had, for he had but one of whom he made friend before, that being Don Garcio, who is of a land that is near to his, and it has been observed that they will not meet since the time when, as it is said, Don Garcio had a——" The speaker, an old gossiping knight, who was too maimed for the wars, and had an usher's duty about the hall, became suddenly aware of the indiscretion he had been near to commit. He was so facile of tongue that he had hardly regarded until that moment that it was La Cerda to whom he spoke. He remembered that the wanton of whom the talk had been that she was found in Don Garcio's room (but whom no one had seen) was said to be one that La Cerda had kept for his own bed.

He added: "There is always talk, which is mostly false, and the rest better unsaid. But it is true that they do not meet, for either will turn aside to avoid that, as I have observed more than once, as I have stood here."

La Cerda thanked him, and walked on. The battery was not far. He could quickly be there. That Francisco had quarrelled with Angelica since they had fought in her room might point to something he had not guessed, and that it would be useful to know. But he saw that the evidence did not go far. If a special intimacy had been noticed between them, it might be policy only which now kept them apart—a discretion that came too late, and that might be most strictly observed when a certain old gossiping knight had his eyes upon them in open hall.

The battery of which Francisco had charge lay, as has been previously observed, outside St. Angelo's wall, on the narrow space that divided the citadel from the harbour waters. It had, in that respect, a position that was specially precarious, mitigated by the fact that it lay so closely under the castle's seaward guns and that it could only be attacked from the water while St. Angelo stood.

It had a further peculiarity, or potential weakness, in the fact that its guns did not point outward across the harbour, where its own danger lay, but were mounted diagonally to St. Angelo's wall, being trained to protect the boom, which closed the inner harbour from hostile attack, and protected the Maltese fleet, which was anchored therein.

The obligations of military discipline can never be more urgently necessary than in a place that is closely sieged, and defended by a mixed garrison in which there is no unity either of language or race, the dangers of treachery or surprise rising under such conditions to their maximum possibilities. It might be said, beyond that, that the exposed position of Francisco's battery, being beyond the main walls of defence, imposed a special obligation of vigilance, for though, as yet, he had commanded no more than an idle post, and might continue to do no more till the siege should end, yet if the call to defend himself or the boom should come, it might be both sudden and vital in its demand.

La Cerda did not expect to find the battery wide open to any who might wish to inspect its guns. Even in time of peace there might have been less freedom than that; but he encountered a rigidity of discipline and precaution beyond anything which he had expected to meet.

Though his dress and demeanour proclaimed him an Italian knight of high rank, and would have enabled him to walk freely through most places within the Christian lines, he found himself challenged sharply before he had even entered the trench by which the battery was approached on its northern side. At the further end of that trench the pass-word and his own name proved insufficient to procure him a further advance until the Captain's will should be known. The sentinel was deferential enough, but his halberd remained lowered across the way.

He was kept there for more minutes than his dignity could lightly endure before Captain Antonio came, so that he had leisure to observe, so far as his position allowed, that the battery was now a larger and more substantial work than he had expected to find, and to hear sounds of mattock and spade proclaiming that its strength was not yet equal to Francisco's desire.

CHAPTER V

CAPTAIN ANTONIO might have come at a better speed had he been otherwise engaged than he was or had he heard any name but the one he did. It was but a few moments before that he had stood at the backs of two men who had not heard his approach, owing to the noise of the excavating at which their companions worked, and at which they should have been doing an equal part.

"But," he overheard, "if it should be she for whom the proclamation is made——" The man's voice ceased, as he became aware that his captain was not more than three paces away.

"Lonzo," Captain Antonio asked, "of whom are you talking now?"

The man became silent, looking confused, and would have been urged by a sharper word, but his companion replied:

"It is that he saw a lady enter the Captain's room, when the moon shone over the scarp."

"Then," Captain Antonio advised, "he should drink less."

"He is not one," his self-appointed advocate replied, for the man said nothing at all, "to drink more than he should."

"To how many has this folly been told?"

"To no other but me, for I am his only friend, and he had mentioned it but a moment before."

"Which was too soon for such talk. Lonzo, I say this to you, and to Pietri alike. There could be no lady enter the Captain's room, for there is none here. I swear that by Our Lady Herself, which is not an oath on which I would be forsworn." He added the names of certain Genoese saints which he was known to revere, feeling that what he did should be done well, and assuring himself that he swore truth, for who could call that slut by the name which God's Mother does not despise?

"No," he said, "no madonna is there. It was the shadows that lied of the passing clouds. . . . But I will give you counsel that you should heed.

"You are men who have been chosen by me, being changed from those who were first here, as you all are. You are well paid from the Order's chest, and you have more beyond that, which Don Francisco supplies. You were chosen thus because there is little that can be said or done, whether in castle or town, of which the Turks do not hear by the next day, and Don Francisco was well resolved that no word should pass out from this place, for which the reason is known to you.

"Now if you should gossip in foolish ways, you would show that you are not worthy of such a trust. You might find yourselves in a worse place and taking a smaller pay. And if you should tell a tale that was false you might end, beyond that, where you would be sorry to be. For it is by such ways that men come to the lash or the prison cell, who are too good for such use.

"And even if you should tell one which is true (but which you need not have seen, had you looked aslant), which you could not do for this time, there being no substance in what you say, should you be the better for that?

"Let us suppose that you had come on traces of her for whom proclamation is made, as you were rashly saying you might have done. Well, it would be your duty to so report. I shall not tell you other than that. But would it be to your gain? I should say not. You would be a witness to be questioned apart. If you did not say all that they would think that you ought to know, or if there should be dispute, so that your tale should become suspect and yourself therefor, would not the thumb-screw be called to aid? He is a man with good eyes who can be blind when he should not see. It is such men who live long."

The man, Pietri, who had seen the wraith in the night, and who had been silent till now, found some words to say when Antonio's lecture was done.

"Captain," he said, "I have eyes which see well in the light" (he could not deny that, for it was as a gunner that he drew pay), "yet it is well known that they are of little avail when the light is poor."

"So I had supposed," Captain Antonio replied, "from that which I heard you say." And as he spoke there was one at his side with a tale that La Cerda was there, and seeking speech with Don Francisco on private affairs, and there was no name that Antonio, who desired trouble neither for others nor for himself, would have been less willing to hear.

"Well," he said, "let him wait, while Don Francisco shall be informed. . . . Or it may be enough that I see him first, for it may be a matter too light to disturb Don Francisco's rest."

And having said that, he went in no haste (for he had some

thinking to do), to where La Cerda waited at the near end of the trench.

He met a man whose patience was not reputed to last overlong, and was near its end, whom he greeted with the deference that his rank required, but without speaking the one word that La Cerda expected to hear.

"I have come myself," he said, "being in command while Don Francisco is taking rest, and he having given me charge that he shall not be called unless there is reason of war."

"The matter on which I came," La Cerda replied, "is one on which I can speak only to him. . . . Do you say that he will sleep long?"

Captain Antonio would have liked to lie, but he was not sure that he would be thanked by him for whom it would have been done. "He is to be roused," he said, "within half an hour of this time."

"Then I will wait, in what comfort you have, making my time his."

"My orders," Captain Antonio replied, in some embarrassment, which was not usual to him, "are strict and exact, that none may enter beyond this point, except at my captain's leave."

La Cerda stared his surprise. "Why, man," he exclaimed, with more contempt for him he addressed than he would have shown at a better time, "do you think I shall stand here? Do you call me Turk?"

Antonio felt a doubt of whether he had been as wise as he wished. Orders were strict, and had a cause which the Grand Master himself would have approved, but he was not sure that they should be applied to one who was a Commander of the Order himself, and whom he knew well by sight. Beyond that he had a shrewd doubt that he was acting as he would not have done but for another thing, which it was equally sure that the Grand Master would have condemned, and of which no suspicion, however faint, should be allowed to rise in La Cerda's mind.

"You will admit," he said, "that in time of war orders may be so framed as to hinder those for whom they are not meant, and that he may take blame who shall interpret them in a better way, being beyond that which he has commission to do. Yet I am assured that this order was not to have held you here, and it shall be my risk that you wait in a better place."

La Cerda was little appeased by an admission that came too late. He said: "You are a wise man," in a tone that proposed a doubt, or at best that his wisdom had been tardy in its advice. He followed

Captain Antonio through a tunnel which had been hewed from the rock, having small chambers along its side, and was again surprised that so much had been done at what he had thought to be little more than a gun-platform outside the wall. He came to where the guns were, and saw two long culverins of the newest make pointing through embrasures which showed him, as in a frame, a picture of the long floating boom and of St. Michael's fort at its further end, and something of the inner and outer harbours to left and right.

"I had not been told," he said, "that you had such weapons as these. I thought that you had but three sakers, such as would throw their discharge to little more than the boom's length."

"So we had," Captain Antonio replied, "and so we have still," and he pointed to where these cannon were drawn aside, "but Don Francisco would have these guns from the *Santa Martha*, which was his own ship, thinking that they might be of more use. . . . It is that which is known to none but the twelve men we have in garrison here, and the seamen by whom they were brought during the night, which must be excuse for the strict orders I have that none shall enter without his leave."

La Cerda was more appeased when he saw that it was something beyond the routine of a leaguered place which had held him back; he unbent enough to discuss matters of warfare by land and sea, on which Captain Antonio had some observations of wit to make and some tales to tell. The time did not seem long before Francisco appeared.

He had heard already, by Captain Antonio's care—though no more than the bare fact—that La Cerda waited him by the guns. He could not guess what La Cerda knew, nor to what questions he might have to make instant reply, and though he came forward in a quiet and confident style, born of his pride and his blood, yet he could not tell, being young, how he should act, nor what he would be likely to say.

La Cerda, having folded his cloak for a seat, had found comfort enough on a stone ledge of the parapet which protected the guns. Captain Antonio stood at his side, in which positions their heights were not so different that they could not discourse with ease. La Cerda rose as Francisco approached, and looked at one who seemed to have advanced in dignity and the qualities by which manhood is known since he had seen him before, more than the short weeks would explain. "War," he thought, laying praise at a wrong door, "may do much for those men it does not kill."

He spoke at once when they met, without waiting to be asked why he had come.

"Don Francisco," he said, "I am still in doubt of whether I owe you thanks, or the word of regret that it may be knightly to speak at times, or no more than a bare sword, such as was between us before, but, by your leave, I will put such questions aside at this time, both because it is hour of war and because you could say that I am unfit" (he looked down at his bandaged arm) "to support my words, and also until I am more fully informed. But I would ask you now, on your knightly word, if you can give me help on a search which I still make?"

"Chevalier," Francisco replied, "it is knightly said, and I will answer it in the best manner I may.

"As to ourselves, there are times when I have the same doubt; but, by your own choice, I will say no more, except that, as I suppose, my honour is still clean.

"As to what you ask, I would ask this in reply: If one should know, or suppose, to where the lady Venetia has made her retreat, is it that which should be told to any without her leave, she being in the great jeopard she is, and there also being proclamation of death against whoever may have taken her in?"

La Cerda weighed the implications of this in a mind that was alert, and with suspicions not buried to any depth. He remembered what he had been told in the last hour, that Francisco had quarrelled with her whom he supposed to have been more close than she was, and that that had been from when they had found him in the room where Venetia lay. It was a simple conclusion that Francisco could tell him where she now was, and a presumption that she was still in the Maltese lines. His doubt of Francisco's faith stirred him to an anxious wrath that he could not lightly restrain.

Yet restrain it he did, remembering the declaration that he had just made; and so, reflecting that it was by patience, if at all, that he would come to the knowledge he sought, he made a reasoned reply.

"As to that—I must conclude that you would not propose it in such a form unless your own knowledge made it to be of something more than idle debate—you may think the Lady Venetia's jeopard to be much more than it is. I have been told by Sir Oliver Starkey himself that she may not have much to dread if she will come forward now, and I should say that her peril is greatly more while she lie concealed, for she will have less mercy to hope if she be dug out than if she will now advance, saying that she did but wait till I should be free to give her support.

"As to the part of who may have been her aid I will say this: It could be told to me—as I think it should, I having the right I have—on my plighted word (which should be assurance enough) that there would be no disclosure without consent, nor such as would bring him to peril he might have missed."

"There would be the question, beyond that, of her own will."

"Which you would ask me to doubt?"

"I mean that she may not agree that she can come forward at little cost, and a mistake would be learned too late."

"But is it not that for her, and for me? Do you propose that I might betray her against her will?"

La Cerda spoke now with an impatience he could hardly repress. Francisco's words seemed to make it clear that he knew where Venetia lay, and his tone to imply that he had a right of decision, and even to speak for her, which gave jealousy more grounds than the position must have contained in its simplest form.

Yet he reminded himself again that, if Francisco had secured her safety when he was himself unable to do so, there might be a debt of thanks to be paid in a better form than the base coinage of suspicions which might be utterly false, and, beyond that, he must have put himself in a peril which was even greater than hers, and that alone must give him some right to say what should be done now. And while he strove to control himself to a temperate mood, and yet one which would still persist—for he was resolved that he would not now turn from that quest, till he had heard Venetia protest her truth with her own lips—Francisco answered with more candour than he had spoken before.

"Chevalier," he said, "I would have you know that I wish to act as a knight should, and I will say that I have no practice in such matters as this, and that I would that the course of honour were more easy to see.

"I will tell you that she came to me, being in a great dread, when she heard that you were powerless (as for that time) to be her support. She asked for aid which I did not refuse, and I suppose that we may have no quarrel for that."

"As to that," La Cerda interposed, "you have thanks." The words were well enough, but they were without warmth, as though he waited to hear that which was still to say.

"I put myself in your hands," Francisco went on, "in the confidence of your own pledge, and because you urge that you have a right to be told, when I say that I may know where she is now. But you must own that my obligation is not to you, but to her. I will see her between now and to-morrow noon, and, if I have her consent, I will then lead you to where she is."

La Cerda heard this, and suspicions stirred with more force in his mind and would not be still. He was not too angry to see that, in the strict logic of the position, Francisco was right; but passion put logic aside to ask with what object he had helped her at all, and why he should be in doubt (as he professed) as to whether she should be willing for him to tell where she now lay. He had to remind himself of his bandaged arm, and of the resolution he had made, as he replied:

"Well, it is but a day, and I suppose there is no doubt of what her answer will be. We will so agree till to-morrow noon, if you will assure me of but one thing, which you will forgive that I ask——"

But the question, which might have brought crisis in its reply, was not asked, the words being drowned in a thunder of Turkish guns which broke out in a sudden fury of storm from every battery round St. Angelo's girth. It was a thunder that did not cease, and La Cerda said: "I must seek my post. I will be here at to-morrow noon."

He spoke to one who had ceased to give attention to him, and went in haste to take boat across the inner harbour to reach his place on St. Michael's wall. He went through a bustle of those who ran different ways with the same object as he, for the noise of the Turkish guns was now drowned in the nearer thunder of Christian reply, and the bells tolled to call all men to their stations upon the walls.

CHAPTER VI

Sir Oliver picked up his sword, which he did not constantly wear. He was slightly bent with his studious toils, so that, as they stood, Angelica's height was little the less and in the supple straightness of youth she might have been held for the better man.

"We must to the wall," he said, "and I would that you had some armour of proof, of which I should have warned you before, though it has been my thought to hold you excused, as long as I can, from the active strife which you should not see, and of which, as I suppose, you will be in no danger to-day. . . . It is the risk of a straying shot."

"You mean that they will not attack our part of the wall?" . .

"Yes. For it is what they cannot do until they have made much further advance, unless it were from the sea, with the fleet to aid."

"And they will not do that?"

"No. It is such a risk as Piali might not scruple to try, but Mustapha would not waste ships and men in so simple a way. It would be stone against wood, and at a short range, and our cannon pointed downward upon their decks. . . . There is no peril of that. . . . The Turks will fire from all sides, that we may be in doubt of where they will throw their strength, yet that is not in much doubt. It is St. Michael that they will pull down, if the fiends are strong."

Sir Oliver went to the wall where he held command, rather in the routine which would not let any part remain unwatched at a time of storm than with expectation that there would be occasion for its defence. He had sent the best part of his own men to the support of those who were more likely to face attack on the Bourg front, but he had little doubt that it was on the southern side that the worst fury of storm would beat for that day.

He went on, as he ascended the winding stair, with Angelica at his side:

"There is a friend of yours who has come, so it is said, to the Turkish camp. I mean Hassan, whom you met on his own deck, and who, by Dragut's death, is now Viceroy of the whole Barbary coast. I should have said on a deck which he had made his, having been ours at the first, and where you made him your jest, as we may suppose that he will not quickly forget. I should say that he would have more lust to meet you again than it would be pleasure to you. Which is a reason (for you) that we guard our walls."

"Is it sure he is here?"

"There is the *Flying Hawk* in Massa Muscetto bay, which he is said to choose for his own ship since he took it from us, finding its speed to be hard to match. . . . There is no doubt he has come, and with him some thousands more of the corsairs that Barbary breeds. He is lord now of all Tripoli and Algiers, and it is said that Dragut's wealth is for him, to augment his own. He keeps Mahound's law so far that he has not Dragut's liking for rum, but that he holds to the Prophet's limit of wives is what I have not heard, though it may also be true."

Angelica laughed in her quick way at a recollection which came with Sir Oliver's words.

"I know not how many he have, nor how few, but I was to be extra to them, unless Dragut should refuse to forego my price for a better deal. . . . I thought it was time that I came away."

It was a danger passed, at which the light spirit of youth could look back in a mocking mood, but there was no levity in the tone with which Sir Oliver made reply.

"The saints keep you from that!—as they doubtless did, with your own courage to aid. But you may well pray that you do not fall to his hands for a second time, which would be no jesting for you."

"Well," she replied, somewhat sobered by this, but still feeling confident against a danger so vague and far, "I suppose I am secure for this time; and I have heard you say that if we fret at a distant fear we are likely to vex our peace for that which will never be. . . . Is St. Michael in peril beyond likely defence? Are we greatly maimed if it fall?"

"I would not say that it is in peril beyond repulse, nor that we are lost if it fall. St. Michael is more strong than St. Elmo was, whether we reckon by weight of guns or by height of walls, or by its nearness to us. But the whole length of the Sanglea is less strong, and that not only where it faces the land but because its southern water is shallow, so that it is said that it may be waded at more places than one, and it is no more than a short gun-shot from shore to shore.

"If St. Michael fall we shall still stand, but we shall have a wound which will bleed much. It is a greater risk that they will cut it off, winning the Sanglea, so that the inner harbour and our galleys would be under their fire, but we may have good hope that they will not prevail, even to that."

They spoke amid a surrounding rumble of guns, and the louder separate thunder of those that fired from the castle walls that were near at hand. It was clear that the Turks attacked with their utmost force, being insurgent on every side. Mustapha, having slain the calf, had now come for the cow, and would not be lightly denied.

Angelica watched from the outer angle of the wall, where her station was, and could see little beyond the smoke of St. Michael's guns and that which rose and drifted over the Sanglea, which, being lower and further from her own front, was beyond her sight, though she could see part of the inner harbour where the Maltese galleys were sheltered safely as yet, and the boom at its mouth was beneath her eyes, as was the battery of which Francisco had charge. She saw him at times, waiting watchful beside his guns, though as yet they could not point at a foe. But it would not be supposed that he should attempt to look up to a place where he did not know her to be, even if he would if he had. . . .

The hours passed, and Sir Oliver came to her side.

"There is little use that I stay here, where we can but watch what we do not share. I have given command to the Chevalier de la Roye, for I have more urgent matters with which to deal. You must stay, for you make one, and give release to a man who can be used at another place. . . . But what are they that come out from the further shore?"

There was a scurry of strife at this time at the entrance to the inlet which was south of St. Michael's fort, which was almost beyond their sight, where Mustapha's swimmers strove with axes to break down the palisade, and Del Monte had called for volunteers to swim out and prevent the damage they sought to do.

He found no lack of those who could swim and who would risk their lives in that way, but the palisades were easier to break down than to mend, and while men fought like sharks in the reddened flood it was broken in places beyond repair. . . .

Angelica, watching from St. Angelo's higher wall, could see ten great boats come out, one after one, from the further shore. They were loaded with men, bearing more than a thousand in all, and they came at a great pace, being propelled by those who knew that a second saved might be no less than the lives of all.

Avoiding all but such guns of St. Michael's fort as could be hastily trained their way, which were neither many nor of much range, they came round toward the gaps in the palisade which had been broken to let them through, aiming to pass under St. Michael's fort and take by storm the long, low water-front of the Sanglea.

"If they succeed in that," Sir Oliver said, "they will thrust a wedge between the fort and those who defend the Sanglea on its landward side, so that those last may be surrounded and sped," and as he spoke a rumble of distant sound arose to further confuse the tormented air, from where, far beyond their sight, Hassan's corsairs swarmed to attack the Sanglea at its southern end.

"Francisco," Angelica said, looking down, "is getting busy at last. But what can he hope to do?"

"Well," Sir Oliver answered to that, "I did not know that he had guns of so great a range, for he was set there to defend the near boom. But if you ask what he can do, I must reply that it will be nothing or all."

Francisco looked out through an embrasure from which pointed the long black muzzle of one of the culverins which he had brought from his own ship and he knew that his day had come.

"Antonio," he asked, "could you reach them now?"

The little captain looked out over the boom, past the entrance to the inner harbour, past the spur which was crowned with St. Michael's fort, to where the ten great boats came on, with trails of following foam, toward the gaps in the palisade which he could not see.

"I could reach them now, but there would be those who would get free, if they were speedy to turn. I will wait yet for a minute's space." He spoke to the man who stood waiting his word at the other gun with his linstock lit: "You said your sight was good in the day? It is now you must prove your word."

A moment later, Angelica, looking down, saw sudden flashes that came as one from the out-thrust muzzles. She saw the great guns leap to the recoil, wrenching their chains. She heard, next instant, the double thunder of their discharge amid the din of encircling sound.

Far out, on the harbour water, a boat sank by the head, spilling its cargo of dead and maimed, and of those who would be unable to live in an element they did not know. Another boat was struggling to turn, pushing frantic oars, while the water poured through a broken side. Below, the two guns were being sponged and loaded anew, and, as it seemed, in no more than a moment's time, they were thrust outward again, sending an even more deadly message of death to boats which had now bunched in a confusion between those who would fall back, those who would still go on, and those who lay on uncertain oars disputing among themselves. But after those second shots, there was but one mind among men who saw that their deaths were near: they turned in flight and, as they did so, the cannon thundered again.

Of the ten boats which set out, bearing about eight hundred of the janissaries which were the flower of Mustapha's troops, and two hundred more of the Tripoli corsairs that Candelissa led, there was but one that got back to the shore; and but two hundred men, including those who were able to swim to land, who would answer their names when the roll would be called on the next day.

Antonio, overlooking the cleaning out of the culverins with a gunner's eye, knew that their work was done for that time and, perhaps, till the siege should end. But it had been enough. It was an example of that which is frequent in the annals of war, of a device which goes beyond that for which it was thought at first; for it was a battery that would not have been erected at all but that the Grand Master had been urgent to protect the inner harbour, where the fleet must be laid up, with an ample boom, and then with guns to defend that. And so it was seen that, with longer guns, it might be used to another end, firing over Isola Point to guard the approach to the Sanglea, which would be likely to be much sooner attacked.

"We shall see no more," Sir Oliver said, "from this point, and I cannot longer remain. But you may have a good hope that St. Michael will not go down for this day, and your cousin has won a praise which, as I suppose, will be the talk of more lands than one."

He went with that word, but the noise of storm that beat on the Sanglea did not slacken till evening fell.

CHAPTER VII

Venetia, clasping small, soft, muscular hands behind her pale-gold head, and lifting a flower-fair face to Francisco's regard, had a thought of content, both for the judgment which had brought her to where she lay and the skill with which she had handled a position which had been novel to her, so that the highest stake for which she could play might still be within her grasp. She had come to a rich market, where the prospects of barter grew better with every day.

Now she listened to Francisco's account of how he had shattered the Turkish boats, and she thought him one who might rise high in the turbulent world she knew. She did not think of it as much more than a fortunate chance (as it was), though the idea of the longer guns had been his, with a boy's desire to make the most of his own command. Actually, he seemed to her, at this moment of conscious triumph, younger, less mature, than she had seen him before, as the excitement of the deed broke through the reserves which were born of shyness and pride, and had been augmented by the restraints which he practised toward herself.

For the moment, it even caused him to forget La Cerda's visit, and that which must shortly be asked of her.

Venetia, surveying the world around her with cool and accurate eyes, did not regard him as a genius of battle, but as a gallant and very fortunate boy, which it was much better to be. For fortune, in her world, was a very tangible thing.

It would have been absurd to compare him, in military experience, in political knowledge, in a score of various abilities, with La Cerda, who had the name of one of the most capable men of his troubled times. But what was the use of that, if it had not kept him from the Grand Master's disgrace, from the peril of St. Elmo's massacre? He was one to whom fortune showed a frown which seemed unlikely to change. . . . And Venetia meant that Francisco should give her more than it could ever be in the power of La Cerda to do.

Her first thought had been no more than to change protectors, when it had seemed that La Cerda's star had been near to set; and had he been later by half an hour when he came on Francisco and her in Angelico's room, she might have put the virtue of the younger man to a test which it would not easily have sustained. But after that she had changed to a bolder dream. To be Francisco's mistress might be pleasant enough, but it would be better to be his wife.

There was nothing in the fact of her known position as the *amie* of a monkish prince to prevent such a marriage, either in civil or ecclesiastical law, or in the social customs that ruled the time. There was more obstacle in the gutter from which she came, but even that was no more than had been overcome by other women who were among the highest in Europe then. Indeed, her position as La Cerda's mistress might be held as evidence that it had already suffered its first defeat. By the code of that day, it was demonstration that she could not be entirely unfitted to become one of the most honoured ladies of Spain. Still—she had far to go, and some high barriers to be overcome.

She did not doubt that she had shown wisdom in her restraint, though she chafed at times that she must not follow her body's will. To be wanton to this proud and very innocent boy (who was nearly of her own years, but was child to her) would have been pleasant enough, and would have held him by a strong cord, but she had resolved that she would be a madonna instead, and was shrewd enough to see that she took a way that held him more strongly still.

So she endured the confinement of the small chamber of stone, coming out only at night, as her safety required, feeling that she had found a safe lair at a very difficult need, and that she was not wasting her time.

None would disturb her there: the discipline was too strict: the movements of the men too straitly controlled. The turn in the stone entrance, which was in lieu of a door, and was intended to secure the occupant from the danger of shot, or flying fragments of stone, was as absolute as a concealment could be, unless one of the men should step in, and look round into his captain's retreat; and who would venture to leave his post for such a purpose as that?

Even so, he might have been silenced or cajoled, either by bribe or threat; but, in fact, none looked, and none but Captain Antonio, who had an adjoining retreat, had suspicion, until she had become careless, and stood revealed to a sudden moon, of which she was still unaware. A few yards from the movements of men, she had been as secure as though separated by dividing miles.

She had used the exigencies of that narrow space, into which Francisco must frequently come, and where he must sleep and dress, with a discreet skill, which would have been beyond the resource of one less experienced in the world's ways, and in the habits and dispositions of men.

He had given up his chamber within the castle, under pretext that he would not leave the battery now that St. Angelo was so closely besieged, but with the further reason that he must be constantly there to secure the privacy for his own cell that it had become vital to have. He must make it his in fact, as well as in name, that the intrusion of others might not be risked.

In this intimacy, she had been careful to maintain a physical distance, a discreet modesty, such as would hold his respect: she had made pretence that she trusted his chivalry as sufficient shield for one who was La Cerda's mistress, not his.

But having established this distance first, she had proceeded to allure him with every weapon she had, either of beauty or wit, as though seeming unconscious of what she did; doing no more in this than to secure redundant victories in a strife she had already won. And gradually, as the days passed, she had hinted in casual ways that she was in no haste to return to La Cerda's arms. Was it wonder if he dreamed, though with slender hope, of a time when she might come to his in a woman's way? That she was seldom out of his waking thoughts? That in his heart he cursed the way that she had come to his power, so that he supposed he could not press her to love without his own honour's loss, unless they should come to a freer time? Understanding which, Venetia smiled in the dark, and was well content. . . .

Now, after she had lain on her couch in that narrow place, listening to the confused uproar that told of the Turkish storm, and then to the crashing discharge of culverins that were not many yards from her own head, Francisco had come to tell her of the effect with which he had been able to use his guns.

"It will be," she said, "a most high honour for you; for which the Order should give you thanks in a public way."

"They will not do that," Francisco replied, being a better prophet than she on that point. "It is not their way. Nor have I done more than to take a chance that came to my hands, and I could not miss. I have done nothing, beyond that I changed the sakers for guns of a better length that were idle in my own ship, it being moored to the inner quay. After that, the praise is for them who laid them well, that they did not miss."

"But that," she said, "even though it were fairly said, is not how honour is paid. It is he who succeeds, from whatever cause, and he who is first in command on the winning day who will take reward.

They would make you Commander, I well suppose, for this and your Uncle's name. But you do not think to take the oath of a Maltese knight?"

There was something more than a casual curiosity in the way in which this question was put, something of the tone of one who has a personal stake at issue on the reply, of which he could not fail to become aware, as she may have meant.

"I have not thought much of that," he replied; "it was my uncle's design, which, had he lived, he would have urged me to do. It is a high honour, and so esteemed in all Christian lands. But I like not the monkish vows."

"The vows," she said, "are not such as can be praised by a woman's lips, be they evil or good. Nor am I likely to love that which has chased me here.

"And the Grand Master," she went on, feeling it to be a discourse that the text required, "may not show his full wisdom in this, that he holds that we who have the high honour to be the consolation of Knights of God, are in ourselves of less honour than ladies should like to be; which is because, as I suppose, if he had his way, they would have no consolation at all, which may be more than men of a living blood will consent to endure.

"But he would see, if his harshness of hate did not cast a scarf round his reason's eyes, that if we be faithful to whom we love, though we be not held in the Church's bond, our honour must stand with those who may be wed in a colder way."

She spoke what she had thought out before, as having a good sound for Francisco's ears, but she was not unaware that it had more than one edge, coming from the lips of her who had little will to be true to La Cerda now. She had a sound instinct that, though she might be legally free to wed, she would have a better chance to win Francisco to that end if La Cerda were not alive. Why would he not die, where so many did? Even St. Elmo had not been able to bring him to that!

Her words brought La Cerda to Francisco's mind in another way, which was as unwelcome to him.

"The Chevalier La Cerda was here to-day," he said, "enquiring for you."

"Leon here!" she exclaimed. "You told him naught? He does not know where I hide?"

Her voice was sharp with a sudden dread, which confirmed the doubt he had felt before as to what she would wish him to do, and gave him a satisfaction therefrom which it would have pleased her to know. But she had little pleasure in his reply, though he could deny that he had done that which was her first fear.

"I said I could tell him naught, unless I have warrant from you."

She saw some implications of that which she did not like.

"Then he must know I am here?"

"He knows less than that. He will conclude that I can see you within the day. That I could not avoid."

Could not avoid! She thought things which it would have been foolish to say. She grew very still, as she would when danger was near. Her face ceased to reveal her thoughts.

As she was not quick to speak, he went on: "I have his promise that he will not make revelation of aught to which you do not consent; and even then it shall be in such form that there will be nothing said of how I have held you here."

"And how," she asked, with some reason behind her scorn, "did he think to contrive that? We are to plead mercy of most pitiless men, and I with my hands red with the blood of death, and we are to elect what we will say, or where we will remain still. It would be to ask for the rack in an urgent voice!"

"I know not what he may have in mind," Francisco replied, feeling that he faced a blame which should not be his, "but he would have it that I presumed too far in that which was his matter and yours, and on which he would let me know that you would come to easy accord if I let you meet. . . . But that his arm is not healed, and that I did not know what you would wish, it had been likely to come to steel, as it did when we met before."

"When will he be next here?"

"At to-morrow noon."

"I will tell you before then what you shall say. We will leave it now. . . . But I have been sheltered here while the storm goes by, and to venture out, when there is no evident need——!"

Francisco felt with her in that. For her to go would be as though the sun should have left the sky; and he could not think either that La Cerda would find her a surer retreat, or that she could now be disclosed without more trouble than it would be easy to overcome. Why must the man come with a bandaged arm? He should have been met with denial of all reply but a dagger's point, and if swords and daggers had soon been bare—well, there might have been some comfort in that!

Even the great deed he had done had come to seem no more than a little thing, nor was he urgent to know whether, in that noise of strife that still thundered to south and east, the Sanglea endured or was overrun. War and love battled for his regard, and he was most aware of the tyranny of a woman's eyes, which might be withdrawn after they had lately softened to him.

He went out to where Antonio watched by the waiting guns that would not be loosed on another prey, or at least not for that time.

CHAPTER VIII

Mustapha, having resolved to attack the Sanglea with all the force that he had, had given Hassan sole command of the operations thereagainst, both by water and land. He had done this because Hassan had come with a crescent fame: he had the vigour of youth: he had the confident manner of those who are sufficient for the crises of life: and his name was one to give valour to doubtful men.

It was also to be weighed that he had had no share in St. Elmo's siege, and its abortive assaults, which had brought no glory to Turkish arms, but only reaped with a hungry sickle the lives of men. He came freshly upon the scene, with an unsullied prestige.

But Mustapha, who resolved all in a subtle mind, had a motive beyond these. The losses of the regular army of the Turks, of the famous regiments of spahis and janissaries whose horsehair standards had been the terror of the Balkan battlefields for the half-century that had seen the Cross go down, and the rise of the Crescent Moon, had suffered losses since they had been landed in Malta two months before, of which he had dreaded to make report.

He knew that Soliman would hear more lightly of the loss of every man that Dragut brought to the war than that one of his favourite regiments had been destroyed. And Dragut had stubbornly and perversely regarded matters in a quite opposite light. If Piali would attack too soon, he had said more than once, it should be Turkish lives that should be exposed to the Christian fire. He preferred that his pirates should live to another day.

Mustapha considered the new levies that Hassan had brought, and he thought that it would be an excellent thing that they should advance on the Sanglea redoubts, and be shot down by St. Michael's guns. But he saw that Hassan might be of Dragut's mind, rather than his, on this point. To ensure that he should not refuse his own troops, there could be no better way than to give him command of the whole operation, to which, indeed, Hassan made no demur.

He agreed to conduct the attack on the Sanglea, and that his own corsairs should lead the assault on the inland side. Mustapha made his mistake when he loaded the boats with the very flower of the Turkish ranks. He had been subtle in that too, not doubting that they would land, and at a time when the Christian strength would have been largely engaged (if not spent) in resisting Hassan's attack, so that the honour of success might be lightly theirs, as he would prefer it to be.

Hassan made no more objection to that. With a seaman's eye, he may have judged the risk of the water attack to be greater than it appeared to one who was more familiar with operations on solid ground. He said that his own lieutenant, Candelissa, should command the boats, for which he was as good a man as could have been found. So it is said that he did. But as he was alive on the next day, we must suppose that he was in the one boat that was left unsunk, or that he found some pretext to stay ashore.

When Piali sulked that the command was not to be his, as Mustapha had expected him to do, he was appeased with words adroit in a falsehood which could not be seen, if at all, till a later day: "This is not for you, whether it may fail or succeed. For, if it fail, it will remain yours to succeed at a better time. And should it succeed is there not St. Angelo standing beyond? It will be your turn for the greater deed."

But in his heart Mustapha resolved that there should be no other name than his own to be linked with that last assault, when the eight-pointed cross should be trampled down from its last footing on Malta's rocks, as he had served it in the fertile garden of Rhodes, forty years before. . . .

Hassan looked with cool and confident eyes on a chaos of strife and blood that spread far around the bastioned trenches of the Sanglea, and from which a confused and dreadful noise rose into the tortured air.

The Christians fought well. So he had expected that they would do. The losses of his own troops must be rising to a high tale. He had expected no less. He knew (as De Broglio said before) that a fosse will feed on the lives of men. But he knew, beyond that, that the cost of failure, at the last count, is always heavier than that which success will ask. He did not intend to fail. He loved the war of the sea better than these bloody scuffles upon the shore, but, if he undertook to storm the Sanglea, he meant that it should be done.

When they brought him the tale (which he had partly seen from afar) of the dreadful loss of the boats, he could afford to take it without despair, seeing how sorely he pressed the Christian lines by that time. He may even have thought: "Well, it is Tripoli will have honour here," with a content that he must not show.

He looked at the Christian ramparts, against which his legions rose like a storming sea. Knightly pennons whcih had flaunted at dawn were no longer there. They were in his own camp, the raped spoil of waves of attack which had risen over the wall. These had been thrown back, but they rose again, and he watched for a higher wave to advance at last which would rise, and rise—and go on.

They who fought to retain the low long ramparts of the Sanglea were not in danger alone from those who made its assault; they were exposed to a pitiless, ceaseless fire from a surrounding circle of foes, who were in number as six to one. They must show themselves to a hail of death, or, if they crouched low, it would be to see the gleam of scimitars rising over the wall.

Hassan said: "It is time to bring this to a right end." He planned well. He saw that the most part of the defenders had been drawn to the eastward ramparts that faced the land, which it was his effort to take by storm. He judged that there would be few left to protect those that faced the inlet, between the land and the fort of St. Michael at the end of the spur. He ordered that the cannon that had bombarded the Sanglea over the narrow inlet, shattering the palisade which ran the length of the middle creek, should prepare to augment their fire. He chose men of good courage, used to water, and to taking ships by the board. He ordered that they should be led by those who knew where the shallow inlet could be waded, leaving their shoulders bare at the deepest parts. The shorter men were to fall out of the ranks at their own choice, should they be unable to swim.

When he had launched these attacks, which he did not expect to succeed, he supposed that they would draw off many of those who were now on his own front, who were few and weary enough as they then were, and so the time would come for the last assault, by which he was resolved to prevail.

He marshalled his best troops, which he had held back till that time, and rode along the front of the fierce turbaned ranks, pointing with his scimitar to the ramparts that had so far endured, but which he thought to be near their fall.

"Sons of the Prophet," he cried, "I point the way of honour and safety alike, for if you allow yourselves to be thrown back now, as you need not be, you must charge again, at a further cost, till that wall is won. The Christian dogs are weary and few. Forward, my children, in Allah's name, and the town is yours."

The fierce dark fanatic faces, lifted to his, burst into a wild barbaric cry, as of a beast that has scented prey. With shouts of God's and the Prophet's names, with clash of cymbals and throbbing of urgent drums, they surged forward to the attack.

The Christians met them with a fire that strewed the ground with the best and bravest who led the charge, but it was one that would not falter nor pause. Gapped and thinned as they were, the ardent ranks swept on, and over the wall. Sword and scimitar, axe and pike, met in a turmoil of bitter strife, where no thought of mercy would be likely to come. Either side might have their own chivalries for themselves, but in this war they slew dogs, such as could not be too quickly sent to their native hells. He who, for the moment, could not meet with an active foe, would seek the wounded, to make an end with another thrust, knowing that what he did would be pleasing to God, and might cancel a score of sins. But such respites were few. Under the meeting ranks, fosse and wall became a shambles of blood and the trampled dead.

Hassan had not led the charge, which it was not his business to do. But he rode forward, urging the rearward rank in support, and reined his horse so close to the fosse's edge that he could observe how each man played his part for honour or blame, which he would not forget to give.

There was, in fact, little danger in what he did, for the discharge of fire-arms had almost ceased on both sides, now that they were locked in so close a broil that no shot could have been aimed at a foe which would not have been as likely to find its rest in a friend's back. He sat there as separate and secure as one who looks on at a show.

As he looked, his face took on a stern satisfied smile, for he saw that his corsairs' fury was not in vain. Inch by inch, they won footing upon the wall.

But the Christian knights, though driven back for some space, were of no disposition to fly. They fought on in a stubborn way, and others came running to their support. The strife swayed backward again. Hassan's face changed. He shouted encouragement to men who were unable to hear: who were most concerned with their own lives, as they struggled to hold their ground, drenched, as they mostly were, either with their own or another's blood.

He saw that it was one of those moments when the issue quivers between victory and defeat, and may be turned by a shout, or a single blow. He rode his horse back for a few yards, and then forward toward the ditch, which he took with a flying leap.

The splendid barb that he rode came down on the curtain's edge as surely as a swallow alights, but the next moment it rolled screaming upon the ground, its belly pierced by a Christian lance. Hassan avoided it as it fell. His scimitar came down in a flashing death upon a man whose lance could not be recovered in time to protect his head. He shouted a war-cry that rose over the clamour of meeting steel and the voices of frenzied men, and his name echoed an inspiration along the strife. The Moorish line was swaying forward again.

La Cerda had been among those who had run to the support of that perilled front. He had been sent, on Del Monte's order, with other knights from a quieter place. They came fresh of vigour and heart among wearied and wounded men. For a moment they had sustained the defence, until Hassan had leapt the fosse. A short distance behind, Del Monte himself, with all the men he could spare from St. Michael's fort, was hurrying to the threatened line.

Hassan saw a knight who was not easy to miss. He showed some freshness of silk, and of polished steel, among those whose armour was soiled and dimmed. He stood firm also, among men who gave ground, who flinched somewhat away. He bore no shield, but had his sword in a single hand, his left arm bandaged against his side.

Hassan's scimitar, keen and curved, cut the air as it threatened the head of the Christian knight, and was parried well. Hassan had a small round buckler on his left arm, to take the point of the straighter sword which was the weapon of Western lands. So it must do now. The two warriors found themselves engaged in one of those duels which were common in the hand-to-hand strife of that day, from which others might stand aside. The difference of weapons and styles of fence made attack more dangerous than defence was sure, and such combats were quickly done.

Hassan gave the first wound. Aiming at the weakest approach, he slashed at La Cerda's left, so that the scimitar's keen thin point cut down the length of the upper arm to such depth that the blood spouted high from the wound. Seeing that he could not endure with that hurt, La Cerda staked all on a downward blow that the Moor was too late to turn. He wore a turban lined with Damascus steel, which was well for him. The fine metal was furrowed deeply, but not cut through. Hassan stumbled forward, and fell at La Cerda's feet.

The fierce hostile crowds that had paused a moment to watch the bout closed in an instant rush to rescue or make an end. Behind them, Del Monte, with a score of knights at his side, charged forward in a rush that regained the wall. The corsairs perished or fled, their inspiration ended with Hassan's fall, but not till they had borne him safely away. In another hour, he was again in control, with no more hurt than a bruised head, and a turban to be repaired.

But Del Monte had bent his knee by a dying man. The arm might have been staunched, and would have proved less than a fatal wound, but La Cerda had taken another thrust from a nameless hand.

Del Monte heard talk that La Cerda had cut down the Moorish leader, so that it was likely that he was dead. It was certain that his valour, and Hassan's fall had held back the tide of attack, giving Del Monte time to arrive.

He would have shriven him, seeing him to be close to death. "You have done well," he said, "for the Cross of Christ, and if you are sped now, as you must know that you are, it is such a death as must give pleasure to God. Have you aught you would now confess? Have you worldly charge that I can make mine, to secure your peace?"

La Cerda spoke from a fluctuant mind, and his voice was low.

"I would have your word," he said, "—for the Commanders will listen to you when the Council meets—I would have your word that he shall do me no further despite."

"If I understand what you mean," Del Monte replied, "as I will not pretend in another way, it is that which is lightly sworn, for the Grand Master will give you honour for what you have done this day, as it is his nature to do."

"I will take your oath," La Cerda replied to that, "though as to what the Grand Master would be likely to do, I should say you misdeem, for he has a venom which will not stay at the gates of death. . . . But I will die content that I have your oath that he shall do me no more despite, either against her, or him who has sheltered her from his bitter hate."

The words were slow and faint, so that Del Monte must bend to hear. As he caught them, he was perplexed with a doubt that he had been taken to swear something more and different from that which he had supposed to be in La Cerda's mind.

So he would have said, or at least that he must be better informed on that which he was expected to do, but he saw that he spoke, if not to a dead man, to one who had become deaf to all earthly words.

"It is the death," he said, "of a good and most misfortunate knight." He made the sign over his breast which the devils fear, and turned to order a strife which was not yet done, though its issue was no longer in doubt.

CHAPTER IX

"He shall be buried," the Grand Master said, "with all the honour his deeds deserve, for it was a most valorous act to so stand his ground when the line sagged, and against one of Hassan's repute, he having, as we may say, but one arm.

"I have a confident hope that God allowed him thus to assoil his soul, putting aside the feeble counsel he gave before, which came, as I suppose, from the lecherous life which he then led, by which devils had entrance to whisper behind his ear. But we may hope that he had also renounced that lechery from his soul, its cause having been vanished away."

He said this in Sir Oliver's room, Del Monte also being there. He was exultant at the great success of the last day, for if they had to provide for the burial of two hundred who had been slain, including such knights as it was pity to lose, yet the attack had been thrown back upon every side, and with such loss that the Turks might not be over-quick to attempt it a second time. It was talked that, including those who had been drowned from the boats, their loss was not far short of four thousand men, which may be hard to believe; but if we suppose it to include such as would soon be healed for another bout, we may say that it is no more than may be the lot of those who set flesh against stubborn stone, if it be defended well from above.

The Grand Master spoke less as one expecting reply, than as giving judgment over the dead, but Del Monte was a man of plain words, though not contentious of mood, and he would make it clear that he did not agree.

"You are right," he said, "as to half, and perhaps more. But as to St. Elmo, and the counsel he gave, I would advise, if you will not take it amiss, that there should be no such words over his tomb, if you should have occasion to speak in a public way when our brothers are laid to rest. For there are many who hold that he said no more than a good knight should, giving honest counsel of war; and he has shown by his end that he did not speak from any faintness of heart, as was said by some at that time.

"And as to putting lechery from his soul, it is between God and him now, and there is no need to say more; except only this, that as he died he made his appeal to me, that I should speak on his part, if you should seek to do him further despite.

"That I said you would never practise to do, and so I lightly swore that I would take his part in such case; but if I should prove to be in error in that, then, by the high Passion of God, I will not be dumb.

"Yet I will say that at the time I swore I did not clearly perceive (hearing but the faint words of a dying man) that his thoughts were on her whom you supposed he had put aside, his petition being made for the wanton who fled away, and for one (as I understood) who had sheltered her from the law's pursuit."

The Grand Master listened to this with a look in which resentment followed surprise, but he controlled himself as a smaller man would have been less able to do.

"Del Monte," he said, "we will have no quarrel for this, and on a day when Heaven's mercy has blessed our arms. La Cerda's soul is with God, and its judgment His, and we have our own, which are still to save. But having sworn such an oath to maintain his part, I will say that you have spoken knightly and well, though it may have been little honour to me. Nor would I be wroth at honest words which are spoken for me to hear, knowing that worse are said when I am further away, by those who are worthy of less esteem. . . . And as to the wanton who could so corrupt the soul of a knight of God, I will go so far as to hope she may not be found. But if she be, I will do justice without reprieve, thinking only of the high office I hold, and neither to favour the living, nor to heed the pleas of the dead."

Having said this, he went out, being more deeply moved even than his words showed, for he thought at times that he was hated by all, and was less than sure that he had such support of God as should make him deaf to the contemning voices of men.

Sir Oliver looked after him, and spoke with a friend's voice.

"I would that he were not so deeply stirred as he often is, for he is not young" (La Valette was sixty-eight at this time), "and he spends his strength in too free a way. He is wrong at times, as we may be tempted to think, but I suppose that he was sent by God to support this hour, and he lives for Malta alone."

"You are his good friend," Del Monte replied, "and have spoken nothing to which I do not agree. . . . I will tell you this, that I was, as it were, trapped to the oath I gave, from which I cannot think that I am therefore absolved, for I do not conclude that La Cerda meant to trap me at all. But he thought of a woman he loved, as a man will at the gates of death, and St. Elmo was in my mind."

"So I have no doubt that it was; yet, if you will heed my guess, the woman of whom you speak, as she is not one to deserve a love of a constant kind, so she did not have it from him. It was pride that stirred, rather than love, in a dying man. It was, in your own word, which I take for his, that the Grand Master should not do him further despite."

Del Monte did not dispute that. He said: "Well, there was one hope the Grand Master had, with which we may both accord. It will be well that she be not found."

It was at this time that Francisco was with Venetia in his rock-hewn cell, and they talked of La Cerda's death. It was a joy to her which she knew she must not show. She had contrived a tear, which may have been slower to fall, knowing that there were no more of its kind to come.

Francisco sat by her couch, and a soft hand fell on his wrist, as though by an idle chance, and was not taken away.

"I cannot grieve," she said, "as I should, having been so friended by you."

Francisco kissed her hand for so kind a word.

His fingers moved on her arm, and were sharply withdrawn, for he had thrilled to a sudden passion at which he feared, lest his knighthood be brought to shame. Yet La Cerda's death had been joy to him, with the birth of a better hope than he had been able to feel before. It was a hope he could not obtrude in this moment of natural grief. . . . But at a near day. . . . When this siege would be done, as it soon might (how many more boats must be first sunk? What a slaughter it must have been to a nearer view!) and when people would come and go in a free way, so that she could be removed without fear—or perhaps sooner than that—he had eager, impatient dreams, over which honour shone, an unclouded star. . . .

An hour later, when they were talking still, between silences which were more pregnant than words, he was roused by Captain Antonio's voice. He stood discreetly without. He said: "Captain, the Grand Master is nearly here. I suppose I am not to hold him at bay?"

Francisco went out with an elation that he found hard to conceal beneath the cloaks of shyness and pride, for he knew that the Grand Master must be coming to inspect the battery which had worked such havoc the day before, and perhaps to give him some tangible honour, or more certain praise for the part which he had been able to play.

He did not meet the Grand Master alone, for Sir Oliver Starkey was there; and three other Commanders of the Order; and a file behind of the gay-uniformed Castle Guards showed that the visit was of an official sort. There was one other that Francisco had not expected to see, for Sir Oliver brought Angelica at his side.

"You shall come," he said; "for it must be pleasure to hear that your cousin will have a merited praise, and to him alike to know that you hear it said."

Angelica would have preferred to have kept away, but she had been alert that Sir Oliver should have no guess that Francisco and she were estranged, lest he should guess further toward the cause, and the same caution had kept her dumb now, being unable to think of a plausible pretext that she would not be glad to be there.

The Grand Master was generous in his praise, and particular in the inspection he made. He must see not only the *Santa Martha's* guns, by which the boats had been overset, but the ways in which the battery had been made strong, beyond the thought of its first design.

"I had no purpose in this," he was frank to say, "beyond to here establish guns of such range that they would command the boom which they overlook. But you have brought guns of a greater range, and made it an outwork of solid strength, so that both harbour and castle are more secure; and, beyond that, you have been able to strike in a vital way from where they thought we had no such fangs. . . . I marvel that it had not been betrayed before now, for there is little they do not learn."

Francisco must answer that with explanation of the care with which he had chosen those who must handle the battery guns, and the discipline which made spying hard, and the Grand Master approved again.

"You are of your Uncle's blood," he said, "and it is pleasure to know that it does not fail. For it draws the venom of death if we can feel that we live again in those that are of a near blood." He sighed, as he spoke, from a private grief, having had his own son (or nephew as he must be called by the etiquette which the Statute of De L'Isle Adam required, and which he had himself been stern to enforce, since he had come to his present power) killed but a few days before, which may be held to show that he had been less austere in his younger days than he now was; but he said nothing of that.

He asked how the guns with which the battery had been first supplied would be put to use, and gave praise again when he was shown that preparations to mount them at a new angle were well advanced.

"By which time," Sir Oliver said, "I must make allotment of further men for this post. Can you give good shelter to such?"

Francisco said there need be no doubt about that, and the Grand Master, who was ever one to see all, to the last item there was, must inspect the excavations in which men might crouch secure against hostile shot, when they were not working the guns.

Venetia heard the voices without, which approached her cell. She could tell they were looking into that which Captain Antonio had, being next to hers. She was in her bed at this time, being the sole one that the cell held, for Francisco would lie on the floor. There she would be most of these days, having no purpose for which to rise. She had lain as they had talked for the last hour, with Francisco on a stool at her side.

Now she looked round in a sudden fear. Was there no place where she could hide from intruding eyes? She sprang out to the floor. As to clothes, she could have had more on, and not much. She ran round, like a trapped rat, seeking a hole that was not there. She heard Captain Antonio's voice without: "There is naught to be seen here, it is like to mine." She stood in the midst of the floor, not daring to move. Was the danger past?

She heard a more austere voice, being that of the Grand Master, though that was more than she knew. "But the angle should be sharper than that, if it is to keep out a fragment of flying stone. Now you observe here——"

Footsteps approached round the bend.

For once Venetia did not know what to do. She stood still.

The Grand Master stopped, as must those behind, who could see less. He may be excused that there was a moment when amazement had made him dumb.

He came from the sun to a cell that was dimly lit, and may have wondered at first if he could be deceived by the sudden gloom. But as his eyes adjusted themselves he became assured that he looked at a woman whose body, supple and young, was reserved from sight by no more than a short shift, and a shawl of price, blue and broidered with gold, that was round her neck as a frame for a pale-gold head.

"Oliver," he said, "what in the fiend's name do we find here?"

The Grand Master did not suppose that Sir Oliver had any special knowledge of this. He simply appealed to him for any information that he required; as it was his habit to do.

Had he not been directly asked, Sir Oliver might have kept still, and the Grand Master discovered no more than that Francisco kept a wanton within his cell. That might have been trouble enough, but it could not have gone deep or far after the service he had just done, for he was not bound by the Order's vows.

But, being so addressed, Sir Oliver made explicit reply: "As I think, it is she who is sought for the steward's death."

"It is shrewdly guessed." The Grand Master had advanced into the cell by this time, and it was half filled by those who crowded behind. He looked round to ask in a sharp voice: "Don Francisco, will you explain?"

Francisco had been at the rear of the group, and, as those of better right followed the Grand Master into the cell, Angelica was left at his side. She knew what was to come some seconds before the Grand Master spoke, for it was what she had been fearing to see. For where else could he have hidden the girl, as she had no doubt he had done?

She had watched Antonio turn La Valette adroitly to his own cell, and then his futile effort to prevent the entrance of that before which they stood. At the moment, all other thoughts were swept back by that of the danger in which Francisco lay.

Standing as though dazed, to await that which he had no power to control, he heard her voice, low and intense, at his side: "Francis, will you not go? There is yet time."

Antonio spoke at his other hand. "There is a boat under the quay, at the hither steps." It was a provision he had made for such a moment as this, though he had said no word of it before.

And it was clearly a chance. There were none around but the Grand Master's Guards, who surely would not oppose his way, and some of his own men. If he could reach the boat, he might row round to some part of the island which was still in Maltese hands. With the help of gold, of which he carried a full pouch. . . . Antonio would have said that a slender chance is much better than none.

There was a moment during which Francisco was unresolved, though it is unlikely that he would have fled, being of too high a pride not to defend that which he had thought fitting to do. But while he paused, he heard Venetia's voice—a cool, insolent voice—and his resolution was made. "I will not leave her," he said, "having done nothing beyond my right."

Venetia had not left it to Francisco to give the Grand Master reply. In that pause of silence she had seen that she was cornered beyond retreat, and her courage rose to the audacity which (as she thought) the occasion required.

"If you will know who I am," she said, "I am here to ask. I am La Cerda's *amie*, as you suppose. I was his who died for your cause in the last day. Would you seek to shame me for that? Is it knightly done, that you do not retire when you see me as I now am?"

Francisco had come forward by this. He faced the Grand Master in the pride of youth and a foolish love, and was neither abashed nor afraid.

"There is not much to explain. I gave shelter to one who came to me in a great need, he who should have been her shield having been jailed for a cause which I do not know. If I may say it with great respect, I am not of the High Order of which you are Head, nor am I under its vows, but I have done in this as my own honour required (or as I so held); and for this you may hold me excused the more if I have been of some service to you, as you have graciously said in the last hour."

The Grand Master heard them both, but did not directly reply. He looked round the narrow cell, and its meaning did not seem doubtful to him, seeing what she had been, and what she was to his own eyes. He saw that the cell had no exit, except that through which they had come. He said to her: "You will have time to be more seemly attired for this hour, and for walking abroad, but you must do it with speed. You are charged with a man's death, and you must first answer to that."

He turned, and those who were there withdrew before him out of the cell, so that Venetia was left alone. He placed two of his guards at the entrance, to make arrest when she should come out. "You will give her," he said, "to the Provost-Marshal's hands, letting her have commerce with none till you have delivered her thus, she being charged with a public crime."

He walked away with no further word till he mounted the castle stairs, letting those follow who would. Then he turned to say: "Oliver, I would be alone. We will talk of this at a later hour."

He saw that he was alone already, except that Sir Oliver had come closely behind, and there were two guards who had followed to the foot of the stair, as their duty was. He went on to his own room, which he still kept for his official affairs, though his lodging was in the town.

CHAPTER X

Angelica, with misery at her cousin's peril warring with other feelings (but with a bright colour in none), lingered at his side, unsure that he wished her there, but reluctant to go. Antonio stood his ground alike, thinking that he saw what must be done, and of a resolute purpose to make it clear.

Francisco stood with no thought now of the flight which Antonio would have urged. His irresolution was of another sort. How could he aid her most? Should he go to her now, to take counsel while there was time? He was unsure whether the guards who stood waiting to make her arrest would regard it as within their duty to bar his way, and he might well hesitate to incur the humiliation of refusal or to attempt a violent entrance.

Antonio, knowing his own mind better than the others knew theirs, was the first to speak.

"If you will take advice from one who has seen more of the ways of men than you have had leisure to do, and can observe where you stand, as has ever seemed to be somewhat beyond your sight, you will use a time which may not be long. You should be away in this hour."

The words brought decision to Francisco's mind, or perhaps rather consciousness of decision already made.

"You may see well," he replied, "with your eyes, but they are not mine. I will neither desert her part at this need, nor will I fly as one pleading a guilt which I do not own. . . . And I may be in less danger than you suppose, for you must see that the Grand Master has passed me by, though he has made her arrest, he being silenced by what I said."

"I have observed you," Antonio answered to that, "to be as guileless as any man I have met, and as no woman could ever be; but, if you can think that, you are more innocent than I had concluded before. He owes you thanks for these guns, and for what they did. He will neither forget that, nor will it turn him aside from the hard methods of war. He will act by the process the law provides, without dally or haste, and if you should use the time to be quickly gone, I would not say that he would be over-much grieved.

But in her case there was process already out, and her arrest is the routine of the law. . . . And he may be the more content that you go, having her safely within the bag. . . . Here is Don Garcio, who was once your friend. He may know more of these matters than we, being in Sir Oliver's grace as few are. You can ask him, if you will, and see whether we do not counsel alike."

Francisco must look at his cousin when this was said, and met troubled eyes.

"Francis," she said, "I would not urge you to flee, if you think it shame, but I am in a great fear. There was proclamation of death against who should do what you cannot deny, and it was said to be without favour to any, of whatever degree. It is time of war, and the Grand Master can be a most hard, though I would not say that he is a pitiless man."

"Be he as hard as he may," Francisco replied, "he has foes enough over the wall, without making others of those who have done such service as I. . . . I would say that it is counsel of cowards, if you will not take it amiss. But we may urge our friends to that which our honour would not allow."

"Then," Antonio replied, "if you call me coward, I will say no more, beyond this. You may go in the next hour, or you will be dead in a week. So in that space you must get all the further honour your life will know."

"That you are wrong in that," Francisco replied, with more confidence than he had spoken before, "I would wager all you could lose, except that, if the loss were mine, I might lack occasion to pay. But, in a word, I will stay here, as my duty is. Only, I will leave you in charge for a short time, for I will see the Provost-Marshal, that she be lodged as her station requires, and have such comforts as gold will buy."

"You may spare your legs," Antonio replied, "for a better cause. For I can tell you that the Provost-Marshal has not so base an apartment to give, but it would be better than was the cellar from which she came."

Angelica did not understand all the implications of this remark, not being aware that Venetia had been born in the next Genoese street to that in which Captain Antonio made his home, but she felt that there was another beside herself who would not have valued Venetia at her own price, at which she was not displeased. She felt also that Francisco was taking the course which honour required, and, if that were so, it must not be her part to turn him aside for any peril it had.

She saw too that dignity and discretion (for even he must see that his friends were few enough now!) might be insufficient to restrain her cousin's resentment at Antonio's contemptuous words, and was the quicker to speak, that she might turn his mind in another way.

"Francis, I would not ask you to play the coward, as I think you know. But will you assent that I see Sir Oliver now, and learn all I can of what the Grand Master will be likely to do? And I will meet you again, and you could then resolve how it may be avoided, or else met."

"Yes," he said, though with less grace than he might, "I will thank you for that, if it can be readily learned, for it will be of avail to know. . . . Can you say a word beyond that, that Venetia be not too straitly confined, she having done that which her honour required, and no more?"

There was a pause during which she was not sure what her answer would be. Venetia's honour? She did not think its requirements could be much, at whatever pass. Much less than even a steward's blood should be spilled to save. Look where she was now! But then she laughed in her sudden way: "Yes. I will say that, if you so desire." She turned abruptly, seeing that Venetia was coming out, whom she was not anxious to meet.

Francisco, when he cast his thoughts in that way at a later hour, was content to feel that the shadow which had lain between his cousin and him was somewhat lifted aside. He associated it vaguely with his having taken Venetia under his protection, which it had been necessary to conceal, even from her. But if she had not known, nor perhaps guessed, till now, could it be that? Then he remembered Angelica's reproach that he had put her in such a position that she had been obliged to appear as his mistress in La Cerda's eyes, lest there should have been more mischief than that. . . . It had been as they came down the stairs that the quarrel had reached its head, though it had been latent before. Its root had lain in his reproaches against herself that she had come in a disguise that he thought shame to the name she bore. . . . Yet he saw that her honour stood, and that she had maintained it somewhat more firmly than he could be said to have done with his to that hour. He saw also that she had shown more loyalty to himself than he had to her (though he would never have loitered to reach her side, had she been in peril that he could aid, as he may have failed to observe), and these were thoughts that he did not like. They abased his pride. He had been grave to rebuke what he thought the unseemly prank that had brought her there, and it was he who was fallen into the pit, while she walked cool and secure.

Yet he was glad to feel that the cloud between them was less, though it had not gone. When he thought of that, he realized, by instinct's rather than logic's aid, that Venetia was the cause, and that she was one whom Angelica was never likely to love. In fact, he must make a choice. Sooner or later, it would come to that, more definitely than now. He did not doubt what the choice would be, for Venetia filled his thoughts, and every passionate hope was centred upon her sharp gay wit, her courageous conduct of life, and the grace of her pale-gold head; but the thought gave him no joy. For, by a paradox which is frequent in the interchanges of human life, as Angelica had become less to him, she had become more. But Venetia was the madonna who filled his dreams.

Turning from these thoughts to his own peril (if such it were), he found that he could face it with less fear than it may have seemed to deserve. Every passion must thrive at the cost of others, which dwindle that it may swell. He thought of what he had done, and could see little to blame, and even less to regret. The Grand Master's proclamation might threaten a felon's fate, but why should such things be proclaimed? Bitter anger and pride strengthened him to fight fear, and to meet any accusation which might be made with a bold front. Had he not sunk the boats which would else have landed those who might have won the centre of the Sanglea, even had St. Michael's fort still flown the eight-pointed cross, which was less than sure? And it had been something more than the competence which every battery commander may be expected to show, that his guns be fired at the best time, and pointed aright. It was through himself alone that there had been guns there of range sufficient to fire across the whole length of the Christian defence on the harbour-front. And his reward was no more than this! He felt that he would not lack words in his own relief, though he was not always known for a fluent tongue. If he had played a boy's part, it seemed that it would be met in a man's way.

He had these thoughts as he walked back from the common jail in the Bourg, where Venetia had been confined. He had found gold to be as potent there as it ever is, whether in palace or slum; though he had paid out less than he would, having had the use of Antonio's wisdom before he went.

For the little captain had not spared his advice, though he thought it to be a fool's errand which Francisco pursued. "You will do less with ten crowns of gold," he had said, "if you pay them down, than if you give one, and show other four which are to be earned in a settled way. But with gold enough that is kept in sight but not pouched, you could put her even to the Grand Master's bed, so that he must sleep on the floor."

Francisco may have gained less for Venetia than for his own peace; for she knew enough of jails on their inner side to have got most that she would, short perhaps of the master-key, but she would have paid in a coin which he would not have been quick to guess; as to which she would have said that it left her as rich as she was before, which we may find to be true enough, if we consider it well.

Francisco was not overlong abroad, but he found that Angelica had come and gone when he got back, having had no more to say than she could ask Antonio to report to him.

CHAPTER XI

"I MUST know," Angelica said, "in what danger my cousin lies, for I can have no peace till I do."

Sir Oliver did not resent the words or manner of this address, which would have been unfitting from whom she pretended to be, and was not much better from whom she was as they both knew, for the sharp anxiety in her tone was easy for him to hear, and his reply was kinder than may be plain in the written word.

"Then you must know something I cannot tell, for there is nothing resolved. But I tell you all that I may when I say that the Grand Master is agreed that he will do nothing alone. There is Council called for the last hour of the day, when the Commanders will consider your cousin's case."

"Then he can be under no restraint till that hour?"

Sir Oliver frowned a little at a question which he thought should not have been asked, and the more so if it were not done in an idle way.

"Why do you ask? It is that which you should be able to resolve in your own mind, without assurance from me."

"I ask because I would have it clear that he will remain of his own will, as having done nothing which should be dispraised in a just mind."

"Can you think that?"

"It is not what I think that can be of any account. It is for him I would speak. He is resolved that he will not go, as he has time to do."

"Can you say where?"

"No. But there are those who could. Of whom he is one."

"You have learnt this from him?"

"There are things I have heard, and I think there are none that I may not say, or at least to you, so that I mention no name but his. He could have gone if he would."

"Well, I will not ask where, which is not easy to see. But I will say that I think him wise. . . . Yet, when I say that, you must not build on it too much, for this is a matter on which I shall have no warrant to deal. It is over me."

"I should be slow to say that. You have a great power."

"You may call it more than it is. And against that which the Council resolve it is nothing at all."

"But you will be there."

"I shall be one among ten or twelve, and there will be some who can speak with more weight than I."

"It is what I will not believe."

"Well, I have said as much as I should. I will not forecast the Council's resolve, nor disclose what my part may be to one who (I suppose) would soon tell it to him. If he remain (as I have said that he should, for it is that, as I think, that his honour needs), he shall have no warrant from me."

"Then I will ask no more at this time, except this, which I have promised to do. Will the woman be so confined that she will have no hardship or shame till her trial come?"

Sir Oliver looked at her with eyes which were less grave than before. "Do you speak as a parrot does, or are you grieving for her?"

"It is a promise I gave. I have said that before. But I will say of myself that I do not think she has done very much wrong; or, at least, it is not for that which she has done wrong that she is pursued, but for that which she would not do, and which she denied (as she must) with a dagger's point. And for one placed as she says she was, I should call it a good way."

"You speak well for one whom I can still see that you do not love. But I will answer you in two words.

"The first is this. She will be fairly tried, and she will be kept in sufficient honour till then (even if she have not had the help of your cousin's gold, which is easy to guess); and this is not an Italian town.

"And the second is this. I know not how the man died, about which it is right, as you must allow, that a proper inquest be made; but the woman is one who will work mischief until she have a knife in her own ribs, for which I should say she is no less fit than you would have me think that the steward was. She will find trouble as a wet sponge gathers the dirt.

"But you shall not say that you have asked a small thing which I would not do. You shall indite a note to the Provost-Marshal from me which I think he will not contemn."

Having obtained all that she could, Angelica went without loss of time to tell Francisco of that, and may have been less than pleased to find that he was away, but she had seen that Captain

Antonio was his friend sufficiently for her to leave a message with him.

"You can tell him," she said, "that the case is one which the Grand Master will not decide on the power he has, as he might do if he were moved by wrathful resolve (for the proclamation, as I understand, gives him power enough, it being a martial time, even to the taking of life), but there will be Council held at the last hour of the day, when there will be debate on what Don Francisco has done. I suppose (though I have no warrant to say) that they will look on the good deed as well as that which they must call by another name, and they should see that the first is of greater weight."

"So it may be that they should," the little Captain agreed, "but do you think that they will? There will be those who will contend that a proclamation so strait and clear cannot be flouted in time of war, lest it be said that there is no rule over those who do well in the field, on which any army would break apart."

"There will be foolish talk," Angelica replied. "That is sure. But we hope that better words will prevail."

"So we will. And so it may be, if you have made Sir Oliver friend."

"He may be of good will. But he says that in this he has little power. We are to build nothing on him."

"Well, I have given my counsel before. I must hope I am shown wrong. . . . Is that all you would have me say?"

"Except that I have obtained that the Provost-Marshal shall have written request that she shall be lodged in a seemly way until the trial is due."

"In a seemly way? I should say that that would not be far from the filth of the middle street."

"That was not what I meant, as I think you know."

"So I do. It is strange how a flower-like face will entrap those who are young, even though it may bring nothing to them."

Angelica laughed at that, though laughter was not near to her heart, for the thought that she had been seduced by Venetia's face to beg a soft lodging for her was a jest which she could not miss.

But when Captain Antonio went on: "Now a score of years will show her better for what she is, so that it will be a book that the young can read," she felt the desire to take the part of one whom she did not love which Sir Oliver had noticed an hour before.

"That," she said, "may be true of all whom God makes, and not only of her. But it may also be that His thought is more surely shown in the freshness of youth than in later years, when the blinds are down, and twilight is on the soul."

"Well," he said, "you take her part, and you may know why, at which I will guess no more."

She thought of why it could be, which had not been clear to herself, and spoke the answer aloud, as she should have been too guarded to do: "It is, as I suppose, that we are caught alike in a world of men." But her voice fell on the last word, as she became sharply aware of the implication of what she said.

She looked at Captain Antonio in a cool way, which it was not easy to do, and found that he was not looking at her. There was a silence the meaning of which was plain for her to guess, but which she was resolved should be broken by him, that she might judge what he knew, and how he would be likely to act thereon.

There came to both their minds (as they could not know, except each for one) a vision of night and a sloping deck, and of two who met in the light of a lantern that hung aloft. The salt water dripped from her doublet's folds: there was a cold wind at her back: and overhead were a few stars.

Then he spoke, and still without looking her way: "It is the gain of those who will wander much that they see things that are strange to tell, or which some would doubt, though they might be sworn in the Virgin's name. And we must see things at times that we do not speak at a later hour."

She considered this, and it was of her nature to take his word in the best way.

"It is knightly said," she replied, "as I should have thought that you would," at which he was well pleased, having some vanity of his own, which was not willing to think himself less than were those of a knight's degree, though he knew that most men would give him a smaller sum.

She went away with the assurance that what she had been careless to show would not be published abroad, and she left a much-puzzled man.

"We see much," he reflected, meaning they who wander on the face of the world, "but the enigmas are hard to rede."

He thought of her as he had seen her first, and of what she had done since to his own sight, and of the position she had come to hold, which was plain to all, at Sir Oliver's side, as one to whom he gave trust, and whom he would yet send on missions from which she might not return.

Why had she come to this peril in such a dress? What was the place she now held, either as woman or man? Was her sex known, and if so to how many, and who were they? What had she been to Don Francisco, or was she now? He had come on a strange vision of life, and its focus was changed by a word, but it was still blurred.

"And why," he thought, "she should be friend to that slut, I see less than before. Is it for the reason she gave? That they are two women snared in a world of men?" Well, so he must think, if it could be solved in no better way. But Angelica did not walk as one snared, but rather, though in a quiet style, as one cool and serene. And though Venetia might be closed in a world of men, he did not think it to be of that she would make complaint, but rather that they were not of a more infidel blood when they looked her way.

CHAPTER XII

THE High Council of the Commanders of the Order of the Knights of St. John met in a formal style, as they had done when they had debated St. Elmo's fate, in the same hall, that was rich and high and of noble size, and furnished in the latest Italian style, so that a synod of cardinals would not have called it a mean place in which to debate the mysteries of the Faith, or the chastising of rebel lands.

But the Grand Master, looking round, thought not of grandeur or pride, seeing the empty places of those who had been there but a month before.

Where was Miranda now? De Broglio? D'Egueras? Medrano? Montserrat? Where a dozen more who had died on St. Elmo's walls? Where Zanoguerra, who had commanded the water-front of the Sanglea, and died at the moment when he had flung backward the last attack? Where La Cerda, the one man who had dared to assert opinion against his own? They were surely with God, having shed their blood to His and the Order's praise, and in the cause of all Christian lands. He did not doubt nor regret, but he saw how high St. Elmo's cost had been in his greatest names.

As to those who had fallen in the storming attack of the last day, he had made oration that afternoon over their flag-draped biers, and among them La Cerda's had not been the least of honour, as he had told himself in a stubborn but honest mind, and with the consciousness that we are all but a poor dust before the Infinite God, which must be felt by all Christian men, as they bend over the dead. . . .

There were others absent besides the dead—knights who excused themselves for weariness or for wounds, or that they must stand to a threatened post; and those who came, being a poor dozen at best, had the look of men who would have welcomed rest more than debate. Yet they had the aspect of stern and resolute men, with will and strength to endure, though the youth of most was a past day.

"Brothers," the Grand Master said, having made but a short prayer, as the time required, "I have called you here for a simple cause, and one, I hope, which may be quickly resolved.

"It is known to all, for it was debated before, that the Chevalier

La Cerda brought to this place, in contempt of his own vows and to the scandal of Christian faith, a certain woman whom he had hidden away in his hired house when he was appointed to St. Elmo's defence.

"This woman, as was likely to be, became a fountain of lust and crime, so that a man was soon slain by her hand, and she fled, to make mischief in new resorts.

"I desire to say little of her, she being now laid by the heels, that she may be justly tried, as our custom is: nor would I have mentioned the Chevalier La Cerda as so debased, he being now dead in a better way, except that the tree which springs from this seed of hell has fruited again, with an evil which is not easy to mend.

"When this woman fled, there was proclamation made, by our common resolve, that none should give her cover to cheat the law, except at the pain of his own life, which should be forfeit therefor, and this alike were he high or low, with lack of favour to all.

"Now it was laid bare to my own eyes, and to others who are now here, that she was so hidden away by one who would not have been soon suspect, he being younger than most, of good name and blood, and being free from the lewd report to which some of our youth will fall when they are not under the Order's vows. I mean, as you mostly know, the youth, Don Francisco, who is nephew to our late brother, the Commander Don Manuel, who so lately died.

"Don Manuel was my friend for fifty years, or but little less to the time he died, and he served our Order as few, under the favour of God, have been permitted to do. Don Francisco alike, seeming to be of his uncle's complexion in this, has done good service to Malta's cause, it being due to him, both in design and control, that the boats of the Turks were sunk, with a loss to them which I need not say.

"That is a matter for which we might give reward with a free hand, either of gold (but that would be naught to him for he does not lack) or in honour that he might put at a higher price; but how can we reward one whom we must apprehend, and put to a quick death, or have it said that we deal justice with partial scales?"

Having put the issue thus, the Grand Master sat down without suggesting a decision he would prefer. He let others speak, which all were not ready to do.

Del Monte sat silently await, conceiving that he was bound by his oath, not as having opinion himself, but as one holding a brief to speak the mind of a dead man, as he must suppose that he would have wished him to do. He waited to hear others first, that he might know what it might be necessary for him to say.

A Commander with a narrow ascetic face, and bright, piercing eyes under penthouse brows, whose name may be left aside, was the first to speak: "There is no choice that I see, but the law must perform its part. For we must observe that this was not an outrage of sudden blood, but that Don Francisco has defied both the law and the special proclamation we made, in a mood of sustained contempt, which is too much to condone in a time of war, when discipline must not fail."

His words were followed by comment of sundry sorts, showing that the Commanders might not be lightly agreed.

For one said: "Yet it was a fault of youth, and of the hot blood that pertains thereto. I say it should not be too hardly judged, he having done the great service he has."

And another: "It is matter to mourn, as is all weakness and sin. . . . It should be most straitly proved that she was hidden of his device, and not secretly there. Yet must the law stand at the last, if it be so sustained. We must pluck forth the offending eye, though the flesh shrink in its human way."

And a third: "It may be observed that Don Francisco is not sworn to the Order's rule, either as serving-brother or knight, and his fault is the less for that."

To which another rejoined: "But that is not the issue with which we deal. He is not charged that he has made lecherous use of the quarters where he is placed, but that he has hidden one whom the law required."

And a fifth agreed: "It was a risk he took, having been warned in a plain way. What can he object, being caught?"

But after that there was a voice of dissent: "It is the temptress who should feel stripes, rather than those whom she brings to sin, and that the more when they are knights who will give their blood for our cause."

And the seventh voice was that of one who agreed: "May we not say that it is shed too greatly by heathen hands for us to spill at this time? That it can be spent in a better way, as such knights are not unwilling to do?"

Del Monte felt that he had heard enough to judge what would be best to say, and that it would be wiser to intervene before differences had become too sharply shown for their advocates to accord with a ready will.

"Brothers," he said, "you will bear with me when I say that

I speak for one who would be mostly concerned, but that he is now dead, and it is his dying charge that I give you now. He hewed Hassan down at his life's cost, when he was over the fosse, and if it be said that but for him I should have lost the Sanglea (excepting only St. Michael's fort) I would call it less than a lie. That being so, I am the more bold to ask you to hear me now.

"As to the woman, she must be tried, as we may lightly agree, and I suppose that La Cerda himself would not have cavilled at that."

"I can tell you," Sir Oliver interposed, "that it was no less than his urgent will that she should be tried, and (as he thought) absolved thereby of the steward's death. . . . And, as I suppose, she would not have fled, but that she was seized with fear when she heard that he was himself held, so that he would not be free to support her part."

"That," Del Monte replied, "was how I thought it to be. And had he not been slain, we may say that she would have come forth by his will, and there had been better end than is threatened now. . . . She must be fairly tried. There is no issue on that. For there must be justice done to the dead, as well as to those who still live, and no less that he who died was suspect, and of mean degree.

"But when we come to the part which Don Francisco has played, of which we know less, as it may have been either at his own will, or as one who would aid a friend——"

"The wanton," the Grand Master said, "was in the single chamber he used. You must face that." He did not speak in a hostile way, but as one sitting above, who would point out that which Del Monte's logic must overcome.

"So I agree," Del Monte replied. "We know not how little it meant, nor how much, and I submit that if we leave it unprobed we may show wisdom in that. . . . But there is one thing you should know, that La Cerda, being at point of death, said that to grieve Don Francisco for this would be equal dispite to him, by which you may say, if no more, that he did not think him to be less than a loyal friend."

"As between themselves," the Grand Master allowed, "it is the best point that you have, and you take it well when you do not urge it too far, for it might break at a higher strain. But this is largely beside the cause which has drawn us here. It is not to La Cerda that Don Francisco must be absolved, nor (as has been said) is he charged with lecherous ways. It is of contempt of law that he stands accused, and can you clear him of that?"

"I do not know that I can. And if he be tried, and let free, or but lightly rebuked, I do not say that respect of law will be fostered thereby.

"I may offer better counsel than that, if I propose that we do nothing at all. For while we do naught, none can tell what is to appear on the next day. And few, if any, will surely know but that we may have witness by which we hold him excused, or even that she was exposed by his own will. There will be sundry tales scattered abroad, and none true; and none will be held by discreet men as more than a likely lie.

"Let us keep this in suspense, and if we drive the Turk from the land at last (to which this is a little thing), then we may review all that Don Francisco has done in another mood, and in the hour of triumph and thanks to God amnesty will seem no more than is timely to give; but if we fail, as we are resolved by the grace of God that we shall not do, then it is all one, and he may better perish by heathen swords than at Christian hands."

There was a voice that asked: "If we accord to that, how will you secure that he will not openly boast that we fear to enforce the law as against himself? From one who has been so hardy in his contempt, it is no less than a likely thing."

"As to that," Sir Oliver said, "I can give some manner of pledge; for I can convey warning to him in a private way, and, if he ignore that, he will not be in the case of a pardoned man, but we can make arrest with a good cause, and his death will be on his own head."

"Is it agreed," the Grand Master asked, "that this matter be put to suspense, to be considered again if the need come, or else not till a further day?"

There were some who murmured assent, and the rest were still. The Grand Master had his way, as he mostly would, whether for mercy or blood, and Del Monte felt that he had got more than he had forecast, and with fewer words, till La Valette addressed him again:

"That this woman be fairly tried, and in accordance with the usage in time of war, there should be one who will put her case, as she can be little fitted to do. Will you take this, as you have so well assumed the part of La Cerda's friend, whose mistress she was?"

There was a short pause, and Del Monte said that he would, though it was plain that he had a poor will. . . .

The Grand Master left the hall leaning on Sir Oliver's arm, as it was becoming his habit to do.

"Oliver," he said, "I may have done well or ill, but I lacked heart to bring one who is near of blood to so old a friend to the shame which would have been surely his, for, if he were found guilty of such a fault, though I might grant reprieve of his life, or even find pretext to set him free, it would be a shame that would mark his life; so that he would be debarred from the companionship of this Order in which his Uncle had more honour than most, and it may be from any high trust or command whether with us, or from the hands of his own King.

"I may grow feeble with age, so that God should cut me off like a rotten branch, as he must at last; but I have a better thought that He will let me endure till the land is free."

"You should take more rest," Sir Oliver replied; "but I say in this that you have done wisely and well."

CHAPTER XIII

"Don Francisco," Sir Oliver said, as one who asks that he already knows; "is not easy to guide?"

"No. He was never that."

"But it may be done best, if at all, by a woman's hand?"

"That is not by me."

"Well, you must choose. For either you must do this, or I will send for him here, and I would prefer to leave it to you."

"Is he to be expelled with his own consent, or to have time to flee in a secret way? He has said that he will not go."

"It is not that. He can stay, or I should say that he must, for he would be shamed to desert, having no cause. All that is required is that he shall be secret as to his having kept Venetia as he did, and that he shall make no boast that the Council do not chastise him therefor."

"There should be few words about that. Is it so condoned?"

"It is less than that. It is in suspense. Yet if his part be observed with care, it is a sword which will not be likely to fall. But you should make it plain that if he fail on his side it will be his death, and there is none who would aid."

"It is more than he could have reason to hope. . . . Can you tell me what they are doing to her? For it is what he will expect me to know."

"She will be tried, as she must; but Del Monte himself will be called her friend."

"We have to thank you for much."

"It is not our rule to speak of what is done when the Council meets, but you must not thank me too far. I did less than I saw done."

"So I must believe, if you say. But I thank you still."

"I may tell you this, that the Grand Master is your cousin's friend, more than you would lightly believe, for he does not forget that he is of Don Manuel's blood. It will be his fault now, if there be more of this either thought or said, for our minds will turn back to the larger things."

"There is her trial to come. He will not forget that."

"That is so. But she is not to be harshly served, beyond what her desert may be shown to be; and I will tell you this for your peace, having watched the world for more years than you have been able to do. When a woman, such as we think her to be, has given all that she can, it is not much, and men will sooner forget than if they had been paid with a grudging hand."

Angelica considered this, but there was no relief in her eyes.

"You think," she said, "that she was mistress to him."

"So I must. I should say that it would be vain to deny, she being caught as she was in their common cell."

"Yet I am not sure."

Sir Oliver considered that she knew her cousin better than he, and he had watched the doings of men enough to know that the obvious is not always true.

He said: "That would be worse."

"So I think."

"Then you shall tell him this. He will be free to attend her trial, or rather that he will be required to be there, though his witness may not be called."

"There is gain in that?"

"Yes. For there will be exposure of what she was."

"He has been told something of that, but he will not hear."

"I would know from whom."

"From Captain Antonio. It is he who——"

"Yes. I know. . . . He may have met her before. He is Genoese. I had not thought of that chance."

"Have I said too much?"

"You have said nothing to vex your peace. But it is my business to know who are here, lest we harbour spies. . . . Captain Antonio may know much. Yet he is a witness we shall not need.

"But you may tell Francisco this, putting it as a warning from me. There will be inquisition made as to who she is, and of what repute before she came to La Cerda's care, and on her answers to that vindication may largely depend. If he would be friendly to her, he should inform himself of these matters by all the means that he may, and counsel her that the truth, though it have some stench, will do her less harm than if she be trapped in a damning lie."

"Can you say how soon the trial will be?"

"It will be publicly held, in three days from now. That is, if Mustapha give us peace, as I think he will, having wounds to lick. So there should be no losing of time by those who would put her case in the best array."

Angelica went to tell Francisco what she had learned, and Sir Oliver turned to matters of more moment than this could be (except to those who were most concerned), until Del Monte came to his room at a later hour.

"Sir John," he said, "has just put that upon me in which I am not skilled, and which is no pleasure to do."

Sir Oliver smiled. "It seemed a right choice, for you would be advocate, as it appeared, whether you were appointed or no."

"You heard the reason of that. . . . I must say that it is a jest for which I do not love him the more. . . . But I am not willing to fail in that which I undertake."

"I am well assured that you will put her defence in the best style."

"So you would say. But I have seen her an hour ago, and I cannot find that she is hotly accused. She has a likely tale, and no other was there, except he whose talking is done. Must not her tale stand? And, if it do, is she not to be acquitted of right, by the laws of our own Order, or by those of Malta, to which she may be more strictly exposed? Or have you more to bring up in a second line when the battle join?"

"I will answer freely on that. I should say that her tale is half false, and perhaps more. But that may be beyond proof, and she may bear it out, if she can tell it in a plausible way, which I should call her practised to do.

"We have no witness, such as you might not suspect, by which we could foil a lie. You can be content about that.

"But you will not be surprised that we shall probe her as to the character that she professes to bear. You should look to that, if you are thinking to bring her clear."

"You mean that you have report against her good name to which she must make reply?"

"We have much."

"It is not of the sort that she was mistress to those whom she could not wed? She is not to be measured by monkish rule?"

"It goes beyond that. We shall say that there is no man with whom she would not have lain for a ducat's pay, though it were one that had been twice clipped by the Jews. That is, if she could not have got more."

Del Monte considered this, and thought he saw a reply.

"You may say that, if you will. You may call it a groat, and I still protest that it should not help you at all; and so, as it has no part in your case, it should not be said."

"If you can argue that, I will listen with care."

"It is simply said. She might have objected for no more cause than that she feared to lose the comforts she had, if La Cerda should suddenly come, and find one in her bed who should not be there. She might have cared no more than that it was not an opportune time, or that she had a pain in her head. Could he therefore rape her of right?

"I should say that it would be strange logic, and a law which we have not heard before now. If you build on that, I should suppose I shall bring her free."

"Well, I shall not be irked if you do."

"But I must still protest that we should not wander so far."

"Which you can put to those who are appointed to judge, but you will find that they will not hear. For it will be a question of how far she should be believed, and when there are questions asked she may be left with no more than a shaken tale. Do you say that we cannot then weigh whom she is who protests that which it has become easy to doubt?"

"That might be; but you go too far, if you so forecast before you arrive. I would still ask that, in this case, we may be content to probe that which has happened in Malta here, to which our laws must apply. . . . I had thought that the Grand Master was of a mind to end this with the least words that are needful to speak."

"I will not dispute about that. I will only say that those who ask overmuch may get less than they had before. . . . But I will be frank to tell you that I have an object in this, for I would show her to Don Francisco for what she is, which he is not anxious to see."

"And if I could take you there by another road?"

"I would be content to arrive, without having chosen the way. . . . But I should still tell you that she must be prepared for inquisition upon herself, which we could not avoid. . . . She must give witness herself, if she is to come clear? You will agree upon that?"

"Yes. She must tell her tale. He having been slain by her bed, and she vanished away, she might be convict if she would not speak. I will allow that."

"And being put upon oath, she must give her name, and whom she professes to be?"

"Yes. That is no more than the common use. It is shortly asked, and soon said."

"And we shall say she is not. We shall give her another name."

"How can you say that, until you have heard what she will swear?"

"I mean, if she say that which La Cerda believed, and which she has told to others, as I can guess."

"And if she give you a true name?"

"She will be well counselled to that. But it is what she will be reluctant to do."

"It is what she will."

"So I supposed, she being guided by you."

"And if she do that . . .? But I will ask no pledge. I will see you again, when I have taken counsel with her. . . . But I will tell you one thing which you might not suppose. . . . She protests that Don Francisco has been no more than La Cerda's friend, and I think in this she spoke with an open mind. You may consider how far it fits the part in which she is dressed by your own reports."

"That may be true, though it will not be lightly believed. But I have been told the same by one who would make a good guess, and the truth is what cannot be known except to the two who were alone in that cell. . . . But if I believe, I should not say she had the more honour, but the more wit."

"Well, I may call Don Francisco's witness on that."

"Which I must hope that you will not do. It would be to stir that which is now still."

"Meaning as against him? Well, I must promise naught. We will talk again."

Del Monte went away with a feeling that he had done more than appeared, for he saw that, if he threatened that he would make Francisco a witness for the defence, he proposed that which Sir Oliver would prefer to avoid. He resolved that he would see Venetia again, for which he must visit the common jail, from which she would not be loosed. But it was not fitting that he should bustle about as though he were a paid tool of the law, and he sent Don Francisco a letter, written in his own hand, proposing that he should come to him, at St. Michael's fort, which he supposed that he would be willing to do.

CHAPTER XIV

ANGELICA did not go to the battery again, which she was reluctant to do. She sent message to Francisco that she could be found at the noon hour at the inn where they met before.

She found him there when she arrived, which she might not have done had she been to her own time, which she had been careful to miss, for she had some pride of her own, though it might not be equal to his, and now that she had found that there was no present danger for him, she had space for thoughts of another kind.

They had come at an hour when there would be few but themselves in the common room, and as he had found a seat in a corner apart, she thought that they would talk there rather than ask for a private place, as though they had secret matters with which to deal.

Before she spoke of the matters of which he had come to hear, she mentioned one which she meant him to know, and which might be overthought if it were left.

"Francis, I should tell you first that Captain Antonio knows what I am."

He frowned at that, as he replied: "Then how many are there who guess now? How did he learn? Is it not what I have always said, that you should not have come?"

"You have said enough. . . . We agree there. . . . Yet that I am here may have been useful to you. At least, it has done you no ill. . . . I was caught by a careless word, such as I should not have said. Did he tell you aught?"

"No. I have not guessed that he knew."

"Then he keeps faith, as I think. I need not trouble for that."

"I would that you could go back, being no more shamed than you now are."

It was a subject which better suited his restless pride than that of which he had come to hear, but it could not be expected that she would look on it in the same way.

"If you call me shamed, it is what no other would do, and it is a word that you should be last to use to one who is so near of your blood, even if you have no care beyond that."

He had the grace to take the rebuke, and to go as near to deny his words as he would be likely to do.

"You took what I said in a wrong way. You have no shame in

yourself, as you could not have; and there should be none to say it aloud while I have a sword which is at your call, as I think you know. . . . You may consider that, if I regarded you no more than as one who chanced to be of a kindred blood, I should not fret that your honour walks on so keen an edge, as you must allow that it does now."

"Well," she said, more mollified by the manner of his reply than she was entirely willing to show, "had I need, I would ask your sword in a quick way, both for a sharp point, and as one that would be bare at the first word, as you need not say. But, till I ask, you may be sure that the need is none."

"It is so I will practise to think. But I suppose that you had other matter in mind when you asked me here."

"I have news, which you may call good, Sir Oliver, as I think, having proved our friend, though he will make little of that. The Council met last night, and debated what you had done, or what else they may have supposed from where Venetia was found——"

"What do you mean when you say that?"

"What I said. It is plain enough. Is it not a matter which all men will judge in the same way?"

"They should consider the urgence with which she fled."

"So they may. Shall we leave that, and come to what they resolved, which it is of more moment to know?"

"I would only say that her honour should not be mired, while she is charged that she was too constant in its defence."

"There is no need to tell me. It will all be said at the right time, for Del Monte will undertake her retort."

"When is the trial to be?"

"In three days, if we are quiet from further attack. But I would tell you first of yourself."

"And I am more anxious for her."

"You will learn all, if you let me speak. As to yourself, the Council agreed after debate that you shall be left clear, if you are silent enough. I suppose that is in reward for the good service you did. Also, the Grand Master proved your friend at the last.

"But it is to be plain, and I am the one that must tell you this, as speaking in Sir Oliver's place, that there is no more than suspense. There is not pardon at all. And the Council will not endure that their forbearance be talked, or that you make boast, as though they threatened that which they dare not do. And if they are stirred to move, it will be in a merciless way, for they consider that what you did cannot be condoned in a time of war; and if you give them such cause, those who had been your friends will not attempt, or will be feeble to aid you more."

"Well, it is what you are charged to say. And there must be those I should thank, as I do you. . . . I will be still from no fear. But it is not my way to go boasting abroad. . . . I am content that I did as I have supposed that a knight should. . . . The Grand Master may see that it was his feud with La Cerda by which she fell."

"So you may think, if you only say it to me; but it may be your death if it enter another ear. Can I avoid dread when you talk in so bold a way?"

"I will be still as a grave. But will you tell me of her?"

"Sir Oliver thinks that the charge against her is not so black in itself but that she should come clear, and that Del Monte is appointed to be her friend may be proof that she is not too hotly pursued. But Sir Oliver was urgent that I should warn you of this, for her own good. Her credit may be straightly arraigned, and when she answers of whom she is, and by what road she arrived, it may break her if she be caught in a wrong word."

"Why should he be doubtful of that? She is not one whose record requires a lie."

"Well, he is. It is a warning well meant, whether it be needed or no. And if you fail to tell it to her, and she stumble when she is asked, you will be the cause of her grief."

"Can I see her again? I was told that there would be much trouble in that, so that even gold might not avail."

"I suppose I could secure that, if I give a good cause. You cannot advise her unless you do."

"I would thank you therefor."

"So you shall. . . . But you would do well for her if you learn what you can first. . . . Captain Antonio knew her before."

"So he will have it to be, but I conclude that he makes a wrong guess. He is Genoese, and it is a town where she never was. He is not her friend."

"But he is yours. . . . If he have the wrong tale, you should not avoid: you should face it, and break it down."

Francisco could not deny that this counsel was good. He said: "If you will contrive that I see her again, I will give her warning of this, of which Del Monte should know. I suppose that she will answer truly when she is charged, and that she will have little to fear, for he will not have her abused."

"If you will meet me here at to-morrow noon, I will bring you an order to see her then, which I am assured that Sir Oliver will not deny."

CHAPTER XV

Francisco did as he had agreed, asking Antonio, when he got back, to tell him why he spoke of Venetia as he did, and promising that, if he said no more than he held for truth, there should be no quarrel thereon.

Having that pledge, Antonio told him enough, or too much, for it confirmed Francisco's thought that he had confused her with another of a like manner or face, as it is easy for those to do who wander about, seeing many in diverse lands.

"Well," Antonio said, "if I have, I have done her a great wrong, which I should be glad to regret. But you should ask it of her."

In the later day, he had Del Monte's letter, and went to him at once. Here he heard much the same talk that Angelica gave him before.

"Let her tell the truth," the Commander said, "and, though it stink, I may bring her free. But if she lie, she may fall in too deep a pit for any rescue to reach, and if you are her true friend you must warn her of that, as I have intention to do. But it is you who should see her first."

"I am her friend," Francisco replied, "and too much so to believe that which is spoken to her dispraise, she being one (if I come through this war) whom I hope to wed. But I will tell her all that you say, for it is right she should know."

"You may recall to her mind that I urged upon her that she should be artless without reserve, but I must tell you that they were words (as it seemed to me) that she was not grateful to hear."

Francisco said nothing to that. But he became more urgent of heart that he should see Venetia himself, both that he might have the relief of assurance from her own lips, and because it seemed that so fair a face had few friends in that monkish hold.

Del Monte saw how she looked to him, and said less than he might, being a man of controlled speech, though he would have words enough for the right time, which he handled as he would handle a sword, using the point more than the edge.

He saw well what had been in Sir Oliver's mind, which he would be glad to support. "Yet," he reflected, "I must practise to bring her clear, putting that before all, for I have pledged my honour thereto. I know not how the steward died, as none will (except she) to the world's end, and as to her, if she spoke in her sleep, she would be most likely to lie. For she is of that sort who should be hanged by one who would govern well (whether for the man's death or another cause, it is no matter for that); in which he would act without malice to her, but as one orders a room."

After that, he had another thought, seeing a plan by which he might protect her, and guide other things to a good end, if Sir Oliver would see it in his way, and could bring the Grand Master to that accord. . . .

Francisco waited till the next day (having no choice), when Angelica met him again, giving him a pass by which he could see Venetia as much as he would, till she should be called to answer her charge; and it was not long from that hour before the key turned in the door of the chamber where she was held, and he was present to her.

The chamber was of a fair size, and, if its appointments were not rich, they were the best the jailer could do; for Francisco's gold had spoken loudly enough, and Sir Oliver's order that she should not be abused had played the same tune, so that the jailer could feel that he was obeying orders by the same means that his pouch swelled, which he was not always able to do.

But she was lodged in the common jail, which was not designed for those of the better sort. A Knight of the Order, or even a serving-brother, being accused either of light or heavy offence, would not have been harboured there, but in a dungeon or tower. The jail had common rooms for those whose purses were lean or bare, and these were noisome enough; and if men fought there for crusts at times, it would not be esteemed matter for scandal against the state, for why should true men be taxed that felons should be able to loose their belts?

But if we think that we live in a better day, we may observe that when Francisco entered the cell there was no jailer beside, nor partition to keep him from her whom he came to see.

The cruelties of those days were most largely of abstinence and neglect, or to a politic end, while those of our own jails are carefully planned to degrade the soul and torture the mind, and are enforced with a bitter and very tyrannous will.

A jail is seldom a place of comfort or peace, though there are few of the world's best, from Christ Himself, who have not entered such doors, but the scrupulous cruelties of design that snatch at a man's clothes, and forbid his speech, and beat him down to a servitude of routine, may be more merciless, as they are more deliberate, than those of dirt and neglect.

Francisco came to a room that was somewhat bare, and its walls were stone, and that only washed with a plain paint, at a time when it was the fashion to have them panelled in wood, or else patterned in paints, if not gay with a pictured scene, unless they might be draped with tapestry in a wealthy hall.

The walls were plain blue: the ceiling bare: the window darkened with heavy bars. The rushes on the floor were too few to soften the tread, and were not clean, having been there for a week, it being a time when rushes were not easy to get. But that, in this time of siege, could have been excused in a better place, and it was at least the best room in the jail, and better than those where the jailer must make his home.

Venetia rose up from a bed, being the place where she mostly was when she could not be active abroad; for she thought that it was so that she nursed the soft contours of youth, on which she depended to make her trade. But she was not soft in a woman's way, being tireless to walk, or to ride or swim, if she should be roused by sufficient need.

Her hatred of Malta (which it would not be easy to overcall) came mostly from how she had been confined, after the first month that La Cerda had brought her there. To her mind, she had not been free from that hour. She had done no more than change jails, and each time for the worse till now, when she might be said to have moved a step up, from the narrow battery cell.

She was not meagrely clad, as we have seen her before, having procured (we may wonder how, but guess with some use of Francisco's gold) a gown of daffodil green, long and slender and straight, being a colour that pleased the pale gold of her hair, and gave her a very simple and chaste allure, as of a madonna in bud.

She had the wary eyes of a cat as the key turned in the heavy door, which changed to a softer glance, as she heard Francisco's voice before he appeared.

"If I am back in an hour's time?" It was the turnkey who could be heard to enquire.

"You can come then, but you must be ready to wait if I am not done."

The man agreed, and there was a sound of the clinking of coins. "I will knock twice," he said, "before I open the door." He wished it understood that he would not appear in a sudden way to the disconcerting of those who might be busy within.

"You are my good friend," she said, "to come thus. I feared that I should be too closely confined, recalling what the Grand Master's malice had said." Her voice was soft, and her eyes added to her words, both in gratitude and appeal.

"I am ever your friend," he replied, any doubt that may have been an undercurrent of trouble in his thoughts during the last day retreating now that her bodily presence possessed him again. "I would be more, if I might."

What did he mean by that? How, she wondered, must this game be played in the best way? She owed much to him. Did he think the time for payment had come? They would be alone for the next hour. She had heard him provide for that. Did he think to play the steward's part, for something better than he had got?

She put the thought aside, and then embraced it again as she considered that he might have taken La Cerda's death to give him more freedom than his honour had permitted before.

He was of another world than that in which she had been bred to bend and cozen and lie, and she would have had some excuse if she had failed to sum his passion, his loyalty, his pride, his knowledge of his own code, and his inexperience of the baser ways of the world, to the total they truly made.

It showed the quality of quick perception, and of a wit that had raised her high from the gutter in which her childhood had sprawled and fought, that she could read one who was so far from herself in standards and ideals of life.

"There is little," she said, "that you could not ask, having done so much."

"It is nothing," he said. "It has been pleasure to me. . . . I would ask nothing of right, which it were unknightly to do. . . . Yet . . . when you have had time to forget . . . I will hope that I can ask more at a better time."

She held out a hand, which he kissed. His reticence wooed her as boldness would have been powerless to do. She came at that time to the threshold of love, which she could not cross, being held back by her own past, the rose of love having fallen in sundry mire.

She said: "You are good to me," and her voice was sincere without need of the art which she would have found it easy to use. But her thoughts, now that she was sure that modesty was the best card to play from a lying pack, returned to that from which they were seldom far, since the Grand Master's eyes had fallen upon her half-draped form in Francisco's cell.

She asked: "But you will be bringing me news? Is it good? Will they let me through? The Chevalier Del Monte was here, and said I had done no more than the law supports, and it should give me quittance of that."

"I have seen him, and had word from Sir Oliver Starkey as well. They speak to another point, and both are urgent that I should put it to your reply.

"I think it needless to do, but I must keep my word, as, except he be clear on this, Del Monte will not undertake your defence in the right way.

"I will tell you what Captain Antonio says, on which he is very sure, and which points to the same danger as they.

"It seems that he knew of a Genoese girl—he is Genoa born and bred—Maria Pezzo by name, of whom he has matter to tell, such as that she was jailed on a charge of robbing seamen who made resort to a house where she was one (he says) of a gang of evil repute.

"He says he knows that she was near to be hanged at another time, though little more than a child, her name being as bad as it was.

"The second time was not more than three years ago, when Doria's galleys were in the port, as he could find men from the fleet here who would witness, and would know her again (which he does not propose to do). He says that she escaped by defect of proof, as was publicly shown, but that, indeed, she bought herself out of the jail by ways he does not scruple to say.

"All this would be naught to us, but that he will have it that you are this girl of his own slums, which he should perceive that you could not be.

"Sir Oliver may have the same talk, or may not, but he is plain that there will be challenge of who you are, and he has warned Del Monte, who says that, let the truth be what it may, if it be told, he has good hope he can bring you off, but he will be cast down by a lie.

"You will forgive that I tell you this, for it is right that you should know what is proposed, that we may be equal to its repulse."

Venetia listened, and there was no sign on her face of the thoughts she had. She saw that she must choose now, either to show what she had been, and to expose the falsehood of that which she had told to him and to La Cerda before, or she must be hardy in a denial which must be sustained when the trial came, lest she come to worse wreck even than the sore back that she had feared since La Cerda had proved too weak to be her defence among these knights where (as she would have said) the manhood was hard to find.

Had it been no more than Antonio's tale, she thought that she might have beaten it down, but there were the two years between the flight from Genoa, and when she came to La Cerda's bed, and what—if she could only guess!—might be known of them . . .? There was the merchant who was robbed and slain in Turin. Her hands, in fact, had been clean of that, but she had been in the house, plying the same trade, even in the next room when they choked his scream, and afterwards they had given her fifty ducats to keep her still. . . . It was by that gold she had made advance. But she knew that three had been hanged for that deed (after a time on the wheel), and that another was wanted, who was not unlike to herself. . . .

"You would think," she said, "that none would believe such tales, which it is wicked to tell. As to Genoa, I was never there in my life days. It is their malice to bring me down, which they cannot do, except they be armed with lies.

"But I will not say that I am not in a new fear, for it is always a simpler thing to propose a lie than to prove that it is untrue. And how am I to do that, we being sieged here as we are?"

Francisco saw some reason in that, but he thought he saw also a way out which she might have missed.

"As to that," he said, "I know not what tale Sir Oliver may have got, but if it be this of which Captain Antonio talks, there should be a confident way. For the Grand Master would not practise to bring you down with a false word, nor would Sir Oliver be a party thereto; and if Captain Antonio will find those seamen he says he can, and they will say (as they must) that Maria Pezzo was different from you, we shall have witness that might be put to Sir Oliver himself before the trial be held, and he would see that he had been wrongly led."

Venetia listened to this, and must look more pleased than she felt. Yet she let a doubt be seen.

"So it would. It is well thought. . . . But what if Sir Oliver have a quite different lie? We should know that first, and I suppose that we must not move in this till Del Monte have consented thereto. He will see me here to-morrow at matin hour, and I will tell him what Captain Antonio would be able to do."

"So it shall be, if you will. . . . But the time goes."

He was reluctant to have delay, but he saw that, if she wished Del Monte to be told first, as having her defence in his hands, it was a wish he could not deny.

She turned the talk after that into other ways, becoming soft of glances and voice, but yet holding him off with his own words: "We will say more at a better time."

He understood that she would give him her love when the charge of murder would be lifted from off her name. He was not likely to give faith to Antonio's tales, judging her both with the blindness of love and as he found her to be.

But she was doing no more than to maintain a position which it could be no profit to lose, though she had ceased to hope it would be her gain. She wanted to think well, which she could not do till he should be gone.

When he left, she lay unmoving for a time which lengthened to hours, her fingers knitted behind her head. Her eyes were distant and hard, and over them at times there came a shadow of fear, and, at others a smile dimpled her face, and passed as a little wind may ruffle a quiet lake, and pass quickly away.

She rose at last, as one throwing off doubt, like a cloak on a summer day. She looked round the room, and said aloud: "Well, there is little to leave," as though there were some comfort in that; and then, more to herself: "I suppose I may come to harbour at last, but the road is long."

She did not think that the harbour for such as she was most often the hangman's cart, for she had courage to meet her need. She had a thing to do now which she had done before in a Genoese jail, when she had been younger and less assured, and she did not expect to fail.

The jailer came in the next hour, bringing the evening meal, which was better than most men had who were free in that time of siege, for there was a promise of gold from Francisco's purse, which he did not intend to miss by any grumbling from her. He had had more now than he should have asked, and as to that which was still to come, he judged that Don Francisco would keep faith, but would not be easy to overbear.

She looked at fish, and a steaming stew, a plate of grapes, and a half-bottle of wine.

"Well," he asked, "are you pleased?"

"It is well enough," she replied; "but you will suppose that I have drunk better vintage than that."

"It is good wine," he grumbled; "you are sore to please."

"It is well enough," she said again. She looked at the man's heavy sensual face in a more familiar way that she had done until then. "I may have other needs."

"Then you must tell other than me." He turned away. He had done enough. It was not she who gave out the gold.

"No," she said, "there is no haste. It is you I must tell. I must have silks bought in the town at an early hour, before Del Monte shall see me here."

He stood hesitating. There might be profit in this, if he would go to trouble enough.

"You should know," he said, "that you must pay first. It is the law of the jail. Can you do that?"

"I do not say but I might. . . . But I have to talk of another thing. Should I have bugs in the bed at the price Don Francisco has paid?"

Anger swelled the veins in the heavy face. Was this a device to cheat him of what was to come, unless he should now dance to her tune?

"There are none such. That I swear," he said in a truculent way. And, indeed, it was a good bed, and the linen sheets were fragrant and clean, beside that it had blankets of wool.

"But if I itch where they bite? I will show you this."

She put a foot on the bed, drawing up her gown to show the inner side of a thigh that was smoothly slender, but rounded well. For a moment's glimpse, she may have shown above that, and his eyes were greedy of what they saw.

He said: "I see naught. There is naught to see." But he came closer, seeing all that he could, at which she flicked the skirt down.

"You may not see," she said, "but I feel." And then: "But there need be no trouble for that. If you get me that which I need, I will pay you all in a good way."

He stood looking at her with heavy lustful eyes, still uncertain what she might mean, and unwilling to show his hope till he were made sure. Besides that, he was half afraid, remembering the accusation that brought her there. But he did not think she would wish to have another dead man laid to her door, with no more than the same excuse.

"You must pay first," he said; "it is the rule of the jail, and after that I will get you the silks."

"Why so I will," she said, "I am in the humour for that. If you will come back at a later hour—and you must bring wine of a better vintage than this."

He looked at her now in a coarse way, seeing her for what she was, or perhaps less.

"Why," he said, "he that was here, did he not feed you full for this time?"

"He did naught but to kiss my hand. But you will know how to deal in a better way."

He was doubtful still, like a wasp that hovers over a candied snare, but he could not resist.

"I will be back," he said, "when the cells are locked, and we shall not be disturbed by any knocks on the outer gate."

He went to his rounds. He would return at an hour when the common rooms would be closed and every prisoner locked away in his own cell till the next day.

After that, there would be two besides himself to keep ward through the night, but the first watch would be his, and they would sleep, unless they were roused by the bell.

She called after him as he went: "You will bring better wine? It is on that that our bargain hangs. . . ."

The next morning, Del Monte saw Sir Oliver at an early hour. He said: "I have looked at this on all sides, and I have a proposal to make. If you take her tale to be true (which you have no witness to overset) I may bring her off; and if you probe her past, I may do it or not, but there is one thing that is sure, I must call Don Francisco in her defence, and Don Garcio also, of whom she tells me that which it is not my business to know, except so far as it may be needful for her relief. But I know you do not want them called at this time.

"Now it seems to me that we each have something with which to trade. Why will you not be agreed to remand her now, till the siege is through? She will do no harm in a prison cell, and you can set her free at the end (as you must now, if I bring her off) when the Turks are gone. You can say now that there is more witness which you must sift, and I will agree for her side, and it will be forgotten amid the thunder of greater things. . . . I came to put this to you, before I see her again."

"Which," Sir Oliver said with a smile, "I am assured that you will not do. She has resolved this for us both, having escaped in the night, none knoweth how; but there is cause to think that she is now in the Turkish lines."

CHAPTER XVI

VENETIA had looked down on a man with whom she had played till he slept in a sated way, being heavy with the wine which she had coaxed him to drink, and of which she had had more than enough.

He had been hard to bring to that point, and she did not think that his doze was deep, or that it would last long, but a short time should be sufficient for her.

She would have liked well to give him a thrust such as that which had gone up to the steward's heart, knowing of none whom she hated more, but she would not do that which might bring her down, if she should be caught at a later hour. Besides that, she had no weapon at all, for the man had been prudent to leave his poniard where it could not be brought into that game, having had the steward's end at the back of his mind. With bare hands, he knew that he could break her across his knee, and he had, in fact, given her bruises that would be black for some days, though in no more than an evil sport, after the manner of such as he when they are brutish with lust and wine.

Her hands were silent and swift as she clad herself with the best she had, and only became slow as she turned the key that it should not grate, for he had locked the door on the inside, as it had been prudent to do for more reasons than one.

She had to trust her own wits beyond that, for he did not carry all the keys of the jail at his belt, as warders would do in the romances which men read at that time, both because it would have been a great burden to bear about, and because it would have been asking men to knock him on the head and go free.

She went along a short passage, and through a door at the end that was standing wide, as he had left it for his return. She closed this, observing a bolt on its outer side, which fell into a socket in the stone floor. As she dropped it, she smiled as one whose vengeance was sure, though it might not come from her hand. He would have much to do (she thought) to explain how he came to be at the wrong side of that door.

After that, she had no trouble at all. She knew the way out, having observed it well as she came in, which those who have been jailed before will have learnt that it is prudent to do. She passed an open door, where a man slept on a bench. She did not see the third man, from whatever cause. She found keys on a wall. It was all as simple as that.

She was sobered by the night air, and the need of caution, which was even greater than when she had been in the jail, but she moved with a settled plan. She was noiseless on the shadowed side of the street, and quick to hide at the sound of a distant step. She came to the quay, and to a place where the skiffs were tied. There was a man set to watch there, and he did not drowse, as she had hoped that he might. He paced the length of the quay, looking out on a water which was covered by a light mist, as it often was in the night hours.

This was the greatest risk that she had. When he was furthest from where she crouched, and near to turn, she crept across, and slipped into a boat, where she lay flat.

He was alert to hear the little noise that she made as she gained the boat. He came back, looking round in a wary way, but she was not seen. When he walked the next time, she unknotted the rope by which the boat was tied, but held it until he had come back and turned again, so that she should have all the time she could at the last. . . . He heard the plash of an oar, and turned to see a boat thrust off from the quay. He pulled out a pistol and fired, meaning at once to hit her if he could, and to give the alarm. . . . Men came then at a run, and boats were pushed out in pursuit, but the mist was her friend that she was not found. It had been more perilous than she had thought, but she did not fret about that, it having been safely done.

She wished to make her way to the corsairs' camp rather than that of the Turks, both because she would rather come to Hassan's than Mustapha's hands, and because she knew that among the men of the Barbary coast she would find those who would understand what she said, which those of Turkey or Egypt would have been less likely to do. There was a jargon talked on the sea-coasts, from Morocco to the Levant, which she knew well enough, having learnt it from the seamen who came ashore at Genoa where she was bred.

It would do well enough for the first of those she would be likely to meet, and it was said that Hassan could talk in more tongues than two. She did not doubt that she would be understood when she came to him.

Here were reasons for what would be best to do, but there was no help in them as to how it should best be done. The Barbary ships lay, for the most part, as did the whole fleet, in the great harbour which was on the further side of Sceberras ridge; but she knew that Hassan's attack on the Sanglea had been at the eastern end, which was on the opposite side of the Turkish girdle which closed St. Angelo in, and it was still there that he would be likely to be. To row up the inlet which was south of the Sanglea would be to invite bullets from either side, as her oars would be heard in the misty light of the dawn. Even in darkness (and if she could find her way) it would be perilous to attempt.

The skiff she had taken was light, being one meant for the harbour alone, and not fit for the open sea. She had been used to boats from her childhood's days, and could control it with ease. She resolved to lie out in the midst, till the night should be further spent, and then pull up to the head of the harbour, and land where (if there were any Turks about, which was less likely than not), they would not be keeping a watch, as they could not be attacked there by the Christians, unless they should sally out from the inner harbour with all their ships, and even then it would not be a place they would choose. The land at the head of the harbour was of no moment to either side, though it would be within the lines of the Turks, which swept round to Sceberras, and to the further harbour beyond. If she landed there shortly before the dawn, she would be well within the lines of the Turks, where no special watch would be kept, and she thought that, with good fortune's help, she might find her way to Hassan's command. . . .

It was two hours after dawn that Hassan sat in his tent, taking the first meal of the day. Most of the Turkish leaders, when they saw how long the siege was likely to be, had found roofs for their heads from the deserted villas which the knights had built in time of peace in all parts of the island. But Hassan would choose a tent when he was not on a moving deck, having the desert ways in his blood, though he had a great house at Tripoli where he kept his wives, and would sometimes be, and Dragut's palace at Algiers, which was splendidly built in the Moorish style, and was now his, and he would spend some time there in the future years, if he did not die at this siege.

He had a pavilion, ample and rich, with partitions within itself, and here he sat on the cushioned, carpeted ground, and ate and drank in a frugal way, for which Dragut would have had a jest of contempt.

A servant entered, and said: "Lord, there is a giaour woman without, who says she has escaped from the town, having been wrongly accused, and fled where she supposes she will be safer than there. She says that she has matter you will be grateful to hear."

"Is she one of a common kind?"

"She has been well-kept, and is white and clean. . . . She is richly attired, and fair enough in the Christian way."

Hassan saw that the man gave grudging praise. He said: "There is one woman who is, as I suppose, in St. Angelo now, whom I would be thankful to get, but I suppose it is not she."

"She is soft of speech, and her hair is paler than gold."

"Then it is not. But I will hear what she has to say. Bring her in, and leave her with me alone."

Venetia came, looking confident in a quiet way, for she was always equal to an event which she expected to meet. With a woman's art, she had contrived to bear little sign of the way in which she had toiled and walked during the night. She was one who would always save that which she wore, at the cost, if not of her skin, at least of a pain which would be less easy to see.

Hassan looked at her with friendly, approving eyes, but she knew too much of Saracen ways to give much value to that. She knew that, if he should order her to the strangler's hands, it would be done in a smooth way, without hardening his voice, as a Christian would be likely to do.

"You have come," he said, "from St. Angelo during the night? By what way did you do that?"

"I came from the quay that is under the castle wall. I took a boat and rowed to the end of the harbour, and then I walked here."

"It is as easy as that? Why have you walked so far from the place where you came ashore?"

"It was to you that I came."

"Why to me?"

"I preferred you to the Turkish leaders, thinking you would listen to what I have come to tell."

"Why should you think that?"

"I was born on Genoa quay."

Hassan considered this reply, which he understood. Mustapha would have been likely to put her to torture as the readiest way of getting the truth from lips which, being Christian, would be likely to lie to him; and when he had done, he would have made an end of a woman's body that was no longer of marketable condition. He might have acted better than that, but it was not a chance that any woman would choose. Piali might have been worse than he. But the corsairs of the Barbary coast had a reputation for destroying little that they would be able to sell. Their mercies were no better than that. But a Christian woman who came to their hands would be stripped and examined with a slave-merchant's eye, and if they cut her throat when they had done, she might be sure that she was of little good, either for man's pleasure or woman's toil.

Hassan looked at her with considering eyes, and there was a silence which was not easy for her to endure. She knew that he would act without haste, but when his next words should come they would be likely to make her fate plain. When he spoke at last, it had the form of a threat, and yet it put a better confidence in her heart than she had yet had.

"I am about to ask you some questions which you will do well to answer with great care; for if you attempt to lie, I do not say you will find a quick death, but you will wish that you had."

"I shall not stumble on that stone."

"Many do. You are Christian?"

"I am Christian born."

"Would you betray those of your race and creed?"

"I seek to save my own life, taking the only way that I have. Had they left me in peace, I had not been here. If their own lives are in more hazard from me, it is no more than they threatened mine."

She spoke the thoughts which had come as she had lain and planned on the previous day, and which were in part what she truly felt, but more largely what she had considered that she must be ready to say. They held a logic which is less likely to be perceived by the rulers of states than by those whom their laws pursue. For a state will make war on the life of a single man who is born on its own land, and think that he should still be loyal to it in separate ways, which is to ask much, and especially so of one whom it esteems unworthy to live.

Hassan asked: "You have no more reason than that?"

"It is said that the Grand Master once rowed as a Turkish slave."

"So he did. What then?"

"Would you have him do it again?"

"Do you mean that you would?"

"It would give me a special joy."

Hassan saw that there might be more in this than he had first thought. It was a fact that La Valette had spent a year of his earlier life toiling on the bench of a Turkish galley, and with a back raw from the driver's stripes. It was an experience such as fell to many of the leaders of both sides in the fierce naval strife that had raged for centuries on the Mediterranean Sea. For, if they were captured, their ransoms would be fixed so high that the money could not be quickly raised, and meanwhile it was held by some that the worse they were served the more their friends would strive to provide the gold.

La Valette had been a captain in the fleet of the Knights of Malta, before any thought that he would come to his present power. He had been a scourge to the Turks, and they had shown him no love when he came into their hands. It may have been his treatment at that time which urged him now (among higher motives than that) to be their so bitter foe.

Hassan had been captive too, and had been one of those slaves who were chained in couples to work at the walls by which Malta was now strong to protect the Cross which its ramparts flew. He also might remember that, when a mood of mercy must be put by.

Now he clapped his hands, at which an attendant came quickly and silently to receive his commands.

"Alif," he said, "I will talk to this woman apart. You will see that none enters here, till you are again summoned by me."

The man bowed without words, and withdrew.

Venetia did not understand what was said, it not being in any tongue that she knew; but as Hassan rose and raised the curtain of the inner pavilion, she could make a good guess at what it had been, and that Hassan did not regard her coming as a matter of no account.

She felt that the first skirmish was hers, but she knew that she had yet to tread on a very perilous edge.

He motioned her to go first, in an abrupt imperative way. He may not have thought that she would have failed to understand what was said before. The precedence was not courtesy to herself, which he would have thought an unseemly thing, even had she been a princess of his own blood, it was no more than the routine prudence of one who did not wish to offer his back to be stabbed by those who might not be friends.

Venetia looked round on a couch and cushions of silk, and on coffers of metal and ivory which she knew to be of a great price, and may have been of the best that the world held at that time. She saw that one, having an open lid, was filled with books which were richly bound, in the style that Morocco had made its own. Her eyes passed over them in a heedless way, as might be excused at the pass at which she then was. But she would have had no use for them at another time, even had they been in her tongue. The world was her book, and she found it to be one of which the last page would be hard to reach.

There were rich arms hanging on the pavilion wall. She saw ewelled hilts, and gilded bucklers finely engraved, and the dark-blue of Damascus steel. In all she saw there was demonstration of culture and wealth.

The pavilion contained other personal, intimate things which she was more quick to observe than a chest of books, but she resolved at the first glance that it was a place where no woman came.

His words sounded as though he had heard her thought: "You may say all you will here without danger of other ears, for I bring no woman to war, no more by land than by sea."

He motioned her to a heap of cushions upon the ground, and stretched himself on his couch.

"And now," he said, "you can tell me much, and by that path you can win safety and ease; for what you sell (if the goods be sound) I will fairly buy. But I warn you again that, if you give me false word, I will have no mercy for that. So when you speak, you should think well."

"I can tell you much," she said, "and I have no purpose to lie. But I have had no food since I left the jail in the Bourg, which was ten hours before now."

"I had thought that, but my time is short. I suppose that you can sit there and not faint; and when I go you can have better food than the town gives, if I am content that you give honest replies. Can you tell me the weakest points at which we could make attack on the town?"

"I could tell you some things it might be useful to know, and of one that may be the best way, but you would judge better than I. I will not boast that I can do more than is true, for (except in the first days) I have been little abroad since I came to Malta when April began, so that there is much that I do not know."

"Then we will leave that, for this time." He began to question her upon many matters which she could not see that it would be much gain for him to know, and on which she soon had reason to think that he knew more than herself, which made her the more careful to answer with exactness, and not to profess familiarities which were not hers.

She was, in fact, in more peril than she could guess, for he was using the knowledge that he had gained when he had been prisoner within Malta's walls, added to and revised by that which he had had from the lips of his present spies, to test both her truth, and her value as to any witness which she might give.

He rose abruptly when these questions were done. "I shall be away," he said, "till the noon hour, or beyond. After that, you shall tell me more."

He returned with her to the outer pavilion. "You can wait my return here," he said. He called Alif, to whom he gave instructions that she was to be well served.

He left her with a sense that she had commenced well. She had not hoped so much as that she would be sheltered in Hassan's own tent, even for some hours of the middle day when he was not there.

When he was outside, he gave commands that she should not be allowed to leave (but this she would have too much sense to attempt, as he might have guessed), and that enquiry should be made as to who she was, and the circumstances under which she had fled from the town. Then he went to join a Council of War that Mustapha had called.

CHAPTER XVII

VENETIA could not know that she had come at a good time for herself, the jealousies of the commanders of the Turkish army having broken out in open dispute since the failure of the attack on the Sanglea. Hassan was determined that he would lose no more men in assault unless at his own time, and to plans that had his assent, while he was not willing that Piali should lead his forces to a success which would emphasize his own failure a week before.

Into Mustapha's heart there had come a doubt of whether St. Angelo would ever be taken by the army he now had, but he would not entertain this, being stubborn in his resolve, with the cold implacable purpose of age, which would not lightly be turned aside. His generals had failed more than enough. Was it in himself to succeed at last? The present Council was to resolve whether there should be further assault, or that they should be content for a time to invest St. Angelo's walls, and bombard it from every side.

Piali was for a continued assault, and, whether his judgment were good or bad, he sustained it at this time with better argument than he always had.

"You talk of caution," he said, "and the lives of men, and I tell you that it is prudence that fears delay, and that you lose more life in the end with this length of siege than if you should drive your regiments against the wall even by firing upon their rear.

"You do worse than that, for you risk that we shall withdraw at last, or be chased away, to the shame of the Moslem lands.

"How long will Europe be still? Do you forget that the allied fleets would be stronger than ours? If we cannot prevail as we now are, shall we do so when a Spanish army is round our rear? Will it be months before the Viceroy is stirred to move? You will find that weeks is a better word."

"You are full of words," Hassan said, when Piali's passionate speech had run down, and after a pause to show that he was not roused to an equal heat, "and some are foolish to me, and some have a better sound. But would you tell us just what you would do, if you have your own way?"

"I would assault," he said, "on every side, and with every man that I have, and I would not cease by day and scarcely by night till the place is won. If they are stubborn and fierce of heart (as I do not deny), I would be more stubborn and fiercer than they, I would bombard with every gun that we have, and I would not cease while we have a keg of powder unbroached."

"It is low enough now," Hassan interposed.

"So it is; but there is more on the way which will soon be here, which is more than the Grand Master can hope on his part. The more we bombard the walls, the more must they reply, unless they would be utterly crushed. Every shot they fire is what they cannot replace.

"I tell you this," he concluded, "of which I am well assured, that if we cannot succeed with our utmost force, as I would have it instantly used, then we shall fail in a slower way."

Mustapha, pulling a white beard, watched him with intent and yet expressionless eyes, and Hassan saw that it was left to him to reply.

He said: "There is one thing for which you do not allow. You do not observe that if we storm upon walls that we do not take, we waste lives that might be used with avail on a later day, when we have beaten their walls to be less defence, and have slain many with constant fire. It is the lesson of every siege that you lose by too early assault. Would you not have those alive now if you could, whom we have lost because we assailed the Sanglea before it was ripe to fall? Should we not be better equipped to succeed on a later day, if we had left that undone?"

"As it is," Piali replied, "I may say yes; but I would have had the assault sustained. We should have been at their walls with the dawn of the next day."

"The men would not have been easy to move. I say nothing of yours, who had been less used, but mine had had enough for that time."

"And was it not the same in the town? We look at our dead at the end of a day of strife, and we feel the ache in our own bones, but we are less aware of those that our foes must feel. It is often that we defeat ourselves rather than that we are defeated by them. . . . But I will ask you, as you ask me. What would you counsel to do?"

"I would not assault again till we have further beaten the walls, unless we can find a weak point of which they are not fully aware. Or, when I do, it should be with every man that we have, the fleet aiding thereto, at which my galleys will not be slack."

"And if the weeks pass, and there be gathering of the Christian fleets, will you say what you would do then?"

Piali looked at him with suspicious questioning eyes, and Hassan was aware that Mustapha was regarding him in a similar way, as though he would probe his mind; and he knew that there was some reason behind the fear that the others had.

His galleys were swift and light, and if there were news that the Christian fleets drew to a head at Genoa or Naples, or even nearer than that, he might not find it too late to embark his men, and with a fair wind at his stern he would not be easy to catch.

Many of Piali's warships were of slower and heavier build. They might be harder to take, but they would also be slower to run, and he had store-ships that were neither strong to fight nor agile to flee, and for which his galleys must be the guard, or they would fall to the Christians an easy prey. He saw that Piali feared for his fleet, and lest, if he should be threatened with a combination of Europe's powers, his position might become worse, because Barbary's galleys would not be there.

Hassan was under allegiance to Turkey, Byzantium being both temporal and spiritual head of the Moslem lands, but it was an allegiance which could not easily have been asserted by Soliman in a punitive way, and especially so with the war of Hungary on his hands; and if his fleet should be destroyed, and that of Hassan remain, the north African coast would be a land to which Soliman's shadow would cease to stretch. If the Christian fleet should approach in a threatening force, and Hassan's galleys should back yards to await their fire, it would be by his own will, and not because Mustapha spoke with his master's voice.

"If," Hassan said, returning the glances which he received in the same deliberate way, "there be mustering of the Christian fleets, I suppose that we must meet them with every galley we have, of which there are some which are not here now, but which I should summon with speed, for, if we were beaten in such a strife, the whole of the inland sea would be no more than a Christian lake. And if you should be so destroyed, and I were not there, it would come to the same end, for how could I singly resist on a later day?"

Piali was silent when he heard this, for he saw that Hassan looked ahead somewhat farther than he, fearing that which would come to pass at Lepanto twenty years after that, which one who sat at that Council would live to share.

Mustapha saw that the time had come when he should speak. He said: "It is well thought, and what I should have expected to hear. And I will tell you now what I think, which is that Piali is largely right, except only that it will not be till a later day, if at all, that we shall have any fear of the Christian fleet. For these blasphemers, for whom one God is too few, and who make God of a man, are now in so fierce a strife of superstition among themselves that they will not unite, even to save those of their misbelief from the swords of the true servants of God. . . . We must press the siege with our utmost power, but we are yet under the shadow of no imminent fear. . . . And there is another ally we have, of which you have not spoken as yet, for there is talk that provision (except corn) is failing within the town."

Piali listened to this, and though his fear was less that Hassan would leave him to be destroyed at the sight of the Christian ships, yet he was still urgent that the siege should be pushed by storm rather than in more gradual ways, and he wished to know (which he thought his right) that he should be in command at such times, rather than Hassan again.

"There is another thing," he replied, "which has not been said, and that is that the summer passes its prime. There will come a day when it is not good to keep an army in tents, and when the seas are loud with contending winds. If you will be counselled by me, we shall then be tied up to our several quays, and unloading the spoil. If you give me command," he turned to Mustapha to add, "with every man that we have, it will not be two days before we are over the walls of the Sanglea, and St. Michael will not be long after to fall."

Mustapha did not return his glance. His eyes were between the two as he answered: "I have had good counsel, on which I shall think well."

He saw that he was weakened by the ambitious hates of those on whom he must most rely, but he could reflect that they were less held apart than were those of the Christian lands. He did not think that the guns of Europe could have thundered round Byzantium's walls and Egypt or Tripoli stood aside in debate of whose part it was to succour those of their own faith, or in a poor hope that the Turks might have single strength to sustain the war. . . .

Yet it was not all Christian men, of whatever faith, who should be blamed at this time, for the spirit of Europe stirred against rulers of colder blood. As the news of St. Elmo's fall, and of the Turkish repulse at the Sanglea was carried from land to land, there was clamour that the Knights of Malta should not be left to perish at infidel hands, and there were prayers in churches of every creed. In the chancelleries of Europe there was frequent debate, and plans were proposed, and put by. For each would ask from whom the cost was to come, or who would gather the spoil, or to whom the glory would be likely to go. They thought less of the rescue thay might have made than of how they would be aligned again on the next day.

Elizabeth said: "They fight well. It would be to our glory to give them aid. Shall the Papists do it alone? For we are all foes of the Turks who are Christian men."

She looked at Burleigh, tapping the board with a restless hand, and he looked back at her, judging her mood, as he was very able to do.

"It is Philip's part," he said; "let him waste his strength before ours. We shall have more peace on the Spanish main."

Elizabeth saw that. Her eyes became distant and shrewd as she schemed ahead for her own land. As she was silent, he spoke again, driving in a new wedge. "There would be a great cost. Do you think Philip would pay?"

"That he would not!" Elizabeth spoke with the contempt that the mean-minded are quick to feel for others of kindred ways. "But the Mayor would support a new tax for so great a cause?"

The assertion had a note of question, if not of doubt. There was much craft to be used in the pretexts for raising taxes at that time, so that men might pay from a willing purse. But Burleigh was cold to that.

"We have other needs," he said, "and what I think is a better plan."

Elizabeth saw that it should be left for that time. "But," she said, "be they papists or no, they are bold men. They shall have a place in our prayers." She gave a charge that news from Malta should reach her hand without pause, be she where she might, either by night or day. . . .

Philip, in his great palace in Seville, which had once been that of the Moorish king, heard that the Sanglea had stood the storm, and wrote to Garcio with his own hand, as his habit was. It was doubtless (he said) by the high mercy of Heaven that these men who denied Christ, and made unholy mock of the Mother of God, should break their teeth as they did on the Maltese rock. The Viceroy should watch with care, and if it should seem that help was required (that is, if St. Angelo would be likely to fall if it were withheld) and if such help could be prudently sent (that is, if there were no danger that it would be less than enough, making no difference to the result, and so being to the shame of Spain, besides that it would be at a cost that no one would be likely to pay), then he might use such force as was near his hand, either of soldiers or ships.

But he must look on all sides, as a statesman should, and also ahead. It would be a great matter to be drawn into a Moslem war. The German Emperor had that on his hands now, and it kept him from being vexatious in other ways. He said again that Garcio must look on all sides, being wary in what he did. . . . But he should let the Pope know that he was preparing help in an ample way. He should receive well all those volunteers who came to Sicily from the northern lands, seeking shipping that they might be transported to Malta's aid. Even if there should be some expenses in their equipment, or entertainment (that the sympathies of Spain should be shown in a public way) Garcio need not fear that he would be expected to pay these from his own purse. He had a generous lord. He could charge them in his accounts, at least so far as they would be covered by the revenues which would reach his hands. . . .

Philip sealed the letter himself as his habit was, and turned his pen to write of matters more near his heart, being of how Egmont was to be weeded out of a land where he had the love of too many men, and the Flanders burghers brought to a humble mood.

Pius IV, the one ruler who wished with a single mind to see Mustapha chased from St. Angelo's walls, strove by pleading, by admonition, even by threats of the Church's wrath, to shorten delay. All the troubled intrigues by which the Vatican paid for its secular power were now centred round the rescue of the beleaguered knights. But he was dealing with statesmen as astute and less scrupulous than himself. They gave fair words and pledges that they were not instant to keep. . . . The weeks passed, and those who watched from St. Angelo's highest tower could see the flashes of the encircling guns, which were never still from this time, having become a girdle of fire, which, like the coil of a constricting snake, drew closer from day to day, but there was no sign of a Christian fleet on the summer sea.

CHAPTER XVIII

Hassan rode back from the Council, revolving many things in his mind, but with a fixed resolve that the event of the siege should subserve his own ambitious designs, as Dragut, as bold but not so careful as he, would not have troubled to plan.

He had seen clearly enough that Mustapha had meant that the toll of losses which must result from the attack on the Sanglea should be taken mainly from his own men, as would have happened had not Don Francisco's guns brought disaster to the Turkish boats. He had accepted that position, which it would not have been easy to refuse, and with some hope that the capture of the Sanglea would have added to his renown. Since it had failed, he had been resolute that he would not be used again as the cat's-paw for Mustapha's plans. The next time that he ordered his men to death, it should be at his own will, both on its occasion and in its design. But there was no need to tell Mustapha that in crude, quarrel-breeding words. He revolved the problem of St. Angelo's capture in a mind that was not accustomed to fail, and he aimed at such a plan as would make its fall to be clearly due to himself, and the wild army that called him chief.

He pondered Malta as an outpost of his own power, rather than as a distant jewel to be set in Soliman's crown, and was not sure that it would be easy to hold, even if it were won. It was too distant from his own base: too near the Sicilian shore. Certainly it could not be securely held unless the naval predominance which the Turks had obtained in the Mediterranean during the last ten years were more absolute than it had yet become. . . . But Malta's capture, with that of the small, but excellent fleet which was warped to the quays of the inner harbour now, would be an important advance to that end. . . . He would not choose to be besieged here as La Valette was now. Better Tripoli or Algiers than that. . . . But the dissensions by which Allah drew the teeth of the Christian dogs. . . . If they should stand idle now, while the stones of Malta crumbled under the ceaseless thunder of Turkish guns. . . . Well, he was young in years. There would be time to go far. . . . And Soliman was still breaking the Christian armies, and was through the mountains beyond Belgrade.

He did not doubt that, if St. Angelo were to fall, it was he that must bring it down. He did not doubt Mustapha's astuteness, and he knew that he was of a vast experience in methods and tactics of war. But he was old, and cautious of habit. Too circumspect in his ways to strike straight and hard, as this occasion required. Hassan agreed with Piali on that, more than he had been disposed to admit. For he thought Piali to be a worse fool than he was. The grossness of the man's size, his truculent overbearing manner of speech, as though he would silence opposition by mere loudness of voice, stirred contempt in one who had more culture, more self-control, and an assurance more confident of itself than Piali's doubtful ancestry and harem breeding had enabled him to acquire. . . .

His thoughts turned to the woman who had wandered that morning into his camp. He did not doubt her to be of a shameless sort, even by the Frankish standards, which revolted his conceptions of the place of women in ordered life. Probably she was criminal too. But she might have knowledge that it would be profit to buy. He thanked Allah that she had come to his tent rather than that of Mustapha or Piali; either of whom, he correctly supposed, would have kept her as secret as he purposed to do.

He thought of another woman who must be, he supposed, within St. Angelo's walls. One whose wit and courage had enabled her not only to escape when she had been in his hands, but by that freedom to bring to wreck the climax of what might have been one of the most splendid and spectacular audacities of a career in which failure was not frequent to find.

Even in that, he had not been without some reason to boast, for there was the capture of the *Flying Hawk*, and then the successful impersonation of the Grand Master's envoy, of which men would talk with little care that he had planned beyond that, and had hoped to lure Don Manuel's galleys to the Formentera trap.

But the fact that he had been so foiled, and by one whose follies of sex and youth had seemed to drop her into his hands like a falling fruit, gave her a larger place in his mind than she would otherwise have been likely to have.

He recalled her as he had seen her first, in the setting of Don Manuel's castle, being that to which she was born, and in the garb which was usual to virgins of gentle blood in the Latin lands. He remembered a pulcritude at which it had been pleasant to gaze, joined to a vivacity of spirit which was not easy to find among the more secluded, restricted women of his own race. But he had not looked at her then with more than a casual admiration, and praised her with courtesies appropriate to the part he played.

He remembered her as she had boarded the *Flying Hawk* in a page's dress, which had deceived him at first. . . . And the spirit in which she had met his recognition, and the knowledge of how she had come by her own will to the jaws of a deadly snare. Had she planned escape from the first? Had she understood the desperate peril she took when she left his deck in the night for the wind-tossed sea? He did not know, and could only guess in a vague way which did not lessen the deed, how she could have come at last to the deck of her cousin's ship. . . . He was not given to the sexual indulgence which was too frequent among the rulers of Moslem lands. Ambition centred his mind. He had Dragut's daughter for wife, a woman to whom he had given honour for her father's sake, and his obligations to him, which he would not lightly forget, even had it not been politic while he lived to keep them before his mind. But for that, she would have tasted more than once the chastisement that such women deserve. For she had her father's passion for the strong drinks that the law of Mahomet will not permit, and if it were either starved or too greatly indulged she would fall into quarrelsome moods, such as women should not be suffered to show to their natural lords. . . .

He had two others who were pleasant playthings at times, but, beyond that, they had no place in his thoughts. . . . He wondered, from what he had seen and heard when a Maltese slave and at other times, what such a wife as Angelica would be worth to have.

He might doubt of that; but that she would be pleasant to beat was no doubt at all. He might admire her for courage and other things, including that she had the look of one who would be likely to bear a good son for the man to whose hands she was fated to come, but the first thought that would fill his mind if she should become his by the chance of war, was that she must be taught that no woman could make sport of his plans without being brought to shame, or a bitter death.

It would be absurd to suppose that the capture of Angelica could appear to him as a major reason for compassing St. Angelo's fall. He had greater dreams; and would have said that there was no woman the world could hold who would be worth the hazard of life, Allah having supplied them in a very plentiful way. But he had resolved that when St. Angelo fell (as he meant it should) there was one who would not escape, nor be included in any amnesty that might place her beyond his power. He would give such orders as would bring her captured and still alive. . . . He had never ordered that a woman should be impaled, as Dragut would sometimes do, but it would have its amusement to see how she would behave in front of that death. . . . He did not resolve that he would order her to be ended thus. It would depend on his mood. But he meant to have her, and to give her sufficient cause to regret that of which he supposed she was boasting now, as a detail that his satisfaction required. . . .

He had this thought in his mind, among larger things, as he rode back to his camp, and enquired what had been learnt of Venetia while he had been away. He found that he had been well served in that, as he mostly was, being one who would be generous to reward, and also just (which is more) both in praise and blame, while having no forgiveness for failure of act or will.

It was proof of the activities and prevalence of Turkish spies in the town that he could be told at once of the charge on which her arrest had been made, with some detail, which did not deviate far from fact, of what she had been, and how she had come to her present pass. He saw that she had not fled without cause, which he supposed to be even more than it was, and somewhat differently based; and when he joined that to the fact that she had endured his first examination without being caught in a mendacious reply, he concluded that she might be one of whom a use could be made.

He went into his tent resolved to question her again concerning herself, and what she had been and done, and after that he would decide whether she would be of more use to him than a slave's price.

Venetia had had her own thoughts in this time. She had been served with better food than she had seen for some weeks, and she was one who was dainty in what she ate, as will often be with those whose childhood did not disdain a scrap of meat that the dogs had left. She knew the difference between that to which she had reached and that she had known in her early days, to which she would not lightly return.

She considered the inquisition through which she had come, which she concluded that she had well sustained. She looked round the comfort of Hassan's tent, and decided that she had arrived at a good place, which she must practise to keep. She knew that Moslems did not regard women quite in the Christian way, and that success might require a somewhat different technique from that at which she had become proficient before, but she did not think that she would prove unequal to that, and she had a sound belief that men are fundamently alike in all lands, when they are snared in a woman's wiles.

She considered what she should tell concerning herself, and why she had fled, and decided that a large proportion of truth would be expedient in itself, as well as saving much trouble to her. Those who live by lies (if it be done with any success) must have learned that the lie is a weapon to use with reluctance as well as care. It is apt to be like the sting of the bee, which might die (as she had been told) through having used it against a foe.

She did not regard the adventures of her life with either scruple or shame, providing that they could be told without rousing interference of law, or losing the regard of those to whom she should speak, as would have been the case if she had exposed herself to Francisco in a bare way, either in body or soul.

But when a woman offers to betray those of her own race to their deadly foes, they do not seek assurance of virtue in her, as making it more sure that she will perform her bond, but rather that she shall give, for that time, no sign of a lying tongue. She decided that Hassan should have as much simple truth as any man could in reason require from a woman's mouth.

"I have one leg over the wall," she said to herself, "and it is my fault if I slip now."

She looked at Hassan as he came in, handsome in the loose crimson and white of his military undress, and she thought him to be one to whom she would not object to belong, though she knew that there were disadvantages in being a Moslem's wife, particularly if he should get another at any time whom he should come to prefer. It might then be necessary, perhaps for years, to live a very continent life, while being neglected by him; with the fear of a bow-string tightening around the neck as the price of an indiscretion so slight that even a jealous Italian husband, whose love had not wandered another way, would not have been much disturbed. . . .

"They have fed you well?" he asked, as he entered, and the question was well enough, as was the good-humoured glance he gave her as she rose up from the cushions on which she had posed herself to await his coming. But she recognized it as being no more than the way in which a man might ask if his dog had been given sufficient meat, or even as he might enquire concerning a creature that was being fattened for his own dish. And he might look at such a beast in just that good-humoured way, as something it gave him pleasure to have. She was shrewd enough to perceive that there was no friendliness in his regard. She must prove her use, if she were to have any favours from him, and then she might find herself shipped for the slave-market at Byzantium or Algiers the next day when her use was done. . . . She had far to go before he would look at her in a personal way.

Well, she had done difficult things before now. She remembered how she had first invited La Cerda's eyes. . . .

He had given orders that he was to be left alone, and he settled himself now to listen at ease, telling her to seat herself in the same way. His power was too great, she was too absolutely in his hands, for him to be careful of the parade of rule. His object was to lead her to fluent talk, that she might reveal herself, and confirm what he had heard, or else be snared in a lie, in which case he proposed to put her in the torturer's hands, while he would stand by to hear what answers the pain would bring.

"I would know," he said, "by what stress you came here, and also what you suppose you can do to earn a life which we do not need. I suppose you know that those Turks who are captured from us are being hanged every day at Notabile market-cross? You must show me why you should be served in a better way."

"I suppose," she said, not being disturbed by a threat which it was clear that (for the moment) he did not mean, "I could show you that, if you are truly desirous to know. For if you should think me of no more worth than a slave would be, a thousand ducats would not be easy to get for what were left when the rope's work had been done."

"You name yourself at a high price," he replied, his eyes wandering critically over her form, which conformed more to the Italian ideals of loveliness than to those of his own race.

"Had he lived, La Cerda would have paid more."

"So he might. Do you grudge that he died by me?"

It was an idea that only came to him as he spoke. Had she found entrance here that she might have revenge for a lover's death? It was a possible thing.

Actually, the idea was new to her, having no substance of fact, and not having been circulated within the Christian lines, though it was a version of the combat in which Hassan had been cut down which had won an easy popularity on the Turkish side; and if Hassan had some cause to doubt it himself (concerning an event on the closing moments of which he had no more than a dazed mind), yet it did not follow that she had not heard the tale, and believed it true.

It was a danger she had not expected to meet that he should doubt her in that way; but she was instant in the adroitness of her reply, in which truth, having been wooed in her imaginations before, was no less than an easy friend: "Did you so? I had not heard that, having been jailed as I was. He is one of whom I will say no ill beyond this, that he had proved unequal to be my shield against the Grand Master's pursuit. . . . I had supposed him dead at St. Elmo before."

"It is of the Grand Master's pursuit you shall tell me now."

"So I will; and you will see that I had no choice but to come here, if I would save my own skin, which I will keep unbruised if my wits can."

"You are one," Hassan said, looking at her in an appraising way, "who would shrink at the whip?"

"I have soft flesh, as you see. . . . I might not be cowardly to cry out, more than most will do. . . . But I have a good hope that I shall compass a better way."

"So you may, if you answer now with a truthful tongue, and if you avoid that you may find that there are worse pains than a whip can give."

"I have no cause nor motive to lie. Having good wares to trade, shall I sell trash? What do you want me to tell?"

"You can tell all you will. I have time to hear."

She told him then how La Cerda had brought her into St. Angelo, and found her lodging in the citadel there, how Sir Oliver Starkey had arranged for her to be sent away, how La Cerda had professed to do that, but had hidden her in his own house, and how he had quarrelled with the Grand Master over St. Elmo, and been sent there in so sudden a way that he could make no further disposition for her.

"I heard something of that," Hassan allowed, being the first time he had spoken since she began.

"So I suppose you might. I heard that there was much talk in the town, and dissension, even among the Commanders, thereon. But I do not say it from my own knowledge thereof, having to lie so close that it was as though I were jailed from before you came."

She went on to her tale of the steward's death, which she had told so often before in one way that it had become fact to her as much as to those who heard, and then, in a briefer style, feeling that she had talked a sufficient time, she added that she had been in hiding since then, till she had been caught by the Grand Master a few days before, and only escaped when her trial had been at hand.

"So far," he said, "your tale has a likely sound, and it makes junction enough with what has reached me from other mouths. Yet I do not see that you have shown cause for so great a dread that you should break jail (and you have not told me how you did that!) to come here. . . . On your own tale, you had cause to push with the dagger's point, as would be allowed in all lands."

"So it may seem to you. But have you weighed the Grand Master's hate against such as I? Or against all women, as I suppose, unless it be a few saints of a bloodless sort."

"There is some weight in that," he allowed, "on your side. For it is a fact, as we all know, that the misbelievers are cursed of God, so that they will not put you to that use for which you are made and meant, and then back in your own place: but they must either raise you to heights which are not for you, or else scourge their own loins, and refuse to touch you at all; which is a marvel of men who are sane in some other ways. . . . I can suppose that the Grand Master was not your friend, yet his repute is not that of one who would have you falsely condemned, and I must still say that your reason was not enough."

"Yet it seemed other to me; and you may better believe when I tell you how they practised to bring me down. I was to be trapped, so I was warned by those who were friend to me, by being required to declare who I was, and from where I came, and when I had told the tale which I had said to Leon—to the Chevalier La Cerda——"

"That being untrue?"

"I had not told him all, as who would in such case as that?"

"Yet being warned?"

"I have told you so far that I will not restrict. I was so caught that there was a ditch on each side, both of which I had no hope to avoid. For if I held to the tale I had told before, they would bring witness to show that I had been born with another name, and if I were first with that, so that their witnesses would sing a stale song, then I must own that I was one whom Turin would be glad to have, with a charge of murder against her name."

"Which we must suppose true, seeing of what you were now charged?"

"Which was not true at all. I was in the house where it was done, in the next room, but I had no part in it further than that, nor knowledge of it before. . . . There were four who knew that for truth, of which three are now hanged for the deed they did, and the fourth, who was with me then, would not speak though the halter were round my neck, for he was one of high rank, and a clean public repute, who should not have been there with me."

"Turin is a far place. Even in time of peace they would not bear you from land to land."

"So it may sound, but Malta is not as most countries are. The

Grand Master has friends in all lands, which he is careful to keep. Yet I will not say I was most fearful of that. I feared that it would be said, as you have said now, that I was one to hang, having murdered before if not then, and so most likely at that time, by a good guess."

"And that is what I must not believe?"

"It is untrue. I suppose there is no reason beside, for you will not care what may have been in Turin, if I can be useful to you; and, if I cannot, you will not give me a soft couch because my hands are clean of all but the steward's blood."

"You may be right there, and yet you may have spoken your bane, for I must tell you that, having heard your tale, which I largely believe, I do not see what use you can be.

"You will say that you know much of the town, and something of its defence. But, if you said all that you can, you might find that I know more. We have good spies, as I have no doubt that the Grand Master has on his side. They are of scanty avail, not being men who hold posts of command, or have keys in reach. They cannot betray that in which they have no trust. But how are you better than they? I should call you less. By your own tale, you have been closely immured, almost from when you were brought to this shore. I suppose that there are few who can know less. . . . Now I will ask you one thing: Have you courage and wit enough that you will go back, saying that you have repented, or what you will, and taking news of that which I will tell you to say? It is for that (and nothing beside) that I will give you gold you will like to have."

Venetia did not like this design, which she weighed in a quick mind, and saw to be beset with dangers on every hand. She saw a tangle of lies in which she might be doubted on either side, and she knew enough of the ways of war to guess that she would not long be safe from a knife drawn briskly across her throat, even from the hands of those she might be preferring to serve. Yet she did not look so downcast as he had thought she would, as she made her reply.

"You say you have spies enough, and, if they content you with what they tell, it is not my part to say they are less than good. Did they tell you much of the cannon by which you lost nine boats of ten, and, as the talk goes, more than a thousand lives? If they did, they were boats that were boldly led."

Hassan looked at her with a quickened regard when she asked that. 'No," he said, "they failed us there, as you have been sharp to see.

They make excuse that the battery was too secretly held. Have you other things, such as that, that you are able to tell?"

"How can I say? Should I have known you were so badly served about that, had not the boats come to where they could be put down?"

"And is that a thing you could have told us before?"

"It was there I was hid for the last days, till the Grand Master must come into a cell where he had no business to be."

"You did not tell me of that."

"I thought I made the tale long enough without talk of each place where I lay close."

"Then I ask you now. Did you so contrive that you could hide in the battery itself, and none know you were there?"

"You misconceive what I did. I was harboured there by Don Francisco of Vilheyna himself."

"By——? What is his post there . . .? He is one I have met before."

"So I heard from him. He is in command. It was his devise to secretly change the guns for those of a longer range."

"Tophet's fiends! We owe that to him . . .? Why did he hide you there? Was he so greatly La Cerda's friend? Or did you pay as a woman can?"

"I paid naught. It was gift from him. He thought me hardly abused."

"Well, so he might. . . . Tell me this, has he one who is cousin to him, woman or man, I cannot tell which, nor what they may call her now, whether Don Garcio or another name?"

"She is man to all but a few. She was not to me, for I hid first in her room."

"Where was that?"

"In the castle itself. In a turret over the part that Sir Oliver has."

"How did you get there?"

"It was where La Cerda had me at first, before trouble began. . . . I fled both to a room I knew, and where I knew her to be."

"And she hid you there, being friend to you?"

There was a tone of puzzled doubt in the query, which Venetia understood, but did not resent. She was ever content to be what she was, and assured that she could be other things if her well-being required. She answered with a candour which may have been more natural to her than the art of lying in which she had brought herself to a trained skill: "She was not my friend. She was never that. But she is not one to betray."

"Do they know you for what you are?"

"She could make a good guess. I am saint to him, unless he changed when he heard me fled."

"Are they not then in accord?"

"Over me? They are far from that."

She told in detail the events which had followed her flight to Angelica's room, filling up with some shrewdness of surmise the gaps where her knowledge failed.

When she had done, he said: "I will think of this, and talk to you again. Meantime you will stay here, for your presence must not be known."

He summoned Alif, to whom he said: "There is no talk that this woman is in my tent?"

"It is known or guessed by two, but they will not speak."

"I will slit their tongues if they do. But if they are still, you can bring me their names on a later day, and they shall touch gold. She must stay here for a time. You will place a guard round the tent, both by night and day, that none may go in or out, except that I so command. If she should do me harm in the night, you will flay her slowly, taking the feet first."

He turned to her, when Alif had gone. "Did you understand what I said? Then I will tell you what will be useful for you to know. You will stay here for this night, and if you mean evil to me you will have the best chance that a woman could. But I gave order that this tent should be circled so that none can go either in or out, and if I should come to harm, they will flay you alive in a slow way, taking the feet first, which (I will tell you as one who has seen it done) you will not greatly enjoy."

He spoke in a smiling way, being pleased to take what might seem to those who looked on an unmeasured risk, as when he had put himself in Don Manuel's power, but which he felt he could control to his own end. Men would say that, having slain La Cerda, and his concubine having found her way to his tent (with what purpose it would be easy to doubt), he had slept with her alone, trusting the Prophet's care as few of the faithful would hazard to do. But in his heart there was a confident hope that Venetia would not seek such revenge, with the surety that she would be peeled alive on the next day. It was more of his own revenge on which his mind was disposed to dwell, and of the larger issue of St. Angelo's fall, as he considered how he could use Venetia's acquaintance with Francisco and his cousin to some treacherous ruse.

Venetia took the threat with a laugh, being content that she was to have a further time during which to win, if she could, the approval of the most powerful man to whom her adventurous youth had yet closely come; though she could not wholly avoid a thought of the hourly danger in which she stood among those who were natural foes, and were ruthless in what they did. She had to guard her life against all with no more to aid than her single wit, and the market value her body bore.

So she laughed with all the courage she had, and gave Hassan a bold reply: "Then I must be glad that you look to be in good health, as one who may live to another dawn, for I would keep my skin where it is most useful to me. Did you doubt lest I would use a knife in the night . . .? I am less of that kind than you may suppose; though you cannot have felt a great doubt, or you had disposed in another way. . . . But, if you will, I can serve you in better sort."

He looked at her somewhat as one will look at a market beast, and she felt a sudden quickening of heart, not of passion, but at the possibility that she was on the way to a new success. She saw that he was not wholly cold to that which her words implied, but when he spoke it was plain that what she sought would be less than simple to win.

"So you could, and so you will, if I wish. You are fair enough in a pale way, but, by your own tale, you are too much of a common kind."

"So I have been," she allowed, "but you could mend that if you would. . . . It is men who alter, not I. . . . I seek harbour that has not been easy to find."

"Well," he said, "you must seek again. For this night, you must stay here."

They were in the outer pavilion when he said this. He went inward, leaving her alone.

She saw that she would have comfort enough, for there were cushions that she could pile to her own will, and rich shawls for warmth. There was a lamp that would last the night.

She lay down and, at first, she was too weary to sleep. Her mind was active to hope and plan. She saw that she had escaped, and come to the place where she now lay, with better fortune than would have been forecast by a cautious mind.

She had been rebuffed by Hassan's last words, and she saw that he looked at her with a contempt the reason of which she did not deny. Those who would come to a clean bed should not be too much mired on the way. Yet, if the storm come, and the rain, and good shelter be hard to find? She took little blame to herself. She was not ashamed before men, and even to God, if He should be hard with her when the time should come, she supposed that she would have something to say. But she did not therefore deny fact. If a ruler preferred to take women only into his bed who were private to him, then a harlot such as herself would not be a likely choice. She must trade at another booth. She would be a fool to complain of that; but if she could overcome his contempt till he should prefer her to those (most probably gross and stupid and fat) whom he now owned—well, it would be more triumph to her.

Her mind turned to the warning threat he had made, and the doubt it showed. In fact, though it did not incline her to seek his life, it fathered the thought, which would not otherwise have been there.

She was one who would always do more in dreams than the waking day. Now she lay lost in imagination of what would be said within St. Angelo's walls, if a tale should reach there that the woman they had harried and jailed had penetrated the Turkish lines and slain the corsair ruler within his tent.

She imagined dispute in which some would say she had broken jail that she might revenge the lover who had fallen to Hassan's sword (she did not doubt that La Cerda had died in that way, having heard no different report), while others would have it that she had been moved by higher zeal for the Christian cause, and had escaped with the noble purpose of ridding it of its most dangerous foe, as well as of vindicating her own character from the imputations that had been cast upon it. She would be Judith to them. Judith was a great name. She wondered what Judith had done in her later years. Probably she had made a noble match with some Hebrew prince, who would be glad to wed with one of such valiant fame, and who had a face to seduce kings. In the day, she would have been queen of the society of her time: and in the night she would have her prince, whose head would not have to be cut off when he had drowsed after their amorous play. . . . She did not think much of the deed itself. She could have cut off the jailer's head easily enough when he fell asleep, and he would have been little loss to the world. She would not have minded doing that, if only he had been considerate enough to bring a sword, as Holofernes seemed to have done. (But what a mess Judith must have made in the bed! Hacking off heads seemed a needlessly sanguinary way to kill men, if it had to be done with good furniture all around.) She supposed Judith had wanted the head. She had heard that version of the tale in which the Hebrew heroine had strolled back to her city swinging Holofernes' head by the hair; and, when she considered that, she saw she had come to the place where the parallel would be sure to fail.

Her imagination became lively on a new path. She had skinned living eels with her own hands. She had seen butchers skin beasts that were just dead, as all men might at that day, when slaughtering was not performed behind solid doors. Men do not greatly change with the years; and it may be error to think that the age in which Malta's agony was endured was more cruel than are those that have been since, or now are. There are cruelties in the laboratories of a later time, at seeing which a fiend might blush to be called a man. But cruelties were open then that are secret now. . . . Venetia was concerned for no more than her own case. If she could have been sure that she would walk up the Bourg swinging Hassan's head by the hair (which would have been short enough to require a good grip that it should not drop) the project might have had attractions which it now lacked.

But she was convinced that it would not end in that way. It would end with her in the midst of a hollow square, surrounded by a crowd of corsairs, very variously and gaily garbed, and all in a silent, eager expectancy to hear how she would scream when the executioners started to peel her feet. . . . No, her skin should stay where it was, as far as that decision might rest with her.

She turned her thoughts to the more practical consideration of how she could earn the goodwill of those in whose power she had put her life. She did not wish to betray her own blood (with some possible exceptions, the Grand Master heading that list), if she could avoid this without risk. She was simply striving to save herself, as most men (she supposed) would think it natural for her to do. Anyway, it was natural to her. She had played for her own hand through more than twenty difficult years, and was not likely to stop now, being among those who might make her back raw for a morning's sport, if she should give them excuse. Her trouble was that she did not see how she was to be of sufficient use to earn a good price in safety and then reward. Hassan's idea that she should go back to cajole the Grand Master with some tale of changing sides again, and betraying the Turkish plans, did not please her at all. She thought (in particular) that Sir Oliver would be hard to fool. The Grand Master might not skin her alive, but he would rack her if he had reason to think she lied, so that she might be a cripple till she should reach the grave, which would be hard to endure. If he guessed that she had come back as a Turkish spy, he would hang her in the next hour, and she would be in fortune if she did not come to a worse pain. . . . She might, of course, decline to fulfil the plan when she would be again under the shelter of Malta's flag. But would the mere fact of that be enough to turn the Grand Master's anger aside? Would he not talk of the law in the hateful way that the strong will, and those in a settled place, as being something above himself, to which he must commit her perforce, though he might grieve with her pain?

She had been adroit to turn Hassan's talk aside with the tale of how she had been concealed in the battery which shattered the Turkish boats. He had been plainly intrigued by her account, for reasons she could not entirely guess; but would he come back to his first idea when he should think of it again?

CHAPTER XIX

"I WOULD be more at ease," Francisco said, "if I could know where she is gone; for I have a hope that she will not have put me out of her mind, and, if I come through this war, I am resolved that I will find her again."

This was to Angelica, a week after Venetia fled. They were better friends now than they had been since she had come into their lives, or perhaps before that. Francisco, being troubled and anxious in mind, would have someone to whom to talk, and Angelica gave a sympathy that was no less true because she had some thoughts, both about Venetia and other things, which she kept unsaid.

As to where Venetia had gone, or even how she had escaped, there was no more than a poor guess.

The jailer had not been found on the wrong side of a locked door or at least it was not known that he had, except by the man who had come to relieve his watch, for they had seen that they would be caught in an equal blame. One had let her escape the cell, and the other had failed to keep watch at the outer door. It was a better tale to say that she had escaped, none could guess when or how, beyond that her place was empty when morning came.

It might not be believed, but it left the blame among three, of whom two might be quite innocent men, and one, in fact, was, being the one who opened her door when the morning came, and his protests that she must have gone in a witch's way had a genuine sound.

It was a good guess that it was she who had fled in the boat which had left the quay with a pistol bullet in swifter pursuit, but it was no more; for she had never been clearly seen in the misty night, and the boat had been adrift the next day near the harbour mouth, being empty then, and the wind carrying it to St. Elmo's point.

The spies brought no word of her having been caught by the Turks, and the most likely guess was that she had got away to some other part of the island, and would there try for passage in a coasting boat, such as would slip over to Sicily in the night. Or it was supposed by some that she had been wounded and fallen out of the boat.

Anyway, she was gone; and Sir Oliver saw no harm in that, and Del Monte thought it a mercy for which his own saint deserved more than common thanks, for he had had no heart in the wanton's defence, which he did not think to consort with his dignity or deserve his care. He thought himself more fitly engaged in command of St. Michael's fort, with which most men would agree.

The defence of that fort and the Sanglea was not a post that allowed of much rest at this time, for it was recognized to be the weakest of the bastioned line which was St. Angelo's outer guard, and the Turks, while they had not attempted further storm during the last week either there or elsewhere, were still pressing closer on every side. They had received some store-ships with extra artillery, and large consignments of powder and shot, and other munitions of war, so that they could still erect more batteries, and maintain fire on all sides both by day and sometimes by night, to which the Christians must make more cautious reply.

It was seen also that the Turkish infantry changed camp in sundry places, so that they lay closer around the walls. None could say when the storm would burst, nor at which point, but there must be vigilance at all, which must never sleep. And every day there came to Sir Oliver's table a list of those who had been wounded or died in the town from the Turkish fire, and in the bicker around the wall; and ever a watch was kept from the highest tower for the Spanish succour which did not come.

The Maltese militia at this time was still holding the most part of the island, except the coasts, with Marshal Couppier in command. They had neither numbers, discipline, nor practice in arms sufficient for them to offer battle to the Turks, but they harassed them both by night and day. Mustapha had held more than one Council to resolve whether he should not divert his strength for a time to strike at Notabile (as it was then called), the ancient town in the centre of the island, which was the headquarters of this guerrilla attack. But the decision was always the same, that though it could be reached, and the whole island overrun, so that the militia would be destroyed, and the remaining population given to slavery or massacre, as Turkish greed or animosity might decide, yet the time which this enterprise would require, and the losses it would entail when operating in a country whose every field had a wall of stone which could shelter an ambushed foe, would be such that, when it would have been done, there would be little remaining strength with which to threaten St. Angelo's walls.

It would be St. Elmo again in a second, fatal event. But if

St. Angelo should be brought down, then the island could be made a more leisured, being a certain prey.

So Marshal Couppier, who had been prepared to resist a Turkish advance till the last man should be dead, found that his task was less hard, though not less needful to do. Up to the time of the great assault on the Sanglea, he had been able, either by water or land, to maintain communication with the Grand Master, so that they would often time operations to vex the Turks at the same hour from their separate sides; but now the Turkish lines were so closely drawn, and so keenly watched, that it was an equal chance that a creeping messenger would be espied, and either shot as he ran or caught to hang in a rope's noose on the next day.

Sir Oliver sent a letter out to tell of Venetia's escape, and to provide that she should be apprehended if she were found, but at this time he had had no reply, nor was he sure that the letter had been safely conveyed through the Turkish lines.

"I suppose," Angelica said on this day, when Venetia came into the talk, "that you will wish that she did not fall into Turkish hands, lest she should have told them things that were best unsaid?"

"She has not done that, as I think," Sir Oliver replied, "for we should have certainly heard. There is not much in the Turkish camp that we may not know if we wish, though the news has become harder to get in the last week. I suppose that they think we are nearly down, in which I should call them wrong. But the scum of men, such as will spy and betray, will ever watch for the winning side and will prefer to barter with them. . . . But as to her whom you name, she could do us but little harm, for what did she know more than a thousand besides? I should say, less. . . . But I perceive that you do not trust that she would not betray those of her own blood?"

"I would not think evil without a cause," Angelica said to that; "but I suppose she would think first of her own skin."

Sir Oliver agreed about that, not guessing how literally it had been, but he did not think her of much account, either to be true or betray. He said: "I suppose you can put her out of your thoughts, as one of whom you will not hear, nor yet see, till your life is through. . . . I am glad to see that, now she is gone, you and Don Francisco are in better accord. . . . I have news for you on another matter, which should give you no pain. You will not have much from Don Manuel's wealth, which the Order claims, but your Segura lands will bring you revenue in your own right, which the Church cannot touch except by your own deed when of full age, so there will be no strife of law about that. You are a ward for the next year, and after that you can freely wed, giving him you choose a great dower. . . . And now you know this to be, I suppose you will leave, if a chance should come that would take you free."

Angelica looked at him with troubled eyes. "Do you think that?" she asked. "I had not thought to hear it from you."

"It is what wisdom would urge, you being free of the doubt you fled, and which held you here."

"Being here, am I less use than my food is worth?"

"You have done your part, and few men have done more, or as much, if I make a full sum, from when you saved your ships from the Moorish trap."

"Had I been a man, would you have said what you did now?"

"Perhaps not. But you are a woman, who should not have come."

"Am I that? I think at times I am neither woman nor man, being less than either. Would you say that a woman's honour must be less than a man should have?"

"No. But it is rooted in other soil."

"And that honour there are those who would say that I did not regard when I came here?"

"That is what I have never said."

"Nor perhaps thought. I did not mean it of you. But there are those who would. There are those who will in the after days. Am I to lose on both counts? By your leave, I stay here till the siege is through."

"I do not refuse. But—do you so decide for no more than the reason you say? For, if you do, I might reply that your honour on both counts is too rooted to shake. But you should ask of your own heart: is it for Malta you so resolve or a nearer cause?"

Angelica took this with a moment's bending of puzzled brows, which lifted again as she gave a candid reply.

"It is Francis you mean by that! What if it should be for him? He is the nearest I have. But I should say it is both. It is also Malta I will not leave while this siege endures."

"Then there is no more to be said, except to pray that it shall not come to such end as will bring you grief, and we must ask that for larger reasons than that you shall steer to a restful sea."

He turned his thoughts to more urgent cares, and she, having done the work she had for that hour, went out to meet Francisco at the tavern which had now become habit to them, and where they knew they would both be at an hour before noon, unless there should be signs of stir in the Turkish camp, such as would keep him beside his guns, or she should have work of another kind which she could not leave.

Now she found that he was seated there when she came. They were alone, for the stringency of the siege had brought such a shortage of food (except only flour) as had caused the Grand Master to take it under his control and ration it in a strict way. There was nothing which could be sold in a tavern now, except a light wine, of which the Grand Master took little account, whether it flowed or ran dry, the water tanks being as full as they were.

Angelica saw at a glance that Francisco was stirred by some instant cause, though whether it were trouble or joy was not easy to see.

"I have had this," he said, "in the past hour," and with the words he passed her a letter, ill-writ on what appeared to be the fly-leaves torn from a large book. "It is for you also to read."

My lord and I think my friend,

I am close held by the Turk, having been caught by them, which I did not intend, when the boat drifted to shore, being beyond control of my hands.

I have made plan to escape, which will be, I cannot say on which night, but the one next after this will be delivered to you.

I shall bring news of such weight as will buy my peace, and some honour for you, but I must entreat and give you my trust in this, that you will tell my coming to none, till I am again in the cell from which I was dragged by the Grand Master away.

When he will know how I have been served, and what I have done for the Christian cause, he may regret that he would have chased me to death, or he may not care even then, saying that I was sent here by the Saints, that I might be used to Malta's avail, which I suppose to be all his care.

I shall come by way of the sea, at the second hour of the night, landing under your guns, being the one place where I am not most like to be met first with an arquebus ball, and after that with a question of who may come in the night from the Turkish lines.

When I plead with you to tell none, and to so contrive that I may gain the cell without being seen except only by you (if that cannot be saved) I do not mean that Don Garcio shall not be told—he not being one to betray. He is one I shall ask you to tell, and he may think in what plight I shall be, having been racked, and had some tortures besides that I cannot write, and being kept in such bareness and dirt as you need not guess. Will you ask him to be your friend to procure such things as I greatly need, and that in the most secret way, to be in the cell when I arrive? And if he can be there himself for my better aid I shall be grateful the while I live.

Your fri—— VENETIA.

The letter ended thus with a broken word, not as though she had written all that she might, but as being hindered by lack of space on the torn sheets which may have been all she had.

Angelica read it twice, saying nothing the while. She had pity at what she read, which she did not doubt, but her heart sank that they were to be so troubled again. When she spoke, it was at first only to say: "It is Arabic book," as she turned the paper, which had been good, but was soiled and torn, and had a brown smear at one place, as of recent blood.

"You will do what she asks?" Francisco enquired, as one who hoped but was less than sure.

"She asks more than enough, and some things that she cannot have."

"You mean that you will not be her friend at so great a need?"

"I meant less. But she must not teach what we shall do. Do you see that she asks your honour, if not your life, that she may cover her own show?—which, I will allow, may be evil enough."

"I see no great risk, if it be shortly revealed, as she must mean it to be."

"She asks what she does not say, that you will draw your men back from the guns. How would you answer for that?"

"It would be but a short time, and a little space."

"Which would be too far and too long. . . . It is time of war. She must find courage to face her shame."

"You think little of her." His face showed the misery of his doubt of what she might have endured.

"You are wrong in that. I will do all that I can that is not hurtful to you, who have gone too near to wreck for her once, which should be enough. . . . She is less than wise for herself at times, being too careful about her fears."

"I should say that she has had high courage, and evil use."

"Which may be true, and yet I may not have said wrong. . . . I will help you in this (unless I change with more thought) on one bargain alone. I must let Sir Oliver know that she is likely to come, bringing news from the Turkish camp."

"It was of my honour you talked. What should I have left if you do that?"

"You would have all that is yours now. How could you lose it by me?"

"She trusts me that I will not disclose."

"You were to tell me."

"And none else."

"But if I do? Could she charge you with that? I think your wits go when you deal with her."

"Then I will say that it is my trust in you which you cast aside."

"Francis, will you hear sense? Have I failed you before? I will only say that she may come, and not when or where. It might be the saving of all (and not least of her) if she should be discovered by chance while she had not been able to disclose herself in her own way."

"Well, if you are so resolved, I cannot prevent. We must trust to you."

Angelica disliked that he should link Venetia's name with his own in the common "we", more than anything that had yet been said, but it was not a feeling which she elected to show. "I will do what I can," she said, "but I think her ways to be such that they bring more trouble to those around than she has herself, and that might be called enough."

She saw Francisco frown at this, which, she became aware as she spoke, had an ungenerous sound, Venetia having suffered so much as her letter showed. She asked: "Am I shrew? Yet I am one to help, as you may have found me before. And if it be more for you than for her (we being so close of blood) you must forgive me for that."

Francisco looked at her in a confused humour which he could not have explained to himself had he tried (which it was sure he would not).

"You are not shrew," he said, "nor unkind. You are the one aid that we have. But you do things in your own way, as you ever would."

He went at that, and had he been asked if he were sorry or glad he would have felt it hard to reply.

Venetia lived. That was good. She was coming back. That was good, too. She brought a hope that she might win pardon, from which his own hopes rose to a new height. She would be here, and La Cerda dead. It should not be beyond him to win her love. He had more pride than conceit of his own worth, but he knew himself to be of a great name, and a great wealth. He had proved he could be her friend, and it was to him that she looked in her present need. There was much in that. He might not be vain of himself, and yet hope she would soon be his, she being cast off by La Cerda's death from a place that had seemed high and secure a few months before, when Malta had not called its victims from every land. . . . But then he thought of what her letter had said. There had been the rack, which could leave men and women crippled beyond repair, though it was not often used to so great extreme. There had been tortures she would not write. And she was now such that she would not be seen except by those she could not avoid. That might be from no worse than dirt, or garments missing or fouled or torn. . . . It was vain to guess. He must wait, striving neither to fear too much, nor to hope too high.

Angelica went to Sir Oliver, who was busy with many cares, and whom there were those who waited to see, not being able to go in by her door.

"I have something to say, if you are not too deeply sunk in matters of greater weight."

"I am not so much that I will not listen to you, let it be on what subject it may, so that La Cerda's mistress do not return."

"But it is of her that I come to speak."

Sir Oliver raised eyebrows of half-humorous resignation, and then showed his more serious mood in the tired sigh of a man who was weary with work which would never cease.

"Well, I must hear. What is it now? She is a cork that will never sink."

"She was caught in the Turkish lines. She has been racked, and had other pains, I know not for what cause. I have to ask this. If she can escape, bringing information you should be grateful to have, will she be received in the right way?"

"How do you know?"

"I cannot say that. I am pledged not."

"Has Francisco been changing letters with her? Will he never learn? She will be his death. . . . I must warn you now that if he helped her escape (of which there has been debate, but there is no proof, so it blew away) he is in more jeopard than she."

"I am assured he did not, for he told me that, and I am one to whom he would be unlikely to lie. Nor has he written to her, nor known where she was, as I have his word, and a better proof."

"It is well for him. But he knows now?"

"If you would not ask what I cannot say?"

"There is no need to say. It is plain without words."

"He was to tell no one but me. You will see how I must stand if I say more."

"But if she makes such query as that——"

"You misconceive. It is not she, it is I who ask."

"And I must know more, or refuse reply. Do you ask with Francisco's consent?"

"I can tell you this. He has had a letter from her, which he had not sought. We took counsel on that, and he agreed that I should ask what I now have."

"You could tell more. How will she get his reply?"

"I have said all that I can."

"Then I will answer this far, and no more. She will be wise to come back, being in such hands, by any means that she may. Being so returned, if she can bring knowledge of great avail, such as the point where they will next make their attack, she will have done service for which we pay. But she must find no promise in that."

"I do not get much."

"Nor do you give with a free hand. . . . I will tell you this. Whatever tale she may bring, we shall not be quick to believe. For a matter of weight would not be opened to her, nor would I trust her at any time."

Angelica looked as though a new thought had troubled her mind. "You think her one who would betray those of her own faith?"

"Her own faith? What is that . . .? If she come back, I suppose she will betray the Turks rather than us, for reasons easy to see. . . . But I do not trust her at all."

Angelica, considering this conversation, felt that she had done well. She had given Venetia any help that she could, which might not be much, but she had not been active for her. She had cleared Francisco of having been in secret communication with her, or having aided in her escape, and as to this letter he had now had, Sir Oliver must allow that he had been promptly informed, and also that Venetia purposed return.

It was not all—it might not be enough for Francisco's defence—if it should afterwards be disclosed that he had disposed his men rather to enable her to gain his cell unobserved than with a single thought for his battery needs, as his duty was, but it was all she could do. She turned her thoughts to supplying Francisco's cell with such comforts as a woman would most urgently need who would come from torture and dirt. She had to use some circumspection in this, and she must visit the battery more than she wished, besides sending a valise to Francisco which was not to be opened except by him.

She blamed herself that she did these things with so poor a will, thinking of that which she supposed Venetia must have endured, but her feelings were less easy to rule than were acts and words.

CHAPTER XX

THE oars moved with long, slow, silent strokes, the muffled blades making no more sound than would be concealed by the lapping of the water on the sea-wall, or the wind would carry away.

The night was dark, and Venetia, sitting in the bow of the boat, could see no more than the dim outline of St. Angelo's towers rising blackly against the sky.

Hassan himself sat at her side. He leaned forward, his eyes searching the night. His presence there may be held for proof of the reckless-seeming courage which had made his name one that the world knew, but there was calculation in what he did.

"You must go slowly," she whispered, "and give me time. It is hard to be exact here, but we cannot be greatly wrong."

"If you fail," he said, "there will be no mercy from me. There shall not be less than one death." His bare scimitar lay at his hand, of which he had warned her before. She was not in a great dread as to that, thinking that she could guide him aright; but it was a threat that she may have required to control her mind to his own will, for she became aware, as the moment neared, that she disliked that which she came to do, more than she thought that she would. Nor was she clear as to what its consequences were likely to be, for she had been plain to him that if the battery should be entered they would be (as it seemed to her) no nearer to the entering of St. Angelo's towers. They would have no more than a place they could not hold for an hour, nor with hope to escape alive when the light should come.

"That," he had said, "is quite clear. Guide the boat there, and do what is agreed when we arrive, and your part is through. I mean no more than to be there for a short time."

Yet if that were true (and she could not see how he could hope to do more), for what use were the boats, laden with men, that she had seen when they embarked, and which were now following silently in their rear? For the battery was beneath and outside the citadel wall, being built on the narrow space between wall and shore.

Francisco was to be caught (so she had been told) and his guns quickly destroyed. There was no design beyond that. And he was needed to save the life of Candelissa's son, whom Marshal Couppier had caught, and was proposing to hang, according to the way of this war. They would be exchanged, and she would have won her reward with less harm to her own race than they might deserve, seeing how they had treated her.

But that fleet of boats, small though they were, and bearing no such number of men as had been in those that Francisco's guns had shattered before, showed that there was a further purpose, of which she had not been told. Well, could she help that? Her first care must be for her own neck. She had no wish to have that scimitar drawn across it, Hassan having shown her, in an idle way, how keen was the shining blade, so that it could sever a cushion which had been thrown into the air. . . .

She could not be greatly wrong if she guided them under the shadow of the main tower, and not too much to the left, by which they would have come to the little quay where the boats were moored —the quay from which she had made escape. If she should go too much to the right, there would be more open sky over the boom which closed the inner harbour that lay between St. Angelo and the Sanglea. . . . She had used all her arts during the past week, and thought she had now some place in Hassan's regard, so that he might be more inclined to keep than to send her away, but she knew he would have no ruth if she should fail now, or if she should not use her voice to betray. . . .

Francisco leaned on the wall, listening into the night, with Angelica at his side. They were intent to watch, for it was close to the time that Venetia had said. The men who should have been stationed around the guns had been withdrawn by Francisco's orders. They lay asleep, or diced by the light of a hanging lamp in their shelter at the battery's rear.

"It is wonder," Angelica said, "that she can handle a boat alone to find her way here in the night (and so that she can say at what time she will come), and that the more that she has been racked and hurt as she says. Nor is it easy to think that she has found those in the Turkish camp who will row her here."

"She is not simple to thwart," Francisco replied. "We do not know how she escaped from prison before."

Angelica made no answer to that, thinking it easy to guess, though she would have guessed wrong. She supposed that it had been with the aid of Francisco's gold, though that might be more than himself knew. She said: "Well, it will soon be shown. . . . What should you do if she should appear with a crew of men, and we here alone?"

"Is it likely she would? But, even then, there is the parapet tc he scaled, and my own men are not far."

"Well, I would it were done."

"So do I. . . . Is that not a boat? Out to the right? Can you not see?"

As he spoke, the great clock of San Lorenzo Church sounded a double stroke, that came clearly through the silent calm of the night, and they knew that the hour had come.

At the same moment, hearing that sound, Hassan said, in his own tongue, which Venetia could not understand: "Pull in now. Pull hard, for the time is short."

The two men at the oars quickened their strokes, and the boat came fast out of the night.

"That is she," Francisco said, and there was excitement in his voice which, to Angelica, was not pleasant to hear. "She has not come with a large crew. There is one at her side, and two who row."

So it was. The boat grounded a short distance away. The man who was beside Venetia jumped quickly out, and helped her ashore. The rowers sat where they were. Venetia came forward with the one man at her side. There was no menace in that, though there might be a puzzle as to why they did not push off, having put her ashore. So Angelica said.

"They wait only to see that she is safely received," Francisco supposed.

Well, so it might be, though she saw little sense in that. It was at least certain that it was Venetia who approached, and, by the way she walked, it appeared that she had not been racked enough to make her slow over the stones.

Hassan was not far behind, having a delicate choice to make. He did not know that he might not be greeted with a volley of arquebus balls, which would be likely to shorten a life for which he had future use. But he had resolved to take this chance in a cool mind, and he would not shrink. If he let Venetia go alone, how would he be sure that she would speak the right words? He resolved that it would be best to follow closely behind. If there were a volley to come, he would be as much covered by her as her smaller size would provide.

Francisco leaned over the edge, and Venetia called from below: "How am I to come up?"

"You must have a rope. There is no other way on this side."

Their voices were guarded and low, for high overhead rose the great mass of St. Angelo's castle, and sentries watched from the wall.

Francisco let down a looped rope. The parapet was not high; and, if she should come round to enter the battery from behind, that she would be seen or heard by the men was a likely thing.

Venetia began to adjust the rope, and Hassan turned away as though his part were done, and he must go back. The two men in the boat began to haul on a rope which had been trailing through the water behind. Its other end was in one of the boats, loaded with men, which the darkness hid. As it tightened, it became a signal to them to pull in, which they were instant to do. Everything had been carefully timed. At ten minutes after the hour the Turkish batteries would open on every side, circling castle and town with an inferno of stabbing flame. But that was still six minutes away.

Venetia came over the top. "Get me to the cell," she said, in a breathless way; "we will talk there."

They crossed the gun platform, and entered Francisco's cell. They could not see that three boats, loaded with men, had come out of the night. They could not know that a dozen more were pulling toward the boom which it was Francisco's duty to protect with the battery's fire.

The men were leaping out before the boats were aground. They had rope ladders with hooks, which they threw up to grip the ledge of the low parapet. They were up almost as soon as the hooks held, Hassan being one of the first.

A voice calling through the night came down from the citadel wall. The commotion had been observed, but its cause was not easy to guess. The sentinel looked down into a darkness in which he thought that men moved, but, if there were hostile attack, why did not the battery show its need?

The next moment he saw the flash of a pistol-shot on the platform below. He called his alarm and St. Angelo sprang alive. But the drama of Francisco's battery was played out before help could reach.

Francisco had looked at Venetia as she had come to the light of the lamp that was in the cell. She had looked pale, and as one who had an excitement that strained control, but there might be no wonder in that. She showed no sign of what she said she had lately endured.

Francisco, seeing her thus, turned to call his men back to their posts. "I will be," he said, "but a moment away."

Venetia's order had been that she should keep him within the cell. This she tried to do, whether for his sake or her own would be hard to guess. But she did not succeed. "It is but a word," he said, "and I am with you again."

Seeing him go, she followed, and Angelica followed her. They saw men clambering over the edge of the scarp. Francisco ran at them with his sword bare, shouting loud for the men who should have been lining the parapet to fling them back. A corsair's pistol flashed, but the ball went wide in the night. Francisco's sword thrust and killed, and it seemed that foes were round him on every side. Yet he was aware that most of them ran for the guns rather than him, and he guessed what they would do.

Angelica heard Venetia's voice in her ear. "You can escape if you run now. But do not say you were warned by me. It would be my death. You were to be caught in the cell, and Francisco both."

She had time to say this, for Angelica stood still, as though she would understand all before she would either remain or fly.

"So you have done this," she said, and wonder was in her voice. But she did not know that Venetia had heard. She had left her side. Venetia knew that there was but one chance for her own life now, and that must be what the Turks would give to one who had partly failed. She had but a moment to run back to the wall, for Francisco's men were swarming in now, with Captain Antonio at their head.

Antonio saw where Francisco fought with a savage fury which made him more than he would have been at another time, for he was aware in that moment's sight of how he had been fooled and shamed, and by whom it had been contrived. He cared not for his own life, having only a lust to kill, and it is a mood before which many will shrink aside.

Antonio ran to his aid, and was shouted away. "Not to me. Guard the guns—the guns." He turned to that which he saw was the greater need.

Angelica saw how Francisco fought, with two men at his front, and one working round to his side. This man made a thrust which might have found flesh, but that Francisco stumbled at the same time over one he had killed before. He came down with his left hand on the ground, and leapt up, facing them again. Angelica remembered, none too soon, that she was Don Garcio, wearing a sword. She ran then to her cousin's aid, feeling that it could not be used in a better way.

The man who preferred to come sideward to those he fought saw that there was one at his own left side. He saw it in time to stay the stroke he would have aimed at Francisco's head, but it was half a second too late for his own avail. Angelica made a thrust under his arm which lacked the vigour which those should use who engage in such deadly play. The point struck the leather baldric, metal-studded, that crossed his side, and had no strength to go through. Feeling that she was foiled, and seeing that eyes and weapon came round to her, she pressed with her full strength. The point slipped off the edge of the belt, and drove in. She felt it sink soft and deep, and would have stayed it in revulsion of what she did, but the sudden strength she had used had done that which she could not change. Through ribs to heart, the keen blade had gone, and it was a dying man who slipped off her sword.

She saw the convulsion that changed his face as he fell, in a flicker of ruddy light that passed over the scene, which was now fought in a red inconstant glare, such as might glow among fiends in a striving hell.

Overhead, the cannon on St. Angelo's walls flashed and thundered into the night. The boom to leftward was lit up with red floating flares which its defenders had set alight to guide them in what they did. Along the line of the boom, swimmers fought in the water; men struggled to defend or capture the Turkish boats: axes laboured to break the boom.

Round Francisco's guns, which should have been raking those boats with a fatal fire, Turk and Christian swayed and struggled in a force that was about equally strong and equally resolute to prevail.

Had Francisco's garrison consisted of none but the twelve men he had had before, as Venetia had told Hassan, speaking truth as far as she knew, there could have been but one end. They would have all been slain, and the guns damaged beyond repair, for which Hassan's men had the spikes and hammers that this office required. But in the last week, the importance of the battery having been better perceived than had been the case before the Sanglea attack, the embrasures for the three smaller guns had been quickly built, and the garrison increased to three times what it had been at first.

Turk and Christian met in numbers that nearly matched, and the strife might have gone on till few were living on either side; but Hassan saw that it could not be many moments before reinforcements would arrive, against which he could not hope to contend.

To that extent, the surprise had failed, though it had given time for the boats to approach the boom without hurt from the battery fire. He was not one to ignore facts to his own death. He looked round to see what there was still time to do. He saw where Francisco fought, and Angelica at his side. He called those men who were near, and whom he could bring to heed in that confusion and din.

Angelica heard Francisco's voice, as he spoke to her without turning his head: "You are mad to be here. You should get clear while you can."

But Angelica had recalled that those who wear a man's dress are expected to do that which a man should. She stood with the dripping sword in her hand, resolute not to retire.

Francisco had but one man facing him now. The other had backed away when his comrade fell to Angelica's sword, the odds changing in a way he did not approve. He had joined the rabble of those who fought round the idle guns. The man who remained was one who could fence with skill. Francisco found him harder to match now he was alone than when he had been one of a crowd. He had a curved scimitar which stabbed at times, and at others would sweep round with a whistling sound. He had a small round buckler on his left arm, which seemed to meet every thrust that the scimitar did not turn, as though it had a magnetic power. Francisco had his dagger out, making it what the buckler was to the Turk, having been trained in that way. It was a duel between those who had different techniques of strife, and might end in any way in that changing light, but Francisco found it too hard to risk turning his head.

Angelica felt her arm seized, as though in a vice of steel. She looked into Hassan's eyes. With a quick effort, she changed her sword to her free hand. In another instant, his violence would have been repaid in a worse way, but other hands were around her now. She was dragged to the wall, crying for help that she did not get.

A whistle shrilled through the strife, calling on the Turks to retire. Francisco felt the sharp pain of a slashed arm, and his opponent was gone. Angelica's voice came from the wall, doubtfully heard in the confused uproar of powder and steel, and the clamour of human cries.

Spanish soldiers were crowding the platform now, from which the last Turks had gone who had legs to flee. Colonna, the head of the Spanish troops, came to where Francisco stood, and saw the fallen around his feet.

"Señor," he said, "you have made a most stout defence."

Francisco looked round. He looked down at a dripping sleeve. He asked: "Has she gone? Is she safe? She was here a moment before."

Colonna thought him dazed by his wound, as perhaps he was.

A voice said: "It is Don Garcio they have got. I saw them drag him away."

Francisco made a quick step forward toward the wall. He seemed to slip on the blood-drenched ground, as it was easy to do. He fell forward, and did not rise.

"Pick him up," Colonna said, "and bear him away. He is sore hurt."

CHAPTER XXI

"BIND her hands," Hassan said. "She is quick to swim."

Angelica was in a mood to have gone overside with her hands bound, trusting that her legs would get her to shore, but she had no chance to lose her life that way, for the man to whom Hassan spoke did his work well. He bound her hands with one end of a good rope, and kept a twist of the other round his own arm.

The boat was fuller than it had been before, having two men to row, besides the one who was Angelica's guard. Venetia sat in the bow, where she had been before. Angelica was on a thwart in the midst.

Hassan, in the stern, watched the scene he left, as the boat moved fast for a few strokes, being followed by arquebus balls from those who now had the battery to themselves, and could look round at their foes.

But that peril was quickly past. The darkness covered them from the search of those whose eyes were in the half-lights of lantern and flaring pitch, and the flashing of frequent guns. The oars stayed at Hassan's word, and he looked back at the wide scene of tumult and fire which had not slackened because he had withdrawn, and those of his men who still lived tumbled out of the battery when his whistle blew, and had pushed off in boats that were round him now.

He was not one to desert such a scene in a careless way. He ordered the oarsmen to turn somewhat toward the boom, that he might better see how the fight went.

When he saw how it was, he said to himself: "The boom may be broken through, and the shipping taken or fired, and after that we shall have the Sanglea, and be near the end. But it will not be done on this night."

He considered that it would be few moments now before Francisco's guns would commence to fire. He rowed boldly toward the boom, giving orders that the attack should cease. As they came into the more lighted space, the battery guns opened, firing across the front of the boom, as they had been first purposed to do. It seemed to Angelica that it would be a mere waste to consider where she would be on the next day. The boat could not endure, and she would have no chance of life with her hands tied as they were.

But the boat did not sink, though a round-shot struck the water so closely that it was near to capsize. Water-logged with the wave it took in, it struggled back into the darkness again, and was baled out by all hands that were free of the oars, except hers, which she could not use. Then it shaped its course to land somewhat south of the Sanglea, being the nearest point that Hassan could choose to come to his own camp. The noise of strife had not ceased at this time, but it was sinking on every side.

Hassan considered the night's events, and, though the attack had failed, he was not wholly displeased. He had added one more to those calculated audacities of which men would talk in a way to augment his fame. He might not have done all that had been in his hopes, but he had stormed the battery that lay securely, as it had seemed, between the sea and the shelter of the citadel walls, and had rendered it impotent during those vital minutes when the boats were approaching the boom. He had a more personal satisfaction in that he had captured one who had outwitted him once before. He had fetched her out of the foemen's lines, where she might have seemed secure beyond any possible reach either of violence or guile. It should be a lesson which would be told through the years, warning those who would thwart his will. . . .

Venetia sat by herself, with some fears which, for that moment at least, she need not have had. She knew that, had she kept Francisco within the cell for even two or three minutes more than she had been able to do, the battery would have been entered, and the guns destroyed before any alarm could have been raised. She knew also that the event would have gone differently had there been no more than the dozen men at call, which, as she had said and believed, were the whole garrison that Francisco had. She did not know whether Hassan would have judged her to have misled him as to the muster of men with deliberate craft, or to have let Francisco come out with a double thought that those of her own race should not be utterly wrecked; or, if he did not really believe, that he might find pretext in these events to deny reward, or even to punish with the ferocity that was the custom of his race and time.

But Hassan thought in a clearer mind. To him, the essential part of the tale she told had been her assertion of influence over Don Francisco, so that he would obey her desire that none should see her arrive. That had been his great risk. Had she deceived him in that, or misconceived her power, as some women do, his own life would have been hard to save, and he had been resolved, in that event, that she should die first.

But, on this vital point, she had proved right: and it was through the use of her power over Francisco that he had entered the battery and returned alive, after doing half his intent, and seizing the captive he most desired.

He was too experienced in the ways of war to expect that all could be made to fall out to an exact plan.

He would have said (had he talked on a matter to which, in fact, he paid little tribute of thought) that the fact that she had come back to his boat as she did was proof enough that she had not attempted to warn Francisco.

So it may be taken to be, though, had she known how matters were likely to go, and in particular that Francisco had not twelve but two score of men within easy call, it may be a good guess that she would have spoken a warning word the first second that she was over the parapet edge, and so gained the name of one who had saved the battery at a great risk, if she could have made it appear in that way.

But she had not known; and with the Turks swarming around, and her treason become plain to those two who had met her first, it had seemed that to get back to Hassan's boat, while the way was still clear, was the best chance that she had. . . .

The boat grounded upon the stones, and Hassan, who had more urgent matters with which to deal, gave a short command: "You will take her," he said to Venetia, and looking at Angelica as he spoke, "to the house where you now are. She is to have her needs, but should she attempt to flee it will be her death, as it would be to any who would help her thereto."

He gave such orders as left little hope or fear that Angelica would escape again. Her wrists remained tied, and the end of the rope was now in the hand of a mounted man. She must move at the horse's speed, but Hassan have given instructions that she should not be ill-used till he should be free to deal with her himself, so that she found the pace was easy to keep.

That was well, for there were three miles to be walked on a rough way by one who had cause to be tired enough before that, but she gave no thought to how she might feel, whether wearied or light of limb, having too much grief of mind to be aware of the body's toil.

Francisco was more likely dead than alive, and if not dead he was shamed (which might be thought worse) beyond hope of a good defence, by a wanton's wiles. He had betrayed his trust, and (if he were not dead) his life might be held forfeit by the usage of war, and he be judged to a shameful end. It would be better that he should have found death from a Turkish sword! So she came even to pray that it might have been. . . . If he were alive, she would not be there to plead his cause as it would be certain to need. . . . She saw that her capture might be laid to his door, and held to augment his guilt. She judged rightly enough that it would not make Sir Oliver more disposed to remain his friend. . . . And when she thought of how much she had told of Venetia's letter she had a fresh grief. Suppose it might not have been known, but for what she herself had said, that Venetia had been there? That even the fact that the battery had been deserted when the Turks scaled the scarp might not have been known or guessed? But she was sure that Sir Oliver would not leave it till now, till he had probed all to the lowest depth. Had her interference not only brought her here, but become the cause that would lead Francisco to shameful death? She forgot herself as she thought of the disgrace which would so surely be his. Or, if her thoughts came to herself, it was only that she must find some escape which would enable her to defend his part—to explain, to excuse, to plead, even to lie, if that would do him avail. . . . There must be a way. Had she not left a moving ship in the night for the open sea? Here on land there must—*there must*—be a simpler way.

They gave Venetia a mule to ride, trusting her to a larger degree, at which Anglica was not surprised, remembering how she had played the traitor to her own friends. It was an old mule and slow, and, had Venetia reined it aside, it would have been quickly caught. But she took what courage she could from the favour it showed, and turned an agile mind to wonder what she could say to Angelica, or what would be said to her, she having betrayed her to such a trap. She had not supposed that, if Angelica were brought away, they would be put into the same place.

The house to which they came was one of those which were scattered over the country-side, having been built by the wealthier knights for more ease in the summer heat than they could find in the crowded town, and at a time when none thought that the Turks would be bold enough to invade the land. It was built in the Italian style, on a ridge of rock, having a seaward view to the east, with a wide belvedere looking that way, and a garden below, which had been well-kept in its day but was now a riot of lawless bloom.

It had been furnished in a luxurious style, which the invaders had abused, but it still had much of comfort for those who might be more concerned that they should lie soft than clean.

Venetia made her way to a bedroom which had been hers for two nights before. She would have been content to have been single there, and would have gone quickly to rest, but Angelica was led in at her back, and the rope loosed, making her aware of how much it had hurt her wrists.

Venetia spoke at once when they were alone, being one to show a bold face to that which she could not miss.

"You will say I have brought you here; but it is what I did not intend."

Angelica looked at her with cold eyes, as at something not worth contempt. But she would be just, as her way was. "No. You warned me to flee."

Venetia had actually forgotten that she had done that. She thought that, after all, she had not much to excuse. She replied, in a more confident tone: "It was all I could; and I did that at a great risk. There is none around in this place who knows (as I suppose) the tongue we now speak, but I will ask you not to talk of it again. It might bring me to death."

"It shall have no mention from me."

"I have been hardly placed, and I would have you know that I am not less than your friend."

"It is more than I should ask you to be."

Angelica turned away as she spoke. She looked out into the night, where a moon rose. She saw the glitter of arms in the garden below, showing that there were those by whom the window was watched. She closed jalousies thereat.

But Venetia would not be so lightly rebuffed. She opened battle again.

"Are you so wroth . . .? It may be that you have not come to so great an ill. . . . I will tell you this. I did not write of my will. Hassan gave me that it should be. He stood there to read. Would you have your skin peeled while you live, from the feet up?"

"It is not of myself I think. It is of one who gave you his trust. You have made him traitor, or naught, who stood well."

"I could not do that. He is what God made him, not I."

"You have likely compassed his death."

"There are many deaths at this time. I had my own life to regard. And I may have saved yours."

"Which you were not needed to do. And I should say it was safer before."

"That is because you have not seen both sides of the wall. Hassan is not one who will fail. In the end, St. Angelo will go up in fire. Have you seen a town sacked? Well, I have not. But I have heard tales. Do you know what these pirates are? There would be a gutter red with your blood. Or, if they knew you for what you are. . . . It would not be to go to a quiet bed with one man, as you are now likely to do."

"There are ways to die before that. But I will not talk. Your thoughts are not mine, and your words have no meaning to me. . . . But you have made a poor guess. The Turks will flee as the summer wanes, and the Cross of Christ will still fly."

"You say what you desire. But I have learned to look more sharply than you. Does a tide not rise because it also retires? Do you not see that each time the Turks are thrown back they are closer in? They say in St. Angelo now: 'We have beaten the Turks again. Did we not see them leap over the battery scarp? Did they not run for the shore?' But would they have reached to there a month past? It would not have been thought. But ever they close in. They are a cord which is drawn more tight till the breath goes. They are a water that rises to overwhelm."

"It is vain to talk. We have different tongues."

Venetia had been throwing off her clothes as she spoke. She answered: "Well, there is one thing you can understand. You should come to bed. The lamp will not last. I suppose you can see that. I will have more oil for another night, if I can contrive that, for the dark is what I have never loved."

Angelica asked in a bitter tone: "You boast that you see much. Do you see yourself as you are?"

Venetia was bare now. She looked in a long mirror against the wall, which was cracked, but still good enough, in the smoky light of a poor lamp, to show her that which it gave her pleasure to see.

"So I do," she said, "I was not made to be peeled, but for better work; which it may be your business to learn. . . . There are no shifts in this place. . . . I have thrown out the flax, which was soiled: we must lie in wool."

There was one bed in the room, of ample size, into which she got as she spoke: "Will you not come? You should rest while you can, and you are more fit for the next day. I have learnt that in harder ways than you have been likely to know."

"We are not for one bed."

"Then has God made you a fool! Will you not sleep, and when you wake you can talk venom again? I know not why I am so vexed. You care nothing for me. You would have had me skinned with a quiet mind. And I gave you warning you would not heed, in the only minute I had."

Angelica said: "I am fool indeed. You have found the word." Her laughter, sudden and short, sounded strange to her own ears.

She drew off some of her clothes, though not all, being in those of a man, and lay down in the harlot's bed.

After that, Venetia was soon asleep, being wearied, and having a conscience at ease. She had done what she could for peace, using words which convinced herself, if Angelica were less easy to move.

"She is stubborn, ignorant fool," she thought, as her eyes closed. "I know not why I care as I do."

CHAPTER XXII

ANGELICA slept late, as the young may when emotion has tired the mind. She waked to the sound of horse-hooves on the gravel below. Memory came back with the sight of Venetia, who had waked earlier, and dressed with care, in other clothes than those she had worn in the night. She had opened the jalousies wide to the morning sun. She looked out at the sound.

"There is Hassan here," she said. "You should rise, unless you will that he see you thus. He will be here for you more than for me, as I hope."

So she did, being still unsure of whether he would approve of what she had done.

Angelica rose in some haste. She saw herself to be ruffled and soiled, which no woman would choose to show, though she may walk in a man's dress.

Venetia said: "There is water here, if you will." There was no doubt that she would be friend, if she could. She gave help unasked, and her movements were light and sure.

It was a short time before one of Hassan's men entered the room, without delaying for leave. He looked at Angelica, and said something in a tongue that was strange to her, but Venetia could understand.

"You are to go below," she said. "I am not for now. . . . It seems," she added, a sudden jealous doubt crossing her mind, "that he could have but short sleep till he must see you again."

Angelica said: "I could have spared him a longer time." Her heart was cold with a fear which she would not show, courage rising to meet her need.

She followed the man down, and found Hassan to be seated on the couch of a salon which had been luxurious once, but of which the furniture had been booted about, and which had not been cleaned since its owner fled.

Seated thus, in a western way, he reminded her, in spite of his different dress, of the Rinaldo she had first met at her uncle's board. He may have thought of her as she had been at that time, but his thoughts were not always easy to guess.

"So," he said, with a smile that she did not like, "you have come to me again."

"I know not," she answered, "why you should go to such trouble to have me here," and was conscious of the futility of the words, even before they were wholly out.

"Well," he said, "as to that, it was not much. And why you are here you may soon learn. But, as I think, you had a wet sword."

"Do you blame me for that? I struck for my cousin's life."

"Which it was your business to save? But it is mine to see that you kill no more, for I have lost a good man."

"I have no wish to use sword, at which I have no skill."

"You have little skill, and less strength. But if you trade as a man, you must pay debts in his coin. . . . Marshal Couppier catches our men, and they hang in his market square. Do you suppose we like that, or that we shall treat those we catch in a better way?"

"I did not make the customs of war, which I would change if I could. But I suppose that they had no gold."

"They would have been worth gold to sell. I say not to your price." He looked at her with eyes that narrowed in an insolent doubting way. "Are you virgin still, after your time in that dress?"

She looked back with an anger that forgot fear. She had a mind not to answer; and then thought that silence would be misjudged. "I am unwed, which should be sufficient reply. But it is nothing to you. I have gold to pay."

"That is well. But there is another matter between us two, which must be balanced before you go. How will you do that?"

"I do not know what you mean."

"There are your cousin's ships, which I should have had but for you."

"It is of him I would know. Can you tell me if he was slain when I was taken away?"

"It is likely enough, but it is more than I chanced to see. I did not ask you of that."

"I will pay for a true tale."

"You can have that without gold. It will all be known in the next hour. But you must think now of that which I asked before. How will you get me the ships?"

"You know I cannot do that."

"But it is what you must, or else pay as you will not like."

"It is wild to ask. Do you think I would betray them to you? I am not as——"

"No. You would be worth less if you were. You are better bred. And you would have me think that you differ in other ways. But, if you show a stiff neck, you may come to the same port. . . . Now I will tell you what I will do. I will set your ransom at 3,000 ducats of gold. That is fair, for you would be worth a high price at Damascus mart, and still more if they should send you further away. You can be set free for that sum. But I must have the ships first, for it is by such means that men will know that I am not one of whom others can make a jest. If I have the ships, you can go free when the ransom is paid, which, in your case, I suppose could be quickly arranged. . . . But if I have not the ships, you have done that which your back must pay. You will be stripped and whipped in a public place, for that is what my honour requires; and after that you will heal, and be worth no less than you now are, and you will be sold in the best market the merchants advise. . . . And when I so resolve, I deal with you in a most merciful way. . . . Dragut would have had you set on an upright stake, for much less than you did, where you would have waited to die."

Angelica thought: "You would have no ships by my word, if I had the power, which it is plain that I have not got." But she checked her speech, for if she might gain no more, the discretion of silence might win some delay, and it was on escape that her mind was set. She said: "I must know first how my cousin fared."

"Do you think you can give orders to me . . .? But you shall know that." He smiled at his own thought.

He said to the man who stood by, and who had understood nothing of this talk: "Take him back, and see that he is guarded with care, for he is one of those for whom men hang, if they get free."

She was returned to the upstair room, where she found Venetia was back on the bed. Under her pale-gold head her hands met in a way she had. She had been thinking of herself, in whom she was most concerned, but she had had a thought of Angelica too, and when she saw that her companion showed no disposition to speak, she addressed her with words that had a sharp edge, although they were said in a smiling, indolent way.

"If we are to be shut here, as we have not sought, there must be one of us who has sense, if not more, and I will give you words that are plain and true.

"If I am one who is shown a rack, I will say all that I can to keep my joints as they are, being those for which I have the first care. If you have things which you would not have me tell, being so abused, hey are best kept in your own mind while we are here. But can you understand that I can be weak to that point, and be still your friend of my will, and one to aid in the smaller things?"

"You have brought one I love to his death, or worse. Can I put that by?"

"I do not know that I have, nor, I think, do you. Will you let me call it a coward's guess, which I had not thought you to be? But you should consider that what I did, if you call it the worst you may, was not of malice either to him or you, whom I would more lightly have helped, being those who have friended me, of whom there have been too few in the right way.

"As I told Hassan when we talked, it is some days back, I do not seek to bring others to wreck, but for a harbour I cannot find. Have you the will to see that?"

"You are one, by your own words, to bring your friends to wreck for your own gain, and it is a thing for which they will not love you the more."

"So I am. And so, I suppose, are many more, or I have watched the world with worse sight than I think I have. But did I ask you for love? I ask you to make common accord, being two in a place of foes. For if you think more of what is past than of that which now is, you are naked to every wind."

Angelica saw that there was some sense in that, but she thought that if two are alone in a world of foes it is a common trust that they both need, and trust was that which Venetia would never have from her again. But it was useless to say. What she said was: "I am not one in whom hate is a strong plant, but you have brought me to bitter dole. . . . Can you show me way to get free? I would give you more gold for that than I suppose you have seen in your life days."

"I would do much for that gold, and something for you, but my skin has a closer claim. Do not speak of it again." And then she added, in so low a voice that Angelica scarcely caught the words: "Unless I speak of it to you."

Angelica understood that Venetia feared, even in that room alone, lest they might be talking for other ears. A faint hope stirred in her heart. Venetia might have a plan which she was too cautious to share. It might be true that she might lose more than she yet had (and there was no margin for that) if she should refuse to meet Venetia on the ground she offered. . . . But she was not one who would feign what she did not feel. . . . '*Forgive us, as we forgive*——' The divine prayer came to her mind. But she had heard it said that such forgiveness is only required to be given to those who ask.

Well, had not Venetia asked? Perhaps, scarcely that. . . . She would try to forgive, but to trust was more than even Heaven would ask her to do. . . . Venetia was speaking again.

"If you will say what he said, I may tell you what it was worth, for I have watched his moods and his ways, even while he thought he was learning me."

"You can know that, if you will. He said first that I could be ransomed for 3,000 ducats of gold."

"That is how they begin. You will proffer one, or else less, and in the end he will take two."

"I did not bicker thereon."

"Then you are not one who should manage your own affairs. You are not (if you will forgive a plain word) worth half the price in any market there is."

"I am not to sell. If any gave that for me, he would wish his gold back in his own pouch. . . . But he required something else which he will not get. He will have our two ships, which he says he would have won on the seas had I not been there."

"How can he get them?"

"So I said. It is vain talk. If they were mine to give, they should not be his. And if I would, it is a thing which the Grand Master would not allow in a session of war."

"He must know that. He does not mean you to go."

"Yet I must. I must find a way."

"Did he say what he would do if the ships are not to be made his?"

"I am to be beaten, and then sold."

Venetia considered this with a frown she was not careful to smooth away.

"You are not to sell, as you said. You were right in that. He will have the ships, or else you. . . . Did I not say that my harbour is still to seek?"

"You will not lose it by me, if you mean that. . . . And I should say you misdeem. Would he beat one who had his regard, in a public way?"

"That he would. He would think you better for that, as a trained horse is worth more than one that is not broken to ride. . . . But you need not fret greatly thereon, for he will not have you beaten more than will heal and will leave no scar. . . . It is queen you may be of all the Barbary coast in a year from now."

Angelica looked at a window which had been open last night, and might be opened again. There might be guards stationed below, but men doze in the night. . . . To drop suddenly, and to run. The height was not so great that she might not come down on her feet. . . . And a poor chance is much better than none. . . . She must watch for hers.

The man who had come to the door before entered again. He said something which she could not understand. Venetia interpreted: "He says it has been learned from the Christian lines that Don Francisco has a wound in the arm, but is not mortally hurt."

Angelica's glance wandered to the window again.

CHAPTER XXIII

THE Grand Master held inquisition of the events of the night. The storm had fallen before the dawn. The boom had been damaged, but not forced. Attacks had been repulsed that had been made on the land side of the Sanglea, and round the Bourg. There was nothing left but to repair damage, to count the slain, and to judge how praise or blame should be given out.

Pompea Colonna had come to Malta in command of four hundred of the Spanish soldiers who had been enlisted when the first peril was known. These men had been lost in strife, or scattered at different posts, till there were not more than a hundred he could array. He had been sent with these to the battery's aid, when it was known that the Turks were over the scarp and its guns were still.

"We ran in haste," he said, "but we did nothing when we arrived, for there was nothing to do. We saw the flight of a beaten foe."

It was generously said. He went on to tell how he had seen Don Francisco fall in the midst of those that his hands had slain, of whom (as he did not know) Angelica should have been thanked for the death of one.

"Yet I see not," the Grand Master said, "how the Turks made so swift a surprise that no alarm could be called till they were over the scarp, if a watch were kept as it was duty to do."

"Don Francisco has the name of one who watched his charge, and would seldom sleep." The words came from a knight of Castile, who felt that all Spaniards should stand as one against the Italian knights who were of more numbers than they.

"So he had," the Grand Master allowed, though with a thought that there had once been a woman found where she should not be. "So he had. But what does he say now?"

"He cannot be asked at this time," Sir Oliver answered. "There is report that his fever is high."

"Then we will hear what Captain Antonio has to say."

Captain Antonio was quite ready to talk.

"I was not on duty," he said, "Don Francisco himself taking the night watch, as he would most often prefer. But I was alert, having been warned that there might be a special need."

His words waked the sharp attention of all who heard.

"Warned by whom?" the Grand Master asked.

"By Don Garcio, as—he—was called. He came to the battery in the late day, when I was in command, and, we having some words, he said that, if he were I, he would be alert for the night, it being without a moon in its first hours, and so inviting surprise."

"Were they no more than words of an idle kind, or did you think that he spoke with a special cause?"

"With a special cause, as I thought, so that I did not unbelt my sword."

"We must know more of this," the Grand Master said. . . . "You say you were there with speed. What did you first see?"

"There was bicker along the scarp, where the Turks came tumbling over the parapet at all parts; and Don Francisco, being nearly alone, was thrusting to force them back. I would have run to his support, but he shouted to me to let him be, and to guard the guns."

"So you went on to them?"

"So I did, with the men that came up with me. . . . There was lively flurry around the guns, to which the most of the Turks ran, having purpose to knock them out, in which they did not prevail."

La Valette looked at him, as he said this, in a more regardful way than before. He saw that one side of his face was black with a great bruise.

"You had a knock yourself," he said. "Are you much hurt?"

"It is naught. I came clear enough, as I often do, being more hard to hit than a larger man."

"Were the whole of the men engaged by this time that you got up?"

"Except those who had been asleep, as their right was at that time. They came tumbling out, as I suppose, with but short delay, for it was soon that they were all there, but at that time I was at no leisure to see."

He went on to tell how he had got the guns to work as the Turks fled, so that they had done their part at the last in driving the boats away that attacked the boom, of which there would have been more sunk had they not fled under St. Michael's fort, and so to the farther shore, skirting the palisades that ran up the centre of the inlet of the Sanglea, and getting some protection from them.

"I can see," La Valette said, "that you did your part. But this is a matter on which the whole is not said. If Don Francisco is not able to speak, we must have this—Garcio, was it?—by whom you were warned."

"That," Antonio replied, "I suppose to be more than you can, for there is talk that the Turks bore him away."

Sir Oliver's voice broke in sharply: "Why do you say that?"

"It is so believed. It is what I did not see, being concerned with those who were round the guns. . . . But it is sure that she was there when the fight began, and was not seen after that."

"Why do you say she?" the Grand Master asked.

"It was a most careless word, but I may suppose that I have done no great wrong, it having chanced as it has."

"It is Don Francisco's cousin," Sir Oliver said to the Grand Master, bringing the truth back to his mind, and then to Antonio: "Why was this not reported before?"

"So I tried to do for two hours, but those who might have heard have been busy with larger things."

There was a new gravity in La Valette's face as he said: "This is evil news, if it be true. There are few I would be less willing to think in those devils' hands." And then his mind went to the core of the problem to ask: "Was she always there during the night?"

"No," Antonio answered, "as I believe, never before. I suppose she was there for her cousin's help, having some reason to fear what the night might bring."

"You are sure," Sir Oliver asked, "that she was there . . .? Sure of that which you did not see?"

"There were those who did. She was there when the fight began. It is said she pushed in to her cousin's aid, he being hardly beset, and using her sword somewhat to his relief. And after that there are those who say that she was dragged over the wall when the Turks fled."

"It seems," the Grand Master said, weighing what he had heard in a careful mind, "that there was no absence of watch, but rather a special care, from what cause it may be hard to enquire. We must suppose that the Turks came with a bold and most sudden rush, or some subtle ruse, and were most gallantly met, by which valour the guns were saved."

But Sir Oliver said, with a grimmer look than he often had, "By your leave, I will enquire when Don Francisco is able to speak."

The Grand Master saw there was more on his mind than he was open to say. "So you shall, Oliver," he replied, "we will leave it so. . . . But I am grieved for one who should not have been here, as we have said before now. She has served Malta well, and if you can find that she still lives, and we can make any exchange, it shall not be grudged—or if payment of gold will do, it must in reason be found if she be poor in her own right."

"She is not that. She can find ransom enough," Sir Oliver replied, "if that will suffice." He asked Captain Antonio to bring those who had seen Angelica to be examined by him in the next hour.

He caused enquiry to be made through the pursuivants who were passing between St. Angelo and the Turkish camp to arrange for exchange of wounded and removal of dead, and other business such as will ever follow a day of strife, asking if one Don Garcio had been taken prisoner in the attack on the battery, for he had a hope that Angelica might not be discovered for what she was.

He had a reply before night. It said that Angelica (giving her all the titles she had in her own name) was in Hassan's hands, and could be ransomed within two days for 3,000 ducats of gold, which could be paid in bills of exchange (in a form which was in common use in the ransomings of that day, for which there was a clearing-house in Amsterdam to which all nations would make resort), and also the two galleons which Don Francisco had brought from Spain. If these were delivered within the time, she would be returned in safety and honour. If the ransom should be more laggardly paid, it would be no less in amount, and she would be delivered in the condition in which she might be at the time.

CHAPTER XXIV

It was late that night, after the Grand Master had disposed of some larger things, that Sir Oliver was able to say: "And there is also the matter of Don Manuel's niece."

He mentioned her in that way to remind the Grand Master of the old friendship he had, but it was without hope, for what was there that could be done?

"Then it is true she was caught? What ransom do they require?"

"Three thousand ducats is named."

"That is absurd. They must come down."

"So they might. But they ask something beside. They will have the two galleys that Don Francisco brought."

"Do they think us mad, or are they? It is not Mustapha's way to jest in such manner as that."

"It is not he. Hassan claims that she was his prey. The ransom, as I conclude, would be gain to him."

"Even so, it is foolish jest. What does it mean?"

"It is not a jest without point. It was through her that the galleys were saved out of Hassan's hands."

"So I recall. It was boldly done. Is he seeking revenge for that?"

"So I suppose. He cannot think the galleys will be given to him."

"In what time must we reply?"

"In something less than two days. After that, the offer is not withdrawn but we must be content to take her as she may then be, without reduction of price."

"Meaning that she will be racked or raped?"

"So we must think. I see not what can be done, unless we could offer such exchange that they could not refuse assent."

The Grand Master pondered this. "There is Candelissa's son. Couppier has him. There is a bargain there to be made, but we should have much more than one girl. . . . If it be two galleys for her, it should be all Hassan's fleet for him. . . . She should not have come, or should have been sent back at the first."

"She has done a man's part, if not more. You must think of that."

"So she has. She is of good blood. And if she be martyred now, as it seems she must, it will not be for naught, she having taken these galleys from Hassan's clutch; and if she be tormented therefor, there should be joy in the courts of God, and much comfort for her when the short time of trial is past and done."

"Shall I offer Yusef?—Candelissa's son?"

"Not surely for her alone! We can do better than that. . . . But I will leave it to you. I am less hard than you think. She is one I would gladly save. But it is my part to bring Malta through."

"I will bargain the best I can," Sir Oliver answered, feeling that he had gained more than he could fairly have hoped, having all left in his hands.

La Valette turned to go, and came back. "Oliver," he asked, "have you thought it strange that she should be there to be taken by Hassan's hands, and he at the right spot? She is one, it seems, that he was singly anxious to have. Was it often that she would be thus exposed, even outside the strength of our walls . . .? And she with premonition of that which came, as is shown by the warning to—to him with the battered face?"

"To Captain Antonio. Yes, I have thought much. She had a place assigned on my own part of the wall, which I could not avoid, she having come with a man's name. But she stood high over the strife, even on the day of the Sanglea assault. When I sent her to take her place, she was in no danger, unless, it might be, from a flying fragment of stone. . . . But the battery was where she had no business to be, nor was ever there, as I am now told, except when she followed me on the day La Cerda's mistress was there revealed, and on this midnight of strife. . . . It is what I will probe more than I have yet done."

"It is Don Francisco's report we must have, and make inquisition straitly thereon. Is he equal to that?"

"He was not to-day, but of to-morrow there is more hope."

"Was he sore hurt?"

"His arm was slashed to the bone. He lost blood. The fever was high, but is now less. . . . He made, as they say, a most gallant fight for his guns' defence."

"So he would. He has done badly and well, so that it is hard to resolve. There was that woman he hid. And now the Turks should not have been over the edge, and he single to drive them back, as the tale sounds. And again there is a woman where she should not be, though I would not join her name with the first. But, apart from these, he had done better than well. . . . Oliver, if it were not too near to a Moslem thought, I would doubt if there can be Heaven where women come."

He went out at that word, leaving Sir Oliver to reflect that there could be Hell where no women were, as in that boiling cauldron of strife which he fed and stirred; and that there was one he would save if he yet could.

He sent a pursuivant on the next day to Hassan, saying that Yusef (whom he mentioned that Marshal Couppier was very anxious to hang) would not be returned alive if Angelica were dishonoured or harmed, and proposing that they should talk of terms in a serious way, which he implied that they had not yet begun. He sent also to Marshal Couppier, asking that Yusef should be cherished with care, knowing that the guerrilla leader had bitter and implacable moods. And having done these things, and others which it is needless to write, he went to the hospital on the north side of the Bourg, where Francisco was nursed.

Francisco lay on a pallet bed, in a ward with a dozen more, for wounded men were easy to find around St. Angelo's walls at this time, and even those of good blood (as so many were) must be content to be herded thus, if they were to have the best physicians around their beds. He looked up at Sir Oliver with eager impatient eyes. He had outfought the fever of the first hours, and the resilience of healthful youth was bringing vigour back to his weakened blood.

He half rose, and sank back, cursing the arm which he had for a moment forgotten, and which reminded him of its needs in its own way.

"They will tell me naught," he said bitterly, "naught at all. It is not this wound by which I am fevered and vexed. It is to learn that which I am not told. Why must men lose all other sense from their heads when they profess the curing of wounds?"

"If you will be quiet," Sir Oliver replied, "and act as you say you are, I will tell you more than the physicians would be likely to do."

"Then I will ask first—were the guns saved?"

"They were not only saved, they were used on a flying foe, Captain Antonio having been stout to belabour the Turks, and then active to run them out."

"You would not be here with a light cause," Francisco shrewdly observed, and his eyes showed his second fear. "Is Angelica hurt?"

"She was not hurt that I know. But there are things I must

ask of you, if you are fit to reply. Did you expect the Turks to come on that night?"

"I had no thought that they would, or they had been met at first in a warmer way."

"Yet it seems that your cousin did. Can you say why?"

"I should say she should answer that."

"So she should. But, for the present, it cannot be asked."

"But you said she was unharmed?"

"That was true. If you will take it in a quiet way, and believe that there is no ill that we may not yet be able to cure, I will tell you all that I know, and after that I will ask you to tell me some things I have still to learn."

Francisco said nothing to this, and Sir Oliver went on to tell him what he had heard of the battery's defence, of how Angelica had been carried away, and of the efforts for her ransom which he had since made.

Francisco was still quiet. He lay so still that Sir Oliver wondered at one time whether he heard all with his mind, though his eyes were not closed. But when the tale came to an end, he said in a low tone: "It is clear now from the first. What do you want to know?"

"It is hard to see how the Turks could so closely approach before the alarm was called. Was it by subtle ruse, or do you blame those who failed to keep a good watch?"

"It was I who failed."

"Then I must ask you to tell me how."

"So I will."

In a low toneless voice, he told of the letter he had received, and so lightly believed, and of the dispositions he made thereon; and how at last he had gone with Venetia into the cell so that the platform was bare of men when the Turks came.

Sir Oliver listened to a tale which was not different from what he had guessed for truth, though he had not supposed that it would be told in so open a way.

His first question was not what Francisco expected to hear, being on a point which was of less moment to him than to Malta's defence, which was Sir Oliver's greater care.

"How did the letter come to your hand?"

"It was given me outside the citadel wall, as I returned to the battery, having met my cousin within the town, by the hand of a half-grown boy."

"Did you see him well?"

"No. It was a bad light. He was one I had no cause to regard, and he was soon gone."

"There is nothing you can recall?"

"He had a scarred chin."

"Should you know him by that again?"

"Unless there be two with such marks."

"You may have done some service in this. . . . Was it with your will that your cousin reported this letter to me?"

"It was her wish. I agreed thereto. . . . She must have had more doubt than she showed to me, or she had not warned Antonio, as you say."

"It was well for you that she did, for Antonio sat with a girded sword, and some men in the same array, or I suppose the guns would have been destroyed. . . . Did you see how your cousin was seized?"

"She came to my aid when I was faced by three, of whom one sought to reach me behind, and him she brought to ground in a bold way, so that I endured to deal with the other two. . . . I called to her to stand back, as I thought she did, but after that there is not much I recall."

"It must have been then she was snatched, for at that time the Turks were turning to flee."

"I have been so fooled that you will say I am not worthy the trust I had."

"That is truth. You are relieved of your command from this hour. Beyond that, it must be left till your wound is closed."

Francisco made no answer to that. He asked: "There is no doubt you will bring her free?"

"So I suppose we may, having this Yusef in pawn. I have a good hope. I will not go beyond that."

"You will let me hear?"

"You shall be quickly told, either of evil or good."

"It is all I ask. . . . I know well you will not fail her part from a slack will."

Sir Oliver went at that, having more matter for thought. He had heard much that Francisco need not have told, and that (unless Angelica should return, and in more mood to talk than before) could not have been discovered in other ways. Sir Oliver had little sympathy with him, and it was his hard resolve to uncover the truth which had kept the matter alive when the Grand Master (knowing less than he) might have passed it by. But at that time he had been careful to say no more than would leave it still in his own hands, lest he should stir more than he could after control. But, since Hassan had mentioned his ransom terms, he saw that the Grand Master's eyes were on the event with a new keenness, which would not lightly be turned aside.

His first duty was to Malta's defence, and he had resolved before seeing Francisco that he should not continue in his command, unless he could give a better account than he expected to hear.

Having heard the tale, he had been instant in his decision that Francisco could not be left in a trust he had twice abused; but, beyond that, on his own confession, he was worthy of death by the laws of war, as they have been at all times.

Sir Oliver might have little sympathy for him, but he did not wish to get Angelica back (which was his greater concern) and meet her with the news that he had been active to bring her cousin to shameful death. Nor was he sure where his duty lay. If Francisco's fault had been widely known, discipline would have rendered merciless punishment almost a necessity of routine, which he would himself have approved, and from which no private feeling would have turned him aside. But it was known to none but himself. He did not doubt that Francisco, if his dishonour were not exposed, might still be more use alive than dead for Malta's defence. . . . None is bound to convict himself. . . . Nor should too much heed be given to the words of a wounded and fevered man. . . . It must be left for more thought, and he would speak to Francisco again.

He was pressed with contending cares when he got back to his own rooms, and it was at a late hour that a Maltese spy, who had got through the Turkish lines, was brought to him to make report.

The man bore no letter, it being held the safer way to trust wholly to spoken words (the Turks thinking the man to be their own spy). He brought account of some volunteers who had landed by night in St. Paul's Bay, and of some stir at Palermo in preparation to send relief (which might be in time, if St. Angelo could endure for another year), and of a good word from Doria, the Genoese admiral, who was ever La Valette's friend, and was now active on his behalf. But when mention was made of Yusef, he said: "Why, I suppose he is hanged by now. So it was to be when I left Notabile this morn. The Marshal was wroth that the Turks dallied to come to terms, having been told the sum that he would not abate. He will have one man hanged on each day, that the folk may see that the vermin are less by that count; and as there was no other caught for this morn, he said that to hang a man of such rank would put those who are weak-kneed in a better heart. Anyway, it was so talked when I came away."

"I must hope," Sir Oliver said, "that a letter I sent may have been in time to prevent that."

"I cannot say," the man replied, "beyond this, that it had not when I left, and Yusef was to be hanged in an hour from then."

"Well," Sir Oliver said, "we can but wait till we hear more." He turned his mind to give the man certain messages for Marshal Couppier's own ear, which must be repeated with care.

CHAPTER XXV

HASSAN listened to what the pursuivant had to say, with a wrath that he must not show, either for him to take back such report to the Christian dogs, or for those around to observe.

He had made an offer to accept ransom for Angelica, in a form to which he knew that the Grand Master would not agree, so that it could not be said that he had not observed the procedure usual on both sides in regard to captives of noble blood; and still more that a wide attention might be drawn to what he had done, as well as what he proposed to do.

He wished to do more than gratify a private revenge. He wished the world to observe how one by whom he had been foiled at first had been captured by him, even from under St. Angelo's guns, and of the fate to which she had fallen at last, though she might be a señorita of great estate, and of the noblest Andalusian blood.

It might sound a jest to ask for the surrender of two of the best galleys in the Maltese fleet as a girl's exchange, and one that must surely be rejected in time of war, but, as Sir Oliver had said, it had not been without point. It emphasized the reason why she had been seized, and that it had been something more than a casual chance of war.

Hassan had supposed that the ransom he asked would be refused (though, in the improbable event of the ships being given up, his pride would have been well served in another way), and that, by his public mention of them, the subsequent stripes which he intended for Angelica's back, and the indignities which were to be hers in the slave-markets of the East, would be recognized as his revenge for her interference to frustrate his plans.

When the pursuivant began by saying that the ransom asked must be regarded as no more than a pleasant jape (which he did with the adroit choosing of words which was the second teaching of the college from which he came, the first being the knowledge of many tongues), Hassan had listened with the inward smile of one who sees his foes dance to a tune which he had chosen before. He expected to hear next of an offer of gold, which he would refuse, be it little or much, to the annoyance of the Grand Master and his Council, who would doubtless wrangle over the proffer of larger sums. He would let them bid up and up, till he saw they would bid no more, and when he had played with them to that end, she should have a whipping she would not like (for he could not omit that, it being little indeed to the tortures he would have used upon one who had treated him with such successful contumely, had he not been disposed to a lenience which he seldom felt), and, after that, he would consider what he would do. There was a Nizam of Central India, he had heard, who would pay a fabulous price for a Spanish virgin of the best blood, if she were of a beauty he could admire, as Angelica could not fail to be (the Turks had spread at this time beyond the mountains of middle Asia, and the crescent flew over Delhi walls), but he might put such thoughts aside, for his wealth was great, and keep her for himself, if she would be docile to him, as he did not doubt he could bring her to be; and she would have Dragut's daughter (now that Dragut was dead) and a score of others, if she desired, whom she could use as she would.

He heard the first part of the pursuivant's speech with an inward smile, which did not disturb the quiet gravity of his face, but when it went on to say that if an offer were made for exchange against the release of Candelissa's son it might be variously received, he found it harder to hear with a passive front, for he saw at once that, though it was a bargain he did not want, it might be hard to decline. It had been to make other provision for this exchange that he had thought to capture Francisco also, and come away with a double bag, for which he had lacked time at the last.

Candelissa had been Dragut's second in command when Hassan had been no more than a cradled child. He was of a great wealth, and in Tripoli he had a great power. He had a reputation for a cunning which brought his foes to an end which it was often hard to lay at his door. He was not one whom Hassan would lightly offend, and, with a common parental perversity, he valued his son more highly than other men (unless Marshal Couppier) were disposed to do.

Hitherto the negotiation for Yusef's release had been in Mustapha's hands, and Hassan had not been directly concerned. It was recognized to be a difficult matter to arrange, for the Marshal was not easily moved from what he regarded as the mission he had from God, which was to kill those of the Moslem faith. If he hanged a Turk, he knew that there was rejoicing among the saints, but, if he let him go for a bag of gold, he was less sure that they would approve. If a man had a trapped rat, would he let him loose in his larder again? Even though he could pay ransom with a portion of cheese? A Turk loosed must be killed or captured again, or, till he was, he would continue to work destruction to Christian men.

Marshal Couppier, being asked the price at which he would let Yusef go, named impossible sums, and did no more than defer his death while he had others to keep the daily hangings supplied.

Mustapha, using his wits to save the youth, if it could be done without payment of sums at which a king might have been overpriced, had promised consideration rather than made rejection of these demands, hoping the while that the chance of war might bring a captive to his own hands, such as the Grand Master would allow to be an equal exchange.

Now it seemed that the chance had come. Hassan (with Candelissa three yards away) could not say that Yusef should hang rather than the girl should be given up.

He sat silent and passive for a time, giving no sign of his thoughts, which was no more than the customed way in which rulers of his race and rank would behave in Council, and still more when they gave audience either to inferior men, or those who represented their foes.

He asked at last: "Yusef would be returned having all his limbs, and in such health as he was on the day when he was caught?"

The question was one which the pursuivant knew to be reasonable, and which Candelissa must recognize as being in the interest of his son. There had been tricks on both sides, at sundry places and times, when prisoners who were not exchanged simultaneously or for whom ransom was paid without adequate care, were returned in such mutilated conditions as the humour of their captors devised. It was the more necessary to be clear on such points, because the offer came from St. Angelo, and Yusef was in Notabile, with which communication was not freely maintained.

"It is so," the pursuivant replied, "that the Grand Master would wish it to be, and he is not one, as I need not say, to do less than his word is pledged."

"He has such a name," Hassan allowed, after a pause of nearly as much length as before, "and that, I do not doubt, he will still maintain. Don Garcio, as it is agreed that our captive is called, is one whom the Grand Master would not lose, which would be (for reasons I will not express) to his special shame. If this exchange be agreed, he will add gold with a free hand?"

"It was rather thought that there would be such offer from you, or the exchange would be less than fair."

"But if Don Garcio be returned with no dishonour of any sort? That is not of an equal weight, as the Grand Master will perceive without explanation from me."

"I must still say that it is on your side that the scale would tilt."

"The offer is not refused," Hassan said, after the longest silence of all, "but you shall come again to-morrow at this time, when I must hope that you will have something to add to make a fairer exchange, and, in the meantime, you will allow that we send to Marshal Couppier in the next hour, having a plain writing from you, that we may be assured both that Yusef is well, and that he will be so kept till this is agreed or it have fallen wholly apart."

The pursuivant made no objection to this, having done most, if not all, at which his instructions aimed, and Hassan felt that he had made the best fight that the position allowed against an offer at which he could not curse aloud, as it would have been a pleasure to do. He cared as much for Candelissa's son as for an old mule, or perhaps less; and he saw the vengeance and vindication which he had designed taken out of his hands for no profit at all, beyond what he could get the old corsair to pay. But, by gaining the day's respite, he had done all that he could to keep the jaws of the trap apart. He had time for thought, and who knows to what thought may lead?

He sent to Notabile, being about six miles away, with a flag of truce, to enquire concerning Yusef's health, as he could not delay to do, and then approached Candelissa, to get what he could out of a lost game, if there were no way by which it could still be won.

Candelissa, a grey old wolf who barked little but would bite in a savage way, turned crafty suspicious eyes upon one whom he regarded as little more than a handsome fortunate youth, who, by Dragut's favour, daughter, and death, had come so soon to a Viceroy's power, to which he himself had the better right, and at one time may have had a good hope to get. They were united by nothing but the belief that it was Allah's will that they should raid the commerce of Christian men, and enslave or slay all who came to their hands, and even in this Hassan had less than the certitude, single and simple, which was dominant in the more primitive mind.

Candelissa knew of a good reason why Hassan should not have agreed the exchange without first talking to him, and that being in the front of his mind, he supposed it to have controlled the event. In fact, it was only after the pursuivant had gone that Hassan considered it at all, though it was one that he would not ultimately have overlooked. The point was that Angelica was Hassan's private property by the usage of war. If she should be given in exchange to purchase Yusef's release, by whom would Hassan be paid for her, and how would the price be fixed?

That, it might be supposed, would be for them to agree now, and for Candelissa to pay, which agreement might not have been easy to reach, but the position was less simple than that.

Candelissa had been resolved that his own son should be released at whatever price, but he had not been equally willing that the gold should be poured from his own stores. He said that the youth had been taken in Turkey's war, and that it was for Mustapha to get him free. This was going further than a jurist of that time would have sustained, but he brought forward some crafty arguments in its support. He made much of the fact that Yusef had been taken on Piali's front, as the commands were set at that time, and as a result of orders he had from him, which (Candelissa said) should not have been given at all, Yusef not being under Piali's control. He hinted that, if the ransom must be provided by him, he might have to go home (with his men) to provide the gold, in which case it would be supposed that Mustapha would not see him again.

To have deserted the siege on such a pretext would have been a defiance of the Turkish power, and of its Viceroy, Hassan, to whom he was more immediately responsible; but Candelissa had looked to Hassan to give him support, as in a matter on which those of the Barbary coast should stand together against Byzantium's domination and greed.

Hassan had taken a middle course, talking to Mustapha and Candelissa in different tones, as the situation required. He gave Candelissa a hope that he would have his support if he would be guided by him, and Mustapha a fainter fear (which was more than enough) that if Candelissa withdrew he would do the same, which would have been the end of the siege.

Mustapha, knowing that Soliman would not lightly forgive if the siege should be abandoned from such a cause, and also that, if a huge ransom were paid under such dispute, it would be likely to be the loss of him from whose purse it should come, temporised, prolonging the argument as to what the amount of the ransom should be, and both he and Hassan may have offered Allah most fervent prayers that Marshal Couppier would cut the knot by twisting one of another kind round Yusef's neck.

Now Hassan saw that, if the youth's life were to be purchased by Angelica's return, there would be need of a clear bargain before as to who should pay her value to him, and even that might leave him no more in the end than an empty purse, and a quarrel upon his hands.

"Candelissa," he said, "you have heard that I did not refuse to give up one for your son's life whom I had purposed to keep, and who is of special value to me. I did that because I would not give you so great a grief to my own gain. But, if I do this, you will not think me less than a friend if I ask a pledge from you that her fair value shall be paid without delay or demur on the day that Yusef is free."

"That," Candelissa replied, "is fair to ask, but it is for Mustapha to grant."

"But if Mustapha will not accord?"

"You have said yourself that it is his part to get Yusef free."

"I do not deny that. But it is for you to bargain with him, not for me. You should buy Don Garcio (who, as you may have heard, is no man) from me, and then ask Mustapha to find her price. Or, if you will say that Mustapha should buy from me, which I do not deny, it is for you to arrange with him."

But Candelissa would not agree to this. He argued in many ways. He talked of obsolescent accounts between the last Viceroy (Dragut) and himself, which a common discretion had resigned to a buried past. He suggested Hassan's power to withhold payments which he should make, in his vice-regal capacity, to the Turkish crown. He talked of many various things, including that they should make common cause to sail away from a siege which was slow to end, and where the plunder at last might not be more than would pay the charges they had to bear. But Hassan saw that these various themes had one feature which did not change. They all meant trouble for him. Loss of prestige, or gold, or quarrels old and new to be on his hands; and the lesson, if not the text, of all was that he had better give Angelica up with no payment at all, beyond such goodwill as it would purchase from Candelissa, which he thought he might value at a small coin, and yet over its worth.

In the end he agreed to see Mustapha himself, thinking that they might devise some compromise which they could unite to enforce, but seeing it to be no more than a poor hope.

Candelissa was the one man who was left with a mind content. He expected to see his son back on the next day, and he thought that he would be a clever man who would afterwards get him to open the secret hoards where his gold was hid.

This conversation took place soon after the noon hour. Hassan knew that it would not be a time to disturb Mustapha, unless for a more urgent cause, for he rested from that time till the sun was further down in the sky. It was a custom born of Egyptian heat, and the habits of age are not lightly changed.

Being alone, he returned his mind to that about which he cared more than the collection of Angelica's price. How could he avoid letting her go? That which he valued before took a higher worth as it became harder to keep.

As he pondered, a subtle thought came. Suppose he could persuade her to remain by her own will? That would be to triumph in a new and even more spectacular way. It seemed fantastic at first, but, as he considered it on all sides, it dressed itself in a garb of reason that gave him a good hope. Rather than lose all, he would bid high, and win a different success from that he had first designed.

CHAPTER XXVI

HASSAN had seen nothing of Angelica since he had told her the ransom he required, and what her fate would be if it were not found. He had no more to say to her till the time should come for her to pay for what she had done. And it may be doubted whether he had given Venetia a further thought, her efforts to reach his regard during the days when she had been confined to his inner tent having borne little fruit to this time.

He had ordered that the two should have freedom within the limits of the house, and had appointed servants to wait on them in more comfort than a Turkish captive would often have. He had surrounded the house with such guard as made escape seem a vain thought. There they could wait, and spend their time in guessing what was to come.

For two to be kept together thus among those of another race, and who were hostile to them, could not fail to establish an intimacy which would be of such kind and degree as their natures allowed.

In a space of two days, Venetia found that she had told her companion more of the adventures of her past life than any living may have heard from her lips before. She had talked thus, having nothing other to do, and by an impulse she did not trouble herself to understand, which sought to justify what she had done by explaining what she had been, and now was. Angelica gave her no confidence in return, but a measure of liking at which she wondered herself, Venetia being, by her standards, despicable in almost all she exposed in her shameless way.

"To understand is to forgive. . . ." It is a proverb of Spain, and of other lands. It is most often less than true, for to understand may be to see that occasion for forgiveness does not arise. Angelica's judgment did not excuse. She saw that Venetia had acted in a base way, bringing others to grief or death for her own gain, and not being greatly ashamed.

She admitted that there might be many who would do the same if it were the only way to escape being flayed from the feet up, though she supposed that most would be afterwards moved both to grief and shame, whereas Venetia would have it that she had behaved as well as she could be reasonably expected to do.

She wondered how she would behave herself under a like threat, and prayed thereon to her own saint, both that she might not be subject to such a test, and that she should not fail if it should come.

Venetia succeeded by her self-revelations so far that Angelica obtained an appreciation of what she was and of what she could never be. Do we blame a tree that it does not dance, or a kitten that it is seldom still? Do we complain that a butterfly lacks size, or that an elephant has no grace? We accept all as they are, and may agree with God when He called them good.

Venetia had a body, slim and soft, that seemed formed for the rites of love, which it was not slow to observe. She had a flower-fair face, and a crown of pale-gold hair, for which many women of better name would have given what soul they had and thought it a low price, as it might have been. She had courage, and a quick wit, and she claimed to be that which she was, and no more. Angelica, to whom she made herself bare both of body and any soul that she had, saw the wisdom of accepting her in the same way. And so they came to accord.

It was while Hassan was arguing with Candelissa, and getting little satisfaction therefrom, that they sat together on the belvedere of the house, being so placed that they could not be overheard in a guarded speech, nor overseen unaware.

"I suppose," Venetia said, "you would get from here, if you could, and if it could be done at less than a great risk."

Angelica was cautious in her reply: "It is not hard to suppose that."

"You will trust," Venetia said shrewdly, but with no sign of taking offence, "where you must, but no inch beyond. . . . I have taught you that (which you were needing to learn), if no more. . . . I will be franker than you, that I would get from here if I could, but I lack gold in a large sum."

"I told you before that I have that, and you said that your skin was worth more to you, as it was likely to be."

"I meant that I would not set you free and remain here, for all the gold that is under the sky. But I have gained a dread of this place, and a fear that it is here I shall end, unless I am soon away. If I knew one to which I could safely flee——"

"How would gold be a help to that?"

"It would solve all, as it ever will."

"Can you show me a plan?"

"There is only one. It is always to bribe. Of the guard and servants around, there is always one. . . . It is to find him, and not to approach those of the harder kind. It is a Greek we need, and it is seldom they cannot be found. A Greek, or a Jew. But to find a Jew here—— Well, it could not be done."

"I would give much to be gone with speed. It is for that I would pay."

"That might be hard to contrive. But there is a question beyond. Where should we go? Or, at least, where should I? Could you give me a pledge that I should not be chastened again if I should arrive within St. Angelo's walls? That you could not! We cannot tell what may be known or guessed of my part when you were seized, even though you should never say.

"But if we could so escape that we should be put ashore on the Italian coast, or even Sicily might do well enough—— You would soon find means to be where you would, either in St. Angelo or another place, and, if I had some gold for my instant needs, I should not long be easy to find."

"It is to St. Angelo I would go by the shortest way."

"Then it could not be with me. Is my offer vain?"

"I have not said that. It may be better to take a long road than to stay here."

Venetia would doubtless have said more to develop her plan, but at that moment there were sounds on the stony path of the approach of a number of mounted men.

"This," she said, "will be with meaning for you. We must hope that you will not be taken apart."

Angelica, seeing that Hassan centred the group, did not doubt that she would soon know more of what her fate was likely to be. She might have surprised herself to observe that Venetia's wish, that they should not be parted now, had a response in her own heart, as though, being so compassed with foes, the woman from whose treachery all her troubles came was a friend that she must not lose.

The riders passed from view, coming closely beneath where they sat. They could be heard to dismount. Shortly, a servant came with the summons they had expected to hear. But it was Venetia who was required.

Angelica, left alone, had leisure to thank herself that she had been guarded in what she said. She did not think that Venetia would betray it, but, if she did, what would it be? Only that, if Venetia fled, she would agree to go too. Hassan would not suppose that she stayed of her own will. It would tell him nothing he would not guess.

But her better purpose was to escape alone, for which she watched at all times like a trapped rat, and on which her mind dwelt, declining to think that it could not be done, though as yet she had seen no way.

She had no desire for the Sicilian shore, from which to return to St. Angelo might be little easier than to escape from this place—especially, she being the woman she was. It was at Francisco's side that she longed to be, taking his part, so that she forgot her present danger at times in the insistence of that desire. . . . But she had seen from Venetia's words that her single escape would be unwelcome as throwing suspicion on the one who remained. Nor could Venetia return with her to St. Angelo, if the chance should appear. She was glad that she had said little of her own thoughts. . . .

Venetia came to Hassan, who was seated in the salon where he had seen Angelica before. He asked: "You would go from here, if you could?"

She was cautious in her reply. "It would be a question of where. I like not a guarded door. I did not fret in your tent."

"There is a felucca sails by night, in four days from now. It would put you ashore on the Calabrian coast. If you were there, with a purse of gold, would you say you had been paid in a fair way?"

It was as though he had read her thoughts. She was about to assent, when he added: "There is one thing more you must do first, which may not be hard."

Her heart sank somewhat at that. Would there always be the one thing more, and the promise moving ahead?

He went on, not requiring reply. "The señorita's ransom has been refused. She is mine for such vengeance as she has earned. I may give her for a plaything for men among whom she will live for a few hours, but not more. I may impale her, or have her skinned. If I do less, she may be whipped, and sold at the market's chance. I may brand her, and make her the jeered slave of my own house.

"Having these powers, I may act in another way, making her my first queen over all my house, with next to a royal rank, and with the riches that women crave. If I should so resolve, I should require one pledge in return, that she would be loyal to me, neither fractious nor sullen of mood, but docile to meet my will. Do you think she would deny that?"

"She would be mere fool if she did."

"How do you stand, after two nights in one bed? Will she take wisdom from you? Have you come to accord?"

"Not so ill. But I am not trusted at all."

"That would be much to require. . . . If she come to this, there will be the felucca for you, and the purse will not be lean."

"If it be more than my power, which I do not think. . . . If I do all that I may. . . . You will let me go?"

"You shall go if you do. It has not a hard sound. You should be content."

She saw that it was all she would get. She said: "It should not be hard. You will see her first? Or do you leave it wholly to me?"

"I will see her now. So you can say; but you need not add what I have said. You can hear it from her."

Venetia went back, saying no more than: "I am to be let loose, but not yet. He would talk to you."

"Did you learn anything but that?"

"Your ransom is not agreed. He said not how they came apart. He seems in a good mood."

Angelica took little comfort from that, thinking that his good mood might be because she was his to bait; but she went down with what courage she could contrive.

CHAPTER XXVII

HASSAN looked at Angelica, as it seemed to her as she entered, with approving eyes. She took what satisfaction she could from that, and from the fact that, though he did not rise at her approach, he did not require her to stand. "You can sit," he said, "if you will."

She had the wit to see that, if he had meant no more than to put her to shame and sale, it would have been done in an open way. When he saw her alone, the idea of some bargain that he would make came to her mind. Perhaps the way in which they had first met may have given her more confidence than she would have felt had she known him in no guise than that of the savage ruler of the Barbary coast. And when they had met for the second time, she had proved the better in that bout—for which it seemed she had now to pay.

"When I talk," she said, in a cooler way than it was easy to feel, "I am not accustomed to stand."

"You might be glad to do that," he countered coldly, "if you were put in another way. . . . It seems that your ransom will not be paid."

"You mean the ships? Did you ever think that it would? It was jest to ask."

"It was none of me. You may call it yours if you will."

She asked boldly: "Then what will you do now? Will you take a price?"

"I will take none. You are mine by the custom of war; which is better than gold."

"Gold will build ships, or will buy."

"But not those two, which I have meant to have. As I will when St. Angelo falls."

"Which it will not do."

"We will change no words about that. If you are wise for the next day, you may live to see. . . . I have said I will have you or the ships, and it seems that you can be better spared."

"What am I worth beyond gold? I can give you that."

"You are worth revenge, and to show that none can flout me and walk secure."

"You have exposed that, for the world to see. You can be content. You can be generous beyond that, knowing that I did no more than I ought on my part. It is the weak who must watch their repute, but you stand too high."

It was shrewdly said, and held a wisdom that he allowed, though it was not of his code. Also, it stroked his pride. But his will was not to be deflected by any words that her wit might find for her need.

"It is so," he said, "that I am able to give you choice. On the one hand, I will not say what I will do, for I have yet to decide; or I may even leave it to you. There is sport if I give you dice for yourself to throw, and as they fall you may be flayed, or impaled, or fastened for ants to eat, or merely whipped, or bastinado'd across the feet. It is for your own wrist to decree. But, in my present mood, the choice will be, on the one side, that you be whipped in St. Catherine's Square, and then sent to a Damascus merchant, who will get me the best price that such as you can command.

"Now against that I will give you a chance that you may pay your debt in a better way, and its condition is only one, of which you cannot complain. I will give you that for which a million women would lick dirt with a ready tongue. I will make you my own wife, wedding you with honour at the eleventh hour of to-morrow morn, and you shall be first of the four which our laws allow (of which I have but three now), and so far as those laws permit, for I am one by whom the injunctions of the Koran are not lightly ignored, they will be servants around your feet."

"When," Angelica asked, desperately fencing for further time, "will you require my reply?"

"It is not a choice that should be hard to decide. . . . But there is a condition that is almost needless to say. If I do this, giving reward to one to whom stripes are due, I must be assured that you will not fail on your part in the duties a wife should yield, but will be docile to please my will."

"It is not thus that ladies are woo'd in my own land."

"Which you have left, and are unlikely to see again. You must be content with the customs to which you come."

"You may see it another way; but it is a hard choice for one who has no purpose to wed."

"Which all women have, who are not sick. You must find different words, or you will have a sore back, if no worse. Would you stand stripped in the sun where the crowd will laugh? Have you seen the whip curl round a woman's thigh? You may dream of that, and give me answer when you awake, which I shall require at the seventh hour, for by noon you will find that you have been either wedded or whipped."

Angelica looked at him in some doubt whether it would be of any avail if she should break into a passion of tearful appeal, which it would not have been hard to do; but she thought it would have no more result than to reduce both his patience and his regard, and, thinking that, her pride was sufficient to hold her in.

"You will be clear," he said, "that it is a loyal wife you would have to be, putting regrets by, and making my country yours."

"You would not require that I change my faith?"

"It is a matter which could be left for this time. You would have instructions to heed. Your faith of a man-born god is for children, not men. You will put it by, when you have been pointed a better way. . . . Yet you should have freedom in that till your own time. . . . There is no more to be said now."

Hassan rose with that word, and walked out without looking at her again. She went back to where Venetia was, being aware, as she climbed the stairs, that her heart beat in a choking way, and that fear had come close to her side, as she had not felt it before. She heard the clatter of hooves on stones, and knew that Hassan had ridden away. She had till seven of the next dawn.

CHAPTER XXVIII

"You are hard," Venetia said, "either to coax or to drive. There was a convent to which you might go, and which you would have ruled at a far day, but it must be another manner of life. It must be marriage for you.

"Now you can be wed to a great prince. You can be the first woman on the Barbary coast, from Alexandria to the narrow Straits, and you say you would liever be whipped. Can I think that? Suppose he change his mind, and yet give you no worse than a rope's choice? Have you seen men hanged? But I have, and some women too. When they are cut down they are not pleasant to see.

"But you know naught. You are not fit to walk in the world's ways. You should be in the cells. I say your uncle was right in that.

"But you are here now. You cannot grow melons and gather figs. You must do what a woman does. Being caught here as you are, you should be glad that you will not go to the rack, or else be raped in a rude way."

"I have thought," Angelica said, "that it is not what may be done to us, but that which we do ourselves, by which we are shamed."

"Well, if you can get comfort from that!"

"I get no comfort at all. I have choice of ills."

"I would give you comfort with a good heart. But who could? You are so stubborn of will. If you dislike to be wife to a Barbary prince, it need not be long. Can you not smile a lie? You could find occasion to get away when he thought you lulled."

"We have a proverb in our land that a lie has short legs. It is a part that I should not sustain, had I mind to try."

"That I doubt. Were you of resolute will, you are one who would lie well. . . . I have heard another proverb of Spain, that truth is for children to speak, or else fools."

"I suppose the meaning to be that, of all mankind, they are nearest God."

"Do you so?" Venetia yawned. "It could be taken another way. . . . But I have heard from a priest's mouth that you are not bound when you swear, being wrongly compelled thereto. It is an oath of duress. I have had much comfort from that, swearing when I am trapped as it may seem wisest to do, and by any oath I am asked, though it be by Bethlehem's star, or the manger that cradled Christ."

"You are versed in much," Angelica allowed, "which I have not pondered till now, but if I wed him at all"—"as you see you must," Venetia interposed—"if I wed him at all, I would practise to keep my vows."

"Well, you could do worse. And it is what I should wish, at the least till I am set free."

Venetia's voice, as she said this, had an accent of sleep, into which she soon after fell, having ease of body and mind, and thinking that she was near the end of as dark a path as she had yet trod.

Angelica lay awake, having more cause. She did not wish to be whipped or slaved, nor did she wish to take the way out that Hassan's offer proposed, concerning which she had some wonder as to why it was made, not being vain enough to suppose that he was drawn thereto by her beauty's power, as some women would have been quicker to do.

Thinking of that, she recalled his courtesies to herself when they had first met.

"The potent arms that you now bear." It had pleased her then. She had thought it sincere. But she knew now that he had been acting a part, which she saw that he had done well.

She remembered then that his face had engaged her thoughts in the night hours. She would have regarded the idea that she should wed him rather differently then from how she did now. But now she knew who he was. The heathen foe of her race and faith. A man with three wives for whom he had so little of love that he offered to put them under her feet. . . . And at that time she had been seeking escape from the dark shadow of convent walls. Something must be allowed for that. . . . And then she had been so young! It was . . . *it was less than four months ago.* It seemed impossible to believe. The quiet, sheltered life, with its many rules, its restraints, its prohibitions of petty things, had the remoteness of prehistoric times. How she had lived in the days between!—And then she must think of that to which it had brought her now.

She had a choice to make, or, as Venetia would have said, with her clear shallow sense, she had really none. Rather, she had a fate to face, to endure, to come through with what honour she could.

But she could not bring herself to regard it thus. She had one dominant thought—to get back to St. Angelo, where she ought to be. Beside that, all other decisions had an aspect of irrelevance. It mattered little whether she were wedded or whipped, if in either case she were foiled of the thing she would.

Indeed, if she were wed, she would be in the worse case, for (she supposed) she would be pledged in honour, if not in words, not to return. Her mind went back to seek way of escape, as it ever would. . . . Francis had a wound in the arm. It was not one (she supposed) by which he would be likely to die. She had greater fear that it would be mended before she could be there, for she judged, truly enough, that as he grew better in health, he would be nearer the day when he must give account of what he had done; and when he did that she did not wish to be far off.

She did not think she could do much of herself, but she felt that Sir Oliver was her friend, and she knew that, even over the Grand Master, he had a great power. . . . He was friend to her, but that he was that to Francisco she was less sure. . . . Francis would be blamed the more that she was not there. And he had called on her to stand back, as she should have done. She had given him the help he required. She might have done more, or withdrawn. But she had done neither of those. She had stood like a fool—like a blind fool—till there had been sudden hands on her arms, and they had dragged her away. Should they blame Francis for that . . .? She might fail to get free, but if she did not attempt, she would be shamed in her own thoughts, which should be worse than to be abused by the violence of infidel men.

She knew that Venetia would not aid her to single escape, nor be willing to risk that she herself should fall either into the Grand Master's or Marshal Couppier's hands. She would be more likely to raise the alarm. But Venetia was sleeping now.

Angelica looked at her as she lay, cheek on hand, in the dim light of the lamp. In her sleep, she had the very innocent look of one whom conscience did not trouble at all. She lived by her own law, and was not ashamed. Her face looked fragile in sleep, though a shoulder, which the blanket did not conceal, was firm with sufficient flesh under its white smoothness of satin skin.

If there were any marks on her face of what her life had been to that day, the night was kind that they could not be seen in that shadowy room. She looked so fair as she lay that it seemed strange that God should so create that which would be destroyed by the malice of time; which may be true alike of the fading of every flower.

"I shall have tried, if I do but walk out, and be driven back," Angelica thought, silently drawing her doublet over her head. And then it came to her mind that Venetia might not escape blame for her flight, and she had a sense of fantastic guilt that she should desert her thus, forgetting how it had come to that pass, and then she thought: "But as yet I am not free!" and there was a sudden laughter to check, which would have come at the wrong time.

Her dressing was soon done, and he spared a moment to wish she had weapon to take, of which there was none in the room, except a dagger Damascus-made, that Venetia had secreted, she would not say by what wile, and which was under her pillow now. Angelica saw its hilt, and thought she could have drawn it out, leaving the sheath still under the pale-gold head, and there came a memory of how Venetia had robbed her room while she slept, at another time. "But," she thought, "I will not go by her code; and it is not weapons but stealth that should get me through."

So she let the dagger be, and went out very silently, closing the door, and down stairs which were half in moonlight and half in shade, and so to the back part of the house, where there was a small window that she thought she might have got through.

She believed that the house was empty at night, the servants not sleeping within, but barring it on the outside, and watching with such patrols through the dark hours that to get out unseen was a feeble chance, though it was one she was bent to try.

But as she entered the kitchen, a man rose, who had been drowsing beside the board. "What is that?" he asked in a sharp voice, and Angelica thought that her effort was soon done.

A shaft of moonlight came from the higher part of a window that was shuttered below. It crossed herself and glittered on a bare sword that had lain by the man's hand, and was now held.

"Telek," she said, "you keep a good watch."

"So I must," he replied, "if I would keep my head where it is. What do you do here?"

"Why, I have no rest. I must walk abroad, as I often do in the night."

"You cannot go beyond here."

"But I will talk to you, if I may."

The man made no objection to that. He was the one she knew best, she being able to understand his speech alone among those who were round the house. But of what race he was she could make no more than a poor guess, and he may have been in nearly as much doubt.

He rose to trim a lamp that had gone out as he dozed, and gave her a better look than he could before. He saw she was fully dressed in a way she would not have been had she meant no more than a walk within doors, having a feathered cap on the black curls which she had shortened to a boy's length, as they were worn in the Spain of that day.

"Why," he asked, in a chuckling voice, "did you think to walk free?"

He was a big man, awkwardly made, having black eyes, under straw-coloured hair, and a large mouth which was used to laugh but could set into cruel lines. Angelica looked at him, wondering whether Venetia would class him among those with whom gold would prevail or as one of the harder kind. Well, it had to be tried.

"I would not turn," she said, "from an open door."

"No," he said, chuckling again, as though at a joke he did not expect her to share. "I do not blame you for that. . . . You will have heard that Yusef was hanged."

"Yusef?" she asked. "Who is he?"

The man showed his surprise. He knew that the Viceroy had visited her after the exchange had been proposed, and before the envoy had come back with the news that it could not be, he having been shown where Yusef yet hung on the gallows that Marshal Couppier had set up in Notabile square. For what purpose should he have come, except to inform her of the proposed exchange on the next day? And would she seek to escape, supposing that her release was so near? He sensed something here that he did not understand, and he knew that heads are sometimes lost by a loose tongue.

"I meant naught," he said, and would say no more.

Angelica had seated herself on the other side of the board. She pushed a ducat across. "There is none to hear," she said, "and it will be silent with me."

"Why," he said, "it is no more than that the Grand Master had proposed that Captain Yusef, whom the Marshal had caught, should be handed over for you. So it was said, and the exchange was to be arranged for to-morrow noon; but the Marshal had been somewhat too quick, and Yusef was hanged this morn, before word could be got to him. That is common talk, and I suppose it is true. But, if you did not know he was hanged, I see not why you should be anxious to quit."

"I had been told that no ransom could be agreed."

"That is how it may prove to be, but there was a different talk on this day, until it was heard at dusk that Captain Yusef was hanged."

"You heard naught beyond that?"

"I heard talk that our General, who is Yusef's father, was wroth, and said there must be as thick a rope for your neck, and the Viceroy said you would be shortly for sale and he could buy you and hang you then."

"So it seems it is time for me to go."

"So it is, if you know how."

"It is that I would ask you." She leant forward, and said in a low voice, as though mentioning that which could not be spoken aloud: "*For a thousand ducats of gold.*"

The man was silent. It was an immense sum to be handled by such as he. Greed and fear strove in his eyes. But he shook his head. It could not be done.

"It is gold I could not collect, nor you pay, being both dead."

"I have better hope."

He quoted an old proverb of many lands. "Live in hope and die in a ditch."

"This is not to hope but to act. . . . There is no haste. You can give it thought."

There was silence for some time after that, except for the sound of a large clock on the wall, of which the single hand was moving upward toward the hour. . . . As it reached the summit, the clock struck—twice.

The man started, and looked at the clock, as though to challenge what it had said. He got up, and pulled a string, by which it would repeat what it had struck at the last hour. The two strokes sounded again.

"I had not thought it had been so late," he said, "I thought it would but have struck once."

"It is so," she said, "when you sleep, as you must have done."

"So I may," he said, "but I wake now. I will not be talked to my death."

"Do you know," she asked, "why I am here?"

"It is some tale of two ships, but I have not heard it all in the right way."

"Then I will tell you now, and you will know that I am one to get free. I have a fortunate star."

She told the tale of how she swam in the night from the *Flying Hawk*, and he stared at her again. His eyes had a bold searching look, as he said: "I was told you were woman under your hose."

"So I am," she said. "I am one of the noblest ladies of Spain, which is why I shall pay you well."

"If it could be done at all," he said in a doubtful way, "it would be when the guard change, but I think you tempt me to death."

He had a new doubt. "How should I be sure of the gold, if I got you free?"

"I will give you a writing now."

"To be my death, if it were found, and I here? No, I would rather trust you than that. . . . It was a thousand ducats you said? Solid ducats of gold of a true mint?"

"So I said. But I will not hold you to that. I will make it twelve. With a home, if you will, in my own land."

He was silent again, wrestling with the temptation, as was plain in his changing face, and she felt that she must bring him to a more resolute mood, lest the night should go.

"When do the guard change?"

"It is at the third hour."

"Then there is a short time to prepare. Will you tell me the plan you have?"

"It is no more than that I shall go out a moment before the hour, holding a light so that you may slip after and not be seen. You will draw into the shade of the shrubs that are by the door, and I will talk for a moment to the man who is near relief. As he is changed, the one who comes to his place will suppose that I am one of the guard who is then relieved. He will not expect me to return to the house, but to walk off. I will hold him in talk for long enough for you to slip by, and will then move away. You must not be too far gone to join me again, and after that we will go to the hills, if we can get through."

"It has the sound of a good plan. Had you thought that to raise alarm on the far side of the house might be a good way?"

The man pondered that. "It might be good at the first, but what start would you get? You would be caught in the larger trap. As I hope, we may get clear before it is known that you are escaped."

"You said that we should go to the hills. It is St. Angelo where I would be."

"Then you must get other guide. I am not mad to that point. We must seek the hills. It is on that side we must get free."

"Then it shall be so, if it must."

He explained, as was easy to see, that the Turkish armies lay so that they had a narrow front of attack and a wider rear. It was toward the rear, which they did not besiege, that there would be the better chance of escape. It would, indeed, have been easy, but for the fear of Marshal Couppier's raids, which kept the outskirts of the Turkish positions in constant, restless alarm.

From this point he made no further demur, and exhibited some intelligence, and a cautious thoroughness in his plans, which gave ground for hope that he would earn his reward if the fates were kind.

He was minute in description of how the bushes lay outside the door, so that Angelica should be able to reach their shelter, on stepping out, without an instant's pause. He calculated how the moonlight would fall. As the hour approached, he extinguished the light, so that her eyes should become used to the dark. He lit a lantern, which he covered behind a bin, till he should require it on going out.

At about three minutes before the hour, he rose up, and unbarred the door. He stepped out, with the lantern aswing on one hand, and the door-key in the other. He laid the lantern on the ground slightly away, and nearer the hinged side of the door. As he turned to lock it, Angelica slipped out. She made no sound, and could not have been seen even a few yards away.

He was hailed almost at once, for there were a dozen watchers around the house, and he shouted back in a great voice, as he moved outward to meet the man who approached him, leaving the lantern where he had laid it down.

"Is all quiet within?" the man asked.

"Within what?" Telek replied. "It is not quiet within me. I have eaten bad fish, as I think. If I could vomit, I might be at better ease. It is for that I am out. But I will not lose sight of the door, though I may be Etna within."

"You will do well, if you can," the man replied. "I have seen one dead in two hours from no better cause. . . . Is the door fast?"

"Yes, and I have left the lantern beside."

The man was one who would leave nothing to chance. He walked up to the door, which it was beyond his duty to do, feeling that it was firmly secure. There was no default in Telek being outside. It was his special duty to guard that door, which he might do from within or without. He had chosen the comfort of a roof and a kitchen chair. The man who guarded the door at the front lay across the outside, knowing that he would be likely to doze during the hours of his watch. He would lean a halberd against it, which must fall with a great clatter if the door should be opened from within, which would not have been easy to do in a quiet way, while its great key yet hung at his belt.

The man, having seen that the door was fast, moved back to his post, shouting to those who were left and right that all was well, which they were anxious to know. Telek walked at his side, or somewhat behind, threatening to vomit at times, which it seemed that he could not do.

"It is worse," the man said, "as I have heard, if you cannot bring it to rise. You should find a leech at the first moment you can."

"I will leave no port where I am put," Telek replied, "while I have legs which will bear me up. But there is a relief due" (they could hear, as he spoke, the steps of approaching men), "and if you will ask the captain——" He stopped in mid-speech, remembering that, if another should be sent to relieve his post, there would be risk that the flight would be discovered earlier than it otherwise might. He changed to: "But no, I will hold on till the dawn. I am somewhat better I think, now that I am in the open air of the night. I will not risk losing this post, and being in the trenches again."

"Well, that is your choice. But to vomit when you have pains is the safer way." Another man came out of the night, and there was changing of pass-words in a perfunctory style. The man who was about to leave appealed to the newcomer: "Here is Telek, who has eaten fish which was bad. I tell him he must vomit or die. Is it not so?"

He went off, having asked that, without waiting for a reply. He had to fall into rank at the front of the house, where those whose duty was done would be marched off.

Telek said: "Well, I may last till I get back." He stood a moment, explaining pain, and then went the same way.

The new guard went to inspect the door, seeing a light. He found that a lantern was on the ground. The door was locked. He thought: "It is to mark where the door is, for us who watch from the outside." It seemed a good way to him. He hung the lantern on the latch of the door.

CHAPTER XXIX

"We must endure," the Grand Master said, "till the autumn days, when they may become weary and go."

"Well," Sir Oliver answered to that, "we may do no less; and, if we can, I suppose it may be enough, for the Turks do not lay siege as do those to whom a month is no loss."

Valette agreed about that. It was plain to all. It gave distant hope, if some increase of present fear. There were signs, even now, in the Turkish lines, that they were preparing another storm. They would not rest in a passive grip of those who must get nearer with every day to when they would starve within. They came storming around the walls as having men to lose, but no time. Doing that, they gave future hope, to balance the present stress.

But the future hope must be faint, for its cause was clear. Mustapha looked north and west for a tempest that did not come; but with a doubt of how long the skies would continue blue.

The menace of Europe was ever before his mind, urging him on. He had had two months incredibly lengthening into three, and Europe had watched, and talked of much which it did not do. But it was a position that might not endure. It was emphatic reason why the armies of Turkey should not camp idly about, as vultures watch round a starving cow.

Europe had heard of St. Elmo's fall, and had muttered, but had not moved. If the next news should be that the horse-hair standards had overwhelmed the Sanglea it might mutter curses again, but would it not conclude that the end was near, and that it would be too late for any succour to reach? So Mustapha might hope, and that the Sanglea should fall he was clearly resolved, though it was not there alone that the tide rose and the tempest beat but at every yard of the leaguered walls. And the Turkish batteries thundered with little rest either by night or day.

"They are in fear," the Grand Master said, "that we may be relieved in a large way, if they dally more. From that cause, there is more fury in their assaults, and we are more pressed at the present hour, though we do our part, and may boast that they bleed well. But will they therefore go when the summer is past, and there is no succour arrived? It is hard to say, but we must still endure as the days pass, not counting toward the end."

He spoke of the powder, of which there was still a good store, but which grew less with each day. Against the tempest of Turkish shot he had ordered before now that there should be no random reply. Each gun must be silent, or trained with care on a mark which would be profit to hit. Now he spoke of rationing every gun, except at issues of active storm.

Sir Oliver said that he would have a plan for that worked out for the next day. The Grand Master said it would be well to do that: he would go to rest now, if there were no other matter of present care.

"I do not know that there is," Sir Oliver replied, "or not one that I see how we can help. You will have heard that the Marshal was overquick to hang Candelissa's son?"

"I cannot blame him for that. I have said that prisoners shall not be fed. He need not have kept him at all; but I suppose it to be cheering to some to see that there is one less on each day. . . . Yet I am grieved that the exchange was not made. Do you know how they have served her to now?"

"She is lodged at the villa near St. Catherine that Le Tonneau built, and she had not been abused up to the last news, which was but a few hours ago. She is companioned by La Cerda's mistress that was, whom Hassan also has in his care."

La Valette frowned at this, in a puzzled way. "Why," he said, "they were together, as I recall, in her chamber before, and it was the same battery in which the wanton was hid that was so sharply attacked, and from which Angelica was secured. . . . Oliver, there is more in this than we have yet probed. It shall not be left till we have turned over the last stone. . . . Is Don Francisco fit to be inquisitioned thereon?"

"I have seen him in the spital where he is laid. He was very frank in his own blame, and, as he was fevered and ill, I put it by in my mind to a better time. . . . But I have given Colonna charge of his battery while he is laid aside, and that appointment I would ask you to confirm in a more permanent way."

"Removing Don Francisco therefrom?"

"So I thought. We should have one there in command of whom we are more sure."

"So it shall be. . . . Have you no further thought that can get her free?"

"I know not what to advise. Beyond that we must bargain anew, offering gold with a free hand."

"We have offered more than her worth."

"Yes. But they may take it at last. . . . There is some hope beyond, that if she be sold the merchants may offer her first to us. I have let the word be passed in the right way that Palermo will give more than the seraglio price would be likely to be. . . . But she must be sold first, as I fear, for Hassan is not looking for gold alone, but to requite the way she foiled him before."

As they spoke, there was a sound at the door, where one would enter whom the usher stoutly withstood.

"What is that?" La Valette asked, with a sharp frown.

"It is soon seen." Sir Oliver went to the door. "So," La Valette heard his voice, "you were right to do. But you can let him in now."

He came back, with Don Francisco following. "Here," he said, "is one who should lie flat. But you shall sit, and tell us why you have come."

Francisco was pale, and his arm was bound to his side, but he was in a mood to forget that.

La Valette looked at him, and a memory came of his own youth, and of a companion who had had the same look forty years before, when he had been wounded, and would still take his place in the breach at a great need, and whose son was before him now.

"Don Francisco," he said, "I have just heard that Colonna has your command while you are unfit, which is well, for it could not be in the hands of a better man. I have been asked to give him that post in a more permanent way, and to remove you therefrom. If it be from that cause you are here, you have but to say that it would be poor justice to you (who did well when the boats were sunk, as I have no mind to forget), and I will reserve all till you are more equal to your defence."

Francisco lifted his eyes to the Grand Master, and it was clear that he found no pleasure in what he heard.

"No," he said, "I do not protest of that. I am justly served."

La Valette's eyes, as he heard that, took on a sterner and more questioning look. "Do you mean me to think," he asked, "that it was by your fault that the battery was surprised, and the guns still, when they should have defended the boom?"

"I must say that, or else lie, which I will not do. . . . But it is of Angelica I must know. . . . There is tale that Yusef is hanged. I must know what you will do now."

Sir Oliver interposed to reply: "There is still some hope that gold will avail, as it mostly does."

"I would be sure, rather than hope, she being placed as she is. Do you know where they have her now?"

"She is not hardly abused by the latest news that the spies bring. She is in a villa some miles away, being there confined with Venetia in the same room."

"With——? It is a fiend's jest."

"Well, so it is. It might be worse, as you can see."

"Is it strongly held?"

"It is nigh three miles in the Turkish lines. There is no rescue could reach, if you mean that. . . . There are armed guards at each door, and a cordon of men is round it both night and day. Hassan does not mean that she shall twice escape from his power."

"Be it what distance it may, or were it held by the whole army of Turks, as you may call it to be, I had thought that she would be for the rescue of Christian knights."

La Valette was stern. "Do you teach duty to me? I have Malta to guard. Should I forget that for a single life, it is there that my shame would lie."

"But I am shamed, if I do not attempt her aid. . . . Will you tell me how this villa lies, when I shall have passed the Sanglea?"

Francisco turned to Sir Oliver, as he put this question, but it was La Valette who replied.

"Oliver, you can be still for the time. It is vain talk, but I will know why he should feel in so shamed a way. . . . Was it by your fault"—he addressed Francisco—"that your cousin came to be there in the night hours?"

But Sir Oliver would not be still. "I can answer that," he said; "for he has told all to me, by whom it shall come to you. . . . But, by your leave, I should let him go."

The eyes of the Grand Master and the secretary met, and La Valette knew it to be one of those times when Sir Oliver would not lightly give way. "But, Oliver," he said, "it is madly vain. Shall he waste his life to no use . . .? But I must trust you in this, as I have trusted in larger things."

La Valette said no more. He stood silently, as having forgotten his purpose to go, gravely regardful, while Sir Oliver drew out a map of the district where the Turkish army was camped, and pointed out where the villa stood in which Angelica was confined. With clear brevity of phrase, he explained the roads and other physical features, and how the Turks were encamped. He spoke as though he were describing that which was within his own lines. When he had done, he looked up to ask: "Can you remember all?"

"Can I forget?" Francisco rose to go. He asked: "Have you a sword?"

La Valette loosed one from his side. "I cannot use it," he said, "as I once did; but in your hand it may yet strike a good blow. It is yours, for the sake of one I do not forget."

Sir Oliver said: "You will need this." He wrote a pass which would enable him to leave the Christian lines by the Bourg gates. "When you show it," he said, "they will point you the way the spies go, where you will not be shot by those who are unaware who you may be."

Francisco said a word of thanks, and went out, silently watched by the two older men, who were not quick to speak when he was gone.

"Oliver," La Valette said at last, "you have let him go to a most sure death, which can be to no gain, either to us, or to her whom he seeks to save."

"So I suppose," Sir Oliver replied. "But it was what I had no choice but to do, for his honour is a soiled rag, both to Malta and her, and I think he has gone in the right way."

After that, he told all that he knew, and more that he guessed, in which he was seldom wrong.

The Grand Master said, when he had done, "I must have hanged him for that, as I have hanged others for lesser things. . . . But God has opened a better way." He sighed at a thought he had. "We may pray for his soul to-night," he went on, "with a good will. . . . I suppose there are Turks who will feel his sword." He seemed to find some comfort in that, but as he went to his bed he had the look of a tired and sorrowful man.

CHAPTER XXX

VENETIA waked to the sound of a closing door, too vaguely heard to judge what it might be. She saw, by the dim light of the lamp, that the bed was empty beside her. She sat up quickly; awake, watchful, alert. Her eyes, swiftly searching the room, saw that Angelica's cap was gone.

Doubt, anger, fear, contended within her, as she swung her feet lightly over the side of the stately bed, and made for the door. She opened it to listen to a silent house. From the kitchen there came the three deep slow notes of the striking clock. Outside, she could hear the noise of the changing guard. . . . What did it mean? Was Angelica still in the house? Should she give alarm? Had she gone two—three—hours ago? How wild Hassan would be! Would it prove pretext enough to send her to the slave-market, if not to the lash, or to more terrible things? She was innocent of any complicity in Angelica's escape, if escaped she was, but she had seen enough of the world's ways to know that innocence might be a detail irrelevant to the position in which she stood. . . . Was it possible that Angelica had not fled, but been fetched away? The idea was rejected. Venetia was sure that she would not have slept through such an event: would not have slept through Angelica's dressing at all, unless it had been noiselessly done.

She took clothes in a quick way, but not so that she was careless of how she might look, if she should meet men before she should regain the room. She lifted the lamp, and put it down, thinking that it might be a fault that any movement of hers should be visible from without. There should be moonlight enough. She opened the door again, and after another moment of listening which returned no sound, she went down the corkscrew stair.

There was silence in the house, and in the kitchen the lamp was out, and Telek gone. Venetia was better acquainted with his habits than Angelica had been. She knew that, though the soldiers who circled the house were changed during the night, the guarding of the doors, which was a duty of those of the inner staff, was undertaken in watches of eight hours, and that Telek's habit was to do his turn on a fireside chair.

The moonlight fell over the table in a slanting line, and showed where a ducat lay. Telek, pondering the huge sum which was his to earn, and then how it could be achieved, had failed incredibly to pouch that which was his to lift.

Venetia did not need to be told more. She had read a plain tale. She went silently back, not failing to pick up the coin.

Should she give alarm? An instinctive habit by which she would be slow to resolve without searching thought, unless she were cornered and forced, held decision back. Then she saw that, if there should be sudden outcry to wake the house, she must not be dressed as she was, and she was quickly back in the bed.

If she knew how long it was since Angelica got away! She wished she had confided in her, but without resentment for that. "Had she so," she allowed in a candid mind, "she had been pure fool, after what she had known me do."

She imagined Angelica, with Telek for guide ("who would be one to trust as you must, but no more") creeping among the rocks, and her natural sympathy for those who were hunted by force or law was an instinct to keep her still.

She was not conscious of any virtue in her resolve (of which we may say there was not much) as she decided at last: "She shall have till the next hour strike, and after that she must use her wits, as I mine." It was after that she began to dream (when would the dreams fail that had brought her far?) that, if Angelica were gone, she might win Hassan's regard, if she could face his first wrath in a skilful way. . . . The hours passed. The guard watched without, and the house was silent within. When the clock struck four, she rose, and put on some clothes in what should appear to be the disorder of haste. She went down, and roused the man who had his watch at the front, with the tale that Angelica was not there.

It was not a thing that had to be said twice to unlistening ears. It seemed but a moment before the house was loud with clamour and search, and little more before Hassan himself had ridden up, and, black with fury, was directing pursuit.

In the next hour it seemed that he had the whole army awake. Horsemen had ridden at random speed to warn the outposts on every side. Not waiting for dawn, far out from the environs of the house, intensive search spread over the moonlit scene.

It was not till all had been done that wrathful energy could contrive that he sent for Venetia, who had courage and experience in such crises of life sufficient to enable her to conceal the fear that reason could not deny.

"You will tell me," he said, "all that you know. It is the one chance that you have, which may not be much."

"So I will," she replied, "and you will see that you owe me thanks. It was I who waked the alarm. Had I slept, as you will not say I was not permitted to do, there would have been no stir till the morn, and if she should now be caught (as I should say is a likely thing) it will be to me it is due."

"I can think such things for myself," he returned, in a cold voice, "and it will be well for you if I shall go by your road. But what I ask is your tale."

"You asked my tale with a threat which I had not earned," she replied, meeting his frown with a quiet front, though her heart beat hard. "I will tell you all I know, which is not much. . . . I was waked by a clock that strikes loud, so that it can be heard through the house, and I saw that her place was bare. She might have left the bed for a light cause, and, had I turned over and slept, I do not think I should have been greatly wrong, the house being so guarded and barred, and I not having been made her watch; but I looked further, and saw that her cap was gone, and on that I did not pause even to dress, but was most instant to raise alarm."

"Then," he said, searching her with suspicious eyes, "you must have had cause to think she purposed to fly, or you had been less quick so to conclude."

"I was so far from that, that I believed she had agreed in her heart that she would do well to be wedded to you. We had talked long on that, and I had so practised, as you desired."

"It would not have been. Yusef is hanged." A new thought came, and he asked sharply: "Had you heard that? It is that which it must have been!"

Venetia's look of puzzled wonder was not assumed, as she replied: "Who is he? I cannot guess what you mean."

"Then there is no need to say more." He did not propose to explain to her that the idea of marrying Angelica had been no more than a last expedient, to prevent her exchange taking her out of his power, and that he had dismissed it at once on hearing that Yusef was dead. He saw, also, at a second thought, that this could not have been more than guessed, whatever knowledge Angelica might have gained, for his motives, or his later change of purpose, had been confided to none. He asked: "She has spoken of flight before?"

"That she had not. Do you think she would be open to me?"

Her tone mocked, and Hassan saw that there was reason in that.

Still he urged: "But you were alone, and no more than two. There must have been talk."

"So there was. But she is one who speaks truth in a frank way, and yet has thoughts that she will not show. I have not met one who at times may be harder to read."

He thought of how Angelica had escaped before, and he did not dispute that.

"There is this Telek," he said, "who is also gone. You will have seen her talking to him?"

"Even that I have not. I am amazed that she could have purchased his help. I should have said that he would not be moved by aught to a great risk of his own skin, nor that he was one on whom to rest faith for any pledge he could give."

"Having sounded him thus?"

"Will you call me so great a fool? Have I fled? Do you not see I am here? And whereto should I go? It is your favour I seek, which is why I stirred as I did the first moment I found her gone."

Hassan considered this, and again he saw that it was a plausible defence, and most likely true. He did not mean that Angelica should escape without all concerned feeling his wrath in a way which would be hard to forget, if he let them live. But though he could be ruthless and cruel, even in fantastic modes, as was the way of his race, yet he had no wish to cut off an innocent head if he could find one that deserved it more.

"I have little doubt," he said, "that they will be caught as the dawn comes, and I will judge all when I have heard their own tale, which the rack may aid." He looked at her with as hard a glance as she had yet had, as he asked: "You swear now that you keep nothing back? It is the one chance you will have. Do you doubt that she fled with this Telek's aid, and has not done him away with some trick?"

"I have told all I know, except one thing that I have been waiting to say. I have no doubt that it was with Telek she fled. I suppose she went in the night, in a secret way, and persuaded him as he sat at watch, for when I went down, there was this coin on the kitchen board."

She produced the golden ducat that she had picked up, and Hassan took it, and observed that it was one of Ferrara's mint.

"Has she a store of these?"

"She had ten or twelve."

"Why did you not let it lie? Was it yours to take? Why did you secrete it away?"

"Let it lie? For how long? When I was calling the guard! I thought it was to be held for your own eye."

He gave her a better glance than before as he said: "Well, you have answered all in a bold way. If you have told truth, and with nothing hid, you need not have a great fear."

He went, leaving her well content. She had not meant to show the ducat, which he had taken away, as she supposed that he would; but, as he had pressed her to tell all, she had felt it to be the safer course. Beyond that, what had she concealed? Her tale had been wrong by an hour. But who would discover that? It was a question of when she waked, and who else could say?

She had overpassed another peril of which her life was too full, by the aid of a cool wit, and having no scruples at all, either to speak or to do.

CHAPTER XXXI

"You must not go out by the gate," Del Formo said, "even by night, for that would be to ask for notice at once, it being a thing which is not done.

"There is a place where the bastion is low, and has been shaken into the fosse more than it should, at which we have winked for reasons I need not say (but if the Turks should choose to rush us at that point they would find it an ill choice), and there you could go down without toil, but, as you have no more than one arm in use, you shall have a rope's help. You will go for thirty paces along the fosse, and you will find the counter-scarp in no better case, and very easy to climb.

"How long you will endure after that is beyond my guess. But I will tell you this. The spies say that they are little observed when they attempt to enter the infidel lines. It is when they return that they must lurk and twist, and that their bellies must worm the ground.

"We understand this, for we are disposed to act in the same way. For if we catch a man coming in, he will have a smooth tale. He will be Christian at heart (that is if he be of Greek blood, as they mostly are), and so deserting to us, or he will pull a script from his caftan's folds, being a letter to one of our own knights. What can we do? We have no sieve that will sift his tale.

"But if we catch him when he is on his way back, we have a man with a full crop. If he have writings, they will not be such as he will be glad for us to see.

"And it will do him no good to say that he was deserting us because he was getting to love Mahound. He can tell few tales that we cannot test, and if he lie he is soon hanged.

"But we might not do that to a known spy, for there are some of these men who can so contrive that none can tell whom they prefer. They have become of use to both sides, being like a post. They are men that neither trusts but both use. It is likely they are loyal to nothing more than their own necks and the coins they get from both sides.

"So you may have a safe start. You may creep the fosse knowing that you will be no mark for our men, who will have warning from me, and after that you will not be shot by the Turks in the gloom, even if you are seen, without they first find who you are."

Francisco thanked Del Formo for this advice, which was better than he had expected to hear. The knight, who was in charge of some length of the bastion of Provence, gave him also the Turkish pass-word for that night, which was something more he had not thought to have, and also a turban to replace the morion which he wore.

"There will be no use," Del Formo said, "for disguise beyond that; for you are not one who could come into the light, and sustain any lie that I could give you to tell. But you must have a turban to meet the moon. I should advise, if you get but a short space from our own lines, that you advance as one owning the earth, with the pass-word to see you through, and may St. Christopher be your guard."

Francisco left him at that, being given to a smaller man to be led to the wall, and Del Formo looked after him with a thought that he had seen him for the last time, but there was not much to stir emotion in that, while men died every day, and your own time was fixed for not more than a month ahead.

Francisco descended the wall, and must stumble somewhat along the fosse, it being more dark than was the open night, and strewn with debris from the round-shot battering of the mound. But he came to the place of which he had been told, and looked up to a light gap where the counter-scarp had fallen in, both lowering itself and raising the floor of the fosse. He clambered out here with little trouble, though with a loud falling of rubble beneath his feet, which would have been his end had he been watched from the wall by those who were not friends.

As he came up to the level land, he thought he saw the movement of one who was not five yards away, and his sword was half out of its sheath, but the man (if one there were) may have wished to be seen as little as he; and so, after a moment of waiting silence, he went on to the Turkish lines.

He heard a sentry's call on his right, and bent his course to the left. Then there were voices out of the night from that side, and he swerved again. The ground was hard and broken, having been ploughed by shot and trampled by many feet. He had to give his most heed to that, lest he should lame himself against rocks, or fall to a sudden pit. . . . He came to a low wall of stone, with a beaten path on its right. It was not quite in the direction in which he wished to go, trending too much eastward, toward the shore, but he thought it best to follow it, till he should come to a road which the map had shown. . . . Out of the darkness he was challenged sharply, in a strange tongue. . . . He shouted back the pass-word he had been instructed to say, and walked quickly on. The voice shouted again a peremptory and yet questioning call, to which he replied with the pass-word again. The voice that called had a note of menace now, but it did not pursue, and it was already some distance behind. The next moment, he had come to the road.

He thought: "I may thank the turban for that. He would not have let a morion by with no more than a wrathful word." But his thoughts were few. He was but aware of the night, and the purpose for which he came. He walked on a silent road, going with an assured mien, as Del Formo had advised him to do. He had no need to ponder or pause, for, now he had found the road, his way was clear by the map he had seen, till he should be near the villa where Angelica was. He remembered each turning, each hill and fall, as Sir Oliver had explained them to be, and the forked road by the little bridge——

He met no one at all, and he was come to the uphill road which approached the villa he sought, when he found that he must shorten his pace, or he would overtake a group of men who marched in a slack way, as they may do in the reality of war, where its pageantry is of little avail, and especially when they move in the night.

He was the more content to have followed, himself unseen, when he found that their destination was his, and that they were halting before the villa, on the side where the ground sank, the front being approached by a flight of steps. The garden rose round the house, becoming level with the door at the back through which Angelica had fled. Before the front of the house, the moonlight gave him a wide view of open country that fell eastward to meet the sea. He looked up, and saw the belvedere, and near to that a dim light, where he supposed that Angelica lay. He stood at the road-side, in a black shadow of cypresses, and saw what the nature of his problem was likely to be. He might succeed with a first blow. He might come out of the night to slay any sentry he might select. He might slay one or two more of those who would be first to come at their comrade's cry. He felt equal to that. But more would arrive. Though he could kill or scatter them all, it might be to earn no more than the right to beat on a barred door. He did not know what watch there might be in the house, but he saw that, if his single arm should be sufficient to foil the outside guard, he would have short time to get Angelica out before there would be wider alarm. . . . There might be no earthly odds that would make him turn, but he had come to save Angelica, not to kill Turks; and, perhaps equally, though he might not observe the impulse that drove him on, to see her, to confess his folly, to gain forgiveness for the fault that had brought her there.

But one thing was clear, whatever might be best to do beyond that. It would be stupid to challenge a double guard. He must stand aside till those who were relieved had marched wholly away, and he saw that they would march back along the road where he stood in a shadow that was black enough, but against a wall that he could not quickly scale with one useful arm. He considered climbing it now, and hiding in the cypresses which grew close on its other side, and then elected a bolder and better way, going forward while the movements around the house would be protection for one who need not be closely seen. He found a small gate, where he entered the garden, which spread wide of the house on that side, and went up a narrow twisting path that was further from the house than the cordon were placed. He had little fear of being perceived, the garden being planted thickly with flowering shrubs, from which the air was loaded with strong scents in the August night, offering quick shelter if he should become aware of a step that might come too close.

He came to the back of the house, as those who were withdrawn assembled below the front. He stopped when he reached a rock-garden that was too open to cross with prudence at such a moment. He drew into a screen of shrubs, through which he could see toward the house. There were two men who talked. Vaguely, uncertainly, for a moment, he thought a shadow passed behind them, coming into the bushes where he was hid. The men's voices were loud. He heard advice: "You should vomit well." Then one turned away. It seemed for a few steps that he would go down by the side of the house, but when the one he left turned to look at the door, he came into the shrubs. Francisco thought: "The man is sick. He is coming to vomit here." He became very still. . . . After a time, there were rustling movements that came close. He perceived that there were two who were coming with a great caution toward the path by which he had approached the house.

He could not tell what it meant, but it was clear that they were as intent as himself that their movements should not be known. Men do not creep through shrubs in the night in a furtive way without cause. They might hunt; but not in a garden which was patrolled. They might burgle; but these men moved away from the house. A wild hope came to his heart, and was put aside, before that which he thought incredible became known for true. Silent, with senses preternaturally alert, as they will be at such physical crises of life, he heard Angelica's voice.

He could not hear what was said, nor the single low word of reply, but after that the two, who had been almost upon him, turned away to the right, so that they would strike the path by which he had come lower than he had left it.

There came a joy, sudden and great, to his heart, with the thought that Angelica had escaped, and the tension of spirit under which he had approached to attempt her rescue somewhat relaxed.

His next mood was a natural doubt, and a fear lest he might do that which would bring ruin on her again. He could not guess who her companion might be, nor what might be the effect of revealing himself; but he saw that, if they should hear him approach, they would think him a certain foe. He would be a fancied danger where they would have real ones more than enough, and might cause them to turn aside from their best way. He saw also that, if he should contrive to follow them at a short distance, he increased the risk of causing discovery and alarm, such as might be fatal to both.

Yet he was reluctant to lose sight of her, when he had come so near, and, if she should be stopped or pursued, his sword might be a good help.

He resolved to follow in a distant and cautious way, risking rather to lose sight than to cause alarm; and then to make himself known by a low call, if they should come to some desolate place where it could be done without fear.

He succeeded in this so far that he did not draw observation from others upon himself, such as would be dangerous to those who were no great distance ahead; and so long, that he was able to learn with certainty that they were not aiming to reach St. Angelo's walls, but rather that part of the island which the Turks had first overrun when they landed in St. Thomas's Bay, and which was now spoiled and bare, not being much occupied by the Turks, nor a place where any of Maltese blood would be likely to make his home.

He did not wholly avoid the suspicion of those he followed, for there came a time when Telek paused to listen, having a vague doubt that they were pursued in a furtive way. But there was silence while they were still, and then, when they started again, and his suspicions recurred, there rose two noises at once to render listening vain. A Turkish battery suddenly opened with all its guns against the Sanglea, as might often be now during the night, when Mustapha would allow his foes no assurance of rest, and there was also the noise of a company of men who were marched to the front line.

At this time, they were on rather high and open ground, which was divided into small fields by low walls of stone. The men who marched were on a road at a lower level than theirs. Telek led in a crouching position, so that they should keep as low as the wall. It was a slow method to choose, and worse for him, he being a large man. But he knew that there was still some time of darkness ahead, and he did not mean to lose either his head or the offered reward. But there were moments when he must rest with an aching back.

It was a mode of progression, however slow, which was not easy to keep in view. Francisco resolved to try to come closely here, and then call Angelica's name, delaying only till the men who marched should be gone, and the night still. He thought to do this by choosing the other side of the wall, and moving more rapidly than they would be likely to do. But when he rose, thinking that they would be near, he could not perceive them at all. He thought that they might have heard his approach and become still. He waited awhile, till they should have courage to move again. Still hearing no sound, he called in a low voice, but had no response. He felt sure that they could not have gone far ahead. He crossed the wall, and crept some way back on the other side.

Here he found an explanation he did not like. There was another wall on this side, at right angles to the one he had followed. Doubtless, they had turned there, while he had gone on, there having been no similar wall on his side.

He followed this, but was soon in doubt. There was a gap in the wall. Had they gone through that, or kept on? Other doubts followed, of a similar kind. He could but keep in the same direction which they had previously held, for which the moon was sufficient guide.

As he went on, the night woke. Behind him, the villa sprang into light. There were noises, and distant cries. It was easy to guess that there had been discovery of Angelica's flight, but had he come no further than that? And what should he do now? It would be hard to escape through the Turkish lines, now that there had been sound of alarm. It would be death to be on such open ground when the light should come. He thought less of his own peril than of those he would aid if he could, but how should he reach them now? It would be their first thought to make themselves hard to find.

Down the road, to which he was now close, a rider came at speed, his loose *burnous* blowing back on the wind. Doubtless he rode to warn the outposts who kept sleepless watch against Marshal Couppier's raids that a prisoner had got free.

Francisco crouched under a wall, doubting what he should do. He knew that he had betrayed his military trust in a way that the Grand Master would not be quick to forgive. He had thought less of that than he otherwise might, because his mind had been obsessed with Angelica's peril, and his equal betrayal of her. He had thought either to die in this attempt, or to bring her back, having redeemed one-half of his offence, and so to face that which he could not change. But it seemed that, if she were to escape, it would be likely to be without aid from him. Even in that, Fate had rejected him as unworthy or unrequired.

He saw now, more clearly than imagination had conceived, that the extent of territory that was occupied by the Turks, stretching from the great harbour to Marsa Scala Bay, was too wide to be closely occupied by an army which may not, at this time, have totalled more than 23,000 men, of whom the far greater part were entrenched in positions of attack, or stationed in support of the batteries that surrounded the Maltese lines. To pass the outposts, either at front or rear, might normally be a dangerous, but it could not be less than a very possible venture. But it would be harder—much harder—now that Angelica's flight had been discovered, and there would be alert watch on all sides for a prisoner of such value, and one whom Hassan would be furious to lose twice. Much harder, also, would it be to find concealment within the lines, where there would be active search. A wild thought came, that he should go back to St. Angelo, and call for volunteers who would join him in the knightly folly of attempting his cousin's rescue from the peril in which she stood. . . . He did not doubt that, after the proof he had made that the Turkish lines could be passed in the night, there would be those of sufficient hardihood to give him support. But reason told him that the hours of darkness were nearly done, that Angelica might now be no easier for her friends than her foes to find, and, most definitely of all, it was a thing which could not be attempted without the Grand Master's consent, which it was sure that he would not give.

To sally out in any force, large or small, was to abandon the strength of stone, on which he relied to outface a foe who must have been five to one at this time, even when what remained of the island militia is added on the Maltese side, and the principle was the same whether it were done with twenty or two thousand men. Knowing the Grand Master, it was absurd to suppose that he would be influenced by the fate of a single life, to deviate, though it were by no more than a yard, from his plans for Malta's defence.

Being in such confusion of doubt, it was an impulse of feeling, rather than a reasoned decision, by which he followed in the direction in which he supposed Angelica to have gone.

Angelica, at this time, was not more than three hundred yards ahead, following Telek down a rocky path to the road with no concealment at all, that being what Telek had told her to do.

She came in doubt and fear, for she saw that, had her companion been the best knight in the world, they were in a desperate case now that the alarm had been loudly raised, and it was plain that he was much less than that.

From the moment that it had become clear that their escape was known, he had sunk to irresolution, and a fear that he could not hide.

He said now that their best chance would be to descend to the road, where they could make more rapid progress than over the fields. Haste was their one chance. She could not say he was wrong, though she failed to see how haste would avail on a road on which warning had gone before. She knew only that she followed a cunning and frightened man whom she could not trust, and in whose power she was in a most absolute way. He was stronger than she. He was the only guide that she had. If she should run, he could probably outpace her for a short spurt. She was weaponless, and he had a sword, and a pistol was in his belt. If he should decide that she would be better dead, it would not be easily avoided by her.

That had, in fact, been in active debate in his mind, as they had crawled over the hill. He thought of the offered reward, for which he had a great greed. But it could not be paid to a dead man. Life is more even than gold, and for his he had now a most urgent fear.

If he were caught, as he saw now to be a most likely thing, the chance that Hassan would spare his life was not worth a groat. He would be lucky if he were not taken alive, for it would be strange indeed if Hassan should give him an easy death.

There came one hope to a cunning, desperate mind. Could he say that Angelica had slipped out by a trick, or perhaps when he dozed, and that he had followed her without giving alarm, knowing that the only hope of mercy for himself would be that he should be the one who would bring her back? It was a poor tale, and a poor hope even if it should be believed, but it was the best he could do. A trapped rat will try to squeeze through a small hole. He remembered the ducat that he had left on the kitchen board. He must spin a tale around that, and, if it had been found, it would give support to less provable words. . . . It was with these thoughts in his mind that he had debated whether it would be best to kill her with a thrust in the back, and say that he had pursued her, and struck to prevent her escape.

Had it seemed best for his skin, he would have done it with no scruple at all, and it was fortunate for Angelica that the probable consequences were ambiguous to his own mind. If she were dead, she could not contradict his tale, which she would otherwise be likely to do. That was to the good. But he had a well-founded belief that Hassan would prefer to recover her alive, rather than dead. A sufficient reason for having killed her would be difficult to contrive. The better plan would be to go on while there might be any hope of getting through the lines, and to be found in the act of dragging back a recovered captive if discovery should come closely upon their heels.

It was with an obscure idea that this programme would have more verisimilitude if it were performed on the road (for how should he, more than another, have discovered her lurking in the dark fields?), but perhaps urged more strongly by the desire to bring the event to a prompt issue, whether for good or ill, which is natural to some natures when nervous cowardice is in control, that he had urged the dubious advantages of the open road.

They had reached it, but had not trodden its stony surface for more than twenty or thirty yards when there came the sound of a running pursuit. After the first horsemen had been sent out to warn the outposts and contain the fugitives, footmen had been scattered in all directions to round them up. Hassan had sent them not by the roads only, but widely scattered over the fields, with promise of rich reward to those who should win the chase. But it was natural that they who came by the roads should make quicker advance than those who spread over pathless fields.

Angelica looked at the man to whom she had given more trust than she would have done at a lighter need. Were they to try the chance of the dark fields again, before pursuit would come up? Even now there was time to get away, it might be unobserved, if no moment were lost. Or was he of the sort to pull out his sword, hearing that there were not many who came? In her desperate fear of being recaptured, and all that it was likely to mean, she felt that she would strike a good blow herself, if she had a weapon of any kind, before their hands should be upon her again.

But he did not offer either to fight or fly. With a sudden movement, he caught her arm in both hands in a brutal grip.

He shouted: "Ho, comrades! Comrades, I have her here! She is caught!"

He snarled at her in a lower voice: "Would you have brought me to death? Will you lie now? Will you say I have not caught you in hot pursuit?"

He shook her in a rough way, though she made no effort to resist, or to get free, having too much pride for a useless strife.

"Would you not rather win the reward," she asked, "than go back to be flogged, as I think you will, if you get no worse?"

"Would you tempt me again," he asked, "as you did with the ducat I would not lift?"

He seemed to be endeavouring to convince his own mind of the tale he had made, or to practise assertion against her own. He began to drag her backward upon the road.

There was time for this, for the men who pursued had ceased to come on. They seemed to have turned to face some trouble upon their rear. Telek slackened his pace as he became aware, by the light of a breaking moon that had been clouded till now, that steel clattered and shone.

A man, turbaned and tall, came forward, with a bare sword, leaving others upon the ground.

Telek stood for a moment in hesitation, doubting what it might mean, as was not easy to guess.

Francisco called: "Angelica, is it you?" in the Spanish tongue, which he did not know.

At that, she wrenched to get free. She called: "Francis, to me!" in a sudden wonderful hope.

Into Telek's mind came a guess that was half true, and an idea by which he might yet save his skin from scars, or his neck from the sabre's sweep.

Here was some rescue intended for her, of which but one man remained, and he, if the faint light told truth, with a bandaged arm. He had a further thought that Angelica must have deceived him as to the details of her escape, which had never been meant to depend on him, nor would he have had any reward. But now, if he could show a Christian dead by his sword (and perhaps others upon the road?) he could make a better tale than he had hoped to be able to tell. He might have not stripes, but reward!

Thoughts are swift, so that he had time for these, for which his life would otherwise have been less than enough. He pulled his sword free, a curved scimitar in which he had a skill he was apt to boast, still grasping Angelica, whom he was unwilling to loose, in his other hand. But Francisco's coming did not pause, as that of a man should when he is met with a bare blade. His sword came straight and swift as a cobra strikes, and when the scimitar swept round to turn it away, it struck a blade that was through Telek's neck, and half a foot out beyond.

CHAPTER XXXII

ANGELICA stood in joy that was careless of the man who bled to death at her feet, or of the menace of farther things.

"Francis, are you hurt? How did you come here? Are you alone?"

"I came to give you aid if I could, you being snared by my fault."

"That I was not. I should have stood back, or taken a better heed. . . . But you are not fit to be here! You were sore hurt, as I heard. . . . Were you single to attack those who pursued?"

"There were but three, on whom I ran at the back. Two are down, and one fled."

"Then we should not stand here."

That was plain, but where were they to go?

Angelica looked down on a man who had become still. She did not regard that his blood had soaked one of her own feet. She said: "There is a pistol we ought to have." In this place to which she had come by her own will, she was not singular if she were forgetting that it was not a Spanish señorita's business to scuffle in bloody bouts. There were few women in St. Angelo's bourg who would not learn in the next few weeks to fight with Turks on a failing wall. . . . There were two hundred children who were being practised with slings, that they might help the defence of the Sanglea at its next assault. . . .

Francisco said: "Yes. We will have that." He knelt down, laying his bare sword on the ground. Angelica saw that he had only one hand to use. She must give him aid.

"It was so," she thought, "that La Cerda fought at the last." Was there an omen in that? She put the dread away with a steadfast will. By Mary's grace, it might still come to a better end, as she would be firm of faith to believe. . . . It was strange that Venetia's two lovers should have been disabled in a similar way. At least—perhaps it was less than fair to give Francisco that name. He must know better now. And then the doubt rose—she was not the only one in the Turkish camp. Had he ventured here in truth solely for her? Or was there another whom he could not put from his heart?

She thought: "I will not be vexed by a false doubt. There should be true words between those who walk as we on the edge of death." She asked: "Francis, did you come in truth only for me, or is there another whom we should save?"

Francisco was handling the pistol with care with his one hand in the faint light of the dawn, seeing that it was loaded and primed. He turned to her with an expression she could not see, but his voice had a bitter tone.

"Can you doubt that? Well, I should not complain. It is what I have earned from you."

"You must not say that! I did but ask that a doubt might die. You know I was ever one for the plain word." Her arm came to his neck, as it had not done since their childhood days. His cheek felt her lips. "Francis, we are friends again—it may be for the last hours?" There were tears from both. But whether they came to a new accord as lovers or friends, it would have been hard for themselves to say.

They rose from the side of the dead man with a new courage and hope, the source of which must have been in themselves, for it had no other nurturing soil. He said: "We must get from here. There will be full light in an hour."

But which way should they go? To attempt to pass the Turkish lines, either at front or rear, did not seem sane to attempt, now that they would be warned and alert, nor could there be much hope that they would stay in the fields unfound.

Angelica had a better thought: "When Venetia fled, she brought her boat to the harbour head, and she landed (that was by night) on a lonely shore. If we could get there—but it is vain, for you could not swim with that arm!"

"We might find a boat. It is the best hope that we have."

They set out over the fields, having for compass the dawn from which they must turn away.

CHAPTER XXXIII

THE Grand Master was in Sir Oliver's room. Assembled here were all the Commanders who could be spared from the walls, for there was news from the Viceroy's court.

Commander Salvago, the Grand Master's envoy at Palermo, sent his own account of a scene which himself had made on the palace steps. Other letters, which had been smuggled in by the same hand, gave various accounts of the stir that had been in the Viceroy's court, and what they deduced therefrom. The Grand Master read, and his own deduction was soon made.

Passion shook in his voice, as he said: "Brothers, I have been silent till now. I would neither give excuse for offence by a petulant word, such as might be swelled in the mouths of men, nor would I think evil of Christian Kings. But I must tell you that which we have to face, and that the word of Spain is a cloaked lie. Would Garcio speak so of his own will? He is one I have known too long. He palters between his master and us, hoping that he may have Philip's smile, and yet save us at last; and he will find that he has worked for a poor wage, for it is on him, when Europe regards our graves, that Philip will throw the shame. Is it not ever the fate of those who let honour go for a king's regard? But I say still that Garcio would not act so of his own choice. He is the tool of a meaner man.

"Salvago says that, being moved by news of how we had bled at the Sanglea, and how the Turks press on all sides, so that it may be said, as it were, that we breathe with pain, he spoke to the Viceroy apart, pleading that the promised aid should be instant to our relief. Might it not well be so urged? Is not Italy full of swords? Does it lack galleys or gold? Is not the day long past when we were promised that their sails should appear?

"So he said, and what answer did Garcio give? If he should come with those who could be quickly arrayed, they might prove too weak, to the shame of Spain. We must not risk that. Shame of Spain! Can it have more than it now has, as the weeks go?

"And then, if he gather an army and a great fleet, such as will be sure to prevail, it may be too late! Should he risk that? It is to be considered with care. He would talk more on another day!

"And when Salvago urged him again, as he was loyal to us to do, what did the Viceroy say then? We have bravely fought, and much honour is ours. Should we not make terms with the Turks, and withdraw, as we did from Rhodes, leaving Malta to them?

"Now, by the passion of God, is it for our honour we fight and die? That would be but a poor gage for men who have sworn our vows. Is it wonder that Salvago was so moved that he walked out, and denounced the Viceroy aloud on the palace steps, so that a crowd gathered and heard? It was not our honour of which he spoke, it was Europe's shame.

"Was Garcio wroth thereat, as one would be who should be so denounced, doing honest part? No, he was smooth still! But he saw such stir at his doors that he knew something must be said, if not done.

"So he has called a great Council of War! All the princes of Italy are to meet to decide whether we are to be relieved, or if they would more wisely leave us to die. And it can be little less than a moon's change before such assembly can be convened and its wisdom heard.

"Brothers, I know not what is to come, which is of the counsel of God, but here I swear, by His Holy Name, that I will yield no inch of this land to infidel feet that is not taken by bloody force, and it is here that our flag shall fly or our Order end."

His voice sank to another note as he looked round and asked: "Do I say well?" His eyes searched sharply for any sign of dissent, as one may look for a hidden snake, and being satisfied with the deep murmur of response from those whom his words had moved to something of his own passionate faith, he went on:

"Brothers, I would not paint with too black a brush, and there is one man who is strong of heart, and constant to be our friend."

He spoke of the Genoese admiral, John Andrew Doria, who had put forward a bold plan, which it was not yet known whether the Viceroy would accept.

Doria had sailed into Messina harbour, bringing such galleys as he controlled, and with a plan for Malta's relief which he pledged his word, being that of one of the best admirals of the day, that he could carry through to success.

He did not ask for a great fleet to destroy that of the Turks, nor for a great army, such as would defeat them in open array. He said: "Give me 2,000 men, and store of all munitions and goods such as men are glad to have in a leaguered place, and enough of light oared galliots to transport them across (and he could name the ships he required, which were then at hand), and I will run them up to St. Angelo's quays before the Turkish fleet will become aware." He would promise to have them there before the Turks would have weighed anchor or cut cables, to come out of their own harbour to block the way.

So he said he would do; and should he fail in the expected surprise, his galleys would be too swift to be overhauled, so what evil could be?

He allowed, should his plan succeed, they might have entered a harbour it would be less easy to leave, and even that they might be destroyed. But he asked, what of that? If the men be landed alive, and the stores tumbled on to the quay, let the galleys go. With such strong support for the valour that Malta showed, it was a likely thing that the Turks would lose heart, and leave. Or, if they did not, then the defence could be stoutly made, and the Turks kept to the outside of the wall.

That was Doria's plan, which had a good sound, and might have come to success. But what the Viceroy did (as the Grand Master would hear on a later day) was to answer him with fair words, and to propose that he should sail to Genoa in haste to collect stores, saying that it would be better that he should be later by a few days than to sail with less than full holds. So Doria hastened north, using oars when the wind failed, and was soon back, thinking that the Viceroy would have assembled men, and been ready to put all aboard.

But what he had done was to send two galleys under a captain whose name is in a doubt which it can be pleased to keep, to sail along Malta's coast, and give his report on Doria's plan, which was no more than that it would be likely to fail: being what he was expected to say. So Doria's galleys were warped again to Messina's quay.

Now the Grand Master told of Doria's plan, not as expecting the Viceroy to give it birth, but as one who would do justice to all. He urged his knights, as he was himself resolved, to put thought of human succour out of their minds. It must be fought out by themselves alone, and to the last sword they had, and the last day that they could endure. If they were to fall, they would fall as St. Elmo fell.

And while they talked thus, looking with clear eyes in the face of death, the door which was at the side opened, and Angelica came into the room.

She was half-clad and drenched, under a borrowed cloak, and there was little of youth in a face that was white with fatigue alike of body and mind, and a fear that she could not still.

She made a motion as though she were in doubt to withdraw, seeing how the room was filled, but Sir Oliver was quick to step forward, and draw her to a seat, speaking with more emotion than his voice would often be heard to bear: "I praise the Mother of God, to whom I have been frequent in prayer," and other voices were not slow to speak in a like way, knowing or guessing who she must be, and having heard how she had been taken away, and for what cause she had Hassan's hate, so that she could feel that she was among friends.

"Are you free from hurt of those fiends?" the Grand Master asked, and with more meaning than his words held, seeing a look in her eyes which should not be there.

"By God's grace," she said, "I have neither shame nor hurt. But I am glad you are here, for it is you I should have been seeking to see. . . . I will ask you now, before all these knights, have I done that which I could for Malta, since you allowed that I should stay here? Am I too bold if I ask a boon which is much to me?"

"You have done more than well," the Grand Master replied, "and as to this time when you were seized, it has not been hidden that it was your warning by which there was rescue near for the guns, which your cousin's treason had cast away."

"By your leave," she said, "that is not the word. He was in a great fault, being beguiled, but treasoned he could not be." She would have risen, but Sir Oliver's hand on her shoulder restrained her from that. "It is his pardon, I ask, as the last boon that I ever will."

"The wrong he did," the Grand Master replied, "is not one to be lightly weighed, nor to be put aside by a woman's prayer. But he has appealed, as I suppose, to a tribunal which will not err. . . . You must tell her, Oliver, what he has so vainly essayed to do."

"You will tell me less than I know," she said. "And that which he essayed was not vain, for you must not think that I have escaped by a separate chance. It is by his sword I am here."

"That," Sir Oliver said, "is a good word, for it will have been consolation to him, who had done you a great wrong."

"Do you say," the Grand Master asked, "that he is here now?" His tone was kindly enough, but with a gravity of reserve which showed that he would not be lightly swayed.

"No," she replied, "I would he were, for it is for his life I fear. But it is by his sword that I am."

"Did he get you forth?" The Grand Master asked. "For to have done that is a most marvellous thing. Brothers," he turned to those around him to ask, "does it not show that, where there is courage to so attempt, God will work beyond the counsel of man?"

"It was not as you may suppose," she replied, "nor quite as he had forecast his attempt; but that he saved me to be here now there are three to prove who lie dead in the Turkish lines."

Sir Oliver said: "You had better tell us the tale."

Sir John de la Fere spoke: "She should have wine before that."

There was a flask found, and a cup, at which she drank once, and let it stand, being forgotten in what she said.

She told shortly how she had been captured and mured, and how she had escaped by her own art, and all were silent to hear her speak, until she came to the alarm that had been roused after she fled, when the Grand Master spoke in a sharp way: "It was that viper again. It is wonder that such can be bred of a Christian stock. She shall see a near death if she come again to our hands."

To which she answered: "So I have thought it was." And then, finding Venetia more fit to forgive since she knew that she had lost hold of Francisco's heart, and her mind being clear, and yet in a tired way which was not easy to rein, she went on about her, saying what she had thought before.

"But I should say there are worse than she. She but seeks an unshaken place, paying the world the while as it was first to pay her. Had she come by a clean road she might have borne a good name, and even lived to the praise of God."

The Grand Master listened to this, which he understood, being one who had given much thought to the natures of men before Malta's need had chased all else from his mind, but he was not complaisant in his reply.

"Had she come by a road where no pits were digged, it is that you mean, and it would be one that no feet have found. Nor while there are fiends that are loose from hell will such ever be, for they are active to dig. But there is one thing I will know. How did you come to be in that battery during the night, that you could be betrayed by your cousin and her?"

"I was not so betrayed, but rather failed, in that I was not fully awake to the quick dangers of war. . . . But I was there with a double cause, both to give succour to one who fled, as she would have had us believe, from tortures she had endured at the Turks' hands, and to be alert if there should be need in another way."

The Grand Master frowned over this reply, and Sir Oliver thought that she would have done better with fewer words, but when Valette spoke he said: "I had guessed the truth, but not that it would be so honestly told. . . . How did you fare beyond that?"

Angelica went on to tell how she had been pursued, and of the betrayal that Telek tried, and how Francisco had come when she would otherwise have been in worse case than before she fled, so that those by whom she would have been caught were either scattered or slain.

Passing over such things as were private to him and her, she told how they had made for the harbour head, finding it to be a bare and desolate way, and meeting none, though they heard voices at times, and had remained very still till they had receded from where they were.

"When we reached the water-side," she said, "it was past dawn, and we could see some distance away, but there was none in sight, nor any boat, such as we had hoped we might find. Francis was unable to swim as I did, his arm being so hurt, but he would have me come, and would not leave me while I remained, so that, as the light spread, my delay made his peril more.

"Seeing that, and as he urged that he would have a better chance, being alone, to come back in his own way, I did not longer refuse. But I have a great fear that he will not survive, for they will be active on every side, and I should say that his strength was about done."

"What is it you ask for your cousin's name?" De Valette's voice was grave, and Sir Oliver, who knew him best, was in doubt of what he would be likely to say.

"I ask, if he return, as I have a great fear that he will not do, that the past may be blotted out, both for evil and good."

"If he die," the Grand Master said, "having bought your life at the greatest price that a man can give, I will say that he has done all that he might to redeem his fault, and in our annals there shall be nothing writ beyond the service he did in mounting the *Santa Martha's* guns where they were potent to vex our foes, and also that when the Turks came he used his sword in a valiant way.

"Shall it be otherwise held if he come back alive, which is, at most, a faint hope? I should say, no; but we will hold that his return is by the mercy of God, which we will not mar." He looked round on the assembled knights and, seeing no dissent, he went on: "The battery which he ruled has passed to another knight. That he has lost. But I will give him a new command, in which I have some hope that he will not fail."

CHAPTER XXXIV

MUSTAPHA had called a Council of War. Angelica's escape, which was much to her, and which disturbed Hassan's mind more than it would have been vexed by a larger loss, was nothing to him. He thought of the passing days, and of the report which Soliman expected to have with each galley he sent home, either for supplies, or with a cargo of wounded men.

Like the Grand Master, he had had reports from the Viceroy's Court, where he had many spies. They were not as sure as those the Grand Master read, being gossip brought from the street and the palace stairs, and observations of those who came and went, and of what galleys were in the ports, and of the enlisting of men.

But they told much, and suggested more; and Mustapha resolved that, for the final stages of the reduction of Malta's knights, there should be plans clearly agreed, so that none of those who shared his command could afterwards say that he had known of a better course.

It was a summons Hassan could not ignore, and he set out for the country house of a rich knight of Auvergne, which Mustapha had made a residence for himself, furnishing it in the Turkish style; but first ordering that the search should not be relaxed until Angelica should be found.

It was to be intensive toward the rear of the Turkish lines, for it was in that direction that Telek and two others had been found inexplicably dead on the road, all having been slain by the straight thrusts of a Christian sword. The man who fled (having a wound of the same kind to justify his retreat) had a strange tale of a giaour with a single arm, who had appeared from the moonlit sky. Hassan called and thought him a fool, but was aware of a thrill of fear, to his own contempt, for there was a vision before his eyes of a Christian sword that was sweeping down, which he would be too late to avoid, and it was in the hand of a one-armed man.

He decided, as Telek had done in his last minute of conscious life, that Angelica must have escaped at a time which had been previously agreed, and by a concerted plan. She must have joined those, one or more, who had been waiting for her. That did not explain why Telek had died when it appeared that he had been aiding her, nor why (as it seemed) La Cerda should have come from the grave for the help of one who had not been mistress to him. But Hassan saw that it was as near the truth as he was likely to get, till he should have Angelica in his hands again and could obtain the explanation from her. This he still had some hope to do, for the horsemen who had ridden first to give the alarm had arrived at the rearward outposts before the time when Telek and those others must have been slain, and by implication it followed that Angelica had not got away when that warning had been received; and after that there was good reason to think that the outposts had not been passed in the direction which it appeared that she must have been aiming to reach. . . .

The Council of War was long, for it was not the Moslem way to debate in haste, and there was much to resolve.

The reports of Mustapha's Palermo spies made it clear that there was no present danger that the Viceroy would assemble either army or fleet in such force as to challenge the Turkish arms. That was good; but the news was more disquieting when it dealt with what might be on a later day. Salvago's oration from the palace steps, and the excitement which had disturbed the city thereon, were indications that Italy might soon be stirred to a mood which even the Spanish King could not ignore. There had been some leakage, too, of Doria's plan, which, if it were to avail, should have been secret and swift, and the possibility that relief should be rushed into St. Angelo's citadel must be considered, and measures taken to frustrate such attempt.

It was agreed, after long debate, that it was a first necessity that the beleaguered garrison should not receive any support, and to secure this result the entrance to St. Angelo's outer harbour must be watched and held, be the cost little or much, and that meant in so great a force that nothing less than an assembly of Europe's fleets would be sufficient to break through it.

Eighty galleys were to be put into fighting shape, even though some men who were now in camp must go back to the sea, and some guns that had been landed reshipped; and these were not to lie at anchor henceforth but to cruise outside the great harbour, except only when tempests blew.

The question of who was to command so large a fleet was not quickly resolved. It was a position to which Piali had the first claim, with Hassan as a clear second. But it was a post which neither desired. The fleet was not intended to fight, but rather to show such force that any probable foe would be frightened away. If St. Angelo should fall by a land assault, it was to those who ordered the storm that the praise would go. There would be little for him who had done no more than make a splash with his galleys' oars in patrol of the Maltese coast. Had there been assembly of Christian fleets, with prospect that the result of the siege might be decided by naval war, there might have been opposite words from those which were now exchanged between the two admirals of the sea.

Hassan said that the command must go to Piali, by right not only of great deeds of the past as leader of Turkey's fleet, but because that fleet was so much larger than that which he had been able to bring from the Barbary coast.

Piali, with weaker logic but equal resolve, said that, had they been in more Eastern waters, it was a right which he would have expected and claimed. On Egypt's or Syria's coasts only Turkey's admiral could command the Ottoman fleet. But here, in waters where Tripoli's galleys were accustomed to represent the combined Moslem power, by the same courtesy he must stand aside.

It was an argument which would have had more force had Turkey and Tripoli been equal allies, or if it could have been supposed that Piali would have consented that Hassan should take command of the whole fleet had there been a major naval battle in view, with himself in the second place.

Mustapha, stroking a beard which hid most of the cynical smile with which he listened while these courtesies were changed, saw that it was time to intervene with the proposal which he had intended before they met.

"I can suppose," he said, turning to Hassan as he spoke, "that you would not willingly leave the Sanglea after the repulses our arms have had until you have brought it down; and I would propose, as Admiral Piali does not desire to assume active command of the half of a fleet which is his to rule as he will, that he should consent to give that to your own lieutenant, Candelissa, than whom one of more veteran valour or knowledge of these seas it would not be easy to name."

It was a solution wise in itself, and to which even Piali could not object; and having resolved that the road of succour to the besieged should be so heavily barred, they went on to discuss the means by which they should complete the pulling down of a weakened prey.

Hassan was to continue to concentrate upon the Sanglea, to which he could not demur if he would, for a change in command at that place, after the failure of the first attacks, would have been dishonour to him, and that the more if it should soon afterward fall, even though that might be from weakening of earlier wounds.

And as Mustapha proposed that Piali should undertake the assault of St. Angelo and the Bourg, he must also show a face of content, having that which might be considered the greater task, and for which he had pleaded before.

That Mustapha did not now take specific control at either front may be held proof enough that he had not less than a strong doubt that the downfall of Malta's knights would not come till they had inflicted a further repulse upon their outnumbering foes; but when he counted their lessening strength, and considered that they would now be isolated beyond relief, he had a confident hope that their resistance would not much longer endure.

It had become a question of the determination with which he would press the attack, the prodigality with which he would use the resources he had, both in weapons and men; and he saw now, in a cautious but very resolute mind, that failure had become the one thing that he could not afford to face. The cost of the invasion had been so great already, its losses so high, that to retire defeated had become an intolerable, as it must surely be an avoidable, shame.

The news from Palermo convinced him that there would be at least some further weeks before the Viceroy would organize relief on a scale which the fleet to be put under Candelissa's command could not easily drive away. It must be his part to use every hour of that time, so that there would be no danger that it would be less than enough.

There was another reason why he should hasten the final agony which St. Angelo was to feel, in the fact that sickness had broken out in his army in what threatened to be epidemic form, and he knew enough of war to dread it more than any hurt that could come from the cannon on St. Angelo's walls. His Arabian physicians, with a degree of knowledge and skill which is not lightly to be despised, were fighting an outbreak of the bloody flux which had already prostrated some hundreds of men.

It was dusk when the Council broke up, having resolved that St. Angelo and the Sanglea should be subjected to four days of intensive bombardment from every side, after which there was to be a demonstration of attack at all points, in which the whole army would be employed with a concentrated assault upon the Sanglea's battered and weakened walls.

CHAPTER XXXV

HASSAN rode away well content with the resolutions to which the Council had come, for he thought that his corsairs had the easier task, the Sanglea having been more weakened than the lines of the Bourg (except, perhaps, some parts of the bastion of Castile), and having been less strong at the first. The siege of St. Angelo might be held to be the most important command, but it would be a poor choice that would fail there rather than succeed at the Sanglea.

Unlike Piali, who had come to the Council as the centre of a gaily-glittering group of lieutenants and guards, Hassan rode alone, being less concerned with the pageantry than the fact of power; and, being content with the resolutions agreed, his thoughts turned the more readily back to that subject which had engaged them before.

There was one question that filled his mind—should he learn, on arriving at his own headquarters, that Angelica had been found, or must he reconcile himself to the idea that she had foiled him a second time?

Bitter as the thought was, he had already accepted its possibility in a fatalistic mind, which, though it might be free from (what he would have considered) the grosser superstitions of Christianity, was yet possessed by belief in the activities of many unseen powers, both evil and good.

When he considered the mystery of those who had been found dead, with Telek inexplicably among them, and the tale of wonder told by the wounded man, he did not assume that there must be some simple reasonable solution to a puzzle of which he had not the key. His mind, even against the efforts of better judgment and conscious will, wandered among dark imaginations of the interference of malignant jinns.

How should a Christian knight—one, at least, who had wielded a Christian sword—have appeared in the night to Angelica's aid, some miles within the Turkish lines? One who had spirited her strangely away, after slaying the Turk who had assisted her escape to that point when his use had ceased?—*One who had but one active arm?*—As had been La Cerda's state at the last, who (as he was now inclined to believe) had died by his own hand a fortnight before, and whose spirit would be active to work him ill.

He recalled that it had never been more than a presumption that Angelica had escaped by swimming from the deck of the *Flying Hawk*. Within a few hours of her disappearance he had been attacked by the Andalusian galleys, and it had been a natural conclusion that she must have reached and warned them by transit of the intervening water. But was it a natural—even a possible—thing for her to have done? And to so have foiled him not once but twice! And each time in a manner which natural explanation would not lightly resolve! Was it strange if he asked himself if she were not befriended by one of the dark spirits of fire, who are said to serve the enemies of the True Faith, to their own ruin at last?

It would be too much to say that he believed the explanation that superstition proposed, but as he rode he pondered it in a troubled mind. . . .

Francisco had spent the day in the hills, in a narrow cleft of rock that was less than a cave, and so placed that it would not attract the suspicions of any searcher who did not stumble directly upon it.

Being resolved that he would not die, if any privation or pain of the passing hours could preserve his life, he had lain there through the whole day till the light should fail. He had been without water or food. For some time, he had been exposed to the direct rays of the midday sun, with but a few inches of shadow toward which he could shrink beneath the hot face of the rock.

As the night darkened, he shook off an intermittent, uneasy sleep, and rose on unsteady feet, to creep, if he could, through the Turkish lines. The night was not too dense for him to look down on the great harbour and to see the black outlines of St. Angelo's towers, in which lights began to appear. Lights twinkled in the hills and over the plain, showing the Turkish encampments, the batteries that now circled St. Angelo and the Sanglea, and the lines that their outposts held.

With ears alert to every sound that the night wind brought, he followed a road that seemed deserted at that hour. It may have been of little use for the ways that the Turks would go, and they who would have used it for their own routine were either scattered or dead. . . . Behind him, there came the sound of a single rider, and a sudden hope stirred in the fatigue of his clouded mind. If he had a horse. . . . It was surely worth the attempt. . . . He drew back into a shadow of wayside trees.

With no more light than was given by stars that had brightened as darkness fell, he looked on a bare road, along which Hassan came, riding at no great pace, for he was lost in his own thoughts. Francisco drew out his sword, and put it back, seeing that he must stop the horse with his one hand, or he might do no more than to make his presence known to a man who could ride away. Better do nothing than that. He staked all on a sudden rush which would seize the rein.

Had Hassan been alert of mind at the time, and aware of surrounding things, it must have come to another end. As it was, having learnt to live on a horse's back even before he had keep his feet on a swaying deck, he was not thrown when his horse reared and plunged abruptly aside, with a high scream of anger and fear. He came down on his feet, but, for the first time in his life, as it was likely to be the last, he ran from a single foe. He had not seen the face of the man who rose under his horse's head, but he saw that he had a bandaged arm.

He paused after a time, having found courage to look back, and seeing that he was unpursued. His heart beat hard from haste and fear, and he had a sense of shame for what he had done which inclined him to the belief, in his own defence, that he had been the object of superhuman arrest.

Yet he went some paces back, with a drawn scimitar in his hand, for even the jinns (he thought) should be met by those who are bold, in the Prophet's name; and what was this but the spirit of one whom in life he slew?

But what use, he thought again, could there be in returning now? If the horse were free, it would follow. There was no question of that. But the road was silent and bare. If it had been seized by a mortal man, he would have ridden away. The bravest of human race cannot be required to vanquish unearthly powers. He thanked Allah that none had seen his ignominious flight.

He walked on to his tent, giving no explanation of why he had come on his own feet. He asked at once if Angelica had been found, and was not surprised at the answer he got. He said: "I will see that other again."

An hour later, Venetia, wary and alert, half hopeful and half afraid, had been fetched from the villa where she had remained since Angelica's flight, and was alone with Hassan within his tent.

She had no key to the mood in which he regarded her now, with his scimitar laid naked across his knees.

"Are you one," he asked, "to know when you are near death?"

"We are all that," she said, trying to force her lips to the smile that was hard to bring, "for death is round us on every side."

"Is there an oath," he asked, "that you are able to swear, which would keep your lips from a lie?"

"There are oaths," she answered slowly, her words advancing like the feet of one who treads a treacherous ground, "which it would be terror to break, but there may be none that would hold me to truth so surely as does the desire to come to a certain rest."

"So you would say, if you had planned to slay me when next I sleep."

"But you have proved me in that."

"So I have," he agreed, the memory doing more on her behalf than she was able to guess, for with that recollection an idea came to his mind that he would regain the self-respect he had nearly lost, if he could have courage to test her now in a final way, being one also (it must be allowed) which it would be pleasure to do.

"Looking," he said, "into the guile which your heart must hide, have you no fear that I may sweep your head with this sword from the neck where it now rests, as with one stroke I should be able to do, and for which purpose I drew it before you came?"

She looked at the keen thin blade, which could go, as she knew, so swiftly through the slender space of her neck, with eyes which she would not allow to flinch.

"I fear death," she said, "with a great fear. But of that you threaten my fear is not much. I have seen men slain in that style, and there are silks here which you would not purpose to spoil; and, besides that, I am one you could use in a better way."

"So I might," he agreed, "if I could trust one of your creed and race; but a viper warmed is one that will be potent to bite."

"Can you not see," she asked, and the petulance in her voice was more convincing than would have been a more reasoned tone, "that I have all to lose, and no gain, if I should earn disfavour of you? Should I go back to those who would jail me again? Who would have my blood in a cruel way, you may call it sure, now that they must know by whose device you entered the battery at their gates? It is your favour I seek to earn, or I am lost on all sides."

He looked at her with brooding, uncertain eyes. Was she a wanton toy for his couch? Or a genie of evil power, such as may tempt the Prophet's sons to the ways of death? Or La Cerda's mistress, perhaps, with a scheme to balance the debt of her lover's life?

He could not be sure; but he knew the shame he felt at his flight of a few hours before, and with the thought his resolution was made, the mixed sources of which—lust, and courage, and pride, and the love of peril which had sailed the *Flying Hawk* to a Spanish port—

would have been hard for himself to weigh. He would prove this doubt, staking body and soul alike on his own courage and wit. For, if he should slay her now, could he ever prove whether wisdom had urged the blow, or a coward's folly, such as will fear a dancing shadow of fire?

There was little change in the brooding doubt of his eyes as he said: "I would see you bare."

She was still in a watchful doubt, but the smile that dimpled the flower-fair face was less hard to wear, as, one by one, her garments slipped to the floor. . . .

An hour later, he looked down with kinder eyes on one who slept in a very innocent way, with a small hand cupping her face, as her habit was.

He had been careful that he should not drowse till her sleep was sure.

"She has wanton's wiles," he thought, "and lips that can lie with ease, but she would be loyal in sheltered days."

He compared her to the darker, fleshier, soon-ageing women of his own race. "She would last better than they, and would always sell."

But he did not know that he would want to do that.

"I must learn your tongue," she had said. "I am quick at tongues. There are many words I have learnt in the last days."

He could understand her without that, having studied the Latin *langues*, and the years he had been a slave in Malta had helped him therein. He had praised her now in words of his own land, and she had tried to use his language in her replies, but it was in her own that she had asked, with a sincerity that his mind had not been active to doubt: "Should you say that I have come to harbour at last?"

He had no thought to make her a wife, being what she was, and also of alien faith and blood. But, if she were discreet in the future days, she might hold the place of a favourite slave.

CHAPTER XXXVI

FRANCISCO stood at the horse's side on the dark road. The animal, nervous and restless at first, had quietened to his voice and hand, and was still now, as, with the rein twisted round his arm, he leaned on the saddle, conscious from that sudden effort that he was near the end of his physical strength.

Alert and conscious of his new master's condition, as a good horse will be likely to be, the animal remained quiet as he gained the saddle with an effort which seemed near to fail, after which control cannot have ceased, for how then should the horse have gone by ways it surely would not have chosen by its own will? But it was a ride which he could not afterwards recall, beyond a dim memory of once having been followed by shouts and shots; and it must have been at a slow pace, or by tortuous ways, for the night was far gone when he came again to the ruined fosse of Provence, from which he had set out on the previous night.

"Now if one should doubt the miracles of the Faith," Del Formo's voice sounded dimly in his ears, as he drank the wine they had been speedy to bring, "he may be assured here by a most wonderful thing. I would have wagered all I have to a nicked groat that you had gone to a quick death."

"Which will be his," said another voice, "unless he come to a quick bed, for you can see that his strength is done."

After that he wakened to whitened walls, and the varied sounds that come from those who are fevered or torn with wounds, some of which are not pleasant to hear, and to know for a better thing that his cousin was at his side.

For Angelica had come, when the day was young, to Sir Oliver's room, having slept little, and he less, there having been warning received, even within an hour of when the council had broken up, and there had been much stir during the night in the Turkish lines, in preparation of that which was soon to be.

Sir Oliver said: "I have an order which you must first write and then quickly obey, which is to transfer you to the infirmary which is for those who are hurt at the north wall, where your cousin lay."

Angelica was neither pleased at this, nor at the way it was said, which was as though he would not be loth to observe her go. She asked :"Will you tell me why?"

"That is simply said. For unless you show openly what you are (for which it might be called a late day) I cannot keep you here, who should be on the wall with a bare sword. Nor can I say that you will long be left to a healer's work, for I have an order in draft by which the hurt must be served by those who are hurt in a less way. Nor can I say that you would be saved for long by a woman's skirts, for we are near the time, as I suppose you can see, when the walls must be held by all who have legs to stand, for, as our numbers shrink, the walls will not contract their girth. . . . There was a woman slain in the breach of the Sanglea who was five months with child, as we did not know till she was dead."

"If you give me a less part than the Maltese women are forward to take, you do me a double shame, I being dressed as I am."

"It is no shame to obey, which you should be more careful to do than your cousin was, having had to battle for him. . . . Which brings me to what I should have been quicker to say had you said less, that you will find him to have come back to the same bed."

"You mean Francisco is back?" Sir Oliver heard the change in the startled voice, and looked at the lighted eyes, and knew for truth what he had little doubted before.

"So I supposed I had said."

"Is he more hurt?"

"I believe no. He had lacked water and food, and his strength was gone. He should survive that, being young."

"Do you know how he got through?"

"Not at all. He is one who should tell you that. But he rode up to the bastion of Provence, to the place from which he had set out, having between his knees a good horse, which, from some signs it bore, had been Hassan's during the last day."

So it came to be that Francisco opened his eyes to see Angelica at the pallet's side, and to tell her what he could recall of how he had come, which was not much; and what he told she did not believe, thinking it to be rather a dream such as fever breeds. For she did not think Hassan would be quick to run from a single foe.

"I should rather think that you cut him down, and that it has left your mind."

"And will you tell me," Francisco asked, "how I could have done that, holding the horse with the one hand that I had? My sword did not come out, and is still bright, as yourself can see."

"Well," she said, "let it be as it may. It is more to him than to us. I am content that you are returned, to which hope had but faintly dared, and that I can tell you this: the trouble there was is a dead thing. I have had that from the Grand Master's mouth; and he will give you a new command."

"Then it is one from which I shall not be withheld beyond a few hours, for I have no need to be here."

"You will lie here for some further days, for that is my charge, in which I am not meaning to fail; but you will not be kept back when you are fit, for the need is urgent on every hand."

And as she spoke, as though to confirm her words, the Turkish batteries opened with a deep thunder of sound from before the bastion of Castile to the southern side of the Sanglea, and across from Sceberras hill. They saw naught of that, in their sheltered place, but they heard the thunder that did not cease.

"I have a doubt," Angelica said, "that you will be sent to the Sanglea, for it is there that the need is worst, and there is report that Del Monte is so sick that he is no longer fit to command, though he is unwilling to come away."

She went on to tell of how a young Knight of the Order, John Anthony Rosio, had devised a bridge of tar-barrels covered by planks to replace the slow ferryboat which had suffered from the Sceberras batteries when crossing to the Sanglea. This bridge was high up the inner harbour, above the quays where the galleys were moored, and men could cross without fear of the Turkish fire, and yet be within the Sanglea lines on the further side. But for that, the Sanglea might have been entirely without support at this time.

"It is said," she went on, "that the bastion which Señor Roubles commands, being at the outmost corner where the water meets with the land, has been so shattered that it is no more than a tumble of stones, which those who make defence will pile anew in the night, to be flattened out again during the day."

The inferno of outer sound increased as they spoke thus, for the Christian guns opened in more measured reply. Powder must be conserved, but the Turkish gunners could not be allowed to train and fire without ducking of heads, and the sight at times of a comrade so torn apart that it could be left to the darker hours to clear him away.

Knowing that this bombardment was to go on for four days and then to end in a rush of foes to the ruined walls, the Christians, all who had strength to lift stone, or to handle tools, whether women or men, laboured without ceasing to rebuild and strengthen the lines on which the lives of all must so soon depend.

In the infirmaries the skilled, but stinted, service strove not only to wait on sick and wounded men, for whom they were too few to do all they would, but to prepare for a coming of many, shot-torn or slashed, who would be certain to be crowded upon them when the assault should come. Even now the influx was steady, and would have been sufficient to strain their resources but for a mitigation which did not cease—the carrying out of the dead. For the peril of those who toiled to keep the walls strong against the constant hammering of the guns was not only from the bombardment itself. Arquebus balls from the long weapons of the Turkish sharp-shooters shortened the lives of many who exposed head or arm during daylight hours, and the besieging trenches had now slanted so near that the old artillery could be used to support the new—bowmen lay below sight, and their arrows, rising into the air, and discharged with the skill of those to whom the bow had been a life-long weapon for sport and war, fell, a silent, infernal hail, over the parapets of defence; and the Christians commenced to answer in the same way. It seemed that the war became more primitive in its form as it approached the final struggle of hand-on-throat which must end the agony of battered castle and ruined town: but in the pitiless ferocity it had already reached there was no lower depth to be probed.

The Christians looked at the nearness with which the trenches, ever advanced during the darker hours, approached them around the bastioned lines which were becoming too long for the numbers by which they could still be manned, and they saw that the siege contracted, grip by grip, like a python's folds. . . . They listened for the sounds of shovel and pick, and arrows rose in the night, to fall on those who laboured, a noiseless death.

Angelica, working to the limit of her vital youth to relieve the wounded and sick, saw another angle of the dark horror of war. It would have been dark indeed but for the fierce, almost fanatic valour which was opposed to privation, pain, and an increasing squalor, against which the high standards of sanitation and decency which had once prevailed in the town went down in a fighting way. In a hundred moods, translated by the nobility or baseness of their own souls, men fought or suffered in a unity of belief that they were the servants of God, striving against His foes rather than theirs, and to be rewarded at last with His gift of eternal bliss. . . .

But amid that pauseless, and often futile, service to maimed and shattered bodies, to which skill and pity could give no more than a lessened agony of decease, Angelica had one comfort which did not pale. Francisco was there, and his wound healed. The physicians, gathering round his bed, and recondite in the Latin tongue, resolved that, though their dressings had been delayed by his absence on such adventure as is not usually prescribed for the healing of wounds, yet the abstinence which had been involuntary on his part, and was a treatment in accordance with the medical practice of the time, must have had a most salutary effect; and now that food was taken again (and somewhat more liberally allowed than the custom was, as antidote to the time when he had had none) he showed a quick returning of strength, and they agreed that the wound would heal in a kindly way.

So he lay for two days, in a quiet which impatience would but prolong, and with leisure to look back and to see himself; and before noon on the third there was a stir at the door, and the Grand Master entered the ward.

There was no wonder in that, for he was ceaseless to oversee, and there was no corner of St. Angelo or the Bourg where his eyes might not be cast in the next hour. He was dressed with more care than when he had laboured among the slaves to make St. Elmo's ravelin strong. That was not because he cared for how he might look at this hour. The time for pomp and pageant was gone by, but he thought that it would be little heartening to those he led if he should appear among them as one distrait. And though he would tire at times with a lengthened day, showing signs of his years, and of the hard life he had led, yet his step now was firm and quick, and he had the look of one who has no care for the protests the body makes, his mind being full of more urgent cares.

Francisco was not surprised that he should have come there, nor would he have supposed that it could concern himself, till he observed that Valette, telling a little group who were with him, including two of his uniformed guards, to remain at the door, came directly toward his bed.

La Valette was never one to waste words. The way he would reach his point was like the thrust of a straight sword. He said nothing now of the past, either to condemn or condone.

"I am told," he said, "that you heal well."

"So I do. I could rise now."

"But you are unfit for the changing of blows, as you must be for a long day. Yet I may have that you can do. Del Monte is sick, and is no longer fit for the command of the Sanglea."

Through Francisco's heart there passed a wild incredible hope that he might himself be considered fit for that high and perilous place, but it sank to its true remoteness as the Grand Master went on:

"I must have one there who will not yield while a stone stands, and who is of the best skill in the defending of leaguered towns. I will have Couppier here, if I can, before the hour when the storm will burst. You are not so ill that you could not sit on a boat's thwart? That you could not ride a mule on a mountain way . . .? So I supposed. Then you will be at St. Angelo's quay when the dusk falls. And you must listen now to what I would have you do, for I shall have no time to see you again."

The Grand Master went on to explain that he wished his orders to Marshal Couppier to be taken by word of mouth, to save the fear that a letter might fall into evil hands, and that that must be done by one of his own Order, or rank, rather than by the mouth of a Maltese spy. For this purpose he chose Francisco, rather than lose an unwounded knight from the defence of the threatened walls.

"You will tell him that we are in good heart and confident to endure, but you will not hide that we are hard pressed upon every side. Our foes swarm, and are bold. I will have him here to command at the Sanglea, if he can get through, which he should do when the night is dark. If there could be devise by which he could bring four or five score of his best men, it would be added strength, which we should be glad to have. But I must leave that to him. He can appoint whom he will to take over his command, but I should say that De Ligny, or else Vertura, would be a good choice. You will take this letter, which is so small that it can be swallowed with ease, as you should do if you are near caught; for if they get it they will rack you for all you know; also, it might be an evil thing in the wrong hands."

Francisco took the scrap of paper, which read:

"Don Francisco speaks with my mouth.

J. DE LA VALETTE."

The Grand Master turned away, having finished the instructions he had to give, and saw Angelica near his side.

"You serve here?" he said. "You do well. But the time is near when all who are sound of limb must scuffle upon the wall. For what avail would there be in the tending of wounds if the Turks should swarm in?"

There was the cold reason in that by which Valette would earn the name of a hard man, such as Angelica did not think him entirely to be. But he was implacable to secure his ends, as are the laws of Nature themselves, which neither forget nor forgive.

She saw that he gave Francisco a chance to serve in a new way, by which he might redeem what was done before. But she saw also that he had chosen him as being best in himself. He was fit by bearing and rank to carry the Grand Master's command: he had shown some capacity to walk in enemy ways: and he had a wound that rendered him unequal to active war. It was a matter of small concern that he might be less than fit for exposure and toil. What he had done for her own release could be done again in a greater cause. So La Valette would have said, and it would be hard to show that he was wrong. He used all to the limit of strength they had, and gave them to death with a firm will, as he had done at St. Elmo before, if it could be to Malta's avail.

CHAPTER XXXVII

THE last days had been hot and still, so that the gun-smoke hung in a heavy circular cloud, as though St. Angelo had been crowned thereby from a baptism of hell, but the night brought a movement of cooler wind. It was not enough to ruffle the surface of the indolent sea, even when the boat slipped under a shadowy hill and so clear of the harbour mouth. But it moved the heavy curtains of smoke and parted a low mist that the waters bred, so that there was more light than the boatmen would have chosen to have.

There were four of these men, one who steered and two who pushed at the oars, while a fourth crouched in the bow, being a man whose sight and hearing were keen and who watched for those they were not anxious to meet. They knew that the light Barbary galleys did not cease to patrol during the night, watching the harbour mouth, and seeking to frustrate any attempts at landing upon the coast. But a galley could be heard or seen before it could take notice of them, and unless they went directly across its path they could slip quietly away. And when Dragut's Point was a mile behind they drew in too close to the shore for any fear that there could be more than a small boat, such as theirs, in the shallow waters beneath their keel. But even such they would not welcome to meet. They crept on, as a mouse creeps in the night, with no thought of escape from the swoop of the silent owl by any challenge of strife, but only to run and hide in shadows and covered ways.

So they came, when they had crossed St. Julian's Bay, and having rowed for some hours, to something less than a cove, a mere dent in a rocky shore, where they could not have approached to land without the leave of a gentle sea, and when they had come ashore here, there was lantern lit, for the path was too narrow and steep to be climbed without light by one who had not known it before. The man who had watched in the bows became Francisco's guide for the land, the other three taking the boat back in the night, for it was not a place where it could be safely moored, nor could there be the risk of a boat being seen there when the light should come. It would have been evil indeed if the landing-place had become known to the Turks, and for fear of that it was never used, nor even approached, in the daylight hours, either by land or sea.

Francisco, climbing the narrow cliff-side path, would have been glad of a second arm, as he would later when he was on a mule's back, riding rough precipitous tracks which would be upward at one moment and down the next, with no warning that he was able to see, but he kept his seat, and his feelings to his own mind, and so, and still before dawn was due, he entered the city which was old when the Phœnicians came to the land.

The six miles he had ridden of rugged ways and terraced hills dimly seen in the summer night, with the constant succession of low stone walls dividing the lower fields, were sufficient demonstration, to anyone conversant with the methods of warfare of that day, of how formidable a task it would have been to attempt subjection of the interior of the island before commencing St. Angelo's siege. And the invaders actually increased this difficulty by the ferocity of their reputation, for the inhabitants, having nothing better to expect, if they should be overcome, and spared from more probable massacre, than that their homes would be burned, and themselves sent into distant and divided slavery, would be expected to fight with the valour of those who have no hope if their arms shall fail. . . .

Marshal Couppier held no state at this time, neither did he regard hours. He must have slept, but it was little observed, and he was as likely to be about in the night as the day. It was, in fact, in the night that most of his work was done.

It was not only that he made attacks on the Turkish lines. It was in the short hours of the dark that he moved troops, that he distributed stores (of which he had reserves in the catacombs of the ancient city, and also in a secret cave of the south), that he sent out and received spies, and that he sought in a score of ways to make the Turks wish that they had gone to another place.

Francisco rode through a beam-barred gate, and up a narrow street where the houses were dark shadows on either side; and having got off his mule, he must bend somewhat to enter a room which was a foot lower than the street, and was half-lit with candles on a table at its far end, where Marshal Couppier sat, with his sword cast on the board, and a secretary at his side.

"It is from the Grand Master you come? You are hurt? But not of this night? Gaspard, a stool."

"I have brought this scroll," Francisco replied, "and I think that what I have to say should be spoken to you alone."

The Marshal looked at the note, which was soon read. He looked at Francisco in a keen way which would believe nothing without proof. Was the letter forged? Has it been stolen, and was Francisco disguised? Was it a plot to stab him, when he should be alone? The Marshal's eyes looked blacker in that light than they were: they would be bright whether in daylight or dark. They were eyes which were quick to see, and no slower to doubt.

Marshal Couppier was an old man, with a great fame. He had taken cities, he had commanded armies on open fields, before he came here at Malta's need, and the Order's call. He did not look old. He had a lean vigour which even years seemed unable to tire. He believed in God and the Saints, and that he had come there to kill Turks, with a mind as simple and clear as that with which a rat-catcher enters a barn. The Order to which he belonged was originally of charitable design, and had become half-monastic, half-military in later centuries. Some of the Commanders whom it had gathered from Europe's bounds were soldiers before all, and their tribute to their Order's vows was to call their wars by the Sacred Name. Marshal Couppier was one of those men to whom war is the sole occupation that fills the mind. Art and philosophy and science are idle toys beside the chessboards of life and death on which they become skilful to play.

Marshal Couppier had a ruthless name, but to call him cruel might be unfair. He took no pleasure in causing pain. He would not order torture without a strong cause, nor further than that cause might require. He killed Turks as a man might kill wolves, being glad of a full bag, and yet with no special pleasure about their deaths. He was not merely ruthless in a blind way, he was sleepless in energy, fertile in design. For the Maltese, fighting to keep their homes unburned and their children alive, he was a leader they did well to revere.

He gave Francisco a short look, which saw much. He said: "Will you follow me?" He got up, and led the way to an inner room, closing a stout door. "You can say what you will here."

"The Grand Master asks that you shall leave one in command, for which he supposes that either of the Chevaliers Vertura or De Ligny would be a fit choice, and come yourself to take command at the Sanglea."

"Is Del Monte sped?"

"He is not wounded, but sick."

"Is there instant need?"

"There is expectation of storm when the bombardment will have endured for four days. He would have you there before that."

The Marshal paced the room with short quick steps, for he was one who could not keep still when his thoughts stirred. He was too good a soldier to question the orders he had received, though he would have preferred to keep the command he had.

He shot out sharp brief questions as to the conditions prevailing at the Sanglea, which Francisco answered as best he could.

"I knew," he said, "that the storm was planned for that day. I had sundry schemes to warm them then on the rear side, but they can be performed without me. . . . Have you more to say?"

"The Grand Master would not desire that you try a too desperate chance, such as might bring men to a vain death, but the defence is becoming somewhat few for the full lengths of the walls, even of St. Angelo and the Bourg, and not only at the Sanglea. Four or five score men, if they could be got through, would not be missed here, and might be there of greater avail."

The Marshal took another turn on the floor. "It should be by boats, if at all. . . . Did you have hindrance to-night?"

"No. But there is talk, so I am told, that the Turkish fleet is being garnished for sea, and that the harbour may be more closely watched, even by the next night."

"So I had heard, but the word came in a doubtful way. We must do other than that."

He thought how quickly one of Piali's galleys might send a dozen boats to the sea-floor, with loss of all. It was a risk that he did not like. Besides that, the hazards of the sea were less familiar than those of the land. Unlike most of the Maltese Commanders, his warfare had been ashore rather than in amphibious struggles with Turkey upon the sea and along the Barbary coast.

"Do you know," he asked, "how closely the lines are manned on the inner side of the siege?—You need not tell me of this."

"I know of one point. I have seen little beyond that."

Francisco went on to tell of his adventure into the Turkish lines. The Marshal did not interrupt while the tale went on, only continuing to pace the room, but after that he asked many questions till he had all the knowledge that Francisco could give.

At the last he asked: "If you were at the villa of which you spoke, could you guide from there to the bastion of Provence?"

"Yes, I could do that."

"In the dark?"

"Not if it were dense. I should need little light."

"There would be eighty lives trusted to that."

"Well, I think I could. I can say no more."

"No. You might be shot before then. It is risk of war, and I think it is not too great. It was done by those who landed from

Cardona's galleys before in a larger way, though the siege then was less tight. Will you say nothing while you are here, either of what has passed now or even that you have been in the Turkish lines?"

Having received this assurance, Marshal Couppier returned to the outer room, where he gave instructions that a good lodging should be put to Francisco's use, being that of a man who had died of wounds a few hours before.

"You shall be served with food," he said, "and if you are wise you will rest through the day, for after that I may ask you to ride again."

Francisco found the advice good, and all that he saw of the ancient town was not much, for he was little awake till he was roused to see that another night had begun.

But Marshal Couppier did not rest. He had the choice that he might attempt to reach his command at the Sanglea by the boat which had brought Francisco, and which would be sent for his use at the same hour of the next night, or that he should attempt to ride through the Turkish host, trusting to darkness and speed, and to the fact that it was something they would not expect him to try.

He thought of all in a thorough way, as his habit was, that nothing might go amiss through indolence or preoccupation of mind, but he may have known himself well enough to be aware that there could be but one end when he had once accepted the idea as a possible thing.

He sent for Vertura and De Ligny, telling them that he needed four score of men, mounted on the best horses they had, and picked with care as not being such as would falter or tire, for a secret mission which the Grand Master had required him to undertake.

"If," he said, "I should be slain, or slow to return, from whatever cause, you will jointly command until a new order arrive, which I know you are well fitted to do." For he knew them to be two who would accord well, having equal zeal, and the one being content to follow the other's will.

He said no more than that, even to them, having a fear of the spreading word which he would seldom forget. "The food," he would say, "should be near your mouth before you let your hand know where it is intended that it shall go."

CHAPTER XXXVIII

Francisco, roused in the late dusk, found that there was a good horse at his door, and another, which a man rode, who was to guide him out of the town.

They rode by rough ways to a hollow field, it might be two miles away, where there was assemblage of horses and men.

Seen by a better light, they would have been but a ragged crowd, sundry of weapons and dress, and with horses as far apart as the heavy mount of the armoured knight, and the light, sure-footed breed that were born among Sicilian hills. Now the saddles were bare, and the men knelt to a priest who assoiled their souls before they rode on a way that might be death to all, and would almost surely mean that some had seen the last sunset their eyes would know.

As they rose, Francisco was led forward to Marshal Couppier's side. "You will keep ever," he said, "at my left hand. There will be one on your other side who will be careful to hold your rein, if we should come to any flurry of strife, that you may use a sword in the hand you have."

There was a bustle now of the mounting and ranging of men, as the Marshal went on: "The password of this night will be 'Peter's keys', which you will see to be one that is not hard to recall for those who ride seeking a heaven of life in St. Angelo's walls. It is not good, if there be a doubt in the dark, that such a word shall not spring to a ready mind."

Francisco said it was a good word, and one he would not forget. The passwords the Grand Master would choose were weighed in a different scale. They must be such as would call men to high endeavour, or contempt of peril and pain, or remind them of their vows and the waiting judgment of God, but Marshal Couppier was of a more practical mind.

Two by two the little force trailed off on to the road. In the van, half-a-dozen knightly lances rose high into the night, but most of the riders were armed, as they were mounted, in diverse ways, and were varied of tongue and race but alike in being those who were more used to a horse than their own feet, and in being fearless of heart, and possessed of a fierce hatred of all who swore by the Prophet's name. Marshal Couppier had picked four score who would ride through the Turks if it were within human power, and might have found it hard among all he had to equal them with the same number again.

The last four rode singly, each with a saddled horse at his side, which would be for the use of those whose own horses might come to ground through wounds, or a false step when they would race through the dark by uncertain ways. It was for such that these men must watch, keeping to what might be safe at first, but must become a very perilous rear. To all but them the Marshal's orders were strict that there should be no pause for the aid of a fallen or wounded man, for they must think first to get through with their own lives, that they might aid defence of the Sanglea walls, being the place where he would prefer them to die.

They moved through the night at a slow trot, which fell to a walking pace at any lift of the road, for the horses must be kept fresh for the later need.

The sky was open and bright with stars, but the best guides they had were the Turkish guns, which did not cease during the night. They were not fully served at all points as during the day, when the gunners could watch their effect, and train them upon visible marks, but they kept up a constant fire from all points, both from around the Bourg and the Sanglea and from the further side of the harbour, so that there was a booming of guns that was seldom still.

But after a time they came to a lower road, where the gun-flashes could not be seen, though the noise endured, and the Marshal turned to Francisco to say: "We ride fast from now, but you will have nothing to do but to keep your seat, and your place here, till Le Tonneau's villa is passed. We are led by those who know the road to that point."

He pointed to where lights flickered somewhat forward and away to their left. "That," he said, "is the outpost which we must avoid as widely as we can do, but there is no hope that we should pass them in such force without being observed, for they have eyes that are never closed. We have planned to surprise them twice, and to wipe them out, which we could not do. It is beyond them, at La Marsa Spring, that the Turks have a great camp for the wounded and sick, who lie in tents or in open air, being the mode of cure that the Arab physicians teach."

Having said this, he gave an order by which the horses were roused to a quick trot, being the fastest pace that such a force would be likely to make, unless scattered in flight. Even when they had walked, the tramping of many hooves had been a sound that carried far in the night, and would be easy to divide from the more distant booming of guns. To the Turkish outpost, knowing that to doze at watch would mean that they would be unlikely to wake at the next dawn, it would be the kind of noise that they did not miss.

It was a strong post, holding thirty men, a low stone house having been mounded and ditched about. Its duty was to watch half a mile of the now desolate land which lay outside the Turkish lines, and to give instant warning of any coming attack, after which they must hold their ground till relief should come from larger forces camped at no great distance away for the guard of La Marsa Camp. There had been a time when they had thrown out chains of sentry-posts each of one or two men as an outer line, but there had been so many deaths from snipers' bullets out of the dark, or the knife of a crawling foe, that it had been hard to get men to face a risk which would mean death in a few nights, if not the first it was tried, and so these posts were made strong, with a chain of sentries further behind.

The horses stirred to a rapid trot, and the line of march curved to avoid the alert watch at the post, so far as it might without rousing the one beyond, which was screened from sight by the broken ground. But they had come to a point now where they must stake their safety on speed rather than secrecy of advance. Every yard gained was a larger hope that they might ride through without the mustering of sufficient force to prevent their way.

The seconds passed with no sound but the clattering hooves, and the boom of the distant guns, until the lights of the outpost they sought to avoid were almost level upon their left, and then those who were at the head of the line were aware of running feet on the stony road, and of a shadow that leapt a wall, and slipped into the night.

"Shall I follow?" a voice asked at the Marshal's side.

"No. Straight ahead." It was the one chance to hold together, and to ride on while there was a clear way.

A moment later, a shot came from the darkness. Most of the troop had ridden past by that time. A horse toward the rear plunged out of the line, and was reined back. Its rider soothed it with a hand on a trembling neck. He could not tell where, or how badly, it had been hurt, but he urged it on. Out of the darkness there came a second shot, and a third.

From the outpost, a trumpet shrilled. The horses quickened to the sound, as though sharing their riders' thoughts, and sensitive to the tension of the event.

Instantly the night became loud with confused noise, through which there was a throbbing of drums. A light which had twinkled ahead became multiplied into half a score.

Marshal Couppier called to the guide, who was at his front. "Can we turn aside?"

"No. We shall be caught in the walls. We must ride through."

So they did, facing some shots, but not knowing clearly what they passed. They saw a low stone house, and carts parked in a field. Horses could be heard to run, either mounted or not. There was no attempt to obstruct their way.

There were many lights ahead now, and the fires of an open camp. It seemed that they rode straight at what must be a more difficult point to pass. The Marshal spoke again. "Must we ride through this?"

But the guide halted here. There was a gate at the right side of the road, which was soon unbarred. They rode into a field.

As they went forward, the ground dipped, so that they lost sight of the camp, which was not more than two or three hundred yards away, but before half the horses were through the gate, they were challenged, and shots followed when they did not reply. Those who came last must pause to look at one who was past their help, and to secure a horse for which there might be another need.

Crossing the field, they came to a gap in the further wall, and turned right on a wider way. Whatever it might have been at the first—field track, or perhaps nothing at all—it was now hard-beaten and broad, being the road by which the ox-teams had hauled the Turkish artillery from their first landing-place at Marsa Scirocco Bay to Sceberras ridge. They closed up here, riding six abreast, and making a better pace. Their course was to the south-east, and had Francisco been alone he would have been likely to turn the opposite way, but the guide knew what he did. They came to an older road bisecting that which had been made for the guns, and swung round to the north again.

The road was good enough, though narrower than that they had left. It stretched ahead, dark and bare. The guide said that Le Tonneau's villa was less than half a mile ahead. If there had been any life on that road in the midnight hours, it must have scuttled away before the sound of the trampling hooves. It was plain that the whole camp was alert, but, for the most part, it was as yet in a blind stir, wondering what had caused the alarm. In all operations of war, to do an unlooked-for thing is to be half-way to success.

As they approached the villa it was natural that Francisco's thoughts should turn to one whom he supposed might still be within its walls. He even wondered whether, if he should tell Marshal Couppier all the tale, he would halt for a sufficient time to break in, and bear her away. It would have been an almost fantastic conclusion to Hassan's exploit, and he would think it to have been the whole intent of the raid. It would be an abuse which it would gall his pride to endure.

But Francisco thought that Marshal Couppier would decline to halt, even for the chance of a better bag, nor was he sure that he would have found any pleasure in such a deed, for though he saw Venetia now for what she was (if not worse), yet he was more bitter against his own folly than her, and even that bitterness was not much, now that he was in accord with his cousin again. But as they rode under the front of the house it became clear that it could not have been done, even though they had come with a settled plan, for it was unguarded and dark, with a clear presumption that Venetia was not there.

But from this point he had not time for other thoughts than that of guiding the rapidly-moving force by the way he had come, with the lives of all, it might be, staked on the accuracy of memory which must trace the path he had found before in a reverse way, which is not always easy to do. If he could do this, it would be to find a way which avoided the Turkish trenches and camps, and which would come at last to the bastion of Provence, where (if a letter which Marshal Couppier had sent by water at the last hour he could choose had got through) they would be expected to come, and would not be met by the fire of their own friends.

To him, from that time, his attention concentrated on his own task, there remained no more than blurred memory of strained sight searching a way through a dark countryside, lit by the dim light of a rising moon, which was past its full, and guided by the gun-flashes from the outer walls of the Bourg. To most, except those who fell, it remained a nightmare of confusion and noise, of struggle and urgent speed.

As the path curved outward to the right, and the forward view was no longer obscured by the higher ground that faced the Sanglea on its southern side, Marshal Couppier saw the blue light on St. Angelo's tower signalling that his message had been received, and, almost at once, there was an outbreak of heavy fire from the batteries of the Sanglea, and such parts of St. Angelo's defences as would tend to draw the attention of the Turks from the road by which he was expected to come. Then there was the sound of horse-hooves ahead, and a single rider, who appeared to have been stationary on their path, galloped away.

"You are sure," Francisco heard the Marshal's voice at his side, "that this is the way?"

It was a moment when he had his own anxiety, for he knew, if he were on the right road, that there was a little bridge to be crossed, to which it seemed they would never come.

"Yes," he said, "is there reason to doubt?"

"There is a large force on the left, almost ahead. If there were a more easterly road——"

"It is the one that I know." The reply came with confidence, for, as they spoke, the road fell, and the little hollow that the bridge crossed was beneath their eyes. He looked up to see the force of which the Marshal had spoken, but the descent had already hidden all forward view. He was disposed to doubt that they could be so opposed, for he knew that there had been no camp in that place but four days before; and how could their coming have been warned and their route guessed, in time for men to have been so assembled to bar the way? The speed with which they had ridden seemed to make it a baseless fear, and that the more because the main force of the Turkish cavalry was known to be stationed further west, on the low ground near La Marsa Spring. It would have been more likely that pursuit would have been toiling upon their rear, of which, as yet, there was none.

Yet Marshal Couppier had done rightly to trust his eyes, which could see far in the dark. But those who moved on their front had not been seeking for them, but were troops who marched in the night to take up a position in reserve for the storm which was to break on the Sanglea when the dawn should come. They were picked troops, meant to be used at a late hour to swarm over a weakened wall. They were to be so placed that they could either advance to the Sanglea, or to the bastion of Auvergne, if the feint attack which was to be made thereat should meet with some unlooked-for success, such as must be supported with speed.

They would, in fact, have been across the road by which Marshal Couppier sought to advance, and it would have been a choice of evils to seek to thrust a way through, or to turn aside to the stone-walled fields, had they not been halted when the first alarm spread a confused doubt through the whole extent of the Turkish lines, and then commenced a more cautious advance when the horseman who had come so close to the column's head had ridden back to tell them what he had seen.

The road was narrow as it fell to the bridge and rose again to a higher ground, but after that it again became wide enough for several to ride abreast.

Francisco, riding now at the head of the troop with the Marshal on his right hand, and on his left the horseman who held his rein, was aware of a broader front, and lances on either side. It seemed a change of formation of doubtful gain when shots came from the darkness on their left hand. The Marshal's trumpeter sounded at that. The horses broke into a gallop. While the road in front remained clear, it seemed that most might get through unhurt. But that hope was vain. The regiment which had been approaching upon their flank had a troop of cavalry detailed to its support. Having ridden round its left flank, they were now filing through a gate on to the road as the Maltese horsemen approached. Stirring to what speed they could as they came out, they charged with a front as narrow as that they met.

Had they been equally matched, there might have been a deadlock of slaughter with stone walls to right and left, and pressure behind of those who waited their turn to slay. The Turks were of the flower of that army which had spread Soliman's power till Vienna shook with alarm; and such delay would of itself have been fatal to the Maltese, with the Turkish infantry closing upon their flank, and firing as it advanced.

But the Turkish cavalry rode lighter horses, and were more lightly armed than were those knights who led Marshal Couppier's line. Filing out on to the road as they did, they could not rouse an equal impetus to the charge they met. The very peril of those in the Maltese rear, whose pistols were making a poor reply to the volleys of the advancing infantry, increased the rush of a charge in which there was none more urgent to get ahead than those who rode at the back.

They pressed forward as toward the only hope of safety they had. By the shock of the meeting fronts, the Christian charge was hindered, but never stayed. Yard by yard, its front a swaying, jostling chaos of cries and blows, it moved on. By sheer pressure it bore the struggling Turkish cavalry backward at a pace which grew more rapid as their horses struggled to turn their heads to the way they were forced to go. They were ridden down at the last, or were swept aside. Those who would have been last to come through the gate were driven back by others who jostled to get back from the jammed inferno of the road, where the wounded fell to be trampled by many hooves, and horses reared and screamed in the press. With reddened lances, the Christian knights rode on at the head of a line which had lessened its pace but never been really stayed.

Francisco, held back from the actual front, with Marshal Couppier still at his side, was glad that the road was straight at this time, and not easy to miss. It was a rush which even the calling trumpet would not lightly have stayed or turned, while the Turkish horsemen were active around its rear. For they were not routed, though they had been ridden through. They were like wolves behind, and on either side of the line. Marshal Couppier was not anxious to check the pace on which safety might depend at the last, but he saw a danger that speed might be converted to random flight.

His voice came to Francisco through the din, asking if the road were still straight ahead, and for how long. Francisco answered as best he could. He remembered it to be so for half-a-mile beyond, or perhaps more. But there must come a time of a slackened pace and caution of where they trod. There was the no-man's land in front of the Maltese lines, through which he had stumbled on foot, but which would be different for a troop of horses; a land of ruins, and ditches, and broken walls, ploughed and shattered by the round-shot of months of seldom-ceasing fire, and through which the slanting advance of the Turkish trenches must be avoided with watchful eyes.

It was fortunate that the Marshal's men had been picked with care, both as being equal to the changing of blows, and such as would be slow to be swayed by a panic fear: fortunate, too, that the road was walled on both sides, and so covered the flanks from the Turkish horse. Their pressure also meant a cessation of hostile fire, which must have fallen alike upon friend and foe. But the rear bled.

The Turkish cavalry were called off, after a time. They rode a bypath in single file, seeking to get ahead to ground where they could operate in a better way. Warning had now gone in advance, and every second lost made it less likely that the little force would get through. Marshal Couppier could guess that; yet he was urgent to slacken pace and have his troop in better control before they should come to the open ground. The horses must be breathed, that they should be fit for the last, and what might be the hardest need.

So when they came to the place where the road must be left for the wilderness ground, they were reined down to a walk, and the Marshal, drawing aside as they rode past, could observe that his losses were yet less than half-a-score, and that for those who remained there were horses more than enough, for more than one kept to the troop though its rider was left behind.

He rode again to the head, where Francisco was. "It is but a short way now," he said. "I suppose we may get through with a good speed. Is it straight ahead?"

"No. We must curve widely toward the right, for there are trenches ahead, and there is a battery not far to our left as we now are."

As Francisco spoke, there was proof of this, for a gun, which had been hauled round, opened upon them, showing that warning had gone before.

"That," the Marshal said, "was a gun ill-laid," for the shot had passed some distance away. "They will not often do that." He considered coolly the distance from which the gunflash had come. Should he ride into the battery, cutting the gunners down, and destroying the guns? He knew it to be a possible thing, for the Turks, confident in numbers, were careful only to protect their guns at the front from St. Angelo's fire. At a battery's rear, now that he was within the lines, there would not be as much as a four-foot ditch to obstruct his charge. It might have been worth the loss, even had he sacrificed half the men that he had. . . . But he remembered that his orders were not to destroy Turkish guns, but to enter St. Angelo's walls. He put the thought out of his mind. There might be trouble enough in doing that which his orders required. He heard Francisco saying that the ground was too broken and rough for much more than a walking pace; and then the Turkish cavalry were upon them again.

It was fortunate that these assailants were few, though they became more, and it seemed that footmen rose out of the night, as though from a sowing of dragon's teeth. They must fight their way from this point, faced more than once by an ordered front, which they must break through unless they would all die, and always vexed on all sides, as a boar when the dogs throng.

They fought on in a group from which it was death to part, the Marshal's trumpet sounding ever to give them a centre to which to draw if they should be sundered for a moment by darkness, or stress of strife, or a stumbling steed.

It may be doubted that they would have got through at the last, had there not come a time when there was another Christian trumpet sounding the charge. Knights who had thought that they would never climb horse again, or put lance to rest, had sallied out of the Bourg gate by the Grand Master's consent, to give them a good aid. And so at last they came through.

It was a triumph of audacious resolve, showing how much may be done by him whose purpose is fixed and clear, as opposed to those who are surprised and unsure.

It did no good to the Turks, who had a night of alarm, when they should have had a good rest for the assault they had planned for the next day, and who had a new lesson in the bold confidence of the Maltese knights, who had put the whole Turkish army to such contempt, which must be to them an ill-omen of things to come.

Francisco, standing weary and somewhat dazed in the guard-room of the Bourg gate, was surprised to see that he held a sword that had lost two inches of point and was wet with blood. He stood in a group which the Grand Master had come to receive, but with no more than a short glance for himself. It was Marshal Couppier to whom the Grand Master would talk. He said: "You shall have two hours rest, if you will, and I will go with you to the Sanglea."

CHAPTER XXXIX

"He has done well in this," the Grand Master said, "and I will forget the past (as I am pledged) with a good will. I have in mind, as a fit reward, that he shall command the bastion of Castile."

"It would be a high honour, indeed," Sir Oliver replied, "and one for which he may soon be fit; but for the time (if you will not cancel what I have done), finding that he was loth to go back to the lazar where he should be, I have given him my own place, on a wall where no attack is yet likely to come."

"And why, I must ask, would you waste him there?"

"Because he is one with a deep wound, which should have occasion to heal."

"We have lines that would hardly be held if none but the hale were there."

"So I know. But, by your leave, he is not to waste, being of more value to us even than some of our older knights. We are here alike to one end, which is to die, as we do; but I should say that his time is not yet (nor for that matter is mine). It is for a week ahead, or perhaps three. . . . And I should say that Castile is in good hands enough for this day, for, if our spies be not greatly deceived, it is on the Sanglea alone that they will storm as men hoping to win."

The Grand Master considered this, and accepted arguments which his mind approved. He knew that Sir Oliver had transferred men from the high wall to defend which had been part of the English *langue*, and which, by the chance of war, was not presently risked, until few but cripples remained. He could not say that it should be wholly divested of men, nor that Francisco might not be of more use after a time of rest than he was now. And as to the bastion of Castile, it might be true that it would be in no extreme on the coming day. But the fact was that the Turks had pressed their attacks at the points that were furthest apart, and De Roubles' bastion at the southern end of the Sanglea, and the bastion of Castile which was at the northern end of the Bourg, were of all places the most battered and flattened out, being little more than heaps of disjointed stones, looking down to a half-filled ditch.

It was morning when this conversation took place. The Grand Master had come from the Sanglea, where he had gone with Marshal Couppier during the night, and to which he purposed return. It was the day which was set for storm, and the Maltese lines were manned in expectation thereof, but the hours passed, and it did not begin. The Turkish guns thundered on, and the noon came. Yet there was no doubt that they had come to the set day, not only from the reports of the spies, but from the movements which had been reported behind the lines.

At midday the Grand Master returned to the Sanglea, crossing by Rosio's bridge. He found that Marshal Couppier, who seemed unaware that he had spent the last night on a horse's back, had brought new energy to a place where it had not been lacking before. There were nearly fifty of those who had ridden in who were either whole, or not too wounded to stand, and he had distributed these where the need was most.

In St. Michael's fort there were few left but those who were serving the guns, and, except at the lazar, it seemed that the Bermola's ruined streets were empty of life; for all toiled alike at the walls, to which they would add strength to the last hour when the storm should come. It was a task at which women and children joined with an equal will, for what hope of life would be theirs if the walls should be found too weak when the tide should rise of that outer sea?

The Grand Master and Marshal Couppier went together to the southern corner where Colonel Roubles had his command. The Colonel met him, a bluff resolute man, who was not of the Order, but had come with Cardona's galleys, as one to whom war was the trade he knew, and having had scent of a fight that he would have been sorry to miss.

When he saw who had come, he was blunt in rebuke. "Why," he said, "do you come here? Would you hearten the Turks with the tale that they have blown you apart? Or do you think me unfit for the post I hold?"

"We are in God's hands," the Grand Master replied, "but it is my part to see all, which I may do without meaning dispraise."

"Well, it is your choice. You may see all you will. But you have come where we learn to duck if we would keep our heads in one place."

The Grand Master could understand that, for there might be no spot in the whole line which had been bombarded with such constant and heavy fire, as it still was. As he stood under the scarp he heard a ball strike, and the rumble of falling stone. But he saw other things that he did not like.

"Why," he asked, "are the guns withdrawn as they are?"

"They are less strong than those that the Turks have been bringing to bear," Colonel Roubles replied, in an easy way. "I would not have them tumbled about, nor would I see my men dead. They are withdrawn for a greater need."

La Valette heard this with a puzzled frown. Report gave the Colonel a good name. "Your men," he said, "are here to be spent in defence."

"And I should say that so they have been. I have lost enough."

Marshal Couppier stood by and said nothing to this; and the Grand Master went on: "I have seen no place where the Turks would be more likely to enter in, or where it looks that they would be less stoutly opposed. Do you think you will keep them out with the dispositions you have?"

"No," the Colonel allowed, "I would not say that. I had fifty men, which was something more than my share for the front I have, of whom nine are down, and I have eight women besides, who will serve the guns, and be of other uses than that. And it is here, as I think, that the Turks have resolved to come. Can I keep thousands out with two score? I should say not. I must make them glad to go back."

La Valette saw that there was more to be understood, and a possibility that his stricture might have been undeserved. But he had been chafed by the Colonel's tone, which was less in deference than he would have from the Maltese knights; and, besides that, he was a tired man, sustained less by physical vigour than an implacable will, and irritation was easy to feel. He said: "You can explain more."

"So I will. They are meant to come and be butchered here. It is a bearpit where they will dance to our tune."

He went on to show a device he was soon to prove, at which the Grand Master frowned at first and was then better content. For he had thought at the opening words that there was to be some yielding of ground, which he was never willing to have, and then saw that he might be wrong.

He walked back with the Marshal through the Bermola streets, in which the houses were mostly damaged if not fallen in by the bombardment of the last month, and was vexed again in the same way, though Marshal Couppier had but mentioned that which was satisfaction to him.

"They may fill the fosse," he said, "they may flatten the wall, but I see not that they will have cause to boast of a great gain. Yard by yard, we can fall back to the fort, and every ruin be bought with blood."

The Grand Master's tone had become sharp in reply: "You think to fall back to St. Michael's fort?"

"I think we can make them overpay for the streets between."

"But I have sworn we will yield no foot. It is of that we have made resolve while our lives endure. For St. Elmo was loss enough."

Marshal Couppier thought that which he was discreet that he would not say.

Seeing him silent, Valette asked sharply again: "You do not think to retire at this storm?"

"I shall not be easy to push."

La Valette must take what consolation he could from the Marshal's tone, and the reputation he had, he having called him to this post, to which he had come in a prompt and almost contemptuous disregard of the dangers that lay between. He was not one who loved Turks, or would be likely to give them ground that he should be able to hold.

La Valette returned to his own post, being at the centre of all, and as he did so the storm broke.

It broke an hour after noon, being a time when the Turks had hoped that the Christians might be somewhat disposed to rest in the heat of the summer day; and it was dusk when it fell. For six hours the Turks swarmed round the shattered bastions of the Sanglea, and were met with bullets and bombs, with stones and arrows, with hoops of fire and with burning pitch, and a dozen other of the hellish weapons of war; but when they fell back at last they had done no more than to penetrate the bastion of which Colonel Roubles had charge, of which they were unlikely to boast.

The Colonel had not abandoned defence of a sheltered front. He had been more subtle than that. He had fired but one gun, as though all others were broken down. He had met the first rush of the Barbary hordes with all the engines and weapons of war that had been prepared, so that they fell back, their courage having paid its heavy tribute of death. But the next time that they came, after the Turkish guns had pounded the broken walls for another hour, they were met with a weaker fire. Hassan, watching this point as that where he had the most hope to win, thought that the hour had come which was to pay for all losses before. He flung forward his bravest troops in a wave which did not recede. It was met with two flanking fires from where the wall was of better height both to right and left, but it went on over a half-filled ditch and a broken scarp, from which the defenders fled as though lacking heart, being so few, to be slain by their swarming foes. They came down to an open space, with ruins scattered about, and the sight of a rising street up which they could see those who were urgent to fly. There was a moment when they thought they had won. They were in the town.

Then the cannon opened upon them which had been missing before. They were the exposed target of a converging fire such as none could sustain and live, and they were powerless to reach their foes. The cannon belched through walls that they could not scale: bullet and arrow fell from windows of houses that had been barricaded below. They drew back from that pit of death, and were delayed by those who were still pouring eagerly in, not knowing to what they came. And when the ground opened beneath the wall in an explosion of earth and fire, leaving a great pit to hinder retreat of those that it did not destroy, they had become sheep that the butchers slew.

CHAPTER XL

It was on the second of August that the Turks were thrown back from the Sanglea, and after that there was the usual truce to remove the dead, and then the guns opened again.

Mustapha, having watched the assault from a backward height, cursed the obstinacy of the idolatrous dogs, but in his heart he was not ill-content. He had gauged the resistance that could still be made at the Sanglea, and he saw, with eyes that had become wise in the warfares of fifty years, that it was not far from its fall. It was like a judgment of doom when he resolved that the next assault should be led by himself, and be made in his own name.

He said to Hassan: "Your corsairs are brave, but this is too hard for any part of our army to win in a single way. It is a matter for all. It must be the whole army shall bear it down, for the time has come when we can endure neither failure nor more delay."

He ordered that the bombardment should go on for four further days, and he resolved that the sun should not set on the seventh day of the month with the Maltese Cross floating over the Sanglea. He chose 8,000 men, being of the best who yet lived, and his judgment was clear and cool that the few hundreds who could still be arrayed on the battered parapets would be unequal to turn them back. "They shall die," he said, "to the last man, before I will allow their retreat, and if we go forward in that resolve there is but one end there can be."

He said to Piali: "I will not hold you back from the honour which should be yours, for I will give you 3,000 men, apart from those that will be under my rule, with which you shall attack the bastion of Castile. I will not ask you to do this before I have advanced upon the Sanglea, showing all the force with which I shall make attack, and when I have drawn to my own front all the might that the Christians can yet array (which cannot be much, for there are already women upon their walls) you can then strike at a point too distant for their return, even had they the strength to outface us both, which I suppose that they will not have when they have buried yesterday's dead."

Piali heard this, and was pleased, thinking that 3,000 should be enough at that time and place, and that the greater honour would fall to him; but Mustapha had a secret thought of another kind. He had little hope that Piali would prevail, but he thought that he would hold the Grand Master back from sending succour to the Sanglea, having a shrewd thought that La Valette, being obstinate in defence of all, would not deplete his lines, at whatever point, in the first hour of assault.

So, this being agreed, there were four more days which went quickly under Italian skies, where Garcio sought a date at which it might be convenient for the princes to meet, but were longer to those St. Angelo held, who must endure the deadly monotone of the guns; and Francisco, pacing a high wall where shots were not frequent to come, had leisure to look back upon things which should not have been, and forward to better things which might be in the future days, if he should outlive the peril through which St. Angelo was now dreadfully crowned with a ring of smoke and converging fire.

Angelica remained for these days in the Bourg spital which was near the north wall, being also a place that was apart from all but a straying shot, and saw there a new angle of the divine horror of war, as she overtoiled in a vain strife against weakness, disease, and pain, watching agony that did not protest, and fortitudes of blinded or crippled men, and faith that transcended death, amidst other things that are less fit to be told, being of baser and fouler kinds.

"If we sustain this day," the Grand Master said, "as I have a confident hope, with St. John to aid, that we shall be able to do, then we may think that the worst is past, for they will try this time, as our spies report, with their utmost strength, and after that there must come a time when they will lose heart, and be reluctant to die."

It was an opinion with which Mustapha might not have been slow to agree, but he would have seen little to vex himself, or for the Grand Master's comfort in that, for he meant that he should not fail.

He looked at the battlements of the Sanglea, of which no more remained than a ragged ruin of stones rising a few feet or less from a fosse that tumbled fragments had largely filled, he considered the fanatic valour of the regiments that he was now moving to the front of war: he weighed the strength (or the weakness, rather) that the Grand Master had, which he could have told within twenty men: he counted the length of front on which defence must be made: and the issue was clear as the day that was dawning then, with a threat of heat, in a heaven of cloudless blue.

He did not wait now till the noon was past, meaning to have full time, as he was ample in strength, for that he purposed to do. The sun was but two hours height from the sea when the first wave of storm broke on the bastions of the Sanglea, and was thrown back by the hail of shots and missiles, of hoops and bombs which Marshal Couppier had prepared.

They came again to the same fate. They were thrown back, and returned. Mustapha, ordering the advance of new troops, as the hours passed, must curse at the growing tale of the dead, but he had a purpose that would not change. He had imagination to see the other side of the wall. He knew the desperate valour of those who fought for honour and faith, or for their own and their children's lives, behind that ragged rampart of stone. But he knew also that there is a point beyond which human strength is unequal to go: he knew that numbers must overwhelm at the last. When his own troops grew reluctant to advance again to that wall of death, he went himself in their rear, and slew with his own hand the first two who turned their eyes in a backward way.

There came a time when Marshal Couppier sent the Grand Master word that he must have help or he could no longer endure. Could he hold out an army with a few score of wounded, exhausted men? It had become an impossible thing. If the Turks came again, as it was clear that they intended to do, there was no doubt they would enter the town.

La Valette listened, but he had every man that he could muster from other points struggling to keep Piali to the outer side of the bastion of Castile. He replied with urgent, confident words; but with no help beyond that.

It was a decision for which he cannot be blamed. The Sanglea—even St. Michael's fort—might fall, and St. Angelo still endure for a time, though it might not be long; but if St. Angelo fell, the fate of the Sanglea must be decided in the same hour. Piali, and his three thousand men, were doing exactly that which Mustapha had intended they should. . . . An hour later, in the midst of the afternoon, the Turks swarmed over the wall of the Sanglea and began a systematic, sanguinary advance through the narrow streets of the town, striving to win all they could while their opponents were weary and might be disheartened men.

Mustapha, slow as he might be to resolve, with the cautious wisdom of age, was not slack when, as he saw, the decisive moment had come. He resolved that he would still press the attack for every hour of light that remained and with every man that he had. The Sanglea his—the inner harbour under his guns—the galleys taken or sunk—he saw that the day could not be far of St. Angelo's final fall.

But as he gave orders for this result, to pour more troops into the streets of the half-taken town, he paused to listen, breaking a sentence that was half-said, puzzled by a distant murmur of dreadful sound.

CHAPTER XLI

It was the night before the great assault that swept over the Sanglea walls that the two commanders of Notabile sat together considering a letter which had been intended for other eyes.

It was, in fact, a draft of the last report that Mustapha had drawn up for his master's regard, and was of no older date than the day before. Their pockets were empty of gold, for it had been bought at a great price, but they did not think it was dear. It told much which was of more value to them to know than of worth to be set down anew, and there was an allusion to themselves at which Vertura's swarthy face creased to a smile, and even De Ligny's showed a gleam of wintry light, though the thin lips did not alter their level line.

Mustapha had narrated Marshal Couppier's transit to St. Angelo fairly enough, though not quite as it would have come from a Christian pen, representing it as an act of desperation in itself, showing the extremity of those in St. Angelo's walls, and as cause for thanksgiving in its results, for the Maltese militia had done nothing, he said, since that night, their movements being likened to those of a snake that had lost its head.

The guerrilla leaders smiled as they read, for that was what they had meant him to think. Since Marshal Couppier had gone, they had done no more then to snipe the Turkish outposts at times, and that in a distant and timid way, so that the change had been too great to be unobserved. It was Mustapha's natural conclusion that the annoyance ceased because the driving impulse had gone. When he gathered force for what he had resolved should be his last attack on the Sanglea, he did not omit arrangements to guard his rear, but he was more frugal in his allocation of troops for those positions, and more confident that it was no more than a perfunctory disposition, than he would have been had Marshal Couppier remained in the Notabile command.

When the attack was at its height, in the latter part of the day, the rear lines, three or four miles away, were more weakly held than they had been at any time since the siege began, and this was particularly the case at La Marsa Springs, where the great open-air hospital of the Turks held over a thousand sick and wounded men:

for this had not been a point Marshal Couppier had previously annoyed, nor had he ever ventured anything which amounted to a serious assault of the Turkish encampments, considering that his untrained militia could be used to more advantage in other ways.

To his two lieutenants, suddenly finding themselves in control where they had been content to take his orders before, there had occurred the audacious project of reversing this policy, and making a sudden and concentrated attack on the Turkish camp at the time when its best troops would be engaged beneath St. Angelo's walls.

To approve this is not to condemn the Marshal's previous sagacity, for it was out of that that the opportunity came. Had the Turks been alert to anticipate the event, they could have made such disposition as would have repulsed it with a loss which might have been tenfold that which it could have inflicted upon them.

But they thought of the Marshal's men as prowlers that might destroy a straggling patrol; as wolves that came in the night. And even that menace had fallen to next to naught since their leader had been required for the defence of the Sanglea.

There were two hundred men who guarded La Marsa Camp. In the heat of the afternoon they dozed or diced, keeping little watch, for they supposed at that hour that the need was none. Those who lifted eyes looked to where the Sanglea was hidden by the Corradin ridge. They listened only for the distant murmur of strife, and were glad that they were not there. Most of them were men who convalesced from sickness or wounds, such as could be excused from the front of war, and yet do that which would give release to an active man. They wondered how the attack fared at the Sanglea, hoping to hear that night that St. Angelo had been brought nearer its fall, and that the time was not far when they would be sailing away, which they were never destined to do. Even those who were diligent to attend the sick did not grudge themselves an hour's sleep in the heat, considering that they would have little rest when the wounded should be brought in during the night and the next day.

There was one who had more reputation for talk than for wisdom of thought, who called out that he saw a flash of weapons among the hills, and was abused for the fool that he was reputed to be. . . .

They came from two points, Vertura with a thousand, and De Ligny with over twelve hundred men. They came to defend their lives and their ruined homes from a merciless, infidel foe who had invaded them in numbers which were far more than their own, and ruth did not enter their hearts. If a Turk were sick, or if he were maimed by a wound before, was he not more easy to slay? Do we make terms with a rat? If a wolf limp, shall it therefore go free? The guard made a short fight, in a dazed way, being confounded by the sudden manner in which they were caught from two sides, and the numbers that came. When it was too late there were some who started to run; but in the end the Turkish army was less by two hundred men.

After that, the Maltese leaders proceeded on a clear plan. The larger part of their force circled inward to take some further detachments of guards in the rear, such as were not too numerous to destroy, and to plunder and burn. They were careful to do the utmost damage they could without going too far or remaining too long for a safe retreat, before Mustapha could turn the scale.

The rest remained to slaughter the sick, which they were very active to do.

It was the cry of this horror which came to Mustapha's ears, and had he known it for what it was, neither more nor less, he could have dealt with it by the despatch of a thousand men, or, indeed, none; for the Maltese had finished and gone before the fastest rescue could reach, being harassed more than enough at the last by some troops of Spahis who had been guarding another point, and charged them in a very resolute style. But there came men running in a panic of foolish fear who cried out that a Spanish army had come to land. Mustapha saw that he was faced by utter ruin, if that were true, unless he could marshal his men to a new front. It was no time for debate, nor to await more definite news than could be heard in the dreadful wail that the wind brought, or seen in the smoke of a burning camp. He ordered instant retreat.

The next day, La Valette gave service of praise to God in San Lorenzo Church, saying that His signal mercy had saved the land, when it seemed that their own arms had been too feeble for their avail.

Mustapha had a bitter wrath as he looked at his ruined camp, and counted the dreadful tale of the dead; but he was not discouraged as he would have been had he stormed in vain against an impregnable wall. He had missed success, but he had proved the weakness of those against whom he fought, and he was at once more implacable and more confident than before that he could bring St. Angelo down.

And though the Grand Master might give thanks in San Lorenzo Church, as he had good reason to do, he could not feel that the event had such an end that Mustapha would be encouraged to go, as he had supposed it would be if the Christian ramparts should still be held when the night came.

He saw that they must look forward to a more desperate strife in the coming days, which they had little strength to endure.

But, for the moment, there was exhaustion on either side. It was toil enough to lift the spades by which they buried their dead.

CHAPTER XLII

VENETIA was at Le Tonneau's villa again. She had been there since the day when Marshal Couppier had ridden through the lines of the Turks, Hassan having resolved that she was out of place in his tent. She was in a somewhat altered state from that she had known before, having two negroid slave-girls under her rule, and the male servants keeping to the outside of the door.

As the hours passed of the last attack on the Sanglea, she listened while the steady boom of the guns changed to a confused murmur of distant sound, and she imagined the flood that rose round the ruined walls, which (as she had little doubt) would overwhelm at the last, and she was glad she was not there.

But she had less comfort in the thought of the place to which she had come, or in that to which she was soon likely to go, as to which she had heard gossip she did not like.

Hassan, so it was said, would ship her to Tripoli by the next galley he had occasion for sending home. It might be false, but it was a tale which had a true sound. She had come upon the difference between the western and oriental treatment of women, of which she had heard before, and she found the experience to be different from the idea and more difficult to be overcome.

She had vaguely supposed that she could make her own way, thinking of herself rather as an individual than as one of a race; and so she had still a bold hope that she would be able to do, but it was less assured than before. To a point, she had succeeded in her design, and her worst danger was past. She was Hassan's accepted toy. If she should use all her wits and wiles, she might become a much-favoured slave. But she was aware of a distance she could not cross, making her experience different from any she had had among western men, and it was a distance which must always keep her wary and in a doubt which might change to fear.

As the dread of St. Angelo's justice receded, she became more sharply aware of her distastes for the new life to which she had come at so small a choice. Now that, in a sense, she had won the game, and in the leisure that success gives it was natural to look at that which was gained, and appraise its worth. This she did; and the more closely she looked the more its value would shrink, till it was not easy to see.

The slender place she had won in Hassan's regard might be gauged from the fact that he should think of sending her to Tripoli now, as something that could wait his leisure for further use, and though she knew its significance to be less than would have been such treatment from Christian hands, it held warnings that one of her wit was not likely to miss.

She thought of what her life would be among Moorish women, who would be likely to hate her before they knew, and of the seclusion in which she would be expected to share their lives, and she could have wished herself back in the Genoese gutter from which she came.

She thought of herself going veiled in the Moorish style, and her lips curved to a contempt that they seldom showed. She supposed that, as being no more than a Christian slave, she might go unveiled if she would. But it was not by such means that she would win a respected place in an alien land. She might go unveiled, it might be, but her status would be that of the dirt.

Hassan, thinking of her as one who would be loyal in easy times, had failed as completely as she to comprehend the distances of habit and tradition and race which must ever keep them apart. Had they come to any alliance of mind it might have been a problem of hard, but not insoluble sort. But even if she could have come to such an accord, it had not entered his thoughts that she should be more than a pleasant sport for his idle hours, being (as he would have said) the best, if not the sole use that a woman has.

So she thought, while she heard the distant clamour of storm that surged into the Bermola streets, till she became aware of a new sound and was waked to a different fear, as the wind brought the wail of a thousand disabled men who were butchered as they would have crawled or hobbled away, or who died in their burning tents.

As she listened, questioning what the sound might mean, rumour ran to the gates, bringing the same tale that was on the way to Mustapha's ears. The Spaniards had come ashore!

Venetia's thoughts became quick and cool, though her face paled as it may not have done at some of the worst perils her life had known. If the tale were true, and a Spanish army were breaking the Turkish rear, then she might be ruined indeed. She saw that such an army, being already at La Marsa Springs, might have cut off the Turks even from the refuge of their own ships. She imagined them in headlong, disordered flight, or making desperate defence while their fleet sailed round to St. Thomas's Bay. What safety, what security, what recognition of whom she was, would there be, in such a flight, for one of her breed?

Or the Turkish army might be obliged to surrender on terms—but would such terms make any notice of her? She would be exposed at the last like a fish in a drained pool! And what mercy from the Grand Master would she have then?

While these thoughts moved in her mind, she prepared for flight, packing what of value she would be able to take away and the slaves be able to bear. She told them that all must be ready for flight if the Spaniards should come too near, or if there should be an order for them to go.

But while she said this, her heart formed a different resolve that if the Spaniards were really near she would fly to them. There would be safety at first, for it could be seen beyond doubt, as it could be heard in her speech, that she was neither Turk nor Barbary Moor. Her tale that she was a prisoner escaping from them would be lightly believed. After that? Her agile mind could still see a hope, if she could face all in a confident mood. She might slip away to some further part of the isle, might even get to sea before her identity would be further probed, in the excitement of greater events. Or—at the worst—might not men be in a generous mood in the hour of victory and relief? She would say that she had escaped back to her own kind at the first moment she could. There would be proof of that which none could deny. She would say that what she had done before had been under threat of most dreadful death, and there was some truth in that too.

She would call Angelica for her friend, who must admit that she had warned her to fly from the battery while it could have been done. At what a risk had those words been said! And she would say, beyond that, that she had heard Angelica leave the room, and the stairs creak as she went down, but remained quiet, though she knew that it must be at her life's risk. It would be hard to prove that the truth in that was not much, and it had a good sound. . . . She might even be praised!

She had not long for these thoughts, for there came soon a more certain tale that there had been no more than a Maltese raid, but they had taught her one thing of which she would have doubted before, and which would remain when the scare was done. . . . She would rather find her way back to her own kind, even at a great risk, than set foot on a boat that would land her on Tripoli quay.

She still had thought of Hassan without active dislike, though he stirred some fear; but, apart from that, she had come to regard him much as she had done La Cerda in those last days when she saw that his star was likely to set. She must find a way to get free.

She pondered how this could be done, and at what time, during the next two days, and then, it being an idle pause for those who controlled the siege, though the army had little rest from routines of attack that did not relax, Hassan sent her word to receive him that night, which she knew that she must be complaisant to do.

CHAPTER XLIII

Hassan would have said that Venetia had no wits to compare with his, and she might have been as confident of an opposite fact, and they might both have been right. At this time she did all that she had planned, her mind working in ways that he did not guess.

That she pleased him well was small praise to her, for that was the trade she knew. It says more for her wits that she told him how she had prepared for flight when there came a cry that the Spaniards were near (of which he had heard before) in such a way that he did not doubt that she would have gone the way of the Barbary ships; and it says much that she drew him to talk of the siege so that she could judge for herself how long St. Angelo would be likely to fly the flag of the Christian cross.

He went when the dawn came, having resolved that he would not send her away while he remained, and he left her pondering what she had learned, which was briefly this:

There was news from Sicily which made sure that no relief would reach St. Angelo for some weeks, with no more than a faint chance beyond that; and the result of the last attack on the Sanglea had left the Turks with a confident hope that the resistance of the Christian knights was coming near to its end. The next assault should see the end of the siege, and Malta a Turkish isle. But for this assault there was no haste for a week, or perhaps more. The trenches had now been pushed so close that the engineers could have the next word. Mines were being tunnelled under the walls. The army was to be rested and prepared for the last triumphant assault, which might be little more than a march through wide breaches which would be blown when the day should come. And meanwhile the remnant of Christian knights, having no respites from daily losses along their walls, or from the useless toil of piling stones that the round-shots tumbled back to the fosse or flung fatally upward among themselves, would have time to consider how weak they were and dread the approaching day.

She listened, and seeing reason behind his words, she had no lust to be back within St. Angelo's walls. . . . But elsewhere in the island might be a much better choice, and she thought that it should not be much longer delayed.

She remained quiet for some days after he left, her mind active with many thoughts behind inscrutable eyes. She did not think that she was confined to the villa's walls within the point that her own prudence would teach, but it was a doubt which she did not put to a hard test, having too much caution for that. She played the part of one who was content in a narrow peace.

The resolve to seek escape by an inland way became firmer as the days passed, but she saw that it would be at a great risk if it were tried either too soon or too late. It should be before St. Angelo's fall, but, within that limit, the longer it were deferred the more suspicion would be quietened to sleep, and the less risk there was that the Grand Master could still stretch out an arm to seize her if she were seeking flight from the island's more distant shore. She did not think it to be better than a perilous chance, but it seemed the best hope that remained.

She had a separate hope that some knowledge might come her way such as she could sell at Notabile to those who commanded there at the price of her own release. She watched ever for this, with a caution that gave no sign, thinking that a mere suspicion might be enough to ensure her death, but she learnt nothing at all, even though Hassan came to take his pleasure a second time.

It was a week later that he did this, and mid-August had come with a heat that was rare and oppressive even to the Maltese, and still more to those who had come from more northern lands, though to the Barbary Moors it was nothing at which to fret.

When he was gone she was disposed to contemn herself that she had been over-careful to avoid showing a curious mind, but it was a matter in which wisdom had ruled, for she had gone as far as she safely could, and she had learnt no more for the good reason that he had had nothing to tell.

The fact was that while Mustapha still pressed the siege with all the artillery that he had, and with bomb and bullet and mine, he neither ordered assault nor fixed a day when it should be. In the secrecy of his own mind he had resolved that the day should be fixed by Don Garcio of Toledo rather than by himself, that being the Viceroy's most direct contribution to the events of the siege for the three months that it had endured. As he had decided to take council with the princes of Italy upon the question of Malta's relief, it was clear that nothing would be done until that Council had met. When it did, it might resolvè that no relief should be sent, and Mustapha could then conclude his work in such leisure as the remaining weeks of summer allowed. Or it might resolve that succour should not be longer withheld. But that could not be gathered in a menacing force by a day or even a week, if it be allowed that it could be mustered to such numbers at all.

Mustapha resolved that he would make no assault until the conclusions of the Council were known, but that if it should resolve on relief he would make it on the next day after the news came to his hands, and that it should then be continued without respite, until the Crescent should float over St. Angelo's central tower.

He did not doubt that he could make the relief too late, nor that he would bring that result before the Spanish Crown would have had time to do more than incur the vexation of some abortive outlay of gold, which its King would be loth to lose. . . .

It was August 17th when the news came, both to Mustapha and the Grand Master in the same hour, that the Council had met, and of the resolution to which they came, on which there had been division and hot debate. For there had been many princes who said that they had been called on too late a day, and that to attempt relief would be to add a second disaster to one which was now impossible to avoid. And this opinion had the more weight because it was put by a good knight, Alvarez de Sande, who had won great repute in warfare upon the Barbary coast. Nor can it be fairly urged that this should lessen his fame, for there was reason behind his words.

"You ask us," he said, "to assemble strength on too late a day, when St. Angelo already totters toward its fall. If we gather in haste, we shall be too weak to make landing against the great fleet of the Turks, and shall but give them the glory of our repulse. Or if we delay while the strength of Spain assembles to our support, we shall be Europe's jest, for the Turk will have laid St. Angelo flat, and have sailed away.

"Had you asked us three months ago, there is none who would have been backward to bare his sword; but now, if you will heed a soldier's advice, who would save you a second shame, you will not attempt that for which your time must be either too short or your strength too weak. You should not delude the Grand Master more with a hope which will prove a mere mock at the last: you will advise him to make terms for his life while he yet can."

These were words which many voices acclaimed, but not all, for Ascanio della Corna, a famed knight of Piedmont (which had been the land alike of De Broglio's birth), made a more passioned reply:

"It is a good word that we should have been called together three months ago, and when you add that we may hasten now and be too late by a day I do not say you are wrong. I say we have bought a shame which may not be easy to miss. But I say, beyond that, that our shame grows with the days, and that there is but one way, and one hope, by which we may put it by, which is to arm at this hour. We must go with what force we have, be it weak or strong, and though it be to no better fate than came to those who fell under St. Elmo's walls.

"But I say that we may yet go with a good hope, for we are not feeble of arm, nor of small resource, even at the call of a day, and if Valette can endure, being so compassed and left alone, shall he fall when our swords are near?

"I say we should still attempt, though we were more likely to fail than I think we are. We have but a partial strength if we move with speed. I will give you that. But if you could see to the Turkish camp, you might view more weakness than you suppose. I should say that they have not more than sixteen thousand men who are on their legs at this hour. And if there were count only of those who are hale and of good heart, I suppose it would be greatly lower than that. Nor could they confront us with such a force and maintain the siege. They would have something worse than the vexed rear that they have now, when we had got ashore, though it were but with a few thousands of men."

"When you have got ashore!" a voice of protest was heard. "Now will you say how you would do that? Do you know the count of the Turkish fleet, that would be watchful to bar the way?"

"I might make answer even to that," della Corna replied; "but there are sea-captains here who should be heard thereon before I."

There was more debate on this point, from which it appeared that the seamen were of a general accord that, though they could not assemble a fleet which would be fit to meet that of the Turks in a set fight, yet if they were asked to do no more than to use darkness and speed to land troops on the island shore at their own choice of the place, it would be a fair hazard of war.

And so at last Don Garcio, having let the talk have its way, put it to the vote, in some doubt of how it should turn: Should they adventure to Malta's aid? And when he found that there was a majority who were of della Corna's resolve, he saw that he must make some show of preparation therefor, though his own had been alike to De Sande's thought, that they had arrived at too late a day.

He wrote to the Grand Master that night that, if he could endure for no more than two further weeks, there should be rescue arrived.

La Valette read the letter to Sir Oliver first, who said: "Well, we may endure for that time." If he had a doubt, it was one which he did not think it useful to speak, but Valette answered:

"For that time? So we must, and for more beyond. For if they say two, we may call it four, and find we have guessed too low."

Sir Oliver saw that La Valette would not admit, even to his own mind, that they could fail to endure for whatever time might be required before the Turks would either be chased away or feel an inclination to go.

Well, need he say a word to disturb that? It is a good mood for one on whom all depend. There is much force in a resolute will.

But in this case the will to win was not on a single side. Mustapha heard, and his mind froze to a cold intensity of resolve. "Two weeks?" he thought, almost in the Grand Master's words in his alien tongue. "We may call it four, and find it under the count—if they come at all, which is less than sure. But two weeks is enough now."

He ordered that both St. Angelo and the Sanglea should be taken by storm on the afternoon of the next day.

CHAPTER XLIV

It was the hottest hour of the day, and Angelica found it hard to sustain in the foul air of the crowded hospital ward, which was not relieved by any impulse of wind. She was not practised to move among death and wounds without the exhaustion of emotional stress adding to the physical strain of service which must cease at times, but was never done.

For in the pause of the last ten days—if pause it can fitly be called while the hail of death drove inward ever from every side—there had been so strait an inquisition into the stations of all who had eyes to see an approaching foe, and could lift weapon to strike him down, and so stringent an ordering of their places upon the wall, as had left her the head of a nursing staff of whom there was none besides who was both able and young.

The sick and hurt must be tended by wounded or crippled men, and by women feeble with age.

And as she toiled thus, the pretence of her sex had failed or been cast aside, as pretences will before the crises of life and death. She had not cast off the doublet that had Don Garcio's name, having, indeed, little leisure for any casting of clothes, but she had become señorita to those she nursed, of which she was careless or unaware.

Nor was she excused from the ultimate risks of war, either by her sex or the place to which she was put, being on the list of those who did the unavoidable civilian tasks, but who must be ready at every hour, on the signal of the three whistles (two long, one short) to catch up weapons and run to their stations upon the wall.

If she had any thought of joy in these days of exhausting toil to mend the bloody wreckage of war, it was that Francisco was still placed, by the grace of a healing wound, on the high wall of the English *langue*, where he was almost alone, and to which the tide of battle was unlikely to rise, unless it should have come to a height which must be fatal to all. . . . But how long could she think that he would be there? For ten days of sleepless vigilance and suspense the meagre line of defenders had crouched behind shattered bastions and connecting walls, or toiled in perilous exposure at rebuilding the tumbled stones. And for these ten days the spies had failed to bring news of the date of the next assault. Certain to come, it had remained an hour of which no one knew.

But this morning there had been word of hope, which the Commanders had passed about. Palermo bustled to send them aid. Messina's harbour would be astir with galleys fitting for sea. In fourteen days, could they endure for that time, there might be slaying of Turks by hands less wearied than theirs. Surely they could endure for two weeks! The word brought a light of hope to the eyes of men both in the hospital beds and crouching under the parapets who would be dead alike by the next day.

And, as the hours passed, it seemed that another sunset would come with no more event that the bombardment which did not cease, and to which there would now be no more than infrequent or spasmodic reply. Mustapha, when he had attacked before with a purpose to make an end, had chosen a morning hour. But this time he had a different plan.

Yet, except for the hour he chose, it began and, to a point, it was to proceed in the same way. "They will expect," he had thought, in a cunning and subtle mind, "that I shall attack at a new point rather than that I shall do the same as before." He, himself, undertook the assault of the Sanglea, and ordered Piali to storm the bastion of Castile, where there was a reason to think that he would not fail.

At two hours after noon, the Turkish batteries suddenly quickened to the discharge of every gun that they had, and the advancing movement of troops could be observed at a score of points.

Angelica, uselessly dressing a festered wound, became aware of the added volume of sound. She heard a boy's voice calling the news in the narrow street, and the noise of a man who ran. She knew that the assault had begun.

After that, for her, there were four hours of suspense. Away at the Sanglea there came a time when the Turks were over the wall as they had been at the last storm. They fought forward from house to house through the ruined Bermola streets, Marshal Couppier finding what satisfaction he could in the price of blood that he made them pay.

At the bastion of Castile, the first wave of storm had been thrown back, and the pressure had increased against the more southern lines of Provence and Auvergne, as though it were there that the final effort would be.

When it might be thought that attention would have been drawn away from the Spanish front, with some consequent weakening of their support, and at a time when the defenders at all points would be wearied with heat and strife, Piali sprang his surprise.

In the last week he had driven mines toward the Castile bastion, one of which had been countermined and destroyed, men having met in the dark passages underground, as rats fight in a sewer. But the second, which burrowed beneath the eastern salient, had been left unguessed. Now there came to those who yet guarded the Castile wall a low rumble of dreadful sound, being the last that would ever trouble their earthly ears.

De Castriot, watching from the neighbouring bastion of Arragon, saw fosse and parapet lifted into the air. They fell in a flattened ruin he did not see through an atmosphere which had become blackened with smoke, and was soon thick with a falling dust. But ditch and rampart were gone, and the gap was wide through which the Turks might enter the town.

It happened, by the blundering chances of war, or, as Valette would have said, by the interposing mercy of God, that the first rush of the Turks was not in too great a force to be stoutly met; for among those who advanced there arose a cry that there was a second mine to be sprung, and that they should stand back for a time, lest they met the fate which they had designed for their foes to feel. They stayed at this, and some of them were not easy for their officers to urge on, till they could be convinced that there would not be a second explosion beneath their feet. But those who came on at once, being some scores, had entered the town before there could be any living of the Maltese who could bar their way.

A certain chaplain of the Order, a man more expert in prayer than with the pike which he had been told to use, saw the inrush of the Turks, and did not doubt that the end had come. As a dog seeks his master in time of fear, so he ran for Valette.

The Grand Master was at his lodging within the town. It was a house, old and large, which he had made the headquarters from which he directed all on a day of assault, and where all knew that he would be found. He had put on his arms at the first call, but had since cast his cuirass aside, being oppressed by the day's heat.

The street that approached the house was steep, and its pavement was a series of steps that gave no ease to a man whose breath was already gone. The chaplain must gasp his tale that the Turks were swarming into the town. His thought was on the narrow safety of the citadel walls. He urged that Valette should be instant to gain St. Angelo's bounds while there was still possible time. He appears to have thought of his master before himself, which may claim some praise which he did not get.

Valette had been at the door, looking for news, for which it had not been easy to wait. He had heard the sound of the bursting mine, which had been an explosion to shake the town. What had happened thereon was not hard to guess, and might have been even worse than it was. He struck the chaplain across the face, so that he fell backward upon the steps he had been so eager to climb. The Grand Master snatched up the pike which had dropped from the hand of a man who may not have known that it was still there. He turned to Sir Oliver, who was at his side, fastening on his own sword. He said: "You must stay here. There must be one to control." He ran down the steps, not regarding that his cuirass had been left behind.

Some guards and attendants came running after him from the house, but he did not look back. He raised a whistle to his mouth as he ran, and the two long blasts and the short shrilled through the street, and were repeated by those whose duty it was to pass such a signal on.

The sound came to Angelica's ears, and she knew that the time had come when all must fight for their lives if they would endure for another day. What use was there in nursing those who were round her now, if they were to be massacred in the next hour? To share the fate of those who had died from the Christian swords at La Marsa's camp?

The Grand Master was right on that. There was no service of any worth unless the Turks could be kept to the outside of the wall. And the call that was shrilling now, even without that preceding havoc of sound, was proclamation that it was no longer simple to do.

With quick hands she reached for Don Garcio's belt, with the sword and dagger which were the only weapons that she had been careful to have, and joined the growing crowd of those who ran to the breach.

It was a motley crowd, of both sexes, of childhood and age, that the whistles called. They varied in language and race, in weapons and in attire, but a common passion was fierce in the hearts of all: the lust to kill the hated invading foe—to kill first, before they should be destined themselves to die. They were not less in number than two hundred of sundry sorts when they came in sight of the breach, and of a drama the first act of which was already done.

For in those first moments, pregnant with Malta's fate, when the Turkish regiment which had been held ready to rush the breach had faltered to the mistaken cry of a second mine, the Spanish knights on either side of the ruined gap had come running to its defence, as blood thickens to close a wound.

Struggling over shattered bodies and tumbled stone, through the mirk of the sulphurous dust-choked air, they had fallen on those few dozens of Turks who had first rushed into the breach with a fury that they had been too few to endure.

As the air cleared, it could be seen that the gap was wide but not so great that it might not be held by the Christian swords, if they would be steadfast to meet the advancing shock. For the Turks had lost that moment when the breach should have been in their own hands, through which their army might have been poured into the town.

Castile and Arragon, Catalonia and Navarre, joining slender numbers to make living wall where the stone had failed, looked out on a rushing regiment of Turks, being one that had made its fame in the Balkan wars. It had been twelve hundred strong when it had disembarked three months before, and might still muster five hundred men.

They came swiftly with double cause, being eager to win the breach, and because the air had cleared enough for them to be in view of the Arragon bastion as their own trenches were left, and De Castriot's guns now scourged their advance with a flanking fire.

As to De Castriot himself, having shown his gunners a mark that they would not miss, he ran to the breach with every man he dare call away from his own part of the wall. When the Grand Master came to the scene it was choked with a jostling, striving crowd of Christians and Turks, who struggled and slew with no certain foothold on the broken masonry that was jagged or slipping beneath their feet.

It was a surface on which men could not move at a quick pace, either to attack or defend, and, broken down though the scarp might be, it still gave advantage to those who would bar the way, both in its own height, and that it now had higher walls both to right and left from which arquebusiers were firing down on the Turks at so short a range as to be able to pick their prey.

The reinforcement the Grand Master brought had such effect both by the weight of its own advance and the inspiration his presence gave, that the Turks yielded some ground, and there was an actual pause in the strife at one time, the Turks falling back some yards from the reach of the Christian swords, unless they should advance beyond support of their flanking walls, which they lacked folly to try.

For a moment it was a matter of flying stones, and worse missiles than they, while the combatants took breath to look at those whom they had seldom seen so closely before.

But it was a moment that could not last. Piali, cursing the slowness of those who had missed their chance, was still without doubt that the town's defence, if not the castle's alike, had come to its last day. He urged the janissaries on again, being himself close on their rear. He ordered up more troops to support their storm and to be ready to swarm into the town when the breach were won.

On the Christian side, reinforcements were gathered fast, and nearly to the denuding of other parts of the wall. Stores of missiles were rushed to the tops of the ragged wall on either side of the breach, to be discharged on the Turks below, so that every forward yard would bring them more under a rain of death from their flanking foes.

For the next hour the Turks came on as though being impatient to die; and with no less courage and bitter hate the Christians refused their way, until the gaps between the tumble of masoned stone were dreadfully levelled up with the trampled dead and hollows brimmed with their blood.

To Sir Oliver, still at the centre of all in Valette's house, careful and cool, and busy with many orders of support and supply, Marshal Couppier came.

"That I am here," he said, "is no reason to fret, for I have left De Roubles in charge, and you could not ask for a better man. . . . But I would hear for myself how matters are like to go, either from the Grand Master or you, for it may change my defence in a vital way."

Sir Oliver at the first was rather cold in reply. "We keep our walls," he said, "as you may suppose that we should. . . . You will not want opinion from me, but I may surmise that the Grand Master, if he were here, would not be pleased that your place is left at a time of storm, be De Roubles the most you say."

Marshal Couppier was unmoved. "You keep your walls?" he asked. "I can boast of less. But do you keep them unbreached? I may be old, and not deaf."

"They have blown a mine at the Castile wall. The Grand Master is at the breach."

"Then they will find it hard to get through. We may pray St. John he come to no hurt. It would be worse than a broken wall."

"We may agree there. What is it you come to know?"

"What I suppose I have learned. That the breach holds."

"Was there so urgent cause to enquire?"

"So I thought, or I were not here. . . . I would not have men die to no gain, and the point is this. We do not boast of our wall. We have let the Turks enter the town. They have half Bermola now, being near to where they will come on some grape from St. Michael's guns, some of which have been turned inward to meet the need.

"I do not fret about that, they having been in the streets for three hours, and losing six to our one. I suppose they may be ill-pleased when they count the slain."

"The Grand Master will be wroth that they have entered the town. He would have them counting the dead with no gain to offset thereto."

"Well, he should not have put me in charge. He has better men. . . . But I fret from another cause. I have but let them enter the town from the south. I have held them off at a great cost from the northern side, lest the harbour come under fire, and the galleys go. . . . I mean at a great cost in the lives of men that I might have used in another way. . . . Now if there be retreat at the Bourg, then is the harbour lost and the galleys gone. It will be St. Angelo for yourselves, and either that for me or to hold out in St. Michael's fort, which I should not be hopeless to do."

"You mean that you would abandon defence of the north side of the town, if you thought that we gave ground at the Bourg?"

"So I should in the next hour."

"For which you would have no sanction from me."

"So I suppose. You are near to say that I shall be blamed that I have not held the whole length of the ditch, which I tell you, as one having some knowledge of war, that I had no longer the strength to do. But that is what the Grand Master will be impatient to hear, for I would say that beside him a mule is a beaten child. Yet he may be more for Malta's avail being wrong, than would another of more placable moods, though with a wisdom that none would doubt. . . . And for those Turks who are in Bermola streets, you may tell him that we have plans to disturb their sleep."

Marshal Couppier went at that, with no more than a parting word: "You should get him back from the wall," with which Sir Oliver was not inclined to debate, except to see that it would not be easy to do unless the Grand Master were of the same mind.

He considered Marshal Couppier's words with more agreement than he had expressed, for he was used to thinking much that he did not say. In fact, the tactics which the Marshal employed (for which De Roubles had been responsible at the first) had enabled Mustapha to achieve his aim more easily than he otherwise would, but had caused its success to be of a very dubious kind.

Mustapha had supposed that the garrison of the Sanglea would exhaust its strength in defence of a wall which had become too weak to be held, and for the length of which their numbers had become too few. He had supposed that he would repeat the success of the last assault in a more absolute form, and from which no false alarm would recall him at last. He did not expect that his troops, after having been slaughtered as they approached the wall, in the unavoidable loss that a storm must mean against a resolute foe, would then be allowed to scale it, to find themselves not in pursuit of a flying rout, but to be entangled among ruined houses and barricaded streets, which had been prepared with much cunning to be traps of death, and were held by bold and very obstinate men. With fanatic valour, and a mirage of success that they could not reach, the Turks fought forward from trap to trap, winning no more than streets that were littered with their own dead, who had fallen beneath the fire of those whom they rarely saw.

Only on the northern side of the town, where the Marshal had given orders that no ground must be lost beyond a line where there had been much ditching and barricading of streets, and mounting of guns that had been withdrawn from the wall, had there been such fighting as took heavy toll of Maltese lives. Here he had put De Roubles in command of his best knights, and they had proved their worth so far that they did not fly, but they could not avoid their deaths. The line was still held as the sun was low, and the Turks still hindered from the inner harbour which they would have been glad to see, but the cost was such as Marshal Couppier had no relish to count, and he would call it evil indeed if it should prove at last that he could have withdrawn, with more loss to the Turks and with less of knights whom he could not spare. . . .

Sir Oliver did not doubt that the Marshal had been wise, both in the decision to fall back to St. Michael's fort and in the manner in which it had been done; but that he had been also right when he had said that the Grand Master would not be content unless the Turks should be counting the dead with no gain to offset thereto had its proof in that which occurred in the same hour, at the breach which the Turks had at last suspended effort to force.

La Valette sat on a stone. A bloody pike lay at his side, he having fought in the front rank, and it being due to those who had surrounded him there, rather than to any care he took of his own head, that his life remained.

"Will you not retire," De Castriot asked, "while we can yet give thanks to merciful saints that there can be no boast of your death? Can you not see that you sit here at a great risk, which is gain to none? For if they cease effort to scale the breach, then will they resume their fire in a short while, turning all their guns on this place, and their sharpshooters alike, as it is simple to guess."

He spoke amid a chorus of those who were urgent that the Grand Master should not remain, but Valette rose as one forgetting the weariness that his face had shown a moment before. He pointed to a regimental Turkish standard which had been planted defiantly on the debris at the further side of the ruined fosse.

"Shall I retire," he asked, "while the Cross of Christ is so flouted and shamed? It were to hear before morn that their standards root where we now stand. I must prefer to abide."

De Castriot gave a short laugh. He looked round on men who were weary with strife, but yet aware of the exultation of having thwarted the Turkish rush and come through with their own lives in a place of death.

"Why then," he said, "it seems we must fetch it in."

He drew out a sword which he had but just wiped and put up. He went out through the breach. Those who stood round stared at first; and then, one by one the Spanish knights, and some others of as much valour as they, followed the way he led. . . . They were fewer when they came back; but De Castriot laid a horsehair standard at the Grand Master's feet.

CHAPTER XLV

Sir Oliver was still at the Grand Master's house when he returned, a satisfied but much-wearied man. It showed the measure of his fatigue that he was content when Sir Oliver gave him no more than a vague word of assent to his query of whether all went well at the Sanglea. He was asleep in a short time, and Sir Oliver would have returned to his own rooms, as it might well have been thought that they had outfaced a storm which would subside till the next day, or beyond; but he observed one thing that he did not like. There had been no request from the Turks for the hours of truce which were usual after a day of strife for the removal of wounded and dead, who must often be drawn by both sides from a common heap.

Considering this, he resolved that he would stay at watch in the Grand Master's house, both to secure that he would not be disturbed by less than an urgent call, and that he should be there himself to make dispositions with speed if there should be alarm in the night.

Brother William, the chaplain whom the Grand Master had struck, had been brought in by his own care and now sat nursing a broken head. Sir Oliver, having no other messenger at his call, sent him to the castle, with a word that he should not return for that night, and sat down to ponder the day's events and to judge of what the end was likely to be.

"The siege must end," he thought, "in short days, either in our common deaths or in a triumph which a few will yet be alive to share; of which few I am more likely to be than is any else, for there may be no man besides me, and scarce a woman or child, who will not have scuffled upon the wall. It is as though I watch a woe which I will not share."

It was from no passion for the blood-shedding of Turks that he thought thus, having another temper of mind, but it was no joy to think that there was hazard of life for all, except only him.

"I suppose," he thought, "that I may be blamed or envied of some, as one who had contrived to keep his own head from under the storm in a careful way. I should not fret for that overmuch, not being one who has practised for praise of men, but I would not be shamed in my own soul. I would do my part at the last."

For it seemed to him that while he held a high place, it was yet no more than that of one who had a mean part in a great day.

As he thought thus, Brother William returned from the errand on which he had gone. He was one whose own place had been one of esteem before the time of the siege, and had seemed soft and secure. Now he had a sore head, and a grief of mind which was more vexatious than that.

He felt that he had been shamed by the Grand Master's blow in a way that his reputation would not survive; and he had a grief of a different kind when he asked himself if it were displeasing to God that he was more zealous to heal the mind than to give the body a wound, even though it were infidel flesh that would feel the sting.

He found Sir Oliver in more leisure for talk than he often was, and in the mood when fatigue of mind will somewhat relax restraint, even in those who are of a settled control.

Brother William began to talk of himself, and of the event that had brought him there, seeking to learn if he might yet have a place in Sir Oliver's esteem. He forgot himself as he went on to discuss questions of doctrine and of the ethics of faith, in which he was more expert than with thrusting pikes. He quotes text: "*Omnes enim qui acceperint gladium*——" to which Sir Oliver replied that it might avoid truth to assert that they did that, unless he spoke of the hired soldiers of Spain; and gave him another text: "*Non veni pacem mittere*——" as to the meaning of which they found also that they were not in accord.

"It may be no merit in us," Sir Oliver said at the last, "that we slay men whose souls (as you will not deny) are doomed to eternal fire, and who would constrain others, even by force, to share the damnations to which they go; but that men should expose themselves to jeopard of their own death that the Christian faith may be buttressed about, is it not that of which the angels of God are glad?"

"By which you mean," Brother William replied, "that I should have pushed forward into the breach, even though I should have been a poor help and been quickly sped, rather than have run to warn others to safety they would not seek?"

"You are one who teaches the Faith," Sir Oliver answered to that, "which I have no title to do. Should you not ask that of yourself, as one who knows the reply?"

"You are more plain," Brother William replied, "than you were before. I will seek my place."

He picked up his pike, which was near at hand, as the Grand Master had brought it back, showing more signs of use than might have been had it remained in its owner's hands. He went to take his place on the wall.

He left Sir Oliver in more thought than before, till he was disturbed by a messenger that De Castriot sent to report a stir in the Turkish camp.

He was not slow to see the meaning of that, and its explanation of why there had been no truce to remove the dead. Mustapha had planned that they should have no peace from that hour till they were taken or slain. There must be another struggle to hold the breach.

He knew that the Grand Master would be wroth if he were not roused, but what purpose was there in that? Would he go again to the front of strife, and a likely death in the night, which would bring joy to the Turkish host, and make the Christians despond?

It seemed to Sir Oliver that he had come to the time of his own chance, and his own test. Should he not do in the dark that which the Grand Master had done in the day? He went out, buckling his sword.

He walked quickly toward the breach, around which the guns were active again, and which was now lit by unquenchable flares flung out from the wall, so that the light would reveal an advancing foe while making the breach darker to those who came. As he walked, he had a great joy in the thought that, whether he lived or died, he would have taken his part that night in the common hazards of war, and a will to maintain the breach as fixed as the Grand Master's could be, so that it would be sure that his life was done if the Turks should enter the town.

But yet as he walked he thought of a score of things which must be required on the next day, of confusions his death would cause, of details that none would know.

He was not of a vain mind, and he knew that the Grand Master was more to Malta than he, but he could suppose that, if Valette lived, there might be no death than his own of which the Turks would be more eager to hear.

Abruptly, he stood still. De Castriot was a good man for that post, valiant, stubborn, and versed in the defending of leaguered holds. Was he needed there of a truth, or did he go as one seeking his own praise?

He went back where his duty was, with sufficient shame, content that he had been near to a folly that no one knew, and to which he would be unlikely to fall again.

CHAPTER XLVI

As Sir Oliver walked back to the place he had left on an impulse which he would find it hard to excuse, if not to believe, on the next day, he heard a growing volume of sound, as the guns of the Turkish batteries, which had been silent before so that the night attack might have the element of surprise, opened from every side, and, one by one, those of castle and town made a more halting reply.

He heard also the deeper rumble of explosions, three or four, that came almost as one, from the direction of the Sanglea, and wondered what Marshal Couppier did, or was done to him, in the disputed Bermola streets.

He saw that Mustapha had begun the assault at a late hour of the day because he had planned to resume it during the night if it were not ended before. It was not a common way with the Turks, their military science at that time not favouring operations during the darker hours, and Mustapha may have counted on that, as making it more likely that the Christians would have been off their guard after the fatigue of their daytime strife. But if that hope had been his, Sir Oliver was glad to think that it had been vain against the vigilance of those whose tired arms had not ceased the lifting of stones to guard their lives as they could for the coming day. Yet he saw that, if St. Angelo were to maintain even for two more weeks, its hardest ordeal was still to come. The first result of the Viceroy's belated movement for its relief had been to rouse a fiercer tempest of storm against its diminished numbers and shattered walls. That might be excused and endured if the promised succour were swift and strong, but it would be evil indeed if it were not more than a half-hearted attempt or an empty tale. . .

He roused the Grand Master when he got back, who took the news in a more temperate mood than he had thought him likely to do. "I suppose," he said, "that De Castriot will not lose the breach in the night hours. You must rouse me with further cause," and returned to sleep as one whose mind was anchored at ease.

His judgment was right in that, as the dawn showed. For the breach stood, and its approach was strewn with Turks who had come too close to get safely away. Also it was partly repaired, De Castriot having driven those who made its defence to labour thereon at all times when they need not be active to slay, to which thay had not been slow, as men who barricaded their own lives were not likely to be.

For the comfort which the dawn brought there was also a good word from the Sanglea, where Marshal Couppier had shown that the undermining of foes is an art of war that both sides can employ. For at the time when the Turks had been about to resume attack, having moved fresh troops into the town, there had been mines sprung under the streets and houses which had been taken by them, having been prepared for that hour even before the Turks had been allowed to come over the wall. And these had been so placed as to be in the rear of those who had made furthest advance in the direction of St. Michael's fort; and those who held the northern streets sallying out at the moment after the mines were sprung, and that in such force that, to make their strength, the fort had been almost denuded of men, there was a large part of the Turks who were surrounded and, being stricken with panic, were either slain, or forced to flee by water, waded or swum, to reach the Corradin shore.

In fact, so well had the Marshal planned the use of the slender forces he had, and with such energy did he counter-attack during the night, that the morning found his wall back in his own hands, and the Turks again on the side where he preferred them to be. So that the Grand Master was not told that there had been Turks in Bermola streets till it was a past tale.

The satisfaction that he could feel in the fact that this last assault had been futile to scale his walls either by night or day was not lessened when there came request from the Turks that there should be a truce of six hours. It was a proposal such as was of the routine of war, as it was waged at that time, and would be lightly agreed where there was exhaustion on either side, but it may have seemed to hold more cause for hope than it did, for Mustapha's purpose was neither to cease assault nor to give respite to the besieged for one avoidable hour.

But men must have some time in which they can sleep and feed, and he had movements and preparations to make for what he thought to be the last act of a drama on which the curtain was near to fall. He thought also to use that truce to his own gain, for he was soon riding along the edge of the ditch to observe what defence of stone had still to be overcome, and all else that could be read by one who was old and crafty in war.

He was ill-content with his own repulse at the Sanglea, and had a bitter wrath that Piali had failed to push troops into the breach in those fateful moments when it could have been his and would have been hard indeed for the ranks of the Christian knights to regain, but he did not see more in these events than a triumph delayed, and when Piali proposed that a summons to surrender should be sent during the hours of truce, as being that which the Christian dogs might now be hoping to hear, and likely, at the least, to produce dissension between the Grand Master, who was known to have a stiff neck, and such as might prefer to make terms for their own lives, Mustapha replied that the time was past for such talk, there being no terms he would give. It had become his purpose to put all to the sword who might still have lives to lose when he should enter the town, unless he might prefer that the Grand Master should have the ignominy of one who toils in chains on the galley-bench, as he had done before in his more vigorous days.

The Grand Master, having no thought of surrender on any terms, whether good or bad, but being resolved to abate any confidence that his foes might feel, was no less alert than the Turkish leader to use the opportunities that the truce allowed.

Being Sunday, there would have been high mass in San Lorenzo Church had it been a time of less urgent stress, with ceremony of burial, each in his own *langue*, of the knights who had died in the last week, but he ordered now that it should be celebrated in the breach itself, and in full sight of the Turks, for which there was double cause.

For he purposed to show the Turks all the strength he had, and as much more as they could be made to guess, to which end, making full use of a risk that the truce allowed, he drew every man he could, both from castle and town, as well as every part of the wall, that they might make such assembly, in numbers and in array, as Mustapha could have no pleasure to see.

It was to be requiem also, and consecration of ground for knights who would never lie in the bounds of the convent church, having been blown apart when the mine was sprung and covered by its collapse, or who had fallen after among the shattered fragments on which they fought, being trampled down and covered by other deaths, whether of friend or foe, and dreadfully buried at last by the stones which those who remained had rolled or tumbled into the breach.

The Grand Master would not have hastened the mass though the earth rose or the heavens fell; but when he spoke himself (as he determined to do, seeing so many assembled there whom he would rouse to his own zeal) he was short of words, considering how much was to be done by few hands during the quick hours of the truce.

"*Gratias ageus Deo, accepit fiduciam*," were the high words of the text he chose, being the record of Paul, after he had left that same isle, fifteen hundred years before that, when he approached Rome in a captive's gyves, and found that he was not forgotten of friends who came out to meet him, and were await at the Three Taverns, on the Appian Way.

It was well said that they should have courage equal to his, seeing that they had endured for the same time, the Apostle having been shipwrecked in Malta for three months before the *Castor & Pollux* sailed (it was likely) from St. Angelo's quay to bear him away, and they now hearing that the Viceroy was stirring to bring them aid; but he was brief about that. He would not have them fight as men clinging to life, and counting only how themselves might come out at the last, for he knew that there will ever be those who crouch low under the wall, having no better impulse than that, leaving it to others to do the great deeds by which all are to go free, through which they may all come to a poor end at the last.

He rather called their thoughts to the vows by which they had become part of the great Order which joined them now, asserting that which he would have them to be in such confident words that it became easy to their belief. He adjured them as men under the inspiration of God to bring down the infidel pride which blasphemed His power before the eyes of the watchful saints.

"We have no lust," he made boast, "for a slothful ease: we have put from us carnal desire: we listen not for the plaudits of men: but before our eyes is the symbol of Christian faith, and in our ears the high trumpet of God calls us to the unfaltering ranks of those who may be martyred but do not fail."

They heard him, and looked out over the half-filled fosse to where Mustapha watched the scene with curious and contemptuous eyes. He rode a milk-white mare that the deserts bred: he was splendid in inlaid armour and crimson silks, and surrounded by those of barbaric glitter that matched his own. Behind him were the trenches which had crept up close to ruined ramparts too weak to control their foes, batteries which had nearly silenced the Christian guns, and regiments forming to make instant assault when the hours of truce should be done; but they looked up to the lifted Cross with the assurance that they were partnered by an Invincible Power, and outward with the fortitude of men who are sacramentally destined to die.

CHAPTER XLVII

Francisco was one of those who had been able to leave his post and had listened to the Grand Master's words, by which he was not unmoved, but his thoughts were on other things which were nearer to him. That most who heard, if not all, would be destined to perish in the next days might have been a most likely guess, and it may be said that, in whatever mood it should be perceived, there could be nothing nearer to him than that. But youth has a sanguine blood, and will plan for life in a very obstinate way.

It was Angelica on whom he had centred his thoughts, being in his sight, though she was one he could not reach till the Mass was done.

He was himself gaily attired, and with care, as his habit was. He was not aware of less vigorous health because he had an arm which must be used, if at all, at more risk to himself than menace to any foe. During the last days he had done little but walk a wall which looked down on Calcara Creek, which had been empty of life. He had had no more than a demi-falcon at his control, which might have been sufficient to sink an enemy's boat, if one had been there, which he did not expect to see.

Calcara Creek was deep enough for the Turkish galleys to have sailed in, if they would have braved St. Angelo's seaward guns (as Piali was now urging that they should do), but if they were there they could do no more than fire upward at walls of stone, and there were more hopeful sides of attack, both by water and land, so that it was left to itself; and as the need grew the Grand Master had ordered that the guns should be removed from that part of the wall to the outer lines of the Bourg, where they would be facing an active foe.

Francisco, being left in this idle place, which had been almost emptied of men, wondered at times if the Grand Master had placed him there as one who had lost his trust, but he recalled the Notabile mission on which he had not failed, and he considered that his wound was still something less than healed, and renewed hope that he might be reserved aside until he should be fit for a better use.

But his impatience stirred to a more urgent resolve when he saw Angelica at a place where he was sure that she should not be, and though he was glad to know that she still bore an unwounded life, he saw other things at which he was less content. For though her eyes met his with a glad and confident look, her face was dark with fatigue which was not of the body alone, but of the ordeal through which she came. And he saw that the clothes she wore were soiled and torn beyond what he would have supposed that she would have endured, though having but an hour to choose for their exchange or either for food or sleep, but now she seemed unaware of the condition in which she stood. . . .

The Mass being done, there were many who hastened to go, some having to reach distant posts in the hour of truce that remained, and most having their own parts of the wall in mind, for the fact that there had been a breach blown in the bastion of Castile did not mean that it would be more easy to make defence of shattered ramparts elsewhere if Mustapha should change his attack. And those who stayed were as urgent to disregard the stiffness of which their own limbs would have been willing to make complaint, as they resumed their work on the tumbled stones before the Turkish guns would open on them again.

Francisco stayed Sir Oliver as he was moving away.

"If I may," he said, "I would have a more active place than I now hold."

Sir Oliver looked at him, and considered that there were many less fit than he who were now at more dangered posts.

"So you will," he said. "And at a near hour. You may be content about that."

Francisco thanked him, but did not give ground.

"I would know," he said, "if it be by order that my cousin is here, or by no more than her own will."

"She is one who must do her part at a final need, and that need was here. But, for the moment, that need is less. There are others who were summoned with her who have returned to their own tasks. She may go back if she will, as I think she should."

"Will you order that?"

"No. For I can neither order all women to leave the wall, we being as few as we now are, nor will I make difference for her. She may go back if she will."

"I may tell her that? . . . It is four hours before my duty resumes at my own post. Can I aid here until then?"

"You should ask De Castriot that, though there is no doubt what he will say. But you must observe that he can give you no warrant to remain if there be renewal of the assault, for which, as I think,

Mustapha is even now making array. For you must then move to your own place, though your hour of rest be not done, for it is there that your trust lies."

Francisco understood a warning in that, which he supposed that he did not need, but he let it pass, having a more urgent question upon his mind. He would have made further request, but Sir Oliver, having other matters on hand, excused himself in a brief word, and hastened away.

Angelica, not supposing that Francisco could stay, had gone back to her own toil. With Brother William, of whom she had made a friend, she sought to roll a great fragment of rock to the edge of the higher wall, where it was broken above the breach, and to poise it so that it could be tipped into the fosse at the right time to fall on a crowding foe. The chaplain's pike was a lever now, which may have been a more congenial use than it first had, but in fact Brother William had shown no slackness of spirit since he had seen the face of his fears.

Angelica looked up with a glad word, and a glance which withdrew somewhat at the sight of her cousin's face. She asked, "Is all well? Are you changed? Are you stationed here?"

"You should not be at that work," he said, without making reply. "Look at your hands."

"So I do," she said. "Or so I might. But there is not much I can see."

She looked at hands which were soiled and skinned, and stained with neglected blood, being too soft for the work they did.

"They are poor hands, as I might have learnt before now, and the stones are rough. But the Turks would be rougher still, and the breach is low."

"You have left that for which you are more fit, and an equal need. Sir Oliver says you can go back."

"Does he say I must?"

"He says you may, which should be the same thing."

"I am not sure. I will go if there be no further assault when the truce is done."

"Which were the more reason to go. Have you been here through the night?"

"I have been here from the first call, when the mine was blown. But you may think too much of my risk, or of what I do. I was one of a crowd. I would not say that I gave no help, but I did little with push of sword, for which others were more forward than I. It is the same jeopard for all, and the need is great. . . . I asked, are you stationed here?"

"No. Though it is what I purposed to ask. . . . But Sir Oliver is agreed that I be released from a place where I do naught. . . . I have De Castriot's thanks that I stay here while I can, though I must go if the Turks come."

They stood talking thus on the edge of the rent the explosion had made, looking down into the breach, that men were toiling to heal. Brother William gave them a glance which saw much, and went on prising the rock. Below them there was a bustle where De Castriot directed the bringing up of a gun which was to be concealed behind a tumble of stones, out of which it would discharge a deadly scatter of grape into the faces of those who should be first in scaling the breach. It was a work which he would have complete when the truce should end, but which he still could not allow to be seen by those Turks who now came even to the further edge of the fosse, seeking to see as much as the terms of truce would permit them to do.

The two stood there looking down at that which they were not careful to see, and forgetful of the urgency of the hour, though it had been the subject on which they spoke.

Francisco was vexed both that she should remain, and that she should be unmoved by his own judgement or wish and even more that, though he had come to long for her when they were apart, they could be of no better accord when they met.

She was aware of the same cloud, but with a fixed will to break it apart. She saw, with a clarity born of the hard tuition of war, and in a situation pregnant with death, that though one might survive by a doubtful chance, that both would was no more than a frail hope, and if they could not part in the right way, it might be to either a burden of long regret which they need not have.

"Francis," she asked, "will you say why you are vexed that I would not go?"

"You are in a danger you should not have, and which is hard to endure. I must think of what happened before."

"Then you waste fear. I shall not be caught twice in that way."

"There are dangers no less than that, which you cannot miss if you stay here."

"So there are. It is as the Grand Master said. We are all likely to die. But if we are bold in holding the wall we have, we may hope for a better end."

"So we hope. Yet I may be anxious for you."

"I expect that, having a dread for you that I cannot still, which will be more when you are gone to a dangerous place. . . But, Francis, in very truth, is it that alone? Do you not think what I do to be both danger and shame? From which you would keep me clean, if I would be meeker to you?"

"I have not spoken of shame. I would have you away from here. I am plain on that."

"So you are. . . . We are of a great house. You do not forget that? We have honour to keep."

"So I think."

"There are Maltese women along the wall. . . . Having come here as I did, would you have me do less than they? Am I to stand further back for fear of death or a fouled hand? It were a poor boast for our house's pride."

He controlled his own difficult pride to answer in words that were not easy to say: "I have been foolish before, and was near to be wrong again. . . . You are one with whom our honour is very sure, and for your safety I can but pray."

He caught a hand at which she had looked down as she spoke, raising it to his lips. He kissed dirt and blood, but she knew it to be a better thing than if he had kissed her mouth, they having been together from childhood days.

Her blood beat fast to a thrill of triumph and of desire as she felt his kiss. There came vision of a lifetime of happy days, which she saw, at her next thought, to be mirage which she had made it likely she would not reach. Yet had she not come thereto by the only road? There would have been no way through the gates of the convent of Holy Cross.

If life were too dear to lose, should she not go back to her work at the lazar, where none would blame her to be?

"Francis," she said, "De Castriot will give you no thanks that we idle here."

CHAPTER XLVIII

MARSHAL Couppier had some cause to be content with the success of the tactics he had employed, having recovered his walls, and that after inflicting a loss upon the Turks which they would be grieved to count; and so he was until he considered the tale of his own dead, which he was worse placed to endure, and that the length of his walls was no less than it had been two days ago, when he had decided that he was too weak to maintain the line.

He could do no better now than to plan that he would fall back as before, asking Mustapha to pay again for that which he had been unable to keep; but he would have been spared some thought, at least for that day, had he known Mustapha's resolve, which was not much less than to leave him alone, as being worth less than the price he asked.

For Mustapha, when he had proposed a truce for the removal of wounded and dead, as it was custom to do, had his plans made, on the assurance that St. Angelo was not far from its fall. He had no mind to entangle himself again in the Bermola streets while Piali broke into the Bourg, and might even bring St. Angelo down, so that the name would be his for the exploit that would bring triumph to Turkish arms. Piali had had his chance for a day and night at the breach of the ruined wall and he had failed to enter the town. Now Mustapha sent him away, with pretext enough, so that he could not object, though he must go in a sullen mood, more being understood on both sides than even Piali would be reckless to say.

For there had been store-ships come into port with equipment both for army and fleet, but especially to refurnish the ships which had been stripped for the army's need. Now that there was talk of the assembly of Christian galleys in the harbours of Sicily, and none knew what fleets might be sailing to join them from further ports, it had become urgent need to refit the ships which had been half emptied both of artillery and crews, so that they might reinforce the squadron which was at sea under Candellissa's command. The fleet was Piali's charge, and the ordering of a naval battle would rest with him. How could he object when Mustapha said that he would take control of St. Angelo's siege, and that Piali should look to his ships?

To Hassan also Mustapha gave a part which he could not decline, and which he accepted without sign of demur, having more control of his thoughts than Piali was ever likely to gain, and those thoughts seeing somewhat further and more clearly ahead.

Hassan had not been idle these last days. Mustapha had had no wish to repeat the blunder which had cost the lives of all who had lain at La Marsa Springs. He had learned that De Vigny and Vertura were no less to be feared than Marshal Couppier had been before, and he had given Hassan charge to protect their rear in a thorough way. This would have meant no more than that some good Barbary troops, and some regiments of Spahis who still had horses for which there had been little use, would have paraded idly from point to point of the Turkish lines, had the Marshal's lieutenants pursued the policy of caution which he had practised and taught. But they conceived, with good reason enough, that the desperation of St. Angelo's plight required that they should take greater risks, to lessen pressure upon its crumbling walls.

They commenced attacks both by night and day, showing valour and skill, but still playing the game that Hassan would have asked them to do.

The untrained Maltese showed a courage none could doubt. They had some success. But De Ligny was ambushed, being betrayed by a Greek spy, and died with a hundred more. There were other encounters in which the Maltese met with disastrous loss.

Now it was known that Vertura was laid up with a poisoned foot. The command at Notabile had passed to the Chevalier Mesquita, a Portuguese of whom little was known, either good or bad, but who had claimed it with no better reason than that he was the oldest knight in Notabile still alive and without a disabling wound.

Mustapha felt that the guerrilla menace was tamed, if not entirely subdued. He proposed to Hassan that he should use the most part of his troops to threaten the Sanglea, so that the Marshal should be too closely contained to consider aiding the Grand Master at any need, but without again attempting to enter the town, unless at such a chance as would offer less costly success than Mustapha himself had won.

"I suppose," he said, "that the first time I was over the wall I should have gone on to St. Michael's fort, had I not been stayed by a lying tale, but the next they were more prepared, and our troops bled.

"It may be now that we shall find the Bourg simpler to win, as it must be the larger gain. But I will leave it to you. You may storm again, if you think well. They must be nearing the end. By every report they are weak and few, and they must get fewer with every day that we hammer around their walls."

Hassan agreed about that, but said that he would be cautious in wasting men. Let the guns resume. There had been a cargo of powder landed the day before. They could fire night and day with no fear of stint, using every gun they had, which the Christians had become unable to do. And their guns on all sides were now six to one, or something better than that.

The Turkish army at this time had been reinforced with some extra regiments, as well as with cargoes of munitions and other stores. Della Corna's guess that they had no more than 16,000 men who could stand on their own legs was too sanguine a word. Mustapha could still count 20,000 good troops whom he could use in a mobile way, without sum of details of guard or supply or the ships' crews that were not ashore. There was a grain ship from Gerbes expected in a week's time, and when it had arrived they would not be short of any kind of supplies, even though it were two months more that the Cross would fly from St. Angelo's tower, which would be a miracle of the Christian saints. . . . The last hour of the truce struck, and the guns opened again.

CHAPTER XLIX

MUSTAPHA had used the hours of truce to remove his own troops from before the Sanglea, where those of Hassan arrived, and with these he increased the weight of attack against the walls of the Bourg.

While the truce endured, he had made open show of such massing of troops before diverse parts of the wall as would make the Grand Master afraid to weaken defence at whatever point, though they might now be no more than a menace of force that the trenches hid. He had been able to rest his men, except for such movements as have been told, while the Christians had toiled on in the growing heat of the day to strengthen their shattered walls, and so it was not without good reasons for hope that St. Angelo had come to its last hour that he ordered that the breach should be stormed again.

The Turkish trenches were now so close to the wall that there was no great space to be rushed, which was well for those who must cross it now, for they must face a hail of shots and missiles of many kinds (but none good) from the preparation of those who knew before where they would be likely to start, and where they would seek to come, and they were exposed besides to the flanking fire of the Arragon bastion, where men had stood by their guns await for the moment when they could be discharged on an emerging foe.

The fact was that when Piali lost the first minutes after the mine was blown, he lost three-fourths of the advantage which such a gap can give in a line which is stoutly and skilfully held. Mustapha was not regardless of this, but he knew how great the exhaustion and how few the numbers must be of the Maltese knights, and he sought to make a quick end. His natural caution may have been somewhat overcome by the obduracy of his resolve that St. Angelo should not escape at last, after the losses he had sustained, of which it might already be said that an army had perished before St. Elmo's and St. Angelo's walls.

The threat of Sicilian succour, vague and weak as it was, also urged him to strike hard while the hour was his. With the numbers he still controlled, if they should be implacably used in assaults which would seldom cease, he did not doubt that he could win all before any aid could appear and, however dreadful the cost, he knew that failure, to Soliman's ears, would be a less tolerable tale.

So it came that as the truce expired, and at the hottest hour of the day, there was a burst of barbaric cries, a throbbing of urgent drums, and the trenches spouted an outrush of dark-faced fanatic forms toward a breach which was now half repaired, and well furnished to fling them back.

So it did; with a slaughter which even this siege could not often have matched, such were the crowding ranks, and such the wanton exposure in which they came. Yet they scaled twice to the breach, and for one perilous moment were within it in a rush against which the reckless valour of the Christian knights was hardly equal to throw them back, even with the aid of the rain of missiles which were directed from both sides of the gap upon those who were climbing upward to their comrades' support.

It was then that Angelica joined with Brother William to send their poised fragment of rock on its dreadful leap upon the turbaned heads of those who were pressing into the breach. It bore down three, wounded or dead, and came to rest on a man's leg, which it broke and pinned, so that it was beyond his strength to get free, in the position in which he lay. He called uselessly to comrades who were now tumbling or slipping down the stones in a desperate haste not to be slowest in flight, that they should lift it and bear him away. A wild-fire bomb, flung wildly after retreating foes, burst beside him, burning and blinding his eyes. A man came to Angelica's side, bending a bow, with which he would have put an end to a tortured life.

De Castriot's voice sounded in sharp command: "Let him be. His cries daunt those who will be told to return." The man lowered the bow.

She felt the air of a missile that passed her face. She could not tell what it was. She realized that it was foolish to stand longer there, having done her part. She turned to say this to Brother William, and saw that he was on the ground. She went on her knees to find a wound from which the blood welled in a tide she could never staunch. He crossed himself with a shaking hand. His lips moved in prayer. He seemed unconscious of her and of what she did.

De Castriot's voice sounded sharply again: "You must not wait. Pull him away." There was one who seized the dying man by the feet, and dragged him roughly aside. They had a cauldron of boiling pitch, which they would place where her stone had been.

De Castriot recognized her as she was drawing aside. "Señorita," he said, in an altered voice, "you should not be here. It is too exposed. You should go below."

"So I will," she said. "I have no more to do here."

He answered: "You did it well," and his attention went back to the cauldron, which he would see with his own eyes to be so placed that it would be of most avail at the next rush.

She went down feeling no horror at what she had seen—she was past that—and little fear for herself. The mind adjusts itself in a short time, and it had become natural to see swords rending in human flesh, and the entrails of those whom the gun-shots tore. She might not have used her own hands to pull a dying man away by the legs, but she understood the tension of those who did. They were obsessed by one overwhelming need—to keep out the Turks, and their own lives had been risked anew in every second they were delayed in that which they were exposed to do.

But as she withdrew from the top of the wall, she became aware that she was exhausted both in body and mind, so that she could do no more for that time. She had leave to go if she would, and she made her way back to her own room in the castle turret, which seemed a haven of peace, even though the noise of the guns was a constant rumble from every side, and at times there would come the nearer thunder of the great cannon on the castle roof, that fired at some distant mark.

When she had changed and cleansed herself of the worst dirt, she went down to Sir Oliver's room, where he was at work, as he always was.

He looked almost as weary as she, but gave her a glance she was glad to have.

"It is well," he said, "that you are safely returned."

"I must sleep. I could do no more. I suppose that they will hold the breach for this day."

"So I think. I should say there are other points that are weaker now, if Mustapha could make the right guess."

There was a tone in that which she heard from him for the first time. She asked: "Can we endure?"

"It is that which we should not doubt, even in our own minds."

"I will practise to avoid that. . . I may sleep long."

"So you should. You will be safe in these walls."

"I was not doubting of that."

She went to rest which was quickly hers, and the agony of the siege went on till the darkness came.

But its events of that day gave Mustapha no occasion to boast, when Hassan came to him with the falling of night, except for the report that La Valette had a wound, which he would be glad to believe.

So he had; having been struck on the leg by a fragment of grenade, when he had been inspecting the bastion of Provence. But as he found that he could still walk, when it had been bound and the blood stayed, he had made nothing of that, and went on to traverse the wall, as he had been doing before, and to encourage a line that was now so thin that they could but wonder, at any point, how they would fare if they should be chosen for storm on the next day.

CHAPTER L

HASSAN had done well enough at the Sanglea, and perhaps more by attempting less. He had kept Marshal Couppier fully engaged, and had made some advance, which he would be unlikely to lose, for he had gone forward no more than where he could lay the defences flat. He had resolved to progress thus in a gradual way, which would be as final as fate, not using his men for what the guns could better do at a short range where there was but feeble reply, and avoiding danger of mines by not bringing on his men too close to the ebbing Maltese line.

He told Mustapha how he had fared, but it was not that of which he had come to talk, but of a new plan.

"If there be relief from Palermo before we have St. Angelo down, where do you say they would land?"

"I suppose," Mustapha answered, "we can be sure of this, if no more. They will not seek to engage our fleet, though we must meet theirs if we can. They will have an army to get ashore. It will be in some quiet bay, where they will hope that we shall not come."

"So I agree. And where will they make their base, if they should come safely to land?"

"At Notabile at the first. They will rest on that, and advance to attack our rear, where we must face round. It might all be done in two days. We must have St. Angelo down before then."

"But if Notabile were ours?"

"They would be worse placed, that is sure. They might not come to land, if they heard that."

"Or they might not put to sea, if they should hear it before they embark. . . . If I should make sudden attack thereon, might it not be a good gain?"

"It should be sudden, so that they have neither time to prepare defence nor avoid the town. . . . And our time is short."

"I could march at dawn, with 4,000 men, leaving enough to hold the front at Sanglea."

"Then you have planned this before?"

"So I have; but I have spoken to none. I would have let it

lapse had our assaults had more gain in the last two days, but I suppose it may now be a good plan."

Mustapha agreed to that. He saw that it might be one of those smaller things by which greater are changed. If Notabile should fall, it would dishearten both those who were in St. Angelo's walls and those who talked of rescue they had not been hasty to bring. And it was a risk which Hassan would take on his own head.

Hassan did not prolong words, having Mustapha's consent. He returned to his own tent, where he would not be alone.

For the fact that he might be marching on Notabile at an early hour of the dawn had not appeared to him to be a sufficient reason why he should not have Venetia's company during the night. Only, as his time would be short for sleep and for her, he had sent her an order to come to his own tent, which she had been pleased to receive.

For though she knew that she lived at a great risk, and might fall by a careless word, having that in her heart which it now held, she saw as clearly that she was not so placed that she could come through in a passive way. Unless she could content herself from that day with the life of a Moorish slave, she must be wise both to think and act in her skin's cause, and to keep her blood where she would prefer it to be.

If she were discreet for this night, she might increase confidence in herself: she might even learn things which it was vital to know. She had gone to a man's bed before then for a poorer price, and he more hateful to her.

She had thought much in these days, which had been quiet for her, though for most around they had held excitement more than enough. She had wondered how the Turkish women endured the monotony of the lives in which they were idly penned, to be called for a man's pleasure at times which must seem seldom enough, being the one event that they were permitted to share. But she had used the time well in her own way, to review how she was placed, and to weigh the chances by which she might hope to come away with her life, and perhaps with a scarless skin.

Now she found Hassan to talk, as she thought, with a free tongue. He told her how they had been foiled in the strife of the last days, but with confidence that St. Angelo was about to fall. He talked of the stores and munitions which had been brought to port in the last week, and of how Piali had gone to the fleet in a sulky mood. He mentioned the grain-ship which was due to arrive in four days' time, and the port from which it had come.

She thought that suspicion had left his mind, and that he talked with less reserve every time that they met, for which she thanked her own discretion, not entirely without a cause. She did not doubt what he said, nor that the end of the knights of Malta was near, and she decided that, if she should delay more, she might find it too late to fly. She had a half-formed purpose at the rear of her mind that she would slip away and take refuge at Notabile on the coming day; but she would not consider that, even in thought, while she was talking to him, lest she should lay it bare in some guardless way, which she would have been unlikely to do.

It was at a later hour, when she heard from other mouths where he had gone, that she saw that his confidence came but a short way. She knew that he must have had Notabile more in his mind than the subjects of which he had spoken to her. She saw also that it must have been harmless to tell her of a march on which he would set out as soon as he left her side, even had she been no less than a practised spy, but it was a matter which he had very secretly planned, and such matters might never be open to her.

She went over all he had said, for which she had leisure enough, seeking something which might be offered for sale at the Grand Master's mart, and found no more than a small thing, of which Hassan himself might have said that it could do neither good nor harm, at that date, for the Grand Master to know. Yet if a small coin be all that your pouch hold——

Beyond that, when she thought of such trade, there was another doubt of equal moment to her. If the Grand Master liked her goods, would he be able to pay? Could he promise her life for more than a few days, even had he a better will than it was easy to think?

She supposed that she must put thought of flight to Notabile out of her mind. She saw that it might be her only course, if she would avoid a great risk, to accept the fate which would ship her away to Algiers. After all, it had been her own choice. (But at how urgent a need!) Yet she would not consent to that till she had tried her cage, bar by bar, for she had come to see that it would be a life which she would find it hard to endure.

Her thoughts turned to St. Angelo again, and though she put herself first, as she would have said that most do, she considered those she had left and betrayed in a different mood from that in which she had fled from their threatened process of law. She may not have observed this, and yet it may have been enough to tip an uncertain scale.

All her life, authority had been her watched and avoided foe. Even wealth was not native to her or to be wooed as a friend. It was to be won, if at all, by violence or subtle wiles. Should it become hers, it must have the look of a captured prey. All the sympathy she could spare from her own needs had been for those who were under the hard heel of the law: whom it caught and baited and jailed in its cold merciless way.

She had not looked upon Malta's knights as being men of her faith and blood : they had been her most powerful and pitiless foes. Secure in a great strength and a great pride, the Grand Master had not quarrelled with her. She had been mere dirt from which he would cleanse his town. And she had repaid contempt with a lively hate, which had yet been short of venom to do him hurt, if he would have left her alone.

That feeling had not changed at the root, for its cause remained. Had she seen the Grand Master chained to a slave's oar, her face might have dimpled into a smile. But St. Angelo had changed from its former aspect of strength, and (from her view) of a too orgulous pride. It had become of her own kind. It looked round for a way to save itself, which was not easy to see. It gasped for life, biting hard the while at the hounds that had dragged it down. Seeing it thus, she became aware that its people were more to her than those to whom she had come. She would have given it help, if she could, at a cost less than her own skin. She had needed all her practised schooling of lips and eyes that Hassan should guess nothing of this when he had talked of its coming fall.

And during the last three days she had observed a vaguely possible way—that is, if she should have any word for the Grand Master that it would be profit to send—which she had considered, and put firmly aside, as being a poor hope and a risk that she did not like. Now, having come back to Le Tonneau's villa, she weighed it again in a more tolerant mind. If she had better hope that St. Angelo would endure—if she had a better message to send—if she were more assured that she might not be at the jaws of a deadly trap—it was hard to resolve. In the heat of the afternoon she strolled out into the road, with one of her negroid slaves at her heels, as she had been making it her habit to do.

The road that ran under the front of the villa had a steep cliff falling away on its further side. It must have been damaged by the heavy traffic which had passed over it during the first weeks of the war. Now a portion of it had fallen away and a slave-gang had been sent for its repair. They were half a dozen men of various origins, war-captives rather than criminals, who were in the charge of an overseer and with two armed soldiers for guard. The men were driven hard, but were allowed two hours for rest and food at the hottest part of the day, which may have been for the overseer's convenience rather than theirs.

At those times he would retire some distance away, as though thinking it unseemly that he should eat or relax with them, but the two guards, who were changed at the noon hour, remained watchful over the resting men.

Venetia had made an easy friend of the overseer, with a gift neither too small nor too large. She could talk to the slaves if she would. It was nothing to him, if it did not hinder the work. Indeed, there had been no need for the gift while it was known that Hassan's favour was hers. She had talked to them, testing the languages that they spoke, and her power to make herself understood; and there had been nothing said (excepting with one, and that little enough) which might not have been shouted aloud. She had been carefully-careless also to tell Hassan of this interest which she had found for her idle days. "I learn tongues," she had said, in which he knew her to have some skill, and quickness to learn, of which she had boasted to him before.

The slave-driver was an easy jovial man, who would do no more, even to one who paused in his work, than to give him a prick with his sword-point, to which a slave should not object. And even that would be done with a jesting word, showing that there was no malice behind the point. It would not commonly go more than half an inch deep, and if some of his charges had more scars from this cause than it would be simple to count, it showed no more than how lazy they were, and how lenient he had been not to have reported them for the lash.

Venetia came to the men, who sat under the narrow shade of citron trees overhanging her garden wall. They ate food which was plain enough, but not stinted, for their owners knew that hard work cannot be got, even by means of the lash, from beasts that are badly fed. After eating well, they would sleep till the overseer should rouse them to work again.

Venetia passed the two guards, whom she had seen before. She gave them a smiling word in their own tongue, which she was learning fast, and which she had assured herself before to be the only one that they knew. She was in no peril from them.

There was one man to whom she could talk in her own tongue, he being Ligurian born. Of the other five, she was sure that her words would have no meaning except to one, a Levantine, of whom she was less sure, and whom she judged to be of the sort who would betray his mother to death for a stale crust if he were hungry enough, but this man was some distance away.

The man of her own land sat as far apart as he could venture to do without the fear of being herded back by the guards. He was not liked, even by those who were fellows in the bondage that he endured, for he was one of morose and passionate moods.

She sauntered on, talking to those she passed in their own tongues as far as she was able to do, and so came to this man, to whom she spoke also of indifferent things, the negroid girl standing by, and understanding nothing at all. There came a time when she said, low, but in a casual tone, and with the smile that should go with a jesting word:

"If I should do all that you ask, would you take a word to the Grand Master for me?"

The man was slow to reply. "How could I do that? I should not be there. St. Angelo is a falling town. I would be loose in the land."

"For the dogs to catch? St. Angelo is the only safety you have. Do you know that Hassan marched on Notabile this dawn?"

"Then there is no safety to find. It would be but few days till they would have me again."

"Not if you have a good wit. When a town falls, there are ever those who get free."

"Shall I have the knife?"

"I will promise naught. There is a low ledge under the wall, as you pass the gate. If you feel there in the dusk—But if you fumble you will be seen."

"I shall not fail. . . What must the Grand Master be told?"

She gave him the message, repeating it twice with care. She went back, passing men who dozed, regardless of what she did.

She had an irresolute mind. If St. Angelo were about to fall, the Grand Master's goodwill, even if it could be bought, would be useless to her. Yet it was an insurance against some possible turns of event which she would be glad to have. But the risk was great. The man might betray her in the next hour. He would be likely to do so if he were caught and tortured, which was a probable end. Should he succeed in escape, he might not enter the town. She had to give him absolute trust, paying first, and in her own peril, for that which she might not get. She would have thought it a less risk had he asked her only for gold. But he must have a knife also, which was to go under the driver's ribs. She saw that revenge, not escape, was the main object that filled his mind. The escape must follow, so that he would avoid penalty for revenge. But to escape while the overseer lived was outside his thought.

She considered it for some time, and resolved: "It is foolish risk, and would be to buy that which I may not get or which may be of no value to me." She put it out of her mind.

At a later hour there was gossip brought to the house. It was vague, and not easy to understand, but it seemed that, on all sides, the Turks had had a bad day.

Hassan was said to be in retreat. A further assault had failed at the Castile breach, and it was said now that it was to be bombarded again, work having been resumed on the construction of a platform or cavalier from which it was to be battered with heavy guns brought almost to the counter-scarp edge. This had been Piali's idea, before he had been sent to his ships, and Mustapha had put it aside.

There were rumours also about Mustapha himself, some saying that he was wounded or dead, or at least that he had been down in a ditch for some hours, from which he did not emerge.

Venetia did not know how much to believe, but she knew that such rumours may show a face of truth which is not properly theirs. They were not the kind of tales which would be scattered about if the Turks were winning the town, or Hassan had carried the horse-hair standards over Notabile's ancient and crumbling walls.

Hearing these things, Venetia came to a different mind. She gave tasks to her girls which would keep them from observation of her. She wrapped a sharp knife with some pieces of gold. She strolled down, and put them where she had said she would. The quick Malta dusk was already near, when the slaves would cease work and be marched away, passing the length of wall.

After all, the risk did not seem over-great. The rag in which knife and gold had been wrapped she had found on a midden heap. The knife would be hard to trace to her. The gold was Italian coin which had come from Francisco's pouch: there was no avoiding of that.

Having done her part, she put it easily out of her mind, after resolving how she would act and speak if suspicion should come, so that she should not be trapped unaware. She had not asked the man's plan for escape, nor how the gold was to be used, having avoided all needless words. She knew only that the knife was for the overseer to feel, which seemed to her as good a use as it was likely to have, and she knew the value of gold, for whatever end.

At a later hour, there was a confirmation of what had been rumoured before. For the most part, the first tales had been true, though their implications might have appeared more than they were.

Hassan had made a march so swift, and with such sudden surprise, that he had come in sight of the walls of the ancient capital of the isle.

As he marched he had surveyed the land with a soldier's eye, and it had become clear to him that he would not have come so far had he not kept his intention secret till the last hour. A few score of men who could shoot from the protection of the low walls that divided the little barley-stubbled fields, and falling back as he advanced, could have inflicted such loss on his ordered ranks as would have been hard to endure. Even to return might be at a great cost, if he should be stoutly opposed.

But he marched over bare fields and by empty roads, with no more to face than some futile shots, as the outposts of the Maltese guerrillas scattered to give him way, and these were no more to him than a score of bees to a bear.

But the surprise, great as it was, did not find Notabile with open gates, which would have been too much to expect. Nor was there any sign that Mesquita was unequal to his command, or that Hassan had come to the spoil of an easy prey. Women joined with men in manning the ancient walls. They showed a bold and confident front.

Hassan rode round the city, surveying its defences on every side. He had no time for a siege. He must storm the wall, or go back. His artillery was no more than two guns, as yet half a mile behind. If he should attempt that which would not succeed, he would have lost men who were needed at the Sanglea, and every hour he remained those might be gathering in the hills who would be active to obstruct his return. The men of Malta might be overcome in the open field, but, being behind the walls, they were foes to fear. He was one who could take a bold risk, if it had his judgment's support. But he did not disguise facts from himself. He said: "They would hold the walls. We should lose men to no gain." He gave orders for instant retreat.

He brought his army clear with a trivial loss, giving the Maltese some reason to boast, but not much.

It was an audacious attempt which might have come to success had the ancient walls been more fallen apart, or been manned in a fainter way. It might have been disaster, had it been led by one less able to see an unwelcome fact, or to act thereon with decisive speed.

Mesquita was not pleased. He said: "Had I known it a day

before, he had paid in blood for each yard he came." But it was of no avail to say that, for the chance was gone.

As to Mustapha, it was true that he had been in a ditch for five hours, but it was not before the bastion of Castile, but at a different part of the Bourg wall.

Being over-bold, or over-confident in surveying a weakened foe, he had ridden too close to a silent wall, and had found that he was under fire of those who were pleased to have so important a mark. He rode off with his staff, who got clear, but his own horse went down, with a cross-bow bolt in its heart. He had a rough fall. As he rose a bullet rattled his scabbard and another tore through the crimson surcoat which he wore loosely over his mail. He was glad to crawl into a half-dug trench, which had been abandoned as being in a too lively quarter for the comfort of those who had started it on a moonless night. Mustapha was glad to be there till the darkness came and he could crawl safely away. He had for company a Turk who had been dead for ten days. He suffered in temper and pride, but the incident did not strengthen St. Angelo's walls.

Before he made that mistake he had ordered that there should be a two-days' cessation of assault at the breach, the guns taking their part again. He had caused a sealed envelope, addressed to the Grand Master, to be thrown over the wall. La Valette opened it when it was taken to him, and read the one word *Thursday* written in the Latin tongue. That was clear enough. It was Monday evening then. The Turkish batteries were to pound them for two more days, after which Mustapha would make an end. He scorned surprise, not acting as one who ordered a battle, but rather fixing a day when the execution would be. Counting the few who yet lived within St. Angelo's weakened walls, it would have been a bold guess to say that he boasted more than he would be equal to do.

CHAPTER LI

It was on Tuesday morning that the Grand Master called a Council of War, for which there had been common request, that all might know how they stood, and what their action should be if the Turks should further prevail. And it was at the same hour, in the great reception hall of his Palermo palace, that the Viceroy of Sicily received the Grand Prior of Auvergne with the honour his rank required, and was insulted by one who addressed him in reply without using the titles which were his, both in his own right and in that of the semi-regal office he held.

"Sir Prior," he asked in a cool way, by which his dignity stood, "do you address me thus of a set will, and, if so, will you tell me why?"

"I have good cause," De Lastic replied, in a voice which was heard even by those that stood at the door, "but should I see you move to Malta's relief, I would call you by all your rights, or by that of Majesty if you prefer."

The Viceroy heard him with an expressionless face. "Sir Prior," he asked, "will you speak to me aside?"

When they had withdrawn to a windowed recess, he said, in an altered voice: "You may be surprised that I give you thanks for words which are good for Malta and me. . . . You are Malta's friend. That is clear. And I can tell you that which I know you will not blazon abroad.

"When I was unable to send the aid which I would have been glad to do—for it is the curse of rulers, as your wisdom will not deny, that we are often hindered from that which our hearts desire—then I sent comforting words, being all I could, and promises which I made loud in all mouths to disturb our foes; but, now that I move indeed, you can give Malta no better help than to protest that I lie still, which we must hope that they hear, and perhaps believe. Yet, if you watch, you may come to another mind, for there are preparations afoot which I cannot hide, as I would be more pleasured to do."

The Grand Prior listened to this, and was in doubt what to believe. "It is true," he said, "that I have heard little of this you do, and have seen less. Yet if you contrive all in a secret way, it is that which is wise in war."

He went in a great doubt.

Yet that which Don Garcio urged was in part true. There were Genoese galleys in Messina harbour, ready to put to sea when they should see assembly of force such as would make it more than a poor jest. There was hurried raising of troops, both in Naples and further north at Milan. The Viceroy saw himself committed to an effort to raise St. Angelo's siege, with no time, nor with support from the Spanish king, such as would enable him to sail with the army which the position plainly required. He might well hope that Mustapha's eyes were not turned this way, nor his fleet alert. He might even had felt relief in his secret heart had he heard report of St. Angelo's fall. For he feared either to be cursed in all men's mouths for a further delay, or to sail with a fleet too feeble to raise the siege, in which case he could see that the shame would be left to him. . . .

Knowing nothing of this, but being in as much doubt as the Grand Prior of what Don Garcio would be likely to do, the Council of Malta met, not now composed of Commanders of the Order alone, as had been the case in earlier days, but of those who, by merit shown or the chance of avoiding death, had come to command at different parts of the wall.

Assault had ceased, except at the Sanglea, where, one by one, with fighting that did not slack, the streets of Bermola passed into the hands of the Moors and were levelled down where they had not been flattened enough before.

But from all sides the batteries fired on the ruined walls, the defenders of which were too few and too worn to repair them anew, as the round-shot shook and tumbled them down. And it was with this sound in their ears that the Council of Malta met for the last time —till the last shot should be fired, and the siege done.

Marshal Couppier was there, with Colonel Roubles from the Sanglea, and Ramegas from his post of guard over the empty ships; De Castriot also, and De Claremont, who had taken over his command of the Arragon wall now that De Castriot had charge of the Castile breach, and Del Formo was there from the bastion of Provence, and others of equal valour from parts of the line which had not yet been subjected to such extremities of assault as it had been their lots to sustain.

The Grand Master had talked much with Sir Oliver in the last hour, and they had not always agreed, but now he gave no sign of his thoughts, nor did he commence with any confident words, as it had been his custom to do.

He looked round on men who were haggard with toil and strife, half of them having bandaged wounds, and almost all more fit for the lazar beds than for that which must face them now. His eyes fell on Marshal Couppier, who may have shown least sign of any there that he had not come from a quiet life. He asked: "Will you tell us first how you fare at the Sanglea, and what men you could spare, if you should hear that we come to a greater need?"

Marshal Couppier was quiet in reply, as one who talks of a meal. "I do well enough, as I think. I am dear to buy. You must not expect beyond that. St. Michael's fort may be hard to take; but I am not yet so far back. I can hold them off from the harbour side for another week, or perhaps more. But if am I to do that, you must not tell me of nearer needs. I cannot spare you a man."

La Valette heard this, and did not look pleased; but he only said, addressing all rather than one: "You have heard how matters stand at the Sanglea. Have you counsel for the Bourg's better defence?"

There was some confused talk thereon, each commander urging the weakness of his own front, and asking assurance that it could be reinforced with speed if it should become a point of special attack, which Cardona interrupted to say: "Chevaliers, if you will listen to one who has spent some years in the trade of war, you have one question first to resolve, on which all must depend. You have two days to dispose, if we have made a right guess of what the Turks are meaning to do; and the first question must be, can we sustain the length of the Bourg lines, or shall we withdraw to the strength of the castle walls?"

The Grand Master spoke as one whose passion was hard to rein: "Do you propose that we yield them walls that they fail to take?"

Cardona was precise: "I proposed neither to stand nor withdraw. I did but urge that we should first be clear on what we purpose to do."

La Valette made no reply. Sir Oliver urged him, in a low tone, which could still be heard by those who sat near: "You must let them speak."

A discussion began in which, while no one urged that they should give up the town, yet they talked of how it could best be done, of how the wounded should be conveyed within St. Angelo's walls, and of other details of such retreat, showing that it must have been thought, and perhaps debated, before.

It went on till the Grand Master could no longer endure. He said: "You will withdraw no yard by my will."

Marshal Couppier spoke, not as one who would argue a course, but as asking the Grand Master a question which would be for him to decide: "There are, in all, twelve hundred men who can stand, or perhaps less. I count some women therewith, and also those I have at the Sanglea. Can you hold the line with that force?"

La Valette was sharp in reply: "Do you, too, counsel retreat?"

"I do not counsel at all. I but seek to know. I have told you what I can do, and how long, on the southern side. But of this side I know less."

"We can hold the line," the Grand Master said, "for we have no choice." He looked round to add: "You have thought of much, but there is one thing you have not observed. Shall we drink of a dry tank?"

There was a moment's silence as they considered this, and saw that there was no answer to make. The castle tank, which collected the winter rain, was of a size sufficient for such a garrison as the castle required and something beyond that. But at this time of the year it was low, as it was likely to be, and now, including wounded and sick, there must be not less than 1,500, besides children, who must be crowded into the citadel walls, unless St. Michael's fort were to be defended apart, which would be separate folly and insufficient relief. They would be dead of thirst in a month, if not less.

They might observe—they might even resent—that the Grand Master's tone had been one of satisfaction, as though the lowness of that tank, which might be death to all who sat there, and many hundreds without, were a special mercy of God: they might feel assured that, had that argument failed, he would have been no less stubborn for his own will. But the fact stood. Retreat to the castle could only be made, if at all, when there were fewer who were yet waiting to die.

De Claremont spoke then, being one who had said little before: "We cannot all drink of that well. We must be equal to hold the town (as we have done to this day) till the Viceroy come. . . . Yet there is much that can be done in two days, if that time be ours, and better now than if the Turks were over the wall. Let the Grand Master take his place in his own state, as he used to be, and let the most precious treasures that the town holds be also conveyed to where they will be more safe than they now are. Let the stores be moved to the castle vaults, and such of the wounded men as cannot walk of themselves, and must be handled with care, be sheltered therein;

and we shall feel, at the worst, that there has been provision made by which some may endure, though the pagans enter the town."

There was some murmur of approval at this, but the Grand Master was not grateful in his reply. "It has," he said, "a most prudent sound; but have you thought that it will hearten the Turks (who will quickly hear) and weaken every arm on our own walls? I should say, if you do that, you will be scaled on the next day. You will make Mustapha right in his date. As for myself, I will stay where I now lodge, where I may still be when the siege is done. . . . But I will tell you that which it will be wiser to do. . . . I will have no men withdrawn to the castle walls. I will send them out to the town. There shall be none that the castle holds by to-morrow noon, save those who handle the guns. . . . If we have strength and time to bear stores therein, or the wounded who can no longer avail, and even the treasures the town contains, will you say that we lack means to make our defences strong? Can we lift all except stones?" His voice rose and shook with the passion that moved his heart, as he said at last: "I tell you we should work as men who blaspheme God, having resolved on our own defeat, which you must see that He does not will."

His passion bore down any opposition there might have been from exhausted men, whose valour was not less than his, though they may have been of a less obstinate faith. The talk turned to the making of a census of all who lived, and allocating them anew, so that there might be equality of strength—or rather of weakness—at every part, with clear order of who should move, and at what stress, to the support of a threatened point. Even the wounded were to be counted in; for, as the Grand Master said, a man may not find it easy to stand, yet he may watch while another sleeps, or be of more active uses than that.

Sir Oliver said that that would be short to do. He had most that would be needed to know in his own records, if not in his own mind.

Marshal Couppier added to that: "It will be shorter yet, for you can leave the Sanglea. I ask naught. I have told you what (or so I think) I can do. But I cannot spare you a man."

"If," the Grand Master began, "it should appear that you have more——"

Marshal Couppier was curt with an interrupting reply: "Then it would prove what you would not be willing to see. . . . If you will hear counsel from me, you will dig trenches where they will shorten your lines. You will fall back, as I do, where you cannot stand, and will not wait to be pushed too hard. It is whether you choose to kill, or yourselves die. It is as simple as that."

La Valette surprised him with a quiet reply. "It is advice I will weigh well."

Marshal Couppier rose. "If you have done, I will back to boil my own pot. . . . Sir Oliver, I would have some words with you before I go."

They talked apart for a few moments on matters of supply at the Sanglea, the Council breaking up the while into little groups of debate. As he went, the Marshal spoke of the Grand Master as one who would see no colour but that which his eyes preferred. He added: "It is he who will save our flag, if a man can. He is of a most stubborn grain. . . . But have you thought there are two?"

"You mean that Mustapha can be as stubborn as he?"

"You are quick to see. You will have had the same thought. . . . Mustapha would not give these two days (of which he was fool to tell) had there not been weary men on both sides of the wall. I should say, if we hold, they are near to break, but I have not said that we can. . . . They have bled much, as we must contrive that they still do. . . . It is good news that Hassan has come back with a drooped tail."

"It had been better had he wasted his strength for no gain."

"He was too careful for that. I call him best of three. . . . Well, I shall have him knocking again. They do not cease at my door. I must get back. Roubles, will you come now?"

De Claremont and De Castriot were also speaking apart. The first said: "I will blow it down if I can. But they build fast. You know what my guns are."

"I cannot hold for a week if they root there. We must face fact."

"It is powder is my most need. Starkey is a Jew about that."

"So he must be. I hear they have scraped the ships. But you must put this plainly to him."

They spoke of the cavalier that the Turks built up to the very face of the breach. Even De Castriot could not think that it would be long held if the stones with which they had piled it up in a loose way were to be blown about from so short a range, with the great guns that the Turks were known to be bringing up.

De Claremont caught Sir Oliver as he was moving away. When he understood what the need was, he gave a frank reply to one whom he knew to be discreet with his own tongue. "It is a great need, as I do not deny. You may have all you can use for two days, besides the ration of course. . . . But I will tell you how we now are. We have powder enough for a month, or perhaps more, if we are frugal in what we fire. If we served our guns as the Turks do, it would be done in six days. I have the most part safe in the vaults here, where it would not be lost, though the town fall in an hour. (You need not tell the Grand Master that. Should he ask, it is his to know). But if you must batter the cavalier, you can have all that you will. You can work your guns night and day for that need."

"I would not ask, were it not a great end, and you will see that it is not for myself."

De Claremont went back to his own place, with a vexed mind. His bastion raked the front of the Castile breach, and his two guns on the northern side were the sole hope of beating down the cavalier which the Turks built. He had a feeling that the advice he had given at the Council had sounded that of a timid man. He saw himself as in a position of safety which might not be equalled elsewhere on the whole length of the wall.

Mustapha might attack at other points of a weak-held line, but, if it were not at the breach, it would be at points far apart. The next bastion was about the last place that he would be likely to choose. It might be said that Castile's weakness made Arragon more sure of a quiet time. De Claremont considered the caprice of Fate, which gave death to one, and to another a quick fame, and to the next to look on in an idle way, though he might not be least as he came (as he surely must) from the imagination of God. He may fret at that, but he should be sure first that he does all that his place permits. . . . As he thought thus, an idea came. . . .

He went back to direct the fire of his two guns, which were served well. They caused the Turks damage and loss, though they had their own ills, drawing the fire of Turkish batteries to which they had no time to reply, by which one was dismounted at last and damaged beyond easy repair. But the cavalier rose, and, as the night came, it could be seen that there was mounting of heavy guns.

CHAPTER LII

"THERE is a name that I do not see."

Angelica was again in Sir Oliver's room. She wrote orders for transfers of men from a schedule he had prepared. Olrig, the last of his scribes, had gone to the wall, come back with a wounded head, gone again when his hurt healed, and was now on the long list of the dead.

"It is your cousin you mean."

"Yes. . . . He is not hurt?"

"When did you see him last?"

"It was three hours ago."

"Then we may suppose not. But there will be no knight left on our English wall. We can spare none now for a place which is not sought by the foe. There will be a woman to sound alarm."

"But he is not on these lists."

"You may suppose that I know that."

She saw that he was not inclined to be more open of speech, and had the sense to wait for what she must soon learn. She saw herself to be posted again to the lazar near the north wall of the town, but, as before, at the call of a sharp need.

She went on with the work she had, and in a short time La Valette entered the room.

Sir Oliver asked: "Would you see these?" showing the schedules of the new orders that would be made, but the Grand Master put them quickly aside. Sir Oliver took up another sheet, that had been under his hand. "There are the thirty here whom I have reserved. . . . Don Francisco is now due."

Angelica heard, with a quick heart-beat she could not still. On what new peril was Francisco now to be sent . . .? But at least she might learn, if she should remain here, as it seemed that she might be permitted to do. She bent to her work, but with her attention on what was said.

The Grand Master paced the room in the way he had when he was troubled in mind. "Oliver," he asked, in an abrupt way, "shall we take the word of that slut?"

"I think in this that we may. For a lie, whether of herself, or being given to her, would have been made in a larger way, and to look more useful to us."

"You think it sounds as of small avail?"

"Of what use can she have thought it to be?"

The Grand Master made no immediate reply. He paced the room again. He broke out: "It may be of the saints themselves, by which they test courage and faith alike, and the scales of God may tremble to rise or fall."

Sir Oliver did not dispute that, though he supposed it might equally be thought a device of devils to detach thirty men whom they could not spare, and whose lack might be the last straw by which they would lose the wall; and this probability did not decrease when he considered the direction from which it came, but he only said: "Well, he should be here soon."

As he spoke, he observed that Angelica had forgotten her work. Their eyes met. She asked: "Is it Venetia again?" Her tone was as though she spoke of an unescapable plague.

"So it is. . . . I suppose you would not trust her at all?"

"Not though she swore by Bethlehem's star, or the manger that cradled Christ. So she told me her code."

"Yet you should hear first."

Her words had drawn the Grand Master's regard. He said: "So you should. You were with her much. You are best to judge."

Angelica saw that whatever cause brought Francisco there, it was not to be hidden from her, and with the thought her cousin entered the room.

He came expecting no more than to take orders in a short way, which he was eager to hear. He was surprised to see not only Sir Oliver but the Grand Master there, and still more when La Valette sat down, as he seldom would when he talked, and pointed him to another chair.

Sir Oliver drew one up for Angelica's use, so that she came from her own desk. They sat round the one table now, and Francisco saw that he must have come to something different from a mere command of where his place would be on the wall, though he could not guess what it could mean.

The Grand Master said: "It is of La Cerda's mistress that we must speak. She is Hassan's now."

To Francisco it was an unwelcome word, besides that it was not what he had expected to hear. Surely that folly was not to be opened again? He had thought it so safely dead. He said foolishly: "She was never mine."

The Grand Master replied in an absent way: "So I am pleased to believe." It was clear that his thoughts were on other things. He added: "Oliver, tell him the tale."

Sir Oliver addressed Angelica equally with her cousin as he began: "The matter is briefly this. There is a slave escaped from the Moors. He is of Ligurian speech. He has scars, old and new, which he could not feign. We think him to be as he says. He tells a tale of one who gave him help to escape, by which Venetia must be meant. He describes her well. He was at work beside the villa where she is lodged. He says she gave him gold and a knife, with which last he slew one he had cause to hate before coming away. With the gold he won free. On his part, he was pledged to bring her message to us, as he truly did. She had charged him to report that a ship loaded with grain is now on the high seas, bound for Marsa Scala Bay, on which provision the Turkish army depends. The message is precise as to the port from which she sailed, and the date due. . . . Now would she do this, and why?"

Francisco found this question hard to resolve, and she was one of whom he was slow to speak in a frank way. While he paused, Angelica asked: "Of what mint were the coins? Did you learn that?"

"They were gold, struck at Ferrera."

"They were of those she had, Francis, from you! They were of some we took from the changers here. The tale has a true sound."

"Even," Sir Oliver smiled, "though you would not trust her at all? Though she would be so lightly foresworn?"

"I say she will lie with ease. She has will and wit, and no conscience at all. But would she not lie in a better way? It sounds that which it is useless to know, we being compassed here as we are."

Francisco objected: "It is not that. It is what Messina would pay to hear."

"Sir Oliver explained: "Your cousin is right in that. It is the kind of tale for which captains will pay, and it might be of much moment to us."

That was simple to see. There were galleys in Sicilian ports that would be quickly loosed at the hope of a fat prize, though they would not be active for war till they should know who would pay their risk, and have either gold in hand or a sure bond.

"I suppose," Angelica said, "she thought we could get message through?"

"So we might. It is still a possible thing. Yet she could not have thought that, for there is no time. For the ship is due in two days, if the winds are kind, as we have known them to be."

"Would she count that?"

"That she would. She was born on Genoa quay."

"Then it is likely true, though it may have no value at all. Would she lay a trap with no better bait?"

"You mean she sends wool, having no silk?"

"So I suppose. Is it of any moment at all—being so near a day?"

"It is nothing, or very much. If we could sink this ship, we should give Mustapha a new reason to go, for the corn will be a great need. But we have first to resolve this—is it lie or trap? For, as you know, she has been used to trap us before."

Francisco said nothing. He was content to let Angelica speak, even though she mentioned how he had used his gold, which he would have preferred to forget. He had been fooled once, to his own shame. It may be excused that he was slow to protest belief for a second time. Yet he thought the tale true, without seeing how it could be of any avail. Had there been time to let Messina know——

Seeing that he would leave it to her, Angelica asked: "How could it be trap to us?"

"It is hard to see, unless she could guess what we are thinking to do, which few would, it having too wild a sound."

"She has a most lively mind."

"She has the devil's help (as we must allow that she may) if she could foresee this."

"What I do not see," the Grand Master—who had been listening to this talk as one who watched for a point which it did not reach—interposed to say, "is why she should seek to help us at all, she being such as we now know her, and her treason naked to us, as she cannot doubt it to be."

Angelica differed there, and was hardy in her reply: "You misconceive from the root up. She would be friends if she could."

"Yet she has gone to a Turk's bed."

"You did not welcome her here. You must weigh that. I can tell you one thing I learnt when I was caught there. She sought a way back that she could not see. She has no love for the Moors."

The Grand Master considered this in an acute mind. He said: "You know her best, as I think, of all here. She is not one you trust, having been caught by her before. If you incline to this tale, I will call it true."

"I should say she believed it true, but it may have been on a poor ground. I will not go beyond that."

The Grand Master spoke in a final way: "We will call it true. . . . The next question is this." He turned to Francisco now, as though Angelica's part were done, and she left his mind. "Can you take the *Curse of Islam* out in the night, avoiding the Turkish fleet, and sink this ship, which you must do as it approaches the Scala Bay? You must not be far out, for a ship is easy to miss on the wide seas, and you must not fail."

"I will do all that I can."

The Grand Master saw the joy of action, of adventure, wake in his eyes, and his voice took a sterner tone. "You must not take this in too light a way. You may lose yourself and your ship, as you are likely to do, but you must not fail. There is but one way that is sure. *You must ram to sink.* Will you do that, though you both drown?"

"Will she have more guns than are mine?"

"You will have none. There is no time to put them aboard, and too many spies. . . . Oliver, you shall explain."

Sir Oliver said: "It is a plan which has been heard by none but we who are now here. It is a risk which is likely death, but it must so stand unless you can offer a better choice.

"You will have thirty men who are seamen proved, and twenty slaves for the oars (which last we can well spare, for they labour ill, and are a curse to guard and feed as we now are). You will go aboard in two hours from now, each man carrying rations and arms, and the boom will be loosed as you cast off from the quay where the *Curse of Islam* is now tied. To take powder and guns aboard were an added risk, for every second's delay after there is stir at the quay will reduce the chance that you find the harbour mouth will be free to pass. But, be that as it may, you are not to fight but to trust to speed.

"We do not know if the grain-ship be armed, nor if it be escorted by ships of war, against which you could not contend, it is a probable guess, had you every gun that your own would bear. But two things are sure. You will not be easy to catch by any ship in the Turkish fleet, if you be once out on the open sea, and the grain-ship will be much slower than you. You must find her first, and then ram to sink, as the Grand Master has said.

"If you aim at that with a single mind, you should not be simple to stay."

Francisco had no better plan to propose. If it were not what at first he had hoped it to be, he allowed no sign to appear. He said: "It is well thought. When the ship is down, we may save ourselves, if we yet can?"

"So we hope that you may."

"There is one thing I will ask. I would have Captain Antonio at my side, where I shall need a good man."

"He is on the list, as it is now drawn."

"Then I have nothing to ask."

"You can be at call in the next hour?"

"Or in less, if you will."

Angelica said: "May I see the list? Is there space for one more?"

Her eyes met Sir Oliver's in a dispute which neither would yield. He said: "There is no space, for the list is closed."

Her eyes went on to La Valette. It was strange to think him the better chance. "Do I ask more than I should?"

"Are you so urgent to go?"

"I am more so than it is easy to say."

"Can you show me cause?"

"It will save a good man for the wall."

"So it will, and you are used to the sea. Oliver, she is in God's hands. We owe her much, as it is. She shall have her way."

Sir Oliver made no further demur. He took the list, and struck out one, Juan Solles, for whom he could find a use. He wrote Angelica's name.

Francisco stood in a doubt. Should he protest? Did he lead her he loved to a sure death? Could he forget that in a selfish joy . . .? He remembered how he had come up through empty halls, which had been filled with a coloured crowd, bright and rich, when he had come to Malta four months before. The Grand Master had done as he said he would. He had emptied St. Angelo's castle of all but those who were serving its guns. Even his own guards had gone from a vacant gate. Who could say that it was not near to its fall, or that Angelica might not remain to a worse and more certain fate? There are graves that are less clean than the sea will give.

"Francis, we must not stand here. We have little time." Her voice had a buoyant tone, as of one who was glad to wake from an evil dream. He felt her hand on his arm. They went out together.

La Valette said: "I send all to death. But there are worse things, as we both know."

It was a ruthless plan, but it was the one which held the best chance of success. He had spared thirty men, when men were his desperate need. They were dead to his use from now, let them live or die. But if the grain-ship should still come into port, they would be a sheer loss, which he must not have.

Two hours later the *Curse of Islam* slipped out of the inner harbour, and the great boom was anchored again. She came out with rapid oars, and sails that felt for the wind. The great harbour was empty and quiet: the night cloudy and dark, except for the gun-flashes that struck inward from every side upon St. Angelo and the Sanglea. Far off, from the Castile breach, the noise of guns was louder than it had been before, showing that the cavalier battery had been got to work; and as the *Curse of Islam* came round to its course for the harbour-mouth the night was lit with a sheet of flame from the further side of the Bourg, and there came a crash of sound that deafened the rumbling noise of the guns.

Captain Antonio said: "They have sprung a new mine at the Castile breach: we may be best where we now are."

But he had made a wrong guess.

CHAPTER LIII

"If we come clear of the harbour-mouth," Captain Antonio said, "I would risk a guess that we get free, being swift and light."

"And," Francisco asked, "does your wisdom say that we shall come clear?"

The little Captain said yes to that, though in a less confident tone. It must hang on the alertness of those whose eyes (if they were open at all) would be turned the opposite way. For the Turks must know that all the ships that the harbour held had been laid up, being stripped of guns and men, and even the powder taken out of their holds. The sole one that had been kept in use, in which Salvago had slipped out to Sicily and back more than once before, had been tied up for the last month at Messina quay.

The Grand Master had been right in judging that the one chance to get clear was to leave at such sudden speed that no sign of preparation could be observed, no rumour surmount the wall, before the *Curse of Islam* should pass the boom.

It might be vain to expect that the mouth of the great harbour would be unwatched. It was known that, night and day, it was patrolled by some of the faster galleys that Candellissa was keeping at sea, and there were the guns of St. Elmo to pass, by which the *Curse of Islam* might be sent to the sea-floor at the first discharge.

But would St. Elmo's gunners stand ready through the night hours beside loaded guns and with their matches alight? It was not a probable fear. St. Elmo would expect warning of the approach of a seaward foe when the fleets would clash in the night, and the guns wake. There would be a watch kept, of course; but if they could be under her guns before suspicion should stir, they might be out of sight, on so dark a night, before they would open fire.

"Yet I should be better pleased," Francisco said, "had I shotted guns at our own bows."

"So should I," Captain Antonio allowed; "for such is the carnal weakness that all must feel who are used to a loaded deck. . . . Yet I will say that the Grand Master is right in that, even for this time; for if we had guns, and came under fire, we should reply, as it would be nature to do, and every flash would show where we are to we know not what other foes.

"What could it avail to us should we rap on St. Elmo's wall or spread death on a Turkish deck? It is our part to take wounds, if we must, in a patient way, and to slip off in the night."

Francisco did not deny that; but he knew that if he had had guns he would have gone on that voyage in a more confident mood, even though his orders might have been what they were. There had been good reason for not waiting to bring them aboard, which could scarcely have been contrived in a secret way, but to call it good in itself was more than he was willing to do.

Yet it made emphatic the purpose for which he sailed and the method he must employ. The sharp bow, fashioned to ram, being the only weapon the galley had, they must close at speed, to shorten the time during which they would be battered without reply; and could he board a well furnished ship, having but a score and a half of men? He saw that the Grand Master's mind would cut straight to its goal in a ruthless way, by which quality failure had been delayed, whether or not they might win to a last success. . . . But he must see that there should be success in this part that rested with him, in which he was resolved that he should not fail by defect of his own will. . . . And his part now must be that of the skulking rat, when the owls are active to seek their prey.

They went down the harbour showing no lights, and keeping as close to the eastern shore as it was wisdom to do on a moonless night. They gave St. Elmo all the distance they could, and though they saw lights on her walls, there was no challenge from her. It would have been hard, at that distance, for the Turks to see that the *Curse of Islam* was not a prowling unit of their own fleet, which they might have said she was almost certain to be.

It was not till the land was falling away at each side of the harbour-mouth that they became aware of the dark shadow of a galley which moved slowly across their way. Its oars were in, and the wind abeam to it, which was fair to them, so that they moved at a better speed.

Captain Antonio, who was conning the ship, must put the helm over in haste, to give it a wider berth. There was no cause of suspicion in that, for had they kept a straight course they would have struck the galley, ramming it in the waist; and that, had they had no larger purpose ahead, they would have been very willing to do. It was a strange chance of the night, such as no scheming would bring.

There were cries from the galley's deck, and shouting of orders which would not have availed, as the *Curse of Islam* came on it out of the night. But she fell off somewhat from the wind, and Captain Antonio handling his ship well, she passed under the poop of the larger vessel, but yet so closely that she could once have been touched with a stretched hand.

There was a man of Malta who had been a slave for ten years, at first in Algiers, and afterwards at the bench of one Dragut's ships, till it had been taken and he released. He had learnt to speak the tongue of the Moors in a native way, and Sir Oliver had put him on the list of the crew to be used at such a meeting as this. Now he answered the shouts that came from the Turkish ship in such a tongue that there would have been no suspicion that they were not one of their own fleet, but that a slave cried from the rowers' bench, giving a warning they could not miss.

There was a challenge shouted over the widening distance of sea, to which there could be no useful reply. Then the oars of the Turkish galley came out in haste. She came round in pursuit, and her guns spoke. She fired at a mark which had become little more than a guess in the dark, and still moving faster than she, so that it was a danger that was soon done; but it had wakened the Turkish fleet.

The *Curse of Islam* could do no more than shape its course away from the land, and trust the darkness to get it free, as at last it did, though it was fired on again from as long a range as the night allowed, from which it took no more hurt than a splintered rail, which an hour would mend.

The dawn found them on a north-westerly course, with Gozo away on the port side, and no sail in sight over the summer blue of a windless sea.

It must be their choice to remain unseen, and their course unguessed, but, beyond that, they were free from a present dread, having no doubt that they were speedy enough to keep far off from a likely foe.

Angelica was early on deck. She was light of heart, having come from that which it was pleasant to leave, to a day of leisure and peace, though she saw that it might be no longer than that; and she was conscious of other things, which, to the young, may be of more value than they. It might be little pleasure to look back, or to look ahead, but the hour was hers.

The day was still cool, though with a menace of heat to come. The sun mounted a cloudless sky.

Francisco had come up a few moments before. He would relieve Captain Antonio, who had been on duty since they had cast off from the quay. The two were talking as she appeared.

She heard Captain Antonio say: "It is one of two, but there is a doubt between them. There must be one to drown. You will flog both, if you will take wisdom from me. When we have loosened their tongues, we shall soon know."

Francisco stood in a frowning doubt. He knew the ruthless code of the inland sea, and that he would not be equal to his command if he let mercy weaken his rule, or failed to subdue himself, with all that he there controlled, to the purpose for which he sailed. It was his mission and his resolve to drive his ship to such goal as would most probably be the deaths of all there, including his own, within two days' time. He would not have scrupled to make an end of the slave whose cry had given alarm to the Turkish ship; but he had some reluctance to order the scourging of an innocent man, as one of the two accused must certainly be.

He knew that hesitation would seem mere weakness to his subordinate in command, and he was not sure that he would be wrong. He could not see it as the strength of one who would not lightly surrender himself, or his independence of will, to the customs to which he came.

He said: "I will see the men."

The slave-master, who was standing await, turned at the order, and went down to the waist to have the two loosed from the bench, and brought up to the poop.

Angelica heard what she did not like. Captain Antonio's words had been plain as she approached, and they were discord to her. Was there no escape from the stench of blood, the horror of death, even for this space of a summer's day, which she thought she had? She was discomfited too by the tone of the greeting her cousin gave. She had not expected more than the situation allowed. She was still Don Garcio: the third officer of the ship. She had not come on deck to be kissed. But his face was a book she knew well, and she was aware (which others would not have seen) that he would have preferred that she were not there.

It was to Antonio that she spoke: "Are we not few enough as we are? Who is to be drowned now?"

"It is no more than he who cried warning last night, when we blundered under the Turk's stern."

She considered this, and was no more pleased than before. "Would you drown him for that? It was no more than nature to do."

"Which it is our nature not to allow." Captain Antonio smiled at the neatness of his retort. "Do you see that it might have brought us to death?"

"From which," she said, "it seems we are never far. Would you grudge us a cloudless day?"

Captain Antonio frowned over this, finding it less easy to understand, and while he paused the slave-master appeared, with the two men between whom suspicion fell.

They came with manacled hands, and were naked for the coming heat of the day, except for loin-clothes of tattered filth.

The one was small, wizened with age, with a stubble of greying hair above a face which might have been that of an ape without requiring a great change. His eyes were reddened by some disease, from which he blinked as one who saw in a mist. His lean muscles must have had some remaining strength, or he would not have been kept alive at a time when there must be no wasting of food.

The other was a much taller and younger man. Misery and toil had not been able to bend his neck, nor to tame the gaze with which he met the little group of officers on the poop. He was lean with the hardships of little food and much work, for St. Angelo's slaves, in recent days, had not been fed as well as those in the Turkish camp; and across his back were the scars of the drivers' whips, confused by that of a wound a flying splinter had dealt, as he had rolled stones to the barricades of the Sanglea a few days before.

Francisco looked at men whom he would have questioned direct, but that he knew nothing of their tongues, nor was it likely that they would know his. He was not ill-taught, knowing (besides his own) the language of Arragon, and to read the three tongues of France; also Italian and Latin to read and speak, and many words of the bastard dialects of the sea; but he felt here an ignorance which he should not have.

He addressed them in the Italian tongue, which they gave no sign that they understood.

"It will do for them," Captain Antonio said, "as well as the devil's patter to which they were bred, for they are fixed that they will not speak. . . . But the slave-master can talk their tongue."

So he could have done himself well enough, but his vanity was reluctant to attempt that which he knew that the slave-master could do much better than he, so that he would listen with critical ears.

Francisco said: "Tell them that silence will be no gain, for we know it was one, and if they are still they will both bleed."

The slave-master repeated this, speaking separately, in different tongues, to the two men; but they remained still. The younger looked about, as one giving no heed to that which he heard. His eyes met Angelica's. She was regarding him as the one who must be destined to die, whom she would have been glad to save. She did not doubt it was he. He had the look of the bolder man. He was likely to have the more voice. He had more to gain if he could win free. . . . She remembered how she had felt as the *Santa Martha* had slipped past her clutching hands. . . . He regarded her in a speculative way, as though judging whether she could be hope for him. His eyes met hers again with a pleading she understood, and to which she dumbly replied. He could not think that there would be much power to aid in a third officer, as he saw her to be, even if there were an improbable will, but he was near to drown, and he clutched a straw. As he looked, his eyes changed to a puzzled doubt which they quickly cleared, and Angelica knew that, with the insight of those who must elbow death, he had put her disguise aside, to see her for what she was.

All this was in an instant of time, while the slave-master said: "They are resolved that they will not speak. Shall I have them tied up for the lash?"

He addressed Captain Antonio, rather than him who was head of all. He meant no offence in that, speaking to the officer who had had the affair in hand at an earlier hour, but Francisco observed it with a sensitive pride. Antonio was the older and more experienced man. It might easily come to be that he would be regarded as the actual captain of the ship, if he himself should prove less equal to the position he held.

Angelica, seeing clearly how the case stood, and with an impulse to save the man if she could, became aware that she must be wary in what she said. She must not act as other than that which she was taken to be, nor so that Francisco's authority would be slurred if he should give her her will. She moved closer to him, as she said, in a low voice: "Francis, will you leave this for an hour's time?"

He heard the urgency in her voice. He asked: "Why, what gain is there in that?"

"I would explain to you apart."

He said: "Take them back to the bench. I will deal with this at a later hour, by which time one may have come to a wiser mind."

When all but the three officers were clear of the poop, he asked: "Why did you wish this delayed?"

"I hoped you would let it be. But I would not plead while others were round to hear."

"But if we do that—can you not see that he brought us all near to death, and the ship lost? If we allow that, how would it be at another chance? There would be a full chorus of who we are."

"It is no more than a wild chance. Would it happen twice?"

"Not, we may suppose, in the same way. But if we are weak with slaves, we are asking for our own throats to be cut. It has been proved before now, both by the Moors and by us, and I would not be one to have to learn it anew."

"It would be a good man lost at the oars, if not two."

"We can make shift to endure that."

"If you owe me aught for past days—which I will not say—I will take this in quittance for all."

"I would do it, you know, for you, without bargain called, but I must put first the duty I have. If I pardon such an offence——"

"Which I do not ask you to do. Let the thing lie. It may be no more than two days and it will matter to none, we being lost or in such triumph that this will be overthought."

As she spoke, a thought came to the minds of both, which she had not meant, of how he had had mercy from such a cup, when he had seemed as surely lost by the hard custom of war. He said: "Well, it can stand for this hour. While they pull on the oars they are gain to us, as you have been shrewd to see. I will do nothing unless I tell you before, but I do not pledge beyond that."

They both knew she had had her way, and were in accord that they had done well.

Captain Antonio, looking on, and hearing all that was said, was discreet to say nothing at all. He went down to his own rest, leaving the two lovers, as he did not doubt them to be, together upon the deck.

When he came up for his next watch the sun was past its height in the sky, and Gozo was the dark line on the horizon behind. The oars were in, and the galley tacking into the wind. She was coming round to a southerly course, meaning to fetch a compass round the islands, and approach Marsa Scala from Malta's southern shore. She was in no haste for this hour, being in that part of her course where she would be least likely to encounter a Turkish ship, and she would make more speed when the darkness fell.

Francisco went below, but Angelica, who was still on deck, was slower to leave. Captain Antonio stood at the poop, looking down into the waist, where the slaves pulled. Angelica came to his side.

"So," he said, "you were potent to let him live. Now will you say why you did that?"

"Him?" she asked. "It was a matter of two."

"But there was one that you were urgent to save."

She considered this. "Did it so appear? Yet I should say you were wrong. I would save two."

"And will you say why?"

"There was once that I came wet from the sea, where I was near to remain."

"You had such logic as that. And there was a time when I could not see you for what you are! I must suppose that my wits failed. . . . But am I bold to ask why you should have come by a way for which you are so unfit, and that not alone by what I know you to be?"

"You would say that I am unfit in a special sense, such as (from what you know) I should not be certain to be?"

"And so you must know you are. Would you not go back if you could?"

"Not a step. . . . I came, as I think, having cause enough."

"Which I should not ask?"

"It is less secret than that. I was too near to a Convent gate."

"Which you would call a great cause? So you came where the dirt was more, and the prayer less."

"It is less simple than that, as I need not say. . . . Nor is it Malta's fault to lack prayer. . . . But I must go below now, for I am to take a watch during the night, which I am equal to do."

Captain Antonio did not question the wisdom of that. He saw that Don Francisco would have them both fresh for the needs of a later hour. Angelica left the deck, and Antonio to his own thoughts, which were on the strange natures and ways of men, and on women the more, and of one most, whom he had come to like and admire.

She had come to that for which she was unfit, by her own word, and which would be likely to end in shame, or a bloody death, which she could have missed for a convent's ease, and she said that she would not go back a step, having come with sufficient cause.

He concluded that she had no love for celibate life. He did not marvel thereat, knowing it to be that which most women will go far to avoid. Venetia would have said the same in another tongue.

Yet to admit that was to marvel with a new cause. He did not doubt that it was for Francisco that she had come, at a peril which was not passed, nor that they had arrived at a common mind. Yet there were two cabins below (being all that the ship had in its after part), of which the smaller had been reserved for Don Garcio's use, and the larger was shared by Don Francisco and himself, "though," he thought, "it is that which his pride will not lightly bear, he being one who will lie alone."

He thought (being their friend) that the cabins could have been better filled. It was as though they should confine themselves by the pretence of a locked door, which they could open at will. And they might go, even now, to tomorrow's death, for which they would be searching with care.

Was there reason in such restraints, until the moment's blessing of life might be snatched back by the jealous gods? Or was it a barren folly of men to deny themselves in that which the kindlier Heavens would not have stayed? Men looked at the open hand of God, and themselves closed it again.

"If it be wisdom," he concluded, "it is not mine. For I would reap while the skies are warm. I would drink, seeing a full cup, and while it stands steady upon the board. Can we take it up, being spilled? Can we go back to a lost day?"

Yet was he sure that they played the game of life by a poor rule? He was less than that. He thought how such as Venetia would jape, mocking that which they lost occasion to do. He looked on at the panorama of life as one may look at a show, and he saw dignity and grace in the control of continent life which such as Venetia could be surely trusted to miss.

He allowed at last that if he were a god, and were peopling heaven, it was among such that he would be likely to choose, and having so come to a verdict of which he was not fully aware, he turned his thought to the horizon which darkened before his eyes, as the sun sank in the backward sky. He had to steer an unlighted ship through the first part of the night, with Gozo on his port bow making a leeward shore, from which the coast lights had been withdrawn at this time of war, and he was content that the night was clear.

CHAPTER LIV

It was four hours after the sun had fallen that Angelica came on deck and Antonio's watch was done.

He said: "You will do well enough, I suppose, for the hours of dark, we being close at call, and there being need of no more than to keep on the present course, for which the helmsman can have your trust, and the present watch, they being men of these seas. You need do no more than to keep the deck, if you will, though (if you prefer to do more) they must be ordered by you."

She answered that she would be content to allow that which went well, without interference from her, and that, if they should give a wide offing to Malta's coasts, she supposed that there was no other danger to fear while they sailed through a lonely sea. He went below, and she remained on a deck where, except in a formal way, she knew that there was no occasion for her to be.

The night-watch consisted of Maltese seamen who could sail the ship on that coast much better than she, and at least as well as Captain Antonio would have been able to do. The night was clear, and a light wind had veered somewhat to the west, making it fairer for them.

She must be alert for the sudden call of a strange sail in the night, but, beyond that, she could fall to her own thoughts. She leaned on the poop-rail, looking backward on a wide wake that shone faintly in the starlit night, and became aware of a sombre fear, which she had refused to feel in the daylight hours.

She had had her day, which was done. A day of quiet peace, during which much had been said on that deck while Captain Antonio rested below, bringing love to a more evident flower. It had been a time during which the pressure of urgent circumstance had relaxed, so that they might have more consciousness of themselves and less of surrounding things, leaving memories which neither would be quick to forget in the after-days. In the after-days? But were they destined to be? For to what were they steering now . . .? It was not that hope should be thrown aside, which it is hard for the young to do. They were seeking a ship that they might not find. There was hope in the core of that, even though they must sail with gunless decks through seas which their foes patrolled. . . . But it was to

Francisco's honour to find that ship, as it must be to Malta's relief. Did she wish him to fail? Either for Malta's need or for his own repute, she would have been slow to say that. The incalculable chances of fate—the unexpected event—she must think of them with what hope she could. . . . And as for Malta, who could say that, let them do all they sought, it might not be too late to avail . . .? She listened for sound of guns which she did not hear. There might be no wonder in that. They must be distant more than ten—perhaps even twenty or thirty miles—from St. Angelo's mortal pain. She could not guess more nearly than that. And the wind was in the wrong quarter to help the sound. . . . She did not know how far that murmur of dreadful noise could be borne over land and sea, but the silence was sinister to her mood. She remembered the rumble, as of a bursting mine, which had come to their ears as they left St. Angelo's quay: the light that had lifted into the sky. Was it already stormed, and those she knew either dead or enduring the ignominy of Turkish chains? Or would it still endure through the coming day—the "Thursday" of Mustapha's insolent warning note? It might well be that they sailed on a useless quest, giving lives that were dear to them, for that which could bring no comfort to those who were already captive or dead. . . . And as she fell in this doubt she became aware, with a quick joy, that Francisco stood at her side.

His hand came on her shoulder first, and as she turned they closed in a strained embrace. She shamed herself with a sudden passion of tears. . . . She gained control of herself, and of lips where kisses had hindered speech, to say: "I am a mere fool. I should not be here. . . . Should you not rest while you can?"

"It was vain to try, remembering where you would be. When he slept, I came up."

He said he would not go down again. He would remain there till the time when he would have been called, and she gone to her own rest. Here were hours of life which they were of accord that they would not lose.

But she crushed emotion down with a steady will. She had not come to weaken resolve, nor to make sorrow he might have missed. She asked: "Are you sure we have time enough? That we need not haste?"

"If—she—have spoken truth on a late day, we have time enough. We must suppose she has, without which we are at no purpose at all. The wind is light, but it moves us on, and must be adverse to them. We can go softly, and rest the slaves."

"Shall you close in to the land?"

"Not at once. It is added risk of our own loss to be there too soon, which would be profit to none. But if we do not quickly find her afloat, I must sail in to view those ships that will be lying in Scala Bay."

"For if it have gone in, there will be no purpose to stay?"

"I did not mean that. It maybe we can ram it there while it will still have cargo to spill."

She had gained that to which she had thought to steer, for he forgot themselves as he spoke of the plans he had, and showed the hard resolve he had formed that he would not fail. She saw that he lost thought of himself—even of her—in the vision of that which he was pledged to attempt, and which he believed that he would be equal to do.

To help Malta at desperate need—to destroy that which would sustain her blood-lusting foes—there was impulse, conscious and strong, and sufficient in itself to have called him to throw his life in the trembling scale; but, beyond that, there were the supporting passions of honour and pride, calling him to vindication of what he had been before, and to the narrow moment of fame that success would bring.

He had done a great thing before by his secret guns, but it might be said that it was only through a fortunate chance that the occasion had come; and that event was confused with others which might have brought him to final shame.

He had done his part in conveying the Grand Master's message to Marshal Couppier, and in guiding him back through the Turkish lines; but—to be a messenger and a guide? It is no high ambition that will be so content, though the message be truly borne, the guidance skilfully done.

Perhaps his greatest exploit had been when he had gone, at the double calls of damaged honour and dawning love, to seek and save from the midst of a thousand foes. But that was private to him and her. That was the price at which he made betrayal a memory tolerable to endure.

But if he could now serve Malta a third and more excellent way, putting his unarmed prow into the vitals of the approaching ship, and bringing privation to her pitiless and exultant foes, he saw that the past must be forgotten in that result, or remembered only so far as it would support his praise.

In the impulse of these mingled motives, urged by the sanguine spirit of youth, he could look to the time when he would drive his prow in the grain-ship's side without too close regard of where he would be likely to be on the next day.

The words of Captain Antonio's somewhat sententious wisdom came back to his mind: "*I have seen many wars, and . . . there is one thing that has never changed. The men who lead at the first will not be there when the triumph sounds and the bells ring. They will be forgotten or cursed. They will be shamed or else dead.*"

Well, if there were no choice beyond that, then death was surely the fairer end. But under the sombre thought there beat the buoyant spirit of youth, and a heart that rejected fear.

CHAPTER LV

CAPTAIN ANTONIO looked at a boat. It was a large boat for the ship's size, or so it would have been viewed by seamen of later times, being designed to take in all the lives of the crew, the slaves falling outside the count. It lay amidships, behind the mast on the low deck of the waist. There were the rowers' benches on either side, and inside of these were two raised gangways of two-foot breadths, running from poop to fore, along which the slave-drivers would parade with whips of sufficient length to reach to the backs they sought; and midmost, between these, there lay the great boat, the lashings of which could be cast loose, or cut at a sharp need. So that, if the ship should sink, in the slow manner of those which are built wholly of wood, the boat would be floated off, even while forecastle and poop might still be high over the waves.

Within the boat was a small skiff, which would be used if an officer should be requiring to go ashore while they were anchored in harbour, or for passing from ship to ship, but which would be thrown aside at a greater need. This was the accommodation which was common in the galleys of that day.

Captain Antonio looked with a careful eye at the lashings which held the boat, and at the gear, the beakers of water, and the provisions which it contained. He might not suppose it probable that it would be a means of life to those who now trod the *Curse of Islam's* decks, but he was thorough in all he did.

In the ship's arsenal there were hand-weapons enough, though she had sailed without mounting of guns; and he had distributed these with the same care, giving to each man those which he was best able to use, and making their duties clear. There were those who must stand by to handle the ship; and others who were to gather upon the prow when the moment came, either to board, or to resist attack upon their own decks; and there were four whom he found to be expert with the cross-bow, who were to be stationed where they would be sheltered themselves, and well placed to shoot over the prow.

Having seen that the great boat was garnished, and would not be delayed in floating clear at a sudden need, he made his way back to the poop, from where Angelica had been observing that which he did. She asked: "Do you count that we may find safety there?"

"It is less than that, but I am one to regard all, lest we come to death by a missed chance, which I would not have. There was a time when I came free by the help of night and a good boat, from a sinking wreck, as those who meant us no good had supposed that we could not do."

"You think we may sink their ship and yet save ourselves?"

"So we may. Though we have done neither as yet, which is the more likely end. . . . If we find her, I suppose that she may go down, and that we shall be in less than a good shape when we have brought her to that. But it is the escort which she may have which we should hold most greatly in fear. . . . If we talk of that we can do no more than to guess, and those who guess what the sea will give are sure of naught, except that they will guess wrong."

It was on Friday morning that this was said. The sun had but just cleared the sea. The night had been windless and warm. Now a light breeze came from the south, but bringing no clouds to the bare blue of the sky, so that the heat of the last week was not likely to decrease with the coming day.

They had sailed far out across the track by which the grain-ship would come, and had approached Marsa Scala as the last evening had waned. Until then they had seen no more than distant sails, which were not those of the ship they sought, and which, if they had surveyed themselves with enquiring eyes, had seen no reason to doubt the Turkish flag which they now flew, or had refused the folly of pursuit of a distant galliot which was plainly faster then they, and would only remain if it were what it professed, and content to be overhauled.

As the dusk fell they had looked audaciously into Scala Bay, going close enough to be assured that the *Flooded Nile*, which was the name the grain-ship was said to bear, had not come to anchor therein. They had gone about as though sailing up the coast to put in at Marsa Scirocco, or St. Thomas's Bay, which was not what a Christian vessel, of their size and alone, would be likely to do.

After that they had cruised backward and forward during the night across the path by which the grain-ship must come, and now, as the dawn had risen, they had so far avoided the land that they might hope to have escaped observation therefrom, but yet remaining so that they would surely observe any sail that might enter the harbour-mouth.

Through the last day they had been near enough at times to hear the low reverberation of the guns that battered St. Angelo's walls, from which they must take what courage the knowledge gave that it had not fallen before Mustapha's appointed day; and what of resolve might come from the thought of its urgent need, which they might do some part to relieve.

Now, in the morning silence, there was no proof that it still endured. Had Mustapha equalled his boast that Thursday would be the end, or had the stubborn courage that the Grand Master felt and inspired been sufficient to throw the Turks back once more to die in the blood-drenched fosse? Was the town still under Christian flag, or were there but a remnant of survivors cooped up in St. Angelo's central towers? It was vain to wonder or ask. They had their own part to play, and must look away from that which they were powerless to change.

And while they watched, the *Flooded Nile* was coming in from the west, with two of the strongest galliots of Piali's fleet, which had met her a hundred miles out at sea, as her escort on either side.

The *Flooded Nile* was a ship built for the bearing of grain. Her hull was deep and large, and her oar-deck high for that space, so that her sweeps were long, and must each be pulled by three men. She was a three-masted ship, and trusted less to her oars than to the wide spread of sail that she could open to friendly winds. Now she came to the end of a perilous voyage which had shown no threat of pirate or storm on the blue of a summer sea, seeing the coast-line of Malta on the horizon faintly ahead. The two galliots that had her in charge can have little blame that they thought that their task was done. They had orders to guide her in, and to join Piali's fleet in Muscetto Bay when they had done this. To this end, they began to draw slowly apart, steering a more northerly course, while she kept straight ahead for Marsa Scala, where her cargo should be discharged.

The captain of the galliots was not less assured that he had brought the *Flooded Nile* safely through the dangers of seas in which Christian pirates were not easy to miss because he saw a small vessel flying the Turkish flag, and drifting lazily northward, as though content that it should move by the way that the wind preferred, and at the pace its lightness allowed, with no more than a mainsail spread. In that sea, on that day, seeing it loiter along, it would seem absurd to suppose it other than one of the hundred-and-eighty sail that were round the island under Piali's command.

The *Flooded Nile* carried a crew of 130 men, besides slaves at the oars. She had four heavy fore-deck guns, and two sakers pointing astern from the lower deck of the poop, where the fighting galleys would be less likely to mount their guns, but she was equipped to spit back at a foe's pursuit.

Her slaves had been driven hard during the night and the last day, and were now sprawled asleep on the benches where they were chained, taking such short rest as their drivers willed, till the whips' cracks should rouse them again, to take the ship through the harbour-mouth. She came slowly on, with close-hauled canvas to use the breeze for her own way.

"It is the mercy of all the saints," Captain Antonio said. "She comes like a pig that pushes open the door where the butcher waits."

Francisco made no answer to that. He looked at the grain-ship's size with a doubt that he would not speak. He had heard much talk of the ramming of ships, by which way the galleys would still trust to resolve a fight, rather than in the cannon upon their decks. It was for that use they were built, with great height and sharpness of metal prows; it was for the clashing of that event that their crews were trained. It was that moment of battle that the chained slaves had most cause to dread, for it might send one ship, if not two, reeling down to the ocean-floor, with them helpless in padlocked chains. . . .

These were matters of which Francisco had heard much talk. There was much that he had been taught. But it is different to see. He knew that Antonio, though he might be under his command, as the difference of rank required, had a long experience of the fighting ways of the sea. He had seen ships rammed, and go down or survive as the Fates allowed. If he looked content, it could scarcely be less than well, and his expression was that of one to whom fortune brings more than his hope proposed.

Yet Captain Antonio looked all sides as they drifted on, and when he saw a galley, with spread of sail and pressure of oars, come out of St. Thomas's Bay, he said: "So it would be. It was beyond reason to hope. . . . Yet I suppose we shall have our will, and the Grand Master will bless our graves."

Up to that moment they had avoided all which might draw suspicion upon themselves. They had even cast off their own garments, above their shirts, lest keen eyes should see that the poop was held by those who wore doublets in Christian style. There were men stationed upon the fore clothed in the loose linen garb that the Turkish seamen preferred. Every second was an added prize as they came nearer their prey, and its escort drew further apart.

"If," Captain Antonio said, "you will take wisdom from me, you will turn to speed, and let caution go."

"So," Francisco replied, "I was thinking to do," and, as he spoke, a gun sounded from the ship which was coming out of the bay.

It was a shot that they were in no range to receive, but it was unlikely that it was intended for them. Its import was that suspicion had been aroused, and that the *Flooded Nile* and her escort were to be waked to alarm; and its effect was instant to see.

The grain-ship stirred to a sudden tremor of life: the two warships came quickly round, like dogs that have strayed too far from the flock when the wolf-pack howls. The *Curse of Islam* cast caution aside. Its sails opened in haste. The whips swung over the rowers' backs. Under the urge of a freshening wind it came fast on its cumbrous prey.

The *Flooded Nile* was futile in blundering effort to avoid that which she was not destined to miss. Her helm went up and then down. But the *Curse of Islam* was first alert, and the fatal seconds were hers. She had the wind at her back, and she could turn more quickly to strike than could the heavier vessel to dodge the blow.

There came a moment when Angelica, standing by Captain Antonio on the poop, saw that they were about to strike their victim amidships with the full force of their driven prow.

As she watched for the crash of impact to come, she was scarcely aware that two of the grain-ship's guns had found time and direction in which to fire, and that a round-shot came over the heads of the straining slaves, to crash through the cabin beneath her feet.

Francisco had gone forward to order those who were gathered to guard the prow. Captain Antonio was left to handle the ship, as he was well able to do. In the last minute, as it became plain that the collision could not be shunned, he directed Angelica how best to hold to the rail, and use the support of a rope's loop, that she should not be cast down to the deck, taking the same precaution himself, as she saw that others did, except only the slaves and those who still lashed them to pull.

The *Flooded Nile* was so much the larger ship, and was built with so high a waist, that their rowers' benches were not greatly below the peak of the Christian prow. Francisco could look into the eyes of men of his own blood, chained to benches through which it drove. It drove through crashing timbers, and cries and blood, and underneath, as the harpoon enters the whale, the sharp ram thrust into the vitals of the great ship, tearing a fatal wound.

The *Curse of Islam* reversed its oars. It strove to back from a wound that it helped to close while it remained wedged as it was and from the danger that it might be drawn down to a common doom if it should be unable to break away.

On the grain-ship, confusion spread. There were men who crowded to clear the boat. There was a gun-crew who remained gallantly at their post, firing, as fast as they were able to load, down on to the Christian decks. The chained slaves shouted, and struggled to break their bonds.

From the Turkish poop, a green-turbaned officer ran forward, calling on all to follow the way he led. He aimed to gain the deck of the *Curse of Islam* before it would be able to draw apart, for he saw that revenge and safety pointed to the same road.

There was a time during which Angelica saw that the two ships remained locked, and were sinking, inch by inch, lower into the sea. The slaves needed no urging now, as they pushed oars in an effort to part the ships on which their lives might depend, and with the added boon of freedom in view, for they saw that the Christian vessel, if it should float, would soon pass from Christian control. There were other Turkish warships in sight, besides the three which were nearing now. At the cannon's call, they had come from Marsa Scala and St. Thomas Bay, and from the spaces of empty sea, as vultures show in the sky when a camel falls.

Angelica had no eyes for them, watching how the Turks swarmed round the prow where Francisco stood. They clambered up on all sides, and there was no relief through those whom the bowmen slew, for there would be ten others pressing behind.

With sword and dagger, with pike and axe, Francisco and the twenty men that were his thrust and hacked to throw them back from the deck that they strove to scale; but they lacked numbers for that. Soon there was a wave of Turks that surged over the side. Pressed ever by those behind, they gained space on the deck, the Christians falling back, yard by yard, amid a clamour of blows and cries.

Captain Antonio looked at that which he did not like. He had had a plan in his mind by which he would have said that there might still be a chance of life for a fortuned few, if the ships had parted at once. But this was thwarting it in two ways. If the Turks should win the ship there would be no hope, even though the next moment should find them moving apart.

He drew out his sword. He said to Angelica: "If we wrench free, you must drive for land. We are swift enough, if the oars ply, and the masts are not shot away. We must beach the ship. There s no chance besides that."

He ran forward along the gangway, calling to those who had been working the ship to join the strife at the bloody prow.

Angelica stood alone on the poop. She watched Antonio pause a moment in the rear of the fighting crowd, and then push in, using his sword in a cool and purposeful way, as one to whom strife was a trade that he understood. She saw Francisco also, still, as it seemed, unhurt, where there had been many who fell. His defensive armour, lightly made, as was the new fashion of war, and useless against an arquebus ball, was yet of good avail in such a turmoil as this: his sword kept his head with a well-taught skill. Yet it seemed that it must be but a short time before resistance must end, and the Turkish wave sweep forward to overwhelm. . . . And then the *Curse of Islam* drew clear of its stricken prey.

As it did so, the grain-ship sank down on its gored side till the decks dipped to the sea. There was a moment when the height of its masts sloped over those of the smaller ship, and their shrouds tangled and snapped.

On the fore-deck, the outnumbered Christians renewed their hope, and smote with a better will, as they saw that they need deal with no further foes than were already upon their board. But at the same time the foremost of the two escorting warships, whose error had brought disaster to that which they were appointed to guard, opened fire from her forward guns.

Whether it were from the wounds they gave, which, at so short a range, the *Curse of Islam* was frail to take, or whether she may have rammed her foe with such force that her own timbers had strained apart, it was plain to see that, though she might not be the first to go, she also was settling into the sea.

Angelica, standing alone on a poop from where there would have been few to heed, had she been competent to command at such a moment as that, said to herself: "I do nothing here. It is vain to stay. I watch a strife which may turn on a single sword." She drew her own, and went forward along the gangway, beside the slaves on the starboard side.

As she went, she came to a new thing. A round-shot had struck the slave-master as he walked the planks, he being one of the few who had kept his post, as his duty was, letting the fore-deck strife go its own way. The shot flung him, a quivering corpse, on to the heads of the two slaves whom he had brought up for judgment on the morning before.

The younger man flung off a body from which the entrails were falling loose, and snatched at the master-keys that his belt bore.

He was so chained to the bench that he could not reach round to release himself, but he was able to bend aside, and use them for setting his comrade free. The man, having gained his limbs, stooped to do the same office for him, as Angelica came forward along the planks. He rose from that to see her feet a yard away from his own head. With a cackle of evil mirth, he reached at them to pull her down. But he was less nimble than she. The clutching hands winced back from the sword's point, and as she pricked them she heard the shouts of the slaves behind, among whom the keys had been passed, clamouring for the freedom that they could give.

She thought: "Francis will be sped with these slaves at his back," and as her eyes met those of the man who clutched at her feet, malign with hatred for all Christian men, whose scourgings had brought him to what he was, she thrust down with a steady hand. The man drew his head quickly aside, but with no gain to his life, the thin blade driving between shoulder and neck with a force she did not scruple to use, as she had done at a former time. She had gone far since that night, but whether nearer to Heaven or Hell it might be hard for human judgment to say.

The man screamed as he sank and the sword came free; and as he did so she knew the voice. It was he, and not whom she had thought before, who had given the warning call in the dark, as they had passed under the galley's stern.

She had no time to consider that, being caught in a different grip from what she could have felt from his ageing hands. The younger slave had her sword-hand's wrist in a grasp that she could not loose. Struggling, she lost balance, and was pulled down from the plank. The memory of how she had been captured before, added to the desire she had to reach to Francisco's side, gave a frantic strength to the struggles with which she fought in the arms of the naked slave. But his grip did not relax. His muscles, hardened by the labour of the bench, were like inflexible steel. He looked at her with mocking eyes, as he twisted the sword from a hand that she could not use. She found that he could speak the Italian tongue, when he had a mind to be understood. "Why," he said, "what a writhing leopard you are."

He bore her to the great boat, and thrust her down under the thwarts. He said: "You are fool to kick. You may live if you lie still. I have a debt that I think to pay."

He drew her hands together behind her back, and bound them with a short cord, doing all in a way that was swift and sure.

As he did this, he looked down on her in a way that she did not like, and she became aware that the ruffed shirt she wore had been torn away, as she had struggled to break his hold. A bare breast made demonstration of what she was.

He cast a piece of sail-cloth over her, so that there was little that she could see. "Now," she heard his voice, "you will lie still, unless you are more fool than you look to be."

She heard the noise of the slaves crowding into the boat, with a clamour of tongues that she did not know. She supposed that he had moved away on his own affairs. She lay as still as the dead, even when she was kicked in a painful way.

She heard the oars go overside, and felt the boat lift to waves that now swept the deck. It rose, bumping against the mast, and over the raffle that strewed the deck. It was washed over the empty benches, jarred on the low bulwark of the waist, and was out on a clear sea.

There came a voice from on high in a strange tongue, to which answers were shouted back. She could but guess that they had passed under the stern of one of the Turkish ships, who had required assurance of those whom the boat held. After that the slaves pulled with a steady stroke.

CHAPTER LVI

FRANCISCO thrust at the back of a flying man, who plunged over the prow. He looked round to find that he stood alone on a sinking deck. Above him, high out of the water, rose the grain-ship's stern. She was going down by the head, and now rose to her final dive.

He looked round on a deck strewn with the dead, and where wounded men crawled for a safety they would not find. Captain Antonio lay on his face. From beneath him, the blood spread. Francisco knelt at his side. At his touch, the dying man lifted his head. He rose on one hand.

He said: "So you live?" His eyes went down to the waist, over which the sea washed. Francisco saw that the great boat was in the hands of the ship's slaves, who were staving it clear of the mast, so that it would float free on the next wave. His eyes went to the poop, to see that Angelica was not there.

Antonio answered his thought. "They have her there, in that boat. It was he she saved." His words were faint, for which he made his excuse. "I lack blood." His head sank. Francisco thought he was dead.

The *Flooded Nile* plunged to her end, and the *Curse of Islam* leaned to the hollow grave, so that Francisco was flung roughly against the rail. He thought her about to go by the same road, but she steadied again, though she was lower than she had been before. He saw the boat tossing on the further side, having floated clear.

One of the galliots was coming close alongside to where he stood irresolute on a sinking deck, on which there was no other erect, if there were any that lived. She fired down at the foundered wreck, as though impatient to make an end. She was the second of the escorting ships, which had failed beyond likely pardon in that which they had been commissioned to do. Her captain may not have wished to go back to port with guns which had not been used.

Francisco looked at the line of the distant coast. He had a doubt that he could swim so far after the toil of the last hour. He looked at the boat where he had been told that Angelica lay, now pulling steadily for the land, and the doubt left his mind.

He stripped off the tattered shirt which he had worn for earlier disguise over his corselet of steel. He cut the corselet lacings down with his dagger's point, being hastened in what he did by a ball which splintered the woodwork a yard away. It would be a poor end to be shot there, while Angelica was the spoil of a Turkish slave.

Having cast the most that he wore, he dived into the sea that had now risen near to the height of the upper deck. As he swam, he became aware that the Turkish sharp-shooters were still making him a target to prove their skill. He dived at that, and the marksmen searched in vain for a head which was no longer above the waves. They concluded that they had shot well, and made some boasting of that, on a ship where boasting was little heard.

Captain Antonio had lifted his head again as the grain-ship plunged to her grave. His lips moved to a smile. He had not the woe of most, to whom failure comes as the companion of death.

He knew that it was not to him that the praise would be loudly paid; but there were those of the sea. He would have good words from the men who knew.

As he smiled, he thought that he spoke aloud, though it would not have been easy to hear: "The Grand Master should be content. He will give thanks to God, and to us but a short regard, or else none."

He crossed himself with a dying hand, having a faith which was sure, though to some its foundations might seem to be weakly laid. After that, he lay still. He did not stir, even when the sea washed over the deck. He was not dead, but his mind dwelt in a day which was real to him as the deck upon which he lay amid the glitter of sunlit sea. . . . He watched the outgoing ships and the sinking sun on the Genoa quay, until his mother found him and bore him in; as some will say that God is unequal to do.

But our concern is with those in whom the trouble of life was not done, of whom Francisco swam through waters that were quiet and warm, and with such purpose to drive him on as left little regard for the length of way, or the weariness that he would have felt at a lighter need; and Angelica lay where she had been thrust, in fear that she might find it no gain to draw observation upon herself, until the boat grounded on a rough beach, and she was uncovered, and pulled erect, by the same slave who had caught her and bound her hands.

Marsa Scala, at this time, was a busy place, being a back-door to the Turkish camp, at which there was much unloading of stores, both of official source, and those which the trading vessels found it good profit to bring.

Merchants' and camp-followers' tents spread widely around the few houses that bordered the narrow bay. Its waters were alive with war-galleys and merchant-vessels busily unloading into boats, if they could find no vacant space at a short quay, which had not been built for such needs.

It was stirred now by the excitement of a sea-fight of which there had been no more than a distant view, and as to the nature and issue of which it could make no more than a poor guess.

The port-officer, a grave, black-bearded man, spendid in crimson and blue, met the boat with a file of guards, who held back the curious crowd with show of pikes that they would not have scrupled to use. He learned no more from his questions than that two ships had been sunk, of which one was a Maltese foe, the slaves of which had been fortunate to come free, as they seldom did from such loss. They did not know the name of the Turkish ship, nor had they any guess of the priceless cargo she bore.

The officer thought it a good tale enough, of which there would be detail to come. His present duty would be to provide for the escaped slaves, who would not all be of the same nation or grade, or requiring the same treatment from him. There might even be Christians among them, put to the bench for some military or criminal cause, who would find they had made no more change than to harder toil and more prodigal stripes. But each man must be examined, his veracity scrutinised, and his treatment graded thereby.

As they came from the boat he gave short questions to each, which were recorded by an officer at his side, and which would be extended and checked at a later hour. In the meantime, there would be provision made for their comfort, including clothing and food, but to say that they could go free would be beyond probable fact, which none, having a conscience at ease, would be likely to put to proof.

Angelica's captor came from the boat leading her by the rope's end which fastened her wrists, and having lifted her to the land in a way she could not resist, being so bound, and to resent would have been folly she would not show.

She had cause to be glad that the crowd were held back by the armed guard, as she heard the chorus of cries, derisive or fierce with hate, which her appearance roused, as she was led thus, wearing the trunk-hose of a man, and with her doublet so torn away as to show the lie that her clothing was.

The port-officer asked: "What have you got there?" He did not wait for an answer, for which there seemed little need. He supposed that he looked on the shameless concubine of the captain of the sunk ship, for whom, if she should prove to be of saleable sort, a different owner must now be found.

He saw something which should be profit to him, being of the perquisites of the post he held, or at least to be shared with others higher than he, with a gold piece (or perhaps two) for the slave who had brought her to land.

He called one of his train to take charge of a merchandise which showed promise of a good price to his practised eye.

The ex-slave did not loosen his grip on the rope. He looked at the port-officer as coolly as though unaware that a soiled loin-cloth was all the finery that he wore. He said: "It is help which I do not need."

The officer's dignity did not flinch. "That," he said, as one whom insolence could not disturb, coming from such a distance below, "is for me to judge."

The answer came with contempt: "So it is; and if you err you must think that your back must pay."

The officer mastered his first wrath, being a discreet and capable man, though he was one to make any place he held lucrative both to himself and those who gave him support. He answered: "I do my part here, in the trust I have, and those who show me contempt do not give abuse only to me, but also to Him in whose name I have authority here, to Whom I am but the dirt on a hog's foot."

The man who had come from the slaves' bench looked down on him who was in crimson and blue (being some inches taller than he), and laughter lightened his eyes. "Now who," he asked, "do you call hog by that word?"

At this question, the officer paled somewhat under his beard, seeing an implication in what he said which he had not meant, and which might be twisted into that through which a good man's neck may feel the executioner's sword. His reply paused. The man was a very insolent rogue, whom he hoped to send to the lash before the sun should be down the sky. But to show that thought, till he was more sure of whom he might be, was a peril his prudence did not permit.

"You misconceive," he said, "in a strange way. I spoke of none but myself, whom I did not boast. But will you say who you are?"

"I am Prince Azov, of whom, among other things, it should be your business to know."

The port-officer stared, letting his dignity go. It was an audacious, incredible claim. Yet, if he were Soliman's nephew indeed, he might crush him, as a man cracks a flea, and forgets next moment what he has done. And if the man made a claim so monstrous which could not stand, his end must be swift and sure and of a nature to content his most bitter foe.

He saw that it was wiser to make mistake, if mistake he must, on the credulous side, and his answer was adroit with the skill of speech which had brought him to where he stood.

"Your Excellency's wisdom may not deny that it is to the protection of those who are of the Prophet's blood that to claim that honour without a proof should not be lightly allowed."

"I can see," the ex-slave replied, "that you are a more discreet man than you gave me cause to think at the first. Does Mustapha—is the Pasha of Egypt here? Then you shall take me to him, by whom you will find I am better known. . . . But I will have a garment which you can spare."

The officer saw that his eyes were fixed on his own gay attire in a way which he did not venture to disregard. He surrendered it with an obeisance that hid the mingled anger and fear that confused his thoughts.

He gave a whispered charge to the captain of his guard to escort the man to Mustapha's headquarters with all the honour due to the rank he claimed. "Abate naught," he said, "for it is on that that our lives may hang. But should he show lack of courage as he gets near—should he prove"—he would have liked to say 'the knave that I hope he is' but that discretion hindered his tongue—"should he prove less than he claims, which must be thought the more probable end, you must make it clear that I have but sent him for His Excellency to deal himself with a most impudent claim. And should he attempt to avoid, either right or left, you will deny him a yard, having no fear; for it is what, if he be that which he claims, he would be unlikely to try."

It came from this that the Prince stood in Mustapha's presence within the next hour, with Angelica still at his side. And that he was such there could be no longer a doubt, when the Egyptian Pasha rose to give him the seat which would put himself in a second place. For it was that which he would have done for five of all that the world held, but not more among living men.

The Pasha was resting in his own house, after the fatigues of the assault of the last day, in which he had taken a more strenuous part than his years were equal to bear.

"I am amazed," he said, "to meet your Highness in such a way, but we may conclude it to be of the dispensation of God that one of the Prophet's blood should be with us now, to observe the end of this pestilent pirates' nest, which we chastise to His will, and the Sultan's praise."

"I am not newly arrived," the Prince answered to this, "it having been Allah's will that I should observe the siege from its first hour. But I may conclude from what you have said that the pirates' nest did not fall on the set day."

There was a hint of sarcasm in this, veiled though it might be in a courtesy of enquiring tone, at which Mustapha felt a resentment he must now show. He answered: "It has not yet come to its last pain, but its state is like to his who bleeds white from so many wounds that it is hard to pick that which may claim his death. Yet is it sure that he will die of all, if not one. . . . It will fall, as I do not doubt, at a near hour, and our travail is almost done. . . . Hassan has the Sanglea till he is near to St. Michael's fort. As he advances, he treads it flat. . . . But will you tell me how you have come, and by what means you have been at the siege for so long a time? And will you not choose that your captive be taken in other charge, than to be led by your own hand?"

Mustapha, having had no explanation as yet, asked the first question with a suspicion that vexed his mind. He knew Soliman's nephew to be one of a romantic repute. He would disappear at times for months, during which his own household did not know where he might be. He was supposed to wander disguised at such times, seeing the ways of the world, after the way of Haroun in the ancient tales. Had his own caprice, or the Sultan's will (which would be much worse) arranged that he should be so present at Malta's siege, as a secret spy upon those who held a command to which success was not quick to come? And to denounce the errors which are so easy to find in the actions of those who fail? It was not a pleasant thought when he considered the waste of life and treasure, the blunders and vacillations which had marked the four months' struggle, against a numerically contemptible foe.

The Prince answered the last question first. He looked at Angelica, around whom he had cast, with a careless hand, a loose upper garment taken from one of the port-officer's retinue, and who now sat on the cushions beside his feet, as the rope's shortness gave her no choice but to do. He said: "She being my present wealth, I will keep her here."

Mustapha asked: "She?"

"There are pointing signs. It will be known when I further explore, as I am likely to do."

"It will be your pleasure to tell me how you have come?"

"It is soon said. I was a caught slave, at work on St. Elmo's redoubt, a week before you were here. I have toiled thus with a shut mouth, lest they should boast whom they had got, at St. Angelo's walls, which I had cause to observe that you battered well, until three days past, when I was put to the bench of an oared boat that slipped from the harbour there, and Piali was too clumsy to catch."

"It was that one, I suppose," Mustapha replied, "which came under the galleys' fire at the harbour mouth. There was some talk that it had been sunk, which I took to be boast or lie. But we learnt on the next day (for there is not much that our spies miss) that it was for Palermo, to beg again for aid which is not likely to come."

"You have spies you trust, and they brought you that? I should say it was a tale the Grand Master gave them to tell. It was our mission to round the isles and sink a ship that was destined here. It was fat with corn, if my eyes were good when its belly slit."

Mustapha heard this with a sudden fear that his practised composure hardly controlled. His hand clutched at his beard in a sudden way.

"Is the grain-ship gone? It is evil news, if it be. For it was the most need that we have."

"Then you may suppose they knew that. For it was with a set purpose they sailed, as was clear to see."

"It is Allah's will. We must make shift to endure. . . . There was cargo of corn, and 300 sacks of the finest flour. . . . It is well that the end is near."

They were interrupted at this point by the arrival of food and wine, which Mustapha had ordered as soon as he was aware of his visitor's rank and the ordeal from which he came.

Prince Azov looked down at his captive's hands. He used the Italian tongue, speaking the first words she had understood since she had been pulled down to his feet. "Will you have sense to be quiet here, if I loose you now?"

"So you said that I had. Was I not quiet in the boat?"

"So you were. You must surely eat, or you will be of a poor use, either to keep or to trade."

She said boldly: "We must talk of that at a better time." She felt him to be an incalculable danger, which she would be fool if she did not fear, but she did not see the cold loathing that Mustapha showed to all of her race or creed, nor would he have the special hatred that Hassan felt. He had talked of a debt which it had been his purpose to pay.

And she saw him now in an inexplicable, bewildering light. It had been strange enough when the port-officer stripped, but that he should turn Mustapha out of his own seat——!

She had had some natural wonder at that, but her mind, as she had sat beneath a flow of words that had no meaning for her, had been possessed by a more urgent doubt, and a more urgent desire.

It had been agreed between Francisco and her, when they had seen the grain-ship's approach and how near to land the event was likely to be, that they should swim for shore if they should be alive when their work was done. She had seen Francisco alive on the fore-deck as she had fought in her captor's arms. That had been near to the end. He had done his work. He would have no scruple of that. She would shut no hope from her heart. . . . But how could she bring him to know that she still lived, and was for rescue again?

Her captor made no further reply. He set her free from the rope. He saw that she was served well. He even regarded her wrists, that were swollen and numbed. He said: "It is what we all feel in our turn. They will soon heal. It is the fortune of war."

She felt that she was in the hands of one who might be less than a foe, and then her comfort turned to a sudden fear, for Hassan's voice sounded without the door.

CHAPTER LVII

Hassan had ridden over on hearing news of the grain-ship's loss. He supposed that he would be first with a tale that Mustapha would not welcome to hear, but which should not wait. He brought details that Prince Azov had not been able to give; but he found two there whom he had not expected to see, and that there was more to learn than to tell.

He knew the Prince by repute, of whom he thought well, as he was also esteemed by him. They met for the first time, in a very cordial way. At Angelica, he gave one glance, and his eyes did not regard her again. She would have been glad to think she was overlooked, but that one glance had been enough to deny hope. She could but wish she could understand talk which might be of much value to know, though, for a time that was long to wait, there was no sign that they thought of her.

They talked first of the grain-ship's loss, on which Hassan said that there was corn in hand to feed the army for six days, or for eight if the rations were somewhat cut. He proposed that vessels should sail before night for Tripoli and Tunis, to gather what corn they could in a quick way, and others for further ports.

They saw that the Grand Master had dealt them a shrewd, though they would not call it a fatal, blow. They had him down, as they thought, but he would bite hard to the last, like a cornered wolf.

"There is a spy," Mustapha said, "that we have not guessed. For the time of its coming was known to few." He added, stroking his beard, "It will be a good day when we watch him die." But whether he spoke of the Grand Master, or of the unguessed spy, was not easy to tell.

The talk turned to the Viceroy's promise to raise the siege, of which the latest news gave them little cause for alarm. There was some stir at Palermo, where the streets were more full than usual of militant crowds. There were galleys at Messina preparing for sea. Perhaps five—perhaps ten. Did they think to face Piali's fleet with that paltry show? It was no more than a flourish of arms which would pass the days till it should be too late by the news of St. Angelo's fall, as, there was good cause to suppose, was the intent of the Spanish King.

The Prince asked how the siege stood, after the assault of the last day, which had been intended to make an end. He mentioned the sound of a bursting mine (as he had thought it to be) which had been heard by all on the decks of the Christian ship, as it had left St. Angelo's quay. He found it to be a subject on which Hassan was dumb and Mustapha bitterly brief. He learnt no more than that it had been the cavalier before the Castile breach which had been destroyed, and that the officer in charge, had he not perished in the event, would have lost his life in a more painful and gradual way.

For the truth was that within an hour of the great guns which had been mounted upon the cavalier being brought to bear on the breach, De Claremont, sallying out with forty men from the Arragon bastion, and leaving his own part of the wall almost bare of defence thereby, had crept through the darkness without discovery, until they had burst into the rear of the cavalier, with a fury before which the garrison had fallen, or else fled in such panic as may come from surprise in the midnight hours.

De Claremont had actually turned the guns on to the regiment which had been hurried forward to recapture the cavalier; and retired at last, after laying a train to ignite the store of powder which it contained, so that the whole cavalier had been blown to wreck and its guns destroyed, with a total loss of not less than two hundred men, including those who had been entering it as the explosion occurred.

De Claremont returned without the loss of a single man, though there might be some who had wounds to dress and who would not be of much avail on the next day; and the incident had been an ominous prelude to the great assault which had been designed for two days ahead. It had, indeed, been a vital part of that plan that the guns of the cavalier should so shatter the breach that the Turkish troops would be able to march through on a level way, and its destruction had reduced the material probabilities of success, apart from its disheartening effect upon men who were only less exhausted than those who defended the weakened walls.

Of the Thursday assault itself, which had only ceased as the sun had set the evening before, Mustapha talked, however, with more content, though it had failed to overflow the obstinate Christian walls.

He said: "They are stubborn dogs, who will sell themselves, as it seems, to the last knight, at the best price they can get; but it will be soon that there will be none who is left to slay."

He gave the spies' tales of those who had fallen along the walls, which were mainly true. For De Roubles, being already crippled with wounds, had gone down under an infidel axe as he had fought at the barricade in the Sanglea which had been built to hold back the Turks from the inner harbour, to which they reached in the next hour, and were now only prevented from attacking the shipping there by the raking fire of St. Michael's guns.

Del Formo had been fatally struck by a random arrow as he had been directing his guns to aid those who were most sharply attacked; and De Claremont, being faced by a sudden rush from the Turkish trenches, with ladders to scale a wall which had been quiet and was weakly held, had been almost alone at his own place, with no more than a cauldron of boiling pitch with which to discourage those who would be first over the rampart edge. He had been sprinkling this in a frugal, judicious way, to gain the minute which was required by those who were running to his support, when his gorget had been driven in by a flying fragment of stone. . . .

Having made those losses their boast, the Turkish leaders came to a more domestic concern, being the lodging that must be found which would be fit for one of Prince Azov's degree, and for the retinue that his rank required.

Mustapha offered his own house, in which they then were, which was politely refused, with such sincerity as the offer deserved. He then remarked that Piali had a good villa near to Marsa Scirocco. It would doubtless be at the Prince's disposal but for the fact that he was at sea, and the offer could not be made.

Hassan saw that his turn had come. The villas within the Turkish lines which would be fit to offer for such a use would make but a short count. There were some which had been good, but were ruins now, Marshal Couppier having been active to burn when his chances came. The contents of some had been roughly used by billeted troops, before good order had ruled, during the first weeks of the siege.

He said that a tent was his own choice; but he had a villa in which was no more than a slave whom his pleasure used, who could be removed at a word. He added, with more politeness than truth, that he had already planned that she should be transferred to his own tent, where he would prefer her to be.

Azov paused in doubt of whether the offer were of no better kind than that which Mustapha had made before, which he had been expected to put aside. But Mustapha gravely gave it assent, as a fitting plan. Hassan found that he had offered that which he would be expected to yield.

Angelica, by the caprice of a mocking fate, was likely to find herself returned to the villa where she had been captive before.

The Prince went on to remark that he was without gold in hand for his instant needs, and Mustapha gave the expected reply.

Hassan, taking up the word, was adroit in allusion to the capture that Azov had made from the deck of the sinking ship. Angelica found at last that there were eyes which were turned to her.

There was value there, Hassan's words implied, which could be turned into ready coin. Azov was casual in reply. How could he price that of the worth of which he could as yet make no more than a vague guess? He had not stripped her as yet. She might prove a rich prize, or one of a meaner kind.

Hassan was casual still: but his offer was firm and fair. He lacked a companion for his own slave. He was willing to buy. As to price, he would not quibble of that. Let the valuers say what her worth would be in a good mart, and he would add ten ounces of finest gold. He was munificent in a careless way. Mustapha, having come to a half-guess at the truth, put in a quiet word to advance the sale.

Azov said: "Well, there is no haste. I will sell to none except I give you the first call, for I see that you will buy in a free way."

Hassan hid the annoyance he felt at a rebuff he had not expected to meet.

"I will suppose," he said, "you are woman-starved, having been slaved as you have. Let me have her to-morrow noon, and you can price her to-day, whether she be virgin or no. Can I say beyond that?" And then, as Azov did not respond: "You can keep her a ten-day time, if you will, so that she be bargained mine from that hour."

Azov said: "You buy with an open hand. I would I had come with a larger choice of the ware in which you are so willing to deal. But you will pardon that I do not sell at this day."

Hassan saw that it would be no gain to say more for that time. He rose up to go.

Angelica could make no more than a vague guess of what this conversation had been, but she was content that Hassan did not take her away.

As he went, the Prince turned to Mustapha to ask: "Is he ever thus?"

"Seeing slaves to buy? Not at all. . . . But I surmise he had special cause."

"He having known her before?"

"So I think. If she be whom I suppose (but I did not see), she is one who did him a quirk, such as it could not be thought that a woman would, and whom he was at some pains to catch on a later day. But she was wanted then to buy Candelissa's son (who was hanged too soon, so that her use fell), and after that she got free for a second time."

"So it is cause of hate that he bids high?"

"It is simple guess; she having done that for which Dragut would have seen her dance on a hot floor, or peeled some skin from her back. . . . But Hassan is of a more sober control. It is hard to say what he would be most likely to do."

Azov looked at Angelica with considering eyes. He had wandered much, and had some wisdom to see the soul that the face betrays. He had supposed her to be of a wanton's trade. She had been friend to an alien slave when his need was sore, and she could have thought of no gain to come. He had seen her use her sword to a man's death in what he had thought to be a cool and competent hand. She was hard to read.

So he said; and Mustapha stroked his beard as he made reply: "The Frankish women are not as ours. They are insurgent of seemly rule, and have the art to be lewd in a cold and impudent way."

The Prince did not debate the wisdom or observation of age. He said: "By your tale, she is hard to hold."

"You are warned. . . . If you will, I will send her to your abode with a guard which she will not break."

Azov thanked him for that. It was agreed that Angelica should be sent on to Le Tonneau's villa, while the Prince would remain to bathe and rest till a cooler hour, and to have new garments supplied.

CHAPTER LVIII

THE two girls faced one another, and the same thought came to the minds of both.

"Am I witched," Venetia thought, "that she must find me again?"

"Is it so narrow a world," Angelica wondered, "that we cannot go by two ways?"

Venetia was first to speak, as was likely to be.

"So you take my room," she said, "as your habit is! I half-guessed it was you when the word came. I am to be gone in two hours, with so much of my gear as can be piled on a mule's back. . . . You will find it a better place than when you were here before."

The tone was friendlier than the words, and Angelica answered without thought of offence therein: "It is not of my will. I would be gone, if I might, in less time than is given you."

Venetia did not heed her reply. She was debating within herself if she should be silent, or risk the peril of speech to learn that which she was anxious to know.

She might have had self-restraint to be still, had she not thought that Angelica was more likely to do her harm in an innocent way than if she were warned before. She asked: "Is the grain-ship sunk?"

"So it was, and our own therewith, which has brought me here."

"Was Don Francisco in charge? Is he dead?"

"I have better hope."

Venetia's voice sank to a lower note: "Was it born of a slave's word?"

"It was, thanks to you."

"If you say that here, you will be my death."

"You need have no tremor for that."

"It was crazed to risk, being here."

"It was to Malta's avail. I should say you have bought your peace."

"It is a peace which is somewhat far."

Angelica made no answer to that. She might have said that she was caught in the tighter net, and much less of her own design, but was there comfort in that? Though it were true, it was best unsaid.

Venetia spoke again, following her own thoughts: "We are

tangled close. It is second time I have brought you here; as I had no purpose to do."

Angelica was not instant to comprehend. She had not thought to blame Venetia that she was captured again. Yet she could not say it was less than true.

If Venetia had not let a slave loose, and sent that message by him, it was sure she would not be there, nor Francisco's life in a doubt which she would not own, lest she be unequal to deal with that which was round her now. Yet it was idle folly to make foundation of that for either blame or regret. Had they not diced with death as they crashed through the grain-ship's side they might have been numbered with those who had fallen yesterday on St. Angelo's shaken walls. They might—— She said: "It is not your blame. You did well. And let them do to us as they may, it is a ship that they will not raise."

Venetia found some comfort in that, but much less than she would have liked to have. When she said that she had had no purpose to have Angelica caught for a second time, she put truth in a modest dress. It was sure that, had she foreseen that risk, a Ligurian slave would still have toiled in fear of a pricking blade, and with murder plotting within his heart at each time that his buttocks bled.

She had blamed herself, it may be a hundred times, for the impulse which had set him free with a word for the Grand Master from her. She had not escaped question upon his flight, and was still in doubt of whether Hassan suspected the part she played. She had been more closely watched than before during the last two days, unless fear had made judgment less, which was not likely with her; and caution had postponed the attempt of her own escape, which was now her settled design.

But if she were suspect, or had been convicted of aiding the flight of one of her own land, it might not have been beyond pardon or easy stripes. When the man had got free she had supposed that her major peril was past. Had the grain-ship come to a safe port there would have been no cause for suspicion to turn her way.

But it was sunk; and in such a way that enquiry was sure to follow as to how it had been betrayed. It would be easy to connect that with the slave's flight, and to look further from him to her, and then for Hassan to recall a confidence which he had thought it worthless to give.

That, at the best, would have been a fine edge of peril, to be trod in a wary way. But that it should have been sunk by a ship controlled by those with whom she had been in contact before! Surely ironic fate had mocked her beyond that which mortals should be expected to overcome.

She said: "That is sure; though it may be more loss to them than to Malta's gain, for it may have come on too late a day. . . . I would give ten years of my natural life to know that I shall have ten days in a whole skin. . . . But, as for yourself, you may be glad to be where you are, for it would be hard to say that you came from a better place."

"As I came from a sinking deck, I will give you that."

"But it was not that which I meant. Did you not come from walls that are near to fall? And you must live here to know how keen is the Pagans' hate. When they break in at the last, it will be fire and pitiless sword, and soft fortune to those who are soonest dead."

Angelica was cool in reply: "I should say they are not yet in, and may never be."

"Because you put your desire before reason's rule, but I was bred in a place where those who do that are most apt to die."

She said no more than her candid thought when she spoke of St. Angelo as a fortress already doomed, yet as she rode to face the ruler whom she had beguiled and betrayed to so sharp a loss, she saw the Bourg jail from which she had broken before as a haven of safety where she would have been glad to be.

"I am a Judith," she thought, "of little fame, and less wit; for I have sent the head, and am still here."

CHAPTER LIX

So Venetia went, and Angelica was left in a house from which Hassan's servants withdrew, and which was astir with those that Mustapha sent.

She took the room for her own use which Venetia had had, and which they had shared before. No one obstructed her freedom in that or other matters within the house, but she saw that the outer doors had a strong guard; and when she had made it clear where she would sleep, a sturdy eunuch stationed himself at the door.

She had been vexed that the only clothes she had were damaged beyond repair, and disinclined to Venetia's ready offer of hers, both because they would have been of a small size, and that she doubted it being a good moment in which to go back to a woman's dress. For escape, in particular, which she must keep in front of her mind, a man's was the better wear. And how should she get Christian clothes, being captive here?

But Venetia had made short trouble of that, when she learnt her doubt.

"Why, what a babe you are in the world's ways! Is there aught that you cannot get if the gold be free . . .? I did not mean the few coins that your pouch holds. It is for Azov to pay."

She found a Jew among the bustle of those who prepared the house for Prince Azov's use, which was more fortune than she had hoped, for it was not a place where they were common to meet, running more risks than they did among Christian men at that time (which is saying much), and having talked to him for a time in a mixture of tongues, it followed that there was choice of doublets within the hour, and much besides that would be useful to have, and no payment asked.

The dusk came, and Angelica barred her door, letting it be thought that she had gone to rest, as she did not venture to do until she had heard Azov come, and the house wake to movement and light. But she was still undisturbed and, after a time, silence fell, and she could have a confident hope that there had come an end to a day of crisis and death, through which she had come alive, as few did from the meeting ships; and so she fell asleep, putting fear from her heart, while the growing silence of night made more audible the steady monotone of the guns that did not cease to beat upon St. Angelo's falling walls. . . .

She waked to the next dawn with the fresh vigour of youth, but to the pressure of sharper griefs than she had felt amid the crowded circumstance of the day.

In the clear light of the dawn, the hope which she had refused to loose when she slept seemed to lack solid foundation of probability. She recalled Venetia's words that she refused to face a reluctant reality when she would not admit that St. Angelo tottered toward its fall. . . . Francisco dead, and herself snared in a way from which she might find no means of further escape, nor an equal heart to attempt it again.

She was undisturbed for an hour, during which she was content to delay that which she could have no pleasure to meet, and gathered back to herself some of the fortitude which she had learnt in the last months, and which she had gone nearly to lose; and then the eunuch's hand was urgent upon the latch, and when she drew the bar, letting him in, he spoke in a tongue which had no meaning for her, but with gestures easy to understand, so that she went down, and found a meal laid in the Eastern style, for herself alone.

The man who had been a slave at her galley's bench was now too changed in his state to think of eating with her, but he came in when the meal was done, seating himself as one who had come to talk in a leisured way.

He looked at her for a time in a silence she would not break, as though he sought for that which the eyes could resolve more surely than words. He may have waited for her to speak, but when he saw that she would not be first, he asked: "You were not hurt by the violence through which you came?"

"I have bruises, but they will go. I was most injured by you."

She looked down at her wrists, which still bore signs of the tightened cord. She added boldly, her lips moving toward a smile: "You told me that you had a debt which you aimed to pay."

She saw an instant's smile in response, which he suppressed, as she thought, as though not wishing to be drawn into familiar or jesting speech.

He asked: "You had Hassan's hate?"

She could not tell how much he knew, nor in what manner it had been told. She met the sudden query in its own way: "Did he say that?"

"Not at all. You are one whom he is most eager to buy."

Her voice was beyond control in its sharp fear: "You would not do that?"

"Can you tell me why?"

"Would you give me death? You spoke of a debt to pay. It was not my word, but your own."

"Which is fully paid at this hour."

"Will you say how?"

"It was life for life."

"You would say you had life from me?"

"So I would. For the man would not have confessed."

"And you gave mine in return? I must say you did less than that. I would have swum to land, as I should have chosen to do."

Azov heard this with an expressionless face, hiding thought which she would have preferred to read, in his Eastern way.

"That," he answered at last, "is beyond probable truth."

"Yet true it is."

"We will leave that. . . . I would hear what you have done to earn Hassan's hate."

"I will tell you all."

She told him the whole tale, which was long, and he gave her no help, being silent, and his thoughts hid.

At the end she said: "If you call your debt paid, we will not cavil on that. Nor need you go short of the gold that Hassan would pay. I am not poor. You can name your sum, so that I go free."

"I am not eager for gold. I have more than I ever need, and its worth is small. . . . You are one of more count than I first thought, and your lover dead."

She checked denial of that. To suggest that Francisco lived might have been to turn enquiry and search toward one who might not be far.

"I can give you naught except gold. I am alien here. Will you let me free?"

"You ask more than you are destined to get. I do much if I keep you from Hassan's hands. He is a pillar of strength to the Sultan's throne, half subject and half ally. I cannot make him wroth for a slight cause. It is a matter of state, which you have a wit that can understand.

"It is plain that he has a fixed will that you shall not elude his power. Can I counter that? I can say you are one whom I desire for my own bed, and I will not sell. There is no answer thereto. But if I loose or sell you another way—no, it is not to be done. There have been wars with less root, if we seek the small sources from which they spring."

"Would you take me against my will?"

"It is captive's doom. But it is yet that which I will not do. You shall have time for your own choice. I will give you ten days, that being his own space, though he meant it another way. . . . It is time enough by all counts, for by that day St. Angelo will be down, and I, if not all, will be in bustle to sail away."

She asked, to gain time for thought: "You say St. Angelo will be down? Can you be so sure?"

"I say what I am told. And what I saw from within the walls until four days back does not give it the lie. The spies report that a third of those who could yet stand were brought low at the last assault, and among them the best names that you had. Can such things endure? Can there be no end? The spies say that there are no longer numbers to hold the walls. We may go in when we will. But as they are still grimly resolved, the Grand Master being of fibre that will not bend, and his knights of a close blood, Mustapha will not haste for our own men to be slaughtered anew. That was the counsel I gave, being asked as one who had seen the inside of the walls. We have guns enough, and powder we can put to no better use. For five more days we batter on ramparts that are flailed too flat, in some parts, for an ample mark—and as the month ends, we go in."

"Then the grain-ship's loss has been futile to change event, even to hasten the next assault?"

"I would not say that. I should say it has found the date. For there is corn enough for the next week, without pulling of belts, and after that we plan to draw from St. Angelo's vaults, for corn is the one food of which they still have a fair store."

"And if they should hold the wall, as they have been potent to do?"

"It is that which has passed their power. When we shall tell the troops where the food is stored—— But you turn aside. Will you choose now, or must you stand till the last day?"

"By your leave, I will take the time which is the most mercy you have."

"So I thought that you would. But I must ask you another thing. On your own tale, you are not easy to hold. Will you be fettered anew, or would you choose that your wrists heal?"

"There is but one answer to that."

"Then will you pledge your word that you will not fly?"

"Except I am rescued by other hands?"

"By whose should that be?"

"I would be blither to know. But I would be careful of what I pledge."

"So you should. . . . Except you be rescued by other hands, you will remain . . . for ten days. That is from yesterday, when you came. I will ask no oath, for I have found that those whose word is infirm cannot be held more surely thereby. . . . You can ask for all you will that the merchants have."

He rose and walked out, as one who had disposed of that which would leave him free for larger affairs. He thought he had done well, and would have agreed in his heart had he been praised as one who had acted a kingly part. She was little more to him than a woman of foreign blood and alien faith, who had done him a kindness which he had tried to repay. He had a sincere and friendly desire to keep her from Hassan's hands. He offered her protection from that, which she must buy at the natural price.

He had offered that which few would have done being as great as he was in his own world, and which he would have offered to few. He had given her time to forget the grief of her lover's loss (which might not be much—could he tell?) and to adjust her thoughts to the idea of a new lord. If she should prefer to be sold or whipped, or perhaps flayed at Hassan's caprice, it would but show her to be of a thankless folly, of which he would be relieved.

This was too plain to him to require the tribute of thought, and she, being quick of wit, was not blind to his own view nor to the nature from which it sprang.

She saw herself to be secure for a few days and to have time to plan beyond that.

She was not wholly at peace with her own heart that she had pledged her word not to seek escape, but her reason told her that she had a real gain at a price which might not be much; for even if a chance of escape might come which she must refuse, it would almost surely be one which she would have missed had her word been withheld, and she would have had discomforts and indignities of restraint, the nature of which she might not exactly know, but which she was glad to avoid.

But, beyond such considerations as these, her decision had been controlled by the hope that Francisco might be alive and not far. Might she not have rescue from him? Would there not be a better chance if she were moving without control? Most of all, would she not be better placed to let him know where she was, which she had given no pledge that she would not do . . .? It was Saturday now. It was on Friday next, the last day of the month, that St. Angelo was expected to yield. She had a day beyond that. There were many chances might be her friends. Suppose Hassan should be killed? Suppose that Francis should come? She would woo hope with a stubborn will.

CHAPTER LX

Venetia, expecting trouble, found, for that night at least, there was none to face. She was not transferred to Hassan's own pavilion, as she had somewhat presumptuously expected to be. He had had her there for his pleasure on single nights, but to do more would have been against the custom of the aristocracy of his own land: to have a woman in constant intimacy being considered to be against the canons of dignity and of decent living, both for himself and her.

There was a double pavilion erected adjoining his own, where she was lodged with the two negroid slaves that were hers, but though he used her for his pleasure during the next night, he said nothing of that which she feared to hear. His thought was fixed rather on Angelica than in suspicion of her, and the one remark he made on the topic which was in the wary rear of her mind was that Francisco was said to have escaped from the sinking ship, by what method could be but guessed, and to be at Notabile now.

"They are hard to drown," he said, and it was plain who other was in his thoughts; "but I suppose they will bleed to a good knife when their time is come."

But, except for that, his time and thoughts appeared to be concentrated upon the attack of the Sanglea, which he would not relax, though the siege had again become no more than an artillery duel at other parts of the line—a duel in which St. Angelo could now make but feeble reply to the Turkish batteries freely-served and outnumbering guns.

Mustapha busied himself with questions of routine, of organization, discipline and supply, and systematic preparation for what he supposed (not for the first time) would be the final assault at the month's end. And Piali, stirred to added activity by the escape of the *Curse of Islam* and its results, had established a close blockade of the great harbour, which he was now obstructing with cables and floating wreckage, and watching ceaselessly both by night and day with a score of his fastest galleys, so that it would have been hard indeed for another ship to get clear or to avoid the fire of St. Elmo's guns.

He was preparing also to launch a naval attack within the harbour at the time of the next assault, it having been resolved that St. Angelo was now so weakened and bare of men that it could do little harm to warships which might yet make such attack on its water-sides as it could not ignore. They would be added weight in a scale that already fell, and might give Piali the boast that he would have some hand in the victory of the final day.

There was the more reason for employing them in this way, as the ships were now at sea with their full crews, and with cannon remounted upon their decks, in preparation for a Christian armada which it was now plain that they need not fear. For with five ships, or with ten, which was the largest number of which they could hear as being equipped at Sicilian ports, they would have no trouble to deal.

But Hassan went on at his own work of laying flat the Sanglea, so that Marshal Couppier, falling back from street to street, from barricade to barricade, would soon be contained within the narrow space of St. Michael's fort if he should be forced to further retreat. It was a contest in which all his cunning and skill could not avoid gradual loss of ground before the well-directed attacks of the far larger forces which were at Hassan's command, and of the superior and well-served artillery on which he relied to blast his advance. Worse than that, Marshal Couppier could not, with all his care, avoid a constant wastage of men, so that the Grand Master, with whatever reluctance, had been obliged to further weaken the Bourg defence to supply his more urgent need.

Hassan, watching his colleagues seize the more spectacular positions for completing the success which was now so nearly within their hands, could yet feel some satisfaction that his alone were the present gains. The others talked of what they would do at the month end, but his corsair forces went slowly, stubbornly forward from day to day. . .

Venetia, looking for tempest, had come to a quiet sea, and then, two days later, she ran into sudden storm, when she had thought it was overpast.

There was a message from Hassan, as the afternoon waned, that he was coming to see her in her own tent. That was in the oriental routine, which would not enter to a woman without notice before, but it was barely observed, for he gave her no time to prepare or to adjust her mind to what she might have to face. He entered on the messenger's heels, and it was clear at the first glance that he came in no friendly mood.

He spoke at once of that which had brought him there, and in a curt way, meaning to give her no time to trim the front of her false defence; but, in her own style, she was more wily than he. She had planned before how she would catch such an attack in a subtle wit.

He said: "There is tale of the grain-ship's loss. The spies tell that the warning went through that slave who had been talking to you. That is what he is plain to say. Did you tell him that, as I recall that you had it from me a few hours before?"

She saw, with an instant alertness of mind that, whether of purpose or not, he had been vague as to the statement the slave was said to have made. Had he accused her? Or had he allowed no more than that he had taken the tale, leaving its source dumb?

But she gave no sign that she saw this, answering with an air of frankness, and as though there were no thought of consequence to herself: "It is what I have wondered myself at times, for I suppose that I might have done it without thought that there would be following harm, he being a slave as he was, and you not having told it to me (as I remember you did, you are right in that) as being a secret thing.

"But when I think, I am assured that it was not said; for we had no talk of that kind. It was of his own land, and of things that had happened there since he was slaved, which I knew to a later year. He did not ask, nor I care to speak, of things that are round us now."

"Yet you will not swear it was not said?"

"So I might, and it would be an oath that must stand, for there would be none to deny, and so I think I would do; but when I answer to you I speak in a freer mood, and it is true that I wondered at first if it could have been said in a careless way, when I heard how the grain-ship was sunk, and how the *Curse of Islam* sailed as soon as the man got into town, but I concluded at last that the word had not come from me. If it were his, he must have found it another way."

"And if he says it was you?"

"I should still say he is wrong, we having had no words of that kind."

Hassan made no answer to this. He surveyed her with brooding, unfriendly eyes. He saw that she either spoke truth, or fenced in a most skilful way, as (he said to himself) if she were in fault she would be likely to do. But in fact she had made him doubt more than firm denial would have availed. To that point, she may be observed to have come best through that bout of tongues.

Her trouble was, as she could not guess, that he did not wish to believe. He had a plan in his mind which required that he should convict, or at least impute betrayal to her.

"Well," he said, as one half-convinced but who must act in a judicial impartial way, "it is for Mustapha to deal. It shall not be said that I keep slaves who betray. You must have trial of him."

He saw her face blanch in a way she could not conceal, though she faced him with angered eyes, in which the most wrath was for her own door, that she should have made such a defence that he would not heed. "Why," she asked, with astonishment in her voice, "would you send me to death? And on so frail a charge, which you do not believe? Nor would I have a great blame had it been true, you having told it to me in so free a way. Am I no pleasure to you, that you send me thus to a cruel end, and with no cause that is worth?"

"If you said naught, should you stand in so great a fear?"

"That I should, as you know well. I shall be their sport. Will they miss revenge for the grain-ship's loss, having a Christian with which to play?" She added shrewdly: "It must be for your shame alike, for it must be said that you told it to me, it being on that that the charge is built."

He was silent at that, not having had any purpose of putting her in Mustapha's hands. It had been a threat to bring her to the mood for that which he would require her to do. But he had been disconcerted by the quickness with which she had seen that he must accuse himself as the first cause, if he should make a public charge against her. Had he believed her guilt, and had no other purpose to serve, he would have been likely to order her death in a quiet way, and one which would give her no option of further speech, as with a bowstring about her neck.

Beyond this, he had a larger doubt than before that one so shrewd and alert would risk her life by sending such a word in a slave's mouth. But he gave no sign of his thoughts, going on as it had been his first purpose to do.

"If I do not send you to him, will you do that which you did before, with your life to win?"

She felt some hope stir in her heart at this, seeing that he held a design that he had not shown, but she thought of all he had required her to do before, and found no comfort therein.

She asked: "Can I tell that till I hear? But will you drive me to pay high for a thing that I did not do?"

"It is doubt for doubt. You may fail now, and if you do you will be tried on that charge. I give you chance to get free. . . I will have Angelica brought to me again, and that in such way that Azov will not trace her to me, nor guess how it was planned. He must not know where she has come."

"She will not trust me again. You can see that."

"That is your trouble to overcome. . . . Can you do this, or will you go at once to Mustapha's hands?"

"I do not say but I might. . . . It would need a most subtle plot. . . . When do you want it to be?"

"It should be before the next day of assault, but not much."

"Which is when?"

"It is the last day of this month. You may betray that if you will. It is open talk."

"It is to be done of my own plan?"

"So that there be no suspicion of me, which I would not forgive."

"I will think what I can do."

"So you should. You have life to win."

He went at that word, feeling that he had done well, and having more belief in the potency of Venetia's guile than belief in the veracity of her recollection of conversations with the escaped slave. His resolution to have Angelica trapped had been made after some talk with Azov had convinced him that she would not come to his hands in a bought way. He knew that she was lost for ever to him, and his vengeance foiled, unless he could catch her now, and his thoughts went beyond that to affairs of state, considering that Azov might come to a great power in the future days, and that it would be no gain to have a woman such as Angelica at his ear, who could have no love for the Viceroy of the Barbary coast.

But against that there was the necessity that what he did should be neither proved nor suspect, for there could be no more deadly offence, by the standards of conduct which were common to both, than to interfere with a woman within the house of another man. It was a matter which he would have hesitated to open to one of his own blood, and in which the loyalty of few would have been sufficient to pursuade them to aid his scheme with a good will. He had seen that Venetia was the one chance that his household gave, and when the rumour had reached his ears of how the grain-ship had been betrayed, the plan had quickly matured in his mind, and he had gone to her before his purpose had time to cool.

When he had said that Angelica must be betrayed before the next day of assault, he had remembered that Azov had said that he would wish to take part therein, but that he might leave on a following day. He would prefer it to be little before that date, thinking that Azov could not be gone too soon after Angelica had come into his hands. He had no doubt that Venetia's mind would be fertile in devising a snare, nor did he fear that any scruple would hold her back to her skin's risk.

But when he left her, her face changed, as she would seldom permit it to do. She paced the length of the tent, which was not her way, with the look of an angry cat.

She hated Hassan at that hour with a loathing beside which her feeling for the Grand Master might be called love. She thought bitterly: "It is Judith I called myself, but they will give me another name, having some likeness of sound, but being that of a man."

But all the time, through the fear she had for herself, and her hatred both of him and that which he had required her to do, there were snares weaving within her mind, as though born without will from her.

After a time, she lay down. She lay very still, as her way was when she plotted against the constant dangers her life had known, or to catch those from whom profit came. Her hands went to behind her head. She thought long, with hard inscrutable eyes. She did not stir till the quick twilight brought one of her slaves to trim her lamps for the night. When she had gone, she rose up.

"I can go to her," she thought, "with no wonder, but certain thanks, having news that she will be glad to have." And having made that resolve, she slept well.

CHAPTER LXI

THE next morning Venetia, having bathed and dressed in the leisured comfort for which she had the keen love of those who have known life of another mode, rode over to Le Tonneau's villa on a good mule which Hassan had assigned to her use, taking one of her maids, for whom a mount was soon found when her will was said. She did not choose to go that distance alone, though there was enough known of herself in the Moorish camp, and of her place in Hassan's regard, both to secure her own safety therein and the quick service of all to whom she might make appeal.

She knew that it did not follow from the readiness with which such service was paid that she might not be watched by some who would have sharp orders for her restraint if she should move beyond narrow bounds; and she had a thought that there would be test in this ride, for, if she were turned, she would have learned that which might be value to know, and she would have afterwards a good defence for Hassan's ears as to where she had been seeking to go.

But, whether watched or not, she rode an unhindered way, and came to the place she sought, to find it a centre of moving life; for Azov, finding a regiment among Mustapha's army which had been recruited from his own land, and of which he was the titular head, had caused them to move their camp, so that they now lay round the house on its seaward side. They were being re-equipped and refreshed by him—to the limit of the resources he could control—to inspirit them for the coming day of assault, when it was said that he purposed to lead them in person to the victory that the hour would bring.

Venetia observed this concourse with an inward disfavour as being a likely hindrance to the plans which were forming within her mind. But she rode unchallenged to the gate, demonstrating thereby what may be done by assurance that knows its way, for it was unlikely that she should be familiar to any of the Turks who looked with curious or scowling eyes at the shameless fair-skinned woman who turned a bare face to the gaze of men, and wore a dress which was bold to discover her body's lines in the infamous Christian way.

Even at the gate, which was guarded well, she was held to no more than a short pause, after she had said who she was and whom she was there to see. The eunuch came to the call, and led her in with words which were hard, and genuflections easy, to understand.

She saw a second barrier down without trouble to her, for she had considered that Angelica might either refuse to see her of her own will, or (more probably) that she might have no liberty to decide. But she was shown to the upper floor, and so through to the belvedere where they had sat on the first morning when they had found themselves to be fellow mice in one trap.

Angelica met her there, still in her boy's clothes, with a greeting which was well enough, though not warm, which Venetia chose to observe.

"I am not one whom you love to see and you make that clear, as your manner is; but when you know why I have come, you may give me thanks in a fairer way."

"You mistake," Angelica replied, thinking that she must have shown more coolness than she had meant; "there could be few, so that they would come with a friend's voice, whom I would not be blithe to see, being mured here as I am."

She judged truly enough that Venetia would be her friend at a free choice, and would even do her any service she could, if the cost were easy to pay. But beyond that—well, she had trusted once and found it a count to high.

Venetia asked: "Have you freedom to go abroad?"

"That I have. Prince Azov is one who trusts in a large way. But, being garbed as I am, I suppose I am better here."

Venetia was puzzled as to the implications of that and hindered therefore in what she had come to say. Her quick eyes had noticed that Angelica wore a sword, which was the natural complement of the dress she assumed, but was not commonly put into a prisoner's hand. She knew also that Angelica had lost her own on the sinking ship, when Azov had twisted it from her grasp. Her poniard was still in its place, not having been taken away, but the sword must have been replaced with a deliberate consent.

She said cautiously, feeling her way: "They do not deny you arms?"

"Azov said that if I walk armed it is clear that I am here with a good right, and I should be less in jeopard of those who may not know how I stand."

"It is of your comfort he thinks well."

She was still in a puzzled doubt. Had Angelica become Azov's mistress to their common content, so that he gave her all the freedom she chose to have? If that were so, she might have come with wares for which the market was done.

She went on: "That could but be if you walk abroad; yet you said you were mured here, so that there could be few you would not welcome to see."

"So I am, by the clothes I wear, and the face I show. I do not know beyond that, for I have resolved that I will not try."

"You would be free if you could?"

"Am I fool? But I am pledged to remain here till—till there be a new bargain made."

She remembered, none too soon, that Venetia was now the petted slave of her special foe. Had she been sent to find how she stood in Azov's regard? She checked her words, and Venetia saw that she must play the one card that she had before Angelica would further expose her own. She said: "Well, I did not come to enquire of matters which are not mine, but to bring you news you might not get in another way."

Angelica felt her heart beat with a sudden hope, which she feared to hold. "It is kindly thought," she said, "for news is welcomed to those who are cooped as I."

"It is of Don Francisco I heard." As she spoke, Venetia saw the light in Angelica's eyes, and did not doubt that she had made a vain guess the moment before, by which deducing she showed perception of the wide gulf that held them apart. She went on: "He escaped the wreck, and is at Notabile now."

"You are sure?"

"I had it from Hassan's lips. Don Francisco was there when the tale came. I cannot say beyond that."

An instinct of suspicion, which was not natural to her but was born of sufficient cause, stirred in Angelica's heart to a sharp fear: "You would not mislead on that which is much to me?"

"It was Hassan's tale. I cannot say more or less. I will swear that, if you desire."

"You told me once you would be forsworn though your oath were by Bethlehem's star, or the manger that cradled Christ."

"That was if I were snared. Being thus, I would lie my way through, if I could, though it were either by way of Heaven or Hell. So would most, as I think, though they may be less honest than I. But I tell you this as a friend, for which I thought to have a good word. . . You may make of it what you will or else naught. I seek neither to aid nor to know."

Angelica felt that she had been ungracious in the reception of that which she took for truth, and which brought a new lightness to her own heart, which was still weighed with sufficient reason for fear. She lacked friends, of whatever kind. If she could only trust——! But she knew that she never could.

She asked: "Can he know I am here?"

"I know nothing of that. You should make the far better guess."

"Then I must suppose not."

Venetia sat as though having no more to say, or waiting for Angelica to speak again. Well, there could be no harm in questioning her. Half-deceiving herself with the thought, she asked: "You would escape if you could?"

Venetia knew that she could reply without fear, even though it should all have been open to Hassan's ears, for it would be simple to say that she had feigned, as part of the plan she had. But she looked round in a cautious way: "There is none can hear?"

"We are alone here, as you know well. It is a place I chose, thinking you would not have come without cause."

"I would escape, if I could. It is hateful here. I suppose Algiers would be worse in a hundred ways. And Hassan is one whom you cannot reach. He takes all, and is distant still."

Angelica heard that which she did not doubt. There was an accent of truth in words which closed in a bitter tone, for it was partial cause of the hatred which had been in Venetia's heart that she could not win Hassan with all her wiles. There had been times when she had nursed hope, but the narrowed distance widened again, and she looked at a stranger's eyes, holding a cold suspicion of her which no art could foil.

Angelica pondered whether she should ask the only aid that she would be likely to get; and as she was slow to speak, Venetia went on: "But where to should we flee, with Malta near to be a Turk's isle?"

"I shall be slow to think that."

"Will it alter for you? It is plain fact."

"Then is the more cause to be free on a former day."

"Before St. Angelo fall? So it is. Do you know when that will be?"

Angelica guessed what she meant. She went as near to guile as her nature was, when she countered with: "Can you tell me that?"

"It is Friday to come. It is the last day of this month."

"That is, if they break in; as they have been unequal to do."

"But as they are equal now, it is wholly agreed. Hassan says the Marshal falls back in the Sanglea, street behind street, as men having no hope to prevail, but who will die in a stubborn way."

"It is Europe's shame."

"So it is. But it is of ourselves we must think. I would walk streets where there is sound of the Christian tongues. . . . The Turks do not go yet beyond three miles of the inland roads. If we further proceed, there will be boats leaving by every creek. They will creep away, being unseen in the darker hours."

Angelica, doubting whether it would be wise to expose her own hopes or fears, found that she listened to one who was content to confide in her. Venetia spoke of that which she had pondered before, and seemed to do so without reserve.

Angelica asked: "Then do you think to get free before Friday come?"

It was Monday now. It was but four days away.

"So I do. I will take the best chance. It is the day before I would choose. Would you make two . . .? We may not come to the same chance. You must think of that. . . . I would give help if I could."

Angelica thought: "I can but ask help that she will not give. Am I worse then than I now am? Could she betray to my loss? It is hard to see."

She saw that there was a chance, if no more, that Venetia might speak from a candid mind, and offer that which a friend could do. Should she cast her one chance aside, because it was no better than that?

"I could not join you," she said, "though the path were clear, for I am pledged that I will not escape, except rescue come."

"And how could that be?"

"There was once it was."

"You mean that Don Francisco came to your aid? It was such a thing as may be done once, but not more. And with this regiment about the gates!"

"So I fear. I but wait and pray, being closely caught. I think at times I were better bound, with no pledge. But I would be free to learn if he lived, and to let him know I am trapped here, as I must contrive that I now do."

"You would have him know?"

"If you could do that!"

"I should say it is less than hard. It is but to make talk that the spies will bear. . . . And I can take the tale in my own lips, if I get away, as I may be instant to do. . . . You think that I have bought peace with the Grand Master and Malta's knights?"

"I should say you have won reward, though I see not how you will claim, nor they pay."

"It is once that we see alike. But I will do what I can, so that it be at no more than a mean risk. It is what I owe for a wrong I did you before, which I did not wish. I may come again, or may not. But, for now, I have stayed too long. There must be excuse. I will take things from the house I forgot before."

She went in a quick way, avoiding the Judas-kiss, and by that manner may have given a better hope that she had talked from an honest mind. She took linen out of a chest for her mule to bear. She asked for a casket, for which there was hurried search, but which could not be found, having no substance outside her mind, where it had been invented a moment before. She said it was of value to her, and she might come on another day. But now she must go, for she would not be abroad when the dusk fell.

Angelica, watching her ride away, had the excitement of joy and a new hope. Thanksgiving had its customed place that night in her prayers, for which a text had been hard to find since she had come to that house for a second time.

Venetia went to her own tent, to which Hassan came at a later hour, as she had thought he would do.

She was not surprised that he knew where she had been. He asked: "Have you trimmed your plot?"

She fenced in reply: "If I do this foul thing, can I come to peace? It is poor service that must be paid with no more than a new toil. Will you say I have served you well, both by night and day?"

"Do you talk of this as a thing done?"

"I am through the worst. She was slow to snare."

"But you have her now?"

"Can I wring the neck of a tame hen? I should say I can."

"It is as easy as that?"

"It was not at first. It is now. It can be done in three days."

"Can you tell me how?"

"Not as yet. But there is one thing on which I must ask your aid."

"I will have no portion in this. So I made it clear."

"It is but that it be talked in the Christian camps that she is in Azov's hands."

"And what avail will that be?"

"Perhaps none. But it is a point on which I would have no doubt."

"You must tell me why."

"But you said you would have no part or knowledge in this?"

"Do you ask no more? Can you contrive that she be here in a secret way, asking no more, besides this?"

"I shall need men of trust on the right day."

"That is vain to ask. I can break in without aid from you. It is violence we must not have. There is no value in that."

"Did I say they should break in?"

"But there must be no violence at all. . . . To seize a woman—even a slave—from Prince Azov's house—it could not be done. There are few I have who could be trusted for that, both to undertake and to be still on the next day. . . . And with that regiment which is surrounding the doors!"

"It will not be there."

"I will risk no talk of a woman seized, be it where you will."

"Is she that, or man?"

"It would become known if she should be ravished away."

"But if she come on her own feet?"

"You mean in a willing haste?"

"So it will be likely to be."

"Then for what do you need men?"

"That were to show all."

Hassan became silent at that. He remained as though lost in thought, leaving her unsure of what he would be likely to say. But he concluded at last: "It is naught you ask. I suppose it to be known before now, both at Notabile and in St. Angelo's walls. But that shall be made sure. . . . You have wit enough to observe my will. . . . When you ask more, there must be more that you will be ready to tell."

"So I will," she said, "on a later day."

CHAPTER LXII

VENETIA had been slow to expose her plot to Hassan's request for the best reason of all, that it was still vague in her own mind, though its outlines were dimly lined. But she had seen that it would be useless to contrive until she had learned how Angelica was confined, and what trust she could have from her.

Now she had a night of short sleep and much thought. She did not fail to observe that when she had asked Hassan for a promise that he would use her thus for the last time he had avoided reply. Hatred stirred anew at this thought, but she was fair enough to allow in a cool mind that she was not punished without offence. For it was truly her word which had sent the grain-ship down to the sea-floor, and if it should come to proof (and who could say what the slave's chatter might be, or that he might not be caught again in the next week?) she would need all the favour that she could claim to secure her life from those she had brought to so great a loss. Even to have betrayed Angelica to his hands for a second time might seem a small thing beside that. . . . Well, to each day its own grief. She had a plot to weave now, which must leave short leisure for straying thoughts. . . . So she came to the dawn.

She set out again before the full heat of the day, riding to Le Tonneau's villa, and taking with her the same maid as before, to whom she had shown a casket which she said was a pair to that which could not be found.

"It must," she said, "have been thrust aside by those who garnished the place for Prince Azov's use, but that it is pilfered I will not think. It will be found at a thorough search."

She went with a mind filled with her own plans, which did not guess, for all the thought she had had, that Hassan might have one also which he had not discovered to her. But when he stood in talk with Azov at a later hour, as they looked down together from Mount Corradin on the ruins of the Sanglea, he said: "There is a white slave of my tents whom I value much. She was owned by one of the greatest of Malta's knights, who had made her first of his house before he came to death at my hands on the Sanglea walls, and she afterwards to my power.

"She was at your villa last afternoon, on a pretext of things she would bring away (I having kept her there till I passed it to you), but the intention was mine, that you might see if she would be one who would please your eyes."

Azov considered this, but with little wonder as to what it might mean. He said: "It was an ill chance that I was not there."

"She has gone again on the same search, if I make a most likely guess."

"Then I may observe her before she leave."

Azov said no more, but it was understood without words that Hassan had made another bid for Angelica's purchase. If gold were not enough, there was to be female flesh tossed into the scale, and that such as some would think to be of a most desirable kind.

It appeared that Hassan would not rely upon one prospect alone, but must assure himself against failure with an alternative plan. So it may have been; but he may have aimed, besides that, to supply a pretext for Venetia's presence in Azov's house, so that suspicion might not turn subsequently to her.

Azov returned more speedily than he would otherwise have done, curiosity being sufficient spur; for he had known more of Venetia than Hassan had thought it needful to say, having had Angelica's circumstantial account.

His education had familiarised him with the habits and appearance of Western women, which had been supplemented by experiences during the Balkan campaigns in which he had taken part, and some subsequent observations from the segregated position of a shackled slave. He was dismounting at his own gate as Venetia came out, having had an interview with Angelica of more than two hours duration, while the house had been searched for a casket which was not there.

She looked at the Prince, splendidly attired, and surrounded by the officers of the regiment which he had made his guard, with innocently provocative eyes, thinking him to be a man of whom she would have been glad to know more at a better time; and had she been aware of the proposition that Hassan had made, it would have appealed to her as a very profitable exchange.

But she did not guess that such a prize was within the rights of her own chase. She was careful, rather, that there should be no tale taken to Hassan's ears such as would rouse the jealousy which is seldom far from the surface of the oriental mind. She remembered also that she had writing beneath her stomacher's hem by which she would be ruined beyond remedy if it should come to the Prince's eyes.

Her own fell demurely before his, and she mounted her mule with a consciousness that she drew his regard, which became entire pleasure only when she had ridden a safe distance away.

This was at midday, and she rested with the satisfaction of work well done, and with a very active regard for that which was yet to do. When the worst heat of the day was past, she sent a slave to Hassan's tent to enquire whether she could come to him, to which he gave prompt assent, but received her in such a manner as to remind her that the accusation under which she lay was still a cloud that he would not permit to dissolve.

"I have short time," he said, but whether of need or policy she had a shrewd doubt; "will you say at the first word if you have brought your plans to a final flower?"

"If I fill you two pokes where you looked for one?"

"Will you be plain?"

"Would you capture him by whom the grain-ship was rammed, and the boats sunk on a former day?"

"Don Francisco? Do you say you can bring me him?"

"Will he not come to her aid, as he did before?"

"He would not take it from you. He was hurt once. He would move further away."

"It is not from me. It is her own hand."

"Which she has trusted to you to bear?"

"It is here to see, if you will."

She passed him a letter unsealed, which he read with care.

"By what tale did you get this, she having known you before?"

"I am the one chance which is hers. . . . But I do not say it was smoothly done. There were tears at times. There were oaths to swear which I might not miss."

He read the letter again, as though being stirred with a new doubt. "What he did before," he said, "was in the cover of night, but this is to be in the full light of the day. Will he be headlong to venture that?"

"But how else would you have it to be? Could she stroll out in the midnight hours?"

"You will need no men, except at the point named. That is clear."

"But I shall. She will not go so far, except under duress. She is pledged that she will not go, unless rescue come."

"It has a weak sound."

"Yet so it is. And there is another cause of as much weight."

"You shall tell me the plan in a clear way."

"So I will, if you have turned to wish that. It is short to tell, and you may find it good if you think long. The letter gives him both place and time where he must be instant to snatch her up. She will go there with me, and such escort as we resolve, who will obey me but not her. She will go as by their duress, they having made show that they seize us both. If we should be stayed by those who suspect our flight, in such a way that we may not get past nor free, so I shall say that it was, and perhaps afterwards that I have said a false word before, having a knife more near to my back than it was comfort to be, and she will be quick to support my word, which will be fact and defence to her. . . . It will be thought that they have taken Don Francisco's gold. . . . Or if you say they will be believed, then it will be plain that we had combined in one flight, she and I, and none will suspect your part, for should you aid her in that, or else me? It would be a folly to say.

"But if we come to where she is to be met, then you take a full bag. You have Don Francisco caught, and she will be one he has rescued and you have captured again. She will be in your hand with some right, even though it be done in an open way, which is for you to prefer."

"Will you tell me this: If I have no knowledge before, how should I be at hand to catch them after they meet?"

"It must be fortunate chance, but if you heed what the letter says you will see I have not been blind. It is a place which your troops patrol, and not those of the Turkish camp. But for that, I could have chosen a better spot."

Hassan pondered this for a time, having forgotten the haste which he had protested before. He said: "You have planned well, and had you done no more than get this letter from her, you would have shown a most cunning art, she having known you before in the way she did. . . . There are some things that I still might ask, but I will conclude that you have not been careless of them. . . . But this letter must not go through my hand."

"I had not meant that it should. But will you tell me how I may find one by whom it will be surely conveyed?"

Hassan gave her the name of a sure spy, with instructions of how he could be safely approached.

"I shall need gold."

"You can have that to your will." He unlocked a coffer. "Take your own sum, so that I know. For I keep a count. . . . But I like not those men that you will have with you at first. It is their tongues from which mischief is like to come, it may be at a far day."

"Yet you will find it safe, if you think well. You will tell them no more than that they are to take orders from me. Can there be after-trouble on that? I am one you trust. Yet if you think them a danger for later days, we are at a place where death is not hard to find. They must be men you can spare."

"How many do you propose?"

"I would have four. They must be enough, if we should be met too soon by those who will question what we may be, to have the front of a proper guard."

Hassan saw that there was reason in that. If the two Christian women were to ride at large through the camp without escort, it was likely that they would soon be questioned and stopped, and that that part of the plot would fail, leaving Francisco for his sole prey; but if they rode with an escort of Moors, they would more easily pass, or could reply in a more confident way. There were still points that he might have questioned, but he saw that Venetia was as capable as himself (if not more) in the details of such intrigue, and she had brought one tangible proof of her skill in Angelica's letter, which he would not have supposed that she would have been able to get, by whatever wile.

There was one point which he would have changed, if he could, but it was no blame to her, for it was a matter agreed between Mustapha and him but a few hours before, and known only to them.

The great, and, as it was expected, the final storm, had been fixed for Friday the 31st. That was freely known in both camp and town. The fact that Mustapha had twice done this before, and had kept his dates, caused it to be regarded on both sides as immutably fixed, whether for hope or despair. But he had now secretly resolved to add the element of surprise to the overwhelming number of rested men who were to swarm over the ruined walls of the Bourg. It was to commence on the afternoon of the previous day. This would make it more difficult for Hassan to arrange for the capture of Francisco and Angelica when they had met, or, at least, for himself to be near at hand.

But he considered that it was a military secret of which he could give Venetia no hint, and to alter the date in Angelica's letter would be a folly that might raise Francisco's suspicions and defeat the whole plot. Finally, he observed that the time had the great advantage that it would appear additionally improbable that he should have had any part in, or knowledge of, a device fixed for an hour when he must be in command at the Sanglea front.

He passed her the letter back. "You must send this, choosing the dusk. . . . You have done well. . . . I will be with you at the tenth hour."

She understood that she was far on the way to forgiveness for that which she was suspected to have done, and to re-establish, if not strengthen, her position with him. She gave him a glance and a grateful word, by which he had no reason to doubt that she would be glad to entertain him that night in her own way. She went back to her tent.

Being alone, she destroyed Angelica's letter with a particular care, after which she went out, following the directions which Hassan had given, to seek the spy who could communicate with the Maltese lines. . . .

When Hassan passed from tent to tent at a late hour, he was addressed cautiously and from a short distance away by a voice he knew.

"You may approach," he said. "What news have you to tell?"

"Lord, there is no news at this hour. But the Giaour woman would send a letter out of the camp."

"Let it go, and in such hands that it will not fail. It is but to bait a trap."

CHAPTER LXIII

MESQUITA sat where Francisco had met Marshal Couppier on a former day. By appearance alone, it might be thought that the Notabile command had passed to the better man.

The present governor had a handsome, aquiline face beneath an abundance of snow-white hair. His skin was the dark olive which is usual among his race. His bushy beard was still streaked with black. The table hid the abnormal shortness of his legs, which rendered him a more formidable knight when a horse parted his knees than when he must do battle on foot, which it was known that he would be reluctant to undertake, nor was he often seen unmounted beyond his door.

His expression now was friendly and suave. There was a verbal deference in what he said which ignored the differences of age and military rank which divided Francisco and him as broadly as the table that stretched between. But his words were as resolved in substance as they were graceful in their address.

"Don Francisco," he said, "I will not suppose that you have done me the honour of visiting me thus for the third time with other object than that which you have urged so ably before. It is one that all the instincts of knighthood would gladly grant, even to one less noble in name than you are, or less illustrious in exploit than the bright sword of your youth has already been. But I am not here, as you will do me the courtesy to agree, to gratify my own will, or the chivalrous impulses either of yourself or of those who may solicit with better right."

"Will you," Francisco returned, with equal deference but no less resolution beneath his words, "be patient to tell me on what grounds you reject my plea?"

"That is what I may not refuse," Mesquita replied, as readily as though he had not set them out, with some elaboration of repetition, on two previous occasions, he being, it may be not uncharitably assumed, one who was not greatly averse from hearing sentences that himself had framed. "You come to me asking consent to release twenty of the best knights and horsemen that I yet have, with the same number of chosen steeds, that they may aid you to rescue a señorita detained in the very heart of the Moorish camp; and you assure me (which I can most lightly believe) that you have their warrant that they will be content to be so assigned.

"Now to what end should I do this? To her rescue? It is not to be thought in a sober mind.

"You say you did it before. That may skirt the edge of exact truth; but, if we allow that, shall it therefore be done again? It is of the order of things which may occur once, but not more. And there is a special folly in this design, in that we are well advised that a regiment is stationed around her doors.

"But if I should agree that you have projected that which is not beyond limit of human power, being of the realm of romances which fed our youth (to which I will not say that this war is not somewhat akin), should I therefore assent to the petition that you are urgent to make? If you think, you will say not.

"Should I not then prefer to pluck Mustapha from out his bed, or bundle Hassan up in the folds of his own tent? Either of which, you must pardon that I observe, should be as simple as to remove this lady (whose plight you will not wrong me so far as to think me slow to deplore) from the well-guarded walls of Prince Azov's house, being in the very heart of the Moorish camp. Could it be as lightly done as you are skilful to urge, should we be content with a single spoil? We should have them both in one night.

"As for yourself, you must lose your life as you will, you being one over whom my authority does not extend; for which, if I must, I will give you a horse that I cannot spare, but I will do no more beyond that."

"You object," Francisco asked, as though unmoved by the lengthy eloquence he had heard, "that she is so distant within the lines?"

"And that not alone, but that she is in a well-guarded place, from which she could not be snatched away (if at all) with the speed for which the occasion would call aloud."

"If those objections should go?"

"Which of their nature they could not do."

"I might so word a request," Francisco replied, "that you would be, as it were, trapped in reply, which I prefer that I should not do, both of courtesy, and having confidence in the high chivalry of the name you bear. But I will ask you only to read this letter which I have had in the last hour."

Mesquita read the letter which Francisco passed over to him. He looked up to ask: "You believe this? How did it come to your hands?"

"It came," Francisco was frank to say, "in a way which I do not like."

"So it would. Will you tell me how?"

"It was by the hand of a boy with a scarred chin, being the same who brought me a note on another day, within St. Angelo's walls."

"Did you catch the boy?"

"That I did. But I gained naught. He denied all that I was most urgent to know, except where he is lodged in the town, which I think I have."

"So have I. The boy is the son of a known spy. He is for sale on all sides. You may put him out of your mind."

Francisco was silent, his mind going back to the way he had been fooled and dishonoured before. But he was free now, and his honour joined his desire to urge a risk which he could not shun.

Mesquita asked: "Do you know the hand?"

"I am most sure."

The Commander's eyes went to the letter again. He read:

> "Rest content that as yet I have had no hurt, but the hours of safety are few. Hassan is eager to have me within his power, and I may not long avoid that, unless at a price that you may guess, but I will not say.
>
> "Also, I am pledged that I will not escape, except rescue come.
>
> "I will not hide that this is by the hand and aid of her of whom you have cause to shrewdly beware, and you must judge as you will; but we are in common attempt, and her oath is not now either by manger or star (of which you will remember that which I told you she said before), but by her own need, which is near to mine.
>
> "If she keep faith (as she will), and if we be not foiled by contrary chance, we shall be by the fallen wall at the tank on the Tarxten road (it is two miles from here) as the sun comes to earth on Thursday, two days from when this is writ.
>
> "There may be Moors also, three or four, who will not be friends. They will be to scatter or slay.
>
> "When you come, it is only speed will avail, and you will know that our horses may not be good."

There was more than this, which Mesquita passed at a short glance, seeing that it was not germane to that which he must decide. He folded the letter, and turned it within his hands, as one seeking a solution he could not reach.

He said at last: "Be it for evil or good, you can have the party you ask, but I will tell you one thing, and there is one counsel that I will give.

"For the first, there are movements within the camps by which I suspect that Mustapha may make his assault a day sooner than he has said, that is to-morrow, when this attempt will be made by you. I will get word of this to the Grand Master, if I can, though it be no more than a guess. But it is no longer easy to do, for the spies lean to those who they think will win, and they judge us down, on which they go more fast than the fact, and may have made a false guess.

"And the counsel is this, that you should keep that letter concealed to your own mind, even from those who will be comrades in what you purpose to do, for though it have been both written and borne in privity and full faith (which are doubts you are cast to take), yet if a whisper stir, by whatever breath, you will be twenty dead to no gain, and she whose rescue you try more closely caught than before. Let your friends (if they must talk at all, as men will) think Le Tonneau's villa your aim, as you have first asked them to do. Let them think that till the spurs strike."

Francisco thanked the old knight, seeing that his counsel was good, though it could have been the cargo of fewer words. He had got that which he asked, as he might have had even though Mesquita had had no further design. But, in fact, the Commander, who was both resourceful and bold, was planning that in which he and his friends would be no more than a gambit of forward pawns, either to live or die.

Mesquita knew that Mustapha's assault would try St. Angelo's strength to its last sword, and that it was urgent that he should give all the aid and diversion he could; and though the undoubtable valour of his untrained Maltese levies did not fit them to meet the professional regiments of the Turkish army in open field, yet he felt that the occasion required that he should risk more than would have been wise on a quieter day. He had a raid planned on the supply camp at Zeitun, further west than the Tarxten road, which was still closed in his own mind. Now he thought: "If Don Francisco succeed, all is well; and if he ride into ambush made, it may well be that, as they dig pits for his death, they will have less thought for our coming another way."

So Francisco and he were each of a pleased mind. And on the next day, when the dusk was near, Francisco rode boldly into the

Turkish lines, with twenty comrades of hopes as bright and wills as hard as the swords they wore, and two led horses therewith.

But, for five hours before that, there had come over the hills a low murmur of customed sound, from where the Turkish regiments swarmed out from gabion and trench, and over St. Angelo's ruined and ill-manned walls, and the barricades of the Sanglea.

CHAPTER LXIV

VENETIA came to the gates of Le Tonneau's villa, as Francisco rode from Notabile by the downhill paths which were least easy to oversee. She had an escort of four dark-skinned Moors of the Barbary coast, mounted on the desert horses that were as native to them as the swaying decks of their pirate craft. She rode a sleek mule, which they could have outpaced by three strides to two on a level ground, and there was another led at her rein.

Prince Azov's regiment had gone, though its horses remained. It went on foot to join in the storm that beat round the Bourg walls. The Prince had a design to rush a part of the bastion of Auvergne, of which his recent slavery had enabled him to observe something on the inner side.

It was a part of the wall that had not yet been a scene of assault, though it had been much flattened by the three-months' battering of the guns. From the slender numbers that must now be spread out to the length of the Bourg walls, it was unlikely that it would be held in much strength. He hoped that a sudden rush, from the covered trenches which now slanted forward almost to the counterscarp of the half-filled fosse, would enable him to enter the town at a small loss, and perhaps give him the right to claim the honour of its surrender, even though he did not propose to disclose attack till the defenders should be hotly engaged at other parts of the wall.

So he had planned; and so it had proved to be. An hour before Venetia came to the gate, a wild horde of Transcaucasian swordsmen had burst out of the trench that fronted the ruined bastion of Auvergne. The rush was sudden and bold: the defenders few. They stood stoutly to their stations along the wall. They met the savage infidel rush with bomb and bullet, with slings and arrows and flaming hoops. They caused more slaughter to those who came than they could have endured though they had died to the last man—or woman—who held the wall. But they were too few to outface the storm. The ramparts became white with the loose-flowing garments of mounting Turks.

Stubbornly, slowly, the thin line of the Maltese knights was borne back, was slain, or was broken through. A word that the

Bourg was won spread far through the Turkish host; and had the first rush been quickly supported by other ranks, it is hard to think that it would have been more than true. But it was a word spoken too soon, whatever might be the hope of a later hour.

When the Grand Master had re-distributed his weakened numbers he had made a slender reserve of the remnant of those Spanish soldiers who had been hired from Italy when the first threat of invasion had come, and who were a separate force, not being of the Order of the Maltese Knights. Of these, they being gathered from the various posts to which they had been scattered about, Colonna could marshal no more than 130 men (of whom all but few had taken a wound) from the 800 who had landed four months before.

It was because this reserve, being centrally placed, was near the bastion of Auvergne that so few had been spared for the special defence of a position which had not commonly attracted the Turkish storm. While these died where they vainly stood, the Spaniards came at a run. The Maltese cry of *St. John*, which sounded ever when the fierce Pagan tide rose round the beleaguered walls, changed to the battle-shout of St. James, the *Close*, *Spain—Close*, *Spain*, which had chased the Moors of Granada back to the Afric shore. The keen scimitars flashed in vain against the hewing of Spanish swords. In a riot of bitter strife, the Transcaucasian horde was driven back, was chased to a wall down which men tumbled with life to buy at a bruise's cost, or were flung dead to the half-filled ditch. . . .

It was as Venetia reined at the villa gate that the news was cried that Prince Azov had stormed the Bourg. There was a flurry of talk, and of servants running out from the house for details they could not get, as Angelica came through the door. She had no cause to think she would be questioned or stayed. She had Prince Azov's permission to go loose on her parole, which she had only been slow to use lest she might come to those who would doubt her tale, and to whom she might have lacked skill of words to reply in a useful way.

The day before, she had walked a short distance upon the road, and though alone, and conscious of watchful and curious eyes, she had not been stayed. Now she would ride with one who had more freedom than she, and with armed Moors upon either hand, who must have instructions for what they did.

But those who had had Azov's first command were withdrawn on this day. The Captain of the day was unsure both of himself and of what he would be right to permit. With some hesitation, but no manners at all, he barred Angelica's way. She was at a loss, not speaking his tongue, nor he hers. She wore a sword which it would have been folly to draw. She stood in a doubt which Venetia was more equal to meet. With the assurance which her position allowed, Hassan's mistress pushed her mule out from the little group at the gates. She became vehement in strange words, yet doing all in a smiling way. She called as witness the chief of the four who were escort to her, and it seemed that he gave her support, though with a look which was short of grace, as though he might have his own doubt, and would be likely to baulk at a high fence.

But his assurance prevailed for this time, and Angelica found herself on a mule's back, in the midst of the little group, and trotting quickly toward the west, where her freedom lay.

Venetia said at her side, low-voiced, in the Italian tongue: "We must show no doubt, but I shall be at more leisure of mind when we have come where we would seek to reach: the man in front is a surly rogue, but he has orders to do my will, which I suppose that he dare not break."

Angelica rode but a short way, as she had had Azov's consent to do, if not more, when she reined up, and said she would return; but the men closed upon her at either side, one taking her rein in his own hand, which he continued to hold, so that she must go on, unless she would use violence beyond her power to win back to a slave's estate, which none could be expected to do.

The men cursed her in their own tongue. They threatened with hands and eyes. It was clear that they had orders to take her the way that they—which was to say that which Venetia—would. From that moment, it could not be said that she had freedom of choice, for whether Venetia served her in good faith, or would betray her anew, it was certain that she would not give the men orders to let her return. Even the casuistry which was taught in the schools of that day could not have shown that she broke parole, it having been defined as at first it had. . . .

They rode on till they came to a place where there was a fork in a narrow road. They turned out to the left-hand track.

There was a sharp cry from Venetia at this. The man who was in control answered in an abrupt way, but did not alter his course.

Venetia said again: "Will you hear? You are on the wrong road."

"I am on that of which there was a word said that I did not miss."

"You were to be guided wholly by me. Those were my lord Hassan's orders to you."

Venetia's protests, and the stubborn spirit in which she had checked her mule, brought the whole party to halt, but they did not turn.

"Why," the man asked, "would you take the wrong turn? There is that here which I do not like."

"You will like it less when the Pasha gives you your pay."

"So I should, if I let you lead me the wrong road."

"Which I could not do. Do you suppose it was called aloud? It is a most secret plot. That is why you were told no more than that you must take orders from me, and while you do that you can risk no blame."

"You would take the road that is most short to the Maltese lines?"

"So I do. She is bait to show. It may fall apart if she be not there, and you may guess that your head will pay."

Angelica saw that something was wrong. She could not tell what was said. In the end, it was plain that Venetia prevailed. They turned round, and took the right, and more western road. She had won, but the man looked at her with scowling, suspicious eyes. He was plainly in doubt, and had become wary of every yard.

Venetia saw the danger that he might be, and her mind was active as they rode on, which they did for a further mile, on a road that had little life for this day, except where some corralled horses had a troop of Spahis for guard, and with the dull thunder of the strife that raged round St. Angelo's walls ever within their ears.

The three other men had come to share the restless doubt that disturbed their corporal's mind. They looked ever ahead with most watchful eyes, but there was nothing to see. When they came to the well and the ruined wall of which Angelica's letter had told, Venetia said: "It is here we halt. You can go back if you will, for your part is done."

The men did not move. Their leader looked at her in a sullen, obstinate way. He said: "I had no orders to leave your side."

She saw that the sun was above the horizon by no more than the breadth of its own disc, and the time was short, whether to lose or win. But she showed no haste as she said: "You were to take orders from me. Must I report that you would do nothing unless it were first explained? Are you so great that you cannot obey on less terms. . .? Yet I will tell you all, and you shall judge whether you should be speedy to go.

"We are here for bait, as I have told you before, and as the sun sinks there will be Christian lances appear on the western road, which you will observe that you cannot see far, so that they will come at the last with a short rush. If they catch you here, will you not be slain with no mercy at all? Do you want that?"

She looked to a ridge of slightly rising ground to the right, and somewhat ahead.

"It is from there, as I suppose, that ambush will burst, to cut off those who think to snatch us away. But will they show they are there till the trap is full? If you stay here, they will not come out at a quicker pace to avoid your deaths. The Pasha will say that your lives are of no account to the game he plays; and if he ask me why I had not sent you away, I must reply that so I did, but you would not go. If your lives are of small value to you, it is to me they are less."

The man looked round on the silent emptiness of the scene, but he did not move.

"Yet," she went on, "if you choose life, you have need neither to die nor to risk blame. You were told to take orders from me, and while you do that, you can do no wrong. It was one reason for this that I should send you from peril when you had done your part, to see that we should not be stayed by those who might not believe our tale." And then, as he still stood in a sullen reluctant doubt: "You had better stay. I take back all I have said. It is less to me than a pig's death."

The man showed no pleasure at this. He seemed as unwilling to stay for her word as he had been to depart before, and the others looked more reluctant than he. They began to bicker among themselves.

Their leader proposed, as though having found a test which would prove her faith: "If we go we must take the mules, for they will be of no use while you stay here."

She answered readily: "So you shall. There will be mounts enough, I should say, when the bout is through."

She slipped off her mule. She said to Angelica: "You must dismount. Be swift, for the minutes pass."

The men took the mules, and rode off, but at a slow pace, and with heads turned to look back.

Venetia said: "It was worth the loss of the mules to get them further apart, though I had thought to do all in a better way. While they watch, we must not dare to walk on. We must hope that Don Francisco may come, and that he will bring better mounts. But there was no speed in those beasts which was worth a tear. A good horse with a double load may be better than they."

The men did not go out of sight. They turned off the road to a rising field, from which they could get better view. They halted there, as though assured that their safety was won, and looking back for a show that they would not miss.

Angelica asked: "What are they expecting to see?"

"They know that Don Francisco is likely to come, and they suppose that there is ambush behind the ridge." She pointed to where she meant. "They think he will be cut off. When they see he is not, I suppose there will be pursuit, which should be too late, if the horses are good. It will be worse if he should not come; for, if they stay, they will take us again, which will be my death."

Angelica said, refusing a fear which was not easy to keep at bay: "He will come, if the letter reached. . . . You are well sure that there is no such ambush arranged?"

"That I swear. . . It is two miles away. If they could look over the ridge they would see no more Turks than there are here, which it is well that they cannot do."

She spoke in a very confident tone, but, as she did so, a line of Turkish cavalry appeared upon the edge of the ridge, and came riding down in single file to the road.

Angelica began: "If you have betrayed us again——" But her voice sank as she saw that Venetia looked at the advancing horsemen with startled eyes in a bloodless face. She realised, as she spoke, that they were not advancing directly upon themselves, and also that, if any had laid an ambush for those who were due to come, they would not have appeared as they did.

"It is what I have not contrived," Venetia replied, but with the voice of one whose mind was on other things. "You must believe that. If we be caught, you may be no worse than before, but I am near to a hateful death."

"It is that we shall surely be."

So it seemed, for they saw now that the advancing cavalry had perceived them, and altered their course. They were coming directly upon them now, though at no pace, being on loose stony ground, which must be descended with care, and still some distance away.

But next moment they halted again. They now looked to the further side. They swung round more to the right, but still so that they were descending toward the road.

Venetia said: "There is rescue comes. It is that they have turned to meet."

"He will have time to turn, and get free."

"Which, if he have the force that you asked, he will not be faint-hearted to try."

Angelica began to walk up the road. Venetia said: "There is short time. It were best to stand."

Angelica saw she was right. She halted again. But she had started that which she could not stay.

The four who had been at uncertain watch had remained puzzled at what they saw. To a point, the appearance of the cavalry had supported Venetia's tale. But they saw, as Angelica had done, that they did not act as an ambush would be expected to do. And they saw also the significance of that which she had not observed, that they were not troops which Hassan would have been likely to send.

The fact was that they were no more than a half-troop of Mustapha's cavalry, which were on patrol duty around a rear that was thinly held. They had turned at once on seeing what looked like a Christian soldier on foot, with a woman of his own race, for it was their part to enquire of all that was not plain at a glance.

When they saw Francisco's spears approaching fast on the western road, they turned to confront the greater menace, and prepared to charge a foe somewhat less numerous than themselves.

The four who watched might have remained still, if the women had done the same, but Angelica's movement resolved the doubt in their leader's mind. He rode rapidly back, with a companion at his side. That they were two rather than four who first came was an occasion to bless the mules. The one that Venetia had been accustomed to ride, having become tired of standing at gaze, or of a mood to return to her, had jerked the reins with a sudden wrench from the hand of a man less careful of what he held than that which he was puzzled to see.

The mule ran down the road, but swerved when it was pursued, and took to the fields. Seeing it go, the other mule became restive to follow. It kicked at the horse of the man by whom it was held. The horse plunged, and it broke away.

Angelica felt a hand at her side. She looked down to see that Venetia, who stood slightly behind her, had drawn her poniard from its sheath.

Venetia said: "You have the sword. You can spare me this. I will not be seized while I live."

"Then there are two of one mind."

Angelica's sword came to her hand. Her fingers strained on the hilt. She had no softness of womanhood at that hour, but a cold resolve that her life should be dearly bought, or be still hers when the rescue came. But shamed and captived again she would never be.

The two Moors came at a gallop now. They could have ridden them down, but their purpose was to prevent escape. They had no thought to kill, nor did they expect dangerous strife.

The first had not even pulled his scimitar out, as he reined his horse back in a sudden way at Venetia's side. As he leapt from the horse, her hand came from behind her back. She thrust upward beneath his belt. She felt the hot blood on her hand as he tumbled upon her, bearing her down. She did not know how much he was hurt, nor perhaps did he, but he had become savage to kill. His fingers clutched for her throat. They rolled over, struggling upon the ground. But Venetia was cooler of wit than he, and his wound was sore. She used the dagger again, and there was no fault in the second thrust. She came up from the bloody bout, soiled with dust and gore, and her throat was an aching bruise.

The man who rode at Angelica came to ground with more care, for he saw one in a man's dress, baring a sword. He dismounted some yards away, and his scimitar shone. Angelica did not withdraw now. She was of a different temper from when Hassan had struck a lighter weapon out of her hand. All the sword-craft she had learnt in youth, when it had been no more than idle play, was her friend this hour. The swords met, and she knew in a moment's space that she was not the one who had cause to fear.

The man gave ground as she passed his guard. The next second, there was blood on her point. He backed further, being mindful to flee.

Down the road behind her sounded the thunder of hooves. She knew that a rider came at his utmost speed. She did not need to look round, not doubting who it might be.

She was aware of Venetia struggling up, and that the two other men, having let the mules go their own way, were close upon her, for rescue or revenge of him who twisted upon the ground.

She called: "Francis, to her! To her!" But he did not heed. The lance flashed by her face as he drove it in. The horse's shoulder brushed her aside.

Francisco dropped a lance that had pierced her opponent through. He wheeled his horse upon those who were closing upon Venetia from either side. He was in time, though by no more than a second's space. His sword shone as he turned, but he offered that which they did not wait. They saw the odds change too quickly for them. They fled separate ways.

Angelica, who had run to Venetia's side, could put up a sword that she did not need. Francisco caught one of the horses whose riders had ceased to live. The second fled, and there was no time to pursue.

Angelica mounted the captured horse. Francisco gave Venetia a hand, and pulled her up to his croup. They looked up the road, and saw the Turks had the worse, and were falling back to the ridge in a ragged way.

CHAPTER LXV

In the quick falling dusk Francisco arrayed his troop for their backward ride. The strife had been sharp, though short, and there was a dead man to be brought away, and some too hurt to ride back without the help of a haler arm. There was a wounded, crawling Turk to be chased and stabbed, for the days of mercy were done.

He put Venetia down, that she might take one of the led horses that had been brought. There was a moment's debate as to which of two roads would be the better for their return.

The Turks they had repulsed did not fly in a panic way. They halted, and came back till they were no more than two or three hundred yards off, standing out plainly on the low ridge, with a dying sunset behind their backs.

There was a moment when Angelica's eyes were drawn to the distant view of St. Angelo's central tower, from which flashes shone in the gloom, showing that it was using its heavier guns against a foe that could be no more than a guess.

She asked: "Are they back in the castle now? Is the town gone?"

Francisco was in the mood for a cheerful view. "No," he said. "They flash more outward toward the sea. It is Piali's galleys on which they fire."

A voice said: "We should not delay. They have firearms that they are meaning to use."

He had good sight to observe that in the growing dusk, but he was not wrong. He had seen an arquebus on its tripod, against the light of the sky, and its match wink. The next moment a bullet scattered the stones.

All this had been in a short time, so that Venetia, who had stayed to cleanse herself of what dirt she could, from when she had been tumbled in dust and blood, was not yet on her horse. There was no trouble in that. She would be lithe to mount in a second's space, which she turned to do.

And as she did this, it seemed that her foot slipped. Her hands clutched the saddle, and slid down as the horse shied away, and she came to earth on her face.

She struggled up on her hands, and half rose, at which there was a scarlet gush from her side, where a bullet lay. She looked down with appalled, incredulous eyes at the sudden fountain of blood, and then her face regained the defiant lie with which she had taught it to face the world. It was a flag that she had not yet hauled down in the presence of any foe, and now Death's victory would be less than that.

She looked at Angelica, whose hand was on her, pressing vainly an unstaunchable wound, and her lips curved to the smile that had done her service at many treacherous times: "Now should you say I have come to harbour at last?"

They rode back with Francisco's arm around a body which they would not leave for the Turks to strip, or the birds to tear, which was the closest she came to him she might have loved had their lives met along fairer paths, and the one of all she had sought to whom she had not been bare in a wanton's way.

They took, of two, the more fortunate path for their safe return, avoiding or out-pacing those who had become active to cut them off.

As she rode at Francisco's side, and the horses came to a walk on the rough side of an upward path, Angelica told how the trick had been played, being of Venetia's design, which had brought them free.

"There were two letters," she said, "that I wrote, of which the one said you should meet me as you have done, and the next that it should be at the limit of Hassan's camp, being two miles away. It was the one letter she showed to him; but the second she sent to you, and at the first place they may still be waiting to be your death.

"I was long to persuade, for I thought it a plan too subtle to reach success, but she was strong in faith she could bring it through, as she has not failed. . . . She is one for whom we should pray long, that she be not hindered from God."

They buried her in Notabile's ancient church, with more honour than came to most at so hard a time, for they said that it was by her bold device that the grain-ship had not come into port, she having been constant to Malta's cause beyond care of her own life, in which we may call them wrong; but it made no difference to her, she being past the plaudits or scoffs of men, or the snares which were spread for those who had grace and wit, and were yet called of a plebeian blood.

CHAPTER LXVI

It was on the morning of the next day, being the month's last, that Don Garcio of Toledo, Viceroy of Sicily, held Council of War in the cabin of his own ship. The galleys were loaded with stores, and their crews aboard. Messina was thronged with troops; its streets a moving pageant of silk and steel.

The army which had been gathered for Malta's relief was of little more than 7,000 men, but it was fresh, well-appointed, and stirred by a most eager desire to achieve its end.

Ascanio della Corna, the Piedmontese, had been given command, which was a choice in which wisdom ruled, he having been most confident that the expedition would reach success and urgent that it should start.

Under him, Alvarez de Sande had command of a regiment that Naples raised; Sancho de Londono was at the head of the Milanese; Vincent Vitelli led the Sicilian troops, to which were joined a regiment of volunteers from more distant lands.

"We can sail," Don Garcio said, "at to-morrow's dawn, if we so resolve; but the wind is of contrary mood, and the seamen look at the sky with most dubious eyes.

"I do not say I would hold anchor for that, the Grand Master being at so fatal a need, but it was yesterday that I had word that the Turks were storming again, and it is a hard doubt that there can yet be strength to keep them without the wall.

"I would not sail, nor would you, on too late a day, to be perhaps scattered by stormy winds, or overwhelmed by the great fleet of the Turks, to give them a further triumph they should not have."

He looked round as though, if he could, he would have thrown decision on other heads. He felt himself as a man trapped, knowing that he had carried out his King's will, so far as it had been made open to him, and yet, if the event should need one to support the blame, he would be condemned, whether for that he did, or he did not do.

De Sande, a valiant man (as had been shown at Gelves in a former year, where he had held a difficult post after those had gone who had more duty to stay; escaping in Doria's galley at last, when it had passed by night through the throng of the Turkish fleet), but being one who had spoken caution before, was now first in a different mood.

"Why," he said, "if you must put it to us again (as I see not why you should be careful to do), I would say that the time for doubting is done. Shall we stand and gaze for a summer wind, thinking of that storm which the Grand Master endures in so stout a way, and which we should draw to our own heads? We may get a name for the world to jeer if Malta should fall in the next days by our unneedful delay. Do Your Excellency but put us ashore, and we have swords enough to make Moslems howl, even though St. Angelo had gone down in fire."

There was a murmur of quick assent to these words, to which Don Garcio saw that he must agree, but at that moment a page entered the room. He gave a scrap of rolled paper into the Viceroy's hand and stillness fell on all there, for they knew what it must be.

Don Garcio looked down on two Latin words, which he read aloud in the vulgar Italian tongue: "Malta stands."

"Chevaliers," he said, "it is short, being sent on a dove's leg, but it is that which we were instant to know. You may get the soldiers aboard, and we will sail with the break of day."

As he said, it was done; and to what result was to be told within four days after that, when the Grand Master held his own Council of War, being of men who showed less of freshness and ease, and were less trimly arrayed.

He limped somewhat as he came in, for the wound he had taken had not been speedy to heal, and sank heavily into his chair. He looked round on the assembled knights, whom he had called in council before the dawn, for it was only then that they could venture to leave their posts on the broken walls. They were few in number, and most had been little known, even to the Order itself, when the siege commenced. There were those present who were commanders only in fact, or were not on the Order rolls. Of the splendid assembly who had first met in the high dignity of the Council Hall, there were few who lived, and of these Del Monte was a sick man, whose fever, from which he was still haggard and weak, may have spared him from falling more surely to the harvest of violent death.

The Grand Master's eyes were heavy from want of sleep, for he was of an anxiety now which did not cease with the dark, so that his times of rest had become fitful and brief; and he must put his hand to all toils, so that none should say that he drove others to more than himself would do.

"Oliver," he said, "you shall tell them the tale we have, for you can harness your words to a yoke that I might not use."

His head sank as he spoke, giving him the look of a beaten man. As Sir Oliver went on to make the statement that they had been summoned to hear, and for some time after that, it was hard for men to judge whether he were alert to surrounding words.

Sir Oliver appeared as exhausted as he. His face had the grey look of one whose food is little and labour much; but his voice was level and quiet, so that men were no more stirred by the news he gave than the facts must cause them to be.

"The tale," he said, "is not good. It seems that, on the failure of last Thursday's assault, of which we may suppose that he had waited to hear, the Viceroy gave orders to venture something for our relief.

"On Saturday the fleet sailed, with himself aboard. They came round Gozo, and from the west, thinking to land their troops on our southern shore, to avoid clash with Piali's ships, as it was wisdom to do.

"The weather was not good, as you know. The ships were beaten somewhat apart. The Viceroy resolved that the sea was of too boisterous a mood for men and stores to be landed in a large way, which alone would have been of any avail. We need not say he was wrong, which we do not know, and there is no profit in bitter words.

"He resolved further that it would be too great a risk to remain at sea, where he might be cut off by the Turkish fleet, it being ten to his one. We cannot lightly blame him for that. He went back, and is in Messina again.

"Only Cardona did not return. Being driven apart by the storm, he made a landing in Gozo, with some hundreds of men. We may suppose that he will contrive to cross in the night, and give Mesquita support."

He finished amid a silence in which men looked at each other as those may who, being doomed to death, have heard rejection of a final appeal. Then there came an outburst of bitter murmurs, amid which one cursed the Viceroy with fluent oaths, and was checked by Del Monte therefor. He stilled the discord with temperate words, speaking with the slowness of a sick man, but as one whose reason was clear, and who would deal justice to all.

"Chevaliers, we cannot say that the Viceroy was wrong, for it was a storm that we did not see, though we have been aware for some days that the waves rise, and that a foul wind has broken the peace of the summer skies. . . . De Garcio has had the name of a good knight, which we need not slur. . . . It is Spain's shame, rather than his, for they were both too late and too few. . . . It may be God's will that we die here in a knightly way, which we should be equal to do, seeing how many have gone before, who were of as much worth as ourselves, if not more."

De Castriot said: "So it may be. Yet Cardona found means to land. Was it a time when men should look at risks with too wary an eye?"

Marshal Couppier, who had listened and watched to this point with the patience of one who is used to wait his time till emotion stills, said: "We may put Spain from our thoughts. For though we curse or condone, it will not alter of how we stand by one man or a shotted gun. We must think what is best to do, by the sound science of war." He looked round as though weighing what strength of arm or courage remained, as shown by those who were round him then.

His words turned the talk to more practical issues: of how they might fall back with the remnant who still endured to the shelter of the citadel walls, and that in so quiet and sudden a way that the Turks would not be crowding into the town before they could make the movement complete. They discussed water and stores, and observed that these problems were less acute now that they had fewer for whom to care.

There was no word of surrender; no suggestion of the possibility of yet making terms by which they might buy life, if no more; no question of secret flight. They sought only to prolong a resistance which had become vain by every canon of war. There was a spirit there for which any leader might thank his saints, and take courage anew. But the Grand Master lifted his head, and looked round as though upon those to whom Judas would be a natural friend.

With a sudden passion, he rose, throwing his hands apart, as though calling witness of invisible powers that the words which had been heard were not his, nor would he be partner to share their shame.

"There are those," he said, "if I may so put it without offence, whom God Himself is not potent to save, nor His marvels teach.

"You may go backward on coward feet, giving that to His Christless foes which they have been futile to take, for you are many and I but one, but it will have no cover from me. If I die, as has happened to better men—for our Brother was right in that—it will be on walls which we have not lost, and which I see no reason to leave."

He sat down, and his head sank again, as though he withdrew in spirit from those who had shamed their faith, and the vows they swore. There was an awkward silence, in which it seemed that none would be first to speak words which all knew that it had become needful to say.

Only Marshal Couppier sat unmoved, his eyes upon the Grand Master in a cool considering way, as though intrigued in mind rather than stirred in heart by the passion he heard, and wondering to what La Valette could be seeking to lead at last.

"Why," he said, when it had become clear that no one else was in haste to speak, "you may curse us for foolish words (if such you hold them to be), but our bones endure. You will find, if you cut deep, that we are not so different from you. It is of dying you talk, to which we are all likely to come, but you must agree that it is not for that we are here. We are for the killing of Turks, that we may crowd a hell that is not yet full. . . . If you can show us that we can do that to the better count from those tumbled walls, where we are now but one man to five yards, if not ten. . . . ! Show us that, and it is there you can have us die. But if you say less, I suppose it is there you can die alone, if you so choose, and we will give the Turks a more perilous climb, being that of ramparts which still remain."

His words were not such as would have been spoken in Council four months before, but was it strange if something of the forms of rank, the courtesies of debate, had fallen from these men who so endured under the stark shadow of death?

If there were a lack of former respect, it was such as the Grand Master did not pause to observe. Rather, the cool logic that edged the words seem to bring him to a more tolerant mood, though there was no change of purpose in his reply.

"You ask," he said, "what I would have you do. That is very simple to say. Is it only we who are worn? Are the infidels still on the outside of their own choice, or have we been equal, by the high favour of God, to repulse their utmost attempts? Do you regard that we have slain the most part of those who have come, both of the great army at first, and those who landed at later times? Or that those who are left may grow weary of wounds and death? That the autumn winds are already here? That the grain-ship was sunk, as it were by a very marvellous chance, the Most High moving even a harlot to work His praise? Should we have tried that, had we weighed all in a careful scale, as those must do who have no comfort in God?

"You ask what we should do? I tell you, if we go back, then our deaths and our shames are sure. If the Turks win the Bourg, they will not go till the last of St. Angelo's stones is broken or overturned, its banners down, and its knights slain.

"Then should we stay where we are? I say, no! We should go forward, not back. We should sally out, and so vex them that they will see that our spirit is so much higher than theirs as our Lord is more than the Arab dog that they make His peer."

Marshal Couppier gnawed his lip. He said: "It has a wild sound, we being placed as we are. . . . But I am not sure you are wrong. . . . Oliver, what do you say?"

Sir Oliver answered: "I should be last to speak, being one of all who is wearing a bloodless sword. But if you will have counsel from me, I say, if the Viceroy make no further effort for our relief, then it is a desperate chance against none. For the Turks are in a force that we cannot longer endure within any walls. We must perish, unless, by a very marvel of God, we can put them in mind to go."

De Castriot rose to his feet in a laughing way. "We have talk at last," he said, "that a knight can hear. By Tophet's heat, I will raid them before the dawn. Oliver, there is none but will take counsel from you. It is this night there are Turks that your words have portioned for death."

Sir Oliver thought: "And not Turks alone," but they were not words to be said. The Council broke up, having resolved to sally out from sundry places around the walls, and harry those that the trenches held, as though impatient to haste the flight of a beaten foe. Had not La Cerda said on an earlier day, "It is too weird for a war?"

But Mustapha, having his own belief as to which side was preferred of God, and having much the more reason to back belief as matters stood at that hour, seeing how closely he drew his bands around the throat of a choking prey, heard the news of De Garcio's abortive attempt with no more than the cynic smile of one who observes that which his reason told him before.

It did not call for confidence in the Prophet's aid to resolve that the end had come. Foiled he had been, it might be no less than a dozen times, and more than once when he had been sure that the crop was ripe—but this time he knew.

He had slain the calf at the first, and had foretold that it would be a harder task to slaughter the cow. But now he saw that the time had come. He need neither loiter nor hasten in what he did. He had had galleys in from Tripoli, bringing grain enough fòr ten days or twelve, which was more time than his leisure asked.

He fixed Saturday, September 8th, as the day when he would plant the Ottoman flag on St. Angelo's central towers.

CHAPTER LXVII

It was on the Friday afternoon that Angelica went to pray in the ancient church where they had buried Venetia.

She knelt there for a long time in a posture of prayer, being less either than truth or lie, for her mind wandered over many things that were past, laying them out, as it were, before Him who created all, and seeking merciful judgment on much that she could not clearly resolve.

It was the confession of one whose words to the priest would ever be brief and vague, for there are those, of whatever practice of faith, who will seek absolution from fault and failure where authority is itself absolute and understanding complete; and where the responsibility of creation lies.

She found peace in prayer, and in the dim quiet of the ancient church, which seemed as unmoved by the violence and hates of men as is the slow patience of God, though she supposed it might be for the Turks to burn in the next week, if St. Angelo should go down.

Facing her as she knelt was a great window of splendid stains, which the Grand Master, De L'isle Adam, had put in, showing John the Baptist preaching at Jordan ford; but, beside that, the windows were narrow and high, so that there was little light, except where the candles burnt, and the mural paintings which warmed the sides of the chancel and nave with tales of the ten virgins, and of the outcast widow who caught at the skirts of Christ, could only be clearly seen when the brightness of middle day was valiant against the gloom, and even then the high pillars rose to a roof that was vaguely dim.

She had given thanks to God for escape from perils to honour and life of which there had seemed to be but a slender chance, and doubly that it had been by the valour and love of him whom she thought to wed as soon as this cloud of horror and war to which she had come by a headstrong will should be lifted from off her life, if it ever should, of which she had a very imminent fear.

She could not come to absolute peace, or a clear joy, seeing the next day as that which might turn all to blackness again; and she had had a quarrel with Francisco, almost over Venetia's grave, more bitter, it had seemed, than those of the earlier days within St. Angelo's walls, because those who have come to closest accord must find it hardest to break apart, though it be for no more than an angry hour.

She had come to a place where the truth of who she was could be no less than a common tale, it having been told to all who had ridden with Francisco to her relief, and she saw that she must be his mistress to many eyes; but if she were now mere woman in what she did, she would be that to all, and no more, which her pride would not endure in a passive way. For to what other end could she have come to this place of war?

She saw that, to keep the skirts of her honour clear, she must be equal to where she was; but she was not moved by that impulse alone, for she thought of those she had left in St. Angelo's walls, and for whom she had learnt to feel too warm a regard to be indifferent to the near peril in which they lay.

She knew that, in the same spirit of desperation in which the remnant of Malta's beleaguered knights were preparing to hold their lines on the next day, Mesquita was marshalling every man he had (and some women therewith), who were to throw aside the caution of earlier days in the endeavour to divert to their own heads some portion of the strength of the Turkish arms. They had had encouragement to this in the success of the raid which had been planned for the time of her own rescue on the Tarxten road, when Mesquita had crossed the Turkish lines near to the eastern coast, and cut off a strong outpost, which he had destroyed to the last man, and made retreat before alarm was spread to any force sufficient to close his way.

Now Francisco had volunteered, with the same comrades who had been with him before, and with some others who were to be added thereto, to act together as a cavalry troop, and to fight in the knightly style in which their youthful training had been.

They were to include none but those who could ride well, and for whom good mounts could be found, and such as were trained in the use of weapons a knight will bear, so that they would be equal to ride into the Turkish lines, not seeking a set strife, but to cause disquiet, now here, now there, such as would engage the movements of troops more numerous than themselves, while they would do all the mischief they could, as occasion came.

But she knew that it was less with any hope of success to their own arms than for relief of pressure upon St. Angelo's walls that their plans were made. It was the spirit by which a dog may spring at a lion's mouth, when his master is on the ground.

She had said that she would be one among these, and when Francisco had made excuse, she had answered with reasoned words, though with an impatience for which she blamed herself at a later hour: "Will you never see where my honour lies? Or that Malta's need is for all it has at this time, to its weakest sword? Is it not on that pledge I continued here, that I would do such part as I could, be it naught or much?

"I may be of little skill and no strength, but it is twice I have used a sword to a man's death, and (which is more) I engaged one who yielded ground rather than I, till you rode him down. Besides that, I can ride well, and I may know more of the roads in the Turkish lines, and of how their camps spread over the land, than any else of your friends. I do not say than you, with whom I will not compare."

And when he would not listen to this, saying only that it was that which she could not do, being unfit, and without training in knightly arms, she said no more, but went to Mesquita himself, from whom she gained consent, using no more than few words, but such as were chosen well.

It was when she told him of this, and that she had a purpose that would not change, that they had quarrelled again in a way of which it was no pleasure to think, for she had said things which she did not mean, which it was seldom that she would do. She had asked him at last if he would have her named for such as Venetia was known to be, and something more which she would be glad to forget, having allusion to his own fault with the one who was dead, and with an implication she had not meant nor seen till the words were said.

Now she judged herself, and was aware of a double fault: for she saw that her motives had not been solely those that she had allowed to him, but that she had been unwilling that he should ride to danger she did not share (which she should have been quick to say); and that his own reluctance was born of no less a thing than his love for her (which she should have been quick to see); and, beyond questions of fault or pride, their common folly was spoiling hours which would not return, and might end at a short sum. At which she resolved that she would not rest till she had come to a way of peace; but as she rose to put this purpose to use she was aware of a trumpet that shrilled high from the western gate, and went forth to face a martial sounding of fifes and drums, and to see a regiment, still in the gay bravado of those who come to a threshold of war which they have not crossed, that was pouring into the town.

CHAPTER LXVIII

It was after the Friday noon, and the sun had turned downward to meet the sea, when Ascanio della Corna dismounted from the back of a sweating mule at Mesquita's door.

He had had a ten-mile ride from Melleha Bay, and the Commander, who had heard a flying rumour of his coming but two minutes before, forgot the lack of length in his legs, and the dignity of the office he held, as he hurried out to meet him.

"We are in time?" della Corna asked. "St. Angelo stands?"

"So it does," Mesquita replied, "being (as I should have said a moment ago) at the end of its last day. But I may revise that, if you will tell me with what force you are here. For I should say that less than an army will not avail."

"There are six thousand men whom the Viceroy now puts ashore in Melleha Bay."

"Then, if they can do battle with Turks who are three to one, if not four——"

"We will do battle with such Turks as are here, be they most or few. I but ask that St. Angelo's walls endure till to-morrow noon, by which time we shall not be far."

"It is a pleasure to hear; for the last tale was that you had gone home after looking over the fence."

"So we did, and by whose design I will spare to say. But being landed in Messina again we had a further Council convened, at which there was talk of disbanding troops which it had been futile to bring to head; but while we were at somewhat high words there was a riot about the doors, for the soldiers clamoured to be led to Malta's relief, and must burst upon us to know that their leaders were not more coney-hearted than they. So it was agreed, whether of shame or goodwill, that we would woo the winds for a second time.

"We left port yesterday noon, and having come southward during the night, we shaped a straight course, with a wind that was fair enough, though somewhat abeam, to Melleha Bay, where we put in, it may be three hours ago, having had no sight of a hostile sail."

"Then you have lost no time that you are here now?"

"I put ashore in the first boat, and rode here as soon as I could find a guide and a beast to bear me along, for I would know to what issue we have arrived. De Sande will overrule the landing of men and stores, in which he has more practice than I can claim."

"Is the Viceroy here?"

"That he is. He is in a galley which would not be easy to catch, if it should have cause to run out to sea. He will see the troops ashore, and go back; which may be less of his will than his King's charge, that he be not tangled too closely in our affair."

Mesquita's lip lifted to a scorn that he had no scruple to show, for he was not of the land or legiance of Spain. "He washes hands?" he said. "It was Pilate's choice. But that which he swills away is the honour he might have had."

"So," della Corna replied, "we may hope it will prove to be. But I would not boast on too soon a day. . . . Will you tell me how the Grand Master stands? Does he still stoutly endure?"

"So he does, in a way. But it had seemed for the last weeks that it is only by the slowness of those who will not be slaughtered more to hasten that which they cannot miss.

"For the Grand Master's losses have mounted to such a sum that he can no longer array his walls. Yet, as their numbers fail, they have snapped in a fiercer way, so that Mustapha has shown no haste to put his fingers between their teeth."

He spoke no more than the fact was, for, two nights before, when the Turks had been lying closely around the walls, as those who shepherded a close-cornered prey, and thinking only of how they could cut its throat without risk of a further scratch from its dying claws, De Castriot, creeping out with two score of his own kind, had entered a battery camp where it had seemed that no watch was set, and when those it held who were not stabbed in sleep had taken to panic flight, they ran on to the swords of another score, whom De La Rosio had led the opposite way.

Forty-seven dead had been the Turkish count in that camp when the morning came, and that was but one raid of five, though they had not all had so great a success, for the Bourg walls had been bared of men for those raids, it being aimed to make the infidel think that they had more strength than their living numbers allowed.

And on the next day there came a new proof that there was still life in those leaguered walls, when the batteries of the Bourg and St. Michael's fort opened with rapid and constant fire, such as they had not opposed for many weeks to the hammering of the Turkish guns. For the careful storing of powder had ceased. "Now, if at all," had been the text on which the Grand Master preached, and all the slender margins that yet remained, both in munitions and men, were being spent in the frail, final hope that they might cause the Turks to lose heart and go, while there was yet a residue of resistance left.

It might be—it was—no more than the last flicker of fire that was nearly out, but it was a proof that Malta's knights could still bite with unbroken teeth, and if it did not decide the date on which Mustapha had resolved to finish the siege, it confirmed, to his mind, the wisdom of the caution with which he moved.

The tale of dead was already more than enough. The faint possibility of relief (he thought) had faded away. Why should he hasten that which was so near to its certain end? He would drink the success which now brimmed to his thirsting lips without more cost of treasure and blood, the spilling of which had already risen to a mark which was beyond simple defence. . . .

Mesquita asked: "Do you plan surprise, or would you have the Turks know you are here?"

"I would let them know with all speed, that it may slacken strain upon St. Angelo's walls."

"We need make no effort for that. To have held it close had been a much harder thing; for the land is sprinkled with spies that we cannot catch, or whom we endure, as being useful to us. You may suppose they will hear all before night is come. . . . And yet. . . ." He paused a moment, and touched a gong, on which a page appeared at the door.

"Catch me," he said, "Juan Goe, if he be in the town, and bring him here with no slackness of foot."

The spy he named must have been near to find, for the two Commanders had sat but a short time, discussing the strength of the combined force they would be able to put into the field and other matters cognate thereto, when a small wizened man, whose lean activity did not appear to have been lessened by the grey bleakness of age which his visage showed, was led in by the page, with two armed Maltese guards at his rear suggesting that there had been little freedom of choice in the celerity with which he had come.

"Juan," Mesquita said, "I have that under my hand by which I could send you to hang when the Turks go, and your use (which is little now) would be quite done."

If the man felt any dread of the threat, it did not appear. His sharp alert eyes moved quickly from face to face, as though they could read the thoughts of those on whom they were cast, so that words were of less moment to him.

"When is that?" he asked. "Will the Turks go?" as though his mind were less concerned with himself than with larger things. He added: "I have done no wrong. I am Malta's friend. . . . What would you have me do now?"

"Here," Mesquita went on, without condescending direct reply, "is the Chevalier Ascanio della Corna, Captain-General of a Spanish army which is landing this afternoon at Melleha Bay."

The man saluted in an absent manner, his eyes bright with observation the while. He was quick to the point: "You would have it known?"

"I would have the truth known. Neither more nor less. Listen, and I will tell you that which Mustapha should pay to hear."

He went on to tell of the regiments which had been landed, and their officers' names, as he had just had them from della Corna. He was detailed and exact. They totalled about 6,000 men (for it was not everyone who had sailed with the first fleet who had been willing to sail again, when impulse and confidence had alike declined), and this number he gave, della Corna sitting the while in silent watchful surprise. But, having finished with them, he went on to mention other troops which had come from the Spanish King, giving as much detail to these fictitious regiments as he had done before to those of substantial fact.

He added: "It was but a feint when His Excellency the Viceroy sailed round the island a week ago. He would not have approached the south coast, where good landings are hard to find, had it been other than that. It was to lull Mustapha to foolish dreams, till he could land, as he has now done, with his full force at the Bay."

The man asked: "They are to know this?" His eyes asked more. They were alive with suspicion of what he heard.

Mesquita countered with another question: "How do you say that St. Angelo stands at this hour?"

The man's eyes seemed to probe for the answer that he was expected to give.

"It is hard pressed," he said. "It is stoutly held, but there are too few to defend its walls. That is known to all."

"And it is to be stormed at to-morrow dawn?"

"That is known alike."

"Has it strength to endure?"

The man did not express any opinion on that. He appeared to regard the question as not needing reply, but as having told him that he had wished to ask. He said: "You would have the Turks warned with speed that this rescue is round their rear, so that they will be afraid to engage the walls."

"Should I tell you, except for that?"

The man did not resent the implication this question held, but he looked troubled in mind. He said: "If I should sell a false tale of so large a bulk——"

"The regiments are now marching here. Before dark, they will begin to enter the town."

Juan considered this. It was hard to say how much he believed. He said: "I will do this myself. They must have a tale that they will not doubt."

Mesquita's hand loosed his purse, but the man's head shook in dissent. "I will have pay from them, or else none. You will know whom I serve."

He went out, and della Corna said: "You think to stop the assault, even before we can have time to arrive?"

"So I do; and have little doubt it is now done. He will take a tale that cousins truth in too close a guise to be refused without proof."

"And if they know our true strength?"

"What would they do then? It is to be guessed, and no more. We may ask what should we do ourselves in the like case. They have perhaps sixteen thousand men, besides the crews of the fleet and without counting the sick."

"They could face us with such numbers as should suffice to hold us in check by the rules of war, and have enough left to enter the town, if they should not stint blood to that end."

"So it looks," Mesquita agreed, "and so Mustapha may seek to do. . . . You will see that I scheme to bring them more about our own heads."

"So you should. It is not numbers that count alone. There are men and men. I have six thousand who will go on, or else die. If it were not too like a boast, I would say I play Gideon's part. We are in more vigour of health and heart than the half of the Turks can be. We must be more fit of body, if not of heart, than are those who still live within St. Angelo's walls. We must draw all we may to our own front. You are right in that."

They returned their minds to discussion of plans for assaulting the Turkish camp, which may be left, for they were to prove as vain as are most of the detailed designs of those who will look ahead, though it be by no more than a day. And meanwhile Juan Goe sat at meat in his own house, that was in some narrow alley of the old town, and with him his three sons, of whom the youngest could be told by a scarred chin, which had not held him back from many ventures into the Turkish camp, and more than once of entering into the Bourg.

Juan Goe was not concerned for his own skin, though he carried on a most perilous trade. His position illustrated the profound truth that they are masters who serve. For, in his own way, he kept faith, he served well. Letters from either camp might be passed to him or his with the certainty that they would reach those for whom they were meant. Whether he had ever sold that to the Turks which could be used for a Christian bane was best known to himself, but it would be admitted by all that he did not peddle false news. He gave worth for the coins he took. He had become useful to both armies alike, and if he preferred either side in his heart, it was a secret he did not speak, or had not till that day.

His safety lay in his sons, as was theirs in him. For it was seldom they would be in one place, as they were now, or could be caught in one net.

If wrong should be done to one, he who acted thus would turn each of four from a useful unsure friend to an open foe, and there could be no profit in that.

Now he spoke his mind in the privacy of his own board. "Boys," he said, "there is yet a hope that Mahound may be brought to earth, and his mouth flavoured with dung. You may help in this, but you must understand that you do no more than scatter a true tale. The Spaniards have come to land in Melleha Bay, and their number is equal to that of the Turkish host, or it may be more."

He gave details, and told each of them where he was to market the news, and how to deck it in an aspect of urgent fear; and as he did so there was a sound of fifes and of throbbing drums, at which they went out to the main street, to watch the Milanese regiment enter the town, with Sancho de Londono at its head, very splendid in steel, and velvet of peacock-blue, and ostrich feathers drooping the wide-brimmed hat he wore for his forehead's ease, a chased-steel basnet hanging against his knee.

That was how Mesquita had said it would be. Juan Goe counted the regiment with careful eyes and unmoving lips. He found the number correct. He concluded that there was more truth in the tale he was pledged to sell than he had been able to think before. Might it all be true? He could not even deny that. At a later hour he slipped down in the dark to the Turkish camp.

CHAPTER LXIX

It was the same evening that Piali came ashore to confer with Mustapha upon the dispositions for the assault of the next day, for which it was designed to concentrate the full strength both of army and fleet.

"For," Mustapha said, "though they be as weak as is rumoured now (which I do not doubt), yet shall we succeed with more ease, and the lighter loss, if we storm inward from every side with force that must overwhelm."

With this purpose, it was planned that Piali's fleet should enter the great harbour in such numbers as it had not done till that hour, and should not only use its guns, but land parties at different points, to vex St. Angelo on its seaward sides.

Hassan, who had continued from day to day his slow, ruthless advance against the barricades of the Sanglea, had now established his trenches close to the counterscarp of St. Michael's fort. From that position, he had driven mines which were ready to fire, with the aid of which he trusted to rush the fort, and so turn its guns upon the inner harbour and the shipping that lay therein and beyond that to St. Angelo and the Bourg, on a side where they were not fashioned to face a foe.

Mustapha's army was to be used for no single assault, but had ladders ready for the attack of every bastion of the outer walls. It was a plan which relied for its success upon the fewness to which the defenders had been reduced. That they could resist, at whatever point, must be less than a confident hope: that they could do so as every one was beyond reason to think.

The Turkish generals did not talk of it now as of a doubtful hazard of war. Mustapha looked no longer in anxious doubt at the strength of the leaguered walls, or talked of assaults which should weaken, if they did not destroy. Rather was he (in the metaphor of his own choice) a butcher who had chosen the date when the cow should die. Does he waste thought on whether the beast's objections will supervene?

The two leaders talked together with more amity than they often felt, seeing success so close, and the time near when they could return to their own lands, and to the plaudits that Malta's destruction would surely bring. They would have been ready to part but that Hassan also should have been there, and courtesy required that they should sit on, conferring in the leisured manner of those to whom time is an unmeaning word, until he should appear or it be clearly resolved that he did not purpose to come.

But when he came, it seemed that courtesy was a garment he had forgotten to wear. He was abrupt to ask: "Do you sit here, as though bewitched by the Christian saints, while the earth quakes underfoot? Is there none to tell you that a Spanish army has come ashore?"

Mustapha looked to be more ruffled by the manner of this address than by the purport of what was said. He asked: "Is an army the word? Do you think I have not heard before this?"

"It is an army, as I am surely advised, of equal strength to every man that we have."

"And at what point did it land?"

"At Melleha Bay."

"Have you heard of those who were put ashore at Gozo a week ago?"

"You believe it is only they?"

"It is not where they would be most likely to land?"

Present anger, and a long-standing contempt, combined to sweep away the pretence of deference and regard which Hassan had rendered until that moment to an older man who was also his senior both in rank and command.

"Allah be your guard for the witless dotard you are! The Milanese were in Notabile streets, it is three hours ago, and Naples marching behind. There is a Spanish army put ashore this day while you have gathered your fleet to the harbour here, leaving them to land on a vacant beach." He looked at Piali, giving him, as admiral of the fleet, the edge of his last words, as he said: "We are fooled for the world to laugh."

The event had indeed, and even in itself, without the Spanish troops with which Mesquita's imagination had swelled the rescuing ranks, an aspect of prevision which its merits did not deserve.

The Viceroy's first futile attempt to land on the southern coast had been as successful in persuading Mustapha that there was no further menace to fear from him as though it had been designed to that end.

The concentration of Piali's fleet for the attack of the next day had left the seas clear for the landing at Melleha Bay as well by the operation of idle chance as though the Viceroy had foreknown it, and picked the hour.

Piali did not reply. His eyes were on the Egyptian Pasha, over whose face a look of age had passed, like a shadow of nearing death. For a moment, as his mind bent to the shock of the adverse news, coming when he had thought that the long travail of the siege, so wasteful in treasure and life and with so little as yet of honour for the great army which had dwindled before its walls, was to end at last in the fall of his insolent hated foes, the dotard of Hassan's abuse did not look to be less than an appropriate word; and, in that moment, Piali's decision was made.

With a colder, more brutal, contempt than Hassan's passion had held, he looked at the aged general who, by the miscarriage of this military adventure, which he had himself been reluctant to undertake, had wrecked the reputation which a score of previous victories had preserved to the average limit of human life.

He said: "You have lost an army here, but the fleet remains, and it is that charge which I will not fail. I take it back to the last ship, in proof that the blunders have not been mine." He was already standing as he said this, and now he turned abruptly away. He went out, throwing back the words: "You must bustle aboard, if you would not stay to be Christian show. I sail in ten hours from now."

Mustapha sat for a moment after he had gone, with the face of a man stunned. He stroked his beard with a shaking hand.

Hassan looked at him with scant sympathy, but he had even less for the one who had gone. He had not come himself to propose flight, but to rouse his colleagues to dress their front to a new foe. Yet, he asked himself, was Piali right? He saw that, in the condition to which the Turkish army had been reduced, it was doubtful that it could resist the attack of an equal number of fresh Spanish or Italian troops, and it was so placed that defeat could not be less than an utter loss. It must offer battle, if at all, with St. Angelo at its rear, and with no retreat except to ships which there might be no leisure to board.

It would have been a great risk; and Piali might have decided with more wisdom than he would often show, even though his resolution came from no more than a moment's impatient contempt for an aged and broken man.

But, be that as it might, his decision left little for others to resolve. If the fleet should sail, it would be plain madness for the army to stay. Nor would Barbary remain for an hour, when Turkey and Egypt had put to sea.

And while Hassan considered this in a mind that was already planning details of the retreat to his waiting ships, something of manhood came back to Mustapha's eyes, as he asked bitterly: "Will you also fly from a foe that you have not seen?"

"I must go, if you go. There is no choice that remains. Will you stay here, and the fleet away?"

"It is at the moment when victory is a flower to be plucked with a light pull."

"So it is. But I ask, do you go or stay?"

"It is Piali's doing, not mine. May he be cursed to hell for this night."

"That is plain enough. Then I must not be slack in getting aboard."

He went with the word, and it was not long before Mustapha regained the self-command he had come nearly to lose; and so, putting fatigue aside and the need of rest that the aged feel, he became active to order the embarkation of troops among whom panic was near to rule, and to make such salvage of munitions and stores, and the lighter guns, as could be in so short a time, with the advance guard of a hostile army, if not its main force, encamped not more than six miles away.

CHAPTER LXX

Sir Oliver Starkey laid down his pen. He had worked long, indifferent to all outward sounds. It must be near to the dawn. He thought: "There may be those who will reach these citadel gates, or else not, we being so scattered about the great length of the outer walls; and, if they do, there may be some further defence, though it cannot greatly avail. But I should say we come to the last day."

His eyes fell on Angelica's chair, at which his mind turned a moment aside to thank God that she had gone clear of what, he thought, was about to be. Yet he would have been glad to see her again.

"She had a spirit," he thought, "that was steel and fire, such as is seldom found in a woman's frame, yet she was without envy, and slow to hate. I would give much that she come at last to her most desire."

He put on a corslet of steel, and belted a sword which, in all these months, he had drawn but once, and then to no use at all.

He had closed his accounts. His records were clear and complete. If he should die, they would be sufficient for other eyes. . . . But it was more likely they would be for the Turks to burn. . . . Such was the futile end of all mortal works. . . . Fires or decay. . . . He could not feel that he greatly cared: he was too weary for that. Rather, he had a sense of great relief that the long struggle was near its end.

"It is not a siege," he thought, "in which the praise will be most loud for those who prevail." He might, had he thought of himself, have taken some credit for that. But he thought of high deeds in which he had had no part. Now he would go out to take the place that his name required in the final strife. He felt as one who moves in a dream, which came as much from fatigue as from the exaltation belonging to such an hour. "We may hope," he thought, "that as we loose hold on life, we draw nearer God."

Being now ready to go, he became more conscious of outer things, and was aware of a low confused murmur of distant noise that came through the night, like that which sounds from within a hive where the bees are vexed. It was silenced at times by heavy fitful firing of battery guns, unlike the long monotone of the Turkish bombardment, which had become so constant that its pauses were more noticeable than itself.

Sir Oliver had a moment of doubt. Had the assault been opened before its hour? Had the Turks entered the town? Had there been default in himself that he had worked there oblivious of outer events? He could not blame himself with reason for that. He was not in active command on a separate front. Every preparation that human forethought could make had been ordered: every commander was at his post. It was the hour that he might have claimed for his own rest that he had given to the completion of the records his office held. . . . Nor was the sound near enough to suggest that the Turks were in, unless it were at the Sanglea. . . . Well, it was vain to conjecture that. He had a place to take at the bastion of Auvergne, and a narrow space of command to which he had put his own name, to replace one who had been killed by a chance arrow the day before. . . . As he moved to the door, it opened quickly. The Grand Master pushed its heavy curtain aside, and entered the room.

"Oliver," he asked, and his voice was vibrant with the excitement which stirred his soul, "can you loiter here . . .? I sent to rouse you from sleep, and they said that your bed had been left unused."

"I had much to do. Is it later than I was aware? I had not thought that there would be stress before dawn."

La Valette stared at him in a surprise to which comprehension came. "*Have you not heard?* The Turks run! They are crowding the ships in Marsamuscetto Bay. They are like bolted rats that the dogs chase. Though it is past wit to guess what the dogs may be. It is the Lord's angel who moves, as we well may judge; even he who fell upon the Assyrian host that was gone when the morning came. God would not suffer them to prevail who jeer the name of His Son. He has but tested our faith to the last hour, that it may be the more plain to see that our rescue is wholly His, amidst the failures of human friends."

"There is no doubt of the fact? It is hard to hear."

"Should I speak so for a guess? They are firing their own camps, that we may not make spoil of that which they are in too swift a panic to bear away. We should have known at a sooner hour had not the Moors made a bold show, opening attack during the night at the Sanglea, and there springing a mine by which there was loss, and a black look at the first. . . . But that is past now, and Marshal Couppier has turned their own guns upon them as they withdrew."

The Grand Master spoke with the conviction of one who had refused doubt on the darkest day, and now came to no other event than that he had looked to see; but Sir Oliver heard in a more sceptical mood. He did not question the interposition of Heavenly Powers, but he knew that it was his part to examine causes of mundane kinds. He looked puzzled, and half incredulous of that which he was unable to understand.

"Have you thought," he asked, "that this may be a most subtle trick to draw us out from the walls?"

It was a suggestion which disconcerted the Grand Master for a moment which quickly passed. "No," he said, "it cannot be that. For it is done in too large a way."

Sir Oliver did not dispute more. He said: "We can see best from the tower." They went up together to the high platform where the great culverins were mounted which could fire to Sceberras ridge, and looked far out over a land of dim movements and flickering fires, through a darkness which was faintly aware that dawn was paling the stars in the eastern sky.

Sir Oliver said: "So it seems. It is a marvel to see. . . . I suppose that the Viceroy has come in a sudden way."

"In such force that they scuttle thus, without battle fought?"

"So it appears. But, if you will take counsel from me, you will issue orders at once that the walls be held and the gates barred till we see the fleet bearing away. It is Mesquita who should explore in the Turkish camp, and we, being so few as we are, should remain on our guarded walls till the doubt is dead."

The Grand Master could not deny the wisdom of this, though he was reluctant enough, as the pause of silence showed before he replied: "I have already given orders of somewhat more courage than that, having sent out those who will explore the trenches from which we suppose that the Turks have fled. Yet I must not say you are wrong. You have been of cool counsel and sound, through all the months of this strife. I will give orders of more restraint till all doubt is done."

La Valette spoke to others upon the tower, for it was a place to which all had come (that is to say few) who were not withheld by the strictness of the orders they had. He sent word to the commanders to hold their walls as though still expecting the rush of a hostile foe, but he did it in a sour voice, as though grudging that he should play so poor a part on a splendid day.

Sir Oliver was aware that he would be judged by the event, and if the Turks were indeed in a panic flight, he would be lightly charged with an overcaution which might ring with a timid sound. He was reminded by the corslet he wore that he had thought to spend the day in another style. If it were true that the Pagans fled, he would not only be the one man who had come through with no wound and a bloodless sword, but he would be stamped with a timidity which would be hard to refute, and which might be held to offer its own explanation of his absence from scenes of strife.

It was an unpleasant thought, though it had no power to deflect his mind from that which he knew to be the sounder practice for a garrison so few and weak as they now were.

He looked keenly over the harbour waters as the quick dawn spread, seeking signs to resolve the doubt, and as his eyes fell on St. Elmo's fort an idea came.

He heard the Grand Master's voice again at his side. He was saying that he was for the Bourg walls, to learn whether the trenches had been explored on the first order he gave, and to what result. He was turning quickly away, as Sir Oliver spoke: "There is one way we can tell. If they feint, they will not loose hold of St. Elmo's fort."

"It is soundly judged. I will send a good boat to prove how it yet stands."

"By your leave, I will take the charge."

"But——" The Grand Master's surprise was natural enough, though it caused Sir Oliver an annoyance he would not show. "Oliver, if you be right, it will be sunk, it is ten chances to one. If the fort be manned, what hope can a boat have when it comes under their guns?"

"Then its approach may well be guided by one whose caution you do not doubt."

"There are a score who could take this doubt, and be better spared."

"Yet it is a favour I ask."

"Then it is one you must have. But you will know that my orders are to push back at the first sign that the Turks are still active upon the Point."

"So you may be assured that I shall be most prudent to do."

It was not more than twenty minutes later that a large boat, containing twenty men besides those who pushed on the oars, passed the boom of the outer harbour, and moved rapidly down to St. Elmo's Point.

At that time, the ships of Piali's fleet were crowding out of Marsamuscetto Bay, and passing beneath St. Elmo's fort on its further side.

CHAPTER LXXI

NOTABILE had not sunk to sleep as the darkness fell. It had stirred ever to louder life as more troops poured through the city gates, and must be billeted for brief hours of rest, until the time came when those who had first arrived must be marshalled to march again, while the dawn was still some distance ahead.

Della Corna, conferring with Mesquita in pursuit of a common plan, and in some doubt of what claim might be made that he was first in command, found that there would be no trouble of that, for the Portuguese leader put forward a plan of strategy of which the most part had been already in his own mind, and which would give them separate points of attack.

The weakness of the Turkish position was obviously the distance that lay between their sea-base at Marsamuscetto and their lines of siege around St. Angelo's walls, divided by the thrust of the great harbour, so that they might be cut off from retreat by an attack aimed at its head and the landward end of Sceberras ridge. It was at this point that it was agreed that della Corna should strike with all the force that he had; while Mesquita, with his less disciplined troops, was to operate on the more eastern position, which would become the rear of the Turks, as they would dispose themselves to face della Corna's attack, and penetrate, if the operations should develop favourably, to Marsa Scala, for the destruction of that subordinate harbour-base.

They could hope that the rumour that they had been careful to spread would delay St. Angelo's storm until they could reach the scene, which they planned for the first hour of the day, and after that they could only hope that the valour and quality of their ranks would avail against the greater numbers of those they met.

The military position was such that it is natural to feel regret that its tactical possibilities were not destined to be exposed, but the plans of the two Commanders went into the limbo of most earthly dreams when a rumour came through the night that the Turkish army was active to put to sea. They saw that Mesquita's device had succeeded beyond reasonable probability, or the intention with which he had sent it forth. . . .

Angelica had gone to rest in a room which remained her own amid the sudden influx into the town, but only so by the sacrifice of Francisco, and two companions of a more impersonal chivalry, who, first claiming that which they had no intention to use, had then contented themselves with the corner seats that a kitchen gave.

She was roused, while it was still night, by Francisco's voice at her door.

"You must up, if you would be riding with us, for there is tale that the Turks fly."

"*That the Turks fly?* How——? But I will be instant to come. You shall tell me then."

"I will have your horse at the door."

She dressed quickly, in haste to know the meaning of that which she did not doubt, though she was unable to understand. It was a marvellous, almost unbelievable, thing. But she had heard the note of excited hope in Francisco's voice, and her heart sang. Were they to come clear at last from this nightmare of cruel danger and dirt and blood, and the constant tale of the dead? Was faith to triumph at last, even as it faltered toward eclipse? Was there to be reward which they would not know for the fortitudes of those who had fallen that Malta's cross might endure to fly?

And her heart was light with another joy as she drew close the belt of a sword which, of itself, she had no longing to wear, for she saw that Francisco had kept, in spirit as well as word, a promise made but few hours before, after they had exchanged regrets, and come back to the contacts of lips and hands dear beyond speech to those who have not broken reserve for the consummation of love.

He had agreed that they should share the dangers of the next day, that they should keep together for loss or gain; but he might have made excuse now that they were to ride out with no more duty, perhaps, than to reconnoitre before the dawn. He might have said that he would not shorten her rest. But she came out to a narrow street that was crowded with mounted men, to find her horse already await, and to gain saddle by the light of the lantern that swung over the iron-bound door.

As the cavalcade moved away, with clash of steel and clatter of hooves, and the rustle that belongs to the motion of mounted men, she became sharply aware that it was she who had been wrong rather than he, more than, even in the frankness of her own thoughts, she had allowed it before. Let her arguments that she must still do her part in a man's way be of all the substance she claimed, it yet remained that, whether as woman or man, she had no right to be there.

She might boast of skill with a slender sword, such as one hand could control, but she was not weaponed in knightly wise. She wore no armour of proof, such as was still the use of those who were the heavy cavalry of the day. Even in Don Garcio's name, she had no proper right to the place she had been stubborn to have.

It was true that the Turkish cavalry was more lightly arrayed, but it was on the extra weight of weapons, the heavier impact of larger horses and larger men, that the Christian knights depended to break through any who might be bold to oppose their way.

Francisco had found her a good horse, such as would be swift at a need, and with the heart to endure, but it was smaller than those that he and his comrades rode. Armed and mounted as they now were, she seemed to ride dwarfed among giant forms, with more difference than the daylight held.

"Francis," she pressed to his side, and looked up to say, "I was wrong to come. I will give you that. The next time you ask, be it what it may, I will grant your will, and we will call it a balanced debt."

There was a time of silence before he spoke: "Do you pledge a word which I know that you do not break?"

"So I do," she said. "I would pay a debt which I can see that I owe." She laughed in her quick way. "But how gravely you put your words! You must not ask for John Baptist's head. We are in the wrong land for that, where all men swear by his name."

"I may ask more."

"You will not ask that I ride back now?"

"I will ask that we wed the day that the Pagans flee, as it is said that they do. I mean the day they have left the land."

After this, the silence was hers. She said at last: "You ask much."

"I ask more than that. I ask all."

"I had thought to wed in our own land, in a good way. And you will regard that I am now ward of our Spanish king."

"Well, I have asked. . . . You shall have your will, as you ever do."

He had asked more than it was likely that he would guess, or she tell, for her own feelings warred in a doubtful mind.

She was of an instinct to take the best things of life in a slow and delicate mood, by which only their full flavour is tasted, their fragrance felt. She was not of those who will spill the cup with a hasty hand, or snatch fruit from a breaking bough. But she had been taught in the royal way that it was in keeping pledge, at whatever cost, that her honour stood. She said: "There is but one answer to that. I will keep my word."

She reached out that their hands met in the dark, and she knew that she had come close to her most desire, as Sir Oliver prayed she should at the same hour. But after that she must have eyes and mind for that which the dawn would bring.

They reined their horses up on a lift of land where they could see far as the light grew, though it was still dim, and night had its rearward stars in the western sky. It was sure that the Turks fled.

There was a moment that Francisco sat in doubt of what he should next do. They could see the Turkish galleys, still burning their masthead lights, one by one passing St. Elmo's Point as they put out to sea, and gathered there as though waiting further orders to go.

Francisco looked down, and his words were not such as she had been expecting to hear: "I would you had not come."

She glanced up, and his look recalled one which she had seen on his father's face, when a great purpose had fired his mind. She said: "You have a high dream, which I am not equal to share? If I were not here, what would you be likely to do?"

"I would ride for St. Elmo's fort."

There was a point in that which she was not unable to see. It would be an evil case for the Turks if St. Elmo should come again to Christian control before they should be clear of the harbour-mouth. But would the Turks overlook that? Who could guess, in the haste of a panic flight, such as it had the aspect to be? Would they think that there would be so rash an attempt to seize it before they should be clear away? It seemed a small chance of a splendid gain, and the counter that must be played was a likely death. Should she let her presence prevent attempt? Should she go back, never, perhaps, to see him in life again?

She made, with laughter, a better choice. "Well," she said, "if you ride or not, there is one who will."

She put her horse to its speed on a downhill road.

CHAPTER LXXII

Sir Oliver sat in the bow of the boat, which moved fast under the impulse of its Maltese rowers who looked ahead as they stood upright to push their oars, the strokes urged by the excitement of a great hope and a failing doubt.

He looked also, with eyes that were cool and keen to search for signs of that he had come to probe, but there was little to see and nothing of certain proof.

The breadth of the harbour waters was empty of any vessel, large or small, except that which was bearing him to St. Elmo's Point. The eastern side of Sceberras was quiet and bare, but there was no strangeness in that, for, except where they had established their batteries on the crest of the ridge, the Turks had been accustomed to keep to the western slope, where their movements would not be seen nor themselves exposed to the fire of St. Angelo's longer guns.

But as he came near to St. Elmo's fort Sir Oliver saw that the flight of the Turks must be something more than the fantastic dream which it had at first sounded to be. There were men moving upon its ramparts, but not as those who look out from a guarded wall. Over the counter-scarp on the landward side there were figures that leapt and disappeared, running down to the harbour beyond. An embrasure was empty, where he knew that a gun had pointed outward, and might have been trained on their own advance.

He hesitated in mind, having learned all he had come to know. By Divine Mercy or human aid, he saw that the siege was raised on what he had supposed was to be its last day in another mode. But he had a new thought. From what he saw, he supposed that the fort might be seized by a bold attempt, the garrison being in act of flight, or at least too occupied with their own fears to be conscious of his approach. He said: "Push on. I am minded to land."

So he did, and went on to the fort, taking all the men that he had and leaving the boat to its own chance. They went by a covered way to the low door through which Angelica had passed more than once before. The door stood wide and they went in, finding no life till they came out on the platform which looked upward toward the Sceberras slope. Here there were signs, such as they had passed before, that the fort had been abandoned in haste. There was a gun on the ramparts still in its place, and another overturned after it had been dragged some distance back from the parapet. Others might have been taken away, as Sir Oliver was unable to tell.

But as he went on to the further side, seeking a view of Marsamuscetto Bay, where the details of flight must be bare to see, there came behind him an eruption of Turks who swarmed up by another stair than that he had used with his own men. Each was loaded with sundry gear, and in a jostling haste to be gone. They were in number more than a score, so that they somewhat exceeded those that he had, before whom, when they saw, they stopped in an abrupt astonished way. There was show of swords, and some would have come on and some backed, with excited talking among themselves.

They could not reach the western exit from the fort unless they should first brush Sir Oliver's party aside, and as they seemed irresolute for the attempt, he advanced on them, with his own men showing a better heart.

But, before they had time to close, another man came in haste from below and shouted something at which they broke apart, with cries of alarm, casting their burdens down and leaping over the wall to the fosse, as though reckless of how they fell.

The words that the men had called meant nothing to those whom Sir Oliver led, but they were plain to him, who was skilful in many tongues.

He called back, in a sharper voice than he often would, those who would have used their swords on the rear of the fleeing Turks. He said to all: "Lose no moment of time. It is life or death. Go back to the boat in the utmost haste that you may. Do not loiter for me, but push back, and say that the Turks are fled. Must I bid you to hasten twice?"

The men went in the haste he said, with a confused thought that he might have feared that the boat would be seized by a flying foe. He started quickly toward the door by which the last of the garrison had come up, and then stopped, seeing a troop of horse who came riding rapidly down the slope, and were now close to the further side of the ditch.

They had ridden hard, and had not come by a bloodless way, for their lances were reddened, or had been broken or cast aside, and there was an unridered horse that ran with a dangled rein at their rear.

He saw that about a score had swung to the left to ride down the fleeing Turks, who were scrambling out of the ditch on the Marsamuscetto side, but a smaller party came straight on, with Angelica in their midst, and Francisco slightly ahead.

He shouted: "Go back! The powder is fired below." But they were not instant to understand, and it must be shouted again, while the seconds passed. When he saw that they understood, and were swinging round, with Francisco's hand pulling hard on Angelica's rein (for she would have stayed, as though to call something further to him), he ran down, seeking where the powder was stored.

He thought: "I should have had time, if they had not come. That is clear now. But I could not tell that. I could not leave them unwarned." He supposed that each second would be his end, but had time to be glad that he had not died before he had come to know that the Turks were down, and the Cross of Malta would fly. He remembered how he had argued once that there may be a special mercy of God for those who come to death by a sudden way. He was glad that he had left his work in such form that it would be clear to another eye. His life was not much, nor would it have much praise from the tongues of men, who have more regard for the deeds of high colour and splendid sound, than for the slow untiring contrivance from which they come. But he had striven much in his own way; and he had sought to deal with an equal hand, and to show mercy at times. Did he assert his own merit to God, to whom all pleas must be folly alike, except the publican's prayer? It was strange how many thoughts may come in the last moment of life, as we run down a dozen steps, expecting each second to face the instant of rending sound which will be the end of our earthly frame. . . . There came the pain of faintly returning hope, as he knew that he had come to the place where the powder lay. . . . Three seconds should now suffice. . . . But he supposed that he might see no more than the last inch of the creeping flame as it would touch the black snake of powder that would be laid to meet it upon the floor. . . . And so he came to a place from which no danger could be, for the match had been damp, or been badly lit, and must have sputtered out, even as the Turk who was to start it had left the vault.

Sir Oliver Starkey became aware of a faintness that he must control with some effort of will, and that he was breathing hard, which may have come from the pace at which he had sought the vault.

He felt some scorn of himself, not having known before that he valued life at so high a sum, and thinking that he must have been a poor sight to the watching saints; and the more so that, if Malta were saved, he might have died in the serene knowledge that his work was not left undone, which is a comfort that comes to few.

But he gave no more time to such thoughts than there had been for those he had had before as he had descended the steps. He recovered rule of himself as he looked down on that futile match, and compared its fate with his own, remembering what he had thought that the day would bring as he had been working throughout the night.

"Well," he said, with a smile, "so it is. We are twins in this. It is one tale till the curtain fall. I neither suffer nor do."

He went up at a slower pace, but it was all in so short a time that Francisco's party had scarcely withdrawn to the distance prudence required, and turned back to look fearfully at the place which might become in the next moment a volcano of lurid smoke and of quaking sound, when they saw him on the ramparts again, signalling them to return.

"I am overcareful," he said, as he met them when they had entered the fort, "having been withheld from the front of war. I feared that there might be laying of mine, or some fiendish snare, but I found that there was no danger at all."

Angelica said: "We must suppose that you quenched the match," and when he denied that, in the tone of one who would not be questioned again, she was puzzled the more; but the others had listened carelessly, if at all, their eyes being upon the sea and the Turkish fleet, of which the last vessels were now clear of the harbour mouth, so that it seemed that the seizure of the fort would bring no evident gain.

But the fleet made no motion to go. It moved in a confused way, like an unshepherded flock, the great galley which was Piali's, and had Mustapha's quarters aboard, lying-to in the midst, and the Barbary fleet having drawn somewhat apart on the western side.

There were reasons enough that the fleet should be in no condition to sail, for as they had loaded all in a common haste, amid the urgence of those who would not be last in leaving the land, they had taken in whatever the ox-teams had first hauled to the quays, or which could be taken into the waist of an anchored ship. It was all salvage, such as they would be loth to leave to fill the maws of the Christian dogs, and they had scrambled it in.

But as they came clear of the land, and had time to look round in a cooler way, and with daylight to aid, they found that some had too large a load, and some were burdened with troops that they could not feed, and some had little water, or none. There were Alexandrian galleys piled with that which should be put off on Byzantium's quay, and men of Egypt on Turkish ships; and so there was much debate and barter, and clamour of tongues, and boats crossing from ship to ship.

And meanwhile, in Piali's cabin, where Mustapha sat, and to which Hassan had come and Prince Azov with him, there was debate more fierce and violent than that which had brought decision the night before.

Hassan, whose way it was to keep cool as Piali raged, said for a third time, and in a fixed tone, without passion of gesture or voice: "It is plain what we must do. We must go back."

"And so," Piali replied, with a contempt that he was careless to show, "you will take St. Angelo, now that it will have been reinforced in so large a way, though you were unequal before?"

"And that I say we were not, it being in act to fall. And you must see that if we are quick to return, they will not have had time to enter the town. We shall but have drawn them down from the hills, as they must think that it has been our subtle purpose to do. If we defeat them first, for which we should be more than enough, I suppose that the Grand Master would yield, for which we could offer terms; for he would have no more to hope, or you might say less, than before."

Mustapha was silent, stroking his beard in the way he had, and watching a quarrel to which he could give victory to either side which would have his support at last.

"It is so," Piali went on, "you would wreck us twice, as we dance to the tunes you play. It was but twelve hours ago that you urged us here, and now you will have us back, saying that it was on no more than a lying tale and that the next is of better worth."

"I have told you," Hassan replied, "that I had a tale from a false spy which outpaced the fact, though it was nearer truth than that Cardona only had come, as yourselves believed. But it is beyond truth that I urged you to put to sea or had had such purpose in mind. It was that of which you must bear the full weight, for we were forced hereto by your single resolve."

"That is truth," Mustapha observed, "which must be told at the right time."

"That," Azov gave his support, "was how I take it to be. For I am assured that Hassan went with no thought but to rouse you to make front for another foe, for we had taken counsel thereon."

Mustapha turned to him to ask: "Then are you of equal mind that we can win all if we land anew?"

"It is chance of war," Azov replied," from which we were craven to sail away. There are 5,000 men, so it is said, or 6,000 at most, and they gathered from sundry lands, and not practised to fight on one field or in one command. Should we say, without trial made, that we are not equal to them?"

Piali was not burdened with wit at birth nor had he gathered overmuch in his living days, but he had enough to perceive that, if he stood out now, he was to be the target of all their blames; whereas if they should land to a new reverse, they must bear that from which his own shoulders would remain free. He said to Mustapha: "Do you ask that the army be put aland? For, if so, it is a right you have, and that which I cannot cavil to do."

"It should be done," Mustapha replied, "with all speed. And of how we come to be here we can talk again at a quieter hour."

CHAPTER LXXIII

The Grand Master received Sir Oliver's message with satisfaction, but as no more than confirming that which he had known before. He ordered that the church bells should ring a triumphal peal, and that all but a slender line of patrols should be relieved from the walls. For the first time in three months St. Angelo became aware of itself, rather than with its eyes on an outward foe, and its plight was evil to see.

The Grand Master was quick to despatch a second boat to learn what Sir Oliver did at the fort, and why he had not returned, and on this boat he went back, knowing how many matters must need his care. He had said first to Francisco, as he stood watching the confusion that showed in the Turkish fleet: "You will take charge of this fort, which you may be said to have won, till further order is made." And to Angelica: "But you, as I suppose, will prefer to return with me, for there will be little of comfort here, either of food or in rooms where the Turks have lain."

"No," she replied; "I may come at a later hour, but for this time I will stay."

She had in mind the promise she had given before the dawn, and what it must mean to her when those ships should hoist sail for their own barbarous lands, as she supposed they would do in the next hour, and till that were resolved that she would remain at Francisco's side.

So Sir Oliver went, and she stayed to watch the restless stir in the Turkish fleet. There was a sack of dates found in the fort, of which she ate, rather than other food, which she was less willing to touch, though some did.

Francisco, who had been busy about the fort, came to her side. He said: "I would stay here, if I could, for it is pleasure both to be with you and to watch them go. But there are other things that it is needful to do, and it is idle to watch them thus, unless they threaten return, which we should be crazed to suppose they will."

"Then you can tell me," she asked, in a puzzled voice, "what Piali's galley intends?"

His eyes followed hers, and saw that the oars of the Admiral's galley were out, and it had come round, so that its bows fronted the land. From its decks, a trumpet sounded an urgent note. Faintly over the water there came a noise of shouting from ship to ship.

It came on at its oars' pace, which was not much, for it was a great ship, and a south wind would have given but little aid, even had it used its sails to the full, which it did not try. But it was plain that it sought return, and slowly, as with a reluctance that could be felt, one by one, the other galleys followed Piali's lead.

Its meaning might not be easy to guess, but it was sure that Francisco had not come on a barren quest.

Such efforts as there had been to remove St. Elmo's guns had been on its landward side, and when it had become plain that time would not allow more to be done, there had been orders to blow it up, so that the long cannon that faced the sea were not removed, nor even disabled for instant use.

Francisco would have chosen to wait till the foremost ships were close to the harbour mouth, and the guns could have opened at a short range. He had not shown Malta's flag, having none to hoist, and the Turkish fleet might have come close under the fort before suspecting the danger to which it drew. But he saw that he must act with a wider purpose than that. If the Turks were resolute to return, the first need was to give warning to St. Angelo, and to those whom della Corna would now be leading to its relief. It was as vital that his own need should be clear, and that St. Elmo should not be invested again while containing less than two score of defenders within its walls.

For both objects there could be no better call than the sound of its seaward guns. As rapidly as they could be loaded and trained, they opened fire on a fleet which was still a long gun-shot away.

The damage caused, if any, must have been slight, but the action was decisive in its effects. When Francisco had thought that he must soon be trusting his rampart's strength against all the weight of guns that a hundred vessels could bring to bear, he saw the whole fleet falter and swerve, as though his shots had been a signal to them to turn away, which they were docile to heed.

Piali's signal trumpet was heard again, and was repeated from ship to ship. The fleet turned, but did not linger again. With the Barbary galleys now in its van, it shaped its course to the north-west, following the line of the Maltese coast, and gathered speed, filling its sails with the southern wind, and with the flashing strokes of two thousand oars impelling its rapid way.

It was a manœuvre that puzzled most who watched it from beach or hill, but della Corna, who heard the news as he rode through the deserted camp, and was within a mile of the ruins of the Sanglea, made the right guess, and proved his fitness thereby for the place of honour he held. He turned his horse at the word, and ordered that the little army he led, which came on in exultation that its foes had scattered away, where it had been looking for blows and death, should make a forced march back by the way it came. He sent horsemen to watch the course of the Turkish fleet, and to inform him of any sign of landing along the coast.

It may be doubted whether Mustapha would have attempted to re-enter the harbour under the fire of St. Elmo's guns, even in default of a better plan, but, in fact, they decided that which he had been debating within himself since it had been resolved to return, he being skilled, as we know, in the strategic gambits of war, which are more than strength of arm or valour of heart, and will often make them of no avail.

Piali, standing sullenly at his side on the high poop of the ship, and watching their approach to the harbour-mouth, saw the flash of the first gun, and its black outburst of smoke, and was not too dull to guess what it must mean, even as the sound followed along the wind, and the heavy shot made spray round his bows from a shattered wave.

"Now," he asked, "will you take St. Elmo again?"

Mustapha ignored the contempt that the question held. He said: "You can tell the steersman to alter course. I have resolved to land in St. Paul's Bay."

Piali stared. There was more here than he was quickly equal to comprehend.

"Why," he said, "I suppose you can do that, if you will. You can land in an empty bay."

"That is how it must be. For which end we have a very fortunate wind, which I must ask you to use, for it is on speed that our hopes depend."

"I must put you ashore at the place you choose," Piali replied, "though it were on the Sicilian shore."

Having said that, he gave the orders for the fleet to alter its course, as it was speedy to do, having guns to face if it went on as it was, and when this had been done he came to Mustapha again to ask, in his sullen way: "Am I to know what you seek to do?"

The Turkish General had no cause to conceal his plan, nor was it gain to him that Piali should be reluctant in his support. He said: "We can be there before they will reach by a landward march, even though they be quick to guess what our purpose is. Should they be slow, we may be first within Notabile's walls."

"Do we gain much, even then? Even though you should defeat them in open field, they will have St. Angelo at their back. They will retire to its walls."

"That will be what we must wish them to do."

"And we bring it down when it is strong with a ten-fold force?"

"We shall but watch that which must fall by its own weight, with no travail from us. We shall contain it, and wait the end, which I should put at a short week. Have you thought that the Italians have come by a hurried march from Melleha Bay, carrying neither powder nor food in a great store, as they could not do?

"Either they must have landed lightly equipped, or they will have much that is still at Melleha Bay, and will be useful to us, for we must cut them off from that base. We shall be on their rear, where they had thought to be vexing ours, and it is to St. Angelo I would have them go."

CHAPTER LXXIV

THE day passed with St. Angelo in a great doubt. There was news at noon that the Turks were landed again in St. Paul's Bay, and were marching inland in numbers far exceeding those with which della Corna could bar their way. There was no comfort in that, and little more in a tale that some of the Turks had been reluctant to leave their ships, so that there had been some violence used in putting them forth.

What might have chanced had della Corna been slow either to think or to do is a vain guess, for he had marched back with such speed that, when he saw the first of the Turks, he had Notabile more than two miles in his rear, and had picked his front on the falling land which looks down to St. Paul's Bay; so that Mustapha must come at those who were better placed, or else stay where he was, which he could not choose.

The next tale that St. Angelo heard was of battle joined, and of fighting which did not slack.

After that it would have waited with anxious ears had the Grand Master given it leisure for aught but toil. But, from the moment when he had heard that della Corna was marching back, he had been implacable, both by example and urgent words, to use the short hours which were surely theirs of freedom beyond the walls.

He had been no slower than Mustapha to see how St. Angelo would be placed if the siege should close round it again with larger forces within its walls. But he supposed that the Turks would not have fled in such sudden haste in the darker hours without leaving much spoil in the camps which would be helpful to meet his needs.

There was none of sound legs and not less than a single arm, man or woman or child, who was not hurried forth to search and load and bring in, with orders to pay no heed to rich garment or gold or gem, but to gather weapons and food, and such things only besides as would be useful to sustain the lives of those who would hold the walls, or to keep the Turks to the outer sides.

It was a toil that only slackened as daylight waned, and there came a sure word that the Turks were in broken flight, with the Christians slaying upon their rear. So it was; and such was the end of Mustapha's exploits on Malta's soil; though there had been a moment when the scale had trembled again, for Hassan, who had judged what the day would bring when he had seen how reluctant the Turks had been to leave ship for another bout, had proposed that his part should be to protect the line of retreat with 1,500 of the best of his corsair hordes; and as the Turks fled and the regiment of Milanese came after in headlong chase, and no order at all, with Naples nearly behind and in no better array, they were taken sharply in flank by such as they had not been thinking to meet, and fell back with a bitter loss.

It was a moment which might have changed the day had the Turks been in better heart, but they had had enough, if not more, and the fact that Hassan had scattered the Milanese meant no more to them than that they could gain the beach with less panting of lungs than had been theirs for a mile before. They were glad at last to scramble into the waiting boats, with Piali's guns firing over their heads, to warn the Christians away. . . .

It was at a later hour, and darkness had covered the wrecked town and the wasted land, when Angelica stood in Sir Oliver's room, feeling as one who had come back to her own place, as from a darkness of evil dream.

"Is it true?" she asked. "Are the Turks fled?"

Sir Oliver was a tired man, but he was of a habit of life by which the body obeys, having found resistance of no avail. He said: "If you will come, I will show you that which it will be pleasure to see, and toward which you have done a part which Malta should not forget."

He led her upward to the roof of the highest tower, where it looked outward toward the sea. The wind had moved to the north-west, and the night was cloudy and cool. The stone parapet was damp to her hand from a fine rain, which had lately ceased. Far out to the east, the lights of the baffled fleet receded upon the sea.

They went down in the silence of those who feel that they have no words to equal the moment in which they live.

"You will find your room," he said, "has been left unchanged. But it has not been cleansed, for there is none living on whom such a charge could have been laid."

With the thought of that room, La Cerda's mistress came to his mind, for whom it had been ordered at first. He asked how she had died, of which he had heard no more than a careless tale. "She was buried, so I am told, as one who had been our friend, both by the news she sent in the slave's mouth and by her plotting to get you free?"

"So it was. She had more honour at last from Mesquita's hands than the Grand Master would have been quick to allow."

Sir Oliver agreed that she had not been one whom La Valette had been eager to praise.

"She might not call for his praise," Angelica said, "yet she was one he should have been laggard to judge, for they were alike in so many ways."

Sir Oliver was surprised. "It is that," he said, "I had not clearly observed. Will you expound to a duller mind?"

"It is plain to see. For they would each seek that which was worth to them with a fierce will, paying costs which they did not count, and that largely in others' woe."

"And beyond that?"

"There are other points, which you might be less instant to see."

"Or admit of one to whom a great honour is due?"

"So it is. For I suppose it is most, under God, by his stiffness of will that we are here as we are and the Turks fled."

Sir Oliver did not differ on that, and the talk died. Their thoughts went their own ways, but they were at the same point when he said, as they were turning apart: "You will be near the time when you will be casting the clothes you wear, as I suppose you will be willing to do."

"So I shall. But they have a use for one further day, which they must not miss."

She gave him no time to seek solution of that reply, but went on to the room which was hers, and had belonged to La Cerda's favourite before.

Her thoughts were still on the dead, but not now to prove that Venetia and the Grand Master had been kindred of soul. She compared herself, and the diverse issues of life which make wisdom vain, and on which the grave is the dumb comment at last. She thought: "I cast prudence aside when I came here, which I did in a most ignorant wise, while she lived with a wary heed, and with more wisdom in earthly ways. Yet is there harbour for me and for her wreck. . . . Or was she right to say that she had won to harbour at last?"

On that thought she prayed long for the dead, and after for those who lived, and for herself last, and had such thoughts that she could not sleep, both of the past, and of many things which she hoped for the future days. . . . But she fell to sleep when the dawn was near, and waked late, as did many else within St. Angelo's walls.

CHAPTER LXXV

It was Sunday, September 9th, when St. Angelo waked to the knowledge that the shadow of death was lifted from round its walls.

The Grand Master gave order that all who had strength to stand should assemble to meet those who had so gallantly come, and at so late and vital an hour, and who had been potent for its relief; and that they should join thereafter to give the thanks that were due to God in the Convent Church, to which the most part of the knights who had come to Malta four months before did not need to arise to reach, being already laid in its vaults.

Della Corna rode through a trodden and blackened land, past half-filled fosse and half-fallen wall, and up the street of a ruined town.

He was met by six hundred of sundry sorts, who were still able to stand. They were hollow-eyed from their sleepless toils: they were sloven of garb and beard: the most of them were maimed or crippled with bandaged wounds.

He looked round when he had greeted the Grand Master, and those who were nearest to him. He asked: "Will you say you have held the town with this remnant of men?"

"They are all here but those that the lazars hold."

Della Corna was silent, being amazed. Then he said: "It is a most marvellous thing, for the heathen dogs must have been held out by their own fears at the last, more than by any strength that you had."

"They were held out," the Grand Master replied, "by our faith in the living God."

Sir Oliver added: "We may say that they were withheld by the valour of those who are now dead. There are eight thousand of Christian graves."

Marshal Couppier said: "They were withheld to the last hour. You had been too late in a day."

Della Corna replied: "I would claim less, having seen that which belies the settled science of war. But it is plain that you must leave here, for I can see that the town is ruin, the land waste. You have neither powder nor walls. And it is known that your treasure was spent to supply your stores when the Turks came. You would be sheep to slay if they should return their fleet with the spring, as they are most likely to do. And, besides that, you are all invalid men. You must get out the ships you have and make sail for a better land, where you can have the comfort and honour that Europe owes to those who have saved her shame."

He said no more than Mustapha would do in another voice, when he would make a boast that Soliman would prefer to accept, rather than disgrace his own arms by degrading him: "I came away, having nothing more to destroy. I left Malta flat."

La Valette said: "We do not think to remain here. We have better plans."

"The Grand Master," Sir Oliver said, "has long held that the castle was not builded where it should have been at first; yet it had seemed a great matter to move the town. But now that it is so battered about, it can be built in a better place."

As he spoke, he looked over the harbour to where the ridge of Sceberras rose, and della Corna saw the meaning behind his words.

St. Elmo should not have been a weak place apart when the Turks arrived, but the spearhead of the central strength of the Maltese knights. They should have built between the two harbours, so that they would have commanded both. But Mount Sceberras, as its name implied, was high and narrow, and too steep for a city site. He said: "You can strengthen St. Elmo's walls, and enlarge its girth, till it be a castle that none could take. But I suppose you must have your town in another place. Sceberras is too steep for the homes of men, as it is simple to see."

The Grand Master said: "Then we must be active to lay it flat."

Della Corna asked: "Do you mean that you will remain here, though your walls are down, and with so wild a project as that?"

"Shall I leave the charge I am vowed to keep? And that when the Cross is high and the Pagans flee?"

Della Corna made no answer to that. He saw in a clear light how it had been that Mustapha had remained on the outside of those fallen walls.

They went on to the church. . .

It is another tale of how the Grand Master planned a new city of impregnable strength, which men would after call by his name, and how he commenced to flatten Sceberras ridge, as he had said he would do.

The Turks had the design that della Corna had guessed, that they would come back with the coming spring; but La Valette saw the one thing that would break their plans, and struck hard and first, as it was his nature to do. He found gold in a great sum for a secret plot, and before the Turks were assembled and fitted forth, there came a night when the great arsenal at Byzantium, which was the first at that time that the world held, rose in dreadful thunder and flame, with utter loss of the thousand cannon and great stores it held, of powder, and of all manner of munitions of war; and the Turks must resign a plan for which they had little left but their naked hands.

So the great street of Valetta was cut from the stubborn rock, and its ramparts rose, and Sir Oliver found that he had still much to control, for there were stores to be brought from far, and thousands of workmen who must be paid, and funds which must be gathered from Europe's bounds, that being hardest of all, for there were many pledges which were not kept; and there would come a day when workmen would call for their wages for which no treasure remained, and they must be paid with tokens of the Grand Master's design—for he would go on his stubborn way, though the gold were none—with NON AES SED FIDES stamped thereon, which would be redeemed on a later day.

And so La Valette would be laid with honour at last in the new church of the city which had been built in his own dream before it rose into solid stone, as must be first with all the makings of man, and as men must have been first in the thoughts of God while the earth still bubbled with liquid heat. And Sir Oliver would write—as may still be seen—the inscription that scrolls his tomb. . . .

Angelica knelt in the church where the psalm of thanksgiving rose, and was aware that Francisco was near her side.

He said, in a low voice that the music drowned, except only to her: "Do you hold your word?"

"So," she said, "you have known me do. But there is one thing I will ask. Am I shamed by the hose I wear?"

"You are one whom no shame can soil, as I should have known at a sooner day. You are as Beatrice was, who walked clean in hell."

"You will wed me, being so clothed?"

"It shall be in what habit you will."

"Then it may be in the next hour. But it shall be so done that it will be noticed of few, for it is a small thing on so great a day."

John P. Marquand
STOPOVER: TOKYO
LAST LAUGH, MR. MOTO
A. E. W. Mason
CLEMENTINA
FIRE OVER ENGLAND
A. Merritt
BURN WITCH BURN
Gladys Mitchell
THE RISING OF THE MOON
ST. PETER'S FINGER
Clarence E. Mulford
BAR-20
THE COMING OF CASSIDY
HOPALONG CASSIDY
Stuart Palmer
THE PUZZLE OF THE BRIAR PIPE
Clayton Rawson
DEATH FROM A TOP HAT
Sax Rohmer
BROOD OF THE WITCH-QUEEN
THE YELLOW CLAW
R. C. Sherriff
THE FORTNIGHT IN SEPTEMBER
G. B. Stern
THE YOUNG MATRIARCH (£2.50)
Phil Stong
STATE FAIR
Rex Stout
RED THREADS
SOME BURIED CAESAR
WHERE THERE'S A WILL
Angela Thirkell
THE HEADMISTRESS
S. S. Van Dine
THE BENSON MURDER CASE
Daniele Varè
THE MAKER OF HEAVENLY TROUSERS
Edgar Wallace
SANDI THE KING-MAKER
Alec Waugh
JILL SOMERSET (£2.00)
P. C. Wren
ACTION AND PASSION (£2.25)
S. Fowler Wright
THE SIEGE OF MALTA (£3.50)
Dornford Yates
SHE PAINTED HER FACE
Philip Yordan
MAN OF THE WEST

CHILDREN'S BOOKS
John Bennett
MASTER SKYLARK (£1.80)
Frances Hodgson Burnett
RACKETTY-PACKETTY HOUSE (£1.30)
Thornton W. Burgess
OLD MOTHER WEST WIND (£1.70)
MOTHER WEST WIND'S CHILDREN (£1.70)
Austin Clare
THE CARVED CARTOON (£1.80)
Howard Pyle
THE MERRY ADVENTURES OF ROBIN HOOD (£2.25)
E. M. Silvanus
THE PELICAN AND THE KANGAROO (£1.80)

Tom Stacey Reprints Ltd
28–29 Maiden Lane, London WC2E 7JP